An

The Midnight War

Book One of

The Midnight Saga

Copyright © 2024 by Andy Lopez

All rights reserved.

No part of this publication may be reproduced, distributed, or transmitted in any form or by any means, including photocopying, recording, or other electronic or mechanical methods, without the prior written permission of the publisher, except as permitted by U.S. copyright law. For permission requests, contact andylpz3@gmail.com.

The story, all names, characters, and incidents portrayed in this production are fictitious. No identification with actual persons (living or deceased), places, buildings, and products is intended or should be inferred.

1st edition 2024

Paperback: 979-8-9901311-0-1

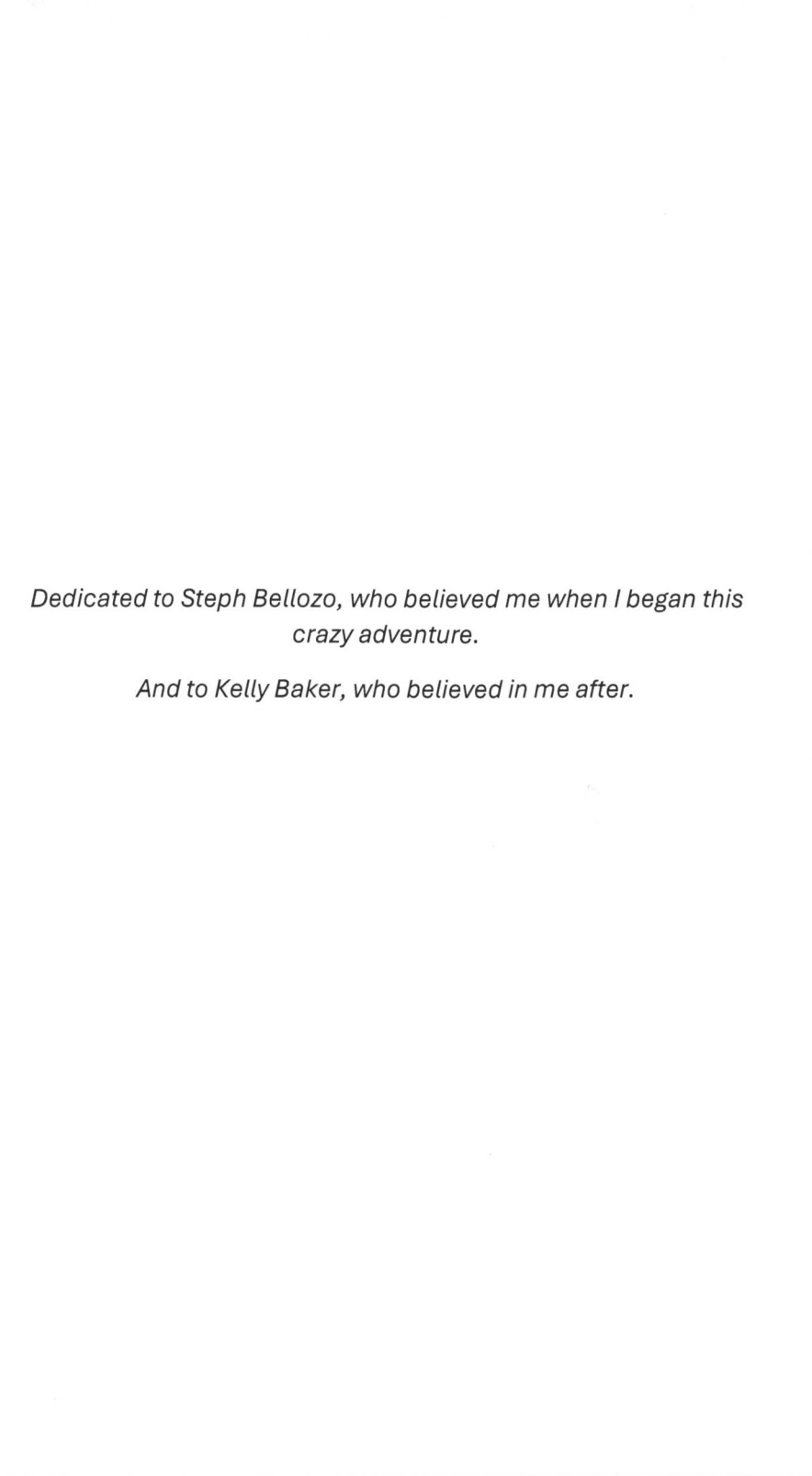

Dedicated to Steph Bellozo, who believed me when I began this crazy adventure.

And to Kelly Baker, who believed in me after.

Andros
Lancaster Lands

Prologue

There was nowhere to hide.

There was nowhere to go.

The sun had already receded into its niche in the dark, leaving a darker feel about the day. The somber light of the moon helped Nevil little with his problem. With his tired eyes, he gazed emptily at the night sky as he reviewed what little options were left.

The King wanted more. Seville was a strong kingdom, but it was faced with great adversity. The ESE could not currently be toppled—all else knew this—but the ESE had many enemies, and worse yet were its allies. All that was necessary was the change in leadership of the ESE, something that was not so cemented. Always it shifted like shadows with flickering light. Three lights governed its dark dance; currently, the Kingdom of Seville was the light which shone brightest, but Nevil wanted nothing else but to leave the other lights in darkness. He knew that at first, the Kingdom hadn't been thought a serious thing. The people scoffed at the idea of this kingdom prevailing, where so many before it had failed. Its time was done; the kingdom was a thing of the past, they said. That was why Nevil needed to be sly and strong.

However, there was little Nevil could do. He served the King, but little did that help without the proper funds. They needed resources—how long ago had they used all theirs? That was why the ESE was established. They needed to gather money through the only means they knew. They knew only of stealing it from the environment and stealing it from others—no matter if they were poor or even dead. *Dead,* he thought sourly, thinking of the executions. He was not opposed to the idea, but deep inside him he wished for a more innovative solution. The kingdom had begun executing people, citing security as the basis for their actions. The reality was that they simply needed less people to feed; less people for which to care. Nevil disliked this solution only on the basis that it attempted to reduce the symptoms rather than curing the disease.

These excruciating conditions dissuaded birthing children. The children could not offer enough in return for the high price of their conception and rearing. Progeny was not the concern. They needed food, and they needed shelter. Like primal beasts they scavenged throughout the land, treasuring any valuables. But even in the scarcity of food, they found within themselves an inner drive to push forward and to toil the land and garner their wealth, and they did all this continuously in search of riches with which to get drunk and forget their problems.

Naturally, Nevil did not belong to this class of people. He was part of the nobility, of those who got drunk because there was no scarcity of food, and no necessity to work the land. He was part of those who laughed when affronted with the circumstances of the people in the Kingdom, and falsely asserted that the Kingdom would last forever and would continuously provide. Nevil knew that these were foolish words, and he was all too aware of the terrible dread that surrounded the land. That was why he searched to improve the land.

Where was he to go? Nevil did not want to fail his King. Unable to break free of the chains that captured the world's minds, he thought only of what he knew. He began thinking of a way, repeated countless times in their past, written in their books of history. He searched for an answer, trying to determine which foreign land they ought to invade, and whose resources to forcefully obtain. They needed to expand, and let the outer filth direct their few treasures to their land. But even so, he had no perceivable choices. They couldn't go to war with others. The Kingdom could cease to exist. Everything would die in fiery retribution.

He left his room and went outside into the chilly night. He was covered in fine black clothing which kept him warm, and though they fought back the ice, he knew, subconsciously, that there was a chill in the air, and he shivered regardless. He walked slowly towards the outskirts of the city, just outside the forest. He would meet with two men in the black of night, away from the prying eyes of the city. He walked slowly, trying inconspicuously to search behind him and ensure no one followed. The only thing he saw repeatedly as he turned was the slow rise of the full moon which glowed in a dull light. The obscured moon gave negligible light to the city behind him, but he could appreciate the light as he left the city and came closer to the forest.

While the moon rose slowly, the wolves readied their cries. The birds flew past—at times blocking the light of the moon. The barks of the dogs broke the silence throughout the land. Other dogs barked at them in response, and they communicated the distress ever-present. The screeching of some unknown animal dominated the skies, and the flutter of predator and prey alike could not be masked in the terrible silence. Despite their attempts, no animal could permanently break that dreadful lack of sound.

A pack of wolves stopped near a river and drank. One wolf stood still in the woods, waiting, scouting. The other wolves approached the water and drank, sometimes being pushed into the water by other parched wolves. The scout waited patiently while its brothers drank to their satisfaction. They finished quenching their thirst and slowly began leaving, but by that time, the scouting wolf had gone deeper into the woods.

He smelled prey. With a quick leap, he sunk his teeth into the human that had traveled into the forest. He smelled of the strange leather and inexplicable nuances that had meant death for so many others. This one specifically smelled heavily of a sort of wheat that had long since expired. Still, despite all these other strange smells, the underlying smell was meat, and the wolf fearlessly snapped at the hand.

The human cried out in anguish, but the scout knew nothing more of this before the other human quickly ended his life. That cry of anguish was the last sound the scout heard. It didn't register the high shriek of agony it gave, which served to express its pain and to deliver a message to its fellow kin. The human quickly disposed of the wolf, as it was inferior. Humans were smarter. Maybe they were not stronger, nor faster, but they had the ability to perceive and register and create. The pack heard its brother fall, for which they entered the woods and prepared to attack. There was fresh meat—the wolves could smell it—but more importantly, they had killed their brother. For this, as even the humans knew, only death could repay.

The humans saw the wolves and with widened eyes they slowly backed away, hysterically breathing rapidly, and turning to one another for support. There were twenty wolves around them now. Why were there so many wolves together? The humans could not say. They grew scared. But, no! They were superior. The ones who should be afraid are the wolves.

The humans turned briefly to each other and drew strength from their scared faces. They had to do something. But as they started to formulate their plans, they grew all too aware that the pack was too numerous. The humans screamed for help but received none. Their wish for secrecy ensured they were too far away from any friendly ears to hear. Nine wolves fell, before the first human—the one who had been bitten—fell. The other continued his struggle and killed another three, but he was then surrounded once more.

The wolves circled around him, and it seemed as though only one wolf was in front of him, walking in circles and producing after-images of itself. The human knew he would have no grave. The wolves would tear him apart on feast on everything. This brief thought enraged him, fueling him with the anger to keep living. He knew he was the superior being. With one motion, four more wolves were killed. Only four remained. One ran away, fearing its death. Another wolf, a female with dark-gray fur, started away, but she caught sight of their biggest warrior, of a muscled male with fur as black as night. It was going to fight. The wolves' instincts told them to run, but the fallen brothers distorted their instincts' call to run and pulled and held them to the ground. The remaining three wolves attacked simultaneously. The human attacked the most imposing of the wolves, but through its power, it continued. The human looked helplessly at its black fur and snarling teeth. The sharp points that opened around him grew more menacing and longer and sharper as they approached, until it finally swallowed his life away. The second human fell, and the three wolves feasted.

    The dripping red liquid contrasted against the dark fur, as the imposing wolf limped weakly to its prey, trying to hide its wound. The pain, however, was too much; the wounded wolf could hold itself no longer and fell to the ground. The soil underneath thumped the imposing jawline, and the soil seemed to demand retribution for all the times it supported the wolves. The impact blurred the wolf's vision and made it forget, temporarily, of its other wound. The wolf knew it could no longer prowl among his pack, but the other two wolves looked at him, deferentially. The wounded wolf looked at the two female wolves, ashamed. He thought of the other male, the one that had run away. The life and strength that wolf had was squandered on his ex-brother. These wolves were stronger, even if not physically. They were more capable. They were better. The two females licked their friend's wounds and rested beside. They could never abandon him, so they awaited his death, accompanying him to the very end. The wounded wolf broke into a howl, and the other two echoed the wolf's cry to the full moon.

    Nevil felt shivers upon hearing the wolves. The long and melancholy cry of the animals had a strange effect on him. The mourning cry seemed reminiscent of the subjects of the Kingdom, and he suddenly wished he had had the sense to bring some sort of drink to calm his anxieties. He asked himself where the others were. They should have been there to meet him. He looked around once more, as if they would suddenly appear before him, and then retreated to his home. He looked up at the sky and stopped. He saw the stars, and he marveled at their beauty. He could not truly appreciate the stars from where he lived, but here, away from the city, it was a magnificent sight. He looked and saw the amazing arrangement of the stars, how they each shone brightly and exceptionally.

Then came his epiphany.

Then came his idea.

He could get resources. The Kingdom of Seville would prosper. If he served right, this would be the end of their woes. The reports were almost entirely unreliable, but Nevil felt something upon looking at the stars, and he knew, as if the fates themselves wished it, that he would succeed. This, he knew, would not be a wasted endeavor. In a mad frenzy, he ran to his home, afraid of forgetting his idea or that a miniscule second would mean the difference between success and failure. He would need to prepare.

Nevil controlled the kingdom, not his pawn, who others called the King. His nephew was a mere formality, while he and Abigail enjoyed the highest confidence of the kingdom's most important members. He remembered sourly that Abigail was no longer available to serve. This abrupt realization left him torn with the decision he now had to make. He could not leave the King to govern the Kingdom alone. He also couldn't leave his task to someone else.

He was cognizant of the significant risk. Not only could he return empty-handed, but he would have wasted a great number of resources and plunged the treasury into even more debt. His stabilizing presence would no longer be there to quash small rebellions and disagreements. He told himself he was not one for desperate gambits. He was for deliberate choices made with the best information possible.

Still, he decided he must be the one who travelled to this far-off land and conquered. It would not do to remain here. He could ensure the kingdom would not fall to chaos, but only as long as they maintained resources and wealth—things that were quickly draining. More preparations, then. He needed to leave strong leadership behind. His mother could serve as primary advisor to the King. Some of his trusted advisors and soldiers would stay behind to maintain peace.

Meanwhile, Nevil would leave his King and kingdom, to travel himself. They had heard continued reports about this land, but its distance, and the exponential costs associated with it, deterred any action. However, they could no longer start fires and hope the rain would not wash it away. Seville was the strongest Kingdom, and they would conquer easily. No one would die. Nevil just needed the rare valuables to be in this land. If he was correct, they would receive riches beyond imagining. He would be a leader. Forever would his stories outlast him; tales of his bravery, his wisdom, and his audacity would inspire the other children.

Nevil gathered the crew that would aid him. They would conquer. They would serve. They would win.

Outside, in the forest on the outskirts of the city, the wolves howled again, mourning their dead brothers. The dark-gray furred wolf continued licking the black-furred one, while the other wolf, a female with fierce eyes and a slender body, lay by its side, no longer acknowledging the wounds. Her head was down, in a terrible fit, and it did not raise its head until a whimper of a noise escaped the wounded wolf. Immediately she shot up and looked at her brother. Another pack approached, and they saw the carnage and knew what it meant. The pack signaled the small remaining pack to join them. This new pack carried on. The wolves that joined the new pack shared their meal, what was left of the humans, while the wolves gave them the security of numbers again. After the meal, they continued. This new pack was bolder, fighting bigger prey, challenging bigger predators, and growling at the other animals of the forest. Days passed and time longer, but it was all the same. They continued in their struggle and fought to live. They reached the outskirts of the forest, where no animal dared to cross, and attacked yet another human. Only two casualties resulted. The pack killed the human quickly enough.

The humans were smarter perhaps. The wolves didn't care. They didn't register the supposed fact. They were fiercer, stronger, more devoted to each other. They could never harm their own or live to see injustice harm one of them. Together, they were better. Not even humans could compare. They would get their meat.

Behind them, a lion roared.

There was nowhere to go.

There was nowhere to hide.

Part I
Calamity

Fire.
Power.
Survival.
The three words had fully encompassed everything he knew. What happened to the ideology that had consumed him in the beginning? He had done everything to serve and given more of himself than he thought possible. He had grown to believe in that man so much that he had stifled his own reservations. Even if that man hates his people, he wholeheartedly believed in what they could do for all the land. He listened to their every order and never strayed.

His was a heavy burden, but no one would deny he was the only one strong enough to bear it. His was a mission no one before had attempted on such a large and dangerous scale. He was fanning the flames of rebellion and hoping the heat would not scorch them. He knew the dangers of the mission he was fulfilling, and he had hoped that he would prove powerful enough to overcome the difficulties. He would have done anything to help that man survive.

He would do so no longer.

They would call him a traitor. It really didn't matter. He would go down in history as something far worse. He didn't care about how they would vilify him. He already saw the image they would see of him. It would be dead eyes of nothingness in a haunt figure. His eyes would be aglow with fire. Only death could ever surround him.

Those were all true, of course. What he wondered was if they would paint him as a power-hungry man who searched for this from the beginning. They could not accept that this might have been thrust upon him. They could never accept it because it required them to acknowledge that any one of them could be infected by the power. They could not believe that it could befall anyone, so they would have to believe that he was always a monster, and that he had always had an inclination for the evil deeds he committed.

It wouldn't matter to him. He loved his old companions dearly. It was the hardest part of the entire ordeal. Despite all the disdain everyone always had for him, and despite their views about him and his people, he never stopped caring. It hadn't been just his friends and loved ones he had cared about, it was everyone. It was all the citizens, all the innocents, all the hard-working pedestrians that tried building their lives in circumstances they could not control.

That's what made him so effective. Unfortunately, for history, that's what would make him so powerful and so dangerous. His passion burned with the fire that was on his fingertips. They had been suppressed for so long, and their plight had been ignored for the sake of stability.

No longer.

He would become a god to the scavengers. They would praise the path he walked, picking away at the carcasses of the dead. He would become a savior to the tormented. They would realize the strength they held, discovering anew the glorious power at their fingertips. He would become a warning for the tyrants. They would learn the fear they instilled in their own subjects, realizing the shortcomings of their ideology.

He looked upon his army, cognizant of what he must do. They would never accept them, and the peaceful resolutions were exhausted long before they were hunted down like savages. He would not be better than the tyrants. They had forced him to join them. Would the tyrants be happy to be proven right?

He began the work. Fire. Fire. Fire. It was the intangible heat of the burning sun. He would bring this fire to the cruel tormentors and see if this new fire would not burn through their oppressive chains. His army rose to a fevered frenzy as they built and built upon the fire. The very forces of nature were at their fingertips, and they could never fail. Would he be killing his compatriots? How many of them would be here?

The power of the force grew. The power was beyond his own. It exceeded anything he could have done by his own merits. The victory, though, was his alone. Only he could have accomplished this. The weight of destiny pulled heavily on his shoulders as he continued his endeavors. He would not fear retribution. He did not fear he was wrong. He only feared how long it would take to create everything anew.

He thought somberly about everyone here. Not one of them would survive. This entire army would be burned away in the scorching sun. The fire would flow and cover them all in ashes. Would they deign to build gravestones there for the individuals of note? He knew already the burden that still awaited him. He alone would survive. He alone would look upon the deaths of so many. Would he let the weight of those souls drown him?

He alone would survive. His alone was this power. His alone was this flame.

And it would burn with a calamitous rage.

Chapter 1
Assassin's Dawn

A faint sound at midnight disturbed the silent night. I opened my eyes to a set of dilapidated walls, with no furnishings and no signs of any inhabitants. The darkness slowly receded as my eyes adjusted, and the lack of furnishings became even more discernable. The extremely bare room only just stood out against the sea of black. No memorabilia lined the walls, nor art nor talismans nor any other personal artifact. It demonstrated the same dismal inn that had lost its customers after death had struck one of its inhabitants years ago. Only the rigid bed remained to decorate the room. I knew the door lay some five and a half steps from where I was, so I immediately went to the door and quietly descended the stairs.

The faint sound managed to rouse me from my sleep. This was perhaps due to the fact I hadn't slept well in too long and had only just begun to muster the strength to continue living, or perhaps I had succeeded in making myself wary, even in sleep. Failing to recognize a potential hazard would not end well, and so I knew I couldn't ignore the sound to some banal cause. I briefly envisioned the various dead assassins that had made attempts on my life, and the enemies that undoubtedly awaited. Perhaps the Benders had prepared another attempt on my life? For a moment, I knew it to be the legendary order from the Telk lands. The unrealistic moment was merely a fantastic thought. Ignoring such ludicrous conjectures, I resumed analyzing. I had thought I had done well to hide what I called my home—I maintained no keepsakes and was wary of anyone following when approaching the abandoned inn. No one was to know where I lived, for fear of who might get harmed.

I continued in the direction of the kitchens, from where I imagined the sound had come. I approached silently, hoping the floorboards would not croak in response. As the inn was abandoned and bare, I had no fear of knocking something down or crashing into furnishings. The chill of the night seemed to be another intruder. The hair on my skin rose in protest, and it took strength not to shiver. It seemed as if the intruder brought with him the chilling attack from the night air. The niggardly quality of my clothing could do nothing about the relentless attack. Upon reaching the door, something precluded me from opening the door, a sort of voice inside my head that incessantly repeated itself: *Do not go in. Do not risk it.*

My hand hovered over the door, ready to open it and reveal what was behind it. Instead, the incessant voice became louder, and changed words. It was strange hearing this voice in my head, as it was not my own. But I knew it was no one else's either, as no one else was talking to me. Though I could not determine what to think of the voice, its message was clear and sapient. The benign voice, full of wisdom, repeated its warning: *This is always the beginning of peril. Do not continue, cease to go forth. You must stay your hand.*

I did not know what to make of the voice; it was strange and foreign, but its counsel was sensible. I was still tired from the arduous day before, and I was still too tired to think properly. Undoubtedly, my fighting abilities would be lacking, and in the very possible case that this was not simply a social call, the outcome would not be favorable. Upon this subsequent consideration, the decision was anything but hard; I withdrew my hand and planned my forthcoming actions. I shuddered at the brief thought of the sequence of events that would have been imminent had it not been for a voice in my head. I considered the risks of attempting to see into this intruder's mind, and decided the potential benefits were sufficiently utile.

The intruder genuflected, facing the floor as another figure, in what seemed like a dark robe, began speaking. "Kevin, I need you to go to Farendor. In the outskirts of the village is an abandoned inn, where you will find a zalphic residing in its shadows. I suppose that is all the description you need, but you will know him by his Telk descent: dark hair and dark eyes, and his Caster metal sword as well."

"I will leave immediately," *responded Kevin.*

"Strike at night. I am certain that even from Markai, word of our "leniency" to zalphics is widespread, but the people of Faldenheim are still hostile. I cannot allow him to be discovered as a zalphic, nor can you allow others to see that you are one as well." *The hooded figure began to walk away, and the scene abruptly changed to an intruder, in front of the abandoned inn. 'Perhaps I may be promoted in rank if I am successful,' he thought.* Kevin knew I was a zalphic, but even that information could not stop the brain. It kept thinking, regardless of its owner's will. In Kevin's mind, I felt the tranquility of the forest, and knew him to be a wood zalphic.

The specificities of the mutations that grant us certain abilities are nebulous. Extraordinarily little is known, even by the Wise Ones. Though the entire order is dedicated to knowledge, they have little consensus on the nature of the mutation, and anything related. However, some abnormal processes, some discrepancies with normal bodily functions, or some disease, determine the variation of the mutation and even the ability to access those powers. The mutation is rare, and those with the mutation are either killed or live short lives.

Great debate arises from its heritable properties. Many Wise Ones have determinedly demonstrated that two parents with the mutation do not necessarily pass the mutation to their offspring. Conversely, two individuals with no history of mutation in their family have produced offspring with the mutation. Others, however, argue that parents with the mutation tend to have more offspring with the mutation. Whichever the case, the mutation continues to arise in the population, in a low, but constant, percentage. There is also debate about its contagious nature. Some Wise Ones could discern no contagious nature in the mutation. People who associated themselves with others with the mutation did not develop it themselves. Others argue that there are rare cases in which someone previously not having the mutation and associating themselves with zalphics have developed the mutation. They argue that these "rare" cases would be more abundant if the mutation itself were not so rare. Regardless, those who would knowingly associate themselves with zalphics were rarer than the zalphics themselves.

Several types of this mutation exist, each with associated stigmas and powers. The first mutation, Z1, is the most mysterious of all. Classified as the *Invincibility* mutation, it is the rarest power, and of questionable existence. The lack of information makes it impossible to classify it any better than Invincibility, with only speculations of their unparalleled power. It is by far the least common; reportedly, only two people had ever had the power. Due to the extreme lack of Z1 zalphics, some have stipulated that the mutation does not exist and is instead a falsified story. Officially, the Wise Ones consider it a valid mutation, and thus assign it Z1.

Z2 mutation is the mutation corresponding to *Telekinesis*. This is the mutation I possess, which allows me to move other objects without direct contact, to read others' minds and communicate with them, manifesting telekinetic energy, and using said energy to manifest other objects and myself.

Z3 is *Fire,* Z4 is *Water,* Z5 is *Earth,* and then Z6 and Z7, the "common group", is *Thunder* and *Wood*. Those with any of the mutations are called zalphics, referring to the deadly disease known as zalphia. Zalphia has had no known survivors and killed infallibly. The idea that they called us zalphics, in association with this deadly disease, had never bothered me personally, but I understood the resounding implications.

1. Assassin's Dawn

Kevin arrived at the inn a few moments before I awoke. I could not understand how he could have been so silent opening the doors and getting into the kitchen. Silent as the assassin, he moved what he could to give him cover. He prepared some sort of crossbow in his hand, though it was smaller than most to which I was accustomed. It wasn't until I saw him preparing his crossbow that I realized I didn't have Telekay, my sword made from Caster metal. I could manifest the sword at will, but that would give away I was a zalphic; at the time, I hadn't a clue who it was, and any non-zalphics would have reacted furiously to the manifestation of my powers. I could not risk lacking caution. Unfortunately, I could not dig deeper into his thoughts without alerting him to my presence. I could not check to see if he had made any inquiries about my abilities or any other preparations that had been made.

I knew I could deliberate no longer. He would soon suspect that I was reading his mind and that I had realized what he was doing. Certainly, I should have now been ensnared in his trap. Without thinking further, I quickly left through the front door of the inn, bringing along a ball, and left the door open. Though the power was possible, I had not yet mastered teleporting somewhere I could not physically see. Without going around the inn, I kicked the ball to curve its trajectory. Quickly, I turned around and teleported into the inn. I ran to the door of the kitchen and reached it as the ball hit the outside wall of the kitchen. Since the distraction had taken effect, I opened the door and prepared to rush the assailant.

As was expected, Kevin was not facing the door, and instead had his head towards the wall. He aimed the miniature crossbow at me and shot, but I had time to move out of the bolt's path. He reloaded, much too quickly for a crossbow, and I realized why it was so small. I teleported out of the way and manifested my sword in my hand. I blocked the next bolt with my sword's blade and continued rushing him. He backed away and reloaded, shooting as soon as he had done so. I used my telekinesis to move the objects around him. I moved some of the cover he had created, leaving him open, then I manifested telekinetic energy and shot a wave of it with my sword. This was known as a pulse slash. Kevin was knocked down and I quickly approached his fallen body, but before I could stab him with my sword, the same voice in my head came back. *Don't kill him just yet.*

    This time, I didn't think about it. I automatically stopped, as if it were controlling me. It surprised me how quickly I decided not to kill him, but I knew he was somehow different from the others. He was not the servant of the Benders, but of someone much more powerful. I knew I could certainly learn something from him—the one who had sent him to kill me, for one. Disregarding my decision to abstain from killing him, I threatened him.

    "I will spare your life Kevin, but in return you must aid me," I said while brandishing my sword.

    "Spare my life? You are not what you make yourself seem if you honestly think it would be so easy." Immediately I considered the possibility that he had been controlling his thoughts, and what I had read from his mind was meant to ensnare me somehow. Or perhaps he had simply left out crucial information. They had to have a telekinetic zalphic among them—if he wasn't sent by the Benders, then that was the only other way to determine I was a zalphic. I didn't know what to do next. Would more people come? Or would he simply unleash his zalphic powers?

    I considered reading his mind but knew it would be folly. I needed to know what he was thinking and planning, but not what he wanted me to think he was thinking. He was still on the ground, smirking, but I could tell that my sword was still making him nervous. I suppose if he was close enough that I could stab him, it wouldn't matter. The benign voice was back. *You need to act.* I knew I would regret thinking too much, so I stopped myself from thinking and acted. I knelt and lifted Kevin off the ground. I manifested telekinetic energy behind me, to act as a barrier in the case that an attack was to come from behind. Nothing seemed to happen. I walked Kevin outside of the kitchen, and then outside of

1. Assassin's Dawn - 17

the abandoned inn. Still, I saw no one nearby, and he could do nothing.

"I spared your life. You have a debt that you *will* pay."

"Don't be overconfident Steven. I've still plenty of options." Suddenly, his fist went towards my left hand, which was holding my sword to his throat. Before I could think to move my hand, the small crossbow bolt he held in his other hand dug into my leg. His fist then hit my hand and I dropped my sword, turning my hand immediately away from him. He bent down as a root lifted his miniature crossbow to him. I had thought it remained in the kitchen, but Kevin was loading the crossbow and shooting bolts. I noticed the mark of the Order of the Bow—a bow with two arrows on either side of it. He was quite far from Markai, the center of the order. Most crossbows took much too long to reload, but this one was much smaller than most, and was consequently easier to reload. Naturally, it wasn't as deadly, but a concentration of them would be sufficiently effective.

He shot a bolt at me, and I only just managed to evade it. He shot another bolt, which I knocked away with Telekay. All the time, I was cautiously looking for any other traps. I couldn't manage to get closer to him, as he kept shooting. He wasn't any closer to hitting me, but I would tire much sooner than he would, and I knew I must do something. I kept blocking with my sword, Telekay, while he continuously shot bolts from his miniature crossbow.

"You're much better than I thought you would be, Steven."

"You shouldn't admire that which shall kill you," I replied.

"As with many others, overconfidence will cause you to err."

"I wonder if it's simple arrogance I have in my abilities, or rather knowledge of my prowess." Vines wrapped around my legs, precluding my movement. Suddenly, he unleashed a volley of bolts from his crossbow. I knew, suddenly, that he hadn't demonstrated his full speed. I dropped Telekay and started controlling it with my telekinetic powers. I used my powers to swing it at the vines, freeing my feet. Still, it was much too late to move out of the way, so instead I simultaneously controlled one of the bolts, turned it on its side, and started spinning it. The other bolts hit the spinning one and diverged from their trajectory. I looked up at where Kevin had been, and quickly discovered that he had moved. I turned rapidly to the left and turned back around to the right. I turned in time to see a bolt coming towards my head. I moved away as quickly as I could but got grazed by the arrow. Blood dripped from my left cheek, but I didn't bother to wipe it. Considering Kevin's speed, I didn't have the time for it.

I abandoned my fighting stance and stood up straighter. Telekay dropped to the floor, as I looked past Kevin. I pretended to look shocked. I backed up, feigning astonishment, and I continued to ignore Kevin and gaze into the distance. Kevin was much too wary to simply look back. He started circling around me, but I quickly moved forward. "Whatever dispute you have with me, we will resolve after I kill that other man." I was aware that Kevin had his crossbow pointing at me, but I ran and hoped he would be fooled. I used my telekinesis to move the sword on the ground towards Kevin. I turned around so I could see him and direct my sword. Kevin had his crossbow aimed at me, so he didn't see the sword which rapidly made towards him.

Then, I heard a sound behind me, and quickly I ducked, jumped to my left, and manifested Telekay in my hand, in time to parry an incoming sword. He swung again, and I backed away. I then felt a pain in my back, and I reached backwards to find one of Kevin's bolts at my back. I turned quickly to Kevin and then the other guy. Though it was dark, with little visibility, I recognized the man in front of me. He had the characteristic features of the Korschers—dark skin, dark hair, short, and strong. Kenneth Bender, descendant of the leaders of those desert people. The Benders were the reason I was at the abandoned inn. I had thought the Benders had nothing to do with Kevin, though certainly that's what they would have liked me to think. Kenneth perhaps hired Kevin, all so he could avenge his parents.

Though I knew I could beat him, Kevin had proven troublesome to handle. Now, with Kenneth here as well, I didn't know what I could do. This was the trap to which Kevin had alluded. Kenneth grabbed his sword and slashed towards my leg. I parried the blow and moved out of the way. A bolt behind me went towards Kenneth's leg, grazing him slightly. I turned my head slightly, so that I could see Kevin. He was limping, and I realized that there was blood on his leg. Telekay must have pierced his leg before I had manifested it to block Kenneth's attack. Kenneth struck again, and again I parried. All the while, Kevin seemed to rest, and lowered the intensity with which he shot.

I had fought Kenneth before, and like Kevin, I knew I could beat him ordinarily. However, with the threat of Kevin and his ranged weapon, along with my general fatigue, I didn't know how well I could continue fighting. In his rage, Kenneth seemed to have forgotten Kevin. He circled wildly around me and struck as quickly and savagely as he could. His anger prevented Kevin from shooting as he wished, and I knew this to be the key. If I could keep Kenneth from thinking rationally, he would move too erratically to give Kevin an opportunity to shoot. "Just like your parents, you will fail." To this, Kenneth responded with an incredible outburst of strength and speed. In retrospect, it was not one of my more concrete ideas. As if Kenneth's increased strength and speed were not enough, and almost in response to my decree, a third assassin appeared.

If it hadn't been for the pain, I would have insisted—with penalty of death—that what occurred next was a dream.

The full moon shone brilliantly against the Dual Swordsman and the other stars of the night. Through the light of both, I could distinguish another face—a ghostly face—which recalled events long past. And from this past, a face with the same proportions arose—a face of muddy brown eyes and delicate features unbefitting to an assassin. Though she was a Korsher, she did not have the characteristic dark skin, and instead it was a light brown. Her rich, straight, brown hair cascaded onto a body that was not too slim to imply a lack of strength, but that wasn't so full that it took away from her attractive proportions. I could still see her, agonizing on the ground as she had been when I saw her last. I remembered her, remembered seeing her die in front of me and having no clue who she was, apart from a name which I had read her mind to learn. Amy. I looked at her fearfully, wondering if I had finally discovered a secret to the taboo question of life after death.

She ran towards me swiftly, but the world itself had all but stopped time, and I saw as each strand of hair moved up and down, to the side and back again, and it seemed that every strand began moving and pointing to me, as if every point attempted to pierce my skin. The light of the ninth moon lit her face, but the light was evil and dark, and its image beautiful and frightening. The dead fought, and the living fought, and those who had all but died fought—and all of them fought to kill me. I remembered my thoughts and emotions when I had seen her die, and I could do nothing but watch her approach me with anger in her eyes and a sharp sword in her hand.

Stunned into paralysis, Kenneth landed a blow on me. My incredulity did not dissipate, and my inert body kept gazing at her. Perhaps I had lost too much blood? She stopped running, and it was only then that my body registered the pain. I knelt to the ground in agony, but the agony of the mind dwarves the meaningless pain of the body. Blood dripped down my sword arm, but I only passingly rubbed it before concentrating on her again. She seemed to hesitate a bit, almost like she was *disappointed*.

"Has the lack of blood affected my senses? I...killed you. I watched you die." Still, she remained silent, coldly watching me from afar with emotions I could not read nor comprehend. I was at a loss. My mind tried desperately to understand what I saw before me, and the futile attempt left me unaware of the ever-closing distance between me and the assassins. Kenneth was beside me. I looked briefly at him, and at Kevin, who had seemingly rested enough, as he was standing, drawing closer, with his crossbow ready. I could handle Kevin alone. Kenneth alongside him, though difficult, I was certain I could have construed a plan to manage them both. I had already begun to make Kenneth move too much to allow Kevin to aid him. But now what hope had I when the dead arose, holding stem and thorn, to beguile me with beauty? I didn't know what to do. If I killed them all, would they simply rise again? Is that how death would seize me, with the help of death? Would my life end at the hands of the Benders? Were they more powerful than I had thought?

As far as I knew, the Korschers were, politically, the weakest of the three major races, and the Bender family that ruled them no longer held so much power. Yet, it seemed Kenneth had enough funds to hire Kevin, and he seemed to have hired Amy as well. Mostly, the thought that bothered me was the reason for this. I had never understood why Amy had targeted me. It was arduous work to survive these assassination attempts, unaware of the lords they served or their motives. What brought the Benders to target me? Why would they want me dead? Or was it someone else? Even facing death, I needed to understand. I needed to demand answers from whomever led them. At the very least, an explanation was required. "How are you alive?" I demanded. Amy looked at me, tears forming in her eyes.

"You killed her," is all she responded. Kenneth started raising his sword. My brain slowed time down, and I thought a million thoughts. I thought about my family, my life, my best friend and my powers, and Amy crept into my thoughts. But at the same time, I envisioned how I could manage to continue living. The sword was slashing down now, towards me. I saw myself in the sword, saw the red running down my arm, saw the eyes filled with fear, eyes as dark as my future. I saw that the darkness which engulfed the sky had engulfed my hair as well, and that's when I thought of it. *Reflection*. I had never attempted such a feat, but it was the only recourse left.

One of the limitations of teleporting was the inability to teleport *through* things. The path needed to be clear to successfully teleport. No walls could be bypassed, no people could be ignored, and attempting to teleport through a sword would simply translate to throwing your body onto a sword with increased speed. Useful for suicide, not so much for staying alive. I found myself on the floor, unable to move, as the sword continued its fearful descent. I couldn't parry the blow; my arm was too injured, and I didn't have enough time to draw or materialize Telekay.

I teleported behind me. My strength was drained from the effort of teleporting; it was one of the more demanding powers. I took quick, shallow breaths, and attempted to focus my vision. I looked up and noticed Kenneth dripped in sweat, something I hadn't noticed even when Kenneth had been right on top of me. Rejuvenated with this knowledge, I dodged Kevin's ranged attack easily. Kevin started using his powers, and incredibly sharp leaves flew past me. I could hear the leaves cutting into the air as they passed me. With Kevin beginning to use his powers, so did the others. I didn't enjoy the idea that this battle would involve our powers. They were too demanding on the body; however, I could not combat their powers without my own. Kenneth shot lightning, but it wasn't towards my direction. I couldn't concentrate on what he was planning to do with this lightning as Amy launched a boulder at me. Luckily my first instinct was to move out of the way, rather than be confused.

Amy didn't have powers. I knew this, I had read her mind. I looked at her again. Had she developed powers? Did the Wise Ones know of her when they spoke of the rare cases in which someone developed powers? I discarded that thought; if they knew of her, she would no longer be alive. Her zalphic powers were much too strong, even if she had developed them. *Twins.* It was the only logical explanation. It was strange: Amy hadn't been a zalphic, but her twin sister was. That was interesting that the mutation could affect solely one of the twins. This resolved so many of my questions related to her, and the feeling was tranquilizing. I silently laughed at the irrational conclusions I reached.

"What's your name?" I asked her with telepathy.

"Jennifer," she answered weakly. There was something about her responses, her attacks, and her determination which I couldn't quite pinpoint. There was something I was missing, something I couldn't quite understand, but I couldn't worry about it now. I teleported out of the way of a ball of sparks, then used a pulse slash to block Kevin's incoming leaves. I noticed a very slight disturbance in the light above me and moved almost immediately. My shoulder was hit, and I saw a bolt that was pointing nearly vertically. The trajectory this would have required validated Kevin's prowess in marksmanship. Water shot past directly in front of me as various high-speed pebbles made their way towards me. The pebbles slowed down drastically thus, and when they hit me, it was nothing more than a slight thud.

I began saying the name before turning around and seeing him. "Maximillius!" Through the dark sky, I could still make out the red cloak he sported. I knew that the inside of the cloak had a sword within a circle, the mark of his order.

"You couldn't handle three people? Ben would be upset."

"My specialty isn't swords," I replied, out of breath.

"Lucky for you, mine is." He drew his Caster sword and took a confident stance, as if his title as a Knight alone would win the fight. He turned his attention to the two furthest away from him. "Kenneth, Jennifer, you fight me." I turned my attention to Kevin, who had not once stopped aiming at me. Though Maximillius had joined me, the strength of my heartbeat did not subside. I grabbed my shoulder, where Kevin had expertly grazed me. Confident as I was that Maximillius and I would win, I knew I shouldn't relax. I tried moving closer to him, but he shot a bolt at me. He wasn't using his zalphic abilities, for which I was grateful. I saw Maximillius approach Jennifer and Kenneth from the corner of my eye. I saw lightning, but it was not coming in my direction, so I stopped paying attention. Kevin now had two bolts in his crossbow. I imagined it was to shoot both of us at the same time, but when he shot them, only one approached me, and the other went flying towards my right, in the general direction of Maximillius, but not towards him.

I recognized that he was trying to get me to go left, so instead I dodged towards the right arrow. Kevin shot again, quickly, trying to force me to go left. I didn't know why he attempted this, but I continued right. It seemed strange. Perhaps he was afraid of shooting one of his own? He was an excellent marksman, but even so, he couldn't anticipate the directions everyone would jump to in the heat of battle. Kenneth was suddenly past Maximillius, sword in hand, and heading towards me. I saw Maximillius turn around, instinctively swinging his sword and getting Kenneth in the back. Kenneth fell forwards a few steps, and Jennifer cried out in anguish. He was on the floor, writhing in pain. I turned towards Kevin, who had his eyes on Maximillius. When I turned towards him, he had a...surprised expression? I couldn't quite tell. "Max!" Jennifer yelled behind him. Maximillius turned towards Jennifer, while Kevin followed Maximillius with his eyes. Jennifer tried running towards Kenneth, but Maximillius stopped her. I looked down at Kenneth.

"I was born in a loving family, caring for little despite our tough circumstances. But you killed them, Steven. I will avenge them."

I closed my hands around Telekay's hilt, ready to silence his audacious words permanently. "It was you and your family who killed the ones I loved." I teleported atop Kenneth, not registering the pain of the teleportation.

"Steven!" I heard Maximillius yell, but it was too late, as I slit Kenneth's throat. What I heard next was a heart wrenching cry. I looked at Jennifer, who, with tears in her eyes, used an explosive outburst of her zalphic powers to split the ground where I was. Before I fell to the ground, I saw the strange sight: from Jennifer's hand, a pillar of rock the size of a sword formed. The rock shattered, leaving behind a sword the color of the black night. *Caster metal!?* I thought, incredulous. The metal was rare beyond comparison. I fell to the ground, all aware that the ground would soon close around me. I concentrated my powers in my palms and outstretched them as the walls began to engulf me. I released the energy, crushing the rock around me. Looking around me, all I could see was the ground which had swallowed me. The walls I had created around me started to shift slightly, and little pebbles bounced from atop, from the walls, and from the ground. The walls rapidly closed around me. I did my best to do the same thing I had done, but the walls closed with too much speed and too much power. My breath was knocked out of me, and I felt the pain of the crushing sensation. Then, the rocky ceiling above me opened into a dark sky. I felt water dripping on my face, refreshing it with its cool moistness.

Death descended from the dark sky. In this form, death was enraged, yearning for its ever-escaping victim. In this form, death struck with ferocity mustered only by every part of its being, or lack of being as it were the case. In this form, the crazed look, the desperate attacks, and even the blind rage, were all overshadowed by its eyes. In this form, death was beautiful. The tears only drew attention to a mesmerizing liquid, shining like a star in the black night. The power of her attacks steadily crushed my wrists, but her face was the only thing on my mind. The brown liquid of her eyes did not look murky, but rather it was a soft stream of sand, silently shifting with a relaxing breeze. The strength behind every blow was surprising, and reminiscent of the strength I surely displayed when I had first learned of her death....

Suddenly, Jennifer fell to the ground after a gasp of pain. I looked up as Maximillius approached the split in the ground and sat down. His sword was not covered in blood, so I didn't imagine he had killed Kevin—he had, undoubtedly, thought better of his circumstances and retreated. "I imagine no more will come," I told Maximillius, eager for him to leave.

"You still have that one in front of you."

"She will do nothing to me."

"She's stronger than you." I didn't reply to Maximillius. I didn't know what to respond to that. She certainly had a lot of strength. I looked again at her sword, made of Caster. It was the lightest and sturdiest metal known. If I had had a sword made of steel, the force of both her strength and the metal would have surely shattered my sword. "Well, I will stay in your telepathy's range. In the case that more appear, let me know." Telepathy: the ability to speak with my mind. As I had done with Jennifer. In my defense, it was not possible to be aware of everyone in my telepathy range. Still, I could have attempted a communication. I should have tried to contact Benjamin and Maximillius. What an idiot I was. Here I was, on the verge of dying, fighting for my life, concentrating only on how my own personal strength and wit could see me through.

I turned to Jennifer and gazed into her eyes.

I needed Maximillius to leave—I could not risk him killing her. Jennifer grasped her sword. Jennifer refused to lie down and accept the loss; she was determined to fight until her last breath. It wasn't the kind of "taking her breath away" I had in mind. In my strange mind, I didn't want to hurt her, so even though I drew Telekay, it was only to preclude her from harming me. The strength of her blows pushed me back, but tactfully I went towards a wall, teleported, then used my telekinesis to keep her against the wall.

I stood there, unable to do anything, and struggling to keep my telekinetic hold on Jennifer while she tried to squirm out of the power. She was frustrated with the hold and tried provoking me. "I have failed my duty to kill you. I don't deserve to live, so finish it, Steven." I didn't have the heart to do that. *She came to kill you. She wasn't hesitating to do just that,* I reminded myself. But something about her, something I couldn't explain—something about her look gave me pause. It was the look of pain. *I won't kill her. I can't.*

"Very well Jennifer. I will kill you...." *A little inside.* I grabbed Telekay and held it in front of me, as if it were a lance. Instead of stabbing her with my sword, I quickly lowered it as she closed her eyes. My hand slammed on the wall next to her face. Her body jerked at the sound, and I stole a kiss from her. I walked backwards as she opened her eyes, surprised, and confused.

Then anger crept back into her eyes. "Sorry, but I must send you away. We will see each other again though, my friend."

"You can't force me to go anywhere," she said, as her Caster sword materialized in her hand. I needed to find out how she did that. Telekay materialized through telekinesis, but she didn't have it.

"Teleportation is a wondrous thing."

"Teleportation requires you to teleport yourself. Even teleporting someone else with you is difficult. You cannot simply teleport someone else."

"Your doubt in my abilities is almost insulting, my friend."

"Stop calling me your friend. I am no friend of yours."

"I didn't call you '*your* friend'; I called you '*my* friend'." At a loss for words, she gave me an annoyed look. Perhaps I should strive to be less of a braggart—but I didn't know what else I could possibly be. The anger crept back into her face, and she swung her sword. I moved out of the way, still conscious that she was very strong. "I apologize beforehand; teleportation is quite taxing the first time." She ignored my words and continued swinging. I blocked with my sword, Telekay, then moved to the right. She anticipated my movement and made to punch me with her free left hand. This was what I had hoped she would do, and I dropped Telekay and grabbed her fist with my open hand. "I'm sorry," I muttered again, and teleported her.

I could almost imagine the screams that would go through her head, or perhaps I simply could recall vividly the expletives and panic that conquered my mind when I first teleported. It was with regret that I had sent her away, but I couldn't bring myself to fight her. Teleporting was an experience very few liked. It was one of the seldom used powers. It felt like falling, almost as if the entire world shifted, and suddenly the sky became the wall and you fell from your original position to the teleported position. But, as the falling commenced, your entire body shattered into thousands and millions of pieces, and every piece fell onto the desired position. The ultimate result is being in a different location, but expending a larger amount of energy than it would have taken to get there through normal means. On top of the wasted energy, the accumulation of the falling sensation of all the pieces of your body was left flooding your mind. With practice, the energy expended was reduced, but never to an amount less than normal means.

I gazed into the horizon, faintly seeing the silhouette of a small form. It collapsed to the ground, where it stayed for a few moments, before shakily getting up and leaving. She wouldn't come back to kill me today. That was as far as my hopes could reach.

I turned around and looked at the abandoned inn. Three assassins in one night. It was no longer safe. But where else could I turn? How could I selfishly intrude on others, at the risk of putting their lives at the mercy of assassins? I returned to my room in the inn, but the restlessness would not leave. I could not sleep; I could not abandon my anxieties. Every miniscule sound—the flapping of wings, the howling of a dog, the sounds of the predators of night—transformed into the cries of my family and friends. I heard screams I had hoped would remain in the past, and when I heard her screaming, I knew I could not remain dormant.

I left the inn, pacing in the chilly night as the light of the moon shone strongly, and I quickly followed the path Jennifer must have taken. The Dual Swordsman had already reached its zenith and had begun its descent. I knew I needed to hurry. As I paced forward, Kenneth's words reverberated in my mind. There would be more. Being a light sleep would not help. Combining my swordsmanship, cunning, and zalphic abilities, I was at the level of a Knight. There were enough Knights in Faldenheim alone that it would be folly to believe someone on their level would not come if the Bender's were truly so determined. The teleportation would have her feeling drained for a while, so I knew if I hurried, I could reach her. I ran out of breath, walked, and ran until I was out of breath again before I finally found her. She almost reached

Faldenheim. She was confronted by someone I hadn't previously met. It was hard to see his face, but the voice was audible.

"Are you going to try to defend your actions? I don't know that I have anything to discuss with you."

"Please, no. It wasn't my fault. It was him...he—I didn't know he would.... Do you understand how I must feel? How was I supposed to know that would happen?" Jennifer was crying, and her tears drowned me in sorrow.

"I can sympathize that it must not have been easy, and what I'm doing is only augmenting your pain, but I can't ignore what happened. You didn't fight back as hard as I thought you would."

It sounded like they were talking about me, so I interjected. "Jennifer. What's happening?"

The one I didn't know turned to me. Now that I could see his face I saw his very light skin, and light blonde hair and blue eyes which seemed to turn to ice. "It seems you have a chance at redemption. But I don't know whether that will be enough." The man opened the ground underneath him and disappeared. What looked like a body also fell into the hole, but I hadn't noticed it so I couldn't tell what it looked like. I was taken by his blatant use of his zalphic powers so close to the castle. If any of the guards had seen him, the guards would all search for him.

"Jennifer, are you alright? I...." I didn't know what to say. She was an assassin. But I was worried for her. "I've come to see you safely to your quarters."

"My answer is no," she replied without hesitation. "Leave or I will redeem myself."

"That guy said that might not be enough. It would be a waste of energy to fight me. Who was he anyway? The one who sent you to the inn? What interest does he have with me?"

"You've killed too many people Steven. My opinion of you will never change. I hate you." I could see tears of hate now, of pain and misery that could no longer stay at bay. "One of us dies now."

"Neither of us dies. That is non-negotiable."

"You are in no position to negotiate. Draw your sword."

"But I'm *not* negotiating. I clearly said "non-negotiable"."

"You are impossible." Her hard eyes softened for a moment—the briefest of moments. Perhaps she fought back a smile too, though that could simply be a projection of my desires. Despite it, I couldn't help but smile at the imagined, lovely sight of seeing her smile. "Why do you smile?"

"It's nothing really. You wouldn't understand." I wasn't sure that I even understood. "I simply wish for you to be safe and go home. You must be drained." Instead, she tightened the grip on her sword. She was angered, all her emotions and movement tried to corroborate that fact, but there was also another emotion, a subtler emotion that I couldn't quite pinpoint. She was clearly perturbed by what the earth zalphic had told her.

"Why did you kill him?" I wondered what Kenneth had been to her. She had reacted violently to his death. Was it his body that had fallen with the earth zalphic?

"Kenneth Bender is the son of the man who murdered someone I deeply cared about."

"You killed the man's daughter. You killed his wife. You killed him. Now you killed his son as well. Your excuse means nothing." Daughter? That was strange. I didn't have much time to think about it though. "Someone you deeply cared about?" She started crying again. The thought of her made me want to cry as well. I could remember all too well the deep sorrow. It had been a while since I had seen her before I heard that she was dead. I didn't get to see her body; I didn't get to see her face. Loneliness and emptiness were now the only thing that came to mind when I thought of her.

Jennifer wiped the tears from her eyes. "Kiss me again, and death will be the last of your worries." With that, she began to walk away. I wasn't exactly sure what I was doing, but I raced after her.

"Can't you simply teleport?" she asked without turning around. At the mention of the word, her whole body seemed to shiver. She must have been thinking about the feeling.

1. Assassin's Dawn - 31

"It is much simpler to walk. Though, it isn't so bad once you get used to it."

"I wouldn't want to get used to it." She stopped walking. She then turned around. I could see the fear in her eyes, the toll that the teleportation must have taken on her. She tried to cover it with anger and sadness. "Leave me, I won't repeat myself."

"I am deeply sorry for what I did. It's a cruel thing to have to go through. I sincerely hope you feel better." She glared at me, anger surely swelling up inside her. I could not shake the idea that she didn't remind me of her sister, even if they were twins. Jennifer was different. She was a very light shade of a typical Korscher. Her soft brown hair and liquid brown eyes looked lovely, though the anger made it impossible to appreciate her true beauty. "I should go now. I apologize."

"This isn't the end," she said, before I could leave. "You haven't seen the last of me."

"I would hope not." She turned around and left, and I could do nothing else but think.

It was a new day, and a new dawn. If the Benders wanted to kill me, I would disappoint them. It wouldn't be so easy. Blood would be spilled, but it categorically wouldn't be mine.

Chapter 2
Telekay

As I was already in Faldenheim, I really should have stayed in the castle. The village of Farendor was far too small for the Order of the Wise Ones. All studies with them were conducted inside Faldenheim, so I always had to travel to the castle for my studies. However, I was much too tired, so I decided to skip them. I knew Aurora would have something to say about that, but I would make it up to her. I walked home slowly since I was in no rush to return to the inn. I thought of Jennifer, and where her home could be. Seeing her in such a state of anger and sorrow had slowly killed me inside, but I knew it would kill me not to see her. I tried to ignore my feelings though and continued walking. I followed the Arjen River which connected Faldenheim to Farendor and continued to the Sehrin Sea. The path was travelled frequently, but the road was not as well kept as the one from Faldenheim to Vernatia.

Judging by the light, I would make it back to Farendor some two hours before the Wise Ones began their lessons. This was a little less than the time required to travel from Farendor to the Wise Ones, but since Aurora would have mounts, she would doubtless wait a bit longer before heading over to Faldenheim. Consequently, I wouldn't see her on the way home. I was slightly relieved that she wouldn't reprimand me, but I desired greatly to tell her about everything that had occurred. I travelled along the road, but I did not see Aurora. When I reached Farendor, I immediately headed towards the abandoned inn, without contacting her.

Upon opening the door, I saw that Benjamin and Maximillius were inside. Maximillius looked tired, no doubt having stayed up late. Seeing him made me realize how tired I was. I had taken a leisurely pace back to the inn, but the three-hour long walk was tiring, and that wasn't taking into consideration that I hadn't slept due to Kevin and the Benders. I entered, but they didn't look up, and they had blank expressions on their faces. I attempted reading their minds, but they easily blocked the attempt, something attainable through training; undoubtedly, they wanted to scold me themselves. However, after a second, it became apparent that something was happening. It was as if I were an imaginary being—the two weren't talking, nor did they acknowledge me, and they were devoid of movements. I couldn't read their faces, nor their thoughts, and I found myself quite perplexed by the situation. Maybe *they* were the ones who were imaginary—they certainly didn't look *alive*. Then, a brusque voice startled me.

"This is but a small fraction of what your power could be. Does that not entice you? Unparalleled power?" There was no one around, but it wasn't through telepathy that I was hearing the voice—at least, it didn't seem that way. "You can become even stronger than I am, who can only distort the perception of the world of another with telekinesis." Still, no other person was around. Only Benjamin and Maximillius were left in front of me, limp and lifeless. There was no one else at the inn.

"Who are you? Do you work for the Benders?" There was no reply. "Were you the one who sent them for me?" It was perhaps when I tried reading their mind that he had interfered with my mind. I had never encountered this type of telepathy. "You were the one who sent Kevin," I said. It was nothing more than a feeling, for this voice and the voice from Kevin's memory were different, but somehow, I felt a connection. "Why do you wish to kill me?"

"You're mistaken. I do not wish to kill you. I want you to join me, in a mutually beneficial relation."

"Then why send Kevin, with the express purpose of *killing* me?"

"To make you stronger. Otherwise, it wouldn't be mutually beneficial."

It was strange not to have a face to look at when speaking. All non-verbal communication failed, so I couldn't properly transmit the exasperation I felt. "How does siding with you benefit me?"

"A home, for one. Or do you think word will not spread of the zalphic living in the abandoned inn just outside of Farendor?"

"What would you have me do, if I were to suddenly hit my head and join you?"

"My order uses the highest discretion in its actions. I cannot tell you now but be certain that this isn't the last time we speak." I wish I could have asked him more, but before I could respond, Benjamin and Maximillius suddenly pounced.

"Steven!" both growled in unison. I stood there awkwardly, uncertain of how to react. "What do you think will happen with Jennifer? She was trying to avenge her sister."

"She'll kill you the first chance she gets. Why did you kill the Bender kid?"

"Firstly, the two things are unrelated. I just...I couldn't bring myself to kill her. I apologize, but nothing can be done now. Even if you are against it, I shall not kill her, so you needn't follow me around."

"Steven, you must think. What makes you think this will end well? She was sent to kill you, there is nothing more to add. If you pursue her, your heart will not be the only thing that is broken." I remembered the words the stranger had said: "I want you to join me." What if Jennifer had some sort of role in that? Regardless, I decided to ignore the thought for the present.

"It doesn't matter. I will not kill her, nor will she try to kill me. That is all that matters."

"Allow me another approach then. Who do you love Steven?" *My family. Kesara. My friends. Aurora.* "Exactly Steven. What would have happened if Max had not shown up? It will not be long before they target our family. Would you risk Aurora's life for her?"

"You must hate your brother right now," interjected Maximillius, "but you know he's right. You changed your name to protect your family, but that farce won't hold out long. Your friends are also no longer secure. Nor any girl you like."

I was getting angered. I knew they were right in some regards, but I couldn't think of any response. If she came to harm, I wouldn't forgive myself. I don't know what I would do in that situation. I resolved myself to protect her, but I thought of the trip to Bravania. What if something happened while I was gone? With nothing in the form of a response coming to mind, I replied with a simple "I'm leaving," and slammed the door behind me.

"Where are you going, Steven? We're at the inn you stay at."

"Let's just go to sleep Ben. I'm tired." I opened the door and teleported past them. I headed up the stairs, to the room in which I slept, while they left. While in bed, I tossed and turned, unable to sleep. It was uncomfortable that others knew where I slept. I abandoned my parents' home because of the Benders. I changed my name in case that would help them. As far as I knew, my family had had no subsequent problems with any others. On top of that, I had to deal with my studies. I studied with the prestigious Wise Ones, as a Scholar, though by all rights I should be an Instructor. It entailed a lot of work, but fortunately I had a propensity for learning. However, the workload often dissuaded me from trying. I looked at the spot with the hidden books. I knew I had some reading to do, but I felt unmotivated to read. I thought of one book, *Strommen and Telkos,* and thought how Strommen was the workload that didn't allow me to cross the Sehrin Sea and become an Instructor.

Telekay lay hidden near me but sleep still evaded me. I was in a much too restless state, and I couldn't calm myself nor lie down any longer. Thoughts of Aurora and Jennifer and Kesara passed through my mind, and the thought of Kenneth angered me. Unable to sleep, I walked around the inn. The plethora of stars had receded, and the great castle in the sky had set. It was a shame. I had always been calmed by the magnificent stars, thinking how small and insignificant I was.

I prepared mentally for anything that could happen. I didn't know what to expect, and this uncertainty made me ironically desire that I didn't have the strength to defend myself. I thought that my life would be much simpler had I not been a zalphic, and without the telekinetic power of Telekay. All the trouble I went through to acquire the Caster sword seemed to be in vain.

&&&

Sixteen years had come and gone, and my powers had already manifested. At that point I had already moved to Faldenheim, but control over my powers still escaped me. I had at that point already learned about the zalphic world, though neither of my parents had the mutation and had been unable to help me get familiarized with that strange world. I was forced, then, to discover my powers and learn what the Z2 mutation entailed on my own. Later I ascertained Benjamin had control over fire. Naturally, he developed this power efficiently. My sister also had the mutation. That had scared me—thinking about how she would be targeted gave me anxiety. I knew she would at least be able to protect herself with her zalphic powers, but the general disdain for us kept me worried. The youngest had still not developed zalphic abilities.

When I first discovered my power to teleport, I sought Benjamin's aid in the matter. As the eldest of the four, and the first of us to develop powers, I thought perhaps he would have knowledge pertaining to other zalphic powers, or other telekinetic zalphics that could instruct me. Instead, what I found was that he was fighting someone, using both his powers and his weapon. The enemy was relentless, and he clearly outmatched my brother. Benjamin was still not a Knight, while this other person was using only his swordsmanship. I felt hopeless as I saw the two of them fight, with skills I didn't have and strength I couldn't match. I could do nothing to help him—I knew that any attempt I made would hinder my brother, so I stood there like a coward. I watched, horrified, and worrying that perhaps he wouldn't prevail. He didn't.

His injuries were worrisome, and the other man just left him there to die. I quickly went to Benjamin and immediately took him to the Wise Ones. While in the room where the Wise Ones were administering their care, I continuously blamed myself for his predicament and found fault in myself for not having a weapon or control over my powers. I should have been able to help him. His wounds were severe.

At some strange moment during my lamentations, I came to a completely idiotic decision. I knew I needed a sword. I needed something with which to protect myself and to protect others. Yet I also decided in cowardice that I should focus on my studies and abandon my wounded brother. There was a blacksmith in Faldenheim, not too far from where I studied with the Wise Ones. Yet, I completely ignored it. Even if the swords were not to my liking, and the steel felt improper in my hands, it would have sufficed. I needed something to use beside my zalphic powers, for I could not use those. Perhaps even a blunt sword would have been better, but I decided instead to travel south, as part of my studies. The great castle Faldenheim had always been on the horizon since we moved here, but soon it became a miniscule point in my vision, and even quicker it disappeared. Naturally, I was accompanying a group from the Wise Ones. Aurora, however, was not present, as she had already completed her required trip. We headed towards the cities around the Desert Lands of Chordola. We first followed the Serpent's River and headed towards Whaldo's Port, from which we were to go to Meliserah.

I kept correspondence with my parents at the time. I had lied to them and said the trip was mandatory, and I could not evade it. Truthfully, I hadn't asked, though with some of them treating my brother, I'm sure they were aware of my circumstances. In one such letter, after their handwriting, another passage, in Benjamin's handwriting read in part: "I promise I will protect you." The words seemed strange, and meditating in them I found the truth hidden in them. The one who hurt my brother—his target was *me*. That was when I decided I would change my identity. I didn't want to endanger my family, so I abandoned the Hewley name. It wasn't too difficult. As a member of the Wise Ones, I spent quite a bit of time in Faldenheim. There was rarely any occasion to give my full name, and the ones at the Wise Ones knew I wasn't wealthy, so they distanced themselves.

My assignment was to learn about medicinal herbs in a certain village between Whaldo's Port and Meliserah. I was aiding in hauling materials for medicine. It was hardly a day to forget. The sky was clear, light shining brightly into the soft sand, and wind gently blowing into the desert. It was a warm day, as if the beautiful weather was supposed to compensate for what would occur next. Nearby in the silent land, a couple cottages had been left abandoned, and the dilapidated road upon which they resided seemed to disappear. Disuse and abandonment meant the road was difficult to see, something unfortunate as the herbs for which I was searching were supposed to be found near the road and the hills. Some hills and trees were visible, but I did not know which hills I was to search. The lonely road said something about me too, I suppose.

Although Amy was Jennifer's twin, she did not feel like it. It's a strange impression I still cannot grasp. Obviously, the resemblance was there, as they were identical, but the aura of their personality was distinct. In my mind, they better fit the description of estranged sisters than that of indistinguishable twins. But minds are crazy, and none have a twin; Jennifer and Amy were sisters, and I had, after all, thought Jennifer was Amy when I first saw her.

"Are you Steven?" In that simple question, I thought about my brother's suffering. I could have lied, but what if they found their way to Kesara? The wound was still too fresh in my mind, so before thinking of a better solution, I answered.

"Yes, I am." Her reply was to pull out two daggers. The daggers meant to intimidate me had instead focused my bravery. I searched calmly within my telepathy's range to check for someone I could contact. No such minds, however, were in the vicinity. Most people I knew were back in Faldenheim. Still, I knew I needn't panic. I was oddly calm in the impending danger. I didn't have the ability to contact anyone through telepathy, and this was due to several factors—my lack of training, the abandonment of the area, and the location of the nearest homes among other things. Regardless, this meant I would be able to use my zalphic powers if the need arose. I didn't know yet who she was, but if she was trying to kill me, I couldn't think of another reason other than that I was a zalphic.

She drew her sword and approached quickly. I positioned myself to react to her movements, but she threw the sword at me. I dodged in a panic, but her muddy eyes and dirt-colored hair flashed with violent speed as she drove a dagger to my side. The blood began flowing, disorienting my vision, and scattering my thoughts. Why would she throw the sword? Why did she warn me of her presence? What would she have done if I had caught the sword somehow? Who was I to her? Weaponless and unable to defend myself, I worried about what I would do in the trying circumstances, afraid of what might be my future. These thoughts engulfed me as I silently cursed myself for undertaking this journey. Had I stayed home in Farendor, I would have been safe; instead, I now worried about this stranger, a girl with a sword and daggers who ambushed me on the empty and dilapidated road.

The pain began making its presence noticed. My movements were heavier, and my discomfort increased with my body's complaints. A darkening cloud passed over my mind, attempting to eclipse my thoughts. It was hindering my ability to think properly. She rushed me again with her sword. When had she picked it up? I took a step back, but my vision spun, and I didn't know which sword I was supposed to dodge. I crouched to the ground and leaped left. She managed to graze my arm, and the sword continued flying past. She had once again discarded the sword and moved to strike me with a dagger. She cut my leg to prevent further movements.

    The finality of the wound, the finality of my senses, and the finality of life and death worried me. She stood there, taking an exorbitant amount of time. She was taking excessively long to finish it. She stood there, staring at me. As much as I wanted to believe otherwise, I knew she wasn't a monster. Perhaps she was a year younger than I, and she was certainly no assassin. I saw the fear in her eyes, the aversion she had to the blood from her dagger. It seemed like it wasn't just the flowing blood either. It seemed she was not comfortable holding the dagger itself. I hated her for that. I hated her for not being a monster. I wanted to hate her.

    I would have enjoyed hating her, seeing the coldness in her eyes and the chill of her gaze. I would have wanted to freeze in her presence and hide from her malice. It would have been great to see her skill with daggers and a propensity to kill. A stoic assassin was what I wanted. Instead, I saw that she was forced into it. That knowledge drove me crazy, almost as much as the lack of knowledge relating to why she did this and who had demanded it of her. I envisioned a sort of test, where she was to kill someone to establish her strength and commitment. By killing me, she would prove she could do what was needed of her and could be decisive despite what was asked of her. But why me? She knew my name; knew I would be here. Who was I? I found myself wondering. I was not rich, nor had I made enemies of the sort that goes around killing. My only offense was being a zalphic—something which I didn't consider to be an offense, and something which they could not discern.

    My strength was diminished, I had no sword, and the wound would prevent me from escaping on foot and would hinder my speed in general. But I knew I was not powerless. I had a wide array of powers available. Yet, even in this situation, I was afraid to use them. All my life I had grown to hate zalphics. When I learned I was one of them, I had already cemented in my mind to fear those powers. I looked around, seeing the same scene four times, each spinning around and converging, and just failing to converge. In the dizzying scene, I did not see anyone except her. I needed to act quickly, with the confidence that no one else was watching.

I grew nauseated from the blood loss. She lifted my head, so that I might see the final blow. The dizziness became the only truth in the world. The next two scenes were beyond my ability to comprehend. Even today I cannot grasp the essence of what transpired at the time. She sheathed her dagger, with the words "it is done" as her only explanation. She turned around, searching for someone or something. I used my telekinesis to bring the sword to me. I heard a sound, but I paid no mind. She turned, jumped backwards, and grabbed her dagger. The exertion of using telekinesis made my vision spin even more, and I felt an overwhelming desire to vomit. I suppressed the feeling and got on my feet. My wounded leg screamed in pain and my side cried in anguish. My strength was entirely gone, but my mind overcame the pain knowing that I needed to stay alive.

The second scene: my eyesight cleared, the duplicates became one, and the pain ceased its nagging. Simultaneously, Amy fell to the ground, collapsing atop her drawn dagger. I felt rested and rejuvenated; the pain no longer existed, and my senses were clear. The dagger seemed to be jammed into her side. I used my telekinesis and moved the dagger. I took it out of her side and slit her throat. I hadn't been sure, but I knew now that she was dead. I took a step and noticed that my leg did not hurt. I looked at it, but the blood still flooded the skin. I inspected Amy but saw no bruises nor wounds aside from those I had given her. She wasn't hit by any physical object, yet she fell atop her dagger.

I concluded that this could only have been the result of the manifestation of some unknown power. As no other person was here, it meant it had to be my own powers. My senses clearing up and the pain receding from my body must have been linked to her body suddenly dropping. I wondered if some hint of this power might have been suggested during my studies with the Wise Ones, but nothing came to mind. As I tried to rationalize the sudden peace in my mind and the collapse of Amy, I became convinced that I had somehow transferred my pain to Amy. Perhaps the pain was compounded and knocked Amy out of consciousness. It was obvious that this was an attack of the mind.

I briefly thought that perhaps this was all I would need. I didn't need to touch them, and the attack could be executed in a crowd, without none being aware that I had used any zalphic abilities. I quickly discarded the thought. An ability that required the user to be injured was flawed. Unless, of course, it had nothing to do with my current state. Then perhaps it could be viable. I wouldn't need a weapon in that case. Seeing as I was not a part of the Order of the Sword, this could avoid suspicions. Perhaps my brother could help me. Even if he didn't have knowledge of the specific ability, he could guide me to another one who had the required knowledge.

Then I realized the folly of my thoughts. If it was possible for me to use the ability, it would be inherently obvious someone else must have the same ability. It was entirely possible that even without the skills and prowess to use the ability, one could learn to block the attack. In that case, I could be confronted by a telekinetic zalphic who could block my powers. Then I would be unable to protect myself if he also had a weapon. Clearly, I would still need a weapon.

I went towards one of the abandoned cottages. I searched for any supplies that could help. I found some bandages, but the wounds were too deep for the bandages alone to fix. I tried resting. At the time, I felt nothing but bliss, but I knew that pain would soon replace it. This new power would eventually dissipate, and the spell it had on me that made me think I was perfectly fine would shatter in a shriek of pain. I needed to cure my wounds, not limit myself to bandage them. I looked out on the road, where a man was standing over her body. I was about to yell for help, but as I had feared, the blissful effect wore off. I collapsed on the ground and grabbed my leg. The man must have heard the thump since he turned towards me and approached. I could not make out what he was looked like. He was saying something, but I could not understand what he was saying. "Wasn't going to.... Killed. Scare. Imply. Telekay." Those were the only words I understood before I blacked out.

I awoke in the apothecary's home. Someone had tended to my wounds. The apothecary did not ask me about the injuries, nor did he seem to care that I had failed to procure the herbs. It all seemed strange. He needed me to get medicinal herbs, yet he was using medicinal herbs to cure me and didn't ask any questions about it. I began then truly wondering who that man had been. He had clearly explained something to the apothecary. I lay in bed, recovering from my wounds and thought about the encounter. I thought a lot about Amy, but I also thought a lot about the mysterious man. What was he trying to say? The broken dialogue I had picked up in my delirious state was too limited.

"Wasn't going to" could refer to any number of things. It was clear though that "Killed" was referencing what I had done to Amy. "Scare." Was he trying to scare me? But it was the last one that stuck in my mind. "Telekay." I had never heard the word before. It was clear that the word had Telk roots and must have some relation with Telkos. Maybe I should have paid more attention to the book *Telkos and Strommen*, though I didn't imagine it would mention Telekay. After I returned to the Wise Ones, I became obsessed with finding Telekay among the History books of Telkos. However, it seemed that there were effectively no writings on it. I could not find anything. I had all but given up when I read *The Shadows,* a book pertaining to folktales and related stories of the ancient Telk civilization. Specifically, it concerned mentions of the dark, ferocious felines known as shadowcats which were indigenous to the land, and the reverence given to them by the superstitious Telks. One of the stories involved a very strong shadowcat, called Khisharat. Khisharat was king of the shadowcats, thrice as large as any other, and with razor-sharp claws that could pierce anything. It could also read the minds of shadowcats and humans alike in some stories. Others said it could speak to all shadowcats through telepathy.

A warrior in search of fame was said to challenge the beast, though the first attempt did not end well. Different accounts supply distinct reasons for the failure. Some say his armor and weaponry were simply ineffective. The potent shadowcat was said to have claws that could compete even with Caster. Thus, the claws of the shadowcat easily ripped through the armor and forced him to retreat when his sword could not keep up. Others link it to his ability to read minds. It was said that every thought of the warrior was considered and countered. Others questioned the warrior himself and found him to be of no skill. The warrior had no fame, and thought he could earn it, so the consensus was he did not possess the necessary skill.

The next part of the story is ambiguous. No attempts to describe how much time passed were made in any of the stories. In any version of the story, however, the warrior returns to face him anew. Each account agrees that this time, the warrior brought with him a Caster sword. The warrior fought against Khisharat once again. The mighty feline roared a terrifying sound. The warrior sometimes quivered, sometimes advanced. The powerful lunge knocks him on his feet anyway. Khisharat has the warrior in its terrifying claws. He reads the mind of the warrior—he plans on cutting one of the claws with his sword. Its powerful jaws open to swallow life and hope, but the warrior just manages to grab the sword and stabs the underpart of the feline's paw. Khisharat lifts his paw up slightly, enough for the warrior to move left. It swipes with its other front leg in retaliation, but the warrior throws himself to the ground and to the left to evade the strike. The feline continues turning and thumps the warrior with its tail.

The warrior gets up and they are now facing each other again. The warrior charges forwards and slightly to the right, so that the massive shadowcat would have to use its weakened paw.

Instead, the clever cat sunders the ground with its powerful claws. A cloud of dirt reduces visibility long enough for the towering feline to strike the back of the warrior. On the ground, the warrior turns his head to see the towering cat. This time, Khisharat takes its foot off him so that the warrior doesn't stab it again. He quickly rolls and tries to get on his feet, but Khisharat has its vicious claws tear the air and almost strikes the man. The man now goes towards the weakened paw and strikes at it, but the feline blocks the attack with its sturdy claws.

    The warrior backs up, preparing his body for the next strike. He no longer thinks ahead to what he will do, but instead relies on his instincts to see him through. Khisharat grows impatient and lunges towards the warrior. The warrior runs straight towards the cat and slides under its weakened paw. With a raised sword, he draws blood from the terrible feline, who smothers the warrior under its large body. The paw, however, is damaged, and the feline licks its wound. This gives the warrior enough space to escape the weight of the feline and cuts off a claw with his sword. The warrior feels no need to kill and goes home with the spoils of the battle. He forges a new sword with the steel of his caster metal and the claw of Khisharat, and he names it Telekay.

    I didn't know where to go from there. I had found a reference to Telekay, but the story did not mention where the warrior went afterwards, or where his grave was. Luckily, the Wise Ones asked me to go to Telkos on another assignment and promised me compensation for undergoing the task. I was to make an analysis of one of their myths. This involved talking to some locals, learning about their beliefs and superstitions, and drawing from their history to make a detailed report. Luckily, I had just the myth in mind, and I travelled and learned of the Khisharat. I learned of the resting place of the one who had finally felled the mighty beast, and I quickly ventured towards the area. Once in the vicinity, I fell under a spell I can only describe as that of delirium.

    I dreamt of a holy land between a sea of black—a blue stone delineated the boundary. The holy land burst into flames, and birds came with beaks full of black water and tried extinguishing the flames. The fire, however, seemed not to harm the holy land, and the fire shot upwards, disappearing from the ground, and setting the birds ablaze in the sky. The panicked cries of the birds were heard and ignored, and they dived for water, only to find that all the water had been irrigated and given to the marvelous trees and the verdant plains of the holy lands. The birds gave a final shriek of terror, and a shadowcat appeared from the now-dry seas. The shadowcat devoured the bird and followed the scent of the bird back to a nest of unhatched eggs. The shadowcat sat on the eggs and kept them warm. It cared for the eggs until they hatched, and it gave them scraps of meat until they were grown. The holy land burst into flames....

The dream switched to a man, clad in darkness and gold and he pointed towards the horizon. As I looked out into the distance, shapes appeared out of nothing, as if teleporting into the scene. Buildings lined my vision, and people walked, and children played, and workers finished their business. A light showed me the path to walk. I avoided the people and followed the path religiously. Mada herself would not have moved me from the line—even if I believed she had existed. Following the path through the town, I saw a barren land. When I looked behind me, nothing was to be found. There was no nearby town, no castles in the distance, and no sign of the previous inhabitants. It was devoid of anything.

Then, ruins lay everywhere. Ruins of what, though, I could not say. A secret passage opened amidst the rubble, though in reality the passage had been hidden in plain sight. Various minerals and precious stones glowed with resplendence. I knew that these precious stones must have once belonged to the Telks. I tried grabbing one of the precious stones, but a force precluded me from doing so. Among the shining artifacts, I saw a sword made of gold and Caster. Its hilt was made entirely of gold, and the strange dark Caster seemed to shine menacingly.

The dream shifted, and I was directly in front of some sort of spirit. The Telk warrior glanced at me, though it seemed more that he was looking through me, as if he were talking to someone else entirely. The words he spoke next would forever be imprinted on my mind:

"This is the sacred ground of the Telks, of the clan that is known as the Madaiites. Word of its location cannot proliferate. Your memory of what you have witnessed will be clouded." I wondered about the sword and its meaning. As if to respond, he continued. "This is the sword of the Seventh Path. Long ago, it was created and served a vile purpose. Mada attempted to use the sword for good, but the evil within the sword fought against her actions. She was forced to leave it and take on her now infamous sword. Those with evil intentions attempted to use the sword, but it was now tainted by Mada's light. It was rejected by the Dark Paths and the Light Paths, leaving none to bear its weight. Now you must take it and keep the memory of the sword for its destined and intended."

I awoke from the trance in front of the burial place of the warrior. He had no inscription on his grave. I looked around, as if I would find the town I had been in, or the barren land, or the ruins. Next to the unmarked grave lay a curiously buried object. I quickly reached down and saw the sword. Very little of the sword was visible, and when I finally pulled it out of the ground, there was no hole where it had been. It was Telekay, I knew, and I hadn't a clue as to what I would write up as my report for my venture into Telkos.

When I arrived, I lurked around Farendor, to make sure no one was watching me, and searched for Benjamin. He was not at home, and he wasn't practicing his swordplay in the training yard. Not finding him in Farendor, I decided to go to Faldenheim. Regardless of whether Benjamin was there, I had drafted my report and wanted to give it to the Wise Ones to receive compensation. While there, I searched in the taverns and streets, and searched for any guards on duty, yet I couldn't find him. I also couldn't find Maximillius and assumed that the two were together. Giving up on finding them, I went towards the Wise Ones to give my report. As I arrived, Lord Horus was leaving the housing quarters of some of the members. Some of the guards stopped me, and I awaited as they left before proceeding. I turned in my work to an Elder and soon walked away with my compensation. I headed back to Farendor, but as I was leaving Faldenheim, a voice from behind stopped me.

"You aren't very bright for someone in the Wise Ones."

I turned around, looking at my brother. "I've been searching for you for quite a while now."

"You could have used telepathy to find me," he teased.

"Well, I suppose I could have done a lot of things differently. However, it is not a crime to want to surprise you, is it?"

"Surprise me with what?" he started asking, as he finally noticed the sword. I eagerly showed him Telekay. I was proud to have a Caster sword, just as he did. I was proud, even if I hadn't done much once in Telkos.

"Where did you get that sword?" He demanded.

"Telkos. While I was off studying. Why? What's wrong?"

I heard him mutter a name under his breath, though I didn't quite catch the name. "Why do you have a sword?"

"I won't let others pay for my mistakes.... I know that assassin was sent to kill *me*. You were forced to spend time in the infirmary because of me. I'm a terrible brother."

"No, you aren't. If you were as terrible as you said, I would have let them hurt you," he said, with a rueful smile. I rolled my eyes. "You shouldn't blame yourself."

"I cannot let others suffer for me. That is why I berate myself. I won't let you come to harm for my actions. You shouldn't have to suffer for them. I will protect myself."

"Your actions? You don't even know why you were targeted. As for protecting yourself, zalphic powers or not, there are plenty of people who could leave you on the ground before you had a chance to think of a course of action."

"Which is precisely why I must isolate myself." Benjamin looked confused.

"That is the *opposite* of what you are supposed to realize."

"I can't let others get hurt because of me again. If Kesara were to be harmed, I would never forgive myself."

"Steven, you can't hide from this."

"I'm not going to hide. I'm simply hiding my family from them. We haven't been in Faldenheim long. They don't know that you and I are brothers. I will pretend to be someone else. Steven Mc.Roy."

"Mc.Roy?"

I shrugged. "It has nothing to do with my past or my family. It means nothing to me. That makes it appropriate—just a random name from a random thought."

"This isn't the point I should be arguing. You can't live on your own. How will you live on your own? And how can you be certain you'll be safe?"

"The Wise Ones provide me with all I need to survive on my own."

"You're going to live in Faldenheim? Any one of Faldenheim's residents can be the one trying to kill you."

"I'm not going to live in Faldenheim."

"Then where?"

"Well, if you don't know, neither will they."

"What if they ambush you on the road to the Wise Ones?"

"I've already fought off an assassin. I can do it again."

"What do you mean you fought one off?"

"In my previous travels. To the village close to Meliserah. I killed her."

"Now you *killed* them?"

"Yeah, that's how I found out about Telekay?" At his puzzled look, I raised my sword, signaling that this was the sword's name.

"If you found out about the sword, that would mean you didn't have it during the encounter."

I nodded my head. "When I confronted her, I didn't have the sword. I managed to use my powers to protect myself." Benjamin didn't say anything about it for a while.

"Are you okay?" He finally asked.

"Yeah. I don't have observable scars, do I?" He shook his head.

"That's not what I mean. Are you okay? It's not so easy to kill someone." I looked back at my brother. I didn't really know what to reply.

"I'm perfectly fine. I was protecting myself. Nothing else really matters."

"How did you do it? Your telekinetic powers are not tailored to killing."

"It was a sort of powerful brain blast. I'm not sure how to explain it. It seemed as if all my problems were sent to her. All the pain I was feeling seemed to be transferred to her and amplified significantly. It seemed to have caused immeasurable pain." Benjamin continued asking me questions about the day, asking for specificities about my encounter. I obligingly answered them all, thinking throughout the interrogation about who Amy was, and why someone had sent her to me.

My walk was soon over. I wondered how long it would take for the mysterious figure to act. He had sent people to kill me, and they had failed. I couldn't help but wonder what he must be thinking, and what his next actions might be. I went towards the entrance of the inn, but before entering I searched with my mind to ensure that no one was around. At that moment, it felt strange. It was like time had slowed down, and I was in a state like the one that had happened in Telkos. My first thought was that I was delusional. The second was that a strong telekinetic zalphic was messing with my mind again.

"Hello Steven, how are you?" The inn and the surroundings seemed vaguely familiar, but there was a haze-like, almost blurry aspect to them. The door, however, was perfectly clear, and when I opened the door, I saw a hooded figure waiting inside. He was not blurry like the rest of my surroundings. I could see him clearly.

I recognized that it was the figure I had seen from Kevin's thoughts.

"You again? What business do I have with you? Why am I so special?"

"You are unique Steven. Extremely so."

"What do you mean by unique? As rare as the Z2 mutation is, telekinesis does not make me unique."

"You don't quite understand."

"Then enlighten me. Tell me so that I can understand."

"There is so much more to you than the Z2 mutation. Just like your brother." I tensed a little.

"I don't have a brother. I alone live here."

He laughed. "I must have confused you with someone else then." He stood in silence, observing me. He seemed to be waiting for my next question, even if he hadn't answered the question I just posed. I was about to ask another question, before he began again: "you have amazing potential. I hope you have more sense than to throw it all away. There are enemies that require our attention, and I need your help to entreat them."

"Enemies? If they are enemies to you, I think I might just get along with them."

"Do not be mistaken Steven. I am not your enemy."

"You will understand if trying to kill me sent the wrong message," I replied dryly.

"I was not trying to kill you. I will show you the true enemy." *Show me?* I asked myself. But before I could give that a subsequent thought, it seemed that I had been transported. There was now a dark room. The man in the center was wearing a robe so I couldn't see his face. Still, I could tell he wasn't normal. He didn't look right; his hands were too small, his arms were too short, his legs seemed oddly cut off. He was very small, and his voice disguised.

> *"I genuflect from under your presence.*
> *Presiding is he who's known as Nevil.*
> *In your genius, we go forth to sentence,*
> *We decree by the Kingdom of Seville.*

*We must teach these people living in dark.
I plead you and beg you not to delay.
They're caught in darkness they view as stark.
This disarray will not be thrown away.*

*Claim the world to your ultimate control.
The road will now return from its dark curve.
Chaotic destruction to all but us!"*

They recited the poem in front of a strange blue sphere. The sphere had some green and brown on it, and some white, but for the most part it was blue. Before I could see more, the vision stopped. I was now back at the inn.

"Who are you? Why are you playing these games?"

"You can call me Jack."

"What do you want with me Jack? You want me to fight this enemy of yours for you?"

"The people you saw are everybody's enemies, not just mine."

I didn't like this. I didn't trust Jack, but his claim that this was everyone's enemy made me pause. I was going to argue more, but then he vanished. I wasn't sure what to do. I ignored the thoughts in my mind and instead attempted to get the rest I desperately required.

Chapter 3
Austin's Assaults

I awoke aggravated and annoyed. After "Jack's" visit, I could not go back to sleep. I spent the entire day tired and spend. When I had returned to the inn, exhaustion consumed me, and I fell into a deep sleep. However, I was awoken and could not recall the subject of the dream. Despite this, I knew it had been a great and gentle dream. Only the feeling of contentedness remained from the slumber. The anti-climactic nature of this annoyed me greatly. I disliked that I had awoken and knew I would yet again fail to get the rest that I required. Even the stressful day had not forced a deep sleep. I closed my eyes, knowing in vain that, try as I may, I would fail to fall asleep. After a bit of trying, I accepted that I would not sleep again until night. I remained in bed, thinking about the events that had occurred, but soon tired of thinking about Kevin and Jennifer and Jack.

Instead, I went to study. After what I had gone through, the safety of books seemed enticing. Catching up on my studies didn't sound like the boring tedious work it was. Luckily, I only had to endure a bit more before I would have a break from my studies. The Wise Ones would soon take off for the Capital, for the Committee of the Wise Ones. Despite my usual disinterest in studying and my propensity to avoid it, I decided to study. I had only a few pages to read from *The History of Andros*.

When King Whaldo Alexander, of the Telks, felt the terrifying effects of the Great Shaking, he embarked on a search for land and glory, and landed on what is now Whaldo's Port. The terrible storm had long precluded sailors to land on Andros, but the godless Whaldo ignored the religious warnings and traveled the Sehrin Sea without trepidation. After landing in Whaldo's Port, he and his people began inhabiting the land, getting closer to the Lancaster Forest. The settlement in Bravania was followed by the new inhabitants cutting down the trees for supplies. They were not aware that people lived in the immense forest, and the natives grew angered. In retaliation, the Lancasters who lived there fought with the precious metal that was abundant in the forest, desperate not to lose any more land than the half that was already taken away in the Great Shaking event. The sturdy metal quickly pushed the Telks back. They fought them back to Whaldo's Port, where they stopped and inhabited the settlements to protect the forest. The Telks moved south along with some of the Lancasters, who were keeping guard.

I could read no more. Apart from not being able to concentrate fully, I already knew all the information I was reading. The Lancasters soon outnumbered the Telks. The Korshers moved away from their mountains to the desert lands. The three groups met in the Capital, to find a ruler for the three. It was pointless to continue reading.

Instead, I reflected on the long day. I thought of Jennifer and her twin sister. I was still intrigued by her powers and what it meant about the disease. No, the *powers*. Her twin sister had not been a zalphic. She had not been a zalphic yet her twin sister Jennifer could control earth. There was something haunting about Jennifer. I remembered the fury in her eyes, and the determination to succeed. I also remembered how she looked at me, at first with sadness, then with false anger. Then unrequited anger. I wanted to learn more about her. Soon, I was lost in the reveries of a foolish heart. Some of the daydreams were concerning my favorite books and remarkable events in my life. Eventually though, they turned into thoughts of the girl. There was the one of a damsel who was crying for help. Admittedly, she was no young maid that required saving. I dreamed that she was in grave trouble, and I alone was the one who could save her. She was given engrims, which nullify the effects of the Z mutation. The Z mutations are normalized—at least for a while. It was truly ironic. They had found a temporary cure for the disease, without even knowing much about the origins or effects. They say *mutations*, but it is obvious they were thought of no more than a disease.

With no defenses, and tied up with a rope, the powerless zalphic was sent off the top of a towering wall. It was the wall of a tremendous castle. Perhaps it was Garrisbrough, as it did not look like the Bravania with which I was familiar. Or perhaps it was a construct of my mind. The grand castle seemed majestic, but it was lonely as well. Nothing could match its grandeur, and in the dream, the castle was empty. Nothing was nearby. The killer smiled and laughed maniacally atop the great castle while the beauty cried and shouted. The immense distance between the top of the castle wall and the ground was to be covered very quickly. I ran with a speed rivaling a direhawk, and for a second, I could have been a Swordsmaster with the swiftness I demonstrated. The dastardly fiend pushed her off, laughing with increased vigor as she sped to the ground. I leaped forward, stabbed my sword into the ground to propel myself forward, then used my telekinetic abilities to soften the impact of her body and my hands. I caught her in my hands, and she smiled a smile that could destroy my world. I kissed her and she kissed me back. I didn't want this moment to die. I wanted to live this moment forever.

I had a certain ambivalence. On the one hand, I felt guilty for envisioning her in any danger, and that she would not be able to protect herself. Yet, it was only a daydream, and nothing would happen to her, so I didn't care. I enjoyed the kiss. I lived in bliss for a few moments.

My reverie was broken when I heard someone think *now is our chance. He doesn't expect a thing. He's busy daydreaming about his little girlfriend. He will soon learn that love does not conquer all. He cannot stop us. Nor anyone.*

I grew wary. Someone among them was a zalphic, though I wasn't sure which one yet. Even with the Telekinetic enhancement Telekay had, I wouldn't be strong enough to take them all on. I tried to read more minds—to find out how many of them there were. There were six of them.

I was a little surprised by the quantity of men. I contacted Benjamin and Maximillius so that they could help me with the battle. I was relieved to find out they were in the range of my telepathy. I also saw that Jennifer was in my range. I was about to ask for her help, but I stopped. I wasn't sure whether she would help me, and I wasn't prepared to learn the answer. Instead, I focused on the current predicament. There were six of them. With Benjamin and Maximillius, that would mean each of us would fight two of them. I grabbed Telekay from under the sheets and gripped it in my left hand. I left the bare room and went down to the equally unimpressive entrance. There was a couch eaten by time, a small table, and a shelf without any books.

I waited and decided to read their minds.

I should probably check to see what he's thinking. Quickly, I tried re-imagining my kissing session. I tried desperately to think of nothing else but the kissing. After I sensed the little disturbance in my mind go away, I got back to my strategizing. I would fight the telekinetic zalphic and another one, while Benjamin and Maximillius each took care of two. If more came, Benjamin and Maximillius would have to take care of them. I was certain that the zalphic would be the hardest one to fight.

"Benjamin, how far away are you from the inn?"

"I'm here already. When you come out to attack, I will attack them from behind."

"Very well. Is Maximillius with you?"

"Yes."

"Look around and think about the place. I'm going to read your mind, so I know exactly where you are."

"Very well." I read Benjamin's mind and saw the advantageous position they had taken. Suddenly, I felt a slight disturbance. I quickly improvised and envisioned myself holding hands with her at the scene. I tried thinking about how soft her hands would be,

3. Austin's Assaults- 57

and the pleasure I would get from having her hands in mine. Then, the disturbance was gone.

This one doesn't stop thinking about her. Perhaps Argus should reconsider his torture methods; making them read his mind will make anyone want to kill himself. Argus? That was strange. I had assumed this had been Jack's doing. Was Argus higher up? Was this a completely different group? Was Argus an underling of Jack? I didn't know of anyone named Argus in the area. There was only the one in Vernatia, but he would have no interest in me.

I closed my eyes and swung Telekay to stretch and prepare myself for battle. I wondered briefly if Benjamin and Maximillius would be doing the same with Infernus and Azure. I wasn't aware of any routines that they had—if they had any at all. Both were Knights in the Order of the Sword, and some of the finest swordsmen I had seen. Naturally, they could not compare to the Bladesman Caspian—but Caspian was the finest soldier in all Faldenheim, and the two had directly learned from him. The title of Knight was the third highest rank in the order and ranked right underneath Bladesman.

Knowing they were skilled gave me confidence. I had learned to wield a sword from them, and they had made certain that I could wield it properly. I decided that I should not delay striking. I tried to read the minds of the assassins, but they had nothing that could help me. They were just...waiting. I tried to think why they would be waiting. Perhaps more would join them? Were they waiting for permission? Perhaps someone was walking at this hour, and they were waiting for them to leave? I knew I couldn't delay much longer. *"Attack now. Don't let them get prepared."* It was the benign voice that had been present the previous day. It again gave sound advice.

"Now!" I was confident Benjamin and Maximillius would react immediately, so I had already pushed the door open and teleported out before I relayed the message. I set up a telekinetic barrier in case there was an ambush. Though it wouldn't offer full protection, it would absorb some of the force of an incoming

projectile, so I focused on the group in front. Despite the lack of light, I recognized Benjamin's silhouette and knew that behind him would be his friend. Two soldiers suddenly fell to the ground. They still moved on the ground, grasping at injured body parts. Some turned around to face the new attackers, and I took the opportunity to send a telekinetic blast. Unfortunately, they were much more aware, and they got out of the way.

"Zalphic!" They cried out. This stopped me momentarily. They didn't know I was a zalphic? I briefly considered what this could mean: one of them was a zalphic, but the others did not know. That wasn't surprising; any zalphic would keep their powers hidden. But that meant this group had been set out blindly to strike me down. Whoever sent them hadn't bothered to tell them anything about me. Presumably the zalphic in their group is the only one that knew. Jack had already used zalphics before, but it was not as if there were an indefinite supply of them from which to garner men. zalphics were rare, and to find them they would need a wide network. I wondered who this Argus was.

The group had a frenzied look in their eyes. They truly did not know I was a zalphic, and even to this despicable group, I was a monster. They all rushed me, but Benjamin and Maximillius quickly reminded them that they still had other concerns. They recovered from the blind rage they demonstrated and split up. Three went towards me.

"Why do you target me? I've done nothing to you."

"No zalphic is free from bloodshed." They hadn't known I was a zalphic, though it didn't seem that mentioning this point would help.

"It is true that almost no one is free from bloodshed. But I only spilled the blood of those trying to kill me, so you see how I take offense to the insinuation that I am some monster."

"*Krills* were monsters, you are something worse." Worse than something whose primary prey was men? I tried not to react to the provocation—even if it wasn't meant to be one.

3. Austin's Assaults- 59

"Since you accuse me of bloodshed, what's one or six more to me then? I do not know why you have come to me, but you will fail to carry out this assignment."

"You think I will go down so easily, zalphic? I am Austin Drost, brother to Kayton Drost." I quickly turned to Benjamin, uncertain of what to do. I had planned to fight two of them, but I realized now that I was gravely mistaken. I would be unable to fight Austin and another by myself. His brother was Kayton Drost. Even if Kayton was the one renowned for his skill with a sword, his brother certainly would have learned something from him, as I had from my own brother. But Kayton was stronger, more-so than *Caspian*. The only blessing from all this is that they hadn't sent Kayton himself. Austin quickly approached, and I had no chance to speak with Benjamin. The two injured ones stood idly while Benjamin took two and Maximillius took one.

I gripped Telekay in my left hand, which disconcerted him a bit. Everyone was used to dealing with those who held their swords with their right hand. Gripping it with my left meant they had to readjust their technique. Still, Austin would be difficult. As if to prove this, Austin bombarded me with a series of attacks. I had difficulty parrying them. He was a skilled warrior, even if he was not up to par with his brother's strength.

Even if my sword skills were as worthy of praise as I thought they were, it was hard to keep up with Austin. He remained on the offensive but could parry when I countered. Maximillius injured the one he was fighting. Austin then yelled at the two men who were resting. The man Maximillius had injured backed away and rested, while the two that had been resting went towards me, and Austin approached Benjamin, who was still fighting two of them. Maximillius went towards Benjamin as well, but at that point I started paying attention to the two. I knew they would not be as strong as Austin, though fighting two of them would make it considerably more difficult.

They did not effectively take advantage of their numbers, and rather fought by alternating. Presumably, they would try to tire me so that they can pounce on any error I made. I parried their lazy blows easily, and counterattacked as best I could. As I imagined, I began to tire from the constant strikes. I knew I must act quickly. When one of them was to strike me, I used my telekinesis to push him forwards. The unexpected force caused him to lose balance, and step forward while trying to regain it. Now that he was closer, I took advantage and landed a hit on his leg. He fell to the ground, and I parried the other's blows. He was trying to constantly strike so that his friend could get up. However, I side-stepped and teleported forward. I struck the one still on the floor in a gap between his armor. After killing him, I turned around to face the other one.

He backed away quickly, retreating into his group of friends. Suddenly, Austin struck me from behind. The mesh of steel helped dampen the force, but I still found myself on the ground, unable to move. The extreme fatigue threatened to prevent me from using my powers, and the pain made it difficult to think. Maximillius was fighting the other assassin, while Benjamin hurried towards me. His path was being blocked by two others, and the injured ones moved to help keep them busy.

Maximillius tried to dispose of his opponent quickly, but it was to no avail. They kept their distance and warily watched his movements. With the other one there to help block his sword, it would be extremely difficult for Maximillius to push through. Austin kept his eyes on my blade, but now he stood towering over me, raising his sword. I took notice of the blue hilt of his sword and the strange red around the tip of his blade. *Blood*. Specifically, my blood. My back must be bleeding—obviously, Steven. Genius.

Time seemed to slow down—no doubt this was but an infinitesimal power of the mind. I prepared for death, knowing that I couldn't move. My legs had given under the weight of my fatigue, and the poison that coursed through my body grew thick and unable to manifest itself. I had already been scathed, and I hardly had the strength to fight back. Then, Austin and his sword disappeared. Teleportation? I was at a loss. An audio cue told me that wasn't what had happened. A strange and small elevated ground now occupied his former position. A crack featured prominently in the ground.

I looked up, glad to see the face that looked back at me. It almost filled me with energy, though my body quickly told me that I was only lying to myself. I still couldn't stand up. Despite this, I was relieved to see Jennifer's beautiful face looking back at me. Both Benjamin and Maximillius were fighting two of them, but upon seeing that Austin was no longer here, they clearly had very little idea what to do. One of the ones Maximillius was fighting went towards Jennifer. Maximillius calmly took his opponent, allowing his opponent to tire himself while he regained some breath. Jennifer attacked the opponent quickly, forcing him to be on the defensive.

Benjamin backed up a few steps and sent a ball of fire. The ones he was fighting got out of the way, but it continued towards the direction of Maximillius. He expertly forced the one he was fighting to reposition and caused the fire to scorch his skin. Now Maximillius sent a jet of water, taking the one who had just been hit and sent him flying towards Benjamin. Unable to do anything while in the air, the powerful jet of water propelled the assassin on a trajectory towards one of Benjamin's foes—the sword flew, acting more like a lance as it impaled a now lifeless body. I wasn't sure if this is what Maximillius had planned, but I knew if that had been the case, he could have made it work.

Benjamin and Maximillius quickly finished their opponents, and then Jennifer came into view. I turned and saw yet another dead body. I turned back to see Jennifer, who didn't have a hair out of place. It was hard to speak with all the pain, so I used telepathy, which had the bonus of preventing Benjamin from hearing what I was going to say.

"Thank you, Jennifer."

"I want you to know the only reason I came is because I have an oath to fulfill."

"I don't believe that. If your words are true, then take me to him."

"I can't. Your friends will stop me from taking you. I can't beat them while I'm carrying you."

"Of course not. Even though you can just leave me on the floor, then fight them.... You're just afraid you won't be able to beat them."

"I don't have time for your ideas of a jest." She walked away into the darkness. I looked at Benjamin and Maximillius, both of whom looked confused.

"I'll explain later. I'm too weak right now. I need to rest." I went back inside the abandoned inn and collapsed on my bed. I closed my eyes, hoping to fall asleep right away. I didn't imagine it would be difficult, considering my weariness and the toll of exerting my powers. I too walked into darkness.

I was in the middle of the forest, alone. Surrounding me were the six assassins with sharp swords and smirks. Behind them were three dead bodies. Benjamin and Maximillius showed immense pain in their faces. I couldn't bear to look at Jennifer's beautiful body. The limp and distorted faces sickened me, but all I could do was stare at Benjamin's face.

The anger threatened to blind all my instincts, so I did my best to not let it overpower me. I knew that if my emotions dominated me, I would lose this battle. Austin came forward.

"Your mind isn't strong enough, give in to the pressure." What was he talking about? After a few moments passed, my mind sensed the pressure he had referenced. It was painful, but it wasn't overpowering. I could still fight. Naturally, I knew the pain would intensify. So, I had to finish quickly and find the source of the pain.

Two assassins stepped forward to fight me. They were stronger than the ones I had fought. Then, three more went forward to attack me. I had no chance against five. I wasn't a Bladesman. I wasn't strong enough. My mind was full of pain. My body didn't feel any of it though. It was as if all my body's pain was transferred to my mind. A sword would stab my side, but I would feel no pain emanating from the area. All I felt was a piercing pain, constantly attacking my mind. I couldn't take the pain. It was killing me. The screeching echoes of a sword drowned out thought and the barrage of swords dominated my vision. Some strikes didn't register, as the constant volley of attacks meshed into one another and formed a wave of constant pain.

Although I was having a dream—more like a nightmare really—it was hurting me. I could still feel the pain crashing into the walls of my mind, shaking, and yelling in frustration. The pain itself was a living being, turning this way and that way, crying out in a deafening roar. It continued its wail, while the assassins seemingly stopped. They all turned to Austin, who had seemingly told them to stop and step aside. Austin then drew his sword and walked towards me. I grasped Telekay, but my strength was receding, and I could scarcely lift the Caster metal sword. He lazily swung his sword, and with great pain I deflected the blow.

He threw his sword away and taunted me. Even with Telekay, I couldn't take him. I was still too weak. He used his power over wood. I was caught in a giant leaf tornado, getting cut by every leaf in the process. Then he sent lightning crashing down. I hit the floor as the lightning struck all around me.

I looked up at him, but as soon as I did, a part of the ground slammed into my face, and I could do nothing. The force of the blow would have been enough to know me out, but I was still conscious. Could you be knocked out in a dream?

"Get back up Steven." When I didn't, he engulfed me it ice-cold water. The water lifted me, and suddenly the only truth in the world was water. I was sustained by it, thirsted for it, and all thoughts revolved around the large expanse of the Sehrin Sea. I was lifted into the sea, drowning in it, freezing in it, until the cold became too much. "Is it too cold for you? Let me warm you up." Then, I was on fire. A scorching heat permeated throughout, and it seemed like every individual member of my body was burning. Each hair on my arm felt the pain of burning alive, and each finger was engulfed in a bright flash of power. The flames glowed in a familiar color—a familiar color of death and pain. The pain was excruciating. The fire extended to my surroundings, engulfing me in flames and smoke. "Is it too hot?"

I silently pleaded with Austin. I silently asked him to stop. He used telekinesis to levitate me. I was helpless. Unable to defend myself, I waited patiently for what was too common. Telekinetic energy hit the small of my back, and I hit the ground with only a fraction of consciousness. He went up to me and now there was white. The bright light hurt my eyes, and I could not face him. From within my body, I felt a strange movement. An orchestra of energy surged through, though it did nothing to strengthen me. I felt it there, just out of my reach, waiting for me to use, but I was unable to reach.

When all hope seemed lost, I finally reached it. The assassins were sent flying. My grip on reality was returned. Austin stopped, everything stopped. My mind was suddenly in a state of euphoria.

Benjamin and Maximillius were silently sitting. I wondered briefly if they might be sleeping, but I soon realized they weren't. Nothing was out of place—though there was almost nothing that *could* be out of place. Before I let Benjamin know I was awake, I thought first of what had happened in the dream. Despite its fanciful elements, it was clear that it was a more real dream than any other I had had before. It was a dream, and yet there was a real sense of pain, and the relief by brain felt was real, and I could feel it even now. I had strength again, and I was no longer burdened by some of the weight my mind had been carrying.

"Care to explain now, bother?" I didn't realize I had made any noise, but my brother knew I was awake.

"Jennifer said that she only came to help me because of an oath she had to fulfill. I imagine it's an oath to some sort of order. I questioned why she didn't take me away if what she was saying was true, but she said she wouldn't be able to take me while simultaneously fighting both of you. You know the rest. She left, I told you that I was too tired to talk, had a nightmare, and here I am."

"Very well. Maximillius, I'll see you soon. Steven...stop getting into trouble," he said ruefully.

"Well. See you. I'm terribly sorry If I've inconvenienced you. You really didn't have to stay until I woke up though."

"You could have been killed in your sleep."

"Well, thank you. That is certainly a possibility, so I hope it consoles you that you saved my life by being here."

"Benjamin looked back. "Now why would that make us feel better? Sounds more of a reason to be sad," he said with a quick smile. I smiled back, and he turned around. Maximillius said nothing. He simply gave me a look and dispersed. I wasn't sure what the look meant. I wasn't sure if it was meant as a reprimand, or a type of comforting look. Regardless, he left without saying much more. For a long time, I just stared into nothingness, almost expecting something else to happen that would govern what I did next. When I realized I had been staring at the wall and not thinking about much, I went down the stairs to get myself something to drink. After the long morning, I needed a drink. After quenching my thirst, I thought about these two different orders. It seemed that Argus and Jack did not belong to the same order. There were no Orders that came to mind which were led by either of these.

I was certain, though, that both were zalphics, and since they had yet to announce that I was one as well, then they were likely trying to keep these matters private. But what were they trying to accomplish? Why were they after me? And would they be the only ones? Should I expect more to come? There could be many of them. There was no telling when they would act. My life is a danger to the life of others.

Why those names? "You can call me Jack." It didn't seem likely that was his real name, and this new name, Argus, seemed to confirm it. Argus was historically the more famous of the two. Argus was a Telk soldier who had travelled to Andros. He served alongside Arjen Elsavar, one of the Telk Royal Guards. Argus formed part of the famous group led by Arjen that protected Whaldo's Port from the Lancasters. Had they failed, perhaps there would be no Telks in Andros.

Jack was a man who had gained fame for fighting on behalf of peasants with no training in combat. Jack was a hero among the peasants, and he protected them from corrupt leaders who would try to falsely accuse peasants and take their goods. Incidentally, Jack was in Whaldo's Port when Arjen and Argus protected the city. Jack walked the streets to prevent panic, and to protect from rioters. Argus famously called Jack another member of that group that protected Whaldo's Port. They were both famous for their righteousness. I wondered if that was the reason for choosing these names. I was exhausted, so I decided to begin thinking of other things.

I went to the kitchen to scavenge for food. I needed to eat something, so I could get some of my strength back. Upon rummaging through the supplies, I thought about the food available to me. I was too tired to make anything. Or perhaps I was just too lazy. I contented myself with stale bread as I continued to think.

I started thinking about the dream. Well, I certainly hoped it was a dream. He was dead. Jennifer made sure of that. Unless...unless she didn't truly kill him. If he weren't dead, he could, in theory, use his powers to mess with my brain. That didn't make sense. He demonstrated a very real aversion to zalphics. He compared me to a Krill. He seemed truly angered when he realized I was a zalphic. Could he hate himself so much that he would convince himself that all zalphics are worse than Krills? Then I realized this was entirely possible.

But that wasn't the only incongruity. He wouldn't be able to penetrate the defenses of the mind while sleeping. I've tried altering dreams. Somehow, for some reason, minds seem equally active when asleep. I could not break through the defenses of the mind, hard as I tried. When the pain from my efforts became too much, I stopped. I would learn later that the Wisest One argues that dreams occur throughout the sleeping process, and not only the moments before waking. He also said the mind was equally active during these dreams as when we were awake since your brain is creating an entire world. I didn't think someone would be able to alter my dreams. Then again, they had succeeded in altering my reality.

Perhaps some were just more gifted than others as zalphics. My powers grew throughout the years, and I became capable of altering dreams. Perhaps, given more time, I could do the same with people's realities. Just as I excelled in Mathematics, someone surely could exceed in telekinesis. Someone with the skill Heramyr had with fire. I thought of his eyes of fire, and the fearful power he wielded, that led so many to their graves. The mutations were a big mystery. But what did Jack say? There's more to me than just the mutation. Like my brother. What did he mean by that? My brother was skilled with a sword. Perhaps he could become a Bladesman. But my abilities were grounded in telekinesis and intellect.

Not for the first time, I came to think about my brother and me—my family at large, really. Two parents, who in all their generations had seemingly never had someone with the mutation, and yet they could give birth to a child with one. Despite attempts to record every case of the mutation in family trees, it was inane to think these would be accurate. I certainly wasn't going to be part of this official record. Just as I hid it, so too did the others. Perhaps it would be more accurate to think of it as two parents who never had any ancestors who were caught and labeled as zalphics.

Two parents who both had the mutation could give birth to a child without it. Experiments seemed to indicate it was unlikely. Jennifer and Amy were interesting in a similar regard: they were twins, yet one of them had the mutation and the other did not. Despite this, here I was, with two brothers and a sister, all of whom were zalphics. How unlikely was *that*?

I laid down on the couch. What does it mean? I closed my eyes, and all that came to me was a battlefield.

I was back in the field, in my fight against Austin and his assassins. Austin stayed back while all his soldiers came forward to fight me. My vitality, strength, and stamina were back. I fought the assassins with a plethora of strength. I parried blows and pushed them into each other. One by one, they fell, until finally only Austin was before me.

Benjamin and Maximillius came.

"Austin, you can't hold up your ground against all three of us."

"Who said anything about fighting three people? It will be four, and it will not be me."

Jennifer appeared. All I could do was shake my head as she went up to Austin and kissed him. It seemed se really had been with him from the start. But what was that about four? It would be two on three now.

I started forward, only to be stopped by a blast that had fire in the center and water wrapping around the fire. I was sent to the ground. Jennifer reshaped part of the ground I was falling on and pierced me through the stomach. This time, my mind and body shared the pain. Benjamin, Maximillius, Jennifer, and Austin attacked me. Benjamin surrounded his sword's blade with flames, and Maximillius did the same with water. Jennifer seemed to have strengthened her sword with her powers. Telekay held up against Infernus and Azure, but the raw strength of Smasher seemed to be too much. The sword was smashing Telekay. I used my telekinetic powers to cover Telekay with a barrier. The power of the blows was reduced, and the noise of steel against steel subsided. My foes were getting ill tempered. The anger was overtaking them. They were beginning to make mistakes. I started shooting telekinetic energy at them.

The blasts hit Maximillius, then Telekay finished him off. Austin hit me right after Maximillius was killed. I blocked Jennifer's boulder attack and barely dodged Benjamin's blow. Benjamin lunged forward; Telekay blocked Infernus as raging fire engulfed us. With his knee, Benjamin hit me in the stomach. I put my right hand over my stomach while holding Telekay with my other hand to defend myself.

I used all the strength I had to send the strongest I could. Benjamin jumped out of the way, but Austin was gliding towards me. The flat of Telekay hit Austin's head, who almost immediately fell over and hit the ground with a loud thump. Jennifer attacked me, but I didn't counterattack—I parried and dodged her blows and stalled. I jumped back to avoid one of Jennifer's attacks. Immediately after, Austin stabbed Jennifer through the heart.

I was confused. I didn't know why he had stabbed Jennifer; she was helping him. I used my powers to loosen Austin's grip on his sword, and made the blade go through Jennifer's body. Afterwards, I launched the sword high in the air. I sent a telekinetic blast towards Austin and teleported to his far right. He dodged—as was expected—so I sent another blast that absorbed the first one and struck him at the same time the sword fell and landed on his neck. He was dead, but to make sure, I stabbed him in the heart with Telekay. I looked around to find Benjamin. I didn't know where he had gone. Instead of my brother, I saw Jack. He came into my mind. I was glad he hadn't made us share our mind.

Inside, he reached out to Austin's mind, and he killed it.

I awoke from the trance, wondering what had happened. I sensed that Austin was gone—he had been gone for a long time. I knew that Jennifer had nothing to do with him.

The problem *now* was that one does not send a Knight to do a Squire's job. Argus must have much more skilled and powerful people he could send. I resolved myself to make certain they die a dire death. It seemed that Argus was toying with me. It was likely he who I had sensed. The one with all the power. When I tried to read someone's mind, he made them think about what I wanted to see. He knew my friends were coming, so he left. But he failed to mention that to the other seven that were there. He left, leaving

Austin instead. That could be why he didn't know what to do. He didn't know how to handle it. He didn't know I was a zalphic. He probably wasn't one either. He wasn't expecting to be in this situation and couldn't react.

So, was it Argus messing with my dreams? Why did Jack show up? It seemed he was helping me by getting rid of Austin. There must be something deeper afoot.

I hated Austin for the pain he had caused me. I imagined the pain he could have caused had he been a zalphic. The ones Jack had sent seemed irrelevant in comparison. Of course, I couldn't get passed Kenneth. Jack had sent a Bender. No one could compare to the emotional pain they had caused me. They could never be forgiven. Austin wasn't a Bender. Austin was a....

Drost? I suddenly remembered. It almost jolted my thoughts. Austin Drost was brother to Kayton Drost, the Bladesman from Vernatia. If Austin was in their service, would they also have Kayton? And what about the other Bladesman of Vernatia, Jacob Victoriano? There were nineteen Bladesman in all of Andros. Caspian was the only one I had met, the only one from Faldenheim. But Kayton was known to be stronger, and Jacob was at a level with Caspian. How could I possibly fight them?

If Austin was a Drost, then he was from Vernatia. This was almost as big a revelation. I realized with a start that perhaps Argus wasn't a false name referencing a hero from around the Great Shaking. He might really be named Argus.

Prince Argus Kingston, first-born of Lord Allister Kingston and heir of Vernatia.

3. Austin's Assaults - 71

Chapter 4
Potential

"Hello Steven."

I turned around, automatically drawing Telekay. "Oh, it's just you, Benjamin."

"I tried to help you, but you were having a nightmare. When I couldn't wake you up, I stepped outside. What happened?"

"Someone used their telekinetic powers to influence my dreams. They caused me *pain*. Physical and mental. They forced me to fight loved ones. And I couldn't do anything about it except fight. You do not understand how horrible it was to fight. I had no wish to kill." Maybe except Austin....

"It's okay Steven. It was a dream, nothing more."

"You don't understand Benjamin. It was more than just a dream. It wasn't just some horrifying nightmare. I felt *pain*. Real pain. Physical, mental, and psychological pain. My world was torn and shattered into innumerable pieces. The pain was unbearable. Argus will pay for all the things he did. If I must swear my allegiance to Jack, so be it. I will fight him. I will kill him as well."

"As well? Who else do you plan to kill?"

"Never mind. Thanks for being here. I really appreciate it. Both of you saved me. Where is Maximillius anyway?"

"He had to take care of...someone."

I wondered who this person could be, but I couldn't and wouldn't read Benjamin's mind. "Business this early?"

"Ask Max, not me."

"Whatever." I looked around. "The inn looks the same." He had a puzzled look. "It still looks the same as it did last night."

"You expected different?"

"I guess with everything that's been going on...I just thought it would look different."

"If you insist, here." Benjamin threw a pillow at me and said: "Happy now? The pillow isn't in the same place anymore."

"I wasn't *that* desperate to have something out of place," I replied while fighting back laughter.

"I know, but it was fun."

"Let's see how fun it is." I threw the pillow at his face, but he grabbed another one to deflect it, then promptly sent that one towards me.

"Come on Steven; give me your best shot." I threw the pillow at his stomach. Benjamin put his hand in front to catch it, but I then used telekinesis to make the pillow rise sharply and hit him in the face. "Hey, now that's unfair!"

"You said you wanted my best."

"Fair...enough." Benjamin trailed off and had an inaudible conversation. As if noticing that I had a worried expression, he addressed me. "Something came up. I must go. Listen, we can talk later but I should hurry."

"Do you need help? Is everything okay?"

"You should rest. I can handle it. See you." Benjamin left—and with him, the only thing that filled the void departed. I felt lonely, and I didn't have anything to do. I scanned the mind of everyone in my range to make sure no other assassin was planning an attack. After quickly scanning the minds of those in my range, I concluded that they had given up...for now at least.

I worked on my telekinetic abilities. By forcing my mind to concentrate for longer periods, and by continuing to learn, I could enhance my abilities. Concentration helped with control and range. I sat and meditated, trying to clear my mind. After meditating silently, I decided to go to Faldenheim. I set off early and took time to ask around and see if I could learn anything about Jennifer. If she was an assassin, it would make sense for Jack to hire her from elsewhere. If she was from the city, would she really

4. Potential- 73

stick around after failing? I tried to envision what she was thinking, but I could not. I would have left as soon as I could.

My first step was to visit the inns in Faldenheim and see if anyone mentioned a foreigner, or someone who left hurriedly. I found very little, but my efforts weren't fruitless. Not many unknown faces had come, though there was word that a small group left the castle. The major topic was the visit from Prince Kingston, heir to Vernatia. He would be here shortly, and I had a feeling this wasn't a strange coincidence. I grew ever more certain that Argus wasn't a false name. I would try to confirm my suspicions the next time I spoke to him—though I didn't know when that would be.

There was also gossip about a guy named John and troubles in his relationship. Another group had gone hunting, but that was not unusual. Traders had come from down south, but this was also not Jennifer, so I didn't care to listen too much. Finding nothing concrete about Jennifer, I went to the Wise Ones for my studies.

Outside, I saw the familiar short stature, and the dark curly hair that belonged to Aurora. I hadn't seen her in a while, and it was great to see her after everything I had gone through. I greeted her with a hug and, catching up quickly, we found it was time to go inside. We would catch up later though. We entered, and I sat next to Aurora and Roy. Whereas Aurora was my best friend, Roy was an acquaintance with whom I had started a friendship—of sorts. He was the only other zalphic at the Wise Ones—out of the fifty or so among us. Another zalphic had been with us, but he had since left the studies.

Incidentally, the subjects of interest for the day were zalphics.

"Rare as powers are, even rarer is to have duo-powers. It has been documented on numerous occasions—some may have multiple mutations." And here Jack told me that I was special. Guess he was mistaken.

"A few records even show ones with *three* powers. We theorize that this is the limit, as the three recorded cases indicate that the side-effects will be compounded...." That was the first time I heard of the effects being compounded. I had known the consequences for a long time, but I couldn't help but think of Benjamin. I tried to repress the thought and continued listening.

"The powers of wood, designated Z7, and thunder, designated Z6, occur the most. Of those few who are zalphics, it seems that almost half of them are either wood or thunder zalphics. The next thirty-five percent are earth and water zalphics, Z5 and Z4, respectively. Z3, Fire, makes up ten percent of their population, while the remaining is mainly made up of the Z2 mutation, telekinesis. The Z1 mutation, known informally as Invincibility, occurs in less than one percent of zalphics."

"Why is it called Invincibility?" asked Erim, one of the students.

"Excellent question. Obviously, they are not truly invincible. The venerable and prodigious Prince Tadeus Banesworth can easily defeat an enemy with any of these mutations. The rarity of power does not correlate directly with the strength of the individual; rather, its rarity represents the *potential* of the power, but its manifestation is another matter completely. The term comes from an ancient Telk language. Its actual translation is closer to "Tempest," in reference to Strommen. The ancient Telks believed these creatures to be so powerful, they could be a personification of Strommen itself, wreaking havoc on the land. Since Strommen means "The Invincible Storm," the fanciful nature of humanity naturally led the term "Invincibility" to resonate with them. This colloquial term became much more prevalent among those hearing about mythical powers. Since it has not been observed, many erroneously attribute endless potential to the mutation.

"Some argue that it's not a real mutation, though we have concluded it is due to Allison. Only two people have been recorded having the Z1 mutation, though we suspect more have been misidentified as either not having a mutation at all or having a different one. Of the two recorded cases, one developed zalphia and died. Consequently, most of what we know is due to Allison Alkarvan.

"She was born some sixty-five years ago. Surprisingly little is known about her—I'll let you draw your own conclusions as to why there would be no information about an Alkarvan. Supposedly, she simply kept to herself and secluded herself from the world. She ran away from Arastaud, and no one has heard reports about her ever since. She's presumed dead; her red hair would be too conspicuous in any town, and it is not an easy task to survive in the woods alone. Luckily, she kept a record of her powers before fleeing Arastaud. She took this with her when she left, but Lady Dalia read her sisters notes beforehand."

She was presumed dead, but not because of the woods. It was because of what the powers did to us, but I didn't interrupt, and left that unsaid. "How old was she when she left?" I inquired.

"She was almost twenty around that time. Likely because she was a zalphic. We only know what Lady Dalia could recall. Luckily, she has an extremely sharp memory." As I thought about this, it started to seem more familiar. I wondered what it was, but it seemed to me that I had heard her name before.

Alkarvan, I knew, was a renowned family name and they had control of Arastaud in the southwest. They were descendants of the Redimer people—former slaves of the Madaites in Telkos—who crossed the Sehrin Sea and claimed their freedom. Arastaud was one of the three great castles, and they were renowned for their auburn hair. But Allison Alkarvan struck me as a name I had heard before. I decided to inquire. "Is she mentioned in many books? Her name seems familiar."

"I do not believe so. Most books omit zalphics. I don't remember you working on anything about the Alkarvans with us. Perhaps you only think you've heard the name. Allison isn't uncommon."

"Well, I'm sure someone recorded the things Lady Dalia remembered. Perhaps I read that copy."

"That's unlikely. There are very limited copies of the text, and...." The Wise One's voice trailed off. He looked at me strangely. "All of you are dismissed. We will resume shortly."

Everyone was confused but started leaving. I looked at Aurora, who was just as confused as me. We started leaving, but the Wise Ones signaled me to stay, so I told Aurora to go along and that I would meet her later.

"Where is this book you might have read Steven?"

"I...I can't say. I tend to keep all my books here, or I read them from your libraries." Truthfully, most of the books I read were with my parents, though I didn't divulge that information.

"The copy of the text is not available to Acolytes or even Scholars. You couldn't have read it in our libraries. Does that mean you have it??"

"My books are standard. All the books I own are nothing special. Except..." Then I remembered a book I had found in the Lancaster Lands. When we moved to Faldenheim from Bravania, I visited the Lancaster Forest, and found a book. I had thought it strange, and thought it a waste to leave it there, so I was going to take it with me to our new home in Farendor. I was curious, so I glanced at a few pages. It had been a diary, which hadn't caught my attention too much.

"I must be imagining things. If I hadn't read it here, I couldn't have read it. I wouldn't have access to it anywhere else." When we were leaving the forest where I found it, I put it in a box with other books and supplies. When we were leaving the forest, we were chased down by a creature from the forest. In our haste to escape, a box fell. Since we were being chased, I didn't have time to retrieve it, but it was a box full of books. I remember being upset that some of my books had fallen.

The Wise Ones seemed to think I knew more than I was letting on, which was true, but they didn't push the subject more. They talked amongst themselves for a while. I just sat there, thinking about the book and Allison Alkarvan. She was dead by now, but she seemed important somehow. I recollected all I knew about the Alkarvans. After the Great Shaking, when the Telks sailed to Andros, they travelled south and founded Arastaud. When the Lancasters, Telks, and Korschers were waging war and trying to

4. Potential- 77

take control of the land, they remained neutral to the conflict and thrived.

The Alkarvans were even opposed to a royal marriage. It was hard to think that even they were susceptible to the bias against zalphics, though I suppose it couldn't be helped since the Madaites were rumored to be the first zalphics. If anything, they would hate me more than any other great castle. This was all that came to mind. I didn't hear much about Arastaud here in the North.

A knock on the door caught everyone's attention. It was Aurora. She was wondering why I wasn't outside yet and what was happening. I too wondered that. They absent-mindedly let me go and continued their discussion. I walked outside and caught up with Aurora. She was one of the few people that could make me forget everything. She also had a way of making me feel stupid, something that for some reason, I enjoyed.

We talked about all the trivial things, the new events in our lives, and then I told her about the assassins. She wasn't a zalphic, but I trusted her wholeheartedly, and she didn't think anything different of me. She treated me kindly and didn't think of me as a freak, like everyone else would have. I especially loved her for that. She was the only non-zalphic I had ever told.

Having told her my tale, she thought me crazy for having come to my studies. "I would have stayed home."

"Yeah, well home didn't seem exactly safe after everything. And this, the study of powers and phenomena and everything, it all keeps me distracted."

She gave me a knowing smile. "You walk around a little too absent-mindedly as it is, Steven," she teased. "Keeping yourself distracted will not end well."

"I enjoy your company, but when you say things like that, I find myself asking why I do."

She rolled her eyes and half-laughing replied, "I'm a girl, that's why." We both laughed a little more. "I'm the one who should be asking why I associate myself with *you*."

I laughed genuinely, something which was much too rare lately. "Come on Aurora. Let's find out why we talk to one another. We'll figure it out—together."

When I returned to the abandoned inn to collect some artifacts, I was not surprised when I was contacted again. I was hoping to clear up what "Austin" did, and who exactly Argus was. However, neither Jack nor Argus were the ones awaiting me.

"Who are you?" I asked, but they did not answer. I stood there, silently waiting for them to answer. Perhaps they were instructed not to answer questions about their identities—and in extension, the identities of Jack and Argus.

"It seems possible to alter people's reality, as well as their dreams. Is that true in general for telekinetic zalphics?"

"In general, no. Without training, it is unlikely to develop these skills. Naturally, there are those with exceeding potential who will learn regardless, though this number is small."

"Which one is harder?"

"Both pose a problem in truth. To alter someone's world while they are awake, it is necessary to shut down their senses; if you sense something that doesn't adhere to what you should be feeling, it is exceedingly easy to cast out the illusion."

"Shouldn't it be easier to target someone who is asleep, then? Since those things seem to be already shut."

"The brain works efficiently while asleep. It is still very active, and there are other security measures to bypass. Changing someone's world when asleep requires very subtle alterations. Little by little, these alterations aggregate, and you get control, though it takes some time. With enough practice, both become simple."

"Can you do both?"

"Yes. I believe that is one of the reasons they had us do this with you." They anticipated my question? Well, both of my questions, seeing as they were not going to answer who they were.

"Do I have potential to learn it on my own?"

4. Potential- 79

"Yes. And the potential for so much more. They believe you can physically alter reality. They have some doubts, but you've shown incredible strength despite your lack of knowledge."

"What do you mean by physically alter reality?"

"What you are experiencing now can be called a hallucination. We are not actually here, and only you can see us. If someone were with you, they would not hear nor hear us, unless we also gave them this illusion. You have power to make things such as this real, though the details of this escape even us." I thought about the time Jack messed with my mind, but as soon as it stopped, Benjamin and Maximillius did not seem to have noticed. To them, I had never had that conversation, and they reacted to me walking into the inn.

"Now Steven, tell us what you know of Invincibility." I understood now that since they had answered my question, I was to cooperate with what they wanted now. Though I disliked this idea, information was as important a tool as a sword, so I accepted. The question still surprised me. I didn't really know what to say, so I regurgitated everything I had heard that day from the Wise Ones, but I didn't mention the name Allison Alkarvan sounding familiar to me.

"And what about this book? Where is it? You must know."

"I don't. It ought to be wherever Allison Alkarvan placed it. Why do you think I would know?"

"No reason. Did you know Allison was the heir to Arastaud? She ran away though—they said Allison had fallen ill. Eventually, her sister Dalia became the chosen leader."

The other one scoffed a little. "Fallen ill. Humph. I supposed that's true enough from their perspective." He looked at me with an expression I couldn't quite read. Fascination pity, incredulity. It was strange. "Tell me something Steven. What's the maximum number of powers?"

It was a weird transition. Still, I answered and played along. "Three." He nodded and seemed to be satisfied. What was that about?

"Do you know what three powers are possible?" Again, another weird question, but I continued to play along. Of the three recorded cases, two of them had Thunder, Wood, and Earth. The last had Thunder, Wood, and Water. Only two combinations of three had been recorded.

"Two combinations," I guessed. "Wood, Thunder, and either Earth or Water." His question must serve some purpose, but I couldn't discern any meaning from it. They had specified I was unique. Could it truly be? But telekinesis didn't appear in either of the two. There was still the possibility that other combinations were available, but not recorded. How would they know I had more powers if I didn't? That didn't seem reasonable.

"Theoretically, any combination would be possible, though I'm sure it is limited by the repercussions of having the mutation. In all three cases, the three zalphics died before reaching the prime of their strength. The oldest one was twenty-eight." Yes, the Wise Ones had mentioned the effects were compounded. "Your family is quite unique. Don't think we haven't taken notice." I immediately stiffened. My family. They can't know who I am. They can't know about Kesara.

"What are you talking about?"

"Let's just say that a wise friend of ours told us something quite interesting." Again, he had refused to tell me. Now I was even more confused. Asking about their friend or how they knew wasn't going to get me anywhere though. That wasn't where my curiosity stopped though.

"You think I have more than one power? What other mutation?"

"Invincibility." They said it so simply. Yet, this was much more serious. I looked at them, wondering if they could be joking—*knowing* they had to be. Invincibility? That was...impossible. It was easier to become a legendary *Swordsmaster* than to have Invincibility. There had been five of them, in contrast to the two with the Z1 mutation. I had telekinesis. That alone was improbable. Invincibility though.... All I could think to say was,

"What?" This seemed surreal. Me? With the Z1 mutation? I couldn't think straight.

"How could you possibly know that?" They didn't respond. I was trying to find answers in the unintelligible mess that was my current state of mind. Could they be serious? How could they know? How would they know I had another mutation? How could they specify it was the Z1 mutation? What were the odds?

How much longer do I have?

"Is that why they are so interested in me, then? They want to know what that power entails?" They simply nodded. It did not seem like they were trying to deceive me. But I still couldn't bring myself to believe them. "When will they manifest?" I couldn't stop myself from asking.

"The answer to those questions probably lies in the original work." They said this almost scathingly. It seemed they knew more than they were letting on. Though, of course, that wasn't hard to accomplish. They weren't saying much of anything. Even if they did reveal this.

Before I could ask anything else, they disappeared. I looked around, trying to calm myself, but my attempts seemed to exasperate my senses. What was this strange sensation? A sort of ringing resounded from the depths of my mind. It was almost far-off, but it was constant. The steady ringing seemed to become louder, and with it, I felt as if the room was shaking. The sound seemed to vibrate the rooms, but these rooms were imagined and contained every single one of my thoughts. Soon my head began to hurt, and the room seemed to fight and attempt to expand. A faint ringing became a vibration, and then this vibration became a nuisance. I wondered what this strange sensation was, but thinking became difficult. My thoughts pounded against this room, and the walls themselves cried in agony. Was it one of the side-effects of the mutations? Was this a unique one for the Z1 mutation?

I laid down on the bed in the room. I figured it might go away, and that I was making asinine hypotheses with these thoughts of the effects of the mutations. I found little reason to be concerned. It might be my imagination, or it might be someone trying to mess with my mind. More likely than not, it was this. Still, the thoughts bounced harder against the walls, and I could feel no other presence. I tried containing the thoughts, but they bounced harder. I tried slowing them down, but they bounced with equal strength, and the entire room was shaking. I rested on the bed, but the pain got worse. I couldn't stop the bouncing, and I could think of no herbs or no method with which to terminate the pain.

It became unbearable. The thoughts thrashed around the room, the walls stretched and screeched with each collision, and the walls sent a throbbing pain to my head. I could not think. I fell to the ground, grasping my head as I fell off the bed. Tears started rolling down my eyes as I pleaded with the crashing to stop. My head. My head was throbbing. I didn't know what to do.

"Argus...Jack...answer me. Benjamin, please help." But there was no answer. The only reply I received came in the form of an engulfing darkness.

I found myself unable to speak. I looked up and saw Jack in front of me, covered up as he always was. My head was still hurting, but it had significantly dampened. I ignored the lingering pain. "What did they do to me?"

"What are you talking about? We did nothing."

"Then what is this pain in my head?"

Jack looked confused. He gave me a strange look, and I felt him trying to go into my mind. He left just as quickly. "No one is doing this to you. Are you sure it's not just a headache?" Again, the pain began to throb. I closed my eyes. There was so much pain.

"What do you mean? I'm a telekinetic zalphic." He looked at me, still confused. "Answer me!" The pain was getting worse. I couldn't help but yell. All he was doing was looking at me with strange looks.

"Have you never had a headache?" I looked up with a confused expression.

4. Potential- 83

"I've never felt this pain. Make it *stop*."

"It's a normal sickness. Everyone gets headaches."

"How is this excruciating pain *normal*?"

Jack seemed to give pause. "I don't know what's happening to you Steven. Honestly. No one is *inflicting* this pain though. I don't sense anything. Everything seems to indicate it is a headache, but I do not know why it is so extreme. Nor do I understand how you could have gone all this time without one."

What does this mean, then? Is there significance to this? "I thought telekinetic zalphics couldn't get headaches. Because of the mutation." The pain was growing, and I scarcely had the strength to stand.

"Having the mutation doesn't stop you from getting headaches." He stood there silently, as if he were also trying to discern significance from this. "You just have to endure the pain." He started walking away, towards the door.

"Get back here!" In an instant, he moved from beyond the doorframe to the space in front of me.

"What?" Jack seemed confused. He looked around, then back at me. "How did you do that?" The pain was slowly increasing, and I had no idea what he was talking about. "You just teleported me." "How?" That was a good question. I had always understood that teleporting through things was impossible, that you had to see where you were teleporting, and that you had to touch everything you wanted to be teleported. Yet here he was. Why was my head hurting so much? "If your telekinetic potential is already manifesting, then your Invincibility powers might manifest sooner."

That's all he cared about. All I cared about was this incessant pain. I wanted to learn what this all meant. No one was there to teach me. "You've had your brother." I looked up, confused. It was clear he was reading my mind. But I didn't feel the disturbance in my mind. Was that because of the pain, or because he could mask his presence so that I didn't know? Probably both, but I didn't respond. "I learned about this cruel world by myself. You study with the Wise Ones. Perhaps you should think of your blessings." There was an uncomfortable silence as I still tried to manage the pain. "Well, it might interest you to know that I didn't know what you did was possible. You teleported me, without touching me. That is extremely interesting. Though now that I know it's possible, it seemed only natural seeing as what we can do with Caster swords." Was he referring to how I materialize Telekay? Or was this referring to more swords than just the one?

"Can you make it stop?"

"No." Jack didn't seem to be lying, but I couldn't tell. "The pain you're experiencing has nothing to do with us, or even being a zalphic, from what I can discern. But once you get past this, we will talk again. Believe me Steven. You will be important. Not only due to your power of Invincibility. You will learn the truth, but you must first develop your powers. You aren't ready."

Truth? What truth? What did they want? It seems they want to use me as a tool to fight someone. What wasn't I ready for? I was frustrated. Frustrated from the pain, from the lies, from the secrecy. I grabbed Telekay by its golden hilt and attacked. Before I reached him, my brain pulsated with pain. I stopped running and fell. It was clear that this was different from the pain I was facing earlier. This was Jack. And it was much stronger. "Your powers are nowhere near mine. Not yet."

"If you are to be believed, I'll grow stronger. Strong enough that you can't control. Then you will know fear."

"With all these japes of yours, it's a wonder someone hasn't already killed you just to shut you up. Your powers aren't as good as you think they are. You need to rest. You have no chance here." I sent a telekinetic ball to his right, intending to ricochet the blast off the wall and hit him from the back. He extended his head and made the telekinetic energy explode. Either he read my mind, or my plan was obvious. "Don't make a fool of yourself." I used my telepathy to move a rod that was behind him, hoping to strike him. He ducked, and the rod went towards me, hitting me square on my chest. "Or maybe you should. That's about the only thing you'll be able to do successfully." Jack gave me something in a bottle. "Here, for the headache. Rest up Steven."

He left, and in my pain, I rationalized drinking what he gave me. It wasn't poison, since he wasn't about to kill me when I had an exciting ability he could use. The pain seemed unbearable, so in my restlessness I drank it. The medicine immediately relaxed the pain. As quickly as the pain dissipated, so did my thoughts.

I awoke thinking about Jennifer. I couldn't remember any dreams I was having, but I awoke to a sense that something had happened to her. I tried seeing if she would be in the range of my telepathy, but she wasn't. I looked at the sky. The half-moon was in the sky, and I knew the sun would soon rise. I should be going to Faldenheim if I wanted to make it to my studies. I decided I would. I wanted to talk to Aurora, and Kesara would be in Faldenheim today, so I could see her as well. I took off and headed towards the castle reflecting on what had happened to me that day.

I arrived at Faldenheim, where preparations were being made for Prince Argus Kingston to visit. I went towards the keep, where the Wise Ones were settled. On my way there, I again searched for Jennifer, hoping to find her in a mess of people. To my surprise, she was near. I debated whether to talk to her and decided that I should.

"*Jennifer, how are you doing?*" Quickly, this turned into something unexpected. "*What have they done to you?*" I looked around frantically, checking that no one was following me. I materialized Telekay and hid, as I figured out what to do. I couldn't teleport to her. I didn't even know where she was. When I read her thoughts, she was thinking only of the punishment Lord Horus had administered. Had they discovered her to be a zalphic? I shuddered at the thought of her being tortured. I didn't know where to look. I didn't know where to go. Growing desperate, I decided to push my limits. "*What have they done to you Jennifer?*" No response, just pain. She couldn't manage more. It seemed as if I too could feel the pain. *"Send me an image of where you are."* It was blurry and indistinguishable. It was much too dark to see who was in front of her, though the stature seemed familiar.

The darkness would indicate that this was a deliberately closed off space. The sun was shining and lit the hallways of the keep. Could they be in the underground tunnels? Or the jail? The room could be anywhere. I concentrated on the image, trying to divine something from any detail. Her vision was too blurred, and the room too dark. Jack believed I had potential. I hoped he wasn't wrong in this respect. Telekinesis was still my main power, and I would need to use it effectively.

I concentrated on the image. Something in me—a voice, a sentiment, a silent mentor—told me I could do it. I teleported there.

I saw Jack and registered only his surprise before I shot him with telekinetic energy. It felt different from a normal blast of energy, but I didn't have time to think about that. I registered that I had lost something, and I went on. I held Jennifer and teleported out of the room, and back to where I had been. Was this another manifestation of my power? I had escaped the room, but I needed to get out of the keep. The guards didn't take much notice of me, so I led Jennifer outside of the keep and towards safety. As soon as we left the keep, the heightened state that had kept me going dissipated, and I started feeling the dreadful repercussions of using my powers. I didn't care.

I turned to Jennifer. She looked at me, scared. I hadn't even thought of what it must be like for her. She must have been terrified. "I'm sorry. I didn't think before I teleported us out. Was it any easier for you this time?" She just shook her head.

"That power is cursed. You shouldn't use it. It does too much to you."

"Nothing in this world comes without a cost. The food we eat can make us fat. Medicine makes diseases more resistant. And our abilities do not come without a cost." Our powers kill us....
"How does it feel when you use your Earth powers? When I use

telekinesis, it drains my strength. But aside from the bodily side effects, something changes. You feel it too, right? A feeling that you give up a little bit of yourself?"

"Yes, I feel it too." She quieted a little. "If that's what teleporting feels like, I do not want to know about your other powers."

"The weaker the power, the weaker the side effect is. I think sharing minds with someone else is the worst of all."

She thought about that. "I had heard mention of it in passing from other zalphics, but what is it exactly?"

I looked at her eyes, possibly trying to emphasize the severity of its consequences. "Teleporting is a pleasant experience in comparison. In the first few seconds, you see a wave of the other's thoughts; they do not even wait upon one another. They clash against each other, each next one getting louder to drown the ones before. After a few seconds, things slow down, and telepathy connects the two minds. Sharing minds allows one to see what the other thinks about things, like telepathy would do, but you also see *why*. You see everything in their life that caused them to think in a certain way. You come to understand them. All these experiences flood your mind instantaneously, threatening to corrupt your own views. But those first few moments only get worse."

She shuddered again. Teleporting was nothing, and no doubt she was thinking about the experience of sharing minds. You lose a part of yourself when sharing your mind with someone else. You opened yourself up; you gave a part of yourself up, only to gain the pain and grief that haunts the other person. "You see the other's secrets. Everything you wish to keep secret, they will see. Maybe the person wouldn't understand any of it. Your whole life's secrets will flash by for only a moment. Still, you give it up, and the other will have them registered in their mind."

After your secrets, all your ghosts, all your pain and suffering. The things that keep you awake at night, the things that drain you of life. Your fears, your pain, your suffering will all come pouring down on the other, and they will feel just that."

She looked up into my eyes, determined and scared. "Do it."

I didn't know why she was doing it. She didn't have to. This wasn't an experience she would enjoy. I shared my mind twice. Despite loving them, it was horrifying. After that, I did not dare to do it again. I hadn't even done that with—I couldn't. I remember thinking it would be easier a second time, but it wasn't. Telepathy was much easier. It was just mental communication. But *sharing* your mind was something else.

But I gazed into her milky brown eyes, and I saw something there, a spark, a strength, a solemnity. Something that told me that this was what she wanted. That she needed to do this. I grabbed Jennifer's hand and made her follow me into someplace no one would be watching. It was the home of a former zalphic, who had been discovered. They had quickly killed him and burned his home. I entered the house, hoping for the best. It was still in disarray. Better yet was that no beggars had made residence there. We were alone. Then, I shared my mind with her.

Kenneth, Patrick, Jessica. Jonathan. Amy. A kid I didn't know. Atkinson, Bender. Me. Much more, so much that I couldn't register. A nomadic people, deserts, mountains, hardships. Graves. A sword. The Chordrun—she was a descendent of the Korschers. Jackson, clouded in mystery. The beating she received. Her family, gone. Her disease. Lord Horus. Teleporting. Sharing a mind. *There's something I need to tell you. Jon—I wished you were Kevin.*

I couldn't share my mind anymore. I broke away. I couldn't take it. Tears started forming in her eyes. She hugged me, and I stood there, trying to comfort her. Truthfully, I wanted to cry too. It didn't get easier. It only got harder. We hadn't even gotten to the ghosts. I stood there, terrified. I listened to the frantic heartbeat of this new companion and registered her quick and hurried breaths.

Between sobs, Jennifer said: "I'm sorry about Jacquelyn." I shook my head. I didn't want to talk about it. "Aurora is very important to you, isn't she? I understand your family would be, but I see she must be special." *Aurora. The other person with* which I had shared my mind. But I didn't break away from her. Nor did I break away when sharing it with my sister Kesara. Kesara....

I couldn't reply to her. Instead, I asked a question of my own: "You wished I was Kevin when you first saw me?" She made no reply either. She just stayed in my arms. We stood there in an awkward mix of bliss and melancholy. Nothing seemed important but us, and we cared to be at peace together, lamenting over our sorrows. "You truly do care. For me, that is." I didn't reply—there was nothing to say. She had seen it. Maybe she hadn't seen everything, but she knew. We walked, trying to let our pain dissipate into the still air. We kept walking and talking, hoping it would serve a better healer than the Wise Ones. Eventually, I saw the guy I had seen her with before: the earth zalphic, Jonathan. He had a strange expression—something like anger mixed with grief, mixed with compassion. I couldn't tell. "Let her be." I didn't want a confrontation. I wiped a tear from her eye, smiled at her, and turned around.

I started my walk to the abandoned inn. I no longer wanted to go to my studies, and I didn't want to distract Kesara since I knew she would be busy. Along the way, Jack contacted me again—by telepathy, which seemed strange. He seemed to have taken a liking to altering my world.

"How did you do that?"

"What are you talking about?"

"That blast...how did you do that? And how did you teleport inside? I don't understand. That takes years of practice. At your level, you should have been lost in nothingness."

"Now you understand the confusion I live with. Perhaps it was my potential unlocking?"

"The blast that you used temporarily negated the effects of my mutation. The legends of an old Telk religion told of such a power, but no one believed it to be true. At this rate, you'll be better than any of us. Even better than Allison or Heramyr." The telepathy ended, leaving me to wonder about my powers.

Telekinesis. Invincibility. What other surprises would they hold?

Chapter 5
Jennifer

Several days passed before anything else happened. The rest of my days were spent with Aurora at the Wise Ones, with Kesara at home, or trying to develop my powers. Throughout the days, I thought about Jennifer and how we had shared our minds. Well, tried to. I couldn't remember much of the experience. It was simply too much information. What I remembered was scattered and it was hard to discern any meaning. It was mostly names and a certain aura of how she felt in their presence. There were plenty of vague recollections of events. Her family, a former lover, the death of her parents, and the Korschers. I hadn't seen her since that day, and I always found myself wondering whether she would be thinking about me.

I couldn't sleep much. I haven't been able to sleep for a while now. I spent my mornings thinking about Jennifer and Aurora and Kesara. People I cared about. I decided I would visit Kesara today. Again, I eventually began to think about Jennifer, and to wonder if she thought about me.

Unfortunately, I found someone *else* had been thinking about me. "Steven. I see you haven't stopped training. That is good to see." What did Jack want now? I didn't want to converse with him. I was still all too aware of what he had done to Jennifer.

"Leave me alone. And leave Jennifer alone as well."

"It's a little too late for that now. You shared your mind with her. You didn't finish, but there is still a lot about you she knows, which *I can easily access.*" It hadn't crossed my mind that through her, Jack would be able to see what I shared. Did that mean he could learn about Aurora's struggles through me? A sudden shiver shook my body. The telepathy ended there. Immediately, I grew worried and headed towards Faldenheim. I grew irritated that I lived so far away as I hurried to reach Jennifer.

After going through the castle gates, I sensed Jennifer's mind. It didn't tell me where she was, but I knew where to find her. I walked in circles to make sure no one was following me. Could Jack read my mind and discover where she would be? Was I walking Jennifer into a trap? I tried to consider the possibilities while I searched for any followers.

They didn't know where she was. I fear she wouldn't be conscious if they knew. So, it stood to reason she was hiding. Would they follow me to her? Why would they think I knew where she would be? It's true that I had saved her from Jack, but we separated. From their perspective, we could have discussed a place to meet.

Then, Jennifer's mind was significantly dampened. I panicked, realizing that it was likely that Jack had knocked her unconscious. My heart started beating quickly. Jack can knock her unconscious without physically being there...I hoped. Perhaps Jennifer's refusals angered him? Regardless, she wasn't safe. They would find her. I had not noticed anyone following me, so I quickly made my way to Jennifer. I went to the former home of the late zalphic, where we had tried to share our minds. She had lit some candles to light the room. I saw her on the floor, with no one else in sight. I quickly ran to her and picked her up. Where should I go? They would easily find me at the abandoned inn. It didn't seem safe to stay in Faldenheim. I couldn't hide her with my parents, nor with Aurora.

I used my telepathy to call Benjamin. I tried to contact Maximillius as well, but he was out of my range. Perhaps he didn't have any Knightly duties today? I wasn't sure. I awaited Benjamin's arrival—I was watching Jennifer in the interim, making sure that nothing took a turn for the worse. I was part of the Wise Ones, but I had yet to take the developed courses that focused on curing. I had read a book here and there to learn some basics, but

I did not know what I could do for her. Benjamin opened the door—I took out Telekay as a reaction.

"Sorry. It's kind of a habit now."

He made no remark about that. He seemed to accept it as an inevitable occurrence. "What happened to her?"

"Jack." He looked at Jennifer and put his hand on her forehead. Jennifer seemed to react to his touch. She seemed to be having a nightmare of some sorts. I didn't know how long it would take her to recover, and Benjamin didn't say anything for a while.

"Put a wet cloth on her forehead. Let her rest for a while. The only way we'll see if she gets better or worse is by waiting." I did as Benjamin told me. Despite me being in the Wise Ones, he had helped my dad during his fits of ailment. He would know more than I about the subject. After putting the cloth on her forehead, I sat down and waited. I returned to Jennifer's side and noticed that she was getting some of her color back.

A few moments passed by before we talked. Benjamin broke the silence when he asked, "So, how did you know Jennifer would be here? And how did you know she was in trouble?"

"Jack implied that he would hurt her. He contacted me via telepathy. I'm just trying to find out what Jack is planning. His plan makes no sense." I hoped Benjamin wouldn't realize I hadn't answered his first question. He probably did. Benjamin perhaps realized part of the reason was that I had taken a detrimental obsession with her. I tried changing the subject some more. "And where is our friend Maximillius? There's something about his absence that's quite curious. You seem to know the answer."

"What?"

"He's usually out of my telepathy range, always has places to go in the morning, and he usually doesn't help me alone. When he helped me with Kevin and Kenneth was the first time, he had ever helped me alone. He always does it with you. You've helped me without Maximillius there. It may sound stupid, but I think something is up."

"I'm your brother. I *should* be helping you more than he is."

"That isn't it though. What is it that Maximillius is doing?"

"You'd have to ask Max, not me. He is doing something important though, Steven. Don't think he wastes his time worrying about a girl that wants to kill him."

Wanted. "I squander my time, do I?" Benjamin just shrugged and continued thinking. Somehow, small talk didn't seem like the normal thing to do. Jennifer had completely gotten her color back, but she was still not awake. She looked like she was just sleeping—no signs of pain or nightmares were apparent. I was starting to get drowsy myself, but I didn't want to go to sleep. I was determined to stay up until Jennifer woke up.

Maximillius walked into the house; I had already stood with Telekay in hand, still all too aware that Jack could come to get Jennifer. "Sorry Maximillius. I guess it has become a habit."

"Well, you better watch that habit," Maximillius said scathingly. That was one of the few times I recalled Maximillius being anything but calm. Benjamin knew what was wrong. I was sure of it.

"What's—" Benjamin immediately blocked my telepathy and shook his head. Perhaps I should try to get Maximillius to tell me. But it was clearly not an appropriate time to do so. "I'm sorry about that." I responded later. After more silence I said "You guys know you don't have to stay here, right? I mean, what's the worst that can happen?"

"Jack shows up to retrieve Jennifer, you don't allow it, and like an idiot you fight him. Then he kills you. Lost in grief, Kesara tries to kill him. He decided the whole family should suffer for your stupidity. Then the world ends."

"It was rhetorical...." It seemed that the negative attitude was rubbing off on Benjamin. I wondered if I had done anything that could anger him. I knew that Benjamin didn't like my preoccupation with Jennifer, but I had done stuff he disagreed with before. I don't think trying to ask him what was happening to Maximillius would anger him.

94 - The Midnight War

"Anyway, we *are* going to leave now. Max is mainly here to meet up, so we can go. Checking on Jennifer's condition was a very minor part of it."

"Why are you answering for me, Ben? *I* can talk." Things were worse than I thought. My desire to discover what was bugging Maximillius suddenly increased. It was an incongruity to act that way towards Benjamin. Benjamin did not seem surprised by Max's reaction. He wasn't in the least part surprised by his actions; something major must have been bothering him. The two of them exited after that bit of awkwardness. As soon as the door closed, the candles went out. It was as if the door somehow caused it. The room became dark, though my eyes quickly adjusted. I knew neither Benjamin nor Maximillius would come back.

For now, I had to be content with knowing that Jennifer would be all right. I checked on Jennifer, who was still sleeping. How long had I been waiting for her to wake up? I considered laying down next to her. What would she think when she woke up? Would she be okay with that? I decided to see what Jennifer was dreaming about. I entered her dreams, but what I found was that it was not a lovely place. The skies were heavy with rain, and all manner of strange creatures of the dark were about. I saw grim looking shadowcats, and krills feeding on the meat of their prey. Direhawks and fellcondors circled the sky, and dead kords attracted the dark scavengers. Regal corpses were abundant, and Jennifer was in the middle of a field, surrounded by beasts that were baring their teeth and clawing at her. Was Jack making her have nightmares? I would have teleported to his location, but he was blocking his mind from mine. I did not have the skills to influence her dreams, and I could not change what she was forced to live through. I didn't know what I could do, and I hoped in vain to be able to do something. I grabbed Jennifer's hand while she slept, trying any method to calm her. She seemed to react to my touch, and in the dream, I appeared, as well as the other earth zalphic. In the dream, I used my telekinetic powers to defend

Jennifer against the animals, while the other zalphic used earth to create unbreakable barriers to protect her from harm. We stopped them from hurting her. We successfully defended her from Jack's assault, but he did not give in, and formed more monsters onto her. A giant fellcondor flew above us, gliding down in an awe-inspiring dive.

We could do nothing against the fellcondor. Neither of us were at the level of a Swordsmaster, and we could do nothing to stop the bird. The animals overtook us, and with all our powers we could do nothing. Still, we did not die, as I think Jennifer must have still felt the warmth of my hand. She must have known she wasn't alone. The three of us tried persevering while beasts charged us with strength we could not match. I withdrew to my own body when I heard a strange sound outside the house. *"Careful now Steven. You are still weary."* The voice was back. I drew Telekay to defend Jennifer and myself from our...visitor. I tried to read their mind, but I couldn't read anything. I realized that it could have only been Jack, and he was here for Jennifer.

But I couldn't let Jack take her. I would not. I wasn't going to let him take her and beat her and give her more nightmares. I put Telekay in its scabbard and picked up Jennifer. I was putting the life of Jennifer and myself in the hands of my telekinetic powers. I exited from the back of the house, hoping that I could buy myself enough time. I went as quickly as I could, using both my strength and my powers to carry Jennifer. I wondered how long it would take Jack to figure out we weren't there, and how much time I would have. He could teleport and catch us in an instant, but he wouldn't dare do that in the middle of Faldenheim. They might be the least severe amongst the great castles, but Lord Horus himself would find himself without life if he were discovered to be a zalphic. This worked especially in my favor. It was a sort of luck. I wouldn't have to teleport Jennifer. After all she had been through, I didn't imagine she would enjoy the prospect of being teleported. I couldn't add this to her burdens. She still suffered some adverse effects. I was used to it already—maybe I had grown accustomed to the pain.

I went into her mind and tried yelling to awaken her. She woke up with a start and looked around. She recognized immediately that she was no longer in the house. "Jack knocked you unconscious. Let's go." We started walking towards the gates. I didn't know if I could trust the soldiers positioned there, so we tried keeping our heads down. I then realized I didn't know where to go. Farendor seemed unsafe. What if we went East? Nerah wasn't too much bigger than Farendor, but perhaps it was large enough that a Korscher girl wouldn't attract attention. We could start heading east until we came up with a better solution. I relayed my thoughts to Jennifer.

"Do you think that will be far enough?" Far enough? I thought it was too far. Was she truly so afraid of him?

"Where did you have in mind? Want to go to Haernaveh and decide from there? Maybe Vernatia?"

"I don't think Vernatia would work out well." Up ahead, we saw a group of travelers. I looked at her, and she shrugged before nodding. We started hurrying towards them, until we caught up with them. They were a group of four. Three males, one female. The oldest were a man and woman, both dark of hair; the male had green eyes while the girl had blue ones. The other two were of a similar age, somewhere between sixteen and eighteen. One was a Telk, with dark hair, and dark eyes.

"Hello." I started off. They seemed wary of me initially, but quickly relaxed. "I was wondering if we could tag along with you. Sometimes the roads aren't safe."

"If you stay with us, we can ensure your safety. We are heading towards Bravania," said the older one with dark hair.

"That's perfect!" Jennifer replied.

I quickly tried thinking of something to add. "One of our closest friends is sick and we need special herbs found only in the nearby forest. We are too poor to afford the services of the Wise Ones, so we volunteered to take this voyage together." They agreed to let us join them. They didn't seem to care about the excuse.

"My name is Lyrus Flores," said the older one with dark hair.

"Rhema Farren."

"Korey Weirack."

"Ferdinand Flores." We introduced ourselves and we went on our way. Bravania? That was much too far. I hadn't planned on making such a long trip. I thought about how far my studies would fall behind. This would be quite the voyage.

The group of travelers were not uninteresting. They seemed very capable and had a strong presence, but my hope to go unnoticed and my preoccupation with Jennifer kept my interest in the group at a minimal.

An interesting aspect though was Ferdinand Flores, a young man who must have been no more than seventeen. He had strong Telk features. I could tell that he was a zalphic, but no one else seemed to know, so I stayed quiet. It was likely he was hiding out. If he didn't know that I was a zalphic, he probably had his suspicions. I wasn't sure whether the group believed our story.

Throughout the trip, Jennifer and I talked more about our upbringing and mundane things. The group did not do anything of note, and Ferdinand did not use his powers. They had come from the Temporary City of Aquareus, in the Detrimental Shores. The Detrimental Shores were so called because the shoreline was ever-changing. The piece of land constantly changed from being completely submerged in water, to being dry as Chordica. The temporary city was there when the land was rich and fertile, and partially submerged in water. From Aquareus, they travelled to Whaldo's Port on a ship, where they restocked for a day and continued to Kelemire. From there, they followed the Arjen River east until reaching Faldenheim.

The trip was uneventful, as we found no bandits or any such troubles. I only lamented not telling Aurora or Kesara. Perhaps Benjamin would understand what I did and tell them. The uneventfulness allowed Jennifer and I more time to talk. We talked quietly about sharing our minds.

She had seen that I had no choice with respect to Amy. I hadn't had a sword, she had daggers, and I had used a power that I didn't know I had. I really did lament killing her. She didn't hate me for it, she was just upset. The sincerity she had felt when sharing minds must have helped her.

She asked me about my family. I found myself talking mostly about Kesara, and she had to ask me about my brothers to get me to talk about someone else. She asked me about Aurora, and I explained to her she was my best friend, that we had met at some party. I told her there was a funny story behind the first time we met, and that I would tell her later. We were nearing a town, and it was best to keep quiet.

After we left the town, I asked a few questions of my own. I didn't bring Amy up, but I asked her about her family. The only reply she had given to me was that they had all died. I asked her about Kevin, and how she hoped I was him when she first saw me. She reddened a little. "I knew "Steven" had killed my sister. I didn't know Kevin. So, when I saw you...I just hoped you weren't the one...." I quickly changed the subject and asked her about her people, and the sort of pressures she had to carry. I knew that historically, the Benders lead the Korschers, and that it was Chordric Bender who led them into these lands shortly after the Great Shaking. I asked her about the Atkinsons, who as it turned out, served as guards to the Bender family.

When we arrived at the outskirts of Bravania, we separated from the group. I said goodbye to Ferdinand, and with my telepathy I told him *"Be careful."* It was unnecessary really, since he brought no attention to himself throughout our brief company, but if felt proper to speak the words. I also thought he deserved to know I was a zalphic as well. I knew it would have bothered me—not knowing if this stranger who had joined my travelling group was a zalphic or if I was just being paranoid. He didn't react. He looked at me and gave me a slight nod. No one else noticed.

"I guess now is an appropriate time to tell you I used to live in Bravania."

"You did?"

"Yeah. I used to live there before moving to Farendor."

"Why did your family move?"

Hmm...I didn't know. "No idea."

"Well, are you going to take me around your hometown?"

"I suppose I will. But first, I will show you something in the Lancaster Forest."

"In the forest?" I signaled for her to follow, and we followed the Okre River until we reached the forest. The trees were almost indistinguishable, but I had been there plenty of times. Despite no longer living in Bravania, I still knew my way around. As I was walking, a curiosity struck me, and I made my way to the general area where I had lost the book all that time ago. I wasn't sure what I expected to find, but I decided I wanted to look. There was nothing remarkable about the place; I couldn't even be sure this was the correct area. Jennifer asked me again why we were in the forest.

"We're going somewhere safe. Somewhere you needn't fear Jack will find you—and if somehow, he does, you will still be protected." We continued walking for a short distance through the verdant forest. *"Two intruders."* I ignored the warning. Soon, we came upon a slight opening in the forest. There was still an abundance of trees, and greenery surrounded us, but for the first time in a while, I could see the bright light of the sun. I went up to one tree, one which had an almost imperceptible difference in color—a subtle nuance of brown that was lighter than that of the other trees. The subtlety of the color was likely ignored by anyone unaware of the ruse; it looked like any other tree in the meadow to an untrained eye. "Follow me, Jennifer."

I approached the tree and kicked its trunk. The false trunk caved in, and we walked through. There were steps heading down and I asked Jennifer to follow. At the bottom of the stairs was a door with a grid on it. "This door works essentially as a false wall, but the wall will not collapse unless you hit the correct places," I started explaining to Jennifer. "The notches serve as a coordinate. You start from the bottom left, and begin moving to the right first, and then upwards. 3:1, 3:14, 14:3, 14:14. That's it." The door opened, and I went through. She had a look of disbelief. I'm certain it was no different than what mine would have been when I first encountered it.

"What is all this?" she asked as she walked through.

"One last step. Say your first and last name."

She hesitated for a second. After giving me a curious look, she spoke. "Jennifer Atkinson." I smiled a little and walked towards one of the rooms.

"What is all this?" she asked again. "What was the point of that, and how did the door open?"

"It's something I created. The first door was just about making holes and cracks in the right place. Putting your finger on the board creates the pressure that is required to open the door. I won't bore you with the details; suffice it to say that the numbers serve as specific pressure points to open the door." It wasn't entirely untrue, though I couldn't explain the details even if I wanted.

"What about my name?"

"Well," I started smiling. She gave me a puzzled look. "I wanted to learn your last name. I didn't know it. We shared our minds—however brief—but it's not like I remember everything."

"You had all the time it took to travel here, and you decide to find out through this game instead of asking?"

"It's more fun this way." She playfully rolled her eyes and inspected the room. "You can stay in this room." This was the room that Kesara usually stayed in. Aurora had also been in this room a few times. Not many other people came. Apart from the two bedrooms, there were two other rooms. One was essentially empty except for a bed. There was also a kitchen, though naturally nothing fresh was stored in it currently.

"This place is yours? She asked.

"It used to belong to my grandfather. I never met him, but my father didn't want it. Benjamin didn't have a use for it, so they gave it to me. I've added some security measures, so we've never had to worry about any unwanted company. It's well protected."

"Protected? How?"

"There's a complex system in place to protect it. I like to think I'm smarter than people give me credit for; and that I've created things that few imagine possible."

"Such as...?"

"I have a...*device* that allows me to keep track of the place. Essentially, it sends a warning if people are in proximity."

"How could it possibly determine if someone is in proximity? Wouldn't we have set them off if that was the case?"

"Yes. It's giving a warning now."

"So why didn't we hear a warning?"

"It...the device does not make an audible warning. It is set up to directly notify through telepathy. I am informed of anything incongruous with the forest life as soon as that happens."

"That's impossible!" Jennifer exclaimed. It certainly would be from her perspective. Apart from Aurora, no one outside of the family knew about it. I certainly had never mentioned it to the Wise Ones.

I decided it would be best to ignore her incredulity. "I can ignore it quite easily; we constantly set it off. Right now, it's warning me that two people are here. It's not immune to me, so it's talking about both you and me. It can pinpoint direction as well. If someone else were to come, I could locate their position. So, you don't have to worry about anyone following us."

"But what if someone else were to come? You wouldn't know because you're ignoring the warning."

"It sends different messages. It would send a new message if someone else came. It's complicated, but it can protect us." For a moment, she just stood there. I also would not know how to take in all this information. I think she was trying to decide if I was making all this up. "I'll leave you to your thoughts Jennifer. I know it's a lot to register." Truthfully, I wanted to stay there, and continue talking. But I needed to give her space. "I'm going to get us some food." She nodded absentmindedly and went to the kitchen. Since I hadn't been here in a while, I needed to check on what was available. I couldn't very well use anything that was spoiled. Despite the various ingredients that were no longer suited for consumption, I didn't need much more to make an entire meal. I went outside and tried locating an animal. After a bit of searching, I finally caught a glimpse of one. I approached the general area and attacked it mentally. Having crippled it, I went up to it, ended its suffering, and returned to the kitchen.

I started the fire and got the various materials I would need. Now that I was making food for someone else, I wasn't being so lazy. I carefully cooked the meat over the flames using telekinesis. I set the food on plates and added some spices. I took some wine out as well.

"Jennifer, the food is ready." She came in, beautiful as she always was. She looked down and seemed impressed with the food—which I didn't know if I should take as a compliment or an insult. I decided to discard the thought, and I sat down. "I hope the food is to your liking Jennifer."

"It smells delicious," she said before taking a bite. "It's as delicious as it smells. Where did you learn to cook?"

"My mother taught me. I always wanted to learn. Often, I would cook with her. I think I might have been a nuisance more than anything, but I learned, to an *acceptable* degree. You should try my sister's cooking. It makes me look like a total amateur."

"Well, you learned well. Your mother must be quite the cook." I smiled and continued eating. All the time, I asked Jennifer about herself, and a simple dinner became more than I could have ever asked for.

Chapter 6
Escape

We stayed the night there, though we did so in separate rooms. I guess the wine hadn't affected Jennifer's judgment, but I was glad she was there. I felt at peace with her around. I went outside, into the forest to let my thoughts run their course. Jennifer stayed inside, resting. The sky was a shade of light green with a blue nuance to it. The color was strange, but I didn't think much of it. I went to the nearest tree and climbed. I sat on the branch and observed the life that was there. The birds were the ones that caught my attention the most. Two of them were flying in circles, in an endless circle. Another was flying almost haphazardly, turning this way and that way, falling, and flying back. I lost myself in the birds, imagining the joy of flying and resting on the wind. The air brushed the hair of my face. But as usual, my delightful time was soon ruined. *"New intruder."* I didn't think it was any of my family members, nor a lost traveler.

"Someone's here Jennifer." She quickly surfaced, sword in hand. "Come on he can't discover this place."

"Well, you said you had this place guarded in multiple forms. Why not use other devices."

"If only it were that simple. The defense system won't have any effect on Jack. Besides, if I activate the defense system, he's going to know he's headed the right way. We must get out of here before he finds us." Or this place.

"It's pretty well hidden." Then she added: "It's not like he'll be able to get in anyway."

"But if he knows where it is, he'll just keep on trying until he succeeds. I'm also not sure he can't force his way in. In either case, we're wasting time. We need to leave." I grabbed Jennifer's hand and made her follow me into the woods.

"You really like this place, don't you?" I pondered on the question for a bit, trying to figure out what she was really trying to ask me; or if there was no hidden question behind it, why she was asking.

"It's a placid place, full of wonders and the forest. It's how the Lancasters wanted to live, which is why they lived in the forests and did not venture out until they were disturbed. It can also be quite convenient at times, as we've seen. I really do like it." We kept walking, while I was still wondering why she had asked. Eventually, I decided that it didn't really matter. The road felt much unrulier; the path was full of weeds, and the holes seemed ubiquitous. Luckily, there didn't seem to be any dangerous animals around. *"I don't see any signs of wild animals but stay wary. I also don't know where the other person is."*

"Aren't we making it easy for someone with telekinesis to realize we're here? Can't they sense telepathy or something?"

"If they can find us through me using telepathy, they can find us another way. It's not so simple to intercept telepathic communications." Of course, it was also not "simple" to alter other people's realities, but I felt that was better left unsaid. I didn't need to worry her, but Jennifer's words made me think. She was right; they might be able to find me while I'm using telepathy. It wouldn't be inconceivable. There was also the matter of what we would do once we discovered who was here. Even for someone like Jack, this was a long way to travel. Is he truly so interested in me?

"You're going to have to distract him." The voice was back again. I couldn't help but wonder if Jennifer saw that when we shared minds. If she did, would she even remember? Did she think me crazy? Well, now wasn't the time for such inquiries. I needed to consider my options. We could try to sneak past our foe. I doubted that would work. Certainly, if they made the effort to search in the forest, they would be aware of their surroundings. If we made a

diversion, we could possibly get out of the forest and run. But that would only work if they came to the forest on foot, and if we had an excellent distraction. We could try fighting. My powers are growing rapidly if they are to be believed. Alongside Jennifer, we could have a possibility of winning. But would we be able to win? Either Jack would come himself, in which case I don't think we would win, or he would send someone who would be able to hold us off. He surely wouldn't send someone we could overpower. The same thing would hold if it were Argus, though I didn't see it plausible that Argus would come down to Bravania.

Fighting was the biggest risk. I still do not have a clear idea of the skill level or the fighting abilities of whoever I would face. I couldn't endanger Jennifer's life like that. I would need more information if I wanted to fight. I couldn't fight.

"Jennifer, we're going to have to create a diversion." She nodded. We continued our walk to adversity. I hadn't the slightest clue if a diversion would work, but it was the most likely to succeed of my plans. I didn't have enough time to thoroughly think things through, so a plan without risks was impossible. During the walk, my mind began processing things at an increased rate. My life no longer seemed to have gone by quickly. Instead, my life seemed long and laborious, with very little to leave me content. The thought of Jennifer dying had some strange effects on my mind. I need to protect her. All I needed to do was help her leave this forest unscathed.

I saw the soil, the grass, the little, tiny creatures that had never truly existed for me. I was always a mountain to them, but now the little creatures squirmed with life, trying not to be squashed by the giant, fighting against an enemy they could never possibly kill. They knew their attacks would go unregistered, so they fled and tried to live. I also took in the trees, the leaves, the branches, and the life that radiated from it. I was to them nothing but a moment, a flash of light that scarcely deserved to be noticed. Mine was a temporary existence. Nature was the only thing there was, and the enemy was those who would disrupt it with their axes and their hoes and their ploughs. It was those who could burn it away with fire, those who steal their water with a swift movement. The enemies tore asunder the very earth they stood on and took what they wanted. I decided it was only logical that Jennifer felt this same way, and her every step registered the precious earth upon which they rested. The effects of our powers were a necessary balancing, a force stronger even than our own mutations, which targeted those who used them.

I looked at Jennifer, who had a façade anyone could see through. She tried appearing relaxed, but I knew if I were to break into her mind, I would find feelings of despair and fear. And yet...there was something about her. Perhaps it was the way she walked, or breathed regularly, or her regular heartbeat. Whatever it was, it served to calm me. It was relaxing. The nervousness I felt was assuaged, and I accepted the feeling willingly without knowing how it worked. I was now more aware of my surroundings and began paying attention to things I would have normally passed off as insignificant.

Jennifer squeezed my hand. I turned to look at her, and she pointed to her head, so I reached into her mind. *"How close is he?"*

"Not too far. But don't worry, everything will be okay."

"Are you sure about that?" I had my doubts. It wouldn't be surprising if this plan didn't work. But I knew that hearing my certainty would help ease her, even if it didn't help me. Then again, she wasn't someone who needed to be protected. I had seen her fight.

"There isn't a guarantee that it will work. It's risky. But that doesn't mean it's destined to fail. If luck isn't on our side, we will have to fight. So just be ready for that possibility." She nodded. At that moment, they stopped moving. Jennifer looked at me in confusion when I stopped. *"He stopped walking. I can't say what he's doing."*

What was he doing? Why stop? Was he devising a trap, or considering a way to make us meet them? Bewildered by the lack of movement, I turned to Jennifer. *"We might need to make the diversion now. I do not wish to give him control of the situation."* Jennifer didn't nod this time; instead, she slowly raised her hand, making a circular motion. I heard a noise, and saw the person turn abruptly; his hands were surging with yellow electricity. It wasn't Jack, then. Jennifer was about to run, but I stopped her. The other one started walking towards the origin of the sound. We walked slowly, trying not to cause any noise. I froze in place when I saw him turning around and walking back. Apparently, he had already discovered it was nothing. I wondered what would become of me and Jennifer.

Could we take on this new adversary? He wasn't going to be as strong as Jack...was he? I knew now that he was a thunder zalphic from the yellow bolts of electricity that surged through his hands. Could he also have another mutation? Somehow, I found it unlikely that he would be able to fight both of us. But if he couldn't, why send him? Why not send someone stronger? It was better to play it safe and make sure Jennifer escaped, no matter the cost. *"Jennifer are you ready?"*

"Yes. Let's finish this." I materialized Telekay, ready to fight.

"You certainly know your way around the forest, Steven. All those years in Bravania must have paid off." It was to be expected that he knew that. "But reduced visibility only serves to my advantage." Before I could react, I was hit by his lighting. "Resisting will only make things harder on Jennifer. Just give up, and we will show leniency."

"Do you expect me to carry out all your whims as well? I'm not going to give up. And you alone can't stop us, so go back to your street thugs and assassins in Faldenheim."

He laughed a little. "You really don't know who we are, do you?" He turned to Jennifer. His face seemed to give her a warning, though I couldn't know what it was. When I looked through the corner of my eyes at Jennifer's reaction, I could tell that she had understood. Her posture stiffened, she seemed to retreat, and her breathing was coming in shorter breaths. "Jennifer, what would your family say?" Jennifer's hand shook. They could hurt people she loved. They could hurt her parents. Patrick and Jessica, I seemed to recall from that moment, brief as it was. She seemed truly worried now. Conflicted.

"Why did he send you, Dart?" Her hand was still shaking. Was she prepared to fight? Or would she be too distracted from the possibility that his companions already could be torturing her family? I tried to read his mind, to see if his thoughts revealed anything. His thoughts were much too guarded, and his defenses against my mental probe were almost impressive. I started running forward—Telekay in hand. I jumped forward, and as if Jennifer knew what I would do, she lifted a piece of the earth underneath and propelled me forward. Dart prepared for the contact by digging his heels in the soil and taking my attack full on. As soon as the swords came into contact, I was shocked by the lightning surging through him. Moving out of the way would have been easier, and he could have still attacked me with his zalphic abilities. It seemed he had stayed to show off his strength.

"Apparently you two are important enough to send me. He's taken an interest in you, Steven. Even if you are still too weak. You alone can't stop me."

"I'm not alone though. I have Jennifer with me." He gave me a knowing smile. I looked at Jennifer, who no longer seemed to have the resolve she once had. He approached me with a cool resolve. I held Telekay in my left hand, but he did not exhibit the usual adjustment and the small bit of unnerve at having to adjust to me using another hand. He showed no discomfort in his style. He slashed with his sword. I parried once... twice... thrice, but each time, I was shocked. My Caster metal sword seemed to do little. I either had to parry his blows or dodge them entirely, but the latter was unsustainable. He launched a thunder attack that I only partly dodged. He quickly wore me out. He was probably the better swordsman as well. I needed to outwit him, but nothing came to mind. He sent another attack which I tried blocking with a telekinetic barrier. The thunder, however, travelled too quickly, and it struck before I could manage to get the barrier up.

"It doesn't seem Jennifer will be of much help to you." I stopped myself from looking at Jennifer. I needed to think. He was trying to distract me with thoughts of Jennifer. I needed to clear my mind. I needed to stop thinking about the ache in my bones. *"Jennifer, you need to leave. I'll fight him. But you need to get away from here."*

"I can't. If I escape.... I just can't. I'm sorry." I wouldn't have run either if I had been in her position. It was still annoying though. Her family was probably back in Faldenheim, much too far for us to do anything. Our bright idea to run away to Bravania seemed to have made things worse. "Join us Steven, and you will avoid all this trouble."

"I will protect Jennifer from you. You're not too much trouble for me." It was an outrageous lie to be sure, but I felt I needed to say it. Maybe I could convince myself if I repeated it. I needed to grow stronger. I teleported, struck with Telekay, and unleashed a blast of energy when our swords clashed. He regained his footing and looked impressed.

"You Hewleys are much too strong," he muttered. I didn't continue the attack as I planned. *Did he just say...Hewley? Hewleys. Plural. He knows my family.* Pictures of my mom and dad raced through my mind. My brothers, swords in hand, on their knees underneath a stronger foe. My sister. She was crying. Anger shook my body. I thought about the time Benjamin spent recovering from his wounds. I had told myself it would not happen again. Now? I wasn't sure I had the strength to follow through. *They knew I was from Bravania,* I remembered. They would know my brothers. They knew he was a Knight, and that did not deter them. The anger gave me new vigor. The aches of my bones disappeared, and as I unleashed a flurry of Telekinetic powers, I didn't feel the repercussions.

I attacked with strength and speed I didn't know I had. I launched my mind at his, and though I didn't break through his mental defenses, it was as if I had struck a dent into his mental shield. I teleported repeatedly towards him, appearing to his left, then right, then behind, all the while launching telekinetic projectiles. He tried turning to his right, but I pulled him towards me as if he were a simple object. The projectiles hit and I swung my sword. He blocked the strike as best as he could, but the awkward angle seemed to have hurt his forearm. I teleported back and launched another projectile. He used his thunder to strike it, but by then I had already teleported twice and was mid-swing. A large amount of thunder came crashing from the sky, and I was forced to abandon my attack as it struck the area where I would have been. Teleporting back, I saw how thunder seemed to now circulate throughout Dart's body, dancing around him, desperate to strike something. The thunder suddenly travelled, too fast for me to react. I was shocked by his strike, and he pushed forward.

I pulled him towards the ground, but he launched his thunder to the ground and propelled himself faster towards me. I teleported behind him and to his left, but he quickly launched another attack in my new location. I teleported again but was still lightly grazed by his attack. It was faster than I could teleport.

More thunder came, and it was still all too fast for me. I teleported upwards, sent some projectiles, then threw Telekay where I thought he would dodge. Then I teleported towards Jennifer, grabbed her hand, and started running. Though she still seemed reluctant to flee, she did not fight me as I led her away. What were they going to do to Jennifer? *"Just run and know that I'll be there to protect you."*

I turned to see a beam of thunder heading towards us. *No. Towards her.* I tried slowing it down with telekinesis, but it travelled too fast and was too strong. The beam headed towards Jennifer and terminated with Jennifer's agonizing scream. Only after did I feel something strike.

When I regained my consciousness, I suppressed my desire to immediately get up and check on Jennifer. I listened for noise, then slowly opened my eyes. I searched my surroundings after finding no one nearby. It seemed that Dart had left me exactly where I had been. Why had he left me here? Surely it would have been better to drag me somewhere, or tie me up? What was Dart doing?

The trees covered the light of the sun, making it feel dark. From the position of the sun, I knew not too much time had passed. There was something slightly amiss, but I couldn't determine what was missing. My thoughts were a jumbled mess, as I was still struggling with Dart's intentions, but there was a weird clarity in my mind—no, that couldn't be the right word. It was a disturbing silence. There was...nothing. There was nothing. No warnings. No ignored messages in the recesses of my mind.

It wasn't warning me anymore. There was no message indicating I was in the area, which meant I wouldn't know if Dart was in the vicinity. Nor would I know where Jennifer was.

I thought back on Jennifer's reaction. She had seemed afraid of him. Or maybe afraid of what he could do to the ones she cared about. It was...logical that she might try to bargain with him. Or maybe there was another zalphic that could read her mind? Either way, it seems she told Dart that I had a way of keeping track of people in the area. She must have told him I could track their locations. I never mentioned the range, so Dart might have assumed it could work from great distances and decided to destroy it.

I made my way back, thinking they could still be in the area. I shouldn't have told her about the device. It was irreplaceable, and now it would be gone forever. What did those few moments of tranquility mean? Were those moments worth it? I struggled with the answer. In that moment, I was all too happy to provide that reassurance. Perhaps I knew it was a bad idea and refused to think about it. But the night spent talking with her meant more to me. Would it have been selfish to let her worry and keep that knowledge to myself?

A small tremor returned my thoughts to my surroundings. Then there was a loud sound—the noise of battle as the earth followed the whims of zalphics. As I got closer to the origin of the noise, it became harder to run. The tremors were challenging my balance. I assumed Jennifer might be fighting, so I tried hurrying.

I got a glimpse of him and recognized he was the earth zalphic who had been talking to Jennifer the other time. I almost jumped in, but then I spotted Dart laying down against a tree. He was relaxed, and unbothered by Jennifer and Jonathan fighting.

"You didn't stop to think about any of the consequences, did you?" Jonathan sent a boulder towards Jennifer, who lifted a wall to protect herself. Perhaps if I could strike Dart while he wasn't focused, we could run.

"I just don't know what I'm supposed to do. I'm sorry I don't have a better answer for you." It looked like Jennifer was trying to open the ground beneath him, but Jonathan was blocking the attempt with his own powers.

"I would give up anything!" He shouted. Dart looked up at the sudden outburst. He also caught sight of me. He seemed surprised to see me standing there. Perhaps he didn't think I would have the strength to run here so soon after being knocked out. I knew we needed to run. I sent a blast of telekinetic energy towards him instinctively.

We will need to fight. There's no other choice now. I needed to help Jennifer as much as I could and fight Dart. This time, I wouldn't get distracted. "She doesn't need to answer to you two," I interjected. Jonathan turned and was visibly angered at seeing me. I had spoken to break his concentration, which allowed the ground to open. Dart blocked my attack and shot lightning towards me. It was difficult to move out of the way in time. It was much too quick.

Dart sent another bolt of lightning. I knew I was going to be too slow to dodge it on my own, so I teleported to his side. He already was preparing a subsequent bolt, so when he turned, I knew I wouldn't be able to dodge. Instead, I committed to striking him with Telekay, which I had materialized the instance I teleported to his side. The lightning coursed through my body as I swung. The force of his blast pushed me back and forced me to miss. I sent projectiles of telekinetic energy, but he quickly created lightning to strike them.

The tremors from the fight behind made us both temporarily lose our footing. I used my strength to pull Dart towards me. This required much more effort than I expected, and I could feel the strength seeping away. As my fatigue increased, I was forced to spend ever-increasing energy to pull. My vision blurred from the exertion, and the bright spots in my vision blinded me to everything before me. I was overdoing it, I knew. I couldn't keep using it like this. My muscles were screaming in protest now as I continued pulling.

I teleported once again. This time, no lightning was in my way, so I went directly in front of him. I made a stabbing motion with Telekay as he once again prepared more bolts of lightning. This time, my path had been too direct for his speed. The force of his blast pushed me back again, but this time I was closer and cut his side.

No thoughts, not anymore. I was propelled backwards.

Land, land, then jump and move forward.

I was falling, but I put my arm forward and pushed against the earth to keep me upright. In that same motion, I started running towards Jennifer, hoping Dart would take longer to recover.

We couldn't fight them.

No fighting.

Run.

Chapter 7
Evade

Jennifer had tears in her eyes. I hadn't heard the subsequent conversation she had had with Jonathan as I faced Dart, but both seemed upset with where the conversation had gone. Jonathan sat on the ground, in the crevasse that had been created during their fight. His hand was shaking, and he was avoiding her gaze.

"Jennifer," I began, as softly as I could, given the circumstances. I turned around to Dart, to see if he was getting up. "You can process this later, but we have to get going." Jennifer nodded her head slightly, though I suspected she hadn't truly heard what I said. My instincts were still yelling at me to hurry and run, but I didn't want to push her too far.

"I'll teleport us," I began. I grabbed her hand, but she immediately pulled it away. That seemed to break her from her trance. She was turning towards me but something behind me seemed to catch her attention. She raised her hand towards me, and instinctively I teleported us away. She tightened her hand around mine, but I suspected that it was getting easier for her. She was beginning to be accustomed.

I went as far as I could, given my wounds. I knew we were still in their eyesight, but it was the best I could do. I started breathing heavily, trying to regain my breath so we could keep going. Jennifer, too, was having difficulties breathing, but we continued moving away as best as we could. We were half walking, half stumbling forward, with thoughts that they would be right behind me if I dared to turn around. I teleported forward again, trying my best to keep moving.

The nausea was overtaking me. The pounding of my heart was demanding all my attention. I needed to rest. I needed to run. An overwhelming urge to vomit was hijacking all thoughts. Jennifer was on the ground—she could no longer keep running. I tried to reach out to her but there were two ever-shifting copies of her on the ground. The disorientation almost caused me to fall on her. Or maybe I would have fallen on the ground beside her. Either way, I stepped and caught myself before I plummeted. Slowly, the two Jennifers began to converge.

I was about to speak, but she nodded her head, knowing I would insist we needed to keep going. I fought the urge to collapse next to her. I wouldn't get back up if I allowed myself the luxury to rest. My body was not too happy about that decision. Breathing was proving difficult as I continued pushing forward. I was uncertain what we would do. We had relative safety in the forests, as it would be harder to see through the trees and foliage. But we would need to make our way back to Bravania. They would likely keep watch of the river road and see us as soon as we left the safety of the trees. Perhaps we could take a detour and go to Oran instead. That seemed dauntingly far in our current circumstances, but the distance was a much better alternative than finding Dart and Jonathan on the road.

I glanced behind, checking if they were close in their pursuit. I could no longer see them, though that didn't fill me with too much relief. How far would they go to chase her and me? How important was I to their plans? This went far beyond the curiosity of a long-hidden power. Why were they so desperate to see what I could do?

Such thoughts engulfed me, with Jack and Argus at the center, as I hit a stray branch. Jennifer laughed, despite herself. Somehow, I didn't care. I was glad that Jennifer was laughing—even if it was at my expense. "Sorry, I couldn't help myself. Are you alright?"

"It's okay. I'm glad to hear you laugh. Especially after everything." I was on the ground though, and as I feared, I couldn't get back up. I was too exhausted, and the ground was all too welcoming. I couldn't trick myself to believe it was a dire situation, even if likely we were still in peril. I was feeling the full extent of depletion, and I had nothing more to offer. "Can we just...sit down and rest for a while?"

"When I want to rest, you rush me, but now that you need it, we're resting? Is that how it is?" But she smiled and nodded, and I felt at peace as she sat down. I wished she had sat closer. She seemed distant still, and there was something else, but I couldn't quite discern what it was. She was ambivalent, that much was obvious. What was it? Fatigue? Shame? Fright?

"Can I ask," I began after a while, "who that was? Why were you two fighting?" He was clearly upset, but it also seemed to me he didn't want to hurt her. She looked away and blinked away a tear. Stupid. I shouldn't have started. I didn't push the subject further.

She grabbed a flower from the ground and twisted it in her hands. "My brother has a neat little trick he does. He impresses all the ladies with it, no doubt. I think you'd like it."

She looked up at me, slightly confused. It was a random jump in the conversation, I knew, but I was hoping to get her talking about something else. "What does your brother do? Something with fire?" Ah, now I understand her confusion.

I smiled a little. "No, not that brother. Not Benjamin, my other brother, Gideon."

"You have another brother?"

"You didn't see that when we shared minds?"

"There was a lot, too much to interpret." Perhaps I would have understood what her relationship to Jonathan was if we had finished the process. It stood to reason she wouldn't understand parts of my story. "Your thoughts focused a lot on Kesara and Aurora." I smiled, thinking of the warmth of having them nearby. They meant so much to me, and maybe Jennifer could as well.

"Let me fill in some of those gaps then. Gideon is the youngest of the four. He is a wood zalphic. The powers recently manifested, but he has a natural gift for arranging the flowers in a way I can't quite describe. He's able to enhance the colors like the best painter would. He's much more creative than any of us."

"Sounds like a nice trick."

Yeah, it really was.

We talked a little, but eventually the conversation came back to our predicament. "We probably need to risk going back to Bravania. I don't think we can make it to Oran, but if we're desperate enough, we can attempt it."

"I think it would be better to go to Bravania." I nodded in agreement. We likely gave Dart too much time already, but there was no getting around needing to rest. "Any idea where Dart is?" I shook my head.

"We've been patiently waiting here." I turned in time to see the blast of lightning.

"Jennifer, you're making this difficult on yourself." I set up a telekinetic barrier in front of us and grabbed her hand again. She squeezed, getting ready again for the sensation. "We," he had said. Jonathan was somewhere around as well. We needed to continue running. I turned and saw the fear in her eyes. I squeezed her hand, trying to reassure her again, and looked towards my path. It would be easier if I stayed in motion. I started running, and then teleported.

My stomach felt the familiar drop, and immediately I felt tired from the effort. Jennifer tightened her hand around mine, but not as much as it had been before. Or maybe I couldn't concentrate enough to tell. Despite the necessity, I lamented that she had to go through the sensation so regularly. If it weren't for me, she might not need to get accustomed to the feeling.

Dart followed this time, not letting us gather ourselves. "Jonathan is somewhere around as well. There won't be much cover now that we're at the edge of the forest. I will distract him."

"You can't beat him. Please don't leave." I cursed my weakness then. If only I were stronger. My brother Benjamin would have been able to. He was always so strong.

"I won't ever leave you," I choked out. It sounded better in my head. I turned back to Dart and teleported to him. Telekay formed in my left hand as I materialized in front of him, and I swung with the strength I could muster after the teleportation. It took Dart by surprise, and he was grazed by the slash.

He sent lightning towards me, and it was much too fast, and I much too slow, to get out of the way. He turned briefly in Jennifer's direction but turned back to me. Good, that's what I wanted.

"How do you think this will end, Steven? You will have to return to Farendor. You cannot run forever." I didn't know how to respond. It was exactly true. It was crazy to go to Bravania to begin with. But we needed money and food, and we couldn't survive on our own without them learning about it, it seemed.

"You haven't caught me yet, so that makes me believe I can escape," I lied. Not very convincingly, it seemed from his reaction. He drew his sword. I prepared for him to strike. "There's a reason he only sent me." This statement, echoing my thoughts, gave me even more pause. It really didn't make sense to only send Dart. Why not overwhelm me? Why go through all of this? If it was this important to chase us down, why not send more? And if we ultimately were not important enough, why send Dart and Jonathan?

Maybe they really had complete faith that Dart could handle it? Was he showing me his full strength? I couldn't imagine that he was holding too much back. His swordsmanship was easily at the level of a Knight. Not quite as good as my brother was, still better than mine. He was much more effective with his zalphic abilities as well. Benjamin skewed heavily to his skills with a sword. Caspian trained him in the use of the sword, not in zalphic abilities. Dart seemed able to control his abilities very well.

"We're only here for Jennifer."

"Then you're here for me, too." I was still tired though and didn't know how I would back those words up. Before I realized anything had happened, I fell to my knees, hurt by lightning. He was heading towards Jennifer.

Get up. Fight. Catch up to him. Go!

I remained on the ground. I wanted to fight my weakness, to get up and chase Dart and never give Jennifer up. I processed logically that I still needed to regain my strength, but there was no time.

If I don't get up....

I can't fail Jennifer.

I can't fail her.

Get up.

Get up!

Breathing hurt. I rested, hopeless. Please.

If they were to find her, what would they do to her? I was breaking a promise I had made implicitly. I couldn't leave her alone. Dart was too strong. Could she hold fight him long enough so that I could recover my strength?

That was a stupid question. She'd be as exhausted as I was. I just needed to stand up and hold a sword. I thought I had recovered enough stamina, but the teleportation had zapped it away. My wounds would not heal as quickly either. As much as I wanted to will it into existence, I was in no condition to fight him off. Even at full strength, I wasn't sure if I could hold my ground against him. Perhaps. But that didn't matter. Current circumstances were such that breathing hurt me. Each miniscule breath tore at my stomach. I felt light-headed. I was probably losing blood.

I won't leave her.

"I won't leave you. But you need to leave me now, Jennifer." I couldn't hold the telepathy any longer. That wasn't a good sign. It wasn't something that took much strength, and yet my powers were so diminished that I couldn't keep it going.

I closed my eyes to see if that somehow helped me. As if closing my eyes would allow energy to be diverted. As if it were a tradeoff between being able to see and recovering. Perhaps it was working, or perhaps I was getting better at lying to myself. The world around me no longer spun in dizzying circles. This helped with the disorientation and nausea. I needed the world to stop spinning. Still, I couldn't help but realize that circumstances would only get worse as I let more time pass by. Jennifer's life was still endangered, and I was increasingly more desperate to go save her.

And yet....

I can't do anything.

I started inching my way towards Telekay. Somehow, I was going to protect Jennifer. I needed to try everything I could. I reached out towards Telekay. It felt good to have my hands around its hilt, but it didn't give me the strength I needed to fight.

Keep moving.

I forced myself up. My hand was shaking from the exertion, but finally I managed to stay upright. I began walking. I couldn't keep teleporting. As quick as it was, it took a lot of stamina. I needed to maintain what little strength I had. I couldn't keep wasting them. I walked slowly, barely doing more than dragging myself forward. This wasn't going to be easy. But I knew this already.

Keep moving.

I had grown too accustomed to my powers, and now they crippled me. It had been too easy to choose to teleport, but always there were consequences. I should have learned that lesson years ago. Yet here I was. I took a deep breath and continued forward. Each step was an agonizing reminder of the strength required to keep someone upright. Every part of my body seemed to gain more weight.

Can't lay down.

Keep moving.

I wasn't going to stop. Now that I was moving, I couldn't stop.

Weary from pain, I almost didn't see Dart.

His back was to me, but he didn't have Jennifer. He was still looking for her. Good. Jennifer was able to hide. I turned into deeper cover. I tried going where the trees were thicker and closer together, so that I could hide as well.

The earth opened beneath me.

Jonathan. I tried swinging, but I felt an arm around my wrist. A hand I recognized. I hand I yearned to have between mine. I heard footsteps above me. They were louder than I thought they would be. Perhaps they were echoing. "Jennifer, I know you are down there somewhere. You also know that I can't return without you. You really need to think this through."

I wasn't sure what we could do. Where was Jonathan? He was around, and he would be able to find us underground, presumably. What could I do with the little time that remained? We had to evade them. I keep saying that, but we really needed to stop fighting them.

The silence extended, casting a shadow over us. The underground area was small, only just big enough for both of us. I didn't complain. "I'm sorry he got past me."

"That's not on you. But I'm scared. He's right."

I needed help. But anyone who could have helped was far away. Benjamin was in Faldenheim, and I no longer knew anyone else in Bravania.

Ferdinand?

He would be in Bravania still, but that wouldn't help. Maybe if we could make it to them, Dart would not risk anything against the bigger group. Even then, getting to them would be hard, and it might not be the answer to our problems. It was stressful trying to figure out what to do. I'm sure Jennifer knew I was trying my best, but it was making me anxious that I didn't have a semblance of a solution. It would be different if it was only me, but there was more pressure since Jennifer was here.

At least breathing was easier now. They would find us, but hiding here was better than fighting up top. A question suddenly occurred to me. "Jennifer, how'd you know that I was above you?"

"Huh?" It looks like she had to think about it a little. "I don't know. Your...steps were different. I think it's because I could tell you were dragging your feet." She shrugged. Maybe we could set up a trap? That didn't make much sense though. Dart knew we were in the area. He wouldn't leave, and trying to move the ground

122 - The Midnight War

would cause too much noise. We couldn't run, we couldn't fight, we couldn't wait, and we couldn't sneak out. What a lovely situation. No one was close enough to help us and I was too tired to help myself.

"Things aren't looking great, are they?"

At least before I *had* a plan—disregarding how effective it was. "No," I admitted. I didn't want this for Jennifer—well I didn't want it for me, either, but it added to the pain that it was happening to her.

Footsteps were growing louder above. The *thump, thump, thump* of impending doom was terrifying. It seemed that I would no longer have to think of a plan. Dart would force our hand. We needed to try and knock him off his feet and then run. There wasn't much else we could hope to accomplish—not in our state.

"Jennifer, when he is right above us, make him fall. *I will try to strike him and then we need to run."* I took a deep breath in preparation, and I heard the ground above opening as light poured down.

I carefully made sure not to use too much strength with the slash. Telekay's Caster metal shone with reflected light of both sun and lightning. Dart's reaction was so quick. I slashed and pushed back with my telekinetic powers, releasing a flurry of pulse slashes. We didn't have much time.

A cloud of dust rose from the ground as Jennifer tried covering our tracks while also confusing Dart. We ran as fast as we could down a cleared trail, trying to get away.

Cleared....

I realized too late, as Jennifer and I fell.

"Fitting that you're trapped in a pit with him," Jonathan said from above. "Seems that you manage to do that to anyone around you."

"Lay off her," I responded immediately.

"Why is it that "smart" people are so easily fooled? Is it because they think themselves so smart that they disregard the possibility entirely?"

7. Evade- 123

"Just what do you mean?"

"You don't know as much as you imagine."

"Imagining how smart people think must be a totally vicarious process for you," I retorted.

"There are worse things. Like losing your intended." He was provoking me, but I couldn't keep the emotions from surfacing. Anger was quickly rising. "Why so quiet? What got on your nerves? You've only brought it upon yourself." He knew. He knew I had lost Jacquelyn—that I had lost her to the Benders. Was this all related? Did she...?

I couldn't hold back. There was something Jennifer hadn't told me. I could face her and let her guilty look break me. I couldn't turn. I had to focus on him. Maybe it wasn't true. Maybe it couldn't be true. "Here I am, ending this before she drags more people." I heard Jennifer sob next to me.

It will end differently. I didn't have the strength to say it. You will not have Jennifer. I couldn't bring myself to say the words.

"We've a war to prepare for, Steven. We really don't have time to waste." Dart's voice was clear, though I still couldn't see him.

War?

"It's why they're so desperate to have you develop your powers. Jon."

"This could have all been behind us Jennifer. But you made your choice. Repeatedly."

"It isn't that simple. I wish it could be."

I drew Telekay. "We don't need to fight. You're tired, you aren't going anywhere, and you are far from home. Jen, I'm only here for you. I can let him be."

"No!"

"Alright," she said, at the same time. I turned to her, but she only shook her head. The ground in the pit moved, and Jennifer was pushed upward. I teleported up, out of the pit, but as soon as I materialized, Dart's hand was on me, releasing a violent current.

"You said you wouldn't!" Jennifer exclaimed. It was the last thing I heard.

I awoke in a daze. That was happening too often now. I wasn't sure how much time had passed exactly, but I knew they would be long gone. I'd have to rest up in Bravania and resupply for the trip back to Faldenheim. I needed to visit my family. It had been too long since I last saw Kesara.

I immediately went to an old healer I remembered from my childhood. He didn't seem to recognize me, and I said nothing of it. Forcibly, I remained in Bravania to recover from my wounds, though I left as soon as I could. There was a party of merchants travelling to Vernatia, taking with them the precious medicinal herbs found in the forests. They saw my sword and agreed to let me travel with them as hired muscle, in exchange for some food. The trek to Vernatia was wholly unremarkable. It would have been faster to go on my own, but also more dangerous. And they were travelling just fast enough that I couldn't complain. As it was a group of merchants, they were keen on travelling quickly and selling their goods, and that suited me just fine. There were no bandits on the way. Perhaps the group of armed men scared them away. When we arrived at Vernatia, I separated from the group. They would go sell now, but I needed to make it back to Vernatia. Perhaps I could use my status as a member of the Wise Ones to secure passage on a river boat? That would significantly speed up travel.

In the distance, I saw a large company entering Vernatia. Guards secured the road and dispersed crowds, and I saw a man in fine robes, so luxurious t was almost obscene. And he had been *travelling* in them.

Next to him was a man sporting a blue cloak: a Bladesman of the Order of the Sword. This confirmed the identity of the other man. Caspian Stoddard was the only Bladesman in Faldenheim— the finest swordsman of the area. This was a different

7. Evade- 125

Bladesman. The company had entered through Vernatia's Western Gate, which received all traffic coming from the river.

I had heard about preparations for Argus Kingston to visit Faldenheim before I left. He must only just be getting back from whatever business drove him there. The Bladesman had to be one of the two that Vernatia had: Jacob Victoriano, or Kayton Drost.

Kayton Drost, brother to Austin Drost. Should I be scared? Should I be hiding? If they saw me, would they recognize me? Or had fancy gotten the best of me? Was the Argus that tormented me a false name, used in reference to the soldier who fought along Arjen Elsavar? Or could it really be that I drew the attention of the heir to Vernatia? I couldn't risk getting closer to Argus. Then I realized that Lord Kingston was a member of the Committee of the Wise Ones. He already exerted great power by being the lord of Vernatia, but his status as a committee member made him untouchable.

What influence would Argus have over the Wise Ones in Faldenheim? Would he receive reports from the members there? My mind started racing through possibilities. Had he been influencing things all this time? Is that perhaps why I was allowed to join the Wise Ones? To their knowledge, I was just an orphan, not someone who would stand out as a potential member.

I had demonstrated my cunning to an elder, and he had taken me in. Was it possible that it was staged? People were being shoved out of the way, and I was all too happy to comply with the soldiers. I couldn't let them see me. I fancifully started thinking I had drawn the ire of Argus Kingston, but the rational part of me pointed out inconsistencies.

Staged or not, I was smarter than a lot of the other pupils. That couldn't have been falsified or planned. They wouldn't have let me in if I couldn't keep up with my studies. It was too far for anything practical. Why would he have let so much time pass? They would have brought me to him, or they would have explained things much sooner. It would have been the logical thing to do.

I needed to get home.

I took a ferry across the river and headed straight to Verrin. I probably wouldn't be able to secure passage on the river boat, and I wasn't going to lose time following the winding river up north. The road wouldn't be as well-kept as following the river, but it would serve well enough.

I lost a lot of times as I spied some bandits stealing merchandise from a trade caravan. I circled around the area and continued travelling until I eventually reached Verrin. From there, it was a simple case of following the river road until I reached Faldenheim.

It had taken much too long to reach Faldenheim. I wanted to hurry and see Kesara, but first I decided to go to the Wise Ones. I hadn't planned to attend the lesson when I arrived, but as I had let my imagination go wild throughout my trip back, I needed to gather some confirmation. I had a much bigger interest in this now.

"And here I thought you had just decided to quit your studies. Would you like us to restart the lesson, since you have so graciously visited?" I didn't really have an answer. This was the first time I legitimately had a reason to miss such an extended period of time. I was potentially being pursued by the heir of Vernatia, who was hiding that he was a zalphic. His hope for me was that I could manifest the rumored power—I still had no clarification on how they knew I have access to the power. But they needed me. For a war? What was the name they had mentioned? The name from the vision. I couldn't quite remember. An enemy from somewhere unknown.

"I have no excuse," I replied.

"Don't interrupt." I quickly assented and looked around. Aurora was not here. Where was she? Aurora ought to be here, how strange. I had longed to see Aurora and talk with her about all the strange things that were happening. I longed to be in her company too. I saw Roy among the group and approached a spot next to him to sit.

7. Evade- 127

He seemed to be thinking of something else, and not really paying attention to what was being said. He always seemed so distant in thought. Sitting next to him was always great though. There was no pressure to socialize, and we could be quiet together, when it suited us. This was especially useful since I wasn't as fluent in conversations as Aurora was, and it was especially hard since I had begun to rely on her too much.

I liked Roy well enough. He was as smart as I was and didn't really need to be here sitting through the lectures. Apart from being just as brilliant, we shared another important similarity. He was a zalphic too. He had Thunder, like Dart, but also had dormant telekinesis. He had the disease, mutation, gift— whatever you wanted to call it. He just couldn't access his telekinetic powers for some reason. I pondered bringing it up to him over the time I had known him, but it always felt like an unapproachable topic. What could I say that wouldn't make him feel awkward about not having access to it? Did he even know? I had never met someone who had the mutation but couldn't access his powers. Some were bad at controlling it, certainly, but they could *use* it. Perhaps I could help him unlock it since I too had telekinesis, but any which way I looked at it, it was a conversation that I didn't want to have. I focused instead on the reading and work that was assigned.

I read the articles we were discussing, but I couldn't focus on what they were saying. Should I have been kicked out of the Wise Ones immediately? Or did Argus tell them to let me resume my studies? They moved on to the mathematics portion of the study, which was my specialty. Circles, ellipses, and hyperbolas. Nothing too fancy today. *"This is kind of a waste of time."* I couldn't stop the voice in my head. It was true though. Everything we discussed seemed obvious.

It was part of the potential the Wise Ones had seen in me. Or "seen" in me. I still wasn't fully certain which it was. In either case, I could easily recall information we had studied ages ago and could connect it to the new concepts they introduced. I never had to work as hard as others. It was always easy for me.

The things that concerned me currently were the recent string of events that had led me to Bravania and back. Where had Dart and Jonathan taken Jennifer, exactly? Did Benjamin and Maximillius know anything? Would they be able to help me? There was so much I didn't know about all of this.

And where was Aurora? I couldn't help but worry about her. Did Argus get her? Do they know how much I care about her? Was their influence so strong that they could get to her as well?

And as I saw the articles and books around, I found myself wondering about that book. Allison Alkarvan. What secrets had she notated? What secrets did the power of Invincibiliity hold? When would these powers manifest? Again, how did they even know I had this power? Was it like how I knew Roy has dormant telekinesis? That seemed likely, but the key difference was I knew what it felt like to contact a fellow telekinetic zalphic. They wouldn't possibly know what it would feel like in my case. Despite what they said, I hadn't exhibited any great or extraordinary power. What could I do? What happened to Allison?

Probably most important of all, who were the strange visitors that seemed to have Jack and Argus on edge? That vision they made me see...where did they see it? I seemed to recall a blue spherical object. I couldn't tell what it was, but it had seemed important. What did the visitors want?

War.

Was that what Dart was referring to? War with them? Or war between Jack and Argus?

Everything revolved around them. Argus and Jack. Fabled heroes of the past. Did they want my powers to manifest so they could fight the invaders? Were they all going to be deformed, like the one from the vision? How large would their army be?

As I sat, doing my work, pondering these questions, I heard people starting to leave. I packed my stuff and headed outside as well. "Hey Steven, are you okay? You look more distracted than usual. And you have been gone for so long." I looked up and saw Roy.

"Honestly, I don't know how to answer that," I began. I looked around, and no one was nearby. "I'm looking for someone, but I don't know where to start."

"They're just like us, aren't they?" he almost whispered. I nodded my head. Yes, she was a zalphic too. That had to be connected as well, right? "I suppose I should let you try and figure it out yourself. There are always people who would need to keep track."

Yes, it really was quite simple.

I needed to do the same thing I had done previously. But this time perhaps plan it out a little better.

I had finished avoiding them. Now, I would be found.

Chapter 8
Rhapsody

"Jennifer?" There was no answer. She was not in the range of my telepathy, though I hadn't expected as much. Dart and Jonathan would have taken her back with Jack. My patience had diminished, and I was going to demand answers. Before I had wanted nothing else but for them to leave me alone, but now I needed them to approach. I needed a way to get into contact with Jack, so that I could find Jennifer.

I continued walking towards Farendor. I really needed to see Kesara and Aurora. I couldn't shake the feeling that something had happened to Aurora, so I needed to verify for myself that nothing had happened to her. It was strange that Aurora hadn't been to the Wise Ones today. Her father always stressed the importance of studies, though sometimes I suspected he was directing the words of wisdom to me, and not to his daughter. Thinking about that made me worry even more. How often had I walked these roads? It had been part of a routine, and as such I found it calming. I walked the path slowly, thinking about how much I had to do, knowing I didn't know how to accomplish any of it. Even at a loss, the walking was soothing. Sometimes that path was winding, sometimes it was straight, but always, it led inevitably to its destination.

Up ahead, a group of soldiers were approaching. As I drew closer to them, I recognized that Maximillius was among them. He sported his red cloak, identifying him as a Knight. There was a man in a black cloak next to him, which identified him as a Warrior, but the rest were desert cloaks. They were jogging, likely trying to keep up conditioning. I stood to the side as they ran. Maximillius stopped but told the rest to continue. I was surprised he stopped and wondered what he wanted to discuss.

"Your family has been worried. Ben has been beside himself," he said in the form of a greeting. Accusatory.

"I...didn't have time to warn anyone. It was a dire situation."

"It didn't do any good, now did it?" That was...how did he know how it had turned out? What did he know?

"I need your help Maximillius. I can't do it alone." It was an unfortunate lesson to learn. "We have to help Jennifer," I continued pleadingly.

"It seems you're obsessed with that girl. I will warn you it will not turn out well."

"Why do you say that?"

"Because your world seems to revolve around her lately. Exclusively. She drags you away for so long, and you couldn't even bother to notify Ben, or the rest of your family?"

"I realize how inconsiderate I've been. But you can't just discard her safety. She's in trouble. I really need your help."

"Yet again, I find myself dragged into your mess Steven. Fine. You and Ben both owe me. If I so much as strain a fingernail, Ben will cover my patrolling duties."

"Why does Benjamin have to compensate for your lack of skills?"

"For someone who wants my help, you have a way of making me not want to offer it."

"They do say I talk too much sometimes," I said in agreement.

"Little brothers tend to be the annoying ones." I looked at him in confusion. He realized only a second later that he was one too. "Not all the time," he added.

"Not all the time," I repeated, nodding in approval.

He shook his head slightly. "So where is she then? What trouble are we talking about here?"

"I'm not sure," I began, hesitantly. I looked around, to make sure none of the soldiers had lingered. "She was taken away by a thunder zalphic named Dart and an earth one named Jonathan."

"Jonathan?"

I nodded. "You know him?" I asked, hopefully. Maybe we could find him and get to Jennifer from there.

"He let you live?"

"They were more concerned with getting her. How do you know him?"

"This is worse than I thought." Maximillius was a Knight, a title received only through merit. What was he worried about? "Dart wasn't trying, was he?"

"Why do you think I couldn't handle him?" I couldn't, but he didn't have to rub it in. The part I was focusing on was that he clearly knew them both. He could lead us there.

"Dart is my superior." *Superior?* Immediately my thoughts jumped to Dart being a Bladesman, but no, there was only one in Faldenheim, his brother. Caspian was the only Bladesman, and as such was the only superior to Benjamin and Maximillius.

"What do you mean? Is he another Knight?" I didn't know all the Knights in Faldenheim, so it seemed plausible enough that there would be a higher-ranking one.

"No," he said, with no further explanation. Why bring it up then? "Did you make your way here directly, or were you seen?"

"I went to my studies."

"The Wise Ones?" he asked, almost groaning in protest. It seems he hadn't realized that I wanted them to come to me. He seemed to think that going to the Wise Ones had been a mistake. They had someone skulking around, checking to see when I would arrive? That worked out well for me. It brought me closer to finding her. "We're going back to Faldenheim then."

"But Kesara is—"

"Kesara is better off with you away from your family," he interrupted my protest. He turned and began walking, expecting me to follow behind. He liked doing that. Maybe it made him feel powerful. Maybe he thought I could practice being meek. Either way, I followed behind.

"Why are we going to Faldenheim?"

"The Benders have been looking for you. We didn't realize Dart was involved, or we would have posted someone in Faldenheim to grab you."

"Who is Dart? Why do you seem afraid of him?"

"We've never been able to beat him sparring." The "we" of course, referring to Benjamin and himself. "Never" implied they had sparred multiple times. Just how often had they fought?

I was about to voice my question but saw a group approaching. Among them, to my great surprise, was Wyatt Stephensen. "Steven?" He seemed just as surprised to see me.

"Mr. Stephensen. Please, I must know! Tell me she's okay," I begged.

"She's the one who has been worried about you. It seems strange that the roles are reversed now." He didn't say this with much humor. I saw the people next to him for the first time. Specialists in medicine from the Wisest Ones. Also, Jonathan was with them. By his posture, Maximillius recognized that something was wrong. He had his hand on his sword already, and I didn't anticipate a pleasant conversation would follow.

"Please," I repeated. I looked into his eyes. They were usually a dull orange, but now his dead eyes seemed even more unremarkable.

"Aurora is just a little sick. It really is nothing to worry about, but you know how fathers can be." Like any loving friend, I immediately imagined the absolute worst. He didn't believe his own words. I didn't need to know the man to see it plainly written on his face. "But I will feel a lot better if we make it back to her soon."

"Please give her my best. Tell her I love her, and I'll go see her as soon as I can."

"She'll be glad to know you're back Steven. It will give her strength." He made his way back to Farendor after those words. Suddenly my actions seemed all the crazier. Shouldn't I go with Wyatt? Shouldn't I go and be with Aurora? She is my best friend, and I wasn't going to be there because...my mind was preoccupied with a girl?

But it wasn't just *any* girl. It was Jennifer. There was nothing I could do for Aurora—no that wasn't true. All she needed was for me to be there. But I couldn't. That's why I couldn't go to Farendor from the beginning. I needed to deal with these people, so that they wouldn't pose a threat to Jennifer nor my other loved ones.

Jonathan and another remained. We waited while the previous group got far away. Jonathan also began to move his hand closer to his sword, though it seemed more precautionary than anything. I could see his mind thinking and trying to find the correct words. He mauled over everything. "Leave her alone Steven."

"I wish I could do that. You don't understand though, I can't."

"I do actually." He turned to Maximillius, who still hadn't drawn Azure. "I can't do anything about it, but it also feels wrong to do nothing."

Maximillius turned in my direction. Just then, Jonathan used his powers to launch himself towards me. Instinctively, I materialized Telekay. I moved to block the strike, only...there was no sword to block. His fist, powered by the speed of his launch, knocked me to the ground quickly. That moment of hesitation when I didn't see his sword was enough for him to land a strong blow.

When I looked up, Maximillius was between me and Jonathan. I tried getting up, but vines wrapped around my ankles. I turned to the other person that had been with Jonathan. A Wood zalphic.

More vines attempted to grab hold of my hands, but I moved them out of the way in time. The vines around my legs grew thorns in response. I materialized Telekay and stabbed downwards, hoping to cut through them, but the vines were stronger than I would have thought. Now the vines reached upward, trying to engulf me. At the same time, the newly formed thorns dug into my legs.

I abandoned any pretense of breaking the thorns and focused my attention on a mental assault. I hammered into his consciousness and forced him to withdraw the summoned roots.

8. Rhapsody- 135

He gathered his wits relatively quickly and retook control, but by that time, I was free to move again. When he tried to resummon them and pin me down, I moved out of the way.

I ran now, closing the distance between us, and swung my sword. Rather than move or try to block with his own sword, he made a tree trunk grow directly in the trajectory of the swing. The sword got stuck in the wood, and my left hand jolted with pain at the unexpected stop to its motion. New roots surrounded me as I tried to set the sword free. My head was beginning to spin, and I started wondering if it was possible to imbue the thorns with poison. "You've caused just a little too much trouble for my employer. Which means it's my problem now."

"Maybe they should stop causing *me* trouble," I retorted.

"You cannot leave alive. Surely, you've realized this by now. The Benders will stop at nothing." It was getting harder to think. The poison was making it difficult to keep coherent thoughts.

He said more words, but I couldn't understand. He turned, looking at Maximillius, who was also under the effects of the poison. That was wrong. Maximillius was strong, stronger than me. He was a Knight in the Order of the Sword. He could not be taken down by this person. This is not how he would end.

My next sliver of consciousness was him drawing a sword. The Wood zalphic approached, and then there was a bright flash. Sparks surrounded him, and another figure now stood in my vision.

Roy Rhapsados.

With a quick and blurry motion, he struck the zalphic and knocked him down. Then he quickly cut through the roots and set me free. Still light-headed, I pushed with another mental assault. This time, he couldn't fight back. I learned his name was Nikko, and he had been sent by the Benders to capture me. Alive. He was to bring me back so I could be tortured.

Roy stuck his hand out and helped me up. I materialized Telekay and immediately stabbed Nikko, killing him. I turned to Roy, expecting to see a strong reaction from him, but he was unphased by what occurred.

I turned back to Maximillius, who was still on the ground, though conscious. I did not see Jonathan anywhere. Had he seen Roy and ran? I wasn't sure. What was Roy doing here anyway?

"Thanks for the help, Roy."

"Why was he attacking you?"

"Jennifer," I replied, as if it were a full answer. "They captured her," I added.

"The girl you mentioned?" I nodded my head. "Is she pretty?"

"That's not the point. She's in trouble and I need to save her." Also, yes, she's beautiful....

"Looks like you could use some help."

"I couldn't ask that of you. I anticipate...trouble."

"I'll take my chances," he said, shrugging. "You just worry about yourself." Like Roy, I wasn't worried about myself either. I had Jennifer to worry about. "What's the great plan now?"

"Roy, you should learn that half the time, I improvise."

"As much as I'd love to talk about how poorly you plan, we have more pressing matters," cut in Maximillius.

The words made me realize that I couldn't see Roy's face. My vision was still unfocused, and it seemed like Maximillius was not faring any better. "Roy...we've been poisoned. We need help. They're in Farendor" Maximillius did not try getting up. If it was obvious to me that his strength was receding, I knew I must have been a gaunt figure approaching death.

Roy worked with apothecaries as much as I did. His training with the Wise Ones would help him. We were closer to Farendor than we were to Faldenheim. I didn't have more strength to give him the details about the ones with Wyatt. I could only hope he would go and get what he needed. Would they have brought what would be needed with them to Farendor? Roy seemed to make up his mind rather quickly. Without wasting any time, he immediately left for Farendor. What would we do if Jonathan came back?

My mind drifted, and I didn't know how much time passed. I was sprawled on the ground now. I didn't have the strength to look towards Maximillius.

More time seemed to skip, and instead of facing the ground, I was now facing the sky. In the bright light, I saw Jennifer's face, and nothing else. All I wanted was to make sure Jennifer was alright. My determination to make that true was absolute. Her face was warm, and the soft sound of the ocean waves behind her was soothing. We were content just staying in each other's presence. A thousand lights shown behind her, but each was insignificant and scarcely important. "I would never let them kill you," she said to me. I know, Jennifer, I know. They could never keep us apart. Nikko wasn't supposed to kill me. The poison was meant to slow me down.

Was it something most zalphics of his type were taught? Maybe Gideon had already learned the basics of this. Maybe I should have been a bigger part of that process. "Max taught me," Gideon said in reply. There was no hint of reprimand. It was pure understanding, and a simple explanation. Maximillius had taken care of him.

"Well, you weren't going to do it, Steven. And Ben is so caught up with his *other* disaster of a brother that he couldn't dedicate his time to Gideon either. So here we are." Quite a disaster indeed, I agreed.

"What kind of poison do you reckon it is?" I asked...somebody.

"The kind that kills, probably." So much for my earlier revelation. "Probably didn't have to worry about it killing you if you were able to produce both the poison and its antidote with your powers."

Seems prone to failure, I'd argue. But what do I know? I don't think I said the last part. Maybe only thought it. I closed my eyes, trying to rest a bit more. I turned to the sound of footsteps. To my horror, there was a shadowcat. The terrifying feline was supposed to inhabit only Telkos. It approached me with no malice. Luckily, I was unassuming enough that it did not feel threatened. I did not want to see the shadowcat snarl, and its claws were terrifying enough from afar.

It approached Telekay, trying to grasp it in its mouth. I put my hand on the blade, stopping the cat from lifting it. It seemed like it wanted the sword, but it was not annoyed by my denial. Instead, it circled me, as if testing my reactions and considering whether I would be adequate prey. The immense shadowcat looked at Telekay with extremely constricted eyes. The yellow eyes were heavily transfixed on the sword now. The shadowcat dug its paw in the ground, making marks with its powerful claws. The markings formed letters, but they were of a language I had never seen before. Perhaps it was an ancient language that was once known. Though they were unintelligible, I could see that it was communicating with me. It tried grabbing Telekay, but I kept my hand there. It motioned with its head to the writing, as if that would explain everything. It saw that I wasn't understanding and started circling wildly. It seemed to whimper, but it was difficult to distinguish the sound from a terrifying roar. It looked in another direction off in the distance and prepared to pounce, but then it swiftly turned its attention back to me.

It looked me in the eye. It looked almost like a person now. No longer was it the vertical slit of a predator. Its eyes told me it wanted my sword. The strange markings reflected in its eyes now. It wanted Telekay. It circled once more, then sat on its haunches. I took that to mean it finally gave up.

A shadow swallowed me, and white fangs engulfed what little vision I had. It was aiming for my neck, and instinctively I raised my hand in defense. With frightening force, it clamped down on my arm....

I awoke light-headed. Roy was standing above, while to the side Maximillius was practicing with his sword. How did he have the strength? So quickly? I was still struggling adjusting. There was nothing abnormal in my surroundings. I looked at my arm, still expecting it to be irreparably mauled. The arm was bandaged, though there was no ripped skin. It seems Roy had given me the antidote there and bandaged the area.

I saw a discarded syringe among other supplied. This was a recent innovation from the Wise Ones. They had made astounding leaps in the medicinal field. Injecting medication into an afflicted area was much more effective than consuming. I wondered who the crazy person was to attempt and discover this. Though that could be said of most innovations.

Returning to reality, I let out a long breath and Roy helped me up. I was still a little dizzy. "Where are we going to improvise to, now?" Roy had an amused expression when asking the question. Where indeed? I turned to Maximillius. Could I convince him to tell me how to find Dart?

"Lucky for us, Maximillius knows how to find Jonathan."

"Not happening," he replied.

"We'll have more fun this way, Roy." Maximillius raised his eyebrows in question. "The Benders have been looking for me, isn't that, right?" He reluctantly nodded his head. It seemed he had a good idea that he wouldn't like the logical leaps I was about to take. "I guess I'll let them find me. Jonathan doubtless informed them about Nikko. Perhaps Dart himself will make another appearance."

"He's too dangerous," Maximillius protested.

"Who's Dart?" Roy asked at the same time.

"Dart was hired by the Benders to bring Jennifer to them. They had people in Faldenheim looking for me. If I let myself be found, they will send more."

"That's big talk for someone who couldn't stand up without help." Even Roy gave a slight nod of agreement.

"Fighting Dart didn't seem to go well for you last time either," Roy mused under his breath. It was a fair assessment, but it didn't make it any better.

"This time I'll have you two." The statement was meant more of a challenge, as if goading them to success, but I saw the quiet confidence in their faces. Maybe it really would be all the difference.

"You still need to rest. The Benders aren't leaving."

I wanted to reject the idea of waiting any longer, but I recognized the wisdom in the suggestion. "It is much too late to travel at this point anyway," added Roy. It's much better to gather our strength and begin our journey tomorrow."

Maximillius didn't wait for me to agree, and instead grabbed his things. "I need to report back. I've been gone for too long. You can find me tomorrow in the training yards." He began walking, but then stopped after a few paces. "Do *not* go to Farendor."

"I need to see them!" I protested. He just walked away. It was more infuriating because he was right. I couldn't let the Benders follow me there.

But I could just be extra careful. It would be obvious if someone was following me, right? I looked around, noticing Roy deliberating between leaving and waiting to continue the conversation. "When are we meeting?"

"Oh yeah," I began, remembering that Roy didn't have the context of knowing the Knight's schedules like I did. "Maximillius should be done with combat lessons an hour after noon. We will meet up then."

He nodded in agreement and went on his way towards Faldenheim.

I was consumed with thoughts of Jennifer. Try as I might, I couldn't help but think of her. At every turn, I heard her laugh, and I saw her warm smile. Those eyes of hers invited me to infinite wonder, and I knew that her hands would be eternal bliss.

I tried focusing on other things, but thoughts of her consumed my living moments. I wanted nothing more than to see her again, to talk to her about inane occurrences. I wanted to be there next to her. Was it too much to ask for her presence?

I wanted more. I wanted to hug her. I wanted to kiss her. I wanted to breathe in her smell and hold her so close to me that no one could ever take her away. And I wanted so much more. I wanted to give into our desires, and I wanted to wake to her visage every morning.

The sun's beauty would be dull if she wasn't there to be illuminated. What good would eyesight be if I could not lay eyes on her? What good would hands be if I couldn't hold her to me? What good would words be if I could not express the feelings bubbling—surfacing—exploding within?

I was going crazy, I knew. Could I feel so strongly for someone so soon?

Yes.

Without a doubt, undoubtedly, unequivocally, undeniably *yes*.

The anxiety kept me up. I could not sleep. I kept imagining conversations with her. Could someone so grand really share those same feelings with someone like me? Who was I when she could have anyone else? It turned my stomach, worrying so much. How could I live up to what she deserved?

I never thought I could feel like this again. It had taken so long to recover from the past. I thought it had left me broken. But now I began to see that those broken pieces were stronger than ever. They were reforged and made anew. Those pieces made me, and now I was leaving them behind. They would never be forgotten—they would always be a part of me. But now they didn't hold me down. They were not the pieces that would cut me, but rather a beautiful mosaic of what I was and what I came to be.

I would give her everything. I would give her all the love I could, and I knew it could be enough. I could be the best version of myself, for her. Indubitably.

I had to find her. I had to know she was safe. I had to know that I was doing everything in my power to bring her the happiness she deserved.

I used to scoff at the stories of star-crossed lovers gazing upon one another and knowing instantly that they were meant for each other. It had seemed ridiculous that such an occurrence was possible. Now I was seeing how the universe itself was mocking me. I couldn't handle the vagueness and tried to determine what it was about her that made her so special, but I failed at doing so. Despite her beauty, it wasn't her physical appearance that captivated me. It wasn't her personality either since I had felt something before getting to know her. It was maddening. Ineffable. I thought about every conversation I had with her, thinking about all the feelings that surged in her presence.

It was no wonder that I found myself pacing around Faldenheim, waiting for Maximillius and Roy. "I see you're deep in thought as always." I looked up as Roy approached. He seemed nervous as he approached. It seemed strange that he wasn't exuding the confidence from yesterday. "Is your friend almost done?" He started looking around, tapping his fingers against his leg.

"He should be here soon." He kept tapping his fingers. Why had Roy agreed to come? It was strange that he would seem so uneasy but still decided to come. Was it because he had said he would earlier? And he didn't want to break his word despite the rash decision to offer his aide? I didn't want him to be beholden like that. I was putting a lot of pressure on Roy. "But Maximillius and I can handle it. We're prepared for what's coming next."

Roy shrugged nonchalantly. "Clearly there's nothing to worry about then." This was more confusing than anything. Roy didn't seem to care. Was he not feeling pressured? He didn't seem worried about the fighting that would take place. He had seen firsthand the poison that debilitated both Maximillius and me. Yet, he didn't care.

Obviously, Roy and I had distinct reasons for being here, but now I began to truly consider them. I didn't care what happened to me, so long as Jennifer was alright. In truth, I thought myself invincible, much like those powers I supposedly had. I was certain that I was smart enough to find my way out of any situation. Did Roy also think himself invincible? In general, he seemed proud of his skill and cunning, but in a much more reserved way than I was.

I had known Roy for a while now. I had conversed with him only intermittently, and we never really went beyond the usual pleasantries and discussing topics related to our studies. Despite this, I enjoyed his company at the Wise Ones. He reminded me of someone in a dream of mine for some reason, but I struggled to remember both the dream and the person. They escaped me, but he felt familiar then.

Roy wasn't scared at all. He might have been tapping nervously still, but this wasn't related to what we were going to do. He was almost too casual about the business, as if it were simply a whim that he was following. It was intriguing. "Are you sure you want to come?" I offered him another chance to escape before we went ahead.

He hesitated to answer, but his body language didn't change. It was more like he was deciding how to answer—but that his decision had already been made. "I'm here already," he said, adding a simple shrug of his shoulder. "Besides, I want to learn how to improvise. I can't very well have every conversation rehearsed." He laughed at himself and avoided my eyes as his tapping increased in speed.

It was a cute little play on the word. I smiled a little. "If only it were so easy," I replied. I was going to add more, but then I saw Maximillius approaching. I pointed him out to Roy. "Thank you for helping me," I said at his approach.

"You didn't give me much of a choice, but sure."

"Speaking of people who shouldn't have a choice, where's Benjamin? I assumed he'd be here."

"Well now you're going to ruin the surprise. You'll have to ask Ben himself. He was going to tell all of you. Your grandparents are coming too." He didn't have to specify which set of grandparents. My father had been abandoned by his father after my grandmother died giving birth to him. My dad's father had apparently left him some land, but he refused it completely. Instead, my father was raised by his uncle and aunt. My dad's father had apparently left him some land, but he refused it completely. The aunt had passed away while I was in my mother's womb, and the uncle passed away a few years after.

It bothered me that he knew this, and I didn't. I wished that I could be a bigger part of their lives. The small bit of information he gave me was interesting. Being able to read people's minds was terrible for my psyche. I wanted to see and learn everything, but I had quickly felt guilty when I would do it to satisfy my curiosity. Instead, I drew my focus to the task at hand.

I nodded in reply to Maximillius. "I'll wait for Benjamin to tell me then. Meanwhile, it seems we'll do this without him." Roy looked expectant, no longer tapping his fingers on his side. Curious how he stopped, when the truth was this is when he should have started to worry. "I've been walking around Faldenheim, going to populated places. By now, the Benders must know that I'm back. Someone has likely sent them word that I was spotted today. I've let it be known that I will be visiting the outskirts in the east."

"You're not as unpredictable as I was led to believe," Roy commented.

"What do you mean?"

"Seems standard. They will know it's a trap. Especially with the bright red beacon here." We both turned to Maximillius, who was wearing his red cloak.

"It stays on," he said simply. At least we wouldn't have to deal with any thieves bothering us once we passed the gates.

"At least we won't have to fight outlaws on top of *them*," Roy responded.

Weird.

"We should..." Maximillius began, but then he trailed off, seeing something behind me. I turned around and almost gasped as I saw Dart casually walking to a tavern. Maximillius started walking towards it, and I turned to Roy, dumbfounded, who didn't know what was going on, but had started following Maximillius.

"I surmise we just skipped through half your plan," he said quietly. I followed now, unsure what we would do in the tavern. In the outskirts, I could demand answers and we could fight him. In this tavern, so close to the training yards, I wasn't sure where the confrontation would lead us. Maximillius had his hand on Azure. At that moment, I felt that the Caster sword would draw even more attention than his red cloak.

Inside, a group of drunks was celebrating loudly. My stomach turned upon seeing them and tried my best not to react to their presence. They are nothing, don't worry about them, just keep walking. It seemed Dart had business with them. Why would Dart, of all people, be talking to zalphic hunters?

The group of drunks specialized in tracking and hunting down zalphics. Now those hunters had four in their midst. "Come join us!" one of them said, slurring his words. Dart smiled amicably but didn't grab the offered drink.

"I'm not here for that, unfortunately. I've got additional orders for you," he said, handing him a note.

"What's this?"

"You can attend it later. I wouldn't want to keep you from your...celebration." The hunters laughed. One of the women grabbed the note and began reading.

"This s—ms like qu, like qu—qui lotofwrk."

"You'll be paid appropriately."

"We still haven't been paid our bonus this month," interjected a much more sober hunter.

"Lord Horus has approved extending the bonus a few months, but I must reiterate that it is not permanent." The bonus, paradoxically, was paid out if no new zalphics were discovered. The hunters didn't seem to hear, as they all immediately cheered upon hearing about the extension, and quickly drank some more.

They broke into a rapturous delight when they heard the bard begin to play "Farah Falls First". It was a catchy song in truth. The lyrics, however, concerned Queen Farah Alexander, the great grandmother of Whaldo III Alexander. They began describing how she fell in love with her husband, but on the day of their very wedding, she met her future lover.

"So she saw him coming right there,

> *Unbeknownst to all who came.*
> *She didn't say it was over,*
> > *Right when it had just began.*
> *It was the first of many others,*
> > *They knew it and felt the pain.*
> *But it was her idea,*
> > *So Farah Falls First, her bed red-stained."*

The song continued then, talking about her love affair with the new man, who truly loved her. He believed that Farah was stuck in her marriage but loved him. But he was heartbroken to learn she had another lover when he came to visit her one restless night.

> *"So she saw him coming right there,*
> > *Unbeknownst to all who came.*
> *She didn't say it was over,*
> > *Right when it had just began.*
> *"It was the first of many others,*
> > *They knew it and felt the pain.*
> *But it was her idea,*
> > *So Farah Falls First, her bliss obtained."*

The first lover is angered by the revelation and plots his murder. He knows he could never approach her with any weapons in hand, so he devises a way to get to her food. After meticulous planning, he is finally successful.

> *"So she saw him coming right there,*
> > *Unbeknownst to all who came.*
> *She didn't say it was over,*
> > *Right when it had just began.*
> *It was the first of many others,*
> > *They knew it and felt the pain.*
> *"But it was her idea,*
> > *So Farah Falls First, her lungs inflamed."*

It always seemed strange that it would be the lover who was so irate, not the husband. But maybe I should let the song live in its own world.

Dart said some more words to them, but I could no longer hear. Then he turned to leave and spotted us. He seemed surprised to see us, but he didn't pause much after and instead indicated that we should follow.

We left the tavern and came to a street that wasn't as busy. "When they told me he had terribly stupid plans, I didn't think they were being sincere." When would this have happened? What plans would they be criticizing? "Since you don't seem aware, I'll let you know there's a very high chance you'll fail."

"You admit there's a chance I'll win, I see."

"That's only because I did my duty and want no further part in it."

"What do you mean no further part?"

"I did what I needed to, and do not need to do anything further. I will not fight you, and I don't care what happens to Jennifer. She's too much trouble, I've been saying this for a while now."

"Then tell us where she is!"

He looked at me blankly, then turned to Maximillius. "Let's make this easy." He started walking towards the training grounds. He grabbed two practice swords and handed one to Maximillius. "First to three."

Maximillius looked at me with uncertainty. I was hoping to find favorable conditions for us. Maximillius had already expressed concerns about how strong Dart was. He likely wasn't going to be strong enough to beat him in a fair contest like this.

"One point. I win, you help us."

"Done," Dart said immediately. "You know what I want if I win." Dart turned to me and smirked. I shot Maximillius a confused glance, but he wasn't looking at me. He was focusing. Dart began warming up. He stretched out his hands and did some basic motions. Confidant as Dart seemed, Maximillius was still a Knight. Dart was taking this seriously, and he too was deeply focused now.

They began with a flurry of blows. It was very reminiscent of when I saw Maximillius and my brother Benjamin sparring. Dart left a small opening, which Maximillius tried to press. Dart continued blocking expertly though, not overstepping his reach. They traded a few more close blows, with neither having the edge.

I looked around, to see if there were others paying attention. I thought, maybe I could distract Dart long enough to get Maximillius to win. I didn't like the idea of cheating, but this wasn't something I would leave to chance. If Maximillius won, Dart had agreed that he would help. This could be the key to getting Jennifer.

Upon looking around, I saw that there were some people who were casually watching, as one does when there's not much else going on. I would have to be extremely subtle if I wanted to help him. Perhaps I could tug at Dart's practice sword with my telepathy. No one would see that.

Maximillius lunged with a quick blow, hoping to catch Dart off guard, but Dart was ready and side-stepped. He followed up with quick strikes which Maximillius had to back up quickly to block. He was a little off balance now, and Dart continued pressing him, moving his sword quickly so that he could not recover.

I needed to hurry. Dart would win soon if I didn't do something. Maximillius needed to win. I needed to get Jennifer back. I needed to see her again. I had been away from her for far too long, and I wanted nothing more in this world than to be at her side. I needed to control the surge of emotions before I did something unwise, but at this point I didn't care. I felt the great impulse to do anything necessary. All these thoughts came instantly, and I prepared to do what I could.

In an instant just as quick as that flood of thoughts, Dart hit him on the chest, claiming the last point.

There was a diminutive applause from those that had stopped to watch. I looked at Dart, at his sword, and at everything around him. I was trying to find anything to say he had cheated. Any excuse to keep my hopes alive. No. I wasn't going to give up on her. I couldn't leave it like that.

"As agreed," began Dart, turning to me. "Steven here must come with me."

"I need to what?"

"That was the agreement. I'll be waiting over there," he said, indicating with a nod of his head. I turned to Maximillius dumbfounded.

"Maximillius—"

"It had to be done," he interrupted. "We weren't going to get his help any other way."

"We didn't get his help *this* way," I fumed. No, this couldn't be it. There had to be a way I could still help Jennifer. There had to be some way I could get to her. "I'm not leaving without Jennifer."

"I agreed to it, and he won. There is nothing to be done about it."

"I wasn't the one who agreed!"

"Just like I wasn't the one who decided we should steal her away in the first place. Yet here I am."

"What does Steven have to do? Why don't I do it instead?" Roy looked a little uncomfortable. I'm sure he didn't want to stand there while we argued. It was an admirable thing for Roy to do. I hadn't gotten far enough to ask what would be asked of me. I just knew it would delay getting to her.

"No, you can't just replace him. They need Steven for this," Maximillius replied.

"I tried to tell you things wouldn't work out as you imagined," Dart teased. "If you want, though, let's have a little fun."

"No," Maximillius said quickly.

"What do you mean?" I asked at the same time. Dart smirked at Maximillius before turning to Roy and me.

"Whatever he's about to say, you have to say no."

"Your words are hurtful Max. I'm giving them fair odds. I just need a little entertainment." I gave Dart a questioning look. "You and Roy, at the same time. Against me. You win, we forget all about this, and I still help you with Jennifer."

"Done," I said, before Maximillius could say more.

This time, Dart waited. I realized a little too late that I had done exactly what Maximillius had done. I turned to Roy. "It makes no difference to me," he began. Just then, a couple of people approached Dart.

"Commander Logan is looking for you. We have troubling word from the prince."

"Commander Logan?" inquired Roy. He recognized the name. Dart stepped aside while he heard the report. I turned to Roy.

"Who is Logan? Who is Dart exactly?" I asked the last question more to Maximillius, but he seemed more concerned with the report Dart was receiving. Roy was examining Dart's face, as if reluctant to believe what he had just come to realize.

"Looks like you were busy, Steven." I looked up, confused. "Devin, you'll have to explain quite a lot to him. I'm going to meet Logan and discuss what we'll need. We will need to go to Vernatia. Possibly Bravania afterwards if things don't go well. Steven, your first assignment is to go with Devin and deal with the problem you created."

First assignment? Problem that I "created"? Before I could think of formulating a question, he started storming off.

"Maximillius, what does he mean by first assignment?" Maximillius looked unsure what to do. Dart already began heading off.

"The wager I made with Dart is in full effect."

"Steven," Roy interrupted. "These people are more dangerous than you can imagine. Logan is directly employed by Jackson Horus."

Chapter 9
Retrieving

Jackson Horus? As-in, related to Hal Horus? They mentioned a message from the "prince". Jackson Horus, the prince of Faldenheim. I immediately rejected the information. Hal Horus had no acknowledged heir. The castle was to go to someone else. But then I realized how strange it was that it was always no "acknowledged" heir. As opposed to no heir. I quickly reviewed the information I knew about Hal Horus.

He was an Elder of the Wise Ones, and formed part of the council that governed the Order of the Wise Ones, along with Allister Kingston and The Wisest One. He was granted lordship of the castle after the death of the previous lord. Before being granted the castle, Hal Horus lived in the Capital, alongside the Wisest One and Allister Kingston. They threw a lavish party for his wedding, and the newlywed couple would move to Faldenheim and begin their role. Tragically, his wife died of illness. He had no children with her before she passed.

"Lord Horus had no son with Lady Malena," I stated, confused. Devin and Roy both looked at me in confusion, as if I should know him.

"Lady Malena had a kid before marrying Lord Horus. Jackson may not be the blood son of Lord Horus, but he is still his son. Everyone knows this." Roy didn't mean it as a slight on my intelligence, but when he said everyone knew, I felt completely ignorant.

"Jackson is Lady Malena's son?" He was a prince. Everything began to come into place. In that instant, the clarity made everything so obvious in retrospect. It was so clear that I began to wonder how I hadn't seen it before. Jackson was the prince of

Faldenheim, the castle I visited for any needs I had. Whenever I needed to go to the market, whenever I needed to buy supplies, and whenever I needed to attend to my studies, I would have to go there. Obviously, such a big place would be a natural center of any operation. They could easily keep track of my whereabouts. *Jack.* He had called himself Jack. What an imbecile I was. Argus and Jackson knew each other because they were both princes. They would even have been childhood friends, based on the timeline.

"Tadeus Banesworth called for the princes of the northern castles to join him to converse about matters of state. Jackson and Argus both went to Bravania to meet with him, which is why Jack is not here. Logan is taking the lead in his absence." I didn't expect Devin to be so forthcoming with information. Of course, there was not much I could do with that information. Even if I was at Bravania, I would not have access to any of them. My status as a member of the Wise Ones would suffice to get me through the gates, but I'd have to be an elder to *maybe* get me access to the lords and princes. I certainly wouldn't be getting there by walking through the doors and asking to be taken to them. I couldn't teleport inside either—not only would they discover I was a zalphic and immediately kill, but even if they didn't, I did not look the part to be walking through the inner keep. I would be immediately apprehended.

"Steven," Roy began again, all his confidence lost, "Logan is a monster that even razebears would fear."

"Logan is none of your concern," Maximillius cut in. "I'm leaving Steven, but you must honor my blunder. I need to go with Dart and get more info." Maximillius started off as well.

"I need to get going, so I need you to follow me Steven," began Devin. "The Benders are going to cause irreversible problems if we don't hurry."

"Roy," I began, "Maximillius has put me in their debt, but you don't need to be dragged along. You are free to withdraw, but I must go with Devin. I appreciate your willingness thus far to help."

9. Retrieving- 153

"I told you already that what happens to me matters little." Roy followed, not saying anything further. We travelled to the gates of Faldenheim, where I was going to head with Maximillius and Roy.

"What are the Benders doing? Why are you so worried?"

"I will answer your question Steven, but we need to continue walking. You're going to want to stop to get more answers, but we need to keep going. You think you can handle that?" His tone made me feel like I wouldn't be able to handle what he was about to tell me.

"What is going on?"

"The Benders abducted Aurora to force Lord Horus into action." Devin preemptively grabbed pulled my shirt, knowing that I would stop moving, and dragged me forward. Aurora, no. They couldn't.

"What have they done to her!" I yelled.

"We have to go find her!" Roy yelled.

"Prepare for the eventuality that the Bender's will force you to make an impossible decision."

"What are you saying?" I was growing more frustrated.

"What happens if they make you choose between Aurora and Jennifer?"

"I will save them both."

Roy looked at me, and with the most discretion he could muster, asked "Who would you choose?" It was grossly indiscreet.

"What do you mean who will I choose? Why are you so certain it would come down to a choice?"

"I mean that if you don't know, you might be paralyzed by a choice in the heat of the moment. Steven, if it comes to it, I will grab Aurora. You focus on Jennifer." It was hard to maintain my frustration when he was speaking in such a somber tone. He was right to think like that. If it came to it, Roy could protect Aurora while I protected Jennifer. It would be better to have this possibility planned out.

"Wyatt Stephensen will not sit idly while his only daughter has been taken. This already is a political nightmare, and we must do what we can to stop any more harm."

"I will kill them all. That will stop all the harm."

"You are not going to kill an entire *people*. We need to prevent further conflict. I know you don't see it this way, but Aurora is the least of our concerns here."

"Yes, you're right about that one thing," I answered.

I hurried Devin along, desperate not to waste any time. Were they to harm Aurora, the political strife of the continent would be the least of their worries. We went past the castle gates without incident and made our way south. We were following the road that led to Jior's Watch, but few travelled this way. Most followed the road to Nerah along the Arjen River. From there, the road from Nerah to Haernaveh was frequently travelled, since too much time would be lost following the winding river up and down again until it finally reached Vernatia.

After travelling down the road for a while, we ran into a group of four that was waiting by the side of the road. On approach, it was clear that they had weapons ready. It seemed this was a group they left behind to deter any pursuers. I recognized one of them, it was Kevin. Why was he here? I thought Kevin worked with Jackson. He had indicated as much when I asked.

"It looks like I have an opportunity to redeem myself." He pulled out his crossbow and aimed it at me.

"I'm here at Jackson's request," I immediately replied.

"You're lying."

"I'm here with Devin," I indicated. Devin shook his head.

"He doesn't know me. He's from Markai." Ah, yes, how could I forget with the crossbow aimed at me. He truly didn't believe me. Two of the others were getting ready as well, but one of them remained on the ground, seemingly aloof. Kevin shot the bolt at me. I blocked the incoming bolt with Telekay and ran towards him to close the distance. In doing so, I sensed a presence trying to attack me mentally. It was a strange feeling, as I could feel the pressure but almost couldn't sense the mind behind it.

Kevin turned to the one who remained. "Stop," he said simply. The remaining person looked distantly towards him, and then turned his head. The strange mental presence shifted continuously. Sometimes it felt like it was receding, and other times it would come forward again. It was hard to describe, almost as if it dispersed into the air at times. Kevin probably wanted to beat me on his own merits and asked the telekinetic zalphic not to intervene. Still, I could not help but be distracted by the strange presence I felt. "Now we continue what I left undone." He stepped forward. I could hear the clash of swords behind me, but I couldn't spare them a glance. It might be my undoing if someone finished their fight and snuck up behind me, but I had to focus on my own battle first.

Kevin sent another bolt. This was saw aimed at my shins, but I lifted my leg in time and jumped to the side with the other. He quickly got a blade out while roots sprouted from the ground and wrapped around my feet.

Kevin hadn't used his zalphic abilities much the first time. He didn't seem as adept with them as Nikko had been. Still, the roots wrapped around my feet would be a problem. I didn't have much time to think of more. Kevin swiped with his blade. I held Telekay in a weird position and blocked as well as I could. It blocked the blow, but the awkward angle and the position I was in made my wrists hurt all the same. I made a stabbing down motion with my sword and kicked with my leg to get as much momentum against the roots as possible. This was sufficient to break free from them, and I scurried backwards.

I was off balance and didn't manage to get off the ground. Kevin aimed his crossbow at me. I looked up at the steel tip of the bolt and imagined it piercing my skull. There was too much I still had to do. I gripped Telekay harder in my left hand, gathering its strength, as I prepared to unleash my powers.

Kevin shot the bolt and I *pushed*. With all the strength I had, I pushed the bolt backwards with my telekinetic powers and repelled it back towards him. My arm felt like it was almost going to pop out and leave my body with the force of the forward momentum. The bolt struck Kevin on his head, knocking him down to the floor. It didn't seem to do more than just daze him. Too much energy had been used to reverse the motion of the steel tip, so it didn't have the speed necessary to do more damage.

"Well, this is quite a familiar scene, isn't it?" The presence entered again, wanting me to stop. How did I know it wanted me to stop? There was no telepathy. There was no substance. Somehow there was so much emotion though. Kevin was out of his daze and looked a little confused, as if unsure why I hadn't killed him. The emotion was strong, hard to resist. I wanted to do it. I wanted to strike down with Telekay and move on. It wasn't him who did it, but he was keeping me from Jennifer and Aurora. He needed to be punished.

As strong as these emotions were for me, they weren't enough. This emotion exuding from the other presence was overwhelming. It was aglow with passion that I couldn't match in my current state. I couldn't risk letting my guard down. I couldn't let the emotions distract me from what I had to do. But the thought of stabbing him now filled me with dread.

Aurora. Jennifer. Kesara. I need to do this for them. I grabbed Telekay and stabbed downwards. The fight with this overwhelming emotion was enough hindrance. Kevin recovered and rolled out of the way. I moved to intercept his motion, but a strong telekinetic force pushed me away. I looked at the one who remained on the ground. He was no longer aloof, but he had not gotten up nor did he prepare to fight. He looked mad and scared.

Still, his presence was *off*. "How are you doing that?" I asked. He looked confused.

"Pierre doesn't understand language well, but that isn't important," replied Kevin. If that was true, why did Kevin tell him to stop? And why did the strange man stop upon his request?

9. Retrieving- 157

Instead of giving further explanations, he shot another bolt. This time, he moved immediately after sending it flying. I dodged the bolt and sent a pulse wave towards Kevin. He moved out of the way, and it flew past him and towards Pierre.

He was angered by the attack and immediately lashed out in my mind. With telepathy, it mostly transmitted words, and with some training you could grow to transmit ideas, without having to expand on them too much. What Pierre was doing was slightly different though. The emotions were overbearing. Perhaps he didn't have the rational functions I was familiar with—or better put, ones that I could understand—but he still had comprehension, and he was transmitting it through his emotions.

And the emotions that struck with blunt force were those of displeasure. He wanted to stop the fighting. He diverted the path of the pulse wave to the ground and kept pressing into my mind. It was fear and anger mixed. It was indignation. A bit of sadness. There was no telepathy as I recognized it, no words being formed, but I was beginning to understand what he wanted to transmit. I was hurting him. Genuinely hurting *him*, and he would stop me if needed. He didn't want to stop it. He didn't like it.

Pierre was still on the floor. Kevin approached with his sword. I turned my attention back to Kevin and intercepted the strike with my sword. A blunt force struck me from behind, and Kevin swung once more with his sword. I blocked with Telekay, but then Kevin took his free hand and punched me in the ribs. It was devoid of most of the strength since I had been pushed into him and he didn't have much space to wind up and gather strength. Still, it hurt.

I set up a telekinetic barrier to my right as I saw another blast coming from the corner of my eye. I didn't know when Pierre had sent the original blast. His mind and his presence had receded, so I mistakenly thought I could focus solely on Kevin. I wasn't keeping track of my surroundings like I should. Kevin and I were still closely entangled, so I punched back and prepared to continue striking.

Kevin swung his sword once again, and I blocked with Telekay yet another time. The physical attack was accompanied by another mental one. Pierre was upset that we were still fighting. The mental attack was unexpectedly strong. Not for the first time, I found myself wondering how he could possibly be so strong and be like...*that*. I assumed telekinetic abilities would be related to the strength of the mind. It was often the case that strong-willed individuals could fight back against mental assaults with ease. Yet, somehow, Pierre was exceptional. Kevin's attacks also made it more difficult to contend with.

"Stop," he said once again. Pierre's attack began to subside again. I risked a quick glance, and saw that Pierre was directing a confused glance towards him. Well, it wasn't much different from his normal gaze, but it's what I imagined. Kevin made a circular motion with his hand. I thought he was preparing to use his zalphic powers, but Pierre copied the motion. Soon enough, a ball of telekinetic energy formed on Pierre's hand. This seemed to distract Pierre now, who made an excited noise and started bouncing it back and forth between his hands. "Let's go." I ignored it the first time it happened, but now I couldn't help but admire his strength. He didn't want to fight unfairly. Maybe he was trying to prove himself. Or maybe there was some other driving force. Regardless, he wanted to beat me. *"Honor will get you killed."* I thought sourly about the oft-repeated words.

Kevin pushed forward with his blade, and I parried his blows. Between strikes he quickly pulled out the crossbow and shot a bolt. When did he have time to reload it again? The distance was too small, so I teleported to the side and managed to avoid it. My body was becoming stiff, but I reminded myself that the pain and slowness were nothing. This wasn't about me. This was about Aurora and Jennifer. They had taken Aurora, and nothing would stop me. Jennifer would return unscathed, but the same would not hold true for those keeping me from her.

I swung Telekay and Kevin swung his sword in response. Before the swords made contact, I stopped the motion of the attack and prepared to block the sword. Upon making contact, I used telekinesis to keep his sword in place against Telekay. He sensed the pull on the sword and grabbed a bolt with his left hand. He went to stab my hand with the bolt. Instinctively, I reached out with my right hand to protect the left hand that was holding Telekay. My right hand gripped the steel tip, so the tip cut my hand open, and blood quickly covered the bolt. My hand was stinging with the pain, but I did not drop it. I dropped my sword and used my free hand to grab hold of his other hand. Then I used telekinesis to control Telekay and slashed Kevin's wrist.

Kevin dropped his sword, and I kicked Kevin on the chest, causing him to back up. As his sword was falling, I used a final spurt of telekinesis to readjust its position. I turned it point first towards him and launched it forward. In the same moment I swung with my left hand, and materialized Telekay into my grip. Both swords made contact at the same time, and he fell to the ground before the strength receded from me. I could feel the sweat. Black spots sporadically appeared in my vision, as everything began to blur. Kevin fell to his side with his sword still stuck to his stomach. Some of the bolts from his side also pierced him. The life of his mind was no more.

Telekay once more fueled me with that strange telekinetic force that gave me strength. It was still far from over. I turned to Pierre, but then heard a cry to my side. "Please, no!" I turned as Roy stabbed the one Devin had been fighting. I turned to the one Roy had been fighting but saw that he was already dead. I couldn't formulate any thoughts on the matter before Pierre let out a cry of his own. The mental attack hit the three of us with abrupt force.

Pierre had tears in his eyes now, and a deep sadness in his gaze. It was hard to tell what had changed in his eyes, but there was something different. I didn't know what I was expecting, but Pierre's genuine reaction made me faulter. Roy approached with sword in hand. "No!" I exclaimed immediately.

Roy barely turned to me. "They're stopping us from reaching Aurora." Devin blocked his path.

"No more," he said, with a shaky breath. Roy turned to me, and when he saw I wasn't agreeing with him, he nodded in assent and sheathed his sword. Another hammer of force struck our consciousness as Pierre lashed out. I would need to calm him. If he could transmit emotion, I could too. I just needed to convey to him that we wouldn't hurt him. That he needed to follow us. I reached Pierre's mind and found a wasteland. It was so strange and different from anything I had encountered before. There had always been a sense of identity pushing back, a natural force of that could sense an intruder and wanted to fight him off. With Pierre, there was nothing. It was a strange environment, not much different from the surrounding air. Hotspots of emotions outlined his consciousness instead. *Peace.* I tried to transmit. *Placidity.* I tried to get him to accept. *Positive.*

I failed.

There was only darkness. Small lights were shining in the distance, but they could do nothing to dissipate the ever-present darkness. It shrouded everything. The light seemed to flicker on and off, and there was a weightlessness that lessened the toll on my legs. It seemed I was levitating, or somehow not standing fully on the surface of the ground. The muscles in my body stretched and contracted, begging me to test the distance I could travel. The lights moved suddenly. Some flickered away, a few grew in intensity, but most flew past me, leaving only a streak of white light. Millions of lights swarmed past as I traversed the darkness, but none gave me respite from its embrace.

As I travelled, the lights continued flying quicker. I saw a familiarly strange blue sphere with various other colors tarnishing its purity. The sphere rotated rapidly, going faster and faster with each spin.

Again, I travelled, and more lights became blurs. I saw two avian creatures flying towards one another. It was the two largest predators known: the direhawk and the fellcondor. The smaller of the two, the direhawk, approached the fellcondor with great speed. As the direhawk approached, it took on the color of polished metal.

The direhawk dug its talons to the fellcondor. The latter simply screeched its reply before turning into the same silvery, metallic color. The direhawk circled the fellcondor, but the fellcondor was still unfazed. Again, the direhawk attacked with its talons, but the fellcondor swiftly moved and avoided the claws. In a precise counter, the fellcondor ripped out one of the direhawk's talons. A bright light seemed to emanate from the direhawk now.

Again, the lights blurred past me, and I found myself in the forests of the Lancaster Lands. There were some subtle differences. The shade of green, the size of the trees, the way the light produced shadows and mixed with the life seemed slightly different. The fellcondor was circling around a nest, filled with eggs from a direhawk. Simultaneously, I could see from another spot in the forest that the direhawk circled the fellcondor's nest. The fellcondor, the stronger of the avian creatures, did not attack the direhawk's nest, and instead left it alone. The direhawk, however, cared little and feasted on the eggs of the fellcondor. The direhawk tried flying away before the return of the fearsome creature. It kept watch of the skies in search of the bird.

Before it managed to fly away, a shadowcat pounced on the direhawk. The direhawk gracelessly fell to the ground, still alive. The direhawk was bleeding, and the shadowcat approached. The cat leaped towards the bird, but the direhawk flew and little and used its sharp talons to close around the shadowcat's throat, until it no longer struggled.

Everything seemed to go in reverse, and I could see the bird imparting life into the cat. The cat released the bird into a nest so that it could fly freely. The bird lovingly repaired the damaged nest and placed eggs in the mended home. The scene played again, and the bird ate the eggs. The cat jumped and scratched at the bird, but this time, the cat unexpectedly stopped. Instead, it was now clawing at something invisible in front of it.

I wasn't sure how Pierre had done that. We were all in the same positions we had been in. I turned to Roy and his look confirmed that he had experienced the same thing. Pierre lay on the ground, apparently lost in thought—or whatever his mind did. He might be too unpredictable to leave alone. Perhaps Roy was right in his initial impression.

I looked at him on the ground. He lacks the cognitive process I have. He does not know what he's doing. The loaf sat there, not knowing what was happening. That made two of us, I suppose. I couldn't bring myself to end it. I tried again, hoping to reach out and help him see what I wanted him too. How much of it was my doing versus his nature, I could never know, but Pierre then relaxed. I indicated to him that he should follow, but he didn't seem to understand my desire. Failing that, I decided to try a simpler approach. I generated telekinetic energy into the shape of a torus. I hoped the roundness would still evoke the playfulness of the ball he was bouncing earlier, but that the whole would add new intrigue that could keep him entertained.

He reached out plaintively to the torus, and I gently gave it to him. He began spinning it, having it go around his fingers. While he was playing, I got him to stand up and started spinning it around my fingers as well, before returning it back to him. We walked down the road, continuing our path in manner. It wasn't as fast as I hoped, but Pierre absently walked down the path and played, so he didn't diverge from the road or slow us down unnecessarily.

Eventually, we caught sight of the other group. They were moving slowly and didn't attempt to hasten upon catching sight of us. The group flanked a slow-moving stagecoach which seemed to have no worries. I hastened upon seeing them, afraid that the stagecoach would burst into high speeds when we were near. No such concerns were valid, as they kept their leisurely pace until we reached them.

"Brandon," Roy said, immediately recognizing one of them. His facial features seemed vaguely familiar, but he had Korscher features, and there were not many people with those around. He had been part of our studies at the Wise Ones. "Brandon, I'm sorry." Brandon turned to Roy but did not respond. "I know I should have done something. I'm...," Roy trailed off, not wanting to repeat vain words. Brandon took out his sword. Roy seemed reluctant to respond with the same gesture. Were they close friends when Brandon was still a member? Curious as I was, a cry of pain caught my attention. I tried running to the stagecoach, but some of the other members of their group raised their swords and stopped me.

"Let her go and live or fight me and die."

"There is no need for that," Devin began. "We were sent here by Prince Jack."

"We're taking the sick girl to Jior's Watch, and our contract ends there. You can do as you wish after. So long as you don't slow us down, I don't much care if you follow," one of them said. I was going to retort, but then I saw *Jennifer* peeking out the side of the stagecoach.

"Jennifer!" I yelled out. She smiled, and that smile alone made so much of the pain worth it. She turned back inside the stagecoach and gave me another faint smile when she looked away.

"What's going on Jennifer?"

"There's quite the story behind this." It seemed surreal to be speaking with her. I had spent so long thinking about this and seeing her again, but I had so many questions and I didn't know where to begin.

"Why are you here with them? Why did you take her?"

"I knew how much you cared," she said, with compassion in her eyes. I looked at the stagecoach, then back at her. "I knew I had to be here with her."

"Jennifer, thank you," I said lamely. I had no words to express the surge of emotions. She was taking care of Aurora because she knew how much I cared for her.

"I promised I would help them if they allowed me to travel with Aurora," she continued. I turned to the people waiting by the stagecoach. They were all paying attention to Roy and Brandon. Roy still hadn't drawn his sword. He would have to handle that situation himself. I walked towards her. You didn't have to Jennifer. I tried saying it, but the words died on my lips. Instead, I went up to her and hugged her. I didn't want to let her go. I hugged with a longing hunger for her warmth, taking in her smell and her stature and all the trivial things that would fill my dreams.

"I'm going to take you both somewhere safe," I said, still hugging her.

"We need to continue to Jior's Watch. It's better if she explains." She made a motion to the stagecoach, and I let go of her despite my reluctance. Inside was someone vaguely familiar, but I paid him no mind after I saw Aurora lying down. She looked *sickly*. This wasn't what I had imagined when I talked to Wyatt. I felt a need to attend to her and cure her. I cursed all the wasted time that had prevented me from getting here sooner. I put my head on her forehead, which was burning up. She had towels for the sweat, but it looked inadequate.

"Aurora," I practically whispered, as if a louder noise would hurt her.

"Steven," she cried out, tears immediately filling her eyes.

"It's okay Aurora. I'm here." I grabbed hold of her hand, comforting her as much as I could. "I'm here."

"Steven," she began again, afraid to say what was on her mind.

"It's okay Aurora. It can wait. Rest up, I'll get you help." This made her cry and she put her face against my chest. I got closer, trying to soothe her as much as I was trying to soothe myself.

"Steven," she began again with a trembling voice. I rubbed her hands, trying to calm her anxiety. I didn't want to interrupt her again, so I continued the comforting gestures until she could say what she wanted. "Steven, I have zalphia."

In an earth-shattering moment, all of time froze. Zalphia was not just deadly beyond imagining, it was death itself. It became hard to see Aurora with the tears that welled in my eyes. I couldn't believe it. I *would* not believe it. It couldn't be happening to Aurora. She was too young and full of life and full of energy.

Zalphia didn't care. In all their efforts, and the great strides the Wise Ones had made for all diseases, zalphia alone was untouchable. The foremost member of the Wise Ones, the Wisest One—who had brought about a veritable medical *revolution* decades ago that showed his brilliance with each passing year—even *he* could do nothing for his best friend's wife. Lord Hal Horus, member of the Committee of the Wise Ones, one of the foremost members of those looking for cures, could do nothing when zalphia killed his wife. No one ever survived. Everyone knew this. Aurora could not have it. I refused the information.

"Steven, I'm going to die."

Chapter 10
Runaway

Anger has a way of fueling someone with energy. The entire world seemed to work in a fallacious manner. There was no reason to act in an appropriate manner when life decided to be decadent and abandoned all civility. What debt did you have to life when it so cruelly plunged a knife to your heart? The revelation that Aurora was sick with a sickness not even one of the most powerful men in the kingdom could cure was *sickening*. My poor friend. She was a beautiful person who showed only love to everyone around her and shared kindness and warmth beyond measure. This same person did not deserve this. Save it for the ones who deserve to die. Fighting Jackson and Argus and whoever else I needed to, however infinitesimal my chances were of succeeding, had seemed manageable.

Zalphia was something else entirely. My arrogance and incredulity had me believe for just an instant that somehow, I could do something, and somehow, I could make a difference. I was smart, and I was almost certain I could do something. The sobering and cold logic quickly chained my thoughts to reality. I would never be able to save her. Lord Horus couldn't cure his wife, and he was an Elder of the Order of the Wise Ones. A member of its committee. Theoretically, he was among the three smartest in all the land. What hope had I to do something different?

As I ran my hand through her hair, I imagined no longer being able to see her, and hold her. I would never be able to run my hand through her hair. I would never be able to tell her about my day and count on the calm of her presence. I would never again hear her cute little laugh, never again hear her funny jokes and her teasing words of encouragement. All that would remain would be memories. She was my best friend, and I imagined the gaping hole that she would leave behind. This couldn't happen.

I looked at Aurora for a sign of hope. I quickly realized it was unfair of me to ask anything else of her. She was tired and sicky, and I could no longer keep looking. I turned to Jennifer, who had a melancholic expression. It was full of empathy.

I hated everything. I hated diseases. I hated the world. I hated whatever energy fueled this nightmare we call life. I hated myself for being unable and inept. Most of all, I hated myself for the cold calculations that would follow: a girl her again, diagnosed with zalphia, already developing these symptoms, and knowing that the old—who are unable to fend off diseases—tended to contract the disease, which would skew the mean time to mortality. This gave her a couple months under the best possible circumstances.

She couldn't die. No, this wasn't possible. Let it take me! I would gladly give my life if it spared hers. Something must be done. Anything. The Wise Ones must be meeting right now, trying to decide how best to counteract the disease. There had been a couple healers with Wyatt. They had seen Aurora. They would know what to do. So why were we here? Away from Faldenheim?

"Jennifer, what are we doing here?" I cried out in helplessness. The Wise Ones must have been working tirelessly to cure the disease. They would have a cure for zalphia. They needed to have one. We needed to go home and get her treatment.

"Jior's Watch is receiving a shipment from Whaldo's Port. It has medicine that will fight off the symptoms for a little while." For a little, she said. No, it had to be a cure that would permanently resolve all her issues. "It's the closest shipment. From there we go to Vernatia. Bravania should be sending some more medication there." I squeezed Aurora's hand lightly. I tried remembering how it felt, but the emotion was too strong, and I could no longer feel what was happening. I was watching my body and saw my hands mechanically stroke her hair and hands. I watched from afar as I swiped at the sweat with the towels and gave her any relief I could. I found there was nothing to talk about. Addressing the disease was too difficult, and conversing about any other topic would diminish the horrid revelation.

Jennifer and the other person stepped outside. I heard parts of a quiet argument, but the stagecoach began to move once again. We needed to get the shipment of medication. The Benders had taken Aurora to help her. I didn't want to think about the reasoning, and instead tried to focus on Aurora.

She was tired and quickly went to sleep. I remained by her side. Roy peaked his head in, observing Aurora's state. He had worry written across his face, so it must have been hard for him too. He seemed to try and detach his gaze from reality. If he was successful, I'd have to ask him how to do it. He didn't say anything, and rather just kept staring and taking it in. I was glad he didn't say anything, as I couldn't have spoken. After a moment, Roy retired as well. I felt powerless as we continued the slow trek. Days passed in this manner, though it seemed a weird mix of a slow slog and a sudden instant.

I went in to talk with Aurora as much as possible, usually answering her questions regarding what I had gone to done in Bravania and what I had been doing recently. I knew she was just trying to keep me talking so I could distract myself. I told her about Jennifer and everything that had happened, while she continued asking questions. I could only hope it was giving her as much comfort to hear me talk as it was for me to talk about anything.

Most of the time, though, I spent walking outside of the stagecoach and letting her rest. Jennifer spent most of her time in hushed conversations with Brandon and the other one who had been with them. Devin and Roy noiselessly walked along. When we reached Jior's Watch, we went directly to ask about the shipment of medication. The mercenaries accompanied the other man who had been in the stagecoach when I had arrived. He provided payment immediately and without further delay, we returned to Aurora and gave her the medication. Zalphia had adverse effects upon exposure, but then usually lay dormant for a few weeks before finally shutting down the body. I had been unsure what this medication was supposed to accomplish, but since there was no better path forward, I hadn't questioned what it was when Jennifer said it was to fight off the symptoms. The medication itself was nothing special, just a generic—though expensive—suppressant. The money that had been provided for the medication was not unsubstantial.

"We've fulfilled our part," began the mercenary leader.

"You'll receive the final portion of your payment upon returning to Farendor and reporting. We have secured passage and will follow the Serpent's River up to Haernaveh." They were given their dues and sent on their way back up the road.

We followed the river and headed towards Haernaveh. We sped up the journey this time around, trying to get there quickly. Aurora was asleep longer due to the medication, but she was no longer having night sweats and was generally looking healthier. Devin spoke about the necessity of getting to Vernatia and reporting back. As we were getting closer to Haernaveh, we saw more and more people walking with supplies, heading to various villages that lay around. It was then that I saw a girl resting by the road. She was coming from the city's direction, but she didn't seem to have any supplies. I would have expected her to purchase supplies or materials, or if she was selling something, I would think she'd have something to help her carry her goods there. Instead, she was empty-handed. Something seemed wrong.

She didn't have a sword, nor a bow. Could it be small concealable weapons, so she wouldn't attract too much attention? She also seemed too uninterested in us. Why wouldn't she show a little bit of curiosity? *"Roy, that girl up there, I think she might be a sentry or something. I'm not sure though. She isn't a zalphic but be prepared in case she tries something. Devin, are you expecting anyone to keep an eye here?"*

"No. I wasn't planning on coming here to begin with. I only decided to follow this way to Vernatia after hearing the situation.

She's not with us." Roy nodded and we continued walking past the road. Roy was on the right, putting himself between the girl and the rest of us. As we walked by, I politely turned my head to her, said hello, and turned forward again. We continued a little before I heard a scream of pain and quickly turned towards her, my hand on Telekay, ready to jump into action.

Roy had stabbed her with his sword, and without pausing further, he went to catch up with the group. I turned around, making sure no one else was in sight, in case she hadn't been alone. I got closer to the stagecoach, for some reason feeling the necessity to draw closer to it to protect its occupants. Brandon drew his sword, and the other one quickly drew his sword and made sure Jennifer was behind him. To them, it must have all seemed so strange.

"I warned Roy that she was looking suspicious. Did she pull out concealed weapons?" I asked, turning to Roy.

Roy did not reply immediately. I think he must have had something else on his mind, but then he said "yeah, she was about to strike. I acted in accordance." Then he nodded and gave another strange gesture. I was more concerned with continuing forward to help Aurora. Brandon didn't sheath his sword.

Even if she couldn't have gotten the word back, Argus would know something was wrong, and when they found she was dead, they would know we came in this way. For now, we had to continue.

"You're killing civilians by your own hand now? I had thought you just let others do the killing." Brandon's words confused me. Civilians? We had just explained that wasn't a civilian. Brandon approached and swung his sword. Roy drew his sword and blocked it.

"Brandon, I'm sorry about what happened. I couldn't do anything back then. You know I couldn't." It seemed whatever had been bothering Brandon was finally coming to the forefront.

"It's your fault she's dead!"

"I'm sorry."

10. Runaway- 171

"Your commiserations won't bring her back."

"What happened?" I found myself asking.

"Expect no help from him when things turn dire," Brandon spat. He continued glaring at Roy, who in turn made no signs indicating he would tell me. "Are you too *scared* to tell him Roy, as you were too scared to do anything? You wouldn't want others to judge you, *surely*."

"I'm not afraid to be ostracized," Roy finally said. "We've all had to grow past that fear early on."

Brandon scoffed. "As if that were the worst of your crimes. You *are* afraid. That's why you didn't say anything when they were killing her."

"Did you want me to tell them I was the zalphic, not her? I couldn't do that. I'm sorry it hurt someone you cared for, but I wasn't going to volunteer that information."

"I didn't just *care* for her. I loved her."

"She didn't know you!" Roy responded in frustration. Brandon remained quiet, seething with anger, but not responding, as if Roy was right. "She didn't know you were a zalphic," he began, softly. "She would have formed part of that mob, filled with all their vitriol had it been someone else."

"You don't know her like I did," Brandon cried out. "She would have understood," he continued, with shaking breath.

"She wouldn't have. No one could."

"Because of people like you Roy. That's why they don't trust us."

"I wasn't the one who branded her. It was the zalphic hunters that did it."

"You were the one who lost control! You used your powers and let them all believe it was her. Do her cries haunt you?"

"You know what would have happened if they discovered I was a zalphic. They would have still killed her."

"And despite that, you chose to be indiscreet."

"She was the one searching out conflict."

"Is that what you force yourself to believe, to maintain a free conscience? You began the fight, not her."

"She instigated," Roy said, under his breath. I wasn't sure if he didn't believe, or if he simply didn't want to tell Brandon. "I really am sorry," he said, louder this time. "Perhaps I should have helped, regardless of the consequences. Maybe I should have thought about a way to help or thought about anything more I could have done to contribute. But those feelings wouldn't have changed what I did. I would have done the same thing now as I did then." Brandon took in his words.

They seemed harsh. I didn't exactly know what was happening, but they had given quite a vivid retelling. There had been a few zalphics discovered by zalphic hunters throughout the years. Naturally, I avoided those events altogether, lest someone discover I could move objects with my mind. The repercussions were swift and unyielding. The dying flower, the crumbling mountain, and the erupting volcano. Those who weren't zalphics thought we were different, and therefore their enemy. Some zalphics thought it a curse, others a blessing, and few as an opportunity to use the powers of nature to further their causes.

Jackson and Argus surely viewed it as the latter. They likely only saw power that could be harnessed. I wasn't sure what I thought about it myself. Like most others, I thought it was a curse, before I developed those powers myself. Even then, I had lived a sheltered life with my parents, and I hadn't seen firsthand the terrible change in demeanor others demonstrated when confronted with us. I couldn't remember ever seeing the death punishment dealt out, though I knew it had happened around me.

"I had to abandon her," Brandon sobbed out. "People knew we were close. They were scrutinizing me, finding monsters anywhere they could." Brandon couldn't continue talking. I wondered if that was why he had left the Wise Ones. Roy couldn't respond to that, and just stood there like the rest of us. Brandon put his sword away. In the palm of his hand, he ignited a flame. The fire surrounded his whole hand, and exploded in a ball of energy as he clenched his fist. He did this a couple more times, with the final time releasing a decidedly orange glow. Benjamin's fire had never taken that color before.

"You were my friend Roy," he said, sadly. "I trusted you. I supposed I was misguided."

Brandon threw the ball of fire at Roy. I had practice against fire zalphics due to my brother, so I knew the heat would be a bigger problem than Roy might initially believe. Even away from his direct trajectory, I could feel the intensity of the blazing attack. Maybe I had failed to account for Benjamin holding back. Brandon wasn't afraid to hurt Roy. Roy launched thunder, which went around Brandon's fire and continued towards his direction. I put a barrier in front of the stagecoach Aurora was in. The barrier went up in time for the scorching heat to disrupt my senses. It felt like I had been burned, and now smoke filled my vision. Eventually, the smoke cleared.

"That you were," Roy responded. He didn't make further moves to attack. "Let them continue Brandon. We've held them up enough. This hasn't any relation to them."

Brandon turned to me. "He seems concerned with not troubling you. I don't have to wonder why that is." He quickly glanced towards the stagecoach and back to me. Instinctively, I wanted to get between him and Aurora, afraid that he might do something to her. "You're right on that account. We've wasted enough time, let's continue." Brandon turned and continued down the road. Devin was also anxious to continue.

"That was an intense interaction," began Devin. I nodded in agreement. "Listen, I need to warn you Steven," he continued, in a hushed tone. "You are still under the command of Prince Jack." I turned to him, confused. "He doesn't want the Benders to run off with Aurora. He might decide we need to take her away once we reach Haernaveh." I didn't really have any plans on what we would do once we reached the city. Aurora's diagnosis had been eating away at me, and I hadn't had many other thoughts outside of it. Could I let the Benders continue with Aurora? They had taken her to get medication and seemed to care what happened to her—at least long enough for it to benefit them.

"Prince Jack needs to prepare for Nevil's arrival, and this business with the Stephensen's could interrupt that."

"Why is Nevil so important? What is Jackson trying to accomplish?"

"Prince Jack and Prince Argus are currently working together to prepare. They're fighting over the best method, but both agree that having you develop your powers is an important safeguard. I haven't been told too much other than that, just that your powers are essential to his arrival. I can't give you much more clarity about that matter. I'm confused myself why they seem so desperate for your powers, when they have other telekinetic zalphics with much more refined abilities. Perhaps they are desperate for a chain of zalphics that can relay information, much like the Teltecs."

I was surprised that Devin didn't know. He had been ready to share plenty of information with me, but I didn't think much of returning the favor. Devin didn't know I had Invincibility. I realized suddenly that I hadn't even told Aurora. Jennifer might know, if that's something that she remembered before I severed the connection between our minds. Devin seemed to be trusted with a lot of information, but they hadn't told him. I wondered who else would know. Argus and Jackson would want my powers to develop, so they could learn what Invincibility could do. Who else had they told, so that they could also help me develop them?

Devin mentioned my powers were a safeguard. Were they truly hoping my powers could defeat Nevil's army? Why were they so reliant on them? I would be unable to make such a drastic difference. The jump between fire and telekinesis was not so vast, so I knew the gap between telekinesis and invincibility would be limited as well. It was still fun to think that it could. No one knew what it could do, so its only limitations were imagination. They couldn't know what powers I would manifest. Neither they nor I could know what difference my power could make until I developed them. I looked at my hands, as if they would suddenly decide to manifest great power. I created a small ball of telekinetic energy, and then it dissipated. I tried doing something with my other powers, but nothing happened.

"See, nothing special. I'm not sure what Prince Jack has in mind." I didn't say much after that. I thought about his words, thought about what I would do when it came time. All that mattered was that Aurora was okay. I could let nothing compromise that.

We finally reached Haernaveh, where we went straight to the Wise Ones. We asked them about any medication that could suppress her symptoms. We were only able to purchase a limited amount in Jior's Watch, as they needed to replenish their own depleted stock. The price the medication had fetched was extremely large. There was certainly a bribery fee hidden in that cost. Now we were all out.

They indicated that no such medication existed. I asked them if they could do anything for her. Was Aurora still in the initial sickness phase? Would she go back to that sickly phase once no more medication was around? Or had it pushed her to the phase where the disease receded temporarily?

Frustratingly, they did not have the answer. They knew little about the interactions themselves. It was to be expected, but nonetheless, I felt annoyed. They quarantined her and asked Aurora about her condition. She gave soft and concise responses.
"Steven."

"Benjamin? You're here?" I asked, confused.

"I came after some moron who decided to go to Bravania to mess with someone much stronger than him. And now he finds himself in another mess. Sound familiar?"

"I see you talked to Maximillius while I've been gone."

"Something like that. Where are you?"

"The sick ward."

"Are you okay!?" he asked with concern.

"I'm perfectly fine."

"*I'll be there shortly. Stay there Steven.*" He ended the telepathy before I could express any further concerns. My hearing focused back to the questions as Aurora continued answering their questions. They grew despondent and saddened by her answers. It angered me that they had given up so quickly after hearing. Shouldn't they have the desire to be the first to treat it? Instead, they told me I needed to let her rest, so I promised I wouldn't keep her up, only stay by her side and keep her company. I also felt that she had been doing too much resting, but I thought it would be odd to argue that point. No one knew what she needed. How would Benjamin react? It didn't seem like he knew about Aurora. He had immediately asked if I was the one that was okay. How would I tell him? The prospect filled me with renewed dread. I had been avoiding the thought and denying the truth. Telling Benjamin about her disease made it real again. How do you tell someone about impending death? How had Aurora done it? She was always so strong. I grabbed Aurora's hand a little tighter, in awe of her strength. How was it that she was stronger than me in this situation? I had grossly revolved her sickness around me, and the effects it would have on me. What about her psyche? What about the great weight that she'd been bearing?

Jennifer walked in, alone for once. "How are you—" she began but cut herself off. The banal question greetings did not fit the situation. She also didn't say that it would be okay. Was I glad that she wasn't lying? Or would I resent that she didn't even attempt to?

"You wouldn't believe it, but I've been better," Aurora said smiling. The joke choked me up a little more. I couldn't quite figure out the emotions, so I did the only thing I could. I deflected from Aurora entirely.

"Benjamin will be here soon," I informed them both. Jennifer seemed to stiffen a little. She laughed nervously before answering.

"I don't think your brother likes me too much." It was probably true. Of course, I wasn't going to admit that to her. My brother was just concerned with my welfare though. His feelings towards her were more a reflection of the situation rather than his feelings towards her as a person. His feelings towards her were likely neutral. Even in my distraught state, I knew that wouldn't be very reassuring.

"Most people don't see it. They think he's uptight like that. But it's not true. He doesn't dislike you. He's just very protective of his family."

"He'll get used to you," Aurora said. "You'll see his capacity to love deeply for those around him. This one gets it from him." She gave me a warm smile. I got flustered.

"I should leave you two, I just wanted to check on you," Jennifer said, getting ready to retreat.

"You should stay," Aurora said on my behalf. I saw Jennifer had her doubts, but Aurora continued. "You don't need to say anything. Sometimes, it's enough you're there."

"Thank you," Jennifer said, understanding immediately what Aurora was saying. She sat with me in silence, her head on my shoulder. Aurora knew exactly what I was thinking when Jennifer was going to leave. I had shared my mind with Aurora. She had been the second one.

When I discovered it was possible to tether minds, I knew that Kesara was the person with which to do it. She was my sister. I had thought that the first time was the hardest, and it would get progressively easier with others. As any power, I assumed it would be easier through use. I knew Aurora was a great candidate to be the second one. It's not that she *wasn't* a great candidate, but I had mistaken the nature of the power, and it had resulted more difficult to go through with her. I was still able to finish the tether though. I didn't have to stop it, like I had with Jennifer. I thought about how difficult it had been with Jennifer. Still, I had experienced so much with her. Although it hadn't been long, I had grown closely attached. They had been quite extreme circumstances. Important people had been searching for us in the Lancaster Lands.

"Overanalyzing everything as usual, I see," Benjamin's voice mocked. I turned to my brother, feeling relief. He was always there to protect me. Maybe it was misguiding and irritating at times, but his intentions were always s honest and pure, and I couldn't help but admire his resolve. His red cloak was a reminder of his strength. I wondered for the first time if that was an intended consequence of the uniform. I had always assumed it was to help identify them as servants of the Kingdom's wishes. He turned to Aurora, on the bed. "Is everything alright Aurora?"

She shook her head. "I'm sick". *Sick.* If that wasn't the understatement of her life...I traced her hand out with my thumb again. Benjamin understood it was a bit more serious than that. I think he was about to ask when he noticed the other person was Jennifer.

"What's she doing here?" Before anyone could answer, he asked her, "Shouldn't you be with Jon?"

"I don't know," was Jennifer's only reply.

"Is that why Devin is outside?" Devin's warning nagged at the back of my mind. What would happen if they wanted to take Aurora somewhere? How would I act?

"Jennifer has been protecting Aurora."

"Protecting her from who? The other Benders?" Answering that would not give the reassurance I wanted.

"Ben, Jennifer has been here to help me with the hardest time of my life." Tears welled up in my eyes as I turned to Aurora. Benjamin respectfully turned to Aurora and stood quietly. "Ben, I have zalphia." I saw the same confused and incredulous face I had when I heard it the first time.

"Aurora," he began, but he was at a loss for words. "I'm sorry."

"We're all doing the best we can do." Benjamin's eyes unfocused for a moment. It was something no one else would have noticed. Someone was using telepathy to communicate with him. That sort of communication never brought good news. Devin walked in shortly after.

"I'm sorry to interrupt. Ben, Steven, we need to get going." I turned back to Benjamin.

"What's going on?" He didn't respond. Was it Aurora's news that had him so stunned, or was it the telepathic he, and clearly Devin, had received? "What's going on," I repeated, this time out loud.

"We need to make our way to Bravania." He turned to Aurora, afraid to say the next part. "Aurora needs to be there."

Chapter 11
Realization

"Aurora is sick." Her last few moments shouldn't be spent going to Bravania. That part I could not say out loud.

"The shipment to Vernatia was re-routed back to Bravania. Any hope you have will be there." I gripped Telekay hard. I wanted to kill him. I wanted to cut out his tongue so he could no longer speak false hopes. He did not believe it would help, and he didn't care what would happen to Aurora, he was just trying to manipulate my feelings to get me to go along.

"I cannot let you take her," Jennifer said, getting between Devin and Aurora.

"I won't leave Aurora's side either," Roy said. I hadn't even seen him come in, but he got close to Devin, ready to act in an instant.

"Do I not get a say in this?" asked Aurora. I felt ashamed by the question. I had assumed I knew what was best for her and responded immediately. "I will not live out my life afraid of this. But my life is not my own. I need to see my parents. I need to go back to Faldenheim. Even if there's no medication to be had."

"Aurora," Benjamin started, "your parents were here. Now I understand why they came in such a rush."

"They're here?" Aurora asked.

Benjamin shook his head. "*Were* here. They're already making their way to Vernatia. They flew on the fellcondors to Haernaveh. They're going to make it to Vernatia within a day."

"Either way," cut in Devin, "everyone is heading to Vernatia, so there's no harm in going there now." I saw Wyatt Stephensen in my mind, and his unwavering dedication. He would stop at nothing to make sure Aurora could be cured. More things were making sense, but I was still confused. He had asked the Benders to help him with Aurora. This seemed to conflict with what Lord Horus wanted. Why?

They prepared for Aurora to receive medication at Jior's Watch. Had the mercenaries returned to Farendor to give a report to Wyatt? How much convincing would it have taken to use the fellcondors? What obscene amount of gold would have been the necessary payment? Even then, they must have flown extremely hard if they caught up with us in Haernaveh and overpassed us. Had they underestimated how slowly we would be travelling due to Aurora? Surely, they would have decided to meet in Haernaveh if they knew. Still, it was clear that Wyatt would be taking his daughter to Bravania. It was the only place with even a sliver of a chance to save her. "Please take me to Vernatia," Aurora said.

"Let's go." Jennifer ran out quickly. She was likely getting her group so they wouldn't be left behind.

"Devin, Steven isn't going to leave her side now. We can report to Logan and meet them on the road."

"Logan?" Roy grimaced.

"We'll see you on the road. Do not stray from there," Benjamin said, not acknowledging Roy's remark.

"We need to take Pierre with us." They grabbed Pierre and went back into the city while the rest of us went east.

As we walked further, we came across a fork in the road. There was the road that followed the Serpent's River, and went to Vernatia, and there was the road to the south that went towards Danika. A group of travelers were coming our way from the road to Danika. The group seemed very familiar, and as I went forward, I saw that part of the group was composed of the travelling group we had joined to Bravania. It was Ferdinand—that boy with the power of wood, and some others, whose names I couldn't remember. They all seemed absorbed with something though, talking to the other members of their group. I saw Jennifer stiffen at the sight of one of them. Her companion also reacted to seeing him.

I couldn't recall much from the time we had shared our minds—when we failed to do so, I should say. I didn't know who she was hiding from, nor why. As our groups crossed, we saluted one another. Jennifer was nervous.

"Jennifer, I'm so glad to see you!" The young boy ran up to her and hugged her. After that, he turned and saluted the one who had been with Jennifer the whole time. "Claudius," he said in greeting, and gave him a friendly handshake. He looked at me, trying to discern something. His group kept walking, not waiting for him, or even acknowledging us beyond the initial salutation. The boy was maybe around Kesara's age.

The group had no insignias identifying him to any orders, but he was clearly a Korscher. He had a big smile, clearly happy to be reunited with the two. He must have been close with Jennifer, but I didn't know who he was. During the tethering process, I saw a kid I hadn't met before. I couldn't recall exactly what he looked like, but it seemed he could be that little kid, a little more grown up.

"Kyler," Jennifer replied. "I'm happy to see you too." She seemed troubled to see him though. I couldn't imagine what it was. Was she just worried that he was travelling? I looked at me again. I didn't want to prolong any silence, so I jumped in.

"I'm Jennifer's friend. Are you two brother and sister?" Is that why his face had been so prominent in those few moments? I was certain about it now. I didn't need a response. "Kyler Atkinson?" At this, both Kyler and Claudius gave me a strange look. Jennifer's face showed panic as well. I furrowed my brows at her, confused.

"What do you mean by Atkinson?" asked Claudius. I wasn't sure what they meant.

"You're her brother, right?" I asked, addressing Kyler. He nodded. "Jennifer Atkinson?" It came out as a question. Somehow, I had been misled.

"She and Amy—Jennifer, what is he talking about?" Jennifer avoided my gaze. "My name is Kyler Bender. That's my sister, Jennifer Bender." I turned to Jennifer, my heart completely dropping. Anxiety filled my stomach as I processed what he was saying. I didn't know what to say. I turned to her, hoping this was all a misunderstanding. She would have *told* me. It would have come up. I had asked, hadn't I? About her family? How well had I really gotten to know her? How much had we really communicated? She couldn't possibly be a Bender. She couldn't be one of them.

Jennifer got between her brother and me, and I didn't know what to do. I felt betrayed. She hadn't told me. I wanted to get angry at her. I envisioned Jaquelyn, with all her beautiful Telk features, but slowly she would turn into Jennifer. I sent a telekinetic blast in frustration. It wasn't really aimed at anyone. It was more of an outlet for the building rage. A wall of earth met the attack.

"Who is he Jen," asked Kyler.

"Jennifer," Claudius said, with a quiet, seething rage. "Tell me this telekinetic zalphic, with Telk features, is not who I think it is." Claudius had his hand on his sword.

"My name is Steven. Steven Mc.Roy." Jennifer held Kyler as he tried to push forward. Kyler was angrier still than the others had been. I looked down and saw my hand had turned red from balling my fist so tightly. I moved my hand to the hilt of my sword.

"You're Steven!?" Kyler exclaimed. I didn't know what to do, so I nodded. He took out his sword. Claudius did too. I turned to Jennifer. Her face reflected deep pain. Kyler and Claudius knew of me. They knew I had killed Amy. Of course, in the grand scheme, it wasn't only Amy I had killed from the Bender family. It was all of them. That had been me. All of them except Kyler. "You killed my sister. You killed my mother. You killed my father. You killed my brother. And now I will kill you." I looked at Jennifer, still not believing that she was truly a Bender. Kyler lunged forward with his sword, but I moved out of the way. He wouldn't stand a chance. Claudius was ready to defend. He watched carefully for any movement.

"Jennifer, why didn't you tell me you were a Bender?" I could scarcely recognize what I was feeling. Anger? Frustration? Betrayal? ...shame?

"Seeing you were so sad about what had happened to Amy, I had assumed the same feeling translated to the others. But I couldn't ask."

"Your mother *killed* Jacquelyn. I didn't know your mother, and still she *killed* her."

"I saw," she said. What had possessed me to tether our minds together? Had I been too overwhelmed by this? Is that why I had stopped it before I could register what I was seeing? I should never have done it. I should have never thought about it but against my better judgment, I had plunged forward. What the hell was I thinking? I heard steps behind me, so I teleported forward and turned around to see Kyler lose his footing, since he was expecting to find resistance. "You killed Amy first." It wasn't an accusation, just an explanation. Somehow, I would have preferred an accusation. I could yell back and unleash the tumult of emotions.

"I really was sorry about your sister. I was protecting myself. How could I know any better? But your mother killed an innocent. I was going to *marry* her, and she took her away from me." I fought back the sobs that were overpowering my voice. I couldn't fight back the tears though. I imagined Jaquelyn, her red blood surrounding her in a bright plea for justice. The red overpowered everything, and it disguised that it was really Jennifer I saw there now. "I never got to see her. I never got the closure. Your mother Jessica simply told me that she had killed her, and I never knew anything of her gain." I took Telekay out. Kyler swung his sword at me, but I parried it and was ready to strike back, but Claudius quickly stepped between us, and then a chunk of earth rose and hit me.

"Stop this, Steven."

"You didn't stop me from killing Kenneth." Jennifer's pained expression lost all composure. She couldn't believe I had just said that. Nor could I. I had blurted it out, not conscious of the things I was saying. She turned, reviled by my presence and ashamed by everything that was happening. Kyler yelled out in anger and came around the slab of raised earth. There was a plethora of different things I could have done. I could have knocked the sword out of his hand. I could have moved out of the way. I could have teleported. I could have likely stopped his attack with my telekinetic powers alone. There were so many things I could have done, could still do, as the sword approached. I parried it, but then used my free right hand to grab the sword. And withdrew it, and I let the sword cut my palm.

Claudius had come around after and was in position to defend Kyler. I let the sword go when Claudius moved his sword between us. The pain felt good. Deserved. Despite my anger, I knew I had gone too far with my comment. I could never take it back. The pain took away from my guilt, but it was not nearly enough. I would lose her forever. I thought I could be happy with her. I had fantasized that we could be together in this crazy world of pain. She had been the one to raise my crushed hopes. She had been everything I wanted. For her troubles, it fell to me alone to bury it. This was not the full retribution owed unto me. The red liquid slowed my thoughts. I was doing too much of that right now. Claudius was still ready to strike, and Kyler was not going to give up. Through the surge of emotions I was feeling, the pain felt right.

I sheathed Telekay and used my powers to fight back Kyler's next attack. I turned to Jennifer to plead silently with her, so that we could leave and go our separate ways. Before any more pain befell us. She was not looking. Kyler struggled forward, but my powers kept him at bay. Claudius still never went on the offensive. I saw the hatred in his eyes too, but he was too skilled to let that distract him. They could probably kill me if they attacked together. But Claudius couldn't let himself be blinded like that. His priority was protecting Kyler, so he didn't risk going on the offensive and being out of position to do so.

"Kyler, come here." We turned to Jennifer.

"Jennifer, you can't ask us to leave. He killed our family," said Kenneth. "You're going to let him leave?" Jennifer didn't say anything.

"I won't hurt him."

"Wait...him?" Claudius interjected. "Is that why Jon didn't want to come? You can't be serious Jennifer. After everything he has done?" Again, I felt a stab of guilt. It had been me. I was the monster. I looked at the bloodied palm. It screamed in pain, but it was not enough. Jennifer didn't say anything in response.

"Jennifer. This is over. It could never be."

"I thought... I thought you could make anything possible."

"I thought I could trust you. We were both clearly mistaken." I turned to Kyler. I recognized the look. It was the same eyes I must have had when I faced Kenneth. The same look I had when I had confronted his parents. What would Jacquelyn have thought? I breathed out heavily. I gazed back and saw that Roy had backed up and taken Aurora a safe distance. I was infinitely grateful for Roy's instincts. I hadn't noticed him move her at all. Aurora is what I would fight for right now. I would dedicate everything to her.

"He cannot leave Jennifer. I cannot allow it. Take your brother with you and leave. I will take him myself. I am honor bound to do so." Claudius spoke with conviction, not pride. If he was honor bound, I had a feeling I knew his story better than I had realized. He was an Atkinson. The sardonic humor of life had made it so Jennifer herself would tell me all about it. The two families were always the greatest of allies since the Great Shaking. Claudius Atkinson would never let this go because it was his duty to protect the Benders. He was Kyler and Jennifer's bodyguard. He would be strong.

Caught up in the fervor, Kyler rushed. I looked at Jennifer pleadingly once more. "Claud, stop him." Claudius did not listen. He moved forward, still prepared to defend Kyler. I teleported out of the way. This time, Claudius swung his sword. I materialized Telekay in my left hand and parried. He was much more skilled than Kyler, and I was backing away and trying to stay on my feet.

I released a pulse blast. Claudius was well-trained and didn't think about dodging the attack. He slashed at the same angle and absorbed the rest of the hit. Behind him, Kyler continued forward, unaware that Claudius would have normally moved out of the way of the attack if he didn't need to protect at the same time.

The ground around me rose. I prepared to jump off, but then it suddenly disappeared below me, leaving a pit where I had been standing. I teleported to stable ground, but Claudius had followed the direction of my eyes and quickly descended on me with his sword. I was out of position with the teleportation, so he knocked me to the ground.

Quickly I sent a wave of telekinetic energy behind, towards Kyler. Claudius tried to intercept the energy, but I had done it too quickly after his maneuver. Jennifer raised a slab of earth to block the energy, but by that time I had backed up and gotten back to my feet. The slab of earth broke into pieces. I used my telekinesis to pull the bits of rock towards me. Claudius saw from the corner of this eye and got close to the ground as Jennifer made everything stop. The bits of rock stopped before they could move further. I stopped trying to pull and teleported forward with a stabbing motion. Claudius still had one knee on the ground from when he was taking cover, so rather than block the attack, he rolled left. I didn't expect him to do it so quickly, and Telekay stabbed harmlessly through the air.

Until it didn't.

I had been facing Claudius the entire time and hadn't even noticed that Telekay stabbed Kyler. Where had he been? I had lost him when Jennifer had raised the ground to protect him. I didn't think surprise had time to register on my face. I didn't mean for this to happen. Everything was happening so suddenly, and just as quickly it had escaped my power to control. Jennifer's wail of agony pierced everything inside me. Claudius was wide-eyed, the shock already reaching his face. He might have seen at the end, after he had rolled. Perhaps he had registered what was about to happen before I even knew Kyler was there. What had I done? Claudius jumped towards me, ready to unleash his fury.

I closed my eyes and heard the clash of steel on steel. I opened my eyes and saw Infernus in front of me. Benjamin's caster metal sword stood gleaming and protecting me. I heard Aurora run forward, and Roy telling her to stay back. Jennifer let out another cry of pain and ran towards her brother's body. This wasn't supposed to happen. Why was this happening? No...this...I couldn't believe it. I couldn't have caused this. Jennifer's tears drowned me in sorrow and guilt.

"What happened?" I asked Roy and Aurora, too numb to say anything out loud. Aurora didn't say anything. What had she seen?

"Kyler thought to use the debris as cover. Claudius didn't see that Kyler had moved forward. He thought he was still further behind. Or maybe that he had finally backed off after realizing he was holding Claudius back. When he rolled, we all saw that Kyler was running forward. You could see his surprise as Claudius dodged."

I had been too focused on Claudius and hadn't seen Kyler among the debris. I hadn't known that he was there when I tried striking Claudius. It was the only opening I had really had against him, so I went forward without hesitation. I had no idea Kyler would be there.

"You monster!" Jennifer was not at the body, holding her brother. There was nothing I could do to make this better. I kept silent as Claudius backed up. She was right. A wall of fire separated us, and Benjamin soon pushed me away. It couldn't stay like this. But Benjamin pushed me forward and I had no strength to struggle against him. How could this be how I left? How could I leave it like this? I looked back. Claudius still had his sword drawn, watching every movement we made. Brandon was by their side now. The smoke began blocking my view. All that was left was the hazy outlines of shrinking people as we went further away. When the silhouettes had become unrecognizable, I turned around and faced forward. If I saw Jennifer again, it wouldn't be her eyes I'd be looking at. It would be the cutting edge of a sword called revenge.

We arrived at Vernatia in a daze. None of us spoke much throughout the trip.

"Where do we go?"

"We need to go to Bravania. We should take her to her parents though. She should be safe with us, but that's what I imagined on your way to Vernatia." He trailed off, realizing it was a little insensitive. A few more words wouldn't hurt me any longer.

"You speak as If I'm not here," Aurora reprimanded us.

"You're right, I'm sorry."

"Do you know where they'll be?" I asked both Aurora and Benjamin, hoping one of them would know.

"They'll be waiting at the Wise Ones. They were supposed to receive the shipment of medication, so my dad would probably be there, setting everything up." That's where we went, and sure enough, Wyatt and Lily Stephensen were waiting impatiently for their daughter to arrive. Naturally, they received her with hugs and kisses and fretted over everything. We left the small family to reunite and enjoy their company.

"We'll be ready to accompany you to Bravania when you are ready." It seemed Roy wanted to stay, but he also felt he was intruding, so he joined my brother and I out. Benjamin led the way into the city. "Where are we going?"

"We are meeting Jack and Logan."

"No," Roy said immediately. "You can go ahead without me. I will be here waiting when you come back."

"I was expressly told to bring you along, Roy," Benjamin said, uneasily.

"How do you plan to force me?" He said it more to himself than as a challenge to Benjamin, but either way he didn't move.

"I'm just a soldier. I do what I'm told." He was lying.

I wasn't sure why I had been so blind to it before, but Benjamin knew a lot more than he was letting on. He wasn't simply a Knight serving his home. I had come to expect the deceptions from Jack and Argus, but not from my own brother. Benjamin wasn't guarding any of the nobles of Faldenheim. He wasn't serving Faldenheim. He was serving *Jackson*.

"Why do you want us to go to him?" I asked defiantly.

"I need to know what we're doing next. Or did you think you'd walk all the way back to Faldenheim now?"

"You're serving Jackson." It wasn't a question, and Benjamin knew it.

"Yes."

"After everything he's done to me?" No, I suddenly realized as I looked at his guilt-ridden face. *Before*. "How long have you been serving him?"

"Steven, that's a complicated question."

"You said you would protect me. Here I am, struggling to stay alive because of someone you serve. What a strange notion of protecting you must have."

"You know that everything I do is for the benefit of our family. Father and mother weren't safe, whether you were at home or at the inn. They would have discovered who your family was eventually. I needed to join Jack and protect everyone."

"Jackson has been trying to kill me!"

"Stop exaggerating. You know as well as I do that no harm was going to befall you. He wants you alive, he wouldn't risk your death."

"I know that now, but I didn't back then. You'll forgive me if I don't see how that helps his past actions."

"Steven, I've been protecting our parents, and I've been protecting Kesara and Gideon.

"You betrayed me. I trusted you."

"Steven, you're not capable of trusting anyone. Not when it really matters. You fail to think about others in a manner that doesn't ultimately concern you. I'm *protecting* our family much better than you could. Whether you see it or not is no longer my problem. You could ask our parents how they've been doing—that is, if you ever bothered yourself enough to visit them without immediately taking off with Kesara." There were further emotions that I wasn't grasping, but I didn't stop to consider the circumstances that were leading to the outburst. Perhaps if I knew what they were, I might agree with him. Instead, his response only served to elicit from me the same emotional response, loaded with the same contempt and haughtiness.

"Our parents think you the perfect child, so much more considerate and lovable than I could ever be. But let me tell you that you are far from their portrayal of you—they love the idea of you, but you spend just as much time away from them as I do. You're simply the one who tries to win their love with gifts from Jackson."

"For a member of the Wise Ones, you are so deficient in any *useful* knowledge."

"It must sting that I was always far smarter than you."

"I think I should leave."

"I'm sorry Roy, we shouldn't air out our grievances in front of you."

"That's not what I was referring to," he said, drawing my attention to a large group that was approaching. At their head, was Jackson Horus. I recognized Dart, and further away from them was Devin and Pierre. The two closest to Jackson, however, I had never seen before. I sensed that one of them was a water zalphic, but he wasn't a member of the Wise Ones, or the Order of the Sword.

"Steven let's get away from these streets. Roy, it hasn't been long enough from your perspective, I'm sure, but I'm sorry to insist that you come as well. You'll need to hear this." We walked towards the keep, where Lord Kingston was housing him. We went to a lavish room. The tables had been moved to the edge of the room, so that there was a lot of open space in the middle.

"Tell me, how are the powers coming along?"

"Terribly." He expected more and stared at me silently. "Luckily I don't need to develop those powers to beat you." I smirked. "Beat" wasn't the word I wanted to use, but I thought it would be prudent not to threaten a prince inside of a keep, even if he weren't really a prince and this wasn't his keep.

"Benjamin is strong, one of the best in my employ. You, though, still have a lot to learn. Just like the rest of your family. Curious how all of you are zalphics isn't it? It comes from your parents. Did you know that's where you all get it from?"

"What? Mother and Father aren't zalphics." Why would they have been so terrified when they found that I was one, if that were the case? Why would I have to learn about it by myself if they knew? I didn't want to believe him, but I saw Benjamin's look. He knew something I didn't, of course. Could this be true? I knew Kesara and Gideon were zalphics. My telekinetic powers allowed me to sense other zalphics, even if those powers were dormant, like Roy's telekinesis. My parents couldn't be zalphics. I hadn't felt anything. I thought of Pierre then, and the strangeness of his mind. His was a much different circumstance, but did that not prove that it wasn't so clear? I thought then of the constant medication my father took. He had always taken them, every day, without fail. It had been so since I could remember. Lately he had been worse, taking in a larger supply.

Could that medication have been some sort of variation on engrims? It could have been something capable of suppressing not just his powers, but the aura that my telepathy sensed. If they were able to completely suppress them, it would stand to reason I would be unable to detect them. I came back to my original thought. If they *were* zalphics, why did Benjamin and I have to learn about this world by ourselves?

"Mom isn't a zalphic," he said, confirming my thoughts. "I told you. I did all this to protect our family." He could tell himself what he wanted. This wasn't how brothers acted. He shouldn't have hidden this from me. He had looked after me all my life, that was undeniable. He risked his life and ended up being treated by the Wise Ones for me. That, at least, had been real. Yet, I couldn't focus on those good moments. Through all the adversity I had faced, he had known all along.

"We really should hurry this along," the water zalphic beside Jackson urged. Jackson nodded his head and approached me.

"You're right. Let's move on. Steven, this is about your sword. It came from the Telks; I'm sure I didn't have to tell you that. It's a sword fitting for the representative of Khisharat. I'm sorry to inform you, but that is not you, Steven. You are not its representative." Representative? What was he talking about? "The shadowcat is the king of the Telk forests. Khisharat, then, is the king of kings. He is the king of those creatures, and only the rightful representative can wield the sword properly. I'm sorry to say, but I cannot let you wield it any longer. Nevil is approaching faster than I imagined, and I need everyone to be ready." He held out his hand, and Telekay made its way towards him. I reached out, trying to stop him with my powers, but he was effortlessly overpowering my resistance.

I made it materialize in my hands, as I so-often had done, but this time it did not obey. It continued inching closer to Jackson despite my efforts. "I'm not giving you Telekay. It is mine," I said, still fighting back.

"It is not for me," Jackson replied, with no further details. "Have you ever tried to use telekinesis on Infernus?" Jackson asked. It was a strange question, but I couldn't let myself be distracted. "It doesn't work when the sword is where it should be. That's how I know it doesn't belong to you. Which brings me to the reason you're here." He turned to Roy. Jackson pushed Telekay to Roy's direction, hilt first. Roy didn't understand how to properly react, and he reached out and grabbed the sword.

I tried pulling it free now, but it felt inert. Normally, Telekay was so full of power. I could feel the energy it exuded, and often it would help replenish my strength. I could no longer feel it. I tried pulling it, but it was as if the sword weren't there. When Jackson was pulling, I could feel his strength holding it at bay, but now I could feel no force pushing against me. It just wasn't possible. I tried pulling Infernus, and the same thing was true. There was nothing to pull. I tried pulling the other sword Roy had, and this started moving easily.

"There's your rightful sword, Roy." He stood there unsure of what to do; he looked at me equally confused. The sword disappeared and then reappeared in his hand. The metal still shone, but now it had a distinct shade of dark purple.

"That is my sword," I answered. "I'm the one who went to Telkos to get it. I'm the one who cared for it for years. The Telk descendant said I could keep it, since I was the one destined to have it. I will not allow you to take it from me like that. You must be doing something to keep it from moving."

"You're subtly changing his words. He said you could keep the memory for the one destined to see. That's quite different. The rightful owner has supreme power over Telekay, and it is clearly not you. It goes to the Khisharat." I tried moving Telekay again, but there was still nothing for me to pull. How was he doing that?

"What do you mean he's the Khisharat? That's a myth from a civilization that died long ago. They have nothing to do with this."

"You can call it a myth if you wish, but its power is real and that matters more than anything you believe. Each of the ten representatives has a destined sword. I thought you would be the Khisharat and arranged it so you could learn about Telekay and recover it. It seems I was wrong on that account, but there are still more swords and more representatives to be found." He looked meaningfully to Benjamin and Infernus. I didn't much care for deciphering his hidden meanings, but this look was clear enough. Benjamin was one such representative. "We still need to find over half of them: Oceana, Rebirth, Strife, Spark, Forester, and Talon."

I ignored what he was saying for the most part, but the bit about "arranging" it so that I could find Telekay caught my attention. I underestimated how long he had been preparing. He intended me to get Telekay. There was never a doubt in his mind that I would serve him. Why did I need to care so much about these invaders? What if they were better leaders? I thought sourly of letting everything fall to them.

I would never serve Jackson. I gathered a ball of telekinetic energy in my hand. Before I could grab much energy, the water zalphic lunged forward and went for my throat. I tried materializing Telekay, but no sword appeared in my hand. A barrier wall of telekinetic energy appeared before me and absorbed the blow, though the barrier shattered as a result. A hollow ball of water surrounded me and immediately it filled with water. The water started filling my lungs, and I had to force myself to stop panicking. I was getting lost in the ocean of blue, but then the water retreated.

"He learned his lesson; I think you can put that away Logan. You too Benjamin." Roy still seemed prepared to launch an attack. Roy made a slight movement, but then I heard a loud screeching noise. I moved my hand to my ear, reacting to block the noise. "I said you were done. You are not safe to have your squabbles here." Roy still looked poised to strike, and I heard the screeching noise again. Where was that coming from? It seemed to only affect me and Roy, as none of the others seemed to react. Was he invading both of our minds and creating that sound? When it stopped, I realized I was on my knee, covering my ears. Roy was also trying to cover his ears.

Jackson had never done that before. I had never heard the screeching sound he produced. He kept reminding me that he was stronger. I was not nearly strong enough. I looked at him with renewed awe, and a bit of fear and hatred. It renewed my previous conviction. I could not serve him. Once I developed my powers of Invincibility, he would not be able to do that to me.

Jackson looked at me with what I thought was pity. He sent a telepathic message, and Pierre approached. "Go ahead and read his mind Steven."

I did as he asked before I realized I should have refused. I felt Pierre's deep connection with Jackson. Hadn't they just met? It was strange to feel how much Pierre cared about Jackson. There was so much positive emotion associated with him. It was hard to remember that I was supposed to hate Jackson. "You're controlling his emotional state. Making him think he liked you."

"I'm not making him think anything Steven. This is what he thinks." What did he mean by that? Pierre didn't truly think. Jackson had clearly overpowered Pierre with his zalphic powers and was controlling him somehow. "I'll leave you to consider everything," Jackson said. He indicated to Benjamin to follow him, and they all left, leaving Roy and I alone.

Roy turned to me immediately. "Here," he said, holding out Telekay. My first impulse was to reach out and grab it, but Jackson's words were annoyingly ringing in my ears. I couldn't feel the sword anymore. The one destined to see it? Is that what the words had been? Jackson should not have known the words transmitted to me, yet somehow, he did. It was meant for Roy to see, not me. He would have to see what I had seen. That meant I would have to let Roy read my mind to see the entire experience. But if I couldn't even remember it fully, how would I show him? Perhaps the measures needed were worse than I believed....

"You heard Jackson, that sword rightfully belongs to you now. It has chosen you." Hopefully the words didn't come out as sour as they did in my head. It was infuriating, but it seemed Jackson was right about this. "Besides, it would probably teleport back to your hands or something." Giving up Telekay hurt.

"I wasn't the one who did that," argued Roy. He opened the hand that wasn't holding the sword and closed it. As it closed, the sword teleported from one hand into the other. Despite expecting it, Roy's hand twitched a little at the sudden movement. "I'm sorry," he said, drawing the sword close to him. I didn't have any words to say, and then he looked down at the sword he had before and offered it to me.

Telekay, one of a few Caster metal swords, forged with the claw of Khisharat, the mythical king of the shadowcats, in exchange for a plain sword. Seemed fair enough.

"There might be a different sword for you," Roy reminded me. He was trying to lift my spirits, but I just wanted to wallow in misery for a bit. "He seems to think you still might be one of the other ones. I'm not sure I understood everything myself. I feel like I'm missing the context."

"You and I have the same amount of context. I'm equally confused." The conversation trailed off. I wanted to ask him about Logan, and why Roy had been so determined to strike him. I really didn't want to discuss any of them further though.

"What now?"

"I'm not sure. I feel like the best I can do is to be with Aurora."

"Let's go," Roy added eagerly. We made our way back. I wanted to give Aurora time with her parents, so Roy and I waited outside the room, standing guard. From that large group that had brought Aurora here, only Roy and I remained with her. There was something almost humorous about that, though I couldn't describe what exactly was so amusing.

They were in the room almost all day, until finally Wyatt stepped out of the room and informed me that they would be taking the fellcondors to Bravania the next morning. He was determined to get here there without losing any more time, and he expressed confidence that she would be able to handle the rough journey on them. He was talking through more details, but they were slowly being drowned out by a commotion from outside. The noise drew nearer to us, and finally Prince Argus Kingston, accompanied by Prince Jackson Horus, appeared.

"Prince Argus," Wyatt saluted, with a slight bow of his head. "Jackson," he continued, with no such movement.

"Wyatt," Argus answered, "we've heard some unfortunate news regarding your daughter."

"Had I known what it was, I would have stopped at nothing to aid you," Jackson added, with surprising sincerity. It was baffling to see him like this. He seemed truly apologetic.

"We didn't know what it was for certain until recently. Please, come in." Wyatt led them inside. I was going to follow, but a man in a blue cloak barred the entrance after Wyatt and the two Princes entered. A Bladesman of Vernatia.

He stood guard while they talked inside. I couldn't hear anything from outside, but there were no loud sounds, and no yelling occurred, so I took it things were going better than my previous conversation with Jackson had gone.

After a few minutes, the door opened, and they left.

"What did they say?" I asked Wyatt.

"They were expressing...their condolences." His voice wavered. "Please keep Aurora company. I must finish those arrangements," he said, stepping out.

I went back in to talk with her.

Seeing her made my mind spiral even more. I wondered what would happen now. I was losing too much. Aurora was sick with a deadly disease. Jennifer thought I had maliciously killed her brother. Benjamin had betrayed me. And now Telekay was in the hands of Roy. It was the least of my troubles, but it was what made it all too heavy a burden. What was next? Kesara? That could not—would not—happen.

"Steven," Aurora said gently. My eyes focused on her. They first focused on the piercing gaze of those two purple circles. Aurora's face came into form from the blurriness. She didn't need zalphic powers to read my mind. Everything I loved was being taken away from me. What will I do when she isn't here anymore? She hugged me. I didn't know why being in the arms of someone who wouldn't be able to do anything was so calming, but I let the touch relax me. I would deal with it later, but for now, Aurora was here, and that was enough.

Chapter 12
Civilizations

I looked out from the window, and the moon shone with magnificent splendor. Midnight was nigh upon the world, and the moon blanketed everything in a luminescent glow. The stars complemented it majestically, creating an intricate masterpiece. The planet Bystra outshone the surrounding stars, preparing to perch in its spot in the Castle constellation. None of the other stars complained about Bystra's glory; the stars continued shining and providing a backdrop to Bystra's zenith.

I thought about home. My parents loved looking at the night sky, getting lost in its spectacle. Would they be looking at these same stars tonight? Were they aware their two eldest children were fighting? Or like most things, did the immensity of the world drown out the small, insignificant moments?

"I know you're a zalphic," I imagined saying. How would father react to the confrontation? Would he deny it? Would he explain? "I found out you were a zalphic through *Jackson Horus* of all people. Not you, not Benjamin. A stranger." Was that partly my fault? Had I been so caught up in my own world that I hadn't dedicated the time to speak with them? When could they have told me about our grandparents coming?

I remembered, now, that Benjamin had news to share with me. Maximillius told me he would share the news when he saw me. I didn't give Benjamin the chance either. Maybe father had wanted to tell me. He would say he didn't have powers, at least not exactly. I could imagine him alluding to the medication. Would he say it outright? He wasn't a zalphic like us though, and his world would be so much different. I'm sure he would describe it in the context of a disease, subtly different in use from the way everyone else said it, but still in the context of a disease. He would say he was a carrier, one with dormant abilities perhaps.

He wouldn't have known what to teach us, or what to say. But why, then, did he panic upon discovering us to be zalphics? "Why were you afraid of us? When you discovered we were zalphics." Even in my imagined confrontation, I couldn't make him say the words I wanted him to admit. It's because you hate zalphics. Just like everyone else. You hate me. You hate us.

"I was afraid *for* you, not *of* you." Did I want to believe that's what would have been his reply? I teetered between the two ends. In my memory, I now pinpointed something I hadn't quite realized before. It was the expression on his face. I thought his face had grown haggard due to the medication and the sickness. Well, technically it *was* classified as one. It was the exhaustion caused by zalphic powers coursing through the body. I projected Aurora's exhaustion onto him, though certainly without the finality.

I thought instead of Kesara now. How would she have reacted to all the madness? She would tell me to forgive Benjamin and my parents. She would say that they loved us, and she harbored in them no ill will for the mistakes they'd made along the way. Well, she wouldn't have classified them as mistakes in the first place. She was always a better person than me, much kinder and forgiving. I wished she was here. She would have teased me endlessly about how desperate I was to figure out what was going on. "You can't know everything," she would say. "I can try," was my standard response. I needed to see her again soon.

I looked back to the moon, and in that moment, I felt connected to everyone else who would be looking at it. How strange that people across Andros, Telkos, Lancaster, and Korsch were looking at the same moon. How strange that people from the civilizations of old looked at it too, and the civilizations of the future would gaze upon it and wonder at all the life that had been captivated by its gaze. The invaders would see the same moon.

I thought about that vision Jackson showed me. How irritating it was that I could not trust him, and yet what falsehoods had he given me? I couldn't immediately recall one. Instead, he worried constantly about the ones who would come. Why was he so worried? I tried remembering what I had seen, tried to remember the words that were said. It was difficult to recall something that had happened so long ago. The same moon I had been looking at slowly turned to that strange sphere I had seen before. The stars faded away as the vision filled my sight, drowning all other senses. I was there, again, seeing the sphere, seeing the robed man with the strange proportions.

> *"I genuflect from under your presence.*
> *Presiding is he who's known as Nevil.*
> *In your genius, we go forth to sentence,*
> *We decree by the Kingdom of Seville.*
>
> *We must teach these people living in dark.*
> *I plead you and beg you not to delay.*
> *They're caught in darkness they view as stark.*
> *This disarray will not be thrown away.*
>
> *Claim the world to your ultimate control.*
> *The road will now return from its dark curve.*
> *Chaotic destruction to all but us!"*

I thought about the recitation. It sounded like Nevil was the leader of the Kingdom of Seville. They were kneeling to him, so at the very least, he was a high-ranking officer. He could be a commander for the Kingdom, rather than its King. At the very least, he sounded very competent based on the third verse. They were going to come to sentence us. What crime had we committed in their eyes?

Kingdom of Seville. I racked my brain, trying to think if I had heard of it. The name didn't sound familiar. Queen Lizer controlled most of Telkos. *"Most"* being the key word there. Multiple regions were resisting, from what I could recall, but they were more local resistance regions rather than an entire Kingdom that was opposing them. I couldn't remember what those regions were called, but Seville did not sound familiar, so I didn't think they would come from Telkos.

I wasn't familiar enough with Korsch, but I hadn't seen anything about Seville when I tried tethering with Jennifer. If anyone knew about potential threats from Korsch, it would be the Benders. I couldn't remember many of the details from that moment, but Seville meant nothing to me in the context of Korsch, and I believed that it would have registered at least subconsciously.

Was it coming from Lancaster? Could the Kingdom of Seville have conquered Lancaster, and ingested Timbergrove as its capital? Timbergrove was one of the three great cities, so it was possible that they could amass a strength large enough to alarm Prince Jackson and Prince Argus. They could have Caster weaponry, which would certainly worry them. They had stressed multiple times they needed my powers so we could fight them. Did they hope I could use my powers to kill Nevil? Or did they expect me to fight against their armies? Were they seeking out war?

The next group of verses were strange. They certainly kept *me* in the dark all the time, but it was strange to claim that we were living in darkness. What "truth" would they give us? How were we living in the dark? I didn't even know what darkness they were referring to, so to claim we viewed the darkness as stark was strange. *They* would be the ones who view our darkness as complete and severe. Maybe those were just some poetic liberties they were taking. How nice of them to liberate us from the complete darkness in which we live—one so dark we don't even realize it ourselves. I suppose everyone needs a justification for what they do. Without that reason, they're just people who are preparing to invade and kill others for the resources, and that would never do for morale.

But then the next verse supports that they believe in what they're doing. They will cause disarray. Perhaps it refers to the chaos of war. If they were to storm the Capital, we would be in complete disarray. Even then, though, the different regions are self-sufficient and wouldn't fall to disorder. Still, I take it to mean it will be panic due to their revelation and "freeing" us from the darkness. They might truly believe they will change our world, and the new knowledge can't be cast away.

At least the next one was self-explanatory. They wanted control, as most others did. I found it rather refreshing that they were clear about what they wanted in this one instance. They want the entire world, which was interesting. Even if they were able to conquer Andros, it was hard to believe Glavaus, *the* great city, would ever fall. I went back to my previous thoughts about the Kingdom of Seville. If they were so confident about their strength, and ability to conquer the world, why had I never heard of them before? Could they truly be strong enough to control it?

Then we have another mention of the darkness, and how they are going to liberate us from the darkness. It could even imply that we were not in darkness before, but had strayed into it, and now they would liberate us. Likely, though, it was just rhetoric. They would come to conquer. Chaotic destruction. They could attempt to disguise their intentions, and attribute nobility to their endeavor, but they were doing nothing more than declaring war and taking from the defeated. Just like everyone before them had done.

It felt more likely that the Telks would invade, and who's to say King Whaldo's reign wouldn't be any less oppressive? I didn't see why I should be more worried about Nevil than any other, real threat. What had that business about the representatives been? Ten representatives, each with their own sword? I reached for Telekay, before realizing it was no longer with me. It was with Roy now, who was supposedly the representative of the Khisharat. Would that mean Roy would oversee the Telk forces? I tried to think of a sequence of events that would lead to Roy holding power over the Telk crown, but that was nonsensical.

It was unlikely he was referring to ten civilizations that would each have their representative. Who would Benjamin represent, if that were the case? Something Jackson said came back to mind, though. One of the swords that was missing was Forester. Everyone in Bravania knew the mythos surrounding the Okran. The Lancasters had always lived in the forests, and showed profound respect to the creatures that called it their home. The ancients spoke of a legendary guardian creature. It was a massive four-legged beast with three horns on its head, a venomous tail, and a mighty roar that could tear off skin, until nothing but bone remained. It had a hard shell of bark protecting its massive form. The most significant aspect, however, was his ability to make the trees and forests grow instantly. It manipulated its surroundings to trap prey, or to conceal itself.

It was said that many foolish men had tried to slay the fearsome creature, but no normal swords could pierce its bulky figure. Only Caster metal swords could get through. One of the foolish hunters forged a Caster metal sword, intending to be the ultimate force. He called the sword Forester, and he managed to skin the sword into the back of the Okran. The venomous tail quickly killed the hunter before more harm could befall him, but the sword was now wedged onto its back, where it remained.

Would the Korschers have a representative? The Chordun had dug the underground tunnels that the Korschers would use when they lived in the mountains. What had I seen about the Chordun in those brief moments with Jennifer? The Chordun had reportedly found a sword during its many excavations and had turned to using it on occasion. It had been a Caster metal sword, named Smasher. Jennifer's sword.

Thinking about this was making me more confused. What seemed more realistic? That the myths of all these ancient civilizations would work together and fight off an invading force? Or that a misguided prince was trying to embed their histories and twist their words so that it appeared to align with his motives?

12. Civilizations- 205

Peering back into the sky, I saw the moon and the blue sphere, constantly interchanging, constantly flickering into one another. *The stars moved, creating a pathway to an unknown location. Turning to the ground, smaller stars directed me towards a path in an unknown mansion. I followed the stars and walked into a dark room with an empty portrait. The darkness was profuse, but the small stars helped navigate and illuminate the ceaseless void. Inside the room, I spotted Telekay. When I reached out to it, it shattered into pieces. Roy's old sword stood to my right now, while Telekay reassembled itself. I ran towards it, but it fled from my grasp and moved around the room. I couldn't catch it.*

I chased and chased as it led me through the mansion. The dizzying maze turned and transformed. A few times, I was forced to retrace my steps and return from my direction of origin, but the intersections of the hallways would be different. I chased it into another room that light could not enter. Despite its lack of illumination, it outshone the rest of the mansion. It was not my eyes that were detecting the glow of power, but something more primal.

I saw an empty portrait. Suddenly the portrait changed, and I saw an image of my grandfather, looking after my father. I had never met the man, but somehow, I knew his presence was in that portrait. His portrait, too, changed and merged from one confusing aspect into another, but all the time I knew it was always him. Then it transformed into someone I didn't recognize. The stranger's face overlooked the Lancaster Forest and stared directly upon that place I had found so much comfort in before. She looked extremely young, but her eyes told a lifetime of struggle she couldn't possibly have lived through. Her hair was the bright red of the Redimer people, far away from her home.

Then, the portrait transformed into my own visage. I looked into eyes that no longer held any hope. The haggard face cried desperately for rest from wicked reality. The portrait, now, seemed to turn into a mirror, as it reflected my surroundings. As I continued to stare, I began to disappear, and could only see the room behind me. Or was it now in front of me? As I continued to stare, I realized that I was now trapped in the portrait, looking out into the room where it was hanged. Lightning struck the mansion, and Roy appeared inside the room. Before him were his old sword and Telekay. I yelled at Roy to help me, but he couldn't hear. I was going to grab his sword—or my sword—it was all so confusing now.

"Choose your sword," I heard my own voice saying. "Choose wisely though." Roy looked around, trying to find me. I tried to tell him I was here, in the portrait, but no sound came out. He looked past it, but he could not see the portrait, or maybe he just couldn't see me. Finally, he grabbed Telekay. I knew that was what he must do. I was starting to believe it more, despite myself. He was the Khisharat. I still didn't know what that meant, but the evidence had seemed clear enough. Moreso, Telekay itself had shown him that it was at his disposal, and even that Roy needed the Caster metal sword.

I continued yelling out, but he still could not hear me. "Very well picked Roy," I heard my voice say again. "You must realize your power." Roy eyes shone and open, as if they hadn't been open before. I yelled again. "Roy, help! It's me, Steven!" The sounds did not carry through, but I did here a booming voice saying "Steven." Had that voice been mine too? It was getting hard to tell. I could no longer hear my inner monologue.

The booming noise startled Roy, and he looked to the ceiling and confusedly searched for the origin of the noise. He backed up towards the portrait and hit the wall. The strength of his crash against the wall caused the portrait to fall. The room quickly flipped, and I found myself falling to the ground, atop Roy. I fell, picking up speed incongruous with the distance to his head. Then, I heard a shattering sound.

The shattering noise roused me from the nightmare, only to awaken to a sky on fire. The world was bright, but I knew it was still night. A man came to me and stretched his hand out. I took his hand and rose to my feet with a gesture of appreciation. He

12. Civilizations- 207

handed me a sword, and when I looked at the man, I realized it was Jackson. I jumped back and sent a wave of telekinetic energy. He used his own powers to disperse it behind him, and then he attempted to invade my mind. I fought off the attempt easily, and he looked pleased at my ability to do so.

"Your powers are growing, and they will continue to do so. You are just starting your ascension. Both powers will carry you to exciting new heights."

I stretched out my left hand. The telekinetic energy surged wildly, like a hurricane of wind that dwarfed Highstorm and Strommen. The power knocked me down to my feet, but the other body was dissolved by the strength. A new voice filled my thoughts, screaming words that I knew I must remember and protect.

The others shall rise, and yet they will fall.
One by one, five shall surely die out all.
The ten beasts shall kill the adversary.
Nonetheless, the sacrifices carry.
Neither more nor less—might one surely laugh?
The great powers of the beasts, split in half.
The path straightens when the five of them die.

"Steven." I turned my head, searching immediately for my sword. I couldn't see anything. My eyes had been blinded by an immense light, and they could not focus on the darkness.

"Roy," I asked, based on the voice.

"Steven, there's trouble." I still couldn't see him, but I pinpointed where he was by his voice.

"What's going on?"

"I don't know. I can't see." It seemed I wasn't the only one. "I can't use them," Roy added. *Them.* I tried reaching his mind with telepathy, but I couldn't feel my own presence. I tried gathering a ball of telekinetic energy as well, but this also failed. What was going on? It wouldn't be good.

Chapter 13
Final Stand

A bright fire illuminated the sky. Lights of red, blue, and green muted the stars that surrounded them. I was able to see now. My zalphic abilities still seemed locked away. I could tell Roy hadn't recovered their use either, by the way he kept glancing at his fingers. I looked back to the lights, a veritable fire that consumed the sky.

"There's no way Nevil could do this. Surely not even an army of zalphics could accomplish this." I said it more to myself than to Roy, but the wonder escaped my lips before I realized.

"Who's Nevil? What do you mean? Why does it look like lightning of different colors is striking the sky continuously?" I liked my fire analogy more.

"It's time you knew Roy," I said, with panic rising in my stomach. "But something is blocking me right now. I'll show you when I can."

"What can possibly be blocking our *strength*." I feared that Nevil might have found a way to weaponize engrims on a grand scale. Was he coming, much sooner than we all realized he would? If he could block our powers, it would cause pandemonium among the forces of both princes. Engrims could nullify the effects of the Z mutation and leave us defenseless. It would nullify my powers, even if I were to develop the power for which they all hoped.

Eventually, the fire—or repeated thunder—began to die down. The dying fire seemed to have a shape, insomuch as all the other constellations had shapes. I couldn't pinpoint what it might be.

"Well, they're back," Roy said, referring to our powers. I was a little surprised at Roy's statement, but then I could feel them again. He was right, I could feel our minds again. "What's going on?"

"I need to show you something Roy. It's clear to me that you need to see all these things." I tried sharing what I had seen, but I could not recall it. I had travelled so far to Telkos, focused on all the thoughts that flooded my mind then, but I could not recall. What were the words Jackson had shown me, and what were the words from the nightmare I had just seen? I knew what they hinted at, but I couldn't recall the details.

As I feared. I had told myself I could no longer go through it. I had told myself I would no longer attempt it. "Roy, this isn't going to be a pleasant experience. We must share our minds. I need to tether yours to mine, and mine to yours." I saw Roy's expression change. I was glad he already knew the implications. Unfortunately, the expression also showed he would never do it. "I know your reservations. Whatever just happened here, it won't be the end, and I know you need to see these things." I could think of nothing to say to convince him.

"Absolutely not." I desperately tried to think.

"Roy, you know we have to do this." I directed his gaze to Telekay. It appeared in his hand. I could feel in his mind that his telekinetic abilities were still dormant. He wasn't doing that with zalphic abilities. He let out a long breath.

"I can never share these thoughts with anyone."

"I understand your reluctance. More than you may know."

"You do not want to understand this pain and these emotions."

I didn't want to. He gave me every opportunity to turn and run. I knew I had to forge ahead, despite my hesitance. "Sometimes you forget that we're all human and go through similar emotions. Some good, some bad, but all part of the human experience. It takes strength to be vulnerable, and very often, the very personal is entirely universal."

"Not this," he said, but I could see him consider the words. "I don't want to." Telekay disappeared from his grip. A pulse of energy touched my mind. It was the touch of the sword, the touch

I had taken for granted. I could see Roy felt the touch too. It reappeared in his hand. Roy gripped it and squeezed it. He started tapping his fingers furiously against his leg, digging deeper and deeper into his leg with every passing second. I let him process what he needed to, until finally, he muttered out his reply. "Very well." I prepared myself for what was about to happen.

His family, there were three of them. Mother, brother, brother. Thunder. Telekinesis. Telekay. So very much more: purple, yellow, the former darkening the latter. Predominant purple. A sword: Telekay again. The Telks. Him, as a child. The Wise Ones, taking him in. Torture. Studies. Brandon and his girl. HB. Losing his powers. Sharing a mind. *Could Aurora ever look at me like that? I never wanted to go with the Wise Ones. I hate myself. I hate my actions. I have—I hate the—I love nothing—I always wonder—kill.* I was forced into his life. My father was killed; I went to the Wise Ones. I still see him sometimes in the shadows. I could have done something, but I didn't. Just as I didn't with the girl. I live by fear. Fear of rejection, fear of incompetence, fear of failure. Why try your hardest? Just believe that if you had tried to your fullest, you would have succeeded. If you fail, it's because you didn't care to try.

I am the Khisharat, the legendary shadowcat of the Telks. Why me? I'm not much. I don't deserve this. Shouldn't Steven be the one? Telekay is now min. The land. I've seen Telkos before. I know where it is. My land. Telkos. A vision, so that I may keep the memory of the sword's origin, for me.

I do not feel the love. They are lying when they say they feel it. Right? How could they possibly care so much for people? Everyone must be faking.

Could I join that secret order? Would I be strong enough?

Pain. Pain, pain and more pain. Why would they do this to me? I am so small, so powerless. Why do they think I will kill them all? I am their prisoner. Logan, please stop. I am only a child.

Mercifully, it was done.

13. Final Stand- 211

I stepped away from Roy, tears in my eyes. He hadn't been exaggerating, he really was trying to protect me. It was worse this time around. It was so much worse. Too many times now: three, and a failed fourth. This was too much. I was losing too much of myself.

I came to realize how much more in common I had with Roy. He was very smart, very much more than I had given him credit for. As smart as me, even. Whereas I didn't worry about trying because I was confident that I didn't need to, he didn't try because he worried that he would fail. I recognized some of that fear in myself, so that I wouldn't challenge the confidence I had garnered. Both roads led to the same destination though, and I knew Roy had had a much harder life. It had shaped him in a completely different way; one that I could see myself following, under those circumstances.

I looked at him with this new knowledge, and I saw him appraising me with his. He never said anything. There was nothing more to say, we knew how each of us were processing those emotions now. I revisited our interactions. He was so quiet during our studies. He refused to comment. If the Wise Ones had a quandary, I wouldn't hesitate to give the answer, to demonstrate my knowledge. He would stay silent, and let me answer, but he always knew the answer as well.

He turned to the sky. "I've never heard of the Kingdom of Seville either. Word would have spread of their strength if they were truly so capable."

"If they didn't have the necessary strength, why were they so certain about invading?" Nevil and the Kingdom of Seville. Something was strange about them. There was also the matter of their disfigured people. Why did they look different? I caught Roy's look as we came to the same conclusion simultaneously.

"Could he really have an army of them?" Roy asked aloud.

"There have only been a few people with this power in *Andros*, but what of other places?" In some parts of Telkos, zalphic abilities were not met with the same disdain. What if Seville did not slaughter—what if they even *encouraged* zalphics to surface? They could have gathered Invincibility zalphics and trained them.

"It's possible that will be your fate," Roy said apologetically. "Each power has its repercussions. Such great power will come at a great cost." The powers kill us, slowly but surely. The stronger the power, the worse the effect. I wasn't sure if it was the tethering, or my own mind agreeing, but what he said was very logical. "How big a price would you have to pay to nullify others' zalphic abilities?" What pain would come from using the strongest power? I couldn't imagine the consequences of its manifestation. Is that what had really happened though? Was that the strength of the final mutation, a display on such a large scale as to affect all of us?

They wouldn't have sent a warning. They would have used it in battle and overwhelmed us. I considered the thoughts rapidly going through my head. "Allison is described as a beautiful young lady; there is no mention of a deformed body."

"She hadn't developed them by the time she ran away," came his answer.

"We are speculating wildly," I said. Neither of us knew what the Invincibility coursing through me would do. What if it was dormant, like Roy's telekinesis, and as such they had never, and could never develop? I tried puzzling out what the power meant for my future, despite telling Roy just now that it would be wild speculation.

"Maybe we should focus on your telekinesis instead. What connection do you have with the Telks?"

"I've visited their sacred land. I saw an ancestor of theirs with the power of telekinesis—he was quite skilled at it."

"Interesting," I replied, confused. Surely the bleeding effect of sharing minds had worn off my now. I knew Roy, and he knew me, but he shouldn't think like me, or confuse my life with his. That had never happened with Kesara nor Aurora. He hadn't had any connection with the Telks. I wasn't sure why I had really asked, but sometimes there was so much information, it was easier to just ask. Perhaps he really had gone through a similar experience.

"I am the Telk Khisharat," he said with confidence. I looked up at Roy. "There are nine more. Jennifer is the Chordun, and Benjamin is one of them too, leaving seven. If Prince Jackson is right, you'd leave six. That vision you saw...."

"Don't think about it. They are just words. They become true because we make them true, but if we try, we can prevent them. We can prevent this war."

"Steven, your sister—" Roy looked to the ground, ashamed. No, no, reject the thought. It isn't true. "We won't be able to sleep, not know what all this means." I couldn't help but admire Roy a little. Why hadn't I gotten to know him sooner? Well, I'd get caught up later. It seemed we were both determined to confront Jackson. Now all we needed to resolve was the small matter of how we would demand an audience of Prince Jackson while he stayed in the keep of Vernatia, somewhere we would not be allowed this late at night.

Up above, we watched as two fellcondors made their way southeast. Had Jackson left? Were we too late? We hurried to where the fellcondors were being held. Wyatt had mentioned that they would depart tomorrow. Had those been commandeered, or were they Vernatia's fellcondors? I wasn't sure how many fellcondors Vernatia owned. Faldenheim had four available to them. Had Wyatt brought one or two of them with him?

We saw a group that was being held just outside the entrance to the fellcondors. As we drew closer, we saw that the guards were arguing with Prince Jackson. Logan stood next to him. "I'm sorry, we have strict instructions not to let anyone use the fellcondors."

"They're *our* fellcondors. Wyatt Stephensen brought them here for our purposes." The guard wouldn't know he was lying. The two guards must have felt uncomfortable in their position. "Are you telling me that I can't take my own fellcondor? Are you prepared to hold Faldenheim's representative prisoner?" Jackson had a way of intimidating people, but the guard still did not let him through. "Are you prepared to be the one to begin this war?" This finally got the guard to relent. "Ready the saddles," he commanded, as they go through. We followed the group as they approached the fellcondors. The guards briefly glanced at us but must have decided we were with Jackson.

"Prince Jackson," Roy called out.

Jackson turned, and upon seeing us, shot the guards an exasperated look. The irony wasn't lost on me, but there were more pressing matters. "I really don't have time."

"All the more reason to answer quickly," Roy said. That was much better than what I was going to say.

"You might be useful," he said, a little unconvinced. "Help us saddle, and you can come." We hurriedly aided their preparations. I had never been so close to a fellcondor. The giant birds were fearsome I still did not understand how they managed to tame such a wild beast. Every time I got close to it, I hoped I wouldn't offend it and get pierced by its talons. Both fellcondors were now ready, and it only just occurred to me to think about who would be going. The giant birds could carry two people comfortably, and three people with effort. Jackson was currently with Logan and three others I did not know. "Fly with Steven and Roy," he indicated to one of them. "You'll have to fly back yourself immediately after we land."

He nodded in understanding and began to climb onto the bird. He turned to another soldier. "Tell Dart to bring the others and head immediately to Bravania at first light. You'll also have to deliver the news to Wyatt. I'm sorry about that part. Tell him we're going to send back the fellcondor and its rider will have medication for his daughter." He started running off, and Jackson called out to him. "Tell him I'm going to help in any way I can. Have Ben stay with them. Better him than an unknown soldier to help them through their grief."

Aurora. I was taking the fellcondor meant for her. Should Roy and I stay here, so that they didn't need to take two of them? They could leave one of them for Aurora and her parents. It wouldn't be

13. Final Stand- 215

right to take it. I didn't have time to think about it longer, because the one who had climbed the fellcondor was yelling at us to get on. Roy climbed up uneasily. Then I climbed, also feeling a bit of that unease. I still couldn't discard the thought that the terrifying bird would decide I was unfit to ride him. It stayed still, allowing me to climb up and secure myself with the saddle.

The fellcondor took off, kicking dust and dirt on the ground below. I felt the rush of wind and the chilling cold of the night. I hadn't felt the night's frosty bite, but up in the sky, it enveloped us. If only the sky was still on fire, maybe it could have heated us and protected us. Instead, I shivered and held on harder to the saddle. I hoped the exertion would help heat my body. Despite the cold, it was a truly remarkable experience. I never thought I would fly on one of these. Underneath me, everything grew small. I looked down on Vernatia, registering in my mind that this is a sight few would ever see. Like me, most would not think to dream about looking upon this kind of world. Atop the bird, I felt that I was also beyond all my worries and fears. I could no longer identify any of the smaller buildings. I flew higher and higher, and Vernatia itself was scarcely becoming visible. We still went higher and higher, until not even the keep could be seen, and there were only clouds below.

The air seemed to speak to me, as if I were meant to be a part of it. The air flowed through me, and I could feel it awaiting my commands. It was no longer siphoning my heat away. The bird flew faster, and the rush of wind excited me. The flap of its wings seemed to order the air to move aside, and I felt at one with its movements. When it picked up enough speed and began gliding, I felt the steady peace of being one with the sky.

I imagined the air piercing into every part of my body, coursing through the bones. My senses were heightened, but I didn't have to worry about using those heightened senses for anything other than enjoyment. The senses were so that I could get lost in myself and in this word. There were no battles to be had, nor war on the horizon. The air seemed to rid my ailments, and I felt the weightlessness in the air that I had associated with the sky. Beneath me, the clouds and the far-off horizon extended infinitely. Above me, the stars twinkled and shone more brightly than they could ever have before.

I could see them so clearly now, and I couldn't help but marvel at their beauty. It was criminal that this visage wasn't offered to everyone. Everything about the sky was wondrous. I felt exhilarated. The fellcondor did not worry, nor did it wonder. It simply flew according to what it knew to be true, and I closed my eyes and imagined myself as the bird. I felt the further flap of wings as it kept us aloft, and I felt the wind rushing at my face. It was refreshing. I experienced gliding through and through, and the whole time, I never tired of the feelings.

After the surreal experience, the fellcondor descended, and I saw Bravania below grow bigger and bigger. We had spent the entire day flying, but it hadn't felt that way to me. It was too brief a moment. The light of the day was already leaving upon our arrival. I didn't want to descend back onto the land, but the heightened emotions left me itching to get off and release my energy. Jackson directed his attention to one of the Bravania guards that greeted them upon landing. Jackson demanded that someone bring the medication they needed. One immediately went to comply while the birds were tended to.

Jackson asked for a room so that he could discuss some affairs. The guards escorted us to a room and stood outside while we entered and closed the doors behind. The room was furnished lavishly. I was strangely getting used to these kinds of rooms. It was like the room that Jackson had used in Vernatia, though it seemed Bravania was just a bit richer.

"What's going on Jackson? What was that thing in the sky?" I asked once we were finally free.

"I don't know all the details," Jackson began. He has been sincere a lot lately. Either something had changed in him, or he was getting much better at deceiving me. I liked to think it was the

13. Final Stand- 217

former. "We were told that there would be an unmistakable sign when the time came."

So many questions arose from that simple statement. It wasn't an explanation at all. I struggled to think of the correct follow up question so that I wouldn't lose the thread of the conversation. "Walk us through that," replied Roy. "The time for what?"

"We were told that is when Nevil would be approaching."

"How did you know that would happen? How did they make that sign?"

"It wasn't them. The sign came from elsewhere."

"Who sent it?"

"It is not my story to share. What's important is that Argus knows. We both know the strange sky was the sign that Nevil is preparing to invade."

"I thought he was already preparing to invade?" I interjected.

"He's been amassing his forces. Now, Nevil will begin his trek to Andros."

"Where is he going to land? Is he really going to attack from Bravania?"

"He's not here yet. It will still be time before he arrives, but it means that the timetables are much farther along than either of us believed. We thought we would have more time."

"More time to do what exactly?"

"To gather the ten and their weapons." I looked to Roy, who immediately put his hand on Telekay."

"Why do you believe so sincerely that they would be the key? That I could be a key?" I asked.

"We believe as we were told. We cannot fight them, Steven. They will kill us if it comes to war."

"Why would the ten make a difference, then?" Roy asked.

"I have blind faith they will," Jackson responded. I wasn't sure if it was conviction in a truth, or the desperate clinging of hope to a lie.

"If they're not yet invading, why were you and Prince Argus in such a rush to get here?" Roy questioned.

"Argus has been preparing for just as long as I. He is preparing to wage all-out war on the invaders. It will kill us all, but he doesn't seem to care. The Banesworths have one of the swords in their possession, Strife."

"How do you know the swords and the beasts and the ten people this falls to?"

"The beasts? I've never used that phrase around you, Steven." He waited for me to continue. The gaze was unjust. Something about the stare and the silence made me want to continue talking and let him know what he wanted. I felt annoyed that I was being manipulated by something so standard. Even aware of what was transpiring, I felt the need to reply.

"I've been studying what they could be. It's obvious with all the context we have now. The swords are tied to the beast, so it comes with the knowledge we've acquired. The truly difficult part is tracking down all the swords. They're all Caster metal swords, most mythical or lost long ago." I was reminded, once again, about how long he had been preparing for this. He had sent me to find Telekay so long ago. He had thought I would be the Khisharat, but he had been wrong about it. "The people are a unique problem. We can only surmise the identity of the representatives—unless we have the sword. As with Telekay, the sword makes it clear whether you are the representative or not. We've verified the identity of three of them. Now, about that word you used," Jackson indicated for me to explain.

"When that *sign* occurred, I saw a strange vision." I explained the relevant part, when I awoke to the sky on fire and the dream Jackson had tested my strength briefly, before telling me those words.

"It was me in that dream of yours? How strange. Not many have heard those words," he observed, more to himself than anyone else. "Well, you can see why it's so important to have them."

"The words imply that we will win. In any case, it seems obvious that we will wage war. So why aren't you also preparing for all-out war, as Argus is doing?"

13. Final Stand- 219

A knock on the door stopped any words that were going to explain his view. Inside came a guard in a blue cloak, accompanying a well-dressed person who was slightly older than me.

"Prince Maekor," saluted Jackson.

"Please accompany me. My brother and Argus were in private conference, so word of your arrival was delayed, but they see it fit for you to join them."

"It hardly suits to send you as a messenger."

"They can't stop me from attending the meeting myself if I bring you in," Prince Maekor smiled mischievously. "I can't let Tadeus take all the glory for stopping this potential war of the north." War of the north? Did they also know about Nevil? It made sense that they would have told Bravania of a potential invasion. Their strength was unmatched by anyone outside of Garrisbrough, far in the south. They would be instrumental in defending the north. Still, the words weren't quite right. It wasn't about protecting the north from an invasion. War *of* the north, not *in* the north. Was this the reason they had been travelling so frequently as of late? Were these those "matters of state" for which Tadeus had invited them previously?

"Let us go at once then, we can't trust them to find any solutions." *"Argus has men outside of Bravania, to the west. Get to them, they might have already gotten the sword."* Logan remained in the room with us as they all left. I wanted to confront Logan about everything I had seen, but I knew it didn't correspond to me. Roy was doing his best to keep his nerves in check around him.

"Should we go?" I asked Roy. Logan didn't seem to care what decision we would come to. He began gathering his things, and then put his ear to the door, listening for any movement. When he was satisfied, he opened the door, signaled for us to follow, and led the way to the western gates.

Logan seemed to know exactly where to go, as he lost no time diverging from the road to Theo's Watch, and instead to a less-frequent path. After a long while, we reached a group of three who had finished their preparations and were preparing to camp for the night. One of them awaited, sword in hand. He looked extremely familiar, but I couldn't place his face. "Don't tell me you've decided to work with Jack," he said to me. I still wasn't sure of my answer. Why was I here? I wanted to learn everything that was being kept a secret from me. I wanted to learn about the powers I had. "Oh well," he said, shooting a burst of lightning towards me.

The strike was too quick, and I knew I wouldn't get out of the way in time. Roy drew away the lightning with his own power. It turned towards him, and electricity visibly flowed throughout, causing spasms all over his body. The soldier was already pressing forward, ready to impale me with a sword. Logan blocked the strike while I jumped back and tried grabbing my sword. He sent a blast again, forcing me to drop my sword due to the electric shock. He continued parrying and striking with Logan. Roy launched lightning towards him, but the soldier let it flow through his body, and he redirected it towards Logan. Logan couldn't move out of the way and was struck by the attack. I sent a ball of telekinetic energy and used my telekinesis to push against his sword. This didn't accomplish anything; rather, he stopped the ball of energy and redirected it towards Roy. He prepared to strike again, but I had gotten closer and parried the blow. The impact was hard on my wrists, and he tried striking again. Once more, Logan parried the blow and stopped the strike. He wasn't holding back with that sword attack. He was ready to kill.

"Doesn't Argus need me? Why are you trying to kill me now?"

"Your question should be why Jackson is trying to protect you so desperately," he replied. "Your Invincibility hasn't manifested, and I don't think it ever will. Either you're one of the ten, and I won't be able to kill you regardless, or you're not, and your last day will be today." He knew exactly what was going on. He knew about the representatives, and my powers of Invincibility. He was also strong beyond belief. He was handling all three of us on his

13. Final Stand- 221

own, and his companions did not look worried. The strength helped me recognize him. Jacob Victoriano, Bladesman of Vernatia. Jacob was a telekinesis and thunder zalphic on top of his overwhelming strength.

"I haven't decided either way," I began weakly.

"I told you, that doesn't matter." Jacob teleported. For a horrifying moment, I had no idea where he went. Instinctively, I put a barrier behind me, and I heard two swords clashing; the strength still crashed and shattered the barrier I had made. I fell to the ground, turning around to see Roy, Telekay in hand, struggling against Jacob's sword. Logan pushed forward, striking with his sword. Jacob was still clearly stronger, but only Logan was able to force him to concentrate on the swordfight long enough that he couldn't keep assaulting us with his zalphic abilities.

The sound of the earth collapsing turned my attention away from Jacob. One of them fell into the hole, while the other just managed to avoid it. They turned to us, and grabbed their swords, but I turned, confused to Roy. The other two didn't waste any time with questions and instead came forward. We would need to finish this fight quickly. Logan could not keep Jacob occupied for long. A stream of water came from their direction, which flew harmlessly past the two that were approaching. Behind them, I caught a sliver of movement, but I could pay no mind as the two went on the attack.

We blocked their blows and began preparing a counterattack when we heard Logan's gasp of pain. We had already taken too long. Logan was down, and Jacob didn't even seem tired by the exchange. He looked up and yelled "Grab the sword. We need to hide."

I looked in the direction he had gazed, but I saw nothing. Jacob left Logan on the floor and approached their belongings. "Where is it!?" The two others looked at each other, and back at their supplies. "Where did you leave it, Agnar?"

"It was there, where you left it," said the one Roy had fought. Agnar, presumably.

"They must have moved it when they made the hole," the other one chimed in.

"What hole?" They both turned to the spot where the hole had been. It was whole again, with no sign of any tampering.

"Their earth zalphic must have snatched it."

We didn't have an earth zalphic with us. He returned his gaze back to the sky. He flew forward, striking Roy before either of us could react. "Where is the earth zalphic?" Roy shook his head, confused. Roy eyes rolled back into his head. I could tell Jacob was reading through his thoughts. "They didn't have one with them. Someone *else* stole it. You will have to explain this to Argus later. We must leave immediately. I can't be seen." They took off in a hurry, no longer worried about us and what we must do. I went towards Roy, assessing the damage from the strike. The wound was severe. I needed to get Roy to a healer. I looked again to ate horizon and saw something moving towards us from the sky. It was blocking the light of the stars behind it at times. How had Jacob seen that before?

Logan was still on the ground, writhing, but the bird would be quickly upon us. I wanted to chase Jacob. If he wanted to leave unseen, the best option would be to thwart his plans. I couldn't leave Roy, though.

Roy turned to Logan and pressed the sword into my hand. I already knew Roy's thoughts on the matter. What would killing Logan and chasing Jacob accomplish? There was still the matter of Strife, which had been stolen from under us. Could we explain we were attacked? We could tell them we were on our way to Bravania and were taken unaware by outlaws. We could even say they stole all our things. I was becoming satisfied with my plan.

"It's better to kill him. They'll also ask why we didn't come from the main roads. We will still be suspicious." I tried to think of an explanation for our strange route. Would they believe it if we said we heard outlaws were on the main road? Perhaps those same outlaws robbed a group leaving Bravania, and they had warned us? That would be sufficient reason to diverge our path. We could have simply run into the misfortune of the outlaws stepping away as well. It would have to do.

"It's still better to kill him," Roy reiterated. "They'd have no reason to believe we'd kill one of our own." I had seen into Roy's mind. I knew this was what Logan deserved. I had killed for less. We would have to hurry.

"You think Prince Jack will believe your story? Do you believe this will not have any consequences?" Logan snarled.

"Jacob severely wounded you. Who's to say you didn't succumb to your wounds?"

"You think if I were so easy to kill that I would be in the employ of the prince? So, before you commit this grave mistake, I'd ask if you're prepared to see this through." As much as Roy—and I now, for that's how the tethering worked—wanted to kill him, Logan was right.

I dressed Roy's wounds as well as best I could while the bird approached. Riding atop the fellcondor was a soldier in full armor. He descended lithely, clearly accustomed to moving in it. "Where is the sword?" he asked, not bothering to ask about the wounds.

I didn't know how to respond at first. "We were attacked by outlaws," I began, ignoring his question and reciting the lie. "We need to take him to a healer."

"Where is the sword?" he repeated, drawing his sword.

"I don't know what you mean," I answered again. "We were assaulted on our way to Bravania and were wounded in the struggle. Please."

"There was a report of three suspicious individuals around the treasury. The sword is now gone, and there were more reports of a suspicious trio leaving Bravania. They were spotted heading here. You truly want to play this game?" He thought it was us who stole the sword. With good reason, sure, but now what could we say?" Those others must have escaped with it. They wanted the reward for themselves. Do I have that right? They won't be able to hide long."

The soldier walked forward, sword at the ready. I drew my sword to protect myself. He wasn't standing down. I positioned myself with the sword in my left hand, as I normally did. The soldier didn't seem fazed at all by the different stance I had. I swung the sword, but he moved gracefully and avoided the strike. That wasn't the skill of a regular soldier. The way he had descended from the bird, the smooth and fluid motions he was displaying, and the certainty of his steps all indicated that he was something more.

I tried striking again, but he parried the blow. He attacked my right side, forcing me to block at strange angles. I thought briefly about striking forward and getting him as he was preparing to swing outward, but I had a feeling that was exactly what he was trying to provoke me to do. I parried and counter-struck, attacking from my left. He parried that easily as well, and it became clear quickly that I would not easily best his guard.

There was something about him that was wrong. He demonstrated incredible skill. The soldier did not stop his attack. I knew I couldn't continue fighting him like this. I needed to get Roy's wounds checked. I switched my sword from my left hand to my right. Using my right hand after so long felt strange, but the movements came to me without hesitation. I struck to my right, stopped halfway, and quickly changed the direction of my strike. The quickness and strength of my strikes increased as I used my dominant hand, and he seemed to realize this quickly. He frantically parried my blows and tried backing up to regain his composure. I tried pressing him so that he wouldn't have time but didn't want to overcommit to the attack. I continued testing his reactions and his weak points. He was quick to protect his right leg, probably because he had a previous wound there.

I made a movement to his leg, which he promptly tried blocking, but I switched the direction of my sword and landed a hit on his side. He groaned in pain, and I struck his sword out of him. I went for his legs, to immobilize him, but he slammed his gauntleted fist into my side. The blow took the air out of me, and he tried grappling for the sword in my hand. We struggled for too long. My heart was pounding from the exertion, but I tried overpowering his grip. He proved too strong and punched me across the face. The world spun until I abruptly hit the ground. He stood standing over me with the sword, ready to claim victory. He thrust the sword down, and I created a barrier of telekinetic energy before me.

As soon as he encountered its resistance, I pushed back with telekinesis. The weight of the armor made him fall backwards, and the unexpected force made him drop his sword as well. "Zalphic," he snarled, though he didn't seem to lose his composure. He went to grab the sword again. As strong as he was, he couldn't counteract my zalphic powers. He knew what I was now, so I would have to kill him. I ran to the other sword. He was prepared for a regular sword attack, but I teleported behind him and swung. He ducked quickly, and the sword bumped off the top of his helmet. He spun around and extended the sword, but I backed up in time. I gathered telekinetic energy in my hand as I did so and launched it his way. He had used his leverage to add power to the strike, so he didn't have much left to get out of the way.

The strike hit and I pushed telepathically. He was on the ground now, but he grabbed the sword and tried getting up. I tried bringing the sword to me, but he grabbed it in time. Instead, I tried pinning it to the ground. He started getting up, pulling on the sword. I released the pressure, causing him to stumble up and forward due to the lack of push. As he came closer to me, I swung my sword. He adjusted his position and arced his back to the ground to avoid the strike. The sword was repelled upward, and I struck the base of the helmet, which was pushed up, off his head. slightly. He fell to the floor and the bounce finished taking the helmet off. I stopped, horrified at the face that looked back at me.

It was Maekor Banesworth.

I thought he had maneuvered his way into that conversation with the three heirs to the North? The second son of Lord Neister

Banesworth was not in the room, speaking with his older brother Prince Tadeus, and Prince Argus, and Prince Jackson. Maekor was here. The second-in line to rule Bravania was *here*, and he had seen that I was a zalphic.

Figure it out later. For a moment, I thought it would be better to stop fighting. Perhaps all those moments where they accused me of being a monster finally chipped away at me—it didn't matter if they hadn't been talking to me specifically. It was numbing, but what could I do? Maekor drew a dagger from his side and desperately tried stabbing me. I teleported behind myself and saw Maekor swipe at nothing but the air. I lifted Maekor with my telepathic powers, and as he hung in the air, hopeless, I forced the dagger out of his hand with my telekinesis.

The dagger spun and spiraled around him, until I finally sent it to his throat, and slashed away. I held the blood there telepathically, not letting it flow down his neck. The blood filled his lungs, surely, while Maekor's life grew still.

As his life stilled, so did everything else. My ears tuned out all the tumult, and my eyes could see nothing except Maekor's face. The eyes hated me and cast aspersions my way. It was nothing I wasn't accustomed to already. Time seemed to stop as I looked into those eyes. Maekor didn't deserve to die. He had that princely arrogance—he didn't even recognize any of us despite seeing us in Jackson's chamber. He hadn't noticed us, who were so beneath him. I couldn't fault him for that. He wanted to prove himself to his brother, and to himself. Just like any of us wanted.

I never imagined anything like this. How far had I fallen? I had killed a prince of Bravania. Who else might I kill to protect my secret? This time, the poison that coursed through my body was acid. The pain and strength I felt was sickening. This had been Maekor Banesworth final stand. I'm sure he had a warrior's mind, and had prepared for an ending like this, but who could ever accept it. In his mind, he had done it protecting Bravania from something he hated.

13. Final Stand- 227

I imagined the entire might of Bravania coming down. All the power of the Banesworths would seek me out and make the punishment to zalphics seem like a playful evening. Prince Tadeus Banesworth, the strongest of all the Bladesman in Andros—the strongest soldier in all the *world*—would make sure that everyone knew the terrifying strength they possessed. I had doomed myself.

I came back to reality as the thrusting force of a lance pierced through me. All at once, I took in the senses I had been ignoring. Maekor's eyes were lost in a world of red and black, as he fell to the ground, no longer held up by my powers. The sound of powerful hooves ran past me and began turning. The sobs of a hysterical girl came into focus as she attempted to whistle, but the shaky breath prevented the proper noise from escaping her mouth. A searing pain yelled out from below, as the jagged ends of a lance were protruding from my body. A ringing in my ears reminded me that I had to continue.

The mount had finished its turn and charged from behind me. I turned to see a young guard atop it. She was determined, and she had seen everything too. Or, at least, she had seen enough. I teleported to the left, as the mount went running past. I drew in a deep breath and pulled with all my strength on the mount's front right leg. The effort was commensurate with the strength and speed of the mount, so for a moment, the pain of the lance was overshadowed by the pain on my shoulders as I had been forced to pull.

The mount's leg broke and fell forward with a terrible cry. The mount whinnied in pain and rolled with a sickening thump. The girl on top of it flew off, but she rolled and continued running away. Again, she put her hand to her mouth, and this time let out a deafening whistle. She followed with other distinctive whistle calls. I could already imagine what they said.

"The Prince is harmed". "The Prince is *dead*". Would they have a call for that prepared? "Zalphic here, gather the zalphic hunters". I reached out with my mind, trying to immobilize the girl.

What would that accomplish? She had already warned the others. I heard other calls in response. I turned back to Roy and Logan as my mind continued to wander forward. The girl was Valerie Landra. She had joined the cavalry at an impressively young age. When Maekor had heard that Strife had been stolen, he took the fellcondor to reconnaissance. Valerie had been one of the first to react and leave on her mount to support Prince Maekor. She did not know about the meeting of the others and did not know why Prince Maekor had gone out himself. How had I learned that so quickly?

I looked at Roy and Logan's wounds. They had not been lethal wounds, but if untreated, they would die regardless. Before, they could have found a way. Now? They would never make it away from Bravania without getting caught. They could not make it to Theo's Watch in such a condition, assuming word didn't get out first, and they were killed on sight.

I turned back in the direction of Valerie and Bravania. Roy needed treatment, and the old man came to mind. I needed to get them to him. They would never expect them to be inside the castle. I put a hand on Roy and Logan and prepared myself. Roy wasn't sure what I was going to do. I closed my eyes, inhaled deeply, and imagined the courtyard the old healer called home. I thought of where I had grown up, searching for a quiet place, hidden away. When I opened my eyes, I saw Roy and Logan looking at me strangely, but I could see them in that place, with me. I teleported inside.

Never had I teleported such a long distance. Immediately, I felt the shortness of breath and exhaustion. I couldn't breathe. The air escaped, refusing to be captured. Black spots covered my blurry vision. I collapsed onto the ground, pushing the broken lance further into my body. I was left with a sliver of consciousness. I started coughing and felt like I was going to regurgitate blood and bile. The black spots covered most of my vision now, and I felt myself slipping away. I couldn't fight, I was too tired, and I could feel a poison coursing through my body, killing me in a slow and effective process. The poison, ever-present, spread rapidly throughout my body. I could see the lifeline of my body withering away, growing weak and being drained of color. I would see a while light diminish, and the purple aura dissipate, I could sense the atrophy that was accelerated by the poison and felt my inevitable metamorphosis into nothing but dust.

I felt my body screaming in protest, the movement of internal parts that seemed to intensify one another: the beat of my heart, the rapidity with which my stomach expanded and deflated, the blood running to the extremities of my fingers and toes, and the frantic searching of my eyes trying to register something. Anything. It was only pain that I could register.

Black spots expanded, but somehow, they were still exposing me to the burning light. The brightness blocked my view of anything, and I was unable to discern anything outside of white and purple and pain. The breathing wasn't coming back to me, I could not breathe, could not participate in the sweet intake of air that could fill me with life again. Breathing was suddenly so foreign a concept to me, that the sweet bliss of inhaling and exhaling was gone. The lungs were all blood. The object rammed into my stomach prevented me from all else. The beathing of my heart accelerated into a pounding frenzy, a crescendo of drumming. I was frantically searching for air, but it seemed the intake would no longer be any concern of mine. The black spots filled with immense light began to blur. Every object converged into a sharp point of nothingness.

Roy could survive now, inside Bravania. Valerie likely hadn't gotten a good look of the others, just me. I heard Roy still gasping for air, or perhaps that was still just me. I exhaled the last of the remaining breath, so that I could no longer utter even a cry of pain.

The light, the darkness, the colors! The white and purples surrounded me. What had I done? My body complained, but my mind knew. It was what I needed to do. That primal fear blocked everything out. I had been so full of strength, hadn't I? It seemed an impossibility now. It withered away, dissipating into nothingness. There was no more pain, no more strength, just that primal fear. It was over.

For my family. For the people I loved. Nothing more now. It couldn't have been for nothing. Kesara. Aurora. Benjamin. Gideon. Mom, dad. Jennifer. Roy even.

"Roy, live on. Live both our lives. You too Aurora, I love you so much. You must live on as well, as only you can do. Kesara, sis, what can I say? I love you most of all. Tell Benjamin I love him, as well as my parents. I forgive them. ...Live on. ...live...on......."

###

Part II
Midnight

Roy Rhapsados struggled to recover from the long-distance teleportation. His wound exacerbated the symptoms, and he breathed heavily to recover. Next to him, Steven was quickly growing paler. A telepathy message filled his mind. *"Roy, live on. Live both our lives. You too Aurora, I love you. Both of you live on. Kesara, sis, what can I say? Tell Benjamin I love him, as well as my parents. I forgive them. ...Live on. ...live...on......."* Roy turned to Steven; he didn't seem to move. Roy struggled to his feet and saw Logan getting up as well. He went towards Steven, but Logan grabbed Roy and pulled him away. Logan dragged him into courtyard, where he spotted an old man sleeping on the streets. Logan pulled him forward, away from Steven and into this crowd. Roy didn't have the strength to fight back. All the time, he wondered about the message. He figured that Steven was transmitting the message to Aurora and Kesara as well. Still, he wondered what Steven had meant by all that. Why was he saying this? They all just needed to get their wounds treated. Roy didn't care for much else. Once they did this, they could ask questions.

When he focused on what was in front of him, he realized that the old man who had been sleeping was now awake and was peering at the wounds of both Logan and Roy. *Steven's wounds too, you must check,* he thought feebly.

His next sliver of consciousness found him with bandages around his wounds. Logan was offering him payment and grabbed Roy. He was quickly taken to the aviary, with the fellcondors. Roy did not have the presence of mind to question what was happening. Logan lifted Roy up, and they took off on the massive bird.

Roy was tired, but he couldn't sleep atop the frightening creature. He was nervous about flying—he didn't feel at ease. It only took a storm or the bird's fatigue to cause them to hurtle down to their graves. Perhaps the fellcondor would find prey and decided to hunt instead of worrying about Roy. The flight gnawed at his unease. The constant wind made him nervous. They didn't belong up here, only birds. He imagined falling off the bird, plummeting towards the ground. He closed his eyes and held on tighter. He wanted to be done with the trip, and it had just begun. The birds went forward at a frightening pace.

When Roy finally landed in Vernatia, he didn't say much to Logan before leaving. They had gone slower, perhaps due to their wounds, so they landed during the light of day. Vernatia was filled with its people, all of them working and trying to make a living for themselves. He went to the sick ward, to get his wounds checked. On his way, he saw Benjamin pacing around. *Tell Benjamin I love him.* Roy supposed he should tell him, but he decided it wasn't his place. He saw Aurora looking out from a window, crying. She must have seen him too, for she quickly went towards him.

"Roy!"

"What's going on Aurora?"

"Did you get that message?" Aurora's eyes started to water again. Roy didn't exactly know what to do. He didn't like seeing Aurora like this.

"I got the message," Roy said, not quite answering the question Aurora was too afraid to ask. He saw how tired Aurora seemed. Ironically, she probably hadn't gotten any sleep since receiving the message, and Roy knew that she needed to rest due to the zalphia. "Come on Aurora. Let's get you back to bed and we can talk there." The wounds could wait a little longer.

Aurora went back to the room she was staying in. The first and only thing he noticed upon walking into the house was how well-off Aurora was. The room had lush furnishings, and though not excessively extravagant, they clearly lived comfortably. Her parents were renting this place temporarily, he imagined. Her parents clearly *decided* to live in Farendor, comfortably having enough money for a home in Faldenheim. Roy hadn't really

Part II - Midnight - 233

considered why Aurora was in the Wise Ones, but Roy knew that those as poor as he weren't usually candidates to join their tanks. The Wise Ones were comprised of lords and princes, and the nobility, and Roy saw that Aurora might have belonged in that world.

She sat down and Roy sat next to her. Aurora fought back tears long enough to ask her question. "Is Steven dead?" *Yeah, he probably is,* Roy thought. Instead, he found a better way to phrase it.

"I don't feel his mind." Roy knew that he wouldn't be able to feel his mind this far away. Affirming her question seemed too harsh, whereas supporting it had seemed the better option. Should he talk her through those final moments? Would she hate him for not doing more for him?

Either way, she started crying. Roy didn't know what to do. He put her hand on her shoulder, but her shaking made him uncomfortable.

"Why!?" Aurora slammed her fist on the nearby table. Her hand turned red crimson, but all she could seem to think about was Steven. Tears came out of her eyes, and the blood was secondary to the tears.

Aurora started crying, which left only Roy. Roy didn't cry for steven though. He felt bad and sad that Steven had died, but he couldn't seem to find it in himself to cry for Steven. They had shared their minds, so it wasn't that Roy didn't know Steven well enough. Roy feared that Aurora would find him a weak survivor. He needed to be strong.

Nevertheless, Roy cried. He didn't cry for Steven, he cried because of the tears from Aurora. Roy hated to see Aurora sad, and he too partook in her grief. Her tears saddened him, until he cried. They continued their lamentation until they were out of tears. Aurora sobbed audibly while tears silently escaped Roy's eyes. Aurora cried over her best friend, and Roy cried over the girl's tears. A knock on the door caught their attention. Aurora wiped her face, and gingerly approached the door. She opened it and saw Benjamin walk in.

He was confused at seeing Roy there, with Aurora. "Roy. Do you know where Steven is? I can't shake this uneasy feeling I have."

"Benjamin, come in." Benjamin walked in, noticing the tears on both of their faces. He turned to Aurora. "What happened that night?" Aurora asked.

Benjamin seemed confused. He hadn't registered that the question wasn't directed at him. Roy began detailing exactly what they had done. "We were outside of Bravania. We confronted Jacob, but he wounded us. When Maekor Banesworth descended upon us, only Steven was able to fight. Steven killed him but got wounded by a guard. Then he teleported all of us inside of the castle walls."

"He killed Maekor *Banesworth?*" Benjamin asked, already sick to his stomach. Roy turned to Aurora, hoping she would be the one to deliver the news.

"Benjamin, steven is...he's dead." Roy saw the shock and fear and anger that entered Benjamin's eyes.

"How do you know?" Benjamin asked, still hoping with naiveté that this was some sort of mistake.

"The wound was severe, and he teleported too far a distance." Benjamin rejected the statement Roy made.

"There was a message from Steven." Aurora started crying again.

"He said that he loved you, Benjamin. That he forgave you and his parents." Benjamin broke out into tears, no longer able to deny the matter. Aurora went into Benjamin's embrace, and Roy felt no sympathy. Instead, he felt a tinge of jealousy.

He looked at Aurora, wondering what she was thinking. *There was an image of Steven. Steven had a purple and a white aura around him. They saw Steven's last instants of lie and saw when he made the telepathy message. There were three lines connecting Steven to the three recipients: Roy, Kesara, and Aurora.*

Steven lost the purple aura, and the line connected to Roy's mind turned purple. The one connected to Aurora's mind was not bright white. Kesara's line had no new color. As Steven breathed out his last breath, the line to Roy and Steven broke. Steven's mind was no longer connected, and the purple color on the line went inside of Roy, and the white light went inside of Aurora.

Part II - Midnight- 235

"What the...?" Aurora asked no one in particular. Benjamin was portably too deep in his sorrow to have even noticed what she said.

Aurora temporarily stopped her tears, and Roy wondered what they had just seen, and why. He had a theory, but to him it seemed much too implausible.

#

Chapter 14
Memory's Troubles

Roy Rhapsados was at his parents' home. He didn't have to go study with the Wise Ones; he hadn't been there since the day Steven died. He had gone to the funeral out of respect. He hadn't said anything to Steven's family, and he wanted to be with Aurora, but of course Aurora was surrounded by Steven's family. The Wise Ones had cancelled sessions in the castle due to an "important matter" they were investigating. Roy knew this matter would be the continued efforts to explain the great thunder in the sky, but Roy liked to think this matter to be Aurora's sickness, and why she seemed to be doing better. Her time should have already come, but she was still around. Roy was glad about that.

The Wise Ones even went out of their way and visited Farendor in order to see Aurora. He didn't know what was happening with the Hewleys; they had a visitor from somewhere if he recalled correctly. They were mourning their loss. Roy wondered how Benjamin must have felt about that.

Roy consequently had little to do but help with the errands of the home and keeping himself busy. He couldn't count on the Wise Ones for a while. Even disregarding their interest in Aurora, the Wise Ones had to prepare the trip to the Capital, so that they may go over any new information they might have found concerning the nature of the world. There was plenty the Wise Ones had to do—a surreal event in the sky, the inexplicable vigor of a girl with zalphia, the all-important Committee of the Wise Ones. Since the Capital was the center of the Wise Ones, that's where they would meet, and where they had historically met all the times before. There lived the mysterious man that headed the organization. It was rumored he was dying. Roy knew that Lord Horus was a friend of that mysterious man.

"Roy, are you ill? I've noticed you seem a tad off lately."

"Mom, it's not something I'd like to talk about."

"Okay honey." Roy's mom said. She knew her son, Roy knew, and she knew that he wasn't one to express his emotions. She walked away, though clearly, she wished to know.

Why did this happen? Roy thought. He was sad, sadder than he thought he would be. Death frightened him more now. *Is this normal? Do Benjamin and Aurora feel this way as well? Not sorrow and grief, but fear?* He was interrupted from his thoughts when someone came to visit.

"Honey, can you see who it is?" Roy walked to the door and opened it. It was Benjamin.

"What are you doing here?"

"Jackson sent me." Roy nodded. Despite the Wise Ones being preoccupied at the moment, Roy was all too aware that the Wise Ones were providing for his family, and as a consequence, he felt obliged to follow Jackson's instruction. Benjamin and Roy walked in awkward silence to the castle. Roy considered asking him his question but did not feel at all comfortable talking about it.

Walking to Faldenheim, they came upon some bandits. Roy knew immediately that they were bandits despite their intent to appear as a group of travelers. Benjamin seemed to notice it as well. *"I've got this handled Roy."*

They passed the travelers and politely nodded. Turning forward, Roy immediately felt a blade at his back. His initial reaction was to get Telekay and kill them all. Instead, he let Benjamin take care.

"Shout and you're dead," one of the bandits said.

"You don't want to kill us," Benjamin replied, factually.

"Why is that?"

"If you wanted to kill us, we would have been dead already. You just want gold and do not care to shed blood. I doubt you've even killed anyone."

The bandit pressed the dagger harder into Benjamin's back and said "you want to see if you're right?"

Benjamin shook his head. "I want no trouble. There are seventeen gold coins in that coin purse," Benjamin said, motioning to the location. The bandit took the purse, clearly delighted, and threw it to one of the others. The bandits walked away, facing them, and went on their way.

Roy turned to Benjamin, confused. "Why did you let them take your gold coins? We could have easily killed them. Even without our powers, Knight."

Benjamin smiled a little. "It matters little. The coins I gave them weren't real. When they try to pay with that coin, the others will see, and they will deal with them in the appropriate manner." Benjamin shrugged. "The punishment for thievery is imprisonment in a public cell, so that they serve as a sign for others."

Roy saw his reason but thought killing them would have been easier. Arriving at the castle, Dart was awaiting, ready to take off. Benjamin didn't seem to care that Dart wanted to take off. He entered the castle and went ahead. Roy dutifully followed and walked in silence. Dart didn't follow, and he instead stood at the castle gates. He was a little annoyed, but Roy figured Dart was giving Benjamin time.

Benjamin made his way to the burial grounds. Steven, having been part of the Wise Ones, and Benjamin having ties with Prince Horus, was given a burial in the castle as opposed to the village. Roy held his breath and looked at the tombstone. The tombstone read:

In Remembering:
Steven Hewley
Born the twelfth day of the ninth month of the 522nd year -- Died the fourteenth day of the thirteenth month of the 545th year.

Roy couldn't make out the writing underneath the inscription, but he wouldn't have read it anyway. His vision seemed to blur, and he experienced the fatigue and faintness associated with using his powers. He was caught up on Steven. He remembered that day, the fourteenth of the final month. A month ago, Steven Hewley had died, and a month ago, Roy himself could not be the same. 522 years after the Great Shaking, Steven was born. 545 years after the Great Shaking, Roy would change.

Roy felt a minor disturbance in his mind, but he thought little of it. He was much too concentrated on Steven. He continued thinking about Steven, and what he had been through. Roy wasn't aware of the surrounding world. He alone was in front of Steven's grave, and he alone felt this strange connection between the two. He was scared of death, scared of being unable to act.

The quiet only accentuated the absolute finality of it all. He rejected the thought with every fiber of his being, and he imagined any possibility in which Steven might still be alive and acting on the forces of the earth.

Roy thought about it all. He found himself floating, going skyward and beyond. When he had gone past the clouds and the sky and the sun, he looked down on the earth as he knew it. A semi-circle rested below him, and off in the distance, the sun burned brightly. The moon was dark, not shining as it always did. Somewhere, sometime, Steven had said you can only shine if you are surrounded in darkness.

Steven enjoyed shining, being in the darkness, but Roy much preferred to be surrounded in an equivalent light. The sun and the moon shot towards each other and crashed violently. The sun seemed to absorb the moon. As Roy examined more closely, it was the moon who had stolen the light of the sun. He looked upon the earth and saw a world of light and shadows, coexisting and forming and dissipating. Roy descended to the earth, back to the grave. The dark crypt that had been previously there, the cold rigid stones that outlined the lifeless body of an impotent form, now seemed radiant with light, trying to escape, and having not one form but four—only one of which was resting, while the other three were busy at work.

Roy found himself scared, but he was for the first time not moved by his fear. Instead, he didn't care and was ready to move forward. The resting form approached him in a slow manner, and he reached out to touch it. Then he felt a pain in another reality.

He recoiled from the shock and grabbed Telekay. Jacob shocked Roy again with his powers and knocked Telekay out of his hand. He put his hand in front of another incoming blast to protect himself, only to find that a barrier in front of him blocked the blast. He shocked Jacob with his powers over thunder, but Jacob just redirected the thunder to him. Roy picked up his sword and ran towards Jacob. He had to protect the girl behind him. He couldn't let her get hurt, so he had to protect Aurora.

Roy found himself asking: *Why's Aurora here?* After that, complete darkness....

###

Aurora Stephensen stared at Roy, scared. There lay Roy's body without any wound, but Roy was convulsing in pain. Benjamin turned his attention to Roy. He didn't know what was happening either. Benjamin seemingly recoiled in pain, and Aurora looked at Benjamin, asking him with her eyes what had happened.

"It's almost a nightmare, but not quite." Benjamin looked around, searching for someone, and then stopped. Aurora turned to the direction Benjamin was looking and saw someone in the distance, but couldn't see him clearly. Benjamin walked towards Aurora, took hold of her arm, and said "come on, we have to go." He took a hold of Roy, teleported somewhere, then teleported back, alone. Aurora didn't know what was happening, but she followed Benjamin when he walked away. They came across some guards and Benjamin approached them. "There's a man in the burial grounds. He seems to be acting suspiciously. I think he might be a grave robber."

The guards thanked him for the information and went to take a look. Benjamin approached someone sleeping on the ground, who Aurora then came to realize was Roy. "Can't exactly carry a limp body without arousing suspicions."

"That's not what I was noticing," said Aurora, as she stared intently at the scar across Roy's forehead. Benjamin kept teleporting forward with discretion, leaving Roy somewhere hidden, and they walked forward, until they reached the Wise Ones building near the keep.

Aurora opened the doors, and Lord Horus and Prince Horus both stood up immediately. Jackson was at first annoyed by the interruption, but saw that it was Aurora, and immediately worried. "Is something wrong, Aurora?" She knew they only cared because they wanted to know if it was possible to survive the illness. As far as they knew, anyone infected died within a few months, and never failed to kill.

She stepped aside and let Benjamin through, carrying Roy. "Roy's been hurt," Benjamin said. Aurora approached Benjamin and helped him carry Roy's body forward. Lord Horus looked at Roy, trying to figure out what was wrong with him, she presumed, while Jackson seemed curious. Aurora figured Benjamin knew Jackson would be busy, so he would only bother him with something important; the matter then became why Benjamin thought this serious.

Another person came from an adjacent room; Aurora knew she had seen him before. He was the one from the underground tunnel. Logan, if she remembered correctly.

"What happened? Shouldn't you be getting Spark?" Logan asked.

"We were in the burial grounds. Roy fell to the ground, grabbing his stomach as if he were in pain. A lot of pain, judging by his motions. I saw Jacob, he was there."

"Jacob Victoriano?" Benjamin nodded. "What is he doing here?" Jackson asked. He looked at his father, Lord Horus, who seemed to understand something no one else did.

Lord Horus spoke up. "That war we have tried to prevent. It will come."

Jackson turned to his dad. "No, that was the whole point of the Bravania meet. Even if they were unsuccessful, Argus will not convince his father to take action." Lord Horus excused himself, and Jackson began to follow. He turned to Logan. "Take care of this."

Logan nodded. Jackson followed him out to the adjacent room. Logan turned his attention back to Benjamin. "So you go to the burial grounds, visit a tomb, then Roy falls to the ground in pain, and you see Jacob in the distance?" When Benjamin nodded, he added: "And you're sure it was Jacob?"

"He did this, but of course he wasn't going to fight me in the middle of a castle where he would immediately be targeted for being a zalphic. So he silently attacked Roy."

"Okay, anything you want to add Aurora?"

How does he know my name? She asked herself, but in spite, she answered. "No, but is Roy going to be alright? The scar on his head seems worrisome." They all looked at Roy's head. Then they all looked at her.

"Are you feeling alright Aurora? Perhaps your illness has resurged, causing you to see things." Aurora shook her head. She looked at Roy's head again. There were no scars. No marks. Aurora was confused.

"Perhaps I just need to rest a little."

Logan seemed more worried at that. He turned to the room, probably considering telling the Horus family, but he decided against it and just nodded. "Very well Aurora. Let me know if you feel exhausted in any way. And yes, he should be fine. Benjamin, take him there," Logan said while pointing to the door that led to the infirmary. "Let Dart know that he is to go to the meeting room here. Spark must wait now."

Benjamin nodded and made way towards the infirmary. Aurora followed, helping him there. The infirmary was scarcely populated with others, and they put Roy in a bed that was secluded. Aurora touched Roy's head, still not believing that there had been no scar. The skin was perhaps not the smoothest, but there were definitely no rough patches that would indicate a scar. She retreated her hand, and Benjamin seemed to be in a conversation, probably talking with Dart through telepathy.

"Ben," Maximillius said behind them. "I can't seem to find Kesara."

"Kesara is at the inn," responded Benjamin. "She said it was something she had to see."

"She isn't there. I can't sense her. Gideon doesn't know anything either."

Aurora recalled the countless hours they had spent crying together. Kesara was the closest thing to Steven, and through him Kesara had grown to become her little sister as well. Aurora thought about where she would have gone. There was clearly only one place.

###

A dark room illuminated the house. Roy was scared. He didn't have his sword with him, and he couldn't make lightning to illuminate the house. He heard a noise and went against the wall. He hit the wall hard and caused a portrait on the wall to hit him on his head. It shattered into pieces.

"Ow!" Roy said out loud. He looked around, and found others in pain and sleeping in beds. He placed himself in an infirmary, but he didn't know where he was. There was a door in front of him. He rose and searched for his sword, but it was nowhere in sight.

Roy looked to the floor in front of him and saw a sword materialize in front of him. "What is this?" The sword he was searching for didn't have a golden hilt. It had a regular black hilt. It also wasn't made of what was presumably Caster metal.

He decided that the sword was better than nothing. He opened the door and saw two guys and a girl he didn't recognize. The girl was pretty, with a skinny build, purple eyes, and black curly hair. One of the guys seemed familiar, but Roy could not place the black hair and sharp features.

"Hey, look who is alive," said the one Roy vaguely recognized.

"Who are you?" Roy looked at the girl and guys with confusion. *Who are they? It seems like I've seen them before, but where?* Roy's head started to hurt.

"Roy, are you okay?" He heard someone say with concern. It was the girl.

"Who are you? How do you know my name?"

"It's me, Aurora. What's wrong? Don't you know who I am?"

"No," Roy managed, confused. He didn't know.

"Are you alright Roy?"

She said she was someone's friend, but all Roy felt was great pain. Someone tried to go into his mind, but the person failed. In the attempt, some of Roy's pain was transferred over to the other, but Roy still experienced enormous pain.

He yelled out "Khisharat!" in desperation, but he felt his vocal cords fail him. Instead, nothing but a desperate groan came out. Despite this, he saw the legendary shadowcat enter his body, relieving the pain, but then blackness engulfed him.

Chapter 15
Fire and Flame

Roy Rhapsados awoke to find he was back in the infirmary. He felt disoriented and had to shield his eyes from the bright light surrounding him. He blacked out for a second, but he saw that the light was receding, and everything was much quieter. He closed his eyes to rest them, and awoke in a world of complete darkness.

He stood up, and felt immediately tired from the exertion. He saw the floor get closer and bigger, but saw only darkness before anything else. Through the haze of his blurry vision, he saw the ceiling and closed his eyes again. He awoke to the sight of a dead body being carried out of the infirmary.

Having repeatedly entered and exited reality, he finally retained a grasp on it on a cold morning where the light that had previously seemed to radiate and harm his eyes was seemingly hiding. Roy steadied himself, not attempting to get up this time. He waited until someone came to see him.

Someone he assumed was studying under the Wise Ones came to check on the infirm, and saw Roy was awake. He asked Roy something, but Roy was still not accustomed to the noise, and had a hard time determining what he was saying. Roy nodded, and closed his eyes. This time, he didn't enter another world, but heard the footsteps of multiple people approaching. He looked up and smiled at his mom and his two brothers. They were saying something, but he was too exhausted to think, and he smiled for them and rested.

Eventually, the Wise Ones asked his family to leave to see if they couldn't better understand Roy's illness. They assented, and the Wise Ones asked him questions pertaining to his health. It reminded him of how the Wise Ones had questioned him in an earlier stage of his life, when he was a broken lad and they were an ominously powerful order. They had trapped him into obedience and exerted their power.

Roy wanted to shudder at the thought, but he considered what the Wise Ones might think of his bodily and mental functions, and instead he decided to brave through the questions.

The Wise Ones left, and the next person to visit him was the girl from before, the one who claimed to know who he was. Roy felt a certain amount of contentedness at that. She seemed hesitant to speak what was on her mind, which clearly wasn't what she asked next. "How are you feeling Roy?"

"I'm good. I don't even know why I'm here."

She asked, knowingly, "When do any of us truly know why?" She looked at Roy's bed in the infirmary, and around at the room. "I remember spending countless days here, sick and dying, not knowing how to deal with the exhaustion and pain and despondence."

Roy imagined being here longer, awake through it all, and again briefly revisited the dark place and his powerlessness. He expelled the thought as soon as he could, and he instead refocused his attention on the girl.

"Clearly, you got better, and that's wondrous. What was wrong?"

She seemed taken aback. She didn't seem to know how to phrase it, and she seemed confused, like he should already know what had happened. "I had zalphia, and had no reason to believe I would live. But here I am, healthy and untaxed by the disease. I'm the only survivor."

Roy felt as if he should be shocked—beyond any sense. Zalphia had never failed to kill, and this news should have been enough to lift him out of this bed in shock. Instead, he felt as though this was information he already knew, and that he had heard the story, just not attached the story to this girl. Zalphia...that was quite the disease.

"They couldn't even cure Lady Horus. What did they give you? Did they find the cure?"

Again, she seemed reserved about the subject, and Roy promised himself not to pry anymore into the matter. "They didn't. I got better. I just slowly got better, and I no longer suffer from it.

Some of the Wise Ones don't even think I had it. Zalphia is deadly without fail, and here I am, *visiting* an infirmary."

"I'm glad you got better; I would have been quite sad otherwise."

"Last time I checked, you didn't even remember I existed." And so they had arrived at the issue she wanted to address.

Roy didn't know how to answer. He was confused, more than she was. For Roy it was a much different experience. These strangers said they knew him, and they didn't seem to be lying. But he didn't know them. He imagined what they might know. Could a stranger know his deepest secrets, aware of the monster he was, or was this girl oblivious to it all?

"I remember...I remember going to Faldenheim with someone. I can't remember who. We were heading somewhere, and we passed Dart at the castle walls. After that, I remember nothing."

"You don't remember the grave? Or Jacob?"

"I don't know what grave you're talking about. As for Jacob, yeah, I know who he is." He was the better version of himself, the one with superior control of his powers, the smarter person, and better skilled with the sword.

"Jacob did this to you. So you don't remember Jacob harming you? You somehow don't remember me anymore. Or Benjamin." She paused for a second. She seemed to think of something. "Roy, do you remember feeling any pain before ending up here? Specifically, a pain on your forehead?" Roy felt his forehead, assuming there was a scar on there, but there was nothing.

Roy couldn't recall any damage to his head. He vaguely remembered something in his mind, but he couldn't recall. Roy shook his head. "I don't remember anything other than a vague pain *in* my head, but definitely not *on* it." She nodded. Roy couldn't talk about the zalphia, and he didn't want to keep talking about what had happened to him, so he decided to change the subject.

"If I remember correctly, your name is Aurora?" She nodded slowly once, and she smiled at him.

"Yeah, Aurora. You remember that much at least. Do you remember all the girls' names? Or just the pretty ones?"

Roy was glad that Aurora was trying to lighten the mood. Roy found himself smiling a little, and he said "Introduce me to some of your friends and maybe we'll see." She seemed to think of

15. Fire and Flame- 247

something else, or someone else. He saw how uncomfortable the statement had made her, and he cursed himself for mentioning it.

"Speaking of my friends," Aurora started, but seemed reluctant to finish. From behind her, he saw someone approach. Jackson was walking towards him, with a girl much younger than him at his side. She seemed vaguely familiar but Roy couldn't place her. The Korscher girl had brown hair and he knew before even seeing her that her eyes were brown too.

Aurora seemed to stiffen slightly, but she stepped aside and let Jackson talk with Roy, though she didn't leave, something for which Roy was grateful. "Roy, glad to see you're doing better. Do you remember anything yet?"

Roy shook his head, wondering what Jackson would do. Surely the Wise Ones wouldn't repeat their previous endeavors. That was what he hoped anyway. "I heard you didn't recognize Aurora here, nor Ben. You also seemed to feel pain when someone else was mentioned." He stopped a little, but then proceeded. "Roy, do you know who this is?"

The girl next to him seemed vaguely familiar. Brown hair, something about her brown eyes seemed familiar, and she had a build not dissimilar to Aurora's, though perhaps with a little more bulk. She seemed uncomfortable at Jackson's side, but she also was defiant somehow. Still, Roy could not place her name.

"This is Jen. She...she really meant something to someone." Roy didn't know what he meant by that, but he didn't have to ponder it long. "Well, I do hope you feel better soon Roy. I'll be around." With those words, he left, and Aurora went back to his side.

"Any idea what that was about?" Roy asked.

"Roy, I don't know what's wrong with you, but it's worrisome, truly. Her name is Jennifer Bender. She...she definitely meant something to someone."

"To whom? Meant something to whom?"

"I'm afraid what will happen if I say his name. Last time, things didn't turn out so well." She emphasized the infirmary to prove her point.

"I'm glad you came," Roy said before he could stop himself. Roy quickly tried to figure out what he could add to seem nonchalant about it. "I don't imagine being alone, recovering, would be very exciting."

Aurora grabbed Roy's hand and squeezed it. "Feel better Roy." He thought of how warm and soft her skin was. Roy thought about how gentle but firmly she squeezed his hand, and how she had gingerly retreated her hand. She didn't immediately retreat her hand, she had kept it in contact.

Roy countered these thoughts by thinking about a sword going through someone's heart, piercing skin and cartilage, and releasing a liquid of relaxing crimson. How his sword firmly pressed against his hand as the sword entered the other's body, and how the blood was warm and flowed gently down.

One of these thoughts sickened him, but he didn't know which.

"Thanks Aurora. Believe me, if I had a choice in the matter, I would feel better and remember everything as it's supposed to be." He wondered what his relationship to Aurora was before this. "Aurora, were we friends before all this? Were we good friends?"

She didn't seem to know how to answer. "Roy, you and I sat together whenever we studied with the Wise Ones. You, another friend of ours, and I were all friends. We went to Bravania together. We went to the Lancaster Lands."

"I'm sorry I don't remember."

"It's not your fault you don't. You said it yourself, if you could, you'd remember, but you can't. But if something made you forget, something can make you remember."

"Yeah, I really hope." Aurora was staring at him, but she wasn't looking at Roy's eyes. She was looking just above them. Roy wondered what she had meant with her question about any pain on his head. Instead of asking though, he remained silent and enjoyed her company. "It's strange, knowing that you know who I am, and not knowing how you know any of it, nor recalling the time we might have spent together."

"I can't imagine how it must feel for you. I feel a little frustrated that you can't recall anything, and I can scarcely put myself in your position." From the corner of his eye, Roy saw guards running back and forth. He realized how much busier the day had become, and how full of activities he had failed to observe. He saw for the first time the light that was making itself noticed, and how even the infirm had a certain vigor. The guards though, that was something that caught his attention.

Aurora noticed this too, and she went to one of the guards. "What's going on?" Roy could hardly hear more of the conversation so he got up and walked towards them. The toll on him was heavy, but he could walk. He heard the guard mention a fire, and the guard was then ordered to go to the meeting room.

Roy turned to the one who had ordered the guard, and it was the same one Aurora had been with before. He noticed for the first time the red cloak identifying him as a Knight of the Order of the Sword.

"Benjamin, why aren't you combatting the fire?"

"There might be a fire, but the chaos that would ensue if people found out I had control over fire would be worse. No, we're fighting this fire off like any normal fire, though I suspect it isn't."

Roy was still lightheaded but he understood the implication. Aurora asked, "You think it's *Argus*?"

Ben shook his head and said "it's impossible to tell. I hope it isn't, but I don't know. Come on, we've wasted too much time. There's a fire." Despite his lack of strength, Roy followed Ben outside the edifice of the Wise Ones and went to the eastern gate. He immediately could see the smoke, and he went on the wagon that the other guy Aurora had been with was already on.

"Took you long enough Ben."

"Sorry Max. Only *they* would ask so many questions after I told them there was a fire." Max chuckled at that, and they were off to fight the fire.

As they got closer to the fire, Roy had trouble breathing. The smoke entered his lungs, preventing him from taking in the air he desired and needed. He had the strong urge to cough uncontrollably, but he knew he needed to keep the façade going—pretending that he was alright and they needn't worry about him. Everything was getting hotter as well, and the noise of people shouting drowned his thoughts.

The frenetic rush of the crowd made Roy feel all the more lightheaded, and he found himself wishing he had stayed at the infirmary. It was too late for such thoughts though, and he saw buckets of water being carried, pouring over the fire. He saw the piles of rock with which they would try to smother the fire. He saw men and women rushing, screaming, and doing everything in their power to protect their home. He saw guards taking off their helms, struggling against the heat and the smoke. The guards had their swords on their hips, and Roy imagined hundreds of guards drawing their swords and trying to fight the flames. *Perhaps they could light their swords on fire and fight fire with fire.*

Max took off, but Ben stayed and told something to Aurora, something Roy didn't hear. Aurora nodded, but Roy continued looking around. He didn't stand up, nor did he think to go help put the fire out, but instead he just observed. *Fallen Castle number two.* But he ignored himself. Faldenheim wouldn't burn. Ben wouldn't allow it, Max and Logan would stop it, and Lord Horus would not be outwitted by a fire.

Maybe that would hold true for a normal fire.

Nothing seemed to be working, and the endeavor of the people seemed to be for naught. They were unable to do anything against the fire, and the desperation was evermore discernable. They would not succeed. The fire would be too much for these people. They needed his help. They needed his powers. They would be unable to protect themselves without using the powers of Ben and Max and Logan. *Would they make that decision?* Roy pondered this, and he knew he ought to do something.

###

Aurora looked at Roy, who just seemed to observe the fire and pontificate. Aurora got off the wagon, noticed that Roy hadn't felt a thing, and followed Benjamin. He knew exactly where he was going, and they found Jackson almost immediately. At his side was Logan and Dart, and they both weren't looking at Benjamin nor her, but instead had their eyes on someone running towards them. Aurora realized he was a scout, coming to inform the prince about something.

Logan stopped the scout, but the other said he needed to see Lord Horus, and that it was vital. Jackson approached the scout, but the scout insisted on seeing Lord Horus. "I am the Prince of

Faldenheim, Jackson Horus. Anything you would like to take to my father can be directly told to me. What is it?"

The scout seemed to hesitate, but he must have figured he wouldn't be able to move on unless he told him. "I saw Prince Kingston on the outskirts of the castle. He clearly didn't want to be noticed. I...it isn't my place to say, nor do I pretend to accuse the prince of anything, but it seemed to me that he...that he has control over fire. And perhaps...he might have had a hand in...this fire." Observably the scout was scared.

Accusing a prince wasn't something you could do lightly, and to accuse him of being a zalphic was not something you said flippantly. Aurora wondered what exactly he had seen that would give him the courage to say these things. He was right, of course, but it seemed all so strange. Jackson signaled to Logan and Dart, and they brought him along with Jackson. They headed towards Lord Horus, and Benjamin and Aurora followed. Benjamin was trying to get Jackson to disperse the people and have him and some other recruits use their power over fire.

Aurora followed Jackson to his father's wagon. There, they relayed the message to his father. "Argus caused the fire."

"You see. The war hasn't been prevented." Aurora remembered what Lord Horus had said, how the meet at Bravania had not prevented the war in the north. The war between Faldenheim and Vernatia. Argus was pushing for war, and this would not be his last attempt.

"We can't accuse Argus. You know what this will mean father."

Lord Horus gave his son a patronizing glance. Aurora kept repeating in her head that he knew this would happen. "Yes, we must keep this quiet. Even if not for the war, we cannot expose his status as a zalphic." Aurora thought that he sounded somehow defeated; Lord Horus knew that war was coming, and he couldn't preclude it. But she also knew that Lord Horus was much smarter than she was, and there might still be something he could do, but Aurora didn't know what that would be.

The scout, who had been maintained a certain distance from the Lord so that he could speak to his son, was signaled to step forward. Lord Horus spoke up. "Explain to me again what you saw, and be not afraid to offer specificities or make observations."

The scout seemed even more nervous talking to Lord Horus, and he looked away. Still, he spoke up. "I was on the outskirts to the southeast of Faldenheim. I saw a robed man walking to Faldenheim from the east accompanied by a young man. I didn't think much of them, they were only two. I went along on my business and left them unperturbed. Later on, I noticed the smoke and was headed to the fire when I saw the same robed man and young man heading away from the fire. I thought it strange. They were heading east, back towards their point of origin.

"I followed them and they met up with a group of people. Perhaps eight men in all. He took off the robe and it was Prince Kingston. He said something to the men, then fire appeared in front of him, from nowhere. I was stunned, and then he closed his hands, and the fire ceased to be."

Lord Horus simply nodded. "Thank you for the information. It is invaluable. I expect you to stay quiet about the subject whilst we deliberate on what is to be done." Lord Horus dismissed the scout and when he was gone, he kept quiet for a while. Aurora knew though that this silence served the construction of his plan. She knew he would think of something. "Allister, forgive me. Argus, you forced me to do this." Aurora was all too aware of the strange demeanor in which he said it. There was something Lord Horus could do, and it wouldn't end well for the Kingstons.

Lord Horus stood up and demanded the people's attention. All around them, the movement stopped as they waited to hear the words of their lord. "As a member of the Wise Ones, and a seeker of the truth and the properties of the world, we have conclusively determined that the fire on the eastern gate has been caused by unnatural means." Aurora held her breath. *Is he going to accuse Argus?* "Furthermore, I, along with others from the Wise Ones, have determined that this fire cannot be extinguished by normal means, as evidenced by the fruitless effort and our inadequacy to stop it. I call upon the fire zalphics to help put out the fire.

"Not for me, not to protect my castle, not to protect your lord from the fire that would engulf him. Instead, I ask you to use your powers to prove that you are not the enemy, that the victims of unwarranted hate deserve peace. That you may use your powers to help your fellow neighbor, that our fear of these abilities is folly,

15. Fire and Flame- 253

and that we owe to you a debt. I ask those with fire, help. I would not have us watch as the home and life of many is destroyed by the hatred that we have so inanely disseminated. zalphics should not be our enemy." Aurora was confused. This wasn't an indictment of Argus. Lord Horus proportioned no blame. He asked for help.

May Allister forgive him? Argus forced him to do this? She didn't understand the relationship between his speech and Argus. Within but a few moments, the streets reverberated with the Lord's call for help. No one came forward though, and Aurora knew this would be the case. Despite what Lord Horus might have said, he wouldn't be able to protect them from the onslaught that would result. Benjamin spoke with Lord Horus. Aurora was too far away, and lost in the fervor from the streets. Lord Horus adamantly shook his head, and Benjamin looked confused.

Benjamin approached her and told her to head to the eastern gate. Aurora figured she knew what this meant. "You're going to take the lead? Show the others that they can and should help?"

Benjamin just shook his head. This took Aurora by surprise. She had thought this was the whole point of Lord Horus's speech. He was trying to get those with fire to help. Why wouldn't he want Benjamin to help? Aurora pondered this, and headed towards the castle gates. Despite what Lord Horus had said, people were still trying to stop the fire, thinking they could, through a collective effort, stop it and protect their homes. They weren't making any progress.

Argus Kingston and his group of men arrived at the castle, running. Alongside him was Jacob. She didn't recognize the others, but they varied in age. Some were younger than she, some were older. Argus immediately went to the fire and helped with the efforts to put it out. The concentrated flames seemed to relax, and the intense smoke lessened.

Aurora watched as Argus and his men put out the fire, and the smug look on Argus that seemed to indicate he thought himself the savior of Faldenheim, something certainly Argus had been planning. He knew that the people of Faldenheim would be unable to cease the fire, and he knew that only when he came would the fire give out. He had planned this. But what had Lord Horus said?

Aurora realized that Argus had just messed up. And by the look of Benjamin's angry gaze, he didn't realize it yet. She heard the murmuring and the repetition of the lord's words. They kept getting louder in her head, and she couldn't believe she hadn't seen this. *That would be why he is an Elder.* Aurora saw the fire die. The fire and flames that Argus had hoped would celebrate him would engulf him instead.

"This is ridiculous," started Benjamin. "I could have stopped this fire, gotten this over with so long ago, but now Argus has come and will take credit for saving Faldenheim."

"It's okay Benjamin."

"How is this okay? Don't you see that Argus is winning the favor of these people, for the start of his war?"

"It won't come to that. Lord Horus has ensured that." Benjamin looked confused, and Aurora motioned for them to join Roy. He was still tired, she knew, and confused about his life. Aurora felt a certain pity for Roy. He didn't belong with Jackson, and he didn't belong with Benjamin.

"Roy." Roy looked up, but somehow was still not broken from his reverie. He glazed over Benjamin and looked back at the castle gates.

"The fire...it's been put out."

Benjamin again got annoyed. "Yes, I can see that Roy."

"I hear from all these people that Lord Horus said someone caused the fire. That someone was using their powers."

"Yeah." In a lower voice, Benjamin continued. "It was Argus. He did this."

"Interesting, but not the point." Roy still seemed so distant, and Aurora couldn't help but wonder what must have been going through his mind. "How are they going to arrest the prince of Vernatia?"

"Arrest?" Benjamin asked. Aurora looked at Roy, surprised. Even through whatever was going through his mind, the fatigue, the amnesia, and all the other burdens of his, he could still see what Aurora saw.

15. Fire and Flame- 255

"Lord Horus said it couldn't be stopped by normal means. He called on those with fire to help. No one came. Only Argus." Benjamin now seemed to understand what Lord Horus had done.

"You mean...."

Roy still seemed in a distant world, so Aurora explained. "Lord Horus knew no one would risk the exposure and help put out the fire. But he mentioned that someone with fire had to put it out. Then Argus came and put out the fire, thereby incriminating himself, letting the people know he is a zalphic." Aurora knew that whatever story Argus told would be ignored. She could imagine the story now. "I was with some men training, when I saw smoke in the distance and I immediately hurried over." No one would believe him now.

After a long while, Roy finally got up. People were relieved, glad there was no fire to worry them now. Argus accepted the people's admirations. They slowly made way to Argus, while the people around them seemed to start realizing what had happened. Aurora noticed a crowd—a mob actually—approach him as well. They were shouting something that she couldn't hear, but she imagined what it could have been. *They're zalphics. They have fire. They're sick. Kill them.* Aurora saw the guards go up to them, swords drawn, and saw Argus as he saw that he wasn't their hero. He was their enemy, and the best part was, he still didn't know why....

Chapter 16
Another Side

Despite the darkness of the keep and the screaming silence, Aurora could see that Argus was in the foulest of moods. *Understandably so*, she thought. Guards circled the group as they moved forward. It was said that those with telekinesis could not teleport through things, so the circle never faltered nor left any open space. Argus didn't speak, didn't invoke his status as a prince, nor his position in the Wise Ones. She didn't think that would do much anyway. They were headed to see Lord Horus, and they arrived at the door. Inside, Jackson, Logan and Dart were next to Lord Horus, who was sitting, waiting to pass judgment.

There were, of course, other officials to hear as well, but Aurora didn't know any of them, nor did she care. The guards that encircled the men continued. Roy was next to her, as was Benjamin and Maximillius, and they were allowed inside on the pretext that they had been there for the lord's plea, and saw Argus fight the fire. Argus addressed Lord Horus without the courtesies due to the lord, and instead expressed himself fully. "Hal, I've done nothing wrong. I *saved* your castle, and your people attacked me. I ought to have my father exercise his power."

Lord Horus stood up. "The castle walls were set on fire by someone with the power over fire—very potent powers at that. We cannot determine that you are free from blame, and so we must keep you and investigate. This is for your own protection Argus. Clearly some—if not all—your men are zalphics, and I cannot allow them to simply leave. The people out there only held back from attacking you because they knew you were a prince. I would not observe how long that status may continue to save you."

"I demand to be taken to Vernatia."

"Your *request* must be denied. This fire was a direct attack on Faldenheim, and leaving is beyond reason."

"I will leave on my own accord then."

"How would you do that Argus? Would you attack us, attack a *lord*, and use powers to escape? That would incriminate you all the more, and of course we are still investigating what could have happened."

"The investigations you speak of are frivolous. I will leave, no one will be harmed, and I will take residence in Vernatia."

"That will not be permitted." At the same time, the guards turned to face the group.

"You allege we are zalphics, but then you underestimate its strength." There was no blink of an eye, no miniscule moment in which darkness had engulfed them, no place in time when Aurora had looked away from Argus, and without any sign, he was gone. Aurora looked around and saw Argus kneeling right in front of the lord, a wicked smile on his face. That was impossible. Argus didn't have telekinesis. He had fire, and that was it. Benjamin had told her, Roy had told her—everyone knew Argus only had fire. But he had just teleported. Upon spotting Argus, some of the guards charged, drawing swords and spears and making to strike him immediately. Lord Horus stopped them by raising his hand. He clearly looked shocked.

Lord Horus turned to Logan and Dart. "Get them out of here." Aurora didn't know who "they" were, but she feared she was part of the group. Logan moved to the other officials, and gathered them, sword in hand, prepared to defend them. Dart followed suit, taking the other men away, all of them but Jacob. "Whatever quarrel you have, it is with me, and not with them. Clearly your powers are strong, and they do not deserve to die for following my orders." Argus nodded, knowing what Lord Horus was doing. Logan directed the guards as well, and they all left—some grudgingly, some with relief.

As soon as they left, Jackson spoke up for the first time. "Jacob. How...?" Aurora realized that it wasn't Argus who had teleported himself, but Jacob who had teleported Argus. She couldn't believe this was possible though. Jacob wasn't touching him. Steven had told her that he had teleported Jennifer once, without teleporting himself, but this seemed even stranger. She suddenly remembered that Jacob hadn't been touching Argus, and he teleported him *through* people. Steven had told her, how he had teleported Jackson and Argus through a wall, and made them appear in front of him. He had told her he had a massive headache, and she had attributed this to a trick of the mind. It must have been true.

She could see Roy looking at Jacob, focusing on nothing else. She turned to Jackson, and Argus stood up. "I'm going back to Vernatia now, but believe me that this isn't even the first of it." Argus got up. He turned to Jacob. Benjamin and Maximillius drew their swords.

Argus briefly looked at Benjamin and then shrugged. Jacob looked at Aurora briefly, and then turned to Roy. Roy seemed to stiffen, and he seemed to want to hide. Aurora wanted to do that too, but there was nothing she could do. Roy had at least the power of thunder, and could try to fight free.

Jacob looked at Argus, who Jacob then teleported to his side. Then he spoke softly into the prince's ear. Of course, Aurora knew that Jacob could have simply used telepathy, told him what was on his mind without having to move Argus. He was showing off his power, demonstrating how strong he was. From Jackson's expression, she didn't suppose that even he could do that. Argus looked up at Roy. "Come with us Roy. Come and unlock your powers, just as Jacob has shown you. Clearly you are held back here."

Roy didn't seem to know what to say. He was shocked, confused that they were asking him to join them. Aurora didn't know what was on his mind, but she thought that Roy wouldn't join Argus. He had too much history here in Faldenheim, in Farendor. Too many things had happened with Steven and her and Roy.

Then she thought of his condition, how he didn't remember, and suddenly Aurora worried that Roy wouldn't deny their request. Roy didn't remember what had happened, and he wouldn't be opposed, but he still had his family in Farendor. He wouldn't leave them behind, wouldn't forsake them.

Roy continued to look at Jacob, and Aurora wondered what could be going through his mind. She wondered what was so important about Jacob.

Lord Horus cleared his throat. "Argus, leave now. I hope you will listen to what Allister will have to say." Argus seemed to tense, but he looked at Jacob. In an instant, Roy kneeled to the ground in pain, grabbing his head, and Benjamin shot fire at him. The fire dissipated before reaching Roy, and Benjamin turned to look at Jacob. Jacob was tired, visibly panting for breath, exhausted from using his powers.

Roy looked at Benjamin, and looked at Jacob, with something like fear in his eyes. Jacob spoke. "You're very strong Roy, but of course you're ill prepared to protect anyone." That seemed to resonate with Roy, and he stood up. "But you're power is unparalleled, and you can learn to use it."

"He's lying Roy," Jackson said, but Aurora didn't think he was paying any attention. Aurora had been sick, suffering from the effects of zalphia at the time, but suddenly, Brandon's words came to mind. *Expect no help from him when someone too strong comes around.* Roy approached Jacob, and turned to Aurora. There was something in his eyes, something like respite. Jacob turned to Benjamin and Maximillius, and Aurora could no longer stare at Roy, so she followed Jacob's gaze. Thunder shot out from him, and Benjamin and Maximillius fell to the ground.

Aurora saw something that gave her at least a bit of hope. Jacob was exerted. He breathed heavier, and she was satisfied that at least, his power wasn't endless. "Jackson, I know as you do that our powers have been limited. He did something to us—I wouldn't admit it, but I know it must hold true for you. That is why I needed all their help, but Jacob wasn't affected, as he wasn't there, and his power will grow, and so will Roy's." Aurora didn't understand the scope of the threat, but she recognized it was one.

Benjamin and Maximillius were starting to get up, and Roy looked at Jacob, as if shocked. Aurora knew that Jacob must have told Roy to do something. He looked at her, looked at Aurora and seemed to say something with his eyes, something like sorry, and then he shot thunder at her and Benjamin and Maximillius.

260 - The Midnight War

The other two fell to the ground, unconscious, but the thunder headed towards her was destroyed. Jacob looked at Roy, and Roy looked at Jacob, confused.

"What are you?" Roy asked. Aurora got mad. He had just joined Argus, shocked Benjamin and Maximillius, tried to shock her, and he was asking what *she* was? Roy was troubled, she knew, but he had issues beyond reparation, something she seemed to realize for the first time at that point. The anger overtook her.

"What do you mean what am I? You just shocked everyone with thunder!" she managed to shout without being scared.

Roy sent lightning towards her, but this time, instead of dissipating, it was redirected toward Argus. He had no time to react. "What the...." Aurora turned to Argus, then looked back at Roy. She didn't know what had just happened, and worse was when she saw Jackson and Lord Horus, the both of them confused.

"She can't be...," everyone turned their attention to Argus.

Roy swallowed something back, but he proceeded to talk. "I'm sorry. I still don't remember you. Maybe we were close. It really seems like we weren't, you didn't seem so believable. But I must go with Jacob."

With those words, Jacob teleported them away. Aurora turned to Benjamin. Benjamin was weak; he managed to get up, only to fall back down. She looked at Jackson, who was still in shock. He looked at Lord Horus, searching for his father's guidance.

"Looks like we're still going to war," Jackson said to break the silence.

"Yeah. Of course, Argus will not be able to change much. He is presumed to be a zalphic, and the people won't follow him. Then all these people already saw Argus teleport, and though he doesn't have telekinesis, people will say he does."

Aurora knew that Lord Horus had no power. His will, his hope for their future, all meant nothing. He was a slave to those he served, and he didn't have the power to do as he wished. There were expectations of him, expectations that he couldn't ignore. Despite what he wanted, Aurora knew he would be forced to follow the will of the people, and these wanted to rid themselves of Argus. They wanted to eliminate the zalphics.

16. Another Side- 261

Even the Wise Ones wouldn't be able to do anything. Eventually, they would have to do the same thing they did with Brandon; he would be forced to leave the order, and soon nothing would protect him. Perhaps if they could prevent the allegations, they could come to an agreement. But if the people believed Argus was a zalphic, Lord Horus would be unable to do anything but declare war.

"What are you going to do about Roy?" Lord Horus addressed his son. It occurred to Aurora that she shouldn't be there, that she should take Benjamin and Maximillius to the infirmary and take care of them, and let the Horuses talk among themselves. They had mentioned Roy though, and Aurora was wondering what they would do, so she remained silent and listened.

"As soon as he gets his memory back I don't think he'll continue fighting alongside Argus. Perhaps someone should take Telekay and try to reason with him." Logan and Dart came in, perhaps at Jackson's directive. They went to Benjamin and Maximillius and lifted them.

Aurora didn't know how long it would take Argus to get back to Vernatia—no one did. They couldn't determine whether they would make the most haste possible, travel at a normal speed, or use Jacob's teleportation to aid them in reaching Vernatia. Regardless of the time, Lord Horus wasted no time making preparations for war. Guards were being trained, men were being outfitted with armor, and the blacksmiths received work.

Benjamin, Maximillius, and Jennifer were with Jackson now, and they were at the part of the keep that housed the Wise Ones. They no longer were preparing their journey to the Capital, and they went over the budgets. "You will head to Vernatia and try to prevent this. I don't know that you'll be successful, but we must try." Benjamin gave an imperceptible nod. "You are to take Max and Jen. Of course, Jon will probably want to go too." Jackson looked at Aurora. There was disdain on his face, something she had started to notice since Maekor was killed.

Benjamin responded softly. "You've nothing to worry about. Max and I will not fail. Jennifer is tough, and she and Jon can protect themselves." Aurora felt weird. Benjamin didn't mean to do it, but his statement made Aurora feel useless, and an inconvenience. The four of them could defend themselves, but what about her? She was the only one unable to defend herself, the only one who wasn't a zalphic.

Aurora stared at Benjamin. She didn't know what to do. She wasn't a zalphic, which meant if she went along, she would be holding them back. But, she didn't want to stay. She saw too many things not to go.

Benjamin, as if reading her mind, said: "Aurora will certainly be of great help to us." Aurora reflected on those words. She didn't know what he meant by that.

"Why aren't we taking Brandon?" Asked Aurora. "Weren't they friends?"

"I need him here." With that terse reply, he directed his words to Benjamin. "Argus wasn't lying. My power has been sealed somehow. His has too. That doesn't mean though, that you should try to fight him yourself. He is still the same swordsman, and he is still stronger than you might think. While you're at it, try and get Roy back. Maybe once he remembers Steven, he will be back to normal."

Aurora thought about Steven, what he would say, what he would do. Aurora felt a great part of her missing, a hole that devoured whatever she tried to fill it with, a hole that let nothing escape and that made everything gravitate around it. Aurora was lost in her thoughts, in how they had shared minds and Steven had revealed all his secrets to her.

"...snap out of it Aurora!" She snapped back to reality. Everyone was looking at her.

Jackson rose, ready to leave, but first he directed his words to Aurora. "You're best friend died; you have to fight on. You don't really get over it, you just try to live with it. You want to keep him alive, I know, but all the work you do will do little to change the reality of it, and you can't let this obsess you. Let Benjamin be an example. He is not cold, he loved his brother, and he feels worse than you that he died, but he can keep his mind focused, you've got to be able to. Otherwise, no matter your strengths and powers and cunning, there will be nothing you can do."

Aurora pondered on that thought, and she looked at Jennifer. She didn't know why, but she felt Jennifer could somehow help her. Aurora saw that she was trying not to think about Steven, trying not to cry, or let her other emotions out. She tried to be calm, but she saw the sadness, the clear withdrawal from reality she still experienced. Jennifer's was different from hers though, she knew, but Aurora thought there was something there.

She looked at Benjamin, who was completely focused, though it was a forced focus. It wasn't normal, like Max's was....

Roy walked alongside Jacob and Argus. It felt weird being there, but not because it was unfamiliar. It was, but with his lapse in memory, there were many things unfamiliar. The strangeness derived from Roy's emotions—that tiny part that here and there annoyed him with demands or shame or frustration. Jacob was strong, and Roy wanted to learn from him. He didn't want to continue the way he was, weak and powerless to do anything. Unable to take control, if he so desired.

Roy had an inherent fear of Jacob's superiority: he was smarter, stronger, faster, and precise. He was an Instructor in the Order of the Wise Ones, compared to Roy's status as a Scholar. Jacob was a Bladesman in the Order of the Sword, where Roy would, at best, be a Knight. *At best*. Jacob could think on the spot, react quickly with his sword, and see all at once the deeper truths hidden in simple events. Roy had to think about these things, slow himself down to analyze and perceive. Jacob had superb control of his powers, shooting precise bolts of thunder to whomever he wished. He could use telekinesis so well, he could control another's mind, even if for only a fraction, and make him shoot fire at someone.

In the distance, he could see Vernatia, the castle of the Kingston's growing larger and larger. The closer the castle got, the more Roy realized what he had done. He wouldn't see his family, he wouldn't see Aurora, nor would he see Ben and Max and all these strange people who seemed to know him. The Wise Ones would still provide for Roy's family, Argus told him, but he still missed his family. They were one of the things that kept him in a world empty of zalphics and secret plots.

Before he realized what he was doing, he checked to see if his brother was in his telepathy's range. He wasn't, and Roy thought how stupid he was. He couldn't talk to his brother like that. His brother wouldn't understand, he would be fearful of his powers. His family had stuck next to him, but they didn't understand the extent of his powers.

He realized with a start that telepathy was something only those with Telekinesis had. He only had the power of Thunder. He looked at a patch of the ground—there were a couple of rocks. He shot thunder at one of them, and the other he moved towards him, with his mind.

Jacob spoke up. "That's interesting. Since when do you have telekinetic powers Roy?"

Roy could only shake his head. He didn't know. It had occurred to him that he hadn't realized the transformation that had occurred. "I don't know. It has just been slowly manifesting. I didn't even realize."

"Since when has it been manifesting?" Roy thought about that. He wasn't sure. He had tried to contact his brother with telepathy, but he didn't think that was the first time. He couldn't remember though, and maybe it was from what he was forgetting—what he couldn't remember as a result of...of something Roy wasn't exactly sure about.

Roy shrugged and shook his head in confusion. "I haven't the slightest clue."

Argus spoke up now. "Roy, would you say you developed your powers *recently*?"

Roy immediately nodded. He couldn't be so certain about his answer, he realized, but he felt that, though doubtful, his conviction was correct. He had answered immediately. "My thunder powers came really early, but telekinesis has fairly recently manifested."

"I see..... He must have given you powers. But how is that possible? Interesting, I need to find out how he did it."

"How who did what?" Roy asked.

"How S—" Argus looked at Roy and seemed to rethink what he was about to say. "How you managed to start using your dormant telekinesis." Argus hadn't answered his question, but Roy hadn't really expected him to. Instead he kept walking, thinking about his powers. He wondered what he would do. For now, he would continue alongside Argus and Jacob. He was afraid. That's what kept him going.

"What are we going to do from here?" asked Roy. Jacob didn't even seem to hear him, but Argus paused for a second.

He resumed his steps and spoke: "Jackson believes that I want to kill anyone that is in my way, and anyone who will prevent me from obtaining my goals. That's half true, but his definition of people in my way and mine are very different. This war that's going to happen, the one against Nevil, we need to prepare for it. We need to protect ourselves."

"So why go to war with Jackson? Why waste resources and men fighting him if someone else is coming? That doesn't seem too bright an idea."

"Jackson is not the recognized heir, but he still exerts much too dominance over others. He cares only for serving his purses and filling them with gold. That is why we have made a plan to overthrow him. We still have time. There are many things we have to do yet."

Roy noticed that Argus hadn't mentioned killing Jackson. He just wanted to take away his power. "What plan is that?"

"It involves a young king overthrowing the rule of an even younger king." Roy was confused. *King.* Roy had thought this was about Faldenheim, but he realized this was much bigger. Argus wanted to overthrow King Whaldo III. Replace him with another king? Who was he referring to? It seemed to Roy that this wasn't the time to fight among each other. This served to demonstrate how imperative this really was, if it was important enough to declare war before an invasion.

"NO!" Roy looked around; the message was a strong voice as if he were travelling among them. Roy thought of the voice. *Who was that? Why did that voice seem so familiar? But...I've never heard that voice before...have I? No, I'm sure I haven't. Could my mind*

be playing tricks? "Roy, you must awaken." Roy's head started to hurt with a great intensity.

Why, why does this happen to me! Roy was not strong enough to withstand the pain. He was again passed out to the world of the brain's fantasies....

There was a twilight being produced by a house. Roy had no idea where he was, but he felt confident. His sword joined him. In a scabbard to his feet lay another sword, a sword made of Caster metal, and a blade of purple.

"Choose your sword. Choose wisely though...." Roy looked up to find no one was in front of him. There was no one in the dark room with him, only darkness. Now he started to feel less confident. Roy had doubts, and he didn't know which sword to choose. Although he felt more comfortable with his old sword, something about this other sword resonated strength. And the way the mysterious voice said it, it made Roy think. He dropped his sword and picked up the other one. There was something familiar about the hilt, the way it weighed, and how strong he felt with it.

"Very well picked Roy. You must realize your power."

Roy woke up with a start. *What the...?* He looked at the sword that had materialized in front of him. *This is Telekay, telekinetic sword of the Telks. It was forged from the claws of the Khisharat, but, how do I know that?*

Argus and Jacob were sitting down, seeming to rest. Argus turned to Roy. Roy tried clearing his head, trying to piece together reality. The castle was much closer than it was earlier, and Roy realized Jacob must have been teleporting them. Jacob was resting, probably exerted from the use of his powers. That, and Roy was unconscious.

"I see you have your sword back. Telekay, blade of the Telks." Argus seemed to be satisfied with this. Roy grabbed Telekay with a gesture of tenure, as if it were a friend he hadn't seen in a very long time.

"Why is Telekay so important? And the other swords? Why am *I* important?"

"I wouldn't know how to explain it to you Roy. The Wisest One warned us of Nevil, and his oncoming arrival. He told us the only way to stop him would be to gather ten individuals who would each wield a specific blade. I don't know why this is, but I trust he wouldn't mislead us, so I gather the ten so that I might be able to stop Nevil."

"How do you know who those ten are, and what swords they wield?"

"Again, the Wisest One has given us the knowledge. Even so, we are still unclear on one of them. He has been able to identify nine of the ten, but the last one eludes him—and by far eludes us. We know the man and the sword because they become one, because only the swords of Caster metal have the properties necessary to materialize like Telekay did with you."

"Who do you think are the ten?"

"There's you, Jen, Jon, Ben, and Max. The five of you have swords that materialize. We think Jacob and Logan are ones, though we can't be sure until we get the sword. The other three, we don't know. The Wisest One determined that each person represents a distinct power. You have telekinesis, Ben and someone else have fire, Max and someone else have water, Jen and Jon have earth, someone has thunder, and someone has wood. We assume the last one is Invincibility."

"Assuming Jacob is one of those ten, and that the other two belong to the Order of the Protectors, that leaves half of those ten with a likeness to Jackson's ideology."

"That is where you are mistaken. Jon serves me, I sent him with Jackson to learn his plans." Roy would never have guessed Jon was betraying Jackson; of course, he hadn't met Jon that long ago, and didn't know much about him. Obviously, Jon would bring Jennifer with him to the Order of the Protectors. Which left Ben, Max, and Logan.

"Ben wants only to protect his family, and as soon as he sees that his goal and Jackson's are incompatible, he'll be forced to join me. Max will follow Ben, as the good friends they are. Hopefully, Aurora follows him as well."

"Aurora? And what if she doesn't?"

"You will be in charge of bringing her to our order."

"How will I do that?"

Argus shrugged. "Emotions tend to run strongly in women."

"You want me to...*convince* her that way?"

"Why not? Jackson used the tactic. Anyway, that leaves only Logan. Logan is second in command, and he'll be hard to convince, but of course, there is the possibility that he isn't the one."

Roy didn't really know what to say to that. He didn't want to keep talking about the plan for Aurora, so he changed the subject. "Before I passed out, you mentioned you wanted to replace the king. Why? Why not keep the current king, wait until Nevil comes? Why is it so important?"

"King Whaldo isn't the leader we need. He won't be able to lead us against Nevil. He isn't even the rightful ruler. The rightful ruler is the firstborn son of the previous king. That isn't Whaldo."

"I don't understand. Whaldo is the first and only son of King Raymond and Queen Serinah."

"Our traditions in no part mention that the son has to be borne of the queen."

Chapter 17
Homecoming

Roy Rhapsados had never been a prince. He would never be familiar with the life of a prince, all the responsibility, power, and weight. He would never understand the relationship between the prince and his subjects. Roy never had to worry about it, nor did he ever fantasize to wield that power and responsibility.

Whatever little thought Roy may have given to the idea and conception of the adoration of subject to ruler was completely shattered upon entering Vernatia. The first thing he noticed approaching the city was how few soldiers were at the castle gates. Roy had never seen such a scarce group of soldiers at a castle gate before. They saw the prince coming and immediately opened the door.

Vernatia was desolate. Few men roamed the streets, and none of them turned to Argus, none of them genuflected nor even acknowledged him. They went further into the castle, and as they got closer to the keep, they began seeing more people. But even before Roy saw them, he heard them, heard their uproar and indistinct chanting. The shouting was unmistakably the cry of anger, of anguish, of uncertainty and fear of the future.

They were all gathered around the keep, and their tremendous uproar drowned out the man standing in front of them, trying to speak. Roy saw the people rise against their lord, and Lord Kingston stood there, trying to placate the people that wanted only death.

Roy didn't actually know what they wanted yet, but couldn't imagine this crowd gathered asking Lord Kingston for a festivity, or tranquility. He heard someone yell out "there he is!" and all at once the entire crowd turned to him, and yelled and protested.

The angry voices and indignant faces seemed to carry in itself a weapon that cut into Roy's being. He was glad that he wasn't a prince—that he didn't have to be the center of all the angst.

Roy realized then why so few guards had been at the gates. He saw the guards, a multitude of them, standing between the citizens and the lord. Roy and Argus and Jacob had no such luck. The people approached them in a current of screams and anger. Argus said something, but despite his proximity, he was drowned by the voice of the crowd.

Roy suddenly wished he could be part of that crowd, lost in the multitude, not needing to stand in front of them. It wasn't the people that scared him, nor their opinion of him. It was what that meant about him that scared him. He felt that he should feel angered too, and he knew that this made him different. He didn't care that the others found him different, but his insides tormented him, told him he wasn't normal, that he didn't belong.

Roy told himself that he didn't want to belong to people as scared as them, but he knew that it was hopeless. He didn't belong in the world of normalcy and uniformity.

The crowd pushed forward, but they didn't attack. Their screams didn't turn to direct attacks, and no one ran forward to hit them. The three of them still had the sigil of the Wise Ones, and Argus was still a prince. Jacob now sported his blue cloak, and no one dared approach the Bladesman. Their anger hadn't elevated enough to strike him. Not yet anyway.

Lord Kingston tried demanding their attention. The people didn't listen. Roy could see guards trying to make their way through the crowd, trying to separate them so they could get close to the prince, to protect him. Roy wondered how the guards must have felt; not only were they certainly in accord with the people, but they had to deal with their potential violence as well. It didn't seem desirable to be a guard at that instance, but they were trained to obey, and that is what they did.

The guards managed to get to the prince, and they proceeded to protect him until he reached his father, all the time being harassed verbally by the crowd, calling him an infected, ill, freak. The people cried out, and the lord slightly inclined his head and put his hand just underneath his stomach, a gesture asking the people to let him speak. *Asking.* Lord Kingston wasn't demanding these people to be silent, but rather he was asking to speak.

The crowd grew quieter. It began in the front, as they were the only ones able to see the gesture, but soon the silence spread, and the people, wondering why others had grown silent, slowly ceased their shouting. Lord Kingston held their silence longer, and turned to his son. "We have all heard word from Faldenheim. All of us are aware that a fire nearly destroyed one of their gates, a fire that was alleged to be started by those with control over fire. Let me not pretend to imply nor play any games. I unreservedly declare that my son, Argus Kingston, is no zalphic, certainly has no control over fire, and that he undeniably did *not* start the fire in Faldenheim."

The crowd began to murmur, but it didn't go past that, since most still anxiously awaited the lord to finish. "Let there be a judgment then, of guilt or innocence, in trial by those of Vernatia. I will not appoint a judge, lest it be said I have paid this judge. Amongst yourselves you must name the most honorable and unbiased among you, and he will determine the evidence against my son."

With those words, Lord Kingston retired to the keep, and Argus followed along. Roy realized with a start that he was still standing there, while the others entered the keep. He hurriedly joined them and the Kingstons retired to the lord's chambers while Jacob headed towards another part of the keep, with some other chambers. Roy followed Jacob and entered the chambers, figuring this was where he would be staying.

Inside were other members of the Protectors. Some of them had been in Bravania, Roy knew, the day that Maekor Banesworth was killed by some outlaw. One of them seemed to remember him as well. "Hey, you're the one from Bravania." Roy nodded. "I'm Javier Lunaer." Roy felt something cold in Javier—not a characteristic, but a chill, a *wetness*. He couldn't quite pinpoint where it was coming, and all that he learned about telekinesis came flowing back. They could tell when other people were zalphics, even what that power was.

Roy felt that coldness in Javier, as he felt something from the others. "This is Joseph," he said, pointing at him. Joseph hadn't been there at Bravania, and Roy had never seen him before, but he felt a natural calmness from him, a relaxing tone. Roy could only associate that with the power of wood. Javier continued introducing the others. Miguel and David also had wood, and Agnar had thunder. These were all advanced members in the Order, not some recruits. It struck Roy that Jacob had decided to bring him to them, rather than with the new recruits.

Over the course of the next few days, they familiarized him with the order and how they functioned. Being part of the Wise Ones, Roy had naturally wondered how many people were training under them, and how the powers divided up. From the recruits, none of them had Invincibility or Telekinesis. None of those present had fire.... Nine had water, thirteen had earth, nineteen had thunder, and twenty had wood.

He knew that this only represented the population that lived close enough to Vernatia, but it satisfied his inquisitiveness, and so he went about his affairs teaching the recruits the offensive, defensive, and passive abilities of thunder. Agnar was still the one in charge of those with thunder, but they were evaluating his abilities as a leader. Roy didn't know how to explain things well, since he assumed that people could make the same inferences he did.

He didn't spend much time outside of the keep, but the few time he did spend, the people still raged on about the trial. They still had difficulties choosing who would be their honorable judge. It struck Roy that Lord Kingston must have known this would happen. Eventually though, they came up with their judge, and the trial commenced.

Lord Kingston was not permitted to defend his son, as it was viewed that his status as lord might persuade the judge. So instead, Jacob presented the case for Argus. Roy was unfamiliar with the person accusing Argus.

They went over the evidence, the statements of Faldenheim and their accusations. They reviewed what Lord Horus had said, how only a fire zalphic could stop it. It was signed with the insignia of the Wise Ones and the Lord. There was no denying that it was truly an uncommon fire. They read the account some of the leaders gave, of Argus teleporting through the guards and kneeling in front of Lord Horus. Things didn't look very well for Argus. All of Faldenheim had identified him as a zalphic, and Roy didn't see the way out.

Jacob spoke up finally. First, he mentioned that there were multiple men, and that it wasn't just Argus. He mentioned how Argus and the men were training, and that they had seen smoke in the distance. The virtuousness of the group demanded that they run and aid to extinguish the fire. Jacob admitted that the fire was not normal, and the Wise Ones were correct in identifying that someone had caused the fire.

Roy wondered what Jacob was doing. He was incriminating Argus. The assent of the crowd grew louder, but Jacob waited until they grew quiet to continue. "However, we cannot take the account of Faldenheim so serious. Now, they say that Prince Argus was surrounded by guards, and he teleported, and didn't just teleport anywhere, but teleported *through* those people. We know teleportation isn't so simple. The Wise Ones have, through countless observation, determined that this is impossible.

"Now, even supposing that what they say is true, that leads us to another problem. They say he teleported through them, so that means Argus has telekinesis. Yet they also say he has the power of fire—is that not why we stand here today? So they would have us believe that, not only does Argus have *fire*, but that he also has *telekinesis*?" The people seemed to falter in their conviction now.

Roy couldn't help but laugh in the inside. "I'm sure I don't have to explain how *extremely* unlikely that is. Those in Faldenheim seem to accuse Argus of everything they can, and see what they might have us believe. Will they say next that Argus is the one who pulls in the tide at the Detrimental Shores? That he is the one that keeps the foliage in the Lancaster Forest? Surely we see that it is not the case he has done this." Roy was amazed at Jacob. He wondered if he had planned this all, if he had teleported Argus without touching him, knowing that this would be his defense, that it was so very much unlikely.

Could Jacob have really thought about that so quickly, so enveloped in the current situation? "If Argus truly was a zalphic, why not kill them all? Why not teleport, and instead of kneeling in front of the lord, stab a sword through him instead? If Argus truly was a zalphic, they could have killed the lord, killed his men, and eliminate any so-called firsthand knowledge of his powers.

"We would like to believe that such allegations have merit. It is the awful truth—that we hope for something so hideous, so that we might talk about it. This scandal would be shocking and unforeseen, and that appeals to the monster inside of us that wishes the ruination of all others. We would like to believe the worst, and these circumstances attract our attention. But we cannot sentence a man because it would be interesting.

"The first time I noticed Prince Argus, he was in the market place. He was going around, seeing what was for sale. He was the prince, and so when he arrived at a wine merchants stand, the merchant offered the prince his best wine without cost, hoping to win favor with him. The prince refused the gift and paid him double the wine's worth. When the merchant refused payment, saying it wasn't necessary, the prince told him it was only fair. He said: 'Why should I receive free gifts of the most quality products? I, who am a prince, rich in coin and not wanting? Why should I receive something at a discount when there are others, without money and poor, who try to celebrate a wedding but can only afford the cheaper products? They need the money but still have to pay more, while I am not wanting in money but still don't have to pay the price?' At that point, I knew that Prince Argus was an honorable prince, who cared about the well-being of his subjects."

Someone from the crowd spoke up, acknowledging that his had actually happened. He confirmed the event, even adding praises of his own. The crowd grew more controlled—they were no longer prepared to strike.

The one accusing Argus mentioned that the fire was still caused by unordinary circumstances, and Jacob agreed. But then, Argus decided to speak. "I was with a group of men. I was not alone, I remind you. I went to Faldenheim to help. I can no longer be so certain of the men's reason. I am not a zalphic, nor did I spawn the fire, but I will not lie. I cannot deny with certainty that my men are zalphics." It was the only thing Argus spoke. It was interesting to Roy. Using the line of reasoning of Argus, you could again accuse him of having telekinesis, then argue that those in his group had fire. Instead, they had already won the loyalty of the subjects, convinced them Argus wasn't a zalphic, and so without thought they accepted his words and ignored the possibilities that it opened.

Roy realized something shocking at that moment. Lord Kingston was not helping defend his son. He had assumed that, though he could not represent Argus in defending him, that he would have a fundamental role in developing the arguments to exonerate Argus. Instead, he saw flaws in the logic, not becoming of an Elder of the Wise Ones. He knew that Jacob had identified these flaws, but had decided that by that point Argus would have convinced the others. But an Elder would not have prepared such flimsy arguments. He wondered what was happening between the Kingstons.

He remembered Lord Horus's words. He hoped Argus would listen to Lord Kingston's words. So then that meant Lord Kingston did not agree with the stance his son had taken, and farther than that, he would not support him.

The people supported him. They no longer resented Argus, and they certainly didn't think him to be a zalphic. Some still disbelieved, Roy saw, and they were wary of Argus. But he had the support of most people now. Slowly, those beliefs would be forgotten, and Argus would not have to worry about this. They had accepted him again as their prince, and the judge agreed that Argus wasn't a zalphic. The people began to disperse; some were still questioning, too afraid of those who were zalphics to let this event be so easily forgotten. Argus went to the keep with his father, and Roy went to his quarters at the Order of the Protectors.

The next day, he went to the recruits, to continue teaching them about powers. He noticed though, that some were missing, and he saw some weren't giving their best effort. Roy didn't care much that they weren't doing as they were told, but he very much wondered why that was. Despite Agnar judging his skills in leadership, he dismissed the recruits before they had mastered the use of thunder as a shield.

He went around the order, listening in on conversations, and saw that they no longer trusted Argus. Roy hadn't thought about the repercussions the statement from Argus would have on the

Protectors. Roy had analyzed it so much for fallacies, he hadn't considered the direct importance to others. He hadn't really considered what it meant for him. He wondered if Argus would accuse him to save his status, then laughed at himself and wondered what he would do when it came to that.

Certainly one of the first things he would do was refuse to follow him anymore—to be part of his Order. Perhaps even leave Vernatia. But it wasn't him that Argus had accused, so Roy wasn't affected by the leader's lack of concern for them.

Over the course of the next few days, tensions rose both between the Protectors, and in Vernatia as well. The Protectors were more and more worried about Argus, and how he had betrayed his men. They worried about what would happen to them, if they would be persecuted by the people. Meanwhile, Argus was stirring the people, trying to make them rise against Faldenheim. Argus attacked the character of those in Faldenheim, calling them liars and questioning their morals.

Argus told the people that they should go to war with Faldenheim. He expressed his concern that Lord Horus, being part of the Committee of the Wise Ones, would utilize his influence to spread more lies against Vernatia, and not just against Argus, but against the people. He let them know that it would not take long for the others to think of Vernatia as another Alexander Castle. That, more than anything, convinced the people that they needed to stop Lord Horus.

Argus demanded for the release of those with fire, and he went on to explain that they should be tried in Vernatia, among their peers. Argus said he wanted them to be in Vernatia, and face the judgment of their fair people—he even went a step further and took the reluctance of Lord Horus to send them to Vernatia as an indictment of Vernatia's ability in judgment. He argued that Lord Horus wasn't sending them because he doubted that Lord Kingston would be able to pass a fair judgment.

Some still doubted him, did not trust that he wasn't actually a zalphic. Most believed he wasn't, but they didn't care for what Argus was saying about Faldenheim, Some though, an increasing group of people, wholeheartedly trusted Argus and echoed his demands. Argus was slowly winning his people back, and maybe he wouldn't successfully get them all back, but he seemed to continually win others.

He didn't seem able to convince the Protectors though, and those who hadn't decided to leave were still all too aware of the prince's betrayal. They didn't want to open themselves to any accusations of being zalphics. Roy tried talking to the recruits, trying to convince them that being among the Protectors would be beneficial. Roy knew that he couldn't articulate his thoughts, and his lack of communication skills seemed evident as he made no progress with them.

Agnar talked to them as well, and calmed them down some, but they still hadn't changed their minds. Almost half the recruits had already left, and Roy knew these hadn't left only because they had nowhere else to go. Roy couldn't think of anything to say to them.

Jacob finally addressed the recruits one day. He hadn't been too interested in the Protectors as of late, and seemed to have just noticed that a lot of the recruits weren't there. "I don't know where the others went, but it was a mistake. We haven't betrayed you, and Argus will still protect those in the Protectors. Think what you will about the man, he stays by those like him, all us zalphics who are trying to survive the increasingly hostile circumstances. That's why he's siding with—" Jacob paused, knowing he was about to say something he shouldn't have. "That's why he's doing whatever's possible to help us.

"He wants to go to Faldenheim. He wants to *rescue* his men over there. Don't you see if he hadn't said anything, the others wouldn't have believed him? Lies must be told even from the noblest of people to get anything done. He's going to war with Faldenheim for them. Granted, not just them, but he's going to war to liberate them and bring them back. You think Argus would just leave them there?"

Jacob was so convincing Roy himself almost believed him. But he knew Argus was going to war because he needed to eliminate Jackson's power. The recruits seemed to believe Jacob. Or, at least, they *wanted* to believe him.

Roy realized now was the time to convince them. "I for one will go to Faldenheim and ensure that they come back to us. I will not leave them to their terrible fate." For a brief second, Roy saw his childhood robbed by the Wise Ones, and he almost shuddered. He saw that the recruits were looking him, and he tried to think of something else to say. "We all know what they are capable of doing, some more than others. That is why we protect each other, why we *must* do this. I will not wait to hear that they have been hanged, or that they have been used to 'further knowledge about powers', and I certainly would not hope that if the positions were reversed, that others would not fight for me."

He saw the recruits assenting, and looked at Jacob, secretly hoping to see gratitude or admiration in his eyes. *"Follow Agnar after you're done here."* With those words, Jacob exited, and he disappeared into the halls of the keep.

Agnar straightened up, cleared his throat, and spoke. "Roy is right. We can't stay here and wait for Faldenheim to decide to kill them. I am going to Faldenheim, I will begin my journey there. I won't hurry, and I'll go at a leisurely pace. If you wish to follow me, you can. I understand if you won't, but I will not let their innocent lives torment my living moments. You don't have to join me today, you can gather supplies, talk to others, and later join me. As I said, leisurely pace. They won't know I go to strike." Roy silently laughed at his argument. To Roy, the idea that the innocent lives would torment his living moments was derisive, but he said nothing and let the recruits believe Agnar.

They both left the recruits, and Roy wasted no time before asking Agnar what Jacob had told him. "He told me to tell the recruits I'd be heading to Faldenheim. I'm going tonight. You won't be joining me, not yet anyway. You will tell the ones who remain that you will claim to be the one who started the fire, and that this would give me the opening I need to save the men there. You won't, of course, but Jacob seems to think this is what will give the recruits the certainty necessary to follow me to Faldenheim."

Agnar went over the general idea of their endeavor. Agnar would go with Javier and Miguel to Faldenheim with as many recruits as would join them. They would pretend to be outraged that Argus wasn't accused. Roy would convince the other recruits to join them, but would be at the keep with Jacob, Argus, and Lord Kingston. He didn't know any more than that.

Roy went back to the chambers, while Agnar prepared the voyage, and he saw Javier and Joseph coming out of the keep, getting ready as well. That night, some of the recruits left, maybe a fourth of those that had remained.

The next day, Roy talked to the recruits, and they all asked him why he hadn't gone with Agnar. He simply told them that he was waiting for them to get closer to Faldenheim, so that he wouldn't be exasperated from the wait. He found that another fourth of the recruits would join them later, but were waiting for one reason or another. Some told Roy that they would go when he went.

He waited another day before telling them that he would claim to have started the fire that burned part of Faldenheim. He went over the reasons he had prepared to give for his decision, telling them it would give the others an opening. Roy could see they were shocked that he was willing to do this, to admit he was a zalphic, so that they could be saved.

"I know all too well what they can do, and I wish it for no one else. Sometimes I would have rather died, and that is maybe what I'm doing now. Dying rather than letting them experiment, but now, not just on me, but the others as well." He thought about the Wise Ones, what they had done to him, all the time he spoke, so that he could sound believable. He was afraid of death though, and was not so ready to give up. He hadn't wished for death, just power to make them bend to his will instead.

His conviction convinced the others. Some here and there still didn't take the cause to heart, but he had convinced a majority, and he had done his job. He asked the recruits to kill some of them, for him, and he retired. He received a telepathy message from Jacob: *"Roy, go meet up with Agnar's group. Something's wrong."*

Outside, in Vernatia, the talk was about Lord Kingston and his decision to address his son's pleas. Roy questioned why it had taken so long. Lord Kingston announced that he believed that Argus was right in demanding the others back.

He also added something Roy was certain that Lord Kinston would omit. He knew Lord Kingston didn't want to go to war with his friend, and Lord Horus didn't seem to want to either. Roy had assumed that Lord Kingston would omit his son's cry to go to war. He instead addressed it, calling it a possible mistake.

But he also expressed that it was necessary, that Argus was also right. He supported his son, supported his ideas, and supported the war.

Faldenheim and Vernatia were now at war.

###

Chapter 18
Haernaveh

Aurora Stephensen saw that there was no way out of war. Farendor, being so close to Faldenheim, and so dependent on them, was expected to provide men as well. Despite her well-to-do family, Aurora was also expected to do some work for Lord Horus. This consisted of going to Vernatia to help prevent the war.

Going on the road to Vernatia, she felt ill at ease. Jonathon never left Jennifer's side, and Aurora was annoyed by this. She wanted to talk to Jennifer, talk to her about what had happened with her and Steven. Instead, Jonathon and Jennifer were engrossed in each other, and Aurora couldn't have the conversations she had imagined. They also refused to show affection, something for which Aurora was glad. She wondered how long they had been together. Seemingly, it had been a while, and she grew sad thinking about Steven, her friend going after some girl who already had a boyfriend.

She had been angered when she had found out, but she figured Jennifer hadn't planned any of it, and though the concept didn't entice her, she accepted it and moved on.

Jackson had told them that they would go to Vernatia, and after having stayed to gather supplies and plan, they had departed. By the time they had departed, the messenger birds would have already arrived at Vernatia. Lord Horus sent messenger birds to describe the fire and the events that led to a "group of brave souls" to travel to Vernatia and try to reconcile the two lords. That was the official reason for this group to travel.

It was true enough, that this is what Lord Horus wanted—to avoid war—but there were still their other purposes. Learn what

Argus was planning, get Roy back, and further anguishing the people. It took a day of travelling for Aurora to realize the last one, but she had pieced it together.

The eldest person of the group was Benjamin, of twenty-seven years, and he didn't have nearly enough authority to speak for Lord Horus and treat with Lord Kingston. No one else came with them, only the original group Jackson had assembled.

Jen and Jon talked the whole time, and Benjamin and Maximillius talked amongst themselves as well. Aurora felt alone, wishing she was with Kesara. She missed her, and hadn't seen her in much too long. Aurora went along in her loneliness, feeling out of place and wanting to be elsewhere.

She heard Benjamin and Maximillius talking about Gideon. Aurora knew this was the time to jump in the conversations, to fight back the darkness of loneliness that threatened to engulf her.

"How's Gideon doing? I haven't seen him in a while. Haven't seen him since the funeral."

"He's doing as well as you could expect. He was our brother, and still can't really accept that he is no longer here. The one we should worry about is Kesara." Hearing that, Aurora felt a certain pain in her chest. Kesara and she were close, and she hadn't been to see her either. She somehow felt that she had betrayed her in a sense, by not visiting, and not being there for her troubled time.

"Last I heard, she had been spending some time at the abandoned inn. Steven didn't keep too much though, I know, and I couldn't imagine she found the sort of closure she was looking for."

"She's going to the Lancaster Lands. She told us a while ago, she had been preparing for it. We had insisted that she go with someone, but she wanted to go alone. She can handle herself, but I still worry."

"So why did you let her go alone?"

"I had no such intentions. I was going to go after her, with Gideon. This was before the fire though, before this impending war. After we reach Vernatia and talk with Lord Kingston about all this, I will continue going forward to the forests. I know where she'll be."

Yeah, Aurora thought. She knew Kesara would end up there. She figured Benjamin would want to get past Vernatia while he could. It seemed so strange that Faldenheim and Vernatia would truly go to war; Tadeus Banesworth had called upon Jackson and Argus, for the express purpose of avoiding it, but that did not seem to do much of anything.

"Can I join you Ben? Can I go with you, to find Kesara?"

"Yeah, of course," Benjamin said, without hesitating. "We'll get her together." Aurora was glad to hear how steadfastly Benjamin agreed for her to join him. She turned to Jennifer, who seemed to be avoiding them. Benjamin didn't like her, and Aurora figured out that he knew about Jonathon beforehand, and that this was why he had asked Steven not to pursue the girl.

Aurora knew he also didn't want to hurt him, and hoped that Steven would decide to forget her before he found out about Jonathon. Aurora felt a weight lift.

She looked around, wondering why. She felt as if she weren't carrying as much, and her hand grabbed at her empty side. She looked down again, and saw that the scabbard was empty. "Ben."

He turned around, and saw the empty scabbard, where Telekay should be. "Where's the sword?"

"I don't know. It...disappeared." Aurora knew she had Telekay not long ago. She wondered if Jacob had used his abilities again, to get the sword. It seemed the only plausible explanation. "You think Jacob took it?"

"I don't know. Perhaps." Aurora didn't know what to do now with Roy. That was perhaps the last thing that could connect him with Steven, and now it was gone. Hopefully, wherever Roy came across with the sword, he would be able to remember. For now, she could only keep moving towards Vernatia to prevent this war, so that she might talk with Roy.

They continued their voyage toward Vernatia, towards preventing war, and came across Haernaveh. They stopped in the city, to get more supplies, and to hear any news about the potential war. Benjamin took off on his own, and so Maximillius took care of gathering everything. Maximillius assured them that Benjamin would return, and Aurora just waited impatiently to leave.

Benjamin returned, and offered an explanation of his absence. "I was in the city, learning what I could of what we've missed since we left Faldenheim." He stopped, seeming almost disconcerted by what he heard. "Vernatia has closed its gates to any travelers. There's a...there is a trial taking place. No verdict has yet been made, but...they're trying *Argus* for being a fire zalphic."

A trial, accusing the prince of being a zalphic—Aurora hadn't seen this coming into fruition. Even a lord's son wasn't exempt from the phobia against zalphics. Vernatia had closed its gates, meaning that firstly, no war would come until at least after this was resolved, and secondly, that their endeavor to prevent war would be halted, and perhaps it would be too late to change anyone's mind. "I've sent a letter to Lord Horus," Benjamin continued, "and we will await his orders as to how to proceed."

Having decided to stay in Haernaveh, there was nothing to do but explore the city. Aurora found it fascinating—the life was nothing like that in Faldenheim. There was something in the city that was familiar, which made it all the more different. The people were much friendlier there, and Aurora lost herself in the shops and places in the city. She talked amongst the people, and implied that a zalphic had recently come to the city. She was saddened to see they still reacted with the malice with which she was familiar.

Still, the place was somehow a peaceful haven. She thought about the impending war, and how it might drag the city into its. She also knew that it didn't necessarily have to occur in that manner. Her thoughts were poisoning her experience, so she let go of her thoughts and lost herself in the city.

Upon the approaching darkness, she returned to the inn at which they were staying. There, Maximillius looked as if he hadn't left the room the whole day. Jen and Jon still hadn't arrived, and Aurora wondered what sort of romantic things they were up to.

The next day, Aurora again explored the city, losing herself amongst its people. Still not convinced that this place could be so similar to others in their disdain for zalphics, she again implied to some of the people that a zalphic had come to the city.

"Are you talking about that one girl that came only recently?" Aurora didn't know what to say to that. She certainly didn't mean to inadvertently accuse someone of being a zalphic. She figured with enough visitors, there would be no one to single out. "She came here alone, a *girl*," said a man. "Young one too, at that. Seventeen or eighteen." Even to Aurora that did sound strange. She wondered if she truly might be a zalphic.

"I don't know who you're talking about. What else can you tell me about her?"

The man thought about it for the second, and shook his head slowly, indicating he couldn't say much. "Some Telk resemblance, dark hair, pretty, short—about your height. She carried a sword. I was a little busy, and didn't have that much time to pay attention. The only reason I know this is because it struck me as odd that she was here. Said something about going east somewhere."

As Aurora thought about it, she sounded familiar. There was nothing else the man could tell, so Aurora continued traversing the city, no longer mentioning zalphics. When she went back to the inn, she heard Benjamin and Maximillius talking. "Yeah, some girl left the city today." She briefly thought if it was the same girl, and then made her presence known. They didn't talk of much after that, but they retired to their chambers, and she went to her own.

The next morning, they got the reply of Lord Horus. He instructed them to go, regardless of what Vernatia was doing. Benjamin thought this would be a waste of time, but he didn't say anything. He made no haste, though, in going to Vernatia, and told the group they would go the next day.

Aurora went around the city one last time, and she visited her favorite shops and places. The city talked about the trial, how Argus had been deemed not to be a zalphic. She never figured Argus would be accused of anything; he was still prince of Vernatia, and had his father, the lord, and the Wise Ones behind him. The news didn't surprise her. She just continued forward, ignoring the trial. She did wonder what Argus was doing now. The delay in the news reaching them gave him a dangerous amount of time to plot.

She continued around the city though, and saw familiar faces. She found the man from before, who had told her about the girl. She greeted him, and he greeted her and began to rush off. He stopped though, seemingly remembering something, and turned to Aurora. "Oh, and I remembered something else about the girl. She said she was from Farendor."

Walking towards Vernatia, she was not worried about who she might find on the roads. Even if she was travelling alone, she would be safe. There were few challenges she could not overcome, and she continued.

Though she was short, she knew how to protect herself, and used short stature as a trap, so that they would take her lightly. She was not worried about bandits, nor did she concern herself with fear of others finding out she could control water, even if she was still careful to keep her zalphic powers a secret.

Kesara continued walking, towards the Lancaster Forest, to where her brother Steven had been. There was a hole no one could fill, and it sucked the life out of her, slowly poisoning her thoughts, wishing she could bring him back, at any cost. *Any.*

She could see Vernatia, and she knew this marked a key point in her journey. After Vernatia, she would go to Bravania, and then to the forest the castle protected. Travelling closer to the place, she found a group of men. They were all armed, each possessing an air of confidence and fear that could only belong to zalphics. Three of them seemed to be leading the group.

They talked amongst themselves as they travelled, and passed her, but one of them stopped. The group kept going, but he stopped, and Kesara found herself stopping as well, wondering what he would have to say.

"Are you going to Vernatia?"

"Yeah," Kesara replied, "just stopping by there and heading to Bravania."

"Where are you from?"

"Just from a small fishing village up north," she lied. "Why all the questions?"

"You just look familiar. What's your name?"

"Why don't you tell me yours first?"

"I am Javier Lunaer, of Vernatia. I work for Prince Argus Kingston." *Argus?* Kesara thought. A sudden rage engulfed her then. Argus had played a significant role in Steven's death. Her brother, so full of life and love, gone much too soon and here was a servant of that evil man.

"What are you doing for Argus? Has he sent you to kill people?" She knew it wasn't the smartest thing to say, but her rage was slowly getting out of her control, and she wanted only to express her anger and anguish and lamentations. The other one didn't seem to take this very well.

"I am on official business, which is not for you to know. Let's not make accusations against the prince."

"Yeah, I hear his own city is doing that for me already." He drew his sword, brandishing the weapon, telling her to silently walk away. She didn't.

"Unless you have a wish to perish, I suggest you go on your way."

I wonder if I do, Kesara thought. "Everyone perishes eventually. But if you mean to threaten me, let me just tell you that you will cease to breathe much before I perish."

"I tend to shy away from hitting girls, but for you I might have to make an exception." He adopted a fighting stance, but waited, still giving Kesara the choice to walk away.

"Scary man with a sword, I am so terrified," Kesara said sarcastically. She drew her sword. "Be sure to use your powers, you'll need them." He seemed to be shocked into place for a second. Kesara knew he was wondering how she had discerned that he was a zalphic

Javier sent water at Kesara, but she annulled it. He approached her with sword in hand, and continued shooting water at her, but Kesara didn't bother to move out of the way of the water. She simply put her hands in front of the water and cancelled its power.

When Javier got close to her, he swung his sword. She spun around, dodging his sword, and quickly hit his stomach with her free fist. With her sword, she pushed him back pressing the sword to his neck. The pressure of the sword against his neck produce a small cut, but not anything too grave. With water, she hit the back of his feet to help trip him. On the floor, Javier shot water at her, but she moved the water to her sides.

She pinned one of his arms with her foot. "Consider yourself dead." With that, Javier closed his eyes, and Kesara grabbed the sword Javier had dropped, and stabbed it into the ground, right next to his face.

From behind her, the group approached Javier, who unsteadily rose to his feet. Javier told them what had happened, something Kesara didn't pay much attention to.

"Who are you, and what is your business in Vernatia? You are no simple traveler from a fishing village," said one of the other leaders of the group.

"I can be of no concern if you do not further bother me. I don't care to kill you." They weren't the ones who had harmed Steven, it was Argus. Only he deserved the retribution due to him.

"What is your name?" Kesara knew she couldn't answer that. Argus couldn't know. "I am Miguel. Who are you?"

Kesara stayed silent. She could offer a fake name, but she also knew that this simple refusal to supply a name angered them, and she could take advantage of that.

"I made Javier stop breathing, and I'm sure you don't want the same."

"He's still alive, he is still breathing."

Kesara simply shrugged. "I didn't say how long it was that he would cease to breathe. I'm sure I made him hold his breath that last instant before he was going to die."

Miguel apparently was done talking, since he took out his sword. The others behind him didn't seem to know what to do. They stood there, waiting for orders, or just wanting to watch, Kesara didn't know which. "Draw your sword, girl."

She didn't, and Miguel decided to lunge towards her. She feigned jumping to the right. She didn't though. Miguel, in anticipation of her maneuver to evade his attack, used his powers to make vines rise from the ground to encircle her.

She wasn't there though, and the vines found no body. The vines circled the air as Kesara circled and hit Miguel in the stomach with her fist, and shot water at his chest to send him back a bit.

Miguel took a few steps back and gripped his sword tightly. He was done fooling around. She merely stood.

Miguel attacked with a cluster of wood, but Kesara used water to keep the wood down, and she moved out of the way. Miguel approached with sword in hand, and she pretended to grab her sword, but then shot water at him. Miguel didn't react fast enough, and the water knocked him to the ground.

He got up and prepared to attack, but the last one told him to stop. Miguel stopped and turned to him. Kesara could now feel the exhaustion, the slow coursing of fatigue.

"You've managed to beat both Javier and Miguel, and that's pretty impressive."

"She didn't *beat* me," Miguel started to protest, but the other paid him no attention.

"And you are...?"

"You don't give us your name and then expect us to tell you ours?" Kesara falsely smiled. "You're clearly from Faldenheim, here to inform Lord Horus about our movements. I see now why the lord of yours is so lenient to zalphics—he uses them to further his cause." Kesara was confused. She didn't know where that accusation was coming from, and he was certainly demonstrating great hypocrisy.

"Roy, go meet up with Agnar's group. Something's wrong." Kesara looked around, confused. She didn't know how she had heard that message; she didn't have the power of Telekinesis. She wondered if someone here was trying to warn her, but she didn't know any of them, and she didn't know what was about to occur.

Even if my conviction should falter, I will not. For as long as I have an ounce of breath, I shall continue, thought Kesara. *I can take anyone that comes in my way. I need to. For myself—for Steven—I must be able to.* She told herself no one was going to stop her from this.

Wherever the telepathy message came from, they seemed to be talking about her, and Kesara was glad she could test if that was truly the case. "Why do you serve Argus? You don't seem like one to idly kill, Agnar." He seemed to stir when she said the name. He was definitely Agnar.

"You will stay with us until we find out what to do." All the others seemed to stand in a more pronounced stance, no longer simply watching. Kesara knew she was strong, but she wouldn't be able to get away from this group so easily. "Now, how do you know my name?"

Kesara shrugged and let herself be surrounded by the group. Javier didn't particularly like her, but she was beyond caring. Her initial rage had dissipated, but she still had no kindness for those serving Argus.

The others were wary of her, but they were awaiting. The only Roy she knew was someone from the Wise Ones—he had studied with Steven and Aurora. Steven had never introduced her to him though. She wondered if this could be the same Roy, but she immediately rejected the idea. That Roy lived in Farendor, and this one came from Vernatia, and obviously wasn't going to be the same one.

Agnar and Miguel were talking, and Javier and someone else seemed to converse between themselves. This other didn't seem like a leader, as the other three were, but he didn't seem to be in equal level with the others from the group. Kesara tried to figure out what she would do when Roy got there.

Kesara saw him at a distance, approaching very quickly. Then, he disappeared, and reappeared in front of them. He stood still, catching his breath, and then looked at Kesara. Kesara sensed that she had met him somewhere. She didn't know where or when, but he seemed vaguely familiar. Perhaps she had seen him from a distance before.

The other Roy was a zalphic too, she thought briefly, *thunder, whereas this one has telekinesis. How strange that two Roy's both were zalphics.*

"Agnar, what happened here?"

"This girl here decided to attack us. She's a Water zalphic."

"Yeah, I could tell," he said, pointing at his head. Kesara felt a little uncomfortable, knowing that he had used his powers and learned something about her.

"I was not the one who first drew my sword, nor did I stop any of you to ask questions." He turned to Javier, but didn't speak. Then he turned his attention to Miguel, and subsequently to Agnar again.

"Where are you from, girl?"

"As I said before, from a small fishing village up north."

Roy looked back at Vernatia. "So the village is in the jurisdiction of Faldenheim, is it not?"

Kesara felt as if the question was a trap, but she didn't know what else to say. It would be either Faldenheim or Vernatia, and she wouldn't be able to name a village around Vernatia, so she nodded. "I'm afraid then, that you cannot go any further."

"Why is that?"

"Faldenheim and Vernatia are now in war. Lord Kingston announced it not too long ago. I suggest you go back to your village—your blood doesn't need to be shed so quickly." *War?* Kesara didn't know what to say. She hadn't expected this. How would she go to Lancaster if she wasn't allowed into Vernatia?

"You can't be serious. I need to go Bravania."

"That is impossible."

"Please, Roy, let me through." He seemed confused, and Kesara realized that she shouldn't know his name. She accidently said it. He seemed to talk to the others with telepathy.

"Do I know you?" Kesara shook her head. "How do you know our names? Why are you truly here, and who is helping you?"

"I am here alone, and want only to go to Bravania. That is no lie." She took her sword out, and the others behind her started to do the same, but Roy stopped them with his hand. "Let's save ourselves from this pointless discussion. I think we both know where this is heading. Just me and you. I win, I get to go."

"Very well," Roy said without thinking much. "Let's go." *"Telekay!"* Roy hadn't said anything, but she heard it clearly in her head. Kesara stopped, unable to do anything but register what had just happened. Not only had Roy made a sword appear in his hand, it was the name of her brother's sword. It looked different, not the same sword with which she had been familiarized, but it was very similar. It was also made of the same Caster metal.

She only just stepped out of the way at the last second, and then Roy shocked her with thunder. Kesara was disconcerted. He had thunder as well, and he had *Telekay*. She also still didn't know why she was hearing these telepathic cues. And he was strong.

More importantly, why in the world does he have Telekay? What's happening? He ran up with Telekay, and Kesara parried the blow. She then asked, "Where did you get that sword?"

"I thought we weren't going to waste our time with pointless banter," replied Roy.

Kesara blasted Roy with water, but Roy was not hurt. He once again sent a lightning blast, and she moved out of the way this time, only to be hurt by a telekinetic blast. That one did hit, and then she was on the ground. He lifted a boulder with his telekinetic abilities, and sent it to her. Kesara rolled out of the way and shot water at him. He teleported out of the way, and she lost sight of him.

She swung her sword and turned around simultaneously. Roy parried the blow, but he stepped back. He shot thunder at her, and she ducked and sent water to him. He used his telekinesis to split the water, and she went toward him and swung her sword, but Roy parried. Roy attacked, and she blocked and then counter-attacked. Roy deflected her counter-attack, and quickly disarmed her.

Kesara hadn't planned what would happen if she lost. She wondered what he would do. He raised his sword, preparing to strike her, but then he stopped. She didn't know why, but he looked at her, confused. Kesara shot water at him and backed away.

He lowered his sword, and then dropped it. As she looked at Telekay on the ground, he began to speak. "What are you doing, Kesara?"

#

Aurora and the rest of the group were walking towards Vernatia. From a distance, she could see a group of people. She wondered what was happening, why they weren't walking and just standing still. Benjamin was looking at the group too. "You think they want to enter Vernatia? That would mean their gates are still closed," she told him.

"Yeah, maybe. We'll ask the group."

"It's a pretty big group. Only reason for a group like that is they all want to go inside Vernatia but can't." She knew though, that this wasn't the only reason. There was also another reason for it: war.

She wondered what was going through his mind. *It's so unfair. Why can't I read minds?* Alas, she couldn't, and she focused instead on trying to determine the reason for the group.

#

Neither Kesara Hewley nor Roy Rhapsados realized that they had met each other. It was the day in which Steven Hewley died, and it was but a brief instant, but it occurred at the abandoned inn which Steven inhabited.

It was only for a moment, for Kesara went to talk with Aurora, and she had only briefly mentioned him by name.

"How...how'd you know my name?" Kesara asked.

"Simple. I...I...." But Roy didn't have an answer. He didn't have one. He couldn't formulate what it was that caused him to guess. He didn't realize that the bond between him and Kesara would preclude him from harming her too much. He hadn't realized that she was Steven's sister. He had only a strange, inane feeling.

"You...who are you?" Kesara was puzzled. The evidence seemed to point to this being Roy, the one Steven had met. But his power of Telekinesis proved otherwise. She didn't know who else it could possibly be. She didn't realize she was right.

"I'm me. I...." Roy wasn't sure of anything. *Where had that name come from?* He had a feeling of strangeness. He let her live...somehow knew her name. He couldn't possibly realize he shared a special bond with her, but nonetheless, that bond was there, and it protected Kesara.

"What's going on? Do you know my brother!?" Kesara, weak from the fighting and dumbfounded by what had just happened, still found hope. That would explain things. He knew her name, and didn't kill her. He had Telekay. He *had* to know Steven in the very least.

"Your brother? Who would that be?" *Do I know her brother? Is that why she seems familiar? But who do I know that has mentioned his sister?*

Kesara hesitated. *Should I really tell him my brothers' name? Some stranger I've never met before? He almost certainly met Steven at some point. If that's so, I need to find out what he knows.*

This could bring me closer to Argus. Maybe he can give me closure. She pondered her thought a bit longer. *Even if he doesn't know him, what would he do with his name? Steven is...there's nothing they can do to him now. I can't let this opportunity pass....*

"My name is Kesara Hewley." Roy seemed to react to her name. He didn't offer a verbal response, but rather just continued to look at her in shock. Roy was beginning to formulate his thoughts, perceiving she was the sister of someone important. He had heard the name Hewley before. Above all, a name came to his mind: Ben, the one with fire. "I've been looking for...I don't know. Something to help wrap my mind around it."

A blast of fire separated the two, and in an instant she heard her brother shout "Step away from her Roy!" Roy turned and saw Ben. Infernus appeared in his hand, as Telekay often did for him.

Kesara looked at the sword Roy wielded. She felt she recognized the sword, that despite the difference in appearance, she saw Telekay. "Why do you have Telekay? That's St—"

"Kesara, please come here, and stay away from him."

"What problem have you with me, Ben?" Roy asked.

"I won't let you hurt her. Kesara."

Benjamin Hewley looked at his sister, who he had parted from to protect. He wished only to protect her, firstly from Roy, and then from her grief. Neither Steven nor he ever wanted this for her.

Aurora Stephensen, from behind, tried putting her hand on Ben, but he ignored her. Aurora looked around at the other people with Roy, people she had briefly seen before. They seemed on edge, hands on their swords, but they had not yet drawn them. Roy tried reading Aurora's mind, but she blocked the attempt easily. Roy seemed surprised; he hadn't expected Aurora to have the strength to block his attempt so easily.

Having failed with Aurora, Roy read Ben's mind, who had a harder time resisting Roy's effort. *I will not let you hurt her.* "I wasn't going to harm her Ben," but Roy wasn't sure what he had planned to do anymore. He resigned himself to sheathe Telekay as Ben grasped Infernus stronger, and approached him.

#

Kesara knew her brother, maybe not as well as she knew Steven, but she knew what Benjamin must have been thinking. He must have been wondering about the family, how they were all zalphics. She had thought of it often as well. She had tried to figure out what made them so special. The possibilities of this are minimal. This shouldn't even be possible, yet it was. Four siblings, all zalphics. Benjamin had Fire, Steven had Telekinesis, and Gideon had Wood. She had Water.

Benjamin looked at her strangely, facing a personal struggle. Then he said something. "I will protect them: Aurora, and Roy. Obviously I will protect you as well, Kesara, that goes without saying. I've always protected you. Roy, I'm going to do what he wanted, and that was to protect you, and some others."

"I don't know who you're talking about, and I don't need protection. Protect your sister, because maybe next time I won't be so forgiving. She beat my friends; I had an excuse to kill her."

"That is nowhere near a valid excuse."

"To me it is. Regardless, we are in war now."

"What?"

"Lord Kingston just announced he supported Argus and his views. Any casualties now are the result of war, and I have no need for justifications."

Ben turned to two others in his group. Kesara recognized one of them to be Jennifer. "Go back to Haernaveh. Send a letter to Lord Horus. Tell him about the war. Go as fast as you can." They left without another word, and left the small group among the bigger group headed by Roy and Agnar.

Kesara looked at Roy. She felt something in him, something familiar. He couldn't possibly be anyone else but the Roy she knew. "What happened between you two?"

"He betrayed us, betrayed Lord Horus. He went with Jacob, helped Argus escape, and proceeded to attack us." Both Roy and Ben turned to Aurora, and Kesara could only wonder why. She had almost forgotten that he was working with Argus. She wondered why Roy would choose to work with him.

"Telekinesis. You didn't have that power before. I knew you only to have thunder."

"It's something I recently acquired."

"Why do you have Telekay?"

"It's my sword."

"No it isn't." Roy seemed to look at her as if she were crazy.

"Kesara, I'll explain all this later. Let's just go."

"If Faldenheim and Vernatia are in war, wouldn't being away from home more safe?"

"You won't be able to pass. You're going to have to go around, and to make that kind of trip, you'll need a lot of supplies—supplies you won't be able to get because of the war."

She turned to Aurora, who seemed to be looking at Vernatia. "Ben, I think it's best if Kesara goes to Bravania. She's right. If you want her to be safe, she can go there."

"How do you suppose she'll get there?"

Aurora paused, as if preparing to say something with which Ben would not agree. "He can take her," she said, pointing at Roy. Roy seemed surprised at the suggestion, but he thought about it and almost seemed eager to comply. She didn't know why.

"You expect me to let her go alone with *him*? He was going to *kill* her!"

Kesara immediately rejected that thought. Somehow, she knew Roy wouldn't. Perhaps maybe he had considered it at first, but she knew he wouldn't now. "He didn't. He stopped, when he had the opportunity to attack." Ben just shook his head.

"She doesn't have to go alone," Aurora offered. "I'll go too." Ben seemed to consider it a bit longer, before he again shook his head.

"Vernatia and Faldenheim are in war. Even if Roy wanted to, there's no guarantee that Argus would let you just go through the city."

"I think I should have a word in this," said Roy. "I realize your frustrations Ben. I can promise to take you and Max to the castle gates. From there, it is impossible for me to ensure anything else. You can ask to see Lord Kingston, but I'll have no say in the matter. I can, however, get Kesara and Aurora across."

"How would you do that?"

"If he thought even for the smallest moment that I could convince Kesara or Aurora to join the Order of the Protectors, he wouldn't hesitate to give me anything I required, or asked for. You will not be able to go though. If you're there, he'll think you're using something to make me do as you ask."

Ben seemed to consider this. Ben looked at her. "Do you know why I left? It was to protect you guys. You know how they treat people like us. They look upon us with disdain, with fear. They do not like us, so what would they say about our parents should others figure out I was a zalphic? I had to run away, to protect them from the backlash.

"That helped little. Steven was a zalphic. So were you. So was Gideon. Have you ever thought why our family was comprised of zalphic children? ...I wanted to save our parents anguish, so I left and took refuge with Jackson. He knew I was a zalphic, and his father was of the Wise Ones. I stayed at his castle, hoping to provide a better life for all of you. I went to work for him, and sent mom and dad money to help out.

"Jackson helped strengthen my powers, and I found out I had Telekinesis under his tutelage. I learned about the Order of the Guardians of Peace, and their plans, and I knew I must join them. I needed to keep the peace, to help our family prosper and be safe. Who knows what they might have done to me if they found out I was a zalphic.

"When I found out Steven was a zalphic, I tried to help him. He went his own way. When I found out you were also a zalphic, I couldn't believe it. I could grasp that Steven and me were both zalphics; unlikely, but completely possible. But then you developed powers, and you went elsewhere. I knew Steven would protect you.

"Then came Gideon. He was the baby of our family, and he too was a zalphic. I sent Max to get him, to help him learn, so that he wouldn't suffer what we had to. Jackson helped me out—in his own self-interest, but nonetheless, he helped. He arranged things so that Steven might join the Wise Ones. I knew he couldn't resist their knowledge. I could keep track of him this way.

"I left, to protect you. Sometimes, leaving *is* the way to protect someone, as leaving is now the best way to protect us. We must leave Kesara. That is what I wish.

"But, you are my sister, and I understand that you want to do this—that you need to. Believe me, I understand your plight. So, if you wish to go, then I cannot possibly deny you this. Go if you must, but I hope you do consider this greatly."

Kesara was moved by her brother. Her brother was telling her to go if she must, and she felt as though she had to. This approval though, caused Kesara to reconsider. She found it harder to discount her brother's wishes, and she also wanted to do as he wished, and to placate him.

Benjamin is my brother. I have to go with him. But…Steven was my brother too. Dead or no, he is an important part of my life. I have to do this. She turned to Aurora. She seemed to want to go, desperate for the same thing Kesara was looking for.

Javier tapped Roy's shoulder and tapped his own head, probably indicating he wanted to talk through telepathy with Roy. Roy then shook his head. Javier seemed visibly angered by this. Agnar then turned to Aurora and Kesara, and shot thunder at them. Roy reacted quickly enough to divert the thunder directed at Kesara, but she saw the other bolt approach Aurora, not stopping.

Aurora wasn't worried though, and then the bolt dissipated before touching her. Kesara was awed.

Already, Roy had taken Telekay and held it towards Agnar. Benjamin had Infernus in his hand, as Max had Azure. All three swords had appeared in their hands, and with the other hands they had blasts of thunder, fire, and water prepared.

Agnar didn't say anything, nor did Miguel. "You will all proceed in the manner that was previously described to you, and going towards Faldenheim. We are still in war, and regardless of what may be happening, war has come, and it is our duty to get back our fellow friends with fire. I will take this group back to Vernatia, where Lord Kingston will decide how to handle the case." Roy stayed quiet for a second, while he looked at the group. "I for one do not wish to fight them. You saw what that girl did to Javier and Miguel." He laughed, while the two tensed. He seemed to be answering something that they were thinking. "She's the least of your worries. Ben there is a Knight, as is Max—the former has fire, and the latter, water. You want to deal with them, truly? Go ahead. I won't stop you, but I don't plan on helping either."

18. Haernaveh- 299

He turned around, sheathed Telekay, and started walking away. Kesara turned to Aurora, then to Ben. He looked at her, asking her whether she wanted to go. He must have seen something in her face, because he started walking with sword in hand, following Roy, and Aurora walked forward with Kesara, heading towards Vernatia.

"Can we trust him?" Kesara whispered to Aurora. "Why is he serving Argus? I'm still confused."

"Roy experienced something quite unusual. He was visiting Steven's tomb in Faldenheim, and someone used telekinesis and altered his mind somehow. He...doesn't remember Steven. He seems to have forgotten the people closely related to him, in one form or another. He didn't recognize me when he awoke, nor did he recognize Benjamin or Max or Jennifer. Something happened to him."

"He can't remember Steven? Even after explaining who he was?"

"There's something even more troubling." Kesara was taken aback by that statement. Completely forgetting someone wasn't the most troubling part? "Whenever we even mention Steven's name, he seems to go in a sort of panic, and he faints."

"By simply saying the name?" Aurora nodded gravely. Kesara wondered what could be the cause. Could someone truly be so strong in telekinesis to do that?

They arrived at the gates of Vernatia, where guards awaited them. She saw the entire castle, garrisoned, and ready for battle. They were preparing for war. Aurora Stephensen watched as Benjamin announced the letter that Lord Horus had given them, about the "brave" company that went forward to Vernatia. Messenger birds had doubtless come and given the same news, but Ben seemed to know what the purpose of the words were.

Lord Horus must have told him the intention of the letter, thought Aurora. Then, she felt bad. *That's not fair. It's entirely possible he could have figured it out on his own.* Aurora knew that by failing to send any real representatives from Faldenheim, and to instead send the only people who were brave enough to go, they were further perpetuating the truth about Argus Kingston's powers, and they hoped this would cause the people of Vernatia to consider again their prince's powers.

They came back with Prince Kingston. He pretended not to know the group. "I know not why Lord Horus plays these games with us and sends people like you to treat with us, but we will not allow you into the city. Go back to Faldenheim. I will not have it said I killed a group delivering only messages on behalf of the lord. You are denied access beyond these gates."

"Prince Kingston," Roy started, "I ask you to allow these two to come through the gates, as I have deemed them useful to our cause and have reason to believe we can greatly benefit from their presence." Prince Kingston agreed to the request and asked that he inform him, in his chambers, how that would benefit them. The guards let Kesara and Aurora through the gates, and they sent Ben and Max back.

They went to the keep, and followed Roy to some chambers. There, they were asked to stay, while Roy went with Argus, no doubt to talk about how they might use the two to further their goals. Aurora didn't care. She was using Roy too, having him help Kesara and her. She hoped she could move on after the trip, as Kesara seemed to think she would. Or maybe she just hoped that as well.

Aurora couldn't quite get over Steven. She wondered how Benjamin was managing, but she didn't ask him for fear that he hadn't, and that she might dig up wounds left buried in his mind. She knew Kesara was having trouble, and she hoped that together, they might learn. She missed him terribly, and it took everything in her power not to cry. Steven had been a part of her. He was like a city in which to lose yourself, and he was gone. Destroyed.

Roy walked in then, not saying a word about the conversation. Instead, he showed them their chambers, and left them off. He said he was going to gather supplies for the trip to Bravania. He didn't bother to say anything else.

After having talked with Argus, Roy seemed tense. He had seemed eager to take Kesara and Aurora to Bravania, but now

Aurora thought she saw Roy more reluctant. They traversed though, making way towards Bravania. Aurora noticed Roy had brought with him finely made clothing in one of the bags. Since his attire was currently the same as his customary choice, Aurora figured this was not intended to "impress" her, or Kesara. She also found something covered in cloth, and he made certain the artifact wouldn't be revealed.

She found no manner in which to address these things, so she kept silent. They travelled, talking about nonsensical matters. Aurora had asked Kesara not to mention Steven in front of Roy, and the eradication of that subject eliminated all other things Aurora wished to ask Roy.

"Why do you want to go to Bravania?" Roy asked Kesara.

She tried to think of something, an explanation that didn't involve Steven. Aurora noticed Kesara's hesitation, and she knew Roy would notice it too. Consequently, Aurora answered for her, embarrassing her in the process, and affirmed "Kesara wants to meet with her lover in Bravania." Kesara looked at Aurora, wondering what she was doing, but Aurora noticed that Roy smiled a little and carried on.

"You don't have to try and hide it from me—I certainly am not inclined to inform anyone of it. You are more than welcome to meet with whomever you wish Kesara." Roy looked at Aurora, seeming to want to ask her something, but he decided against it.

"What is it Roy? What would you ask me?"

Roy seemed disconcerted. With the same rapidity Aurora had used when supplying Kesara's answer, he asked a question to divert her attention. "Do you have any family in Haernaveh?"

"No," answered Aurora. She knew it wasn't the question he had had in mind. "Why do you ask?"

"Haernaveh is being taken."

Aurora stopped immediately, not able to believe the news. "Taken? What do you mean?"

"Agnar took Haernaveh. Vernatia took the first of its Faldenheim conquest." Haernaveh. She had liked the city—enjoyed it so much, really. *Wasn't Jon supposed to send word to Lord Horus? How could they take it? Lord Horus wouldn't have let Haernaveh be taken so easily.* Aurora wondered how much strength Vernatia actually had. She had always assumed Garrisbrough, Bravania, and Arastaud were the great castles. After the three, she thought Faldenheim was above Vernatia and Markai. Could Vernatia truly win?

#

Chapter 19
The Wise North

Roy Rhapsados had at first been content that he would take Kesara and Aurora to Bravania. When Aurora had first proposed that Kesara go with him to Bravania, he knew immediately that Aurora would go as well. When he reached Vernatia, Roy had hoped, with some naïveté, that Argus would allow him to go to Bravania with Aurora and Kesara, thinking that Roy could convince them to join his efforts. Argus had not been so easily convinced, and now Roy travelled to Bravania to converse in secret with Prince Tadeus.

Aside from refusing to see him in the first place, Roy had no hope of convincing Lord Banesworth to join Lord Kingston. Instead, Argus had instructed Roy to talk with Prince Tadeus, and convince him to join them. Prince Tadeus would then talk with his father, and the prince would convince the lord to go to war.

Roy had asked how he planned to do all this, and they had tediously gone over the specificities. Aurora had survived zalphia—the only known person to do so—and Tadeus would not be disinterested in seeing her. Then, he would inform Tadeus of their plan to attack Faldenheim, and that with the Bravania forces behind them, they could easily conquer.

Prince Banesworth would inevitably ask why he would comply with the wishes of the Kingstons, and Roy would inform him about his brother, Prince Maekor's death. Roy had known that some outlaw, yet to be apprehended, had killed the prince. He would reveal that he knew who had killed him, and show him Kesara and a portrait he was carrying of Ben, wrapped in cloth to cover the painting.

The prince would order the guards who had seen Maekor's killer to examine the portrait, and they would assent that the portrait, though not the killer, showed great similarities to him. This, of course, was because Ben and Kesara were brother and sister to the real killer.

This obviously required no gift in the ability to reason. The killer was undoubtedly Gideon, the only other brother of Ben and Kesara. Argus hoped that Prince Banesworth, giving into hatred and vengeance, would assent to attack Faldenheim after Roy told him the killer lived in Farendor. He would, of course, also imply that it had been Lord Horus who conspired to kill Maekor. This would hopefully lead Tadeus to convince his father to attack Faldenheim.

Tadeus would undoubtedly fall to their wishes. The problem would be convincing Lord Banesworth. If Prince Tadeus resulted unable to convince his lord father to join Vernatia, there would be another to make the alliance a reality.

Roy was displeased that his voyage had turned so much more of a war effort than a trip for two lovers to meet. Roy wondered whether Aurora had a lover there too, or why she wanted to go there. Aurora had told him that she, some other friend of theirs, and him travelled to the Lancaster Lands together. Was she perhaps meeting this friend in Bravania? He wanted to ask her, but he couldn't. So, when Aurora told him to ask the question that was on his mind, he was forced to divert their attention.

He had not planned to tell them about Haernaveh. He had learned this from Jacob, who through telepathy had informed him that Haernaveh was taken, and that this was to be reiterated when talking with Tadeus. Having no other question that came immediately to mind, he asked if they had family in Haernaveh. To Aurora's further questions, he informed her that Agnar had taken the city for Vernatia.

She seemed shock, and Roy wondered what she was shocked about. Roy wondered if it had to do with the message that should have been delivered, with the loss for Faldenheim, or some other thing he didn't understand.

"It seems surreal that the two lords are in war."

"Yeah," Kesara started answering, "are they not supposed to be friends?"

Roy hadn't really considered this friendship. "They are both members of the Committee of the Wise Ones. Even the Wisest One is rumored to be from the Lancaster Lands, which would mean all three have in some form or another an interest in the north. People have referred to this area as the Wise North, seeing as Faldenheim, Vernatia, and Lancaster are all in the north. They certainly have ties stronger than most other lords."

"So why do two lords, friends with one another, go to war?"

"The Alexanders have always ruled over us. When the Firion Calamity removed all but a few Alexanders, their rule was much more unclear. We named the only remaining male the king of our land, even though he hadn't been born. There's still another Alexander, one more suited to rule us, and Argus would seat him in the throne rather than King Whaldo."

Aurora hadn't known this, Roy saw. He hadn't either, until Argus had explained it to him. "They're called the Wise North and they would wage war to name a different Alexander King. What illness infects those that leads us, whose symptoms include inane disputes and folly?"

"Normally, I would agree with you Aurora. Most often do not change many things, and instead wish only to placate those that give them support and power. This King, however, is different in a very fundamental level."

"I doubt he is. Why do you say that Roy?"

"Because he, unlike all others, is not afraid of change, or difference. He does not hold with disdain those who, through a simple accident of birth, scare others with their abilities. He doesn't believe there ought to be a division between them, and he would make this world better."

"It's obvious that he only says this to get us behind him. We are the army with which he would overthrow others, so why not tell us what we want to hear," asked Kesara.

"Perhaps being part of the Wise Ones has made Roy and I structure our thoughts alike. He is not saying that this new king is a noble man, who believes that is what's right. He's saying this new king is a zalphic, that it is for this reason that Argus supports him. A zalphic king would not hastily kill other zalphics." Kesara considered these words, almost seemingly shocked.

Roy wanted to transition to another subject, but he knew he had peaked their interest too much to shift the conversation. "This new king is a zalphic, and Argus would put him on the throne. I see why Argus would do this, but why is Lord Kingston agreeing with his son? Surely he knows of a different resolution," Kesara said.

"This too surprised me," Roy began to reply. "What few understand is how little control even lords have at times. They are at the mercy of their people, and are forced to placate them. Without the support of those that give them power, they're just individuals who were arbitrarily chosen to give their opinion."

Aurora nodded, knowing this to be true, as if she had already thought about the subject. "I thought," continued Roy, "that if any two lords could avoid going to war with one another, it would be Lords Horus and Kingston."

"Argus was the one who started the fire. He caused this." Roy shook his head.

"The conflict between Faldenheim and Vernatia was already escalating before the fire. Before Maekor was killed. When Hal Horus became lord of Faldenheim, and Allister Kingston the lord of Vernatia, there were those in the castles who objected. Lord Horus and Lord Kingston were friends already though, and so they helped each other, so that they could prosper, and so they may placate those who did not regard them as the rightful lords. It stems from the lack of need for an heir. Lord Horus doesn't have a recognized heir to the castle. If he were to die, either King Whaldo III will follow his mother's initiative and name a new lord, or Faldenheim itself would find the most agreeable lord, based on honor and merit. Since Lord Horus was named by the queen, the people of Faldenheim didn't feel properly ruled. Faldenheim had almost unanimously elected a new lord before that. He forced the would-be lord outside of Faldenheim, it seems."

"That's not true." Roy wondered what Aurora knew that he didn't. He looked at her, expecting her to continue. "Not wanting to give Lord Horus any problems, and trying not to undermine his decisions, he chose to leave Faldenheim."

"That seems idealistic. Something probably made the man leave Faldenheim. A threat, or some sort of agreement."

"He moved to Farendor by choice. I know."

"How did you know he went to Farendor? Is he...is Wyatt your father?" Aurora nodded her head. That explained why Aurora was well-off, and why she was part of the Wise Ones. She was to be a princess.

"Regardless. The same holds true for Vernatia. Some didn't enjoy Allister Kingston's status as lord. When he proved to be a just and competent lord, they backed him, deciding to forget the ordeal. I'm sure some still feel reservations, but the lords do well in their responsibilities.

"Bravania has always been held by the Banesworths, and they didn't relish the idea that should they die, another might be named. They wanted their closest family to become lord, so that the Banesworth continued to rule—just as the king ought to be an Alexander. They didn't want the people to get the idea that a lord named by the king could do well, so they refused to treat with the north. They disbanded the Wise Ones—despite being one of the great castles, they hold no Elders in their walls.

"This caused Vernatia and Faldenheim to treat with one another even more. With their visits to the Capital every five years, for the committee of the Wise Ones, they became even closer. The others thought they held too much power. Vernatia and Faldenheim merely had to push for a change, and with the Wisest One as their close friend, they could succeed in changing anything they wanted.

"Bravania wanted another three Elders be named part of the committee. An Elder from Arastaud was to be named immediately, and they would then decide on the other two—so that the Wise North would not control all the land. The Wisest One steadfastly refused."

"Why?"

"I've not the slightest clue. I do know that The Wisest One, Lord Horus, and Lord Kingston are all good friends. The Wisest One was a central figure in the upbringing of Jackson and Argus. Perhaps he thought the committee as his family, and didn't want anyone else in it. I know not. However, this displeased Lord Banesworth.

Queen Serinah had just given birth to Whaldo, and was indisposed—so the Wisest One ruled the land for that brief instant. Lord Banesworth could do nothing.

"To avoid Lord Banesworth's further anger, Lord Horus and Lord Kingston decided to have a false argument. They hoped this would, at least temporarily, make Lord Banesworth see that Lord Horus and Lord Kingston were not in accord in everything, and they would consequently not control the land together.

"The proposed argument had to be big enough that they didn't see it as a petty dispute. Lord Horus took the bold step of calling for the end to the harassment of the zalphics. He made it clear that he didn't want to accept them into important occupations, but merely that the violence toward them be minimized. Lord Kingston kept the stance of the rest of the land, not caring whether excessive force was used to eliminate them. Faldenheim became much more tamed in their demonstrations of violence.

"The territories under Faldenheim are more passive against zalphics, though the latter group might not think so. Regardless, Faldenheim took their stance, and Vernatia had a distinct opinion. Lord Banesworth seemed to think the dispute was authentic, and they became much less hostile against the two lords, as he no longer thought them to be a point of concern. Bravania began trading with Vernatia again, and the castles grew. Every so often, Faldenheim would revisit this difference with Vernatia, to remind the others that the "Wise North" was simply an imagination of others, and they didn't have control.

"The lie got out of hand though. Argus and Jackson want nothing more than having us coexist harmoniously. The people of Faldenheim still disliked zalphics, but with a lord that didn't care to exterminate them, their aggressive tendencies lowered. The people of Vernatia, however, grew even more restless when it came to zalphics. They were more violent, and the difference in ideology between the two grew tensions between them.

"Argus visited Faldenheim to come to an understanding with Lord Horus a few months ago. This was for the benefit of the people, as the two really had no difference it their way of thinking. They no longer cared about keeping the façade, but the people had already been lost to them. The meeting was fruitless, as they could not think of a manner in which to change the people's attitudes. The best they could do was to lessen their own aggression to zalphics.

"Tadeus Banesworth soon after called for a meeting of the princes. As they would be the future lords, and since they could treat with their fathers, Tadeus thought that this meeting could help their future prosperity. Jackson is not the official heir, but he is the closest to one as there is in Faldenheim. Tadeus was trying to prevent the war that seemed inevitable with their difference in ideology. The people of Vernatia certainly didn't regard those in Faldenheim well. They thought Faldenheim had become too permissive, just as the Alexander Castle had become permissive before it fell. Those in Faldenheim thought those in Vernatia were excessively cruel. Strange, as both of them wanted nothing to do with us either way, but petty disputes are disputes nonetheless."

Roy stopped talking for a bit, thinking about what he had said. It was tragic really, how this all started, and how it had gone out of their grasp of control. "That isn't cause for war," Kesara interjected, interrupting Roy's thoughts.

"This alone, no, it wasn't enough for them to go to war. Two other events though, made this war occur. There is the king that Argus wants to put on the throne."

"Why is Jackson against putting him on the throne? Wouldn't he want a zalphic king, to help other zalphics?"

"There is also the second matter. Those who are coming to invade. Jackson thinks we ought to focus on the invaders, then worry about putting a king or not in place. Argus thinks that first we need to put this king on the throne, so that he might decriminalize zalphics, and then we can use our powers to fight off the invaders. Argus believes this to be the only way, but the only manner in which to go about this is to remove Jackson's influence.

"He may not be the recognized heir, but he is still rich and the son of the lord. Argus started that fire with the intention of being Faldenheim's savior. He wasn't going to let the fire get out of control, so he knew no one would die. He also knew that by stopping the fire, the people would support him. Having saved Faldenheim, he was going to subjugate Faldenheim without going to war, and instead winning the favor of the people, and having them support his cause.

"Well, we know how that turned out.... When Argus came back to Vernatia, and he was accused of being a zalphic, the people nearly killed him. I was there, and I saw first-hand how all those people were angry. Had he not been a prince and a member of the Wise Ones, the guards would have slit his throat upon seeing him. Jacob convinced the people that Argus wasn't a zalphic, and most abandoned all their suspicions of him.

"The problem is, accusing someone of being a zalphic is very serious. Should he have been found to be one, they would have killed him. Failing to be found thus, Argus had only one option. If he didn't show anger at the accusation, it would have been thought peculiar in the least. He called for war in consequence, and the people listened, as they still had no favor for those in Faldenheim. Had he asked to go to war with Bravania, they would not have assented so easily. Yet, he exploited their disdain for those in Faldenheim, and Lord Kingston declared war."

Aurora looked at Kesara, who seemed to be processing it. She knew some of it already, but some of the matters were not supposed to have been spoken. "The people get what they want. And they wanted war." *Aurora is absolutely right,* thought Roy.

When Kesara Hewley, Aurora Stephensen, and Roy Rhapsados arrived at Bravania, there were guards expecting them. They let them through the gates and took them immediately to the keep, where Prince Tadeus Banesworth and Princess Fayrah Banesworth were conversing with their father, but who then left his children to speak with Roy.

"Lord Banesworth," Roy genuflected and watched him leave. "Prince Tadeus Banesworth," Roy saluted him, and turned to Aurora and Kesara, to introduce them. "I believe you know one of my beautiful companions already."

"Of course, how could I forget one such as you? Aurora Stephensen, how do you fare? You radiate beauty."

"As opposed to radiating the illness of zalphia, like last time?" Aurora replied in an amiable and jovial tone.

Tadeus laughed. "I am glad to see you are doing well. I was concerned for your condition the last time you visited us here. It is truly a miracle you have survived to grace me with your presence today."

"You speak too kindly, prince. This is my friend, Kesara Hewley."

"Are all those of Farendor so beautiful," Tadeus asked, while turning to Kesara. There was something about the compliment that made Kesara feel warm. Though she thought it was simply the expected gallantness, she had never been complimented so by a prince before.

"I am certain some more beautiful than I approach you every day."

"That is surely impossible." Kesara smiled at the compliment again, and Tadeus turned to Roy. "Lord Kingston sent a letter, informing me that someone from Vernatia was coming to see me. Might I inquire why it is to me you speak, if it is my father who rules this castle?"

"I ask we save the conversation until I am more rested and better suited to carry this important discussion. I assure you, though, that what I have to say, mirroring the attitudes of the Prince and Lord of Vernatia, will be of interest to you. I ask, as I am unaware of the efforts of war since leaving Vernatia, with the utmost haste, that you inform me of the war between Faldenheim and Vernatia."

"There is not much to tell. Faldenheim has mobilized its army, and already has met the Vernatia army in war. Vernatia's army is in Haernaveh. We have received no messages of late, and I am unable to tell you much else."

"I am grateful for what you have shared with me. If you'd excuse us though, we are tired from our journey, and would like to rest. Might we be directed to the chambers you have so graciously offered us?"

"All our comforts are yours. Sister, lead the ladies to their chambers."

"You honor us too much, Tadeus," said Aurora.

Fayrah led Aurora and Kesara to the chambers they would inhabit. It was all much more than Kesara was used to, and she couldn't help but revel at the lushness of the accommodations. They exchanged pleasantries and made polite conversations with Fayrah before she left.

"What do you think they're talking about," asked Aurora after Fayrah had left.

"Who?"

"Roy and Tadeus."

"Didn't Roy go to the chambers? I thought he was tired?"

Aurora smiled, knowingly. "Roy didn't want to talk with Prince Tadeus because he didn't want to converse in front of us. Leading us to our chambers was his justification to get rid of us. I assure you, Roy and Tadeus are discussing the matters for which Roy was allowed to come to Bravania instead of participating in the war."

Kesara hadn't thought about that. "So he's trying to convince Tadeus to help Lord Kingston in his war?"

Aurora nodded. "Yes, that would seem the obvious reason. How do you think he'll go about convincing him?" Kesara didn't know. Perhaps the truth was held in something Roy had told them about the Wise North.

The people of Bravania were famous for their hatred of zalphics. Coupled with the predisposition to hatred, Maekor's death caused Bravania to further target anyone with the Z mutation. Aurora Stephensen saw this first-hand among the people. Since Kesara had come on the pretext of meeting someone in Bravania, they both left the keep often. On one of those occasions, Aurora and Kesara saw as a zalphic used his powers of wood inadvertently.

The reaction was almost immediate. The zalphic hunters appeared faster than an emergency team would have. Gathering a crowd, so that they could all testify that the young boy was a zalphic, they stripped his clothes and shouted at him. One of the hunters grabbed his well-maintained sword and drew a volcano with his sword's tip. The volcano was painted red with the young boy's blood, all the while the boy was screaming in pain. "The volcano erupts," a different man said, and with another sword, he made cuts originating from the volcano's top, and went towards varying locations. The blood made it truly look like an erupting volcano, and Aurora felt uneasy at the sight. They then lynched the fourteen- or fifteen-year-old only after having all of them hit him.

The guards separated the crowd and took the body down. Aurora hadn't heard the cry of any parents, and she wondered if that was because the parents were afraid or angered. Kesara returned to the keep, visibly troubled by the event. Prince Tadeus saw them enter and seemed confused.

"I thought you were visiting someone?"

Kesara was still a bit disconcerted, so Aurora answered instead. "We just saw a young zalphic boy stripped and lynched. They chose the erupting volcano. We lost our desire to explore."

"Ah, yes, you of Faldenheim are so much more lenient against these...*people*. What is the customary consequence for zalphics there?"

"They are harassed. Certainly not stripped and lynched, and not imprinted with any of the three symbols."

"Kesara, you seem so unsettled by the event, as if you weren't accustomed to such violence." Aurora noticed again how Tadeus was much less courteous to Kesara. He was much less gracious and had grown rude in his treatment of them. Still, Tadeus was a Prince, and was expected to be polite, and so his statement superficially reflected only genuine confusion.

"I am not. Faldenheim has its share of problems, but I've seen no such things."

"Kesara speaks truly. This was a horrid thing to do to this young boy." Tadeus didn't say anything. They needed to get out of there, out of Bravania.

"Prince Tadeus, I would take this moment to be indiscreet and request we be allowed to go to the Lancaster Forest."

"Might I inquire why you would like to go there?"

"We wish to escape the dark manner we use to treat with others, and surround ourselves in the peace of the forests."

"Do you mean to say the people of Bravania are cruel?"

"I mean we are *all* cruel, and in the face of such cruelty, I would ask to go elsewhere."

"I will consider. I must speak with my father—surely you understand that with this war, we wouldn't want you ladies to travel needlessly." *The war is to the west, not here,* thought Aurora, but she said nothing and assented.

Aurora and Kesara went to the chambers, and didn't do much searching around the castle for the rest of the day, and the day after. Finally, Tadeus went to visit them.

"My lord father has assented to your request, but would ask for a few things in return. First, he would wish to send an escort, who will not travel alongside you, so that you may converse privately, but will go to protect you two in these dire circumstances. He also wishes to ask you of your state Aurora."

"My state?"

"A few months ago, you had zalphia, and now you seem well. He merely wants to be certain you feel well, and would have me ask about your previous condition." She feared Tadeus was withholding the final request that was the true request they wanted. She agreed nonetheless, explaining in detail when she was diagnosed, and how the Wise Ones checked her and did all that they could. She recalled going to Bravania, meeting Tadeus.

Tadeus seemed placated by the information. "I hope that you might enjoy the respite of the forest. Please do not stay too long, so that I do not worry." *Your final request is that we come back to Bravania. Just say it Tadeus.* The Prince, with these words, excused himself and left them alone.

"I'm glad we can go to the Lancaster Forest."

"Yes, but we can't visit Steven's sanctuary. There will be guards. I don't think you want them to find it. There is also the matter that we are captives now, and he sends this escort to make sure we return to Bravania."

"I never thought of it that way." Aurora didn't directly oppose staying in Bravania, but she worried what Lord Banesworth might ask in return for their stay, and this request made her nervous. She didn't have much political power, nor was she a zalphic, but she still wondered what Lord Banesworth could and would ask her to do.

Regardless, they prepared for the trip to the Lancaster Forest. Aurora walked around and saw Roy. He seemed worried, and lost in thought. He seemed to lighten up when he saw Aurora. With some discernable worry still in his voice, he mentioned that Vernatia was in retreat. Faldenheim had retaken Haernaveh. Aurora didn't know why he was telling her this. Roy then asked her if she was ready for the voyage to the Lancaster Forest.

"You know about that?"

"I'm the one in charge of the escort. Well, I suspect one of them will be in truth my superior, but in name I will lead them." It felt strange to Aurora that Roy should be amongst the Bravania escort, while she and Kesara talked amongst themselves. "Why don't you join Kesara and me? We will appreciate the extra company."

"I would like that," said Roy, with no more of the anguish and worry in his voice. "Are you sure you don't wish to first speak with Kesara about the change in arrangements?"

"She won't mind, don't worry."

"I'll go tell the lord then." Roy dismissed himself, and Aurora went back with Kesara.

"Roy is going to join us."

"He's going to be part of the escort?"

"No," started Aurora. "I asked him to join us. We won't be able to go anywhere. We might as well try to get Roy to remember." Kesara assented. Aurora figured if she had wanted to talk with her, she could have done it throughout all the time they were together. Being in the Lancaster Forest would change nothing, and since they couldn't go where Kesara wanted to, the voyage itself would be in vanity.

###

Chapter 20
Alliance

Roy Rhapsados spoke with Kesara and Aurora throughout the voyage. Mostly they recounted any experiences they had shared, and to Roy's surprise, he hadn't met Kesara before. He was naturally confused by this, as he felt strongly that he had met her before, that he knew her somehow, since he had known her name without her telling him.

Aurora and he were part of the Wise Ones at Faldenheim. She also lived in Farendor. Roy recalled—for one reason or another—having entered Aurora's home, and seeing lucrative decorations. "Have I been in your home before?"

"Yeah. Just once."

"Why was I there?"

"It was to mourn the death of a friend." Roy figured that this friend was the one with which they had gone to the Lancaster Lands, and why he hadn't met him as of yet. He had thought Aurora would meet him in Bravania, but she only ended up travelling around aimlessly with Kesara.

"Things are coming back to me, though not all details. Some still elude me. I do remember you. We would sit together in our studies of the Wise Ones. I had seen you around here and there."

"I hope you get your memory back. It must be troubling to not be able to recall."

"There is something about having all my cognitive processes working well, yet not remembering people and events. Whilst I have trouble remembering these things, I can remember with ease the properties of Caster metal, everything there is about the Z mutation, the history of Andros, and a plethora of trivial information."

"You'll get there Roy." *Say thank you. Say it.* But he couldn't. He let the silence prolong, and he felt awkward at the extended quiet. *Say something, anything. Prolong the conversation. ...Come on. Just say "Why did you want to go to the Lancaster Forest." That's all you have to say.* But Roy found himself unable to speak. *She probably thinks you're a freak. Say something you idiot.*

"Roy, might I ask you something?" Roy looked at Kesara, who seemed to be staring intently at a high branch. Without waiting for his reply, Kesara continued. "That boy that got lynched—how did you feel about that?" This was worse for Roy. He didn't know what he could say. *I guess the boy doesn't like hanging around so much anymore.* Luckily for him, he wasn't saying the things that came to mind. "There is a certain brutality in the action—is this really how they feel about the zalphics? Has Faldenheim guarded us so much against the atrocities?"

"That's why Argus wants the new king to rule—so that he may preclude such actions." *No idiot. Don't bring up Argus. Why would you do that? Just have a normal conversation.* He hadn't answered the question, and he figured Kesara would notice this, but she didn't seem to care.

"I hate Argus. At least...I want to hate him." *See why did you bring up Argus?* Roy desperately tried changing the subject.

"Let's not worry about Argus," Aurora said. "We came here to avoid all that, so let us enjoy the forest."

"Your brother is a Wood zalphic, right?"

"Yeah," Kesara nodded. "Gideon is ironically the only one of us who hasn't been to the Lancaster Lands." *What else can I say? Why must I be so introverted?*

Suddenly, Kesara drew her sword, and Aurora looked around, startled. Roy didn't know what was happening, and he noticed that Aurora wasn't quite so sure either. Only Kesara determinedly looked at a particular direction. He knew Kesara must have heard something.

Now the sound grew clear: a distinctive crunching of branches and leaves, and the sound of someone gasping for air while he ran. He soon came into sight.

Behind him was a feline who was chasing him. The young boy ran since he had no form of defense.

Only...he *did* have something with which to defend himself.

Kesara called out to the boy, who immediately ran their way. Roy could see the boy fleeing from the feline, but he could also see his mistrust. He didn't need vicarious means to know it was the mistrust that all zalphics have. They weren't liked very much.

The boy ran towards them. Roy figured the boy wasn't running for help, but to keep himself alive. It's what he would have done: run towards them to get the beast to eat the others while he kept running. He would have used his powers first, though. Then he got a good look at the boy.

Kesara soaked the ground with water, causing the boy to slip. The boy looked at Kesara with fear in his eyes, wondering why she had betrayed him in that way, and let out a cry as he turned around to the leaping beast behind him. Kesara blasted the feline with water as it leaped, and landed with a cry and prepared its growling. Roy used his telekinesis to grab a branch and crush the beast's head. As the whimpering of the animal died down, Kesara turned to the young boy. "Why are you here?"

"I was running away. You should know something about that." He looked at Roy too, but Roy turned around, making sure none of the guards had seen them. They hadn't.

"So running away is the only option?"

"You know how it is for zalphics. They treat us like monsters. They do not care for us or our lives. They refuse to feed us, refuse to converse with us. How was I supposed to live there when no one would even look at me?"

"So you thought it better to run to the woods, where the wild animals would eat you. And instead of protecting yourself, you ran. Is that right?"

"I...I don't want to die. Whatever...*this* is, it kills us. Maybe if I don't use it, I won't end up with the same fate."

I can feign indignation. "Really now? Smart boy. Don't use my powers in a situation where I will be killed, to save myself from being killed by my powers."

The boy looked at him, not knowing what to say. They hadn't rehearsed this.

"I know you are zalphic, I can sense it. You ran away because you were afraid of what they'd do to you, but I can help you harness your powers."

"I don't want to harness my powers, I want to escape them."

"What is your name?"

"I'm Ferdinand."

"Well Ferdinand, you ought to learn what you can about your powers. Regardless of whether or not you want to, learning won't harm you."

Neither Aurora nor Kesara said anything to the boy of seventeen. Instead, they stood silent. "I'm not certain why you offer this. What do you have to gain by doing this?"

"You are a zalphic, and I know one or two things about that. I can help you, because I know what it's like."

"And in return, what would you request?"

"All you need to do is return to Bravania with me. Prince Kingston might ask you for your compliance, but you have no need to obey." Ferdinand nodded.

"I hope they don't persuade you to do something you shouldn't do," Aurora finally said. *The kingdom and its people have already done that to him.* Roy saw that she was still wary of Argus.

The guards, who had heard something, approached the group. At seeing Ferdinand, the guards drew their swords. "It's alright," said Roy before they went any further. He was much too important to let Ferdinand be taken. He hadn't expected Argus to send Ferdinand to Bravania, but now Roy had to play his part. "This is Ferdinand Flores, and he will join us." He turned to Aurora and Kesara. "Unless you wish to stay longer, I believe we have been in the Lancaster Forest for an adequate amount of time. Would you object to heading back to Bravania now?"

They didn't vocalize any objections. Roy knew that Kesara mentioning the lynching meant that she was still not ready, but he had to get Ferdinand to Bravania, and he couldn't concern himself with Kesara's reservations. *She will still have all the time it takes to get back to Bravania.*

#

Aurora Stephensen had thought it strange at first, how the usually reserved Roy had suddenly decided to help the zalphic they had met. Aurora wasn't a zalphic though, and to this she attributed her inability to understand Roy's decision.

Then Roy mentioned Prince Kingston, and Aurora suspected at that point that Ferdinand knew, at least, Argus. The manner in which Roy mentioned Argus was strange; he told Ferdinand to go to Bravania, and that Prince Kingston would ask for compliance. There was no reason for Prince Kingston to be in Bravania, nor any reason to mention him, unless mentioning a separate request—something which Roy wasn't doing.

When the guards had approached them, she knew that Roy and Ferdinand had met before. Ferdinand had offered no last name when Roy asked, yet he introduced him to the guards with the name. He wasn't supposed to know that information. Even if Flores was the name given to bastards, Roy should not have attributed this name to the boy. Now she wondered who Ferdinand was. This had all been an elaborate manner in which Roy could get Ferdinand an audience with Lord Banesworth.

Roy wanted to get Ferdinand to Bravania almost immediately. She knew how Roy thought too well for him to deceive her. He was somehow similar to Steven, though certainly not as cynical. *I wonder who this Ferdinand is. Roy attempted too intensely to get him to Bravania with the utmost haste.*

Consequently, when they arrived at Bravania, and Roy and Ferdinand were taken directly to the audience chamber to speak with Lord Banesworth, she was not surprised. She went to the chambers, to rest. Aurora explored Bravania while Kesara stayed in her chambers. Aurora understood Kesara's decision, but she could not stay in there any longer, letting her thoughts overshadow her. She needed to distract herself. Her thoughts had assaulted her for much too long now, and she sought for an alternative state of mind.

This continued for a couple of days. Kesara explored Bravania more, but primordially stayed at her chambers, while Aurora distracted herself with everything Bravania had to offer—mostly consisting of talking with the people.

Returning to the keep on one such exploration, she ran into the princess, Fayrah Banesworth. She seemed excited, and Aurora asked her the reason for her excitement.

"Oh, Aurora. I am engaged!"

"And who is the lucky lord? I cannot immediately recall any prince suited to your age."

"Why don't you guess," offered Fayrah, smiling. *It isn't Faldenheim. There is also nothing Roy could have said to convince Lord Banesworth to marry Fayrah to Argus. I don't imagine it is the Leisiter Castle either. That leaves just two castles.* "Is it Prince Elsamar Bastion? Or do you like them so young that you want the princeling Oskar Alkarvan? I cannot think of any other prince your age."

"Neither. He is even greater than these two." *Greater than a prince of the great castles? No castle was greater than Garrisbrough, which would only leave....* "You don't mean to say...you are to marry the King?"

Fayrah let out a shriek of joy and smiled widely. *King Whaldo should marry the Bastion girl though, Hellen. She is of his age, as is Fayrah, but she is a Bastion. They have the strongest ties to the Alexander crown, and would give King Whaldo the greatest support, from the strongest castle.*

"That is tremendous news. You must have been shocked upon reading the letter."

"Reading the letter? How ill-suited it would be to ask for my hand through a *letter*. No, silly, he is here, and personally came to ask for my hand."

"King Whaldo Alexander is *here*? That's impossible." Aurora was entirely confused.

Fayrah let out another laugh. "Not *Whaldo*. The rightful king. I am to marry King Ferdinand Alexander."

"Ferdinand? *Alexander?*" Aurora's thoughts flooded with Roy, and going to the Lancaster Lands. How Roy was worried about getting Ferdinand back to Bravania. The reason for his voyage to Bravania. This would definitely be considered important enough to excuse him from the war effort.

"Yes, I am engaged to Ferdinand Alexander. My lord father supports his claim to the throne." *But, Argus also supports his* claim to the throne. Aurora hadn't seen this coming. *That makes Bravania and Vernatia allies. Faldenheim....*

She congratulated Fayrah, communicating only the most cheerful of expressions, and hurriedly went with Kesara. Before getting to the chambers, she ran into Roy. He stopped, and clearly didn't know what to say.

"Aurora. I...how are you doing?"

"I've just heard that Fayrah is engaged to Ferdinand. Strange, as I didn't know there was another Alexander."

"He is son of the former king, and rightful heir to the throne."

"Whaldo is his first son."

"Maybe with the Queen, yes." *A bastard then?*

"Was that the whole point of the voyage? To marry Fayrah to Ferdinand?"

Roy looked at her for a long second. "I was supposed to convince Prince Banesworth to pressure his father into helping Vernatia and attacking Faldenheim."

"That seems overly-complicated."

"I convinced Prince Banesworth, but he was unable to convince his father." *Is that why Tadeus has been so rude to Kesara and me?* "Lord Banesworth was not convinced. Then, we ran into Ferdinand."

"He married Fayrah to get Lord Banesworth to support him. How do you think this will end Roy? Before, it was just Faldenheim and Vernatia at war with each other. Now, Bravania and Vernatia are in rebellion to the Kingdom."

"Arastaud won't do anything, and Garrisbrough is too far away."

"They can travel by ship."

"And land where? Whaldo's Port is Ferdinand's." *Whaldo's Port has ceased to support King Whaldo? That's ironic.* Of course, it wasn't the same Whaldo, but Aurora thought there was something about that. *Aquareus is currently flooded by the Detrimental Shores. That only leaves Bloodpool as a major port city. Ferdinand is about to control the North.* Any other harbor further north belonged to Faldenheim, so Aurora knew Whaldo's Port would have been essential. "How did he get Whaldo's Port?"

"He hasn't been idly waiting."

"You seem so sure this will work. King Whaldo won't idly wait either. There is still the Capital and Markai. Lady Callisto Leisiter and Queen Serinah are sisters. Markai won't abandon the Capital."

"The most difficult challenge is to take Faldenheim in time—before the forces from Markai help. With Bravania's forces, I don't imagine that should take long."

Roy's withdrawal from the subject was strange. He didn't seem to care about Faldenheim or Vernatia. He was telling her what he knew, and didn't demonstrate pride or resentment at what was going to happen.

"Was this your plan the whole time? Is this why you volunteered to take us to Bravania?"

"I wanted to take you. I didn't want to serve Argus—I didn't want to help with the war effort. I wanted to go to Bravania with you, and talk, and enjoy your company. I didn't want any of this. Things have a way of being thrust at me though, and I do what I must. I wanted to take you to Bravania and help you escape the war."

Aurora knew that Roy could be cynical, and that he could be indifferent to many things. But she also knew he had a hard time expressing himself, and she heard the sincerity in Roy's voice. This helped her not punch Roy. "You have to get to Kesara. I have to get you out of here."

Aurora looked at Roy. *I've been wanting to get out of here since the beginning.* "Bravania is now in war with Faldenheim. He won't let you leave so easily. I have to get you out now." Aurora had been too caught up in the shock with Ferdinand, and Fayrah, and the fate of Faldenheim. She hadn't thought about herself, and now that Roy had brought her fate to her attention, she realized he was right. She needed to get Kesara. She started walking towards her.

"How do I know you'll help us?"

"You have only a few limited choices. Trust me, then, either I help you escape or betray you. If you don't accept my help, you must find a way to escape by yourselves—something even *you* might not be able to do."

"How would you get us out? You can't use your telekinesis." *You're too afraid.* "There is nothing you can do that I won't be able to do myself."

324 - The Midnight War

"I put you in this position. I'm going to get you out."

Aurora felt frustrated. She knew she could give Roy too many chances, and always he would fail. She didn't imagine he would change. Still, Roy demonstrated an intense desire to help them. "What would you suggest we do? We're prisoners now."

"Kesara holds no power as a prisoner. Except...." Aurora prepared herself. She knew he was about to say something she wasn't going to like. "Prince Tadeus had taken a...*special* interest in her."

"Why?"

After a few moments of silence, Roy stopped walking. This only annoyed Aurora more, as she needed to get to Kesara. "He knows her brother killed Maekor," Roy whispered. *Well, damn.* The anxiety started rising in Aurora. That would be why Tadeus had been less and less courteous. She started running towards Kesara. Approaching the chambers, she saw Tadeus walking away, with guards holding onto a prisoner. *Kesara.*

"Leave her alone Tadeus." The Prince turned, and saw Aurora.

"You cannot tell a Prince what to do," he said, no longer feigning friendship. "I've been waiting much too long to do this. Unfortunately, it took my lord father a bit more convincing. Guards, seize her too."

"You're not going to do that," interrupted Roy.

"Who are you to deny this?"

"Lord Kingston sent me here with these two, so that we might make an alliance and overthrow Faldenheim. These two are still prisoners of Lord Kingston, and therefore must be taken back to Vernatia. I'm sure King Ferdinand will agree this is the correct manner to address this issue." *You may have saved us from being tortured by Tadeus, but we are still prisoners.* Still, Aurora knew this was the best Roy could do. It was more than she would have been able to say.

Tadeus, visibly angered by these words, nonetheless said "very well. Prepare for travel. We are going to Vernatia."

###

Chapter 21
Retribution

Faldenheim will fall, thought Kesara Hewley. With the Bravania forces, Faldenheim was in retreat. The Bravania forces went to aid Vernatia much sooner than Lord Banesworth set out to the castle.

Forces had been sent to aid Vernatia whilst the royal wedding was prepared. It was extravagant, and certainly would have been a jovial event if Kesara wasn't preoccupied with the inevitable trip to Vernatia.

Under Roy's protection, Tadeus hadn't mistreated her or Aurora, but she saw the hostility in his eyes, and the demeanor in which he treated with them. Clearly, he wanted to discuss her status as a prisoner of Argus Kingston with Lord Kingston.

Unfortunately for both Aurora and her, they had now arrived at Vernatia's gates with the rest of the Bravania forces. The war would resume, and her fate would soon be sealed. She wanted to be with Lady Melisa Banesworth, back in Bravania, so she wouldn't be with Tadeus in Vernatia. She didn't contemplate any reason for Lord Kingston to deny the Banesworth's request to leave her in their hands.

Aurora demonstrated confidence, but Kesara knew she was doing this for her benefit. She didn't feel the confidence. Kesara felt only the dread of the upcoming conversation between Lord Banesworth and Lord Kingston. There was nothing they could do.

Immediately they were sent to the keep, and the entourage of guards did nothing to alleviate Kesara's worries. She didn't feel safe. To her side, Aurora walked, undeterred by what they knew was going to happen. Kesara admired Aurora. She was strong, even if she might not realize it. Kesara thought Aurora was stronger than her, even if Aurora was not a zalphic. She survived zalphia, evidence enough that she was strong.

Roy walked with them, not saying anything, but plotting in his head. Kesara wondered what Roy could be thinking up. He reminded her of Steven sometimes, how pensive and away from the world he could get. Prince Banesworth didn't look at them, and he went forward with a haste that implied urgency.

She knew that Tadeus knew who killed Maekor. He knew Steven killed his little brother, and there was nothing she could do that would stop him from taking his frustrations out on her.

At least Steven can't face this anger, she thought bitterly. Arriving at the chambers of the lord, Kesara, Aurora, and Roy were stopped and instructed to wait outside—along with most of the others. Only King Ferdinand, Queen Fayrah, Lord Banesworth, and Prince Tadeus were allowed through.

They continued speaking for a while, and Kesara grew ever-more nervous. Roy hadn't said anything, and Aurora kept her façade, trying to soothe Kesara. She appreciated Aurora's effort, but she thought it was unfair for Aurora to have to keep it up. She should be able to cry and show her fear, though it occurred to Kesara that perhaps she didn't want to.

The growing anxiety culminated when the guards called Kesara, Aurora, and Roy forward. They entered the chambers and respectfully bowed to the King, and the Lords. Neither Kesara nor Aurora addressed Prince Tadeus, and instead began a spiel about Fayrah's beauty.

Soon enough, there was nothing left to do but continue with the affairs that were to be addressed. King Ferdinand cleared his throat. "Kesara Hewley, Aurora Stephensen, Roy Rhapsados. You have all been called forward because the decision to be taken directly affects you, and I believe that each person has a right to hear *as* their fate is decided—not to hear what has already been concluded."

He turned to Prince Tadeus. "My King, Roy Rhapsados is a soldier dedicated to Vernatia, and under the service of Prince Argus." Argus nodded, confirming this was true. "Roy came to Bravania, as part of the war effort, to seek allies against Faldenheim. Roy came with these two prisoners from

Faldenheim, Kesara and Aurora. Roy revealed information pertaining to my brother, Maekor, and so I petition to Lord Kingston to transfer these prisoners to my care."

Yeah, care, thought Kesara. "My King," started Aurora. Kesara turned to her. *What is she going to say?* Ferdinand signaled for her to continue. "I find it unfair that we are but prisoners of Lord Kingston."

"It is the way of war. Fighting for Faldenheim has made you our enemies."

"My King, if I may, Roy is also from Faldenheim, yet he chose to serve Lord Kingston."

"I must agree; Roy has served me well, taking care to do as I've asked him," added Argus.

"And as such, must we not also be afforded the same luxury? I've raised no arms in favor of Faldenheim. I made no attempts to hinder the efforts of Vernatia. Instead, I travelled to Bravania along with Roy, who was acting in accordance to Prince Kingston's wishes." *We're to be...traitors?* Kesara didn't know how to feel about that. She was from Farendor, and belonged to Faldenheim. Her brothers were there, as was her family. *I won't have to fight for Vernatia, will I?* Then, she realized fighting for Vernatia did not fit. *Fight for Ferdinand, against King Whaldo.*

"Lord Kingston, Prince Argus, is it true that they did not raise arms for Faldenheim?"

"Unfortunately, she speaks lies. Kesara brawled with some of my men: Javier, Miguel, and Roy himself."

Immediately, Roy offered a reply: "My King, it is true that Kesara fought Javier and Miguel, and even myself. However, at the time that this occurred, Kesara was unaware of the war. The Lord had only just made the declaration of war. When Kesara drew her arms, she was acting in her personal defense and interests."

"She had no knowledge of the war?"

"No messenger birds had been sent, as the declaration was so recent." This seemed to anger Prince Tadeus. He was looking at his father, trying to see what could be done.

"How is it, then, that they came to be thought of prisoners?" asked King Ferdinand.

"Since she had attacked some men, and attacked me as well, I informed her of the war, and told her I would take her back to Vernatia. When I conversed with Prince Kingston, he directed me to Bravania, instructing me to take Kesara and Aurora to Bravania with me, and to try to make an alliance."

The King turned to her and Aurora. "Is there something that Roy is omitting, or has misrepresented in one manner or another?" They shook their head. Kesara held on to the hope that they would no longer be prisoners. "It seems clear that before we even consider Prince Banesworth's petition, we must first decide whether you are a prisoner from Faldenheim, or a supporter of Vernatia.

"You didn't help with the war effort, let's make that clear. It was Roy who tried to make the pact—you two were simply accompanying him. Now, you were outside of Vernatia's gates when you attacked these men, is that correct?" Kesara nodded, not knowing how to further address the King. "War had been declared, and whether or not you knew it, Vernatia was in war with Faldenheim. Someone from Faldenheim, attacking men of Vernatia, whether under war or not, is unacceptable. I therefore have to assert that you are prisoners of Lord Kingston." And like that, Kesara's hopes were shattered. She turned to Aurora, who seemed a bit surprised as well.

It was clear this was what she had been planning, and it had failed. "Now, Tadeus, your petition may be valid, but at this point you are asking Lord Kingston to give you his prisoners. Why? What is it that you learned about your brother, Maekor? Why the interest in these two?"

Prince Tadeus seemed reluctant to speak. "My King. Roy informed me that the outlaw who killed my brother lived in Farendor." Kesara turned to Roy, who was avoiding her gaze. "You must understand that I would want Kesara as my prisoner."

"He would torture us," Kesara interjected without thought. "My brother did not mean to kill Maekor. In any case, he is dead." A sense of sadness invaded Kesara. Roy turned to her, seemingly surprised—as though he didn't know that Steven was dead. Kesara couldn't concentrate on that.

"Your brother is dead?" asked Roy shocked.

"Roy, could you leave? We have no need for you to be here anymore," Argus said. Kesara didn't look up, but she heard Roy's footsteps grow fainter, and a door opening and closing behind her.

"It seems to me that I have no need to decide for the Lords. What would you say to this Lord Kingston?"

"I have no objections to this change." Kesara felt hopeless. Aurora had tried to free them from being prisoners to Tadeus. Roy had even tried to help as well, though he had told Tadeus about her brother killing Maekor, which would be the reason why Tadeus wanted her as a prisoner.

She could already imagine the treatment she would receive. She turned to Argus. He was looking straight at her, something she hadn't notice before. She wanted to hide the fear she surely was portraying. "My King, if I may." Kesara looked at Argus. "Kesara Hewley is the sister of Steven Hewley, the one who transgressed direly. She, however, had no part in this, and as such should not be punished for this. Steven is not her only brother. Benjamin and Gideon Hewley are also brothers of hers, and the former might be persuaded to join our cause. This will not happen if I do not have Kesara under my care."

"Steven?" The King seemed to be lost in a reflection. He then inspected Kesara more closely, and nodded his head in confirmation of something he was thinking. "I see the resemblance," he muttered. "Kesara," he started, unexpectedly loud, "what would you have me do?"

Kesara looked at Aurora, and back to King Ferdinand, confused. "Free me?"

"You answer me with a question?" He paused. "Would you have me name you prisoner of Argus, or Tadeus?" Kesara felt this was a trap. "I would go with Prince Kingston."

King Ferdinand nodded his head. "And that is how it shall be." Tadeus, visibly irate, tried his best not to shout. "My King, surely you agree that being of relations with my brother's killer, I ought to have her as my prisoner. I would ask what importance bringing her brother to our cause brings."

"I'm sorry, but I will do nothing. They are rightfully Lord Kingston's prisoners, and as you heard from Prince Kingston, they are to be used to further the war effort. That is all that's important."

King Ferdinand dismissed them, and Argus asked to leave for a brief moment.

"I will not help you Argus. I will not trick my brother into serving you. There is nothing you can do to me to change my mind."

Argus seemed unfazed by the words and addressed Roy at first. "Tadeus will not leave this issue alone, and he will continually try to make Kesara and Aurora his prisoners. You two need to get out of here. Go to the Lancaster Forest."

"Why would we go in the direction of Bravania? And why should we listen to you?"

"Tadeus will search for you two. Scouts will inform him if you're trying to escape to the south. He won't expect you to go to Bravania. Roy isn't going with you. He'll think you three are together, as you're all going away at the same time, but Roy will be elsewhere. He'll be searching for a party of three, and hopefully this will buy enough time. Go to the Lancaster Lands. That's where you wanted to go anyway, right?"

"Why are you doing this?"

"You seem to think I do things only so that I might benefit from it."

"That is exactly what you do."

"You can always argue that is true. Everything ultimately can help you or hinder you. I do this so that you aren't hindered." He tossed them some coins. "Get some supplies. Despite the war, this should be enough to pay for all you'll need. Roy, come along."

With that, Argus left, and Kesara turned to Aurora, wondering what had happened, and wondering what they were to do.

###

It was not the case that Roy Rhapsados had been trying to avoid the battlefield. He would have had little pause to go to war; instead, he had been concerned with Aurora and Kesara, and the plan to form an alliance with Bravania, and to marry Ferdinand and Fayrah had been coincidental. But Roy had now joined the Vernatia forces—and Bravania forces—and began the fight to retake Haernaveh.

Jacob, as a Bladesman and an Instructor, was assigned forces, and Roy was assigned as part of Jacob's forces. They were the only two zalphics of the forces. They fought their way through the lines of the Faldenheim forces at Haernaveh, who were in retreat.

Roy, though he formed part of a bigger force, felt solitude in the battlefield. He paid no mind to those around him, nor did he think of Jacob or Argus, or King Ferdinand or King Whaldo. Instead he looked at the battlefield and felt the desire and need to kill. There was no one to his side, no one behind, there was only what was immediately ahead of him. No thoughts hindered his movements, and no emotions guided his actions.

He saw the soldiers in front of him, and felt the strength of Telekay as it slashed and blocked and cut, killed and precluded death, and as it felt the resistance of steel and flesh. He felt the sturdiness of his shield, as it blocked projectiles and swords, and as it remained a firm and constant presence. Roy saw rivers of red, flowing through the landscape of death—the bodies fell, from somewhere in his side, to in front of him, and beyond the fields of his vision.

He blocked an incoming strike, spun forward, and, being behind him now, slit his throat. Without pause, without thinking about having killed someone or checking for something that wasn't there, he continued forward, stepping to the side as an arrow breezed past him. He constantly stayed in motion, not needing breath, as adrenaline—as The Wisest One so called it—coursed through him and focused his skills.

He raised his shield and kneeled as a volley of arrows flew towards them. In this position, he noticed blood on his arm, and didn't know if it was his or someone else's. He felt no pain, though he knew in his state, that didn't mean anything. The arrows having stopped, he went forward, and saw the wave of warriors in front of him. He didn't think about how he would kill them all, or what his fellow warriors would do. He went forward with Telekay in his hand, and felt the resistance and the desperate attempt to stay alive.

He stepped to the side, and an arrow flew past him, striking the man behind him. Roy didn't turn around—he only registered the cry of pain, and continued forward. He blocked a strike with his shield, and as another soldier made to strike him, he blocked the sword with Telekay. He then charged one of the soldiers, shield first, and used his telekinesis to strike with a fallen man's sword. When the soldier turned momentarily to the direction of the blow, Roy felt as Telekay went through the sturdy flesh of his enemy. The other soldier, perhaps having seen Roy's powers, determinedly went to strike Roy. From the side, Roy saw a sword go through the soldier.

Roy didn't turn to his comrade to thank him. He wasn't convinced he had even needed help. He continued forward into the streets of Haernaveh. He continued, striking enemies and evading swords. He saw a man with a bow, and he used the nearby debris as cover, as he went forward.

Thrice Haernaveh had seen war, and the ubiquitous destruction corroborated this fact. Roy could not go forward, as the bowmen precluded him from doing so with the constant volley of arrows. Turning around, he realized he was separated from Jacob and the others. He was only worried that they would reprimand him when he got back. Looking at the corpses, he saw a man lying on top of a bow.

He moved towards the other direction, then quickly turned around as soon as he knew the bowman had released an arrow. He ran to the body, shield between him and the bowman, and launched himself to the ground. An arrow flew above him. Arriving at the body with the bow, he soon realized that no quiver lay nearby. He turned to look for arrows, but saw none close enough.

Roy stood up and held his shield, hoping that it would catch an arrow. Instead, the arrow caught him on his left leg. He kneeled in pain, and again hid behind some of the debris. He saw the blood pouring from his leg, and felt pain screaming from it. He used Telekay to rip the steel tip from the arrow, and pulled it out of his leg. His screams of pain were heard only by the bowman, but he got the arrow out. Now possessing an arrow, he grabbed a rock and threw it in the general area of the bowman. Then he drew the arrow and shot it where Roy had previously been, at the dead body from which he got the bow. He took off his shield, and slowly rolled it that way as well, as he backed up, turned around, and ran the opposite direction.

Roy knew the arrow flying to a different direction would attract—if only momentarily—the bowman's eye. Then, the shield would offer another distraction while Roy went to cover. Running, he saw that some debris was hanging precariously from a nearby roof. Roy knew he could use his telekinesis to knock it down and get rid of the bowman, but he chose not to do it. Instead, he climbed and got a rock from a roof. The bowman thought Roy was trying to flank him, so he wasn't looking at the roof, and was rather aiming elsewhere. Roy measured the weight of the rock by throwing it up in the air a few times, and then threw the rock at the bowman. Roy immediately jumped down, and as the bowman turned to him, to shoot the arrow, the rock hit him, and disoriented him.

Roy moved forward, despite the pain from his leg, and closed the distance rapidly. He knocked the bow out of his hands and struck him with Telekay. Roy picked up a shield, the bow, and a quiver of arrows, but he didn't stop to rest his leg. Instead, he moved on, keeping weight off his leg. There were others fighting. Roy grabbed an arrow and aimed it at one of the enemies. He shot the arrow, and hit the one he was aiming for, though not at the spot he was aiming. He grabbed another arrow, but by then he saw the soldiers could defend themselves, so he went onto a different street and moved forward. A group of three soldiers were heading towards him, and Roy limped towards them.

They all paused to look at his leg, but Roy grabbed Telekay and struck at the one to his right. He moved out of the way, and the others started attacking his side. He blocked both with his shield, then struck with Telekay. Since his sword was made of Caster metal, the shields and the swords of the others started to fragment. The three started an onslaught of blows, from his sides and from the front, and Roy blocked with his shield and struck with Telekay. One of the soldiers raised his sword for too long, and Roy quickly stabbed him in the side.

Though he was still alive, the blow slowed him down, and Roy focused on defending himself from the constant blows. He backed up, almost tripping over a body, then stepped over the body and continued going back. When the soldiers stepped over the body, Roy went on the offensive unexpectedly, and one of them tripped. Roy struck both his feet, then blocked the other's blow. Roy hit the soldier's shield with Telekay, and it finally gave way to the superior metal.

Without defense, Roy made quick work of him, and then killed the other two wounded soldiers. Roy turned and saw a little girl, prepared to cry. Somewhere he registered but ignored the feeling that one of the three might have been her father. She let out a cry and Roy went towards her. Hidden behind her was a dog. The dog sensed the girl's distress and ran towards him, barking. Roy grabbed the barking dog and put his sword to its head. The girl started crying more, and Roy tried not to care.

Despite his attempt, he could not bring himself to kill the dog in front of this little girl. He told himself to do it, that it was but a dog, but he couldn't. He saw the crying girl, and hated that he couldn't go through with it. *There's no reason to keep it alive.* Still, Roy didn't feel at ease. *What happened to the man who could kill a girl for no reason on the road from Bravania? Who can kill men without thought and care little for the consequences?*

He hated that he couldn't do it, so he let the dog go and walked away. The cries of the girl echoed in his head as he continued forward. The scream got louder in his head, and he needed something to calm him. The pain from his leg seemed insignificant at the point, and though he was unconsciously limping, he felt no need to keep weight off his leg.

Going further, back into the primordial battleground of the war, he saw a sea of death, inviting him to drown. Instead, he went forward, noticing the fatigue of all those in his position, and feeling himself robust. He wasn't the only one injured, but he didn't show it as so many others did.

Roy faced the onset of enemies, but soon enough, no faces with life looked back at him. Though he knew it was an irrelevant relationship, he saw that the Vernatia forces were doing much better right when Roy had joined the fighting.

Continuing the fight, Roy encountered the first zalphic of the Faldenheim forces. Devin Gallious was approaching him. Roy let a long breath out and prepared to fight. Roy was fatigued, and using his powers would result in more weariness. There were also all the others around him to consider. If they saw him use powers, they would all try to kill him. Friend or foe, it mattered naught.

Roy gripped Telekay and struck as Devin blocked with his sword. Again, Roy struck, and again Devin blocked with his sword. Roy struck at his shield, and still Devin blocked with his sword. Roy discerned that Devin did not want to block—perhaps he had relied on his shield too much during the battle, or had even sustained a wound on that arm. Roy struck, and Devin blocked with his shield this time, showing a little pain in his face. Devin countered, but Roy blocked in turn with his shield. Roy kept constant vigil to see if Devin would use his powers of Wood. He didn't, perhaps because he was too tired, or because there were too many around. Regardless, Roy backed away and hid behind his shield as he grabbed an arrow from the quiver on his back and dropped it on the floor. He attacked with Telekay some more, and hid again behind his shield. He grabbed the bow on his back and dropped it as well.

Roy then went on the offensive, striking quickly with Telekay and using his shield to go forward. Devin was defending himself well, though, and Roy couldn't break through his defense. He backed up, dropped Telekay on the ground, and grabbed the bow and arrow he had dropped. He drew the arrow and shot it at Devin's head. Devin raised his shield as Roy dropped his bow. Devin staggered a bit, after the blow to his injured hand. Roy went forward and brought his hand to the ground. Telekay appeared in his hand, away from the view of the others, and he struck Devin at a weak point on his greaves.

Devin fell to his knees, and Roy rammed his shield on Devin's shield and caused him to fall on the ground. Roy found an opening in the armor and struck downwards with Telekay. Instead of flesh, the sword struck bark that Devin had produced to defend himself. He withdrew Telekay and left Devin on the ground. It would be too dangerous to keep fighting Devin, for he was worried they would inevitably use their powers without properly concealing them.

He went elsewhere, and continued fighting. Roy went forward, finding Jacob. *"I thought you had deserted us—that all the death was too much."*

Roy didn't look at Jacob, and instead went up to a man, moved out of the way of the incoming strike, and struck him down with Telekay. Roy killed him quickly and cut the face of the man, imprinting onto the dead face a sword within a circle—the sigil of the Order of the Sword. *"Death is only too much if you're not the one killing."*

Chapter 22
Rain

"By decree of Whaldo Alexander, son of Raymond and Serinah Alexander, King of Andros: Faldenheim, Vernatia, and Bravania are to cease this conflict, and Lords Horus, and Kingston are to travel to the Capital immediately. Failure to do so will result in a swift response from forces of the Capital and other castles."

The decree was worthless, Roy knew, but Whaldo still had hope that it would work. He didn't yet know that Vernatia and Bravania now genuflected to a different king. The only interesting part of the decree was the swift response promised. That meant that King Whaldo was already amassing his forces. Roy wondered how long it would take him to realize Whaldo's Port would deny him access to the harbor.

Ferdinand's forces took Haernaveh, the city located at the midpoint of Faldenheim and Vernatia. The fighting would slow them down, but Faldenheim was also very far from Markai.

While others talked about war tactics and the specificities of their attack, Roy wandered through the ruins of Haernaveh. Despite the destruction, he saw the life that once was there. He saw the ruins of shops, imagining what life must have been like before the War of the Wise North. He continued walking through the streets, looking at the decrepit taverns and the dilapidated homes.

Haernaveh still showed life, as the dwellers of this city labored to reconstruct the thrice destroyed city. It was hard for Roy to tell which ruins belonged to which attack. He saw a sector of the city in shambles, which was likely not reconstructed after the first or second attack. Roy thought about his home in Farendor, and his mother and brothers. He was glad Farendor didn't lie on the path to Faldenheim.

He walked through the city, taking in the tears of those affected, seeing corpses moved away from sight, and feeling the silent cry of the streets. Roy retreated from himself—not worrying about his thoughts or his feelings, and instead focusing on what was in front of him. He continued in this state, and he found himself lost in an array of ruins and shops and homes.

Roy noticed that the sky was darkening, and the busy activity of the day had been gradually dwindling. The lack of light did nothing to take away from Haernaveh. Roy greatly enjoyed the place, and he decided he would visit the city again when there was no war and the city was how it should be. Soon, the star-filled sky gave it a magnificent color, and the shining moon was in the middle of the sky. It was a quaint city.

Roy teleported to a roof, and stared at the stars. *They're beautiful. Aurora would love the stars, surely. If she were here, what would she say? Would she remark on the apparent shift of the light, or would she speak of the formations visible in the stars? Or why not note the simplistic radiance?*

How many others must be looking at these same stars? They could be different people, with different backgrounds and different events governing their lives, but they all see the same stars.

Roy lay on the roof, observing the stars. He wondered about their secrets, wondered how life may be on other places. Roy paid no attention to the events of that day, nor did he care to think more about Aurora. He was oblivious to his surroundings, and fell asleep.

#

Aurora looked at the stars. She felt small and insignificant, and she saw how frivolous the war truly was, when there was such a vast world to consider. Staying in Vernatia had been risky, she knew, but Kesara was convinced Argus was planning something by sending them to the Lancaster Lands.

They had stayed in Vernatia, with King Ferdinand and Lords Kingston and Banesworth. The princes had gone to Haernaveh, though she didn't know how much battle they saw. In Vernatia, the effort of war was manifested with the blacksmiths making weapons and armor, and supplies being procured by the Wise Ones.

It was night, and so she was resting from her work in gathering supplies for one of the blacksmiths. Aurora would be most helpful amongst the Wise Ones, but she feared that Prince Tadeus would have people looking for her there. So instead, she had gone with the blacksmith, while Kesara trained with legions that were held back to train further, and to supply the war effort with fresh soldiers.

They had no intention of helping Vernatia conquer Faldenheim, but too much suspicion would arise if they did nothing. Aurora headed toward an inn that Kesara and she had paid for with the gold Argus gave them. She wondered throughout the trip to the inn what would happen to Faldenheim. The news wasn't good; Faldenheim was in retreat, Haernaveh had been captured, and the forces of Ferdinand were sitting in Haernaveh, planning their approach to Faldenheim.

King Whaldo Alexander had issued a decree, asking the North to cease their fighting, but she didn't have any hopes the fighting would stop. She was interested to know what Lord Kingston and Lord Banesworth would reply. They weren't going to stop the war, and this would be a slight on the King. Would they declare their support for Ferdinand?

If they did that, they would be in open revolt, and the forces of Markai would be amassed immediately to aid Faldenheim. Roy had explained it all to her already though—would the forces be able to arrive before Faldenheim fell?

Aurora arrived to the inn, and found Kesara asleep in one of the beds. She smiled at little Kesara sleeping, seeing the younger sister she never had. She was five years younger than her, and six years younger than Steven. She was the same age as King Ferdinand. That was a strange thought.

Aurora stayed up late that night, haunted by her thoughts, hoping that sleep would come, and that the nightmares could give her respite. She missed Steven terribly, and she couldn't help get lost in thought and emotions when thinking of him. He was her best friend, and he was gone.

There was nothing she could do. There was nothing anyone could do. Not her father, nor her mother, her friends, the Wise Ones or the Wisest One—no one could save her from this. Jackson had told her that you never really get over it. Perhaps that was true. She wondered why Jackson told her that. Aurora felt that Jackson didn't particularly like her—ironically, the only prince who seemed to like her was Argus. Not that she'd met a lot of princes, but it was still strange.

I wonder what I did to Jackson. Would he hold a grudge for being my father's daughter? My dad was going to be lord of Faldenheim, but he has been nothing but courteous to Lord Horus.

Aurora discarded the thought, thinking it unimportant. That wasn't the issue she should ponder. Unable to sleep, she left the room and walked around in the black of night. Guards made their patrols, and Aurora brought with her some papers—so that it would seem she was delivering important messages throughout the night. She walked around, processing in her mind the restlessness that seemed resultant from the war.

Aurora soon realized that she passed more and more guards, and she saw that she had unconsciously walked toward the keep. Aurora noticed some of the guards watching her, and saw a guy that was continually looking in the direction of the keep, then looking around impatiently. Aurora paused, not exactly sure what to do. She couldn't go into the keep, and walking away so quickly would look conspicuous. She had decided she would go talk to the one waiting when she saw a girl leave the keep.

She seemed to be hurrying towards the guy, who must have been waiting for her. Aurora was closer to the girl, so they crossed paths first, and Aurora noticed that it was someone she knew. Of all the questions that came to her mind—all the things she wanted to know, all the things that had caught her curiosity—she found herself asking "Jennifer, what are you doing in Vernatia?"

Jennifer stopped—the unexpected question from Aurora had paused her attempts to get to the guy. *Jon.* "Aurora? Weren't you supposed to be in the Lancaster Lands? Or shouldn't you be in Faldenheim?"

The same could be said of you. Instead, Aurora voiced only surprise. "I didn't expect to find you here." *What are you doing exiting the keep at this time at night?* "I've been separated from Kesara. She is in the Lancaster Lands, and currently I have no place to be but home—somewhere that, at present, I cannot reach."

She heard footsteps behind her, and she knew that Jon must have approached Jen rather than wait for her. "So if I'm not mistaken, you two were supposed to go to Haernaveh, and send word to Lord Horus about the war. You didn't, and Haernaveh was taken."

"We should leave now Jen."

"Jon is right. He and I have to go now. It was nice seeing you."

"It is very dark. Shouldn't you rest?" Jennifer turned to Jonathon, not sure what to say. Aurora tried devising a way to get them to talk. "Where are you going?"

"We're going to meet up with my uncle."

"And where is he?" Jon looked eager to leave, but he didn't say anything. Aurora was trying not to make any accusations, but she found it was getting more difficult to hold in her thoughts. "The Korscher Mountains?"

"Yes. My uncle is in the Korscher Mountains. My people have been in the mountains, living there after the Great Shaking stopped being a tragedy and became rather a story."

"So is that why you came here, to Andros?"

"Yes. My uncle is a Bender, and the leader of the Korscher people. He sent his little brother, my father, to see who might treat with us, so that we could establish ourselves again in Chordica—and the rest of Andros."

"Why not just come? The territory is yours—no one would fight you."

"We needed a guarantee that we would be treated as equals. Without fair prices, we won't be able to survive. That's why I went to Faldenheim. Lord Horus promised to ensure the Wise Ones would support us."

"Then why did you betray him? Why did you betray Faldenheim?"

"Faldenheim is not where I belong, and I owe it no allegiance. I'm not from Faldenheim, like you. I am a Bender of the Korscher people, and it is to them that I owe my allegiance. Lord Horus promised much, but he is only a third of the committee of the Wise Ones—and not even the one with all the power. Lord Kingston could stop his attempts, so I needed to make sure we could trust him as well. I couldn't trust Argus though."

"But you could trust Jackson?"

"No. You're right—I couldn't. But there was someone I *could* trust. Ferdinand."

"Ferdinand?" *She knows Ferdinand. That's why Claudius and her brother were with him.* "So thinking the new king would provide you with what you want, you opted to aid Vernatia in their war and let Haernaveh get destroyed?"

"I don't owe you an explanation Aurora. Know that the Korschers are returning to Andros." *So Ferdinand has the North and the East.*

"And you Jon? You chose to go with Jennifer?"

"My heart made it impossible to go anywhere else."

"That's the funny thing about the heart. It makes you believe what it immediately feels, and then in the future you're left with a decision you never should have made."

"What are you implying? That I will regret this? I can assure you, I won't." He turned to Jennifer and grabbed her hand.

"I wasn't exactly talking about you." Aurora looked at Jennifer, who was staring back at Jon. Aurora had no more to do there. "Jen." *Love and life are mortal adversaries.* "I hope your love may triumph over everything." With that, Aurora turned around and walked away. She returned to the inn at which she was staying, and did not wake Kesara when she went to sleep—or rather, went to the thoughts and helplessness that occur in the middle of the night with a lack of sleep.

The next day, much of the same process reoccurred. Aurora went to work helping the blacksmith, and Kesara trained with the other soldiers. Aurora, unable to sleep, again traversed through the night, with letters. The guards stopped her, asking what she was doing, and she explained her lie. This time, she didn't see Jennifer.

A couple of days later, she heard the response from the North to King Whaldo's decree. "Lords Kingston and Banesworth, of Vernatia and Bravania, remove our support of Whaldo III Alexander. Instead, we respect the authority of the rightful King, Ferdinand Alexander, firstborn of the former King, King Raymond Alexander, with Urimé Jeram, of Whaldo's Port, prior to King Raymond's marriage to Serinah Leisiter. As the rightful King of Andros, it is the duty of all Lancasters, Korschers, and Telks, to support his power.

"I, Ferdinand Alexander, claim my birthright to rule as your King, and have the support from the honorable peoples of Bravania, Vernatia, Whaldo's Port, and Chordica. My half-brother Whaldo—through no blame of his own—has ruled with false authority over these fair lands."

###

Roy Rhapsados ducked as an arrow bounced off a sword intended to decapitate him. The other now had left his side unprotected, and so Roy drew red liquid from the side, and Telekay was bathed in crimson. Not stopping to think about what had just happened, he continued to raise his shield as another soldier intended to strike him.

The sword bounced off his shield, but not before producing a small pain in his shield arm. Roy did not grimace, and instead went to counter-strike, only to find a shield blocked Telekay as well. The shield slowly splintered away as the Caster metal continually struck at the shield. The other saw that his shield was splintering away, and he parried one of Roy's strikes, but not using his shield caused him to leave his shield arm in the open, and Roy quickly brought Telekay down.

Before the blood had soaked the ground, Roy raised his shield and rammed into the warrior. No longer with secure footing, Roy struck with Telekay again, and though he blocked the strike with his shield, the warrior fell. Roy stepped on the sword before the warrior could do something, and struck him before he could bring his shield between them. The shield soon fell to the ground, and Roy was grazed by an arrow as he withdrew Telekay from the flesh.

The armament on his arm reduced the pain, but he still felt the annoyance of the arrow. This time he was more aware of his allies, not straying too far away from them, but he still continued fighting without the hindrance of thought.

He was weary, but he could not fool himself; he lived for this—he lived to be a soldier, to be in a battlefield where he could fight. He didn't need money, nor did he need to command others. He was content being a soldier. All he needed was control. With sword in hand, Roy could control and fight—he wasn't subject to a greater force. He didn't have to worry about anything—no fear paralyzed him. Roy was in the battlefield, fighting and killing, living and prevailing.

Off in the distance, he noticed Brandon fighting. Though he didn't think about it, he did what his conscious mind would have done: he headed towards Brandon's direction.

He fought with others on the way, sometimes killing them, and sometimes going past them and fighting someone else. When he got closer to Brandon, he saw him fighting with another. The other was clearly a skilled warrior, as Brandon was having trouble keeping up with him. Brandon blocked a strike with his shield, but when he started a counter-attack, the soldier brought his shield up to the sword, as if striking with his shield, and then struck his sword arm.

The other soldier went to strike Brandon, but Roy used his telekinetic abilities to change the trajectory of an incoming arrow and shot it towards the soldier's arm. Brandon took advantage of this distraction to go on the offensive again.

Brandon struck, and the other soldier just got his shield up in time, but he staggered and Brandon struck again towards the soldier's greaves. When the soldier lowered his shield, Brandon stopped his strike and punched with his shield hand over the soldier's shield, making contact with the soldier's helm.

Soon, the cry of "Zalphic!" caught everyone's attention. Roy, shocked from the sudden shout, could not take his eyes off of Brandon. Around him, the swords and shields lowered. Brandon towered over his opponent, frozen in place—as if wondering if he had accidentally used his fire. "Zalphic!" Roy and Brandon turned, and faced the zalphic that had caught everyone's attention.

He formed part of the Faldenheim forces, and all his allies seemed to distance themselves from him. "See! Faldenheim supports these *creatures.*" *They said, as they were preparing to commit an atrocity.* "Get him!" Roy walked slowly towards him.

The zalphic, fearing for his life, immediately encircled himself in thick roots. The Vernatia forces gathered themselves around the zalphic boy, and began to strike the roots with war axes and swords and whatever they could find. Roy looked again at Brandon's direction. Brandon looked relieved. Roy had at first thought it had been Brandon they were yelling at. Not able to withstand the constant blows, the trunks gave way, revealing the boy. Hands grabbed at him. They were all armored, and he couldn't use the thorns that Roy would have thought to use.

Soldiers from both Faldenheim and Vernatia grabbed the boy's arms and legs. The Vernatia soldiers took off the boy's armor, cut his hair, and then cut some of his fingers off, while the Faldenheim soldiers held him in place. The cries of the zalphic boy drowned the distant clash of steel on steel from those who were unable to hear the initial cry of zalphic.

Will they choose the dying flower, the crumbling mountain, or the erupting volcano? They ripped the shirt of the boy and began to draw in red blood a flower that was bending downwards with a lack of force. "All flowers need rain," said Roy. He went up to the zalphic and slit his throat, causing a shower of blood to fall towards the flower.

Roy did not relish the idea of killing a zalphic. It didn't bother him, but despite everything, zalphics needed to stand together. He knew though, that if he hadn't done that, the others would have let him suffer longer.

"Charge in three, two, one," someone from behind him shouted. After all, they were still in war, and a city still had to be taken. Fighting almost to compensate for the warless period, the soldiers again fought with a ferocity that fire alone could describe. The fighting consumed them all, and Roy killed more people than he bothered to count.

He was certain he had bruises on his arms, but he could not feel any of them and was instead lost in a world of battle. He fought his way back to Jacob's men. He was fighting Devin. Jacob knocked him down, but he stabbed his sword into the ground next to Devin's fallen body. He lifted his sword and went forward to fight another.

Jacob didn't want to kill a fellow zalphic. Roy didn't know how to feel about himself, and how he would have killed Devin if it weren't for him using his powers. Roy concentrated instead on the war, killing and surviving. The war might soon be over, but Roy's battle had just begun.

Chapter 23
Faldenheim

Faldenheim was in sight, and Roy Rhapsados knew this would be a difficult battle. Worst of all, they had heard that forces in Markai were already in route. By Roy's calculations, they had three days to take the castle. He didn't know if they would be able to do it. The time remaining indicated that King Whaldo had not waited for the reply of Lords Kingston and Banesworth, and had instead sent the Markai soldiers towards Faldenheim. Roy didn't imagine that Lord Kingston had anticipated this, and the lack of time meant they would have to take unnecessary risks in order to conquer.

Faldenheim was also well equipped. Though they certainly lacked the people of Vernatia *and* Bravania, they were wealthy, the wealthiest of the North, and had resources to arm every last man. They were also defending and had the luxury of hiding behind their walls. Throughout the war, the lords certainly had considered how they would conquer Faldenheim, but Roy had been absent for those discussions.

He knew that soldiers would be joining them that had been previously training. The fresh soldiers would certainly help, but it didn't matter if they couldn't get past Faldenheim's gates. Roy drew Telekay and examined his sword. It was still in great battle condition, having experience little wear and tear—Caster metal was much sturdier than the other metals. Roy spun the sword around and looked at his reflection. He could see signs of his Telk heritage—the dark hair and dark eyes, and the slightly darker tone than that of most Androsii. He didn't see the vulnerabilities that gave him pause, and instead saw the traits of a warrior.

The time was near for him to battle. He was scared of death, and therefore had no intention of confronting it that day. He looked at the impending castle, with all its walls and people. He turned to his fellow soldiers. Jacob was staring at Faldenheim as well. Behind him, the indistinct chatter died down.

He turned around, and saw King Ferdinand approaching. All around, people bowed their heads respectfully, and Ferdinand looked around before speaking. "Today, we fight Faldenheim. Officially we are here to claim Faldenheim to my rule. I realize that perhaps not all of you have the same conviction as your lords, and perhaps you might not care who rules you from the Capital. Some of you fight only because you live in a city governed by Vernatia or Bravania, and have come only because your lords demanded it. I don't blame you.

"I am King by heritage, yes, and King in name, but I am not yet truly a King. That I can only become after I rule. I will not be truly your King until I demonstrate to you that I *deserve* to rule. My brother grew up in the Capital, separated from all the castles and cities. His mother does not allow him to leave in fear that those who killed our relatives might try to kill him. I am here, joining you in battle. I travelled and met Lord Kingston and Lord Banesworth. I've seen the bandits that stalk the roads, and the guards who help those bandits in exchange for lumps of coins.

"Change must be had, but change can only come if we do something. We cannot sit idly and expect change—so I ask you, not as a King, but as a man. Fight for change, and fight for a better life for us all. With Faldenheim, we can become a free North. My brother has done nothing for you—he has only hid behind his lords and laws. One castle separates us from a better world. After that, I shall demonstrate what a true leader does for his people." Roy was impressed by King Ferdinand's words. He almost believed them himself. The soldiers cried in agreement, and they began their march towards Faldenheim.

From the distance, Roy saw Faldenheim's gates open. The confusing sight gave rise to murmurs amongst the men. The two men that walked outside were accompanied by a couple of soldiers with white flags on them.

Approaching closer, Roy saw that it was Lord Horus and his son Jackson who had exited Faldenheim and was waiting for something. Roy also noticed that the men atop the walls had arrows drawn, ready to protect their lord, or to attack preemptively.

The army stopped, and they quieted, almost expecting an explanation for the strange situation. King Ferdinand approached Lord Horus, along with Lords Kingston and Banesworth.

"Allister, Neister. I've been expecting your company. I don't believe we have met, Ferdinand." Roy noticed that Lord Horus didn't address him as a king.

"Lord Horus. I've heard many a great thing about you from Lord Kingston. I do hope that you have exited your castle to come to my service."

"I cannot do that Ferdinand. I am subject to the King of Andros, King Whaldo III Alexander."

"I am the rightful king."

"King Whaldo was the firstborn child of King Raymond Alexander and Queen Serinah. Do you deny this?"

"No I do not deny that, but—"

"It is he, then, who is rightfully king."

"I am the firstborn of King Raymond."

"But not with Queen Serinah."

"The law states only the firstborn of the King is to be his successor."

"Lamentably, we have deteriorated since the days of the first King Whaldo. Do you think a bastard should inherit the throne?"

"I am King Raymond's firstborn, and by the law established by King Whaldo, it is to me that the throne belongs."

"King Whaldo had in mind that a King would be honorable and have no children outside of his marriage."

"'The successor to the throne of Andros shall be the firstborn child of the Alexander King or Queen. If the Ruler has no children, the throne passes to the eldest sibling. If an eldest sibling does not exist, the royal line goes to the eldest sibling of the previous Ruler—the last Ruler's Uncle or Aunt, and to their children. The throne shall not pass to another family unless no family member closer than first cousins to the previous Ruler, the Ruler before him, or the Ruler before *him* exists. If no such cousins exist, a decision similar to the voting on the day of the Great Shaking where Abigail Alexander was named Queen shall be observed—or alternately, a majority decision of the Great Castles.'

"It says King *or* Queen. Not King *and* Queen."

"It says King or Queen because only one of those are of the royal line of Alexanders, and if the firstborn is a daughter, she is an Alexander Queen. An Alexander King *and* Queen are not both necessary."

"I am the firstborn, and am the rightful King."

"All of you support a false king. I stay true to King Whaldo III. You should stand down." With those words, Lord Horus went back to his castle. The soldiers abandoned the white flags before entering the gates, and two archers fired shots, hitting the two white flags. King Ferdinand retreated behind the lines, and the two armies stood anxiously. From the high walls of Faldenheim, a sword was thrown to the ground.

Roy anxiously awaited as he gripped Telekay quickly for comfort, and drew an arrow. As soon as the sword hit the ground, Roy released the arrow, and a volley fell towards them. The battle for Faldenheim had begun.

Kesara Hewley was heading towards Faldenheim, along with many others who had stayed behind. Kesara had been told they would train longer, but upon hearing that the Markai forces had already begun their march to Faldenheim, training was cut short, and they were mobilized.

Kesara couldn't help but think she would go to the battlefield and find her brothers Ben and Gideon, or her father, or someone she knew, and they would be dead. The thought took a darker tone as Kesara imagined that they realized her brothers were zalphics. She expelled the thought and focused on the war in general.

She didn't know what she would do when she got there. She was of Faldenheim, and certainly she would encounter familiar faces in the war—a baker, a merchant, or a cook. Anything really.

Kesara wanted nothing more than to have Aurora at her side. Since Kesara was a soldier, and Aurora would be a healer, they were separated and had to march alone. Kesara listened vaguely to what her fellow soldiers were saying. At their marching rate, they would arrive in Faldenheim in the beginning of the second day of fighting. On the latter part of the third day, the Markai forces would arrive.

The river extending to the east in Faldenheim would trap Ferdinand's forces between the waters and the Markai forces. Kesara wondered if she could use this river to her advantage. She was a Water zalphic, but she didn't have to reveal her powers to use it.

She wondered again what Gideon would be doing in the war. Ben was a Knight, and he would certainly fight. Gideon was not a member of the Order of the Sword, nor did he form a part of the Wise Ones. He was fifteen. Kesara wanted to know what he would do. He was a male though, and the thought of him fighting others who were much more experienced than him gave Kesara pause. Max had been training Gideon, she knew, but that did nothing to alleviate her anxiety.

"It's a lovely day to kill those zalphic-loving people, isn't it?" a voice behind her asked. Kesara didn't turn around and continued walking, assuming that the voice was addressing someone else. "My only question is, if we take Faldenheim, what will you do if some of the soldiers decide to ravage Farendor?"

To this, Kesara could only turn around. She saw that the voice that had been addressing her belonged to Agnar. "Kesara Hewley. You seem so shocked that a servant of Prince Kingston would be travelling to war for Vernatia."

"I would have thought you'd be in Faldenheim already. Why are you here, and what do you want of me?"

"I can't be expected to fight in every single battle. Argus wanted me to stay behind for various reasons."

"Why haven't you informed Argus that I'm here?"

"When did I say I didn't?" Kesara looked around immediately, but saw no one. He laughed sardonically. "I've no need to harm you."

"You tried striking me with lightning last time I saw you."

Agnar smiled. "Roy wanted me to do that, so that Ben might trust him a little more. I never harmed you Kesara. I never fought you either." *Roy? Did he really plan that?* Kesara didn't know what to think.

"Why are you being kind to me?"

"I have my doubts about what Argus is planning, and even what Ferdinand desires. I don't agree with what Argus Kingston is doing."

"Then why not join Jackson?"

"I'll let you know a secret Kesara. No one is how they would like you to believe, and what you believe often is mistaken due to the things they decide to hide." Agnar smiled a little. "Good luck escaping, Kesara Hewley," and with those words he left.

###

On the second day of the fight for Faldenheim, new forces came to aid the weary soldiers from the first day. As Roy Rhapsados hid behind his shield, he felt the arrow on the other side of the metal bounce away. To his right, a soldier fell to the ground with various arrows penetrating his armor. He felt the heat of the flaming arrows scorch him as he helped ram the gate for what must have been the seventy-fifth time that day. The gates were unyielding, and Roy wondered what they would do.

The gates of Faldenheim were much too sturdy. Roy knew they would have to find another method. They would be unable to destroy the gates. The only option Roy could see was someone getting above the walls and then opening the gates. He looked at the war ladders that were erected to climb the gates.

The Faldenheim soldiers simply pushed the ladders off the walls. *"Jacob, we need to get over the gates. We won't be able to destroy them."*

"Yes, I realize that. How would you suggest we continue?"

"The war ladders are the only option." Roy looked at another war ladder, and a giant boulder was thrown down the ladder, killing some of those climbing.

"Very thoroughly considered I see...." Roy again helped the continued ramming of the gates, but to no avail.

"The ladders—we're placing them to the top of the gates. What if we placed them under, so that they can't push the ladders down?"

"What about the boulders? And even if you could get past the boulders, what then? A soldier in armor will have a hard time climbing, and they would be immediately killed upon reaching the top of the wall."

"Anything we can plot must be better than what we are currently doing. ...What if there is a zalphic?"

"A zalphic will be immediately killed—more likely worse."

But Roy was convinced that a zalphic would give them the necessary diversion. Roy abandoned his post among the men ramming the gates, and headed towards the war ladders. Roy headed forward and upward, convinced of what he would do.

Roy saw an arrow approaching and moved as best he could. The arrow passed him, and hit someone further down the ladder. Roy again started climbing. He looked up and saw as a boulder was about to be thrown downwards. He decided to evade the boulder by switching to the other side of the ladder. The boulder passed by him, nearly crushing his fingers as they held on to the ladder, and felt the vibrations on the ladder that the boulder had caused. The ladder had not been destroyed though, and he went back to the other side of the ladder and climbed with the utmost rapidity.

He was nearing the top, and he again switched sides of the ladder. Arrows rained past him, showering his allies beneath him with steel and fire. He caught his breath in order to do the next part of his plan. With all the concentration he could muster, he looked at the soldier at the highest point of the war ladder, and teleported him atop the wall.

The cry of "Zalphic!" rang vociferously, and if Roy didn't know he was fatigued, he would have thought it was that cry that made him lose his footing and let go of the rung on the ladder.

Beneath him, a force held him up and attached him to the ladder. As Roy's vision came to him, he saw Jacob holding Roy, but felt Jacob's telekinetic force keeping him on the ladder. Roy could see the sweat on Jacob's brow, after which he took a hold on the ladder and held himself up.

Those on the ladder raced up. The soldier was denying that he was a zalphic, but no one believed him. He had just teleported in everyone's sight, and there was no denying his abilities. Roy caught his breath and slowly, Roy went up the ladder, and upon arriving to the top he saw the "Zalphic" soldier was dead, and that Roy's fellow soldiers were defending access to the ladder.

Roy put up his shield and kneeled as a volley of arrows tried to kill the men that were appearing. Roy noticed the men from other parts of the wall came to aid in killing Roy and the men climbing the ladder. Roy knew that if they could hold the ladder, other men on other ladders might be able to successfully climb due to the decreased number of defending soldiers.

Ferdinand's forces stayed put, trying to keep the war ladders safe. Roy was still tired from the effort, and so he had his shield raised to protect him. More soldiers kept climbing the ladders, making the effort to defend them progressively easier.

Roy saw as another group of forces successfully climbed a war ladder, and were beginning to defend it as well. If the Faldenheim forces didn't eliminate these two groups quickly, more and more soldiers would climb the ladders. Roy knew they had to push forward, but he was much too tired, and the other soldiers had decided that it was more important to defend their position.

The men on the other side did not think it was more important to defend their position though, and they pushed forward. They weren't getting too far, as the Faldenheim forces were still well-placed and well-armed, but seeing the group of soldiers push forward made the other group push forward. They were a bigger group, and they weren't so easily held back.

Roy heard the cry of alarms as the Faldenheim forces realized they could not contain the group. The other group was still pushing forward, forcing Faldenheim to split its forces a bit. The soldiers fought their way through the forces. Roy pushed one of the boulders down towards the forces defending the gates, and he continued defending his fellow soldiers. The fresh soldiers greatly aided the group, and they fought and continually pushed forward and down the walls of Faldenheim, heading towards its southern gate.

23. Faldenheim- 355

There were too many soldiers for Faldenheim to contain; the additional forces that had arrived steadily climbed the war ladders and joined the groups pushing forward. A great system of red rivers and bodies imprinted the ground on top of the walls.

The difficulty of the path towards the gates did not deter the group, and the ever-increasing force pushed forward. When finally they had reached the gates—among other forces fighting on other parts of the wall—the group rejoiced in their endeavor and opened the gates. Ferdinand's forces charged into Faldenheim, and Roy saw Tadeus Banesworth amid the front lines. Roy followed his trajectory and saw how in the course of but a few seconds, he killed five soldiers with a violent speed that he would have thought only possible in a dream.

The blood flowing down his body was about the best aspect of his injuries. Aurora Stephensen applied some bandages to the wounds, but she knew the wounds were too deep for bandages to improve. She knew he would die in the tent, along with some of the other soldiers who had suffered from battle wounds. Aurora again looked at the arm of the soldier, where a sword had nearly cut his arm off; the skin on his shoulder was split, revealing blood-tainted muscle and bone.

Aurora brought him water and injected him with a vial that the Wisest One had procured to reduce pain. At that point, the only thing Aurora could do was minimize his pain. She moved on to another soldier whose wounds were not as severe.

To him, Aurora did not give the vial—as there was a limited supply—and instead, injected him with a different substance to reduce some of the inflammation. She kept constant vigil on the soldiers, making sure none of them had unexpected complications.

The frenetic rush of soldiers being brought in and out, and the Wise Ones going from soldier to soldier to offer aid, was distressful, but it gave Aurora a task to perform. She was still worried about Prince Tadeus, but if he were to come there, he would be in too much pain to pay attention while Aurora hid.

Notwithstanding, she kept a constant vigil on the incoming soldiers as well.

Aurora went throughout the day in a constant flurry of motion—healing and watching and worrying. She worked and worried for the better part of the day, when she saw someone come into the tent carrying a wounded soldier. The wounded soldier was carried to a bed while the worried soldier who carried him turned to those around him, hoping for some reassurance of the wounds.

Aurora had a nagging feeling that she had seen the soldier before—the worried one. He had typical Androsii features, but she knew she had seen him before. She tried to recollect her memory as she went over to aid the wounded soldier.

The wounds—under optimal circumstances—were treatable, but she was not confident with what she could do given the limited supplies and inadequacies of the tent. "You can go back to battle—we'll take care of him here."

"I'm not abandoning him here—he's my brother." Aurora looked at the worried soldier, still unsure where she had seen him. "I'm not going anywhere while he might...." He trailed off, but Aurora concentrated on the wounds. The armor was cutting into his stomach, shattered from some sort of war hammer. She needed to clean the wound and remove the armor, but removing the armor would exasperate the wound.

At this point, the soldier lost consciousness, and the worried soldier next to him began his lamentations. Aurora calmed the soldier, letting him know that his brother was only unconscious and still with life. She didn't know how much longer the latter would hold true though, so she began preparations to remove the armor. She collected the soldiers sweat with a moist towel and took apart the straps and joints of the armor, until only the shattered steel plate remained. The soldier came back to consciousness, muttering unintelligible phrases to his brother when he wasn't screaming.

Perhaps he understood what was being said. Aurora hoped this was the case, as she saw now that it was a hopeless endeavor. The wound was worse than she had previously thought. The other soldier listened carefully to the wounded soldier, while Aurora fetched some pain medications. It was a small dosage, but it was all Aurora could do.

She injected him with the vial, and turned to the waiting soldier. "The armor was shattered, and there is no way to safely remove it. I've given him something for the pain, but I'm afraid there is nothing more I can do." The soldier took it all in, searching longingly at his brother who was now between consciousness and death. He let out a cry and went closer to his brother. The tears streaked down his face, flowing down past dried blood, and collecting on his jaw. Teardrops fell as the soldier talked to his brother, telling him they needed to live to see so much still.

The wounded soldier looked dreary, and, taxed with the medication given to him, could scarcely raise his voice over a murmur. Still, Aurora heard the distinct fear in his voice as he spoke to his brother for what might have been the final time. "Joseph, I love you." Joseph only held his brother more tightly as Aurora saw the life drain from the wounded soldier.

"I do too. That's why you have to live." But the soldier knew that wasn't going to happen, as Aurora knew it wasn't going to happen. He gave his brother a lamenting smile and rested his eyes for the last time.

It had all been simpler when Faldenheim's gates were still closed to Ferdinand's forces. Kesara Hewley didn't have to worry about killing someone she knew, or actively taking part against her home. The soldiers from the day before had been unable to penetrate the walls, and for the entire morning, the same had held true on the second day with all the new soldiers as well.

When the walls had been climbed and the gates had been opened, the task was much more difficult for Kesara. She had strategically stayed near the river, trying to find a possible entrance through a sewage system or a gate for water. She knew they would find none, and that Faldenheim was almost impregnable. Only once had Faldenheim been sieged—when the Lancasters came from the forest to attack the Telk invaders four-hundred years ago. They had an abundance of Caster metal then, and most suspected that it was only due to this that the Lancasters were successful. The metal was much scarcer now, and she didn't think it possible to breach the walls.

Now soldiers from Faldenheim fought soldiers from Vernatia— once staunch allies now racing to kill each other. Ferdinand's army gathered at the gates to invade, while the forces of Faldenheim scrambled to defend itself.

At the river, Kesara had noticed the details even those from Faldenheim might not notice: how the current was stronger than usual, how the water level was off, and the strange man-made holes observable from parts of the river.

She abandoned her thoughts of the ocean and went to the now open gates of Faldenheim. There, she stayed towards the edge of the castle walls, defending herself from the volley of arrows and keeping vigil for anyone she might know. She noticed that, despite having penetrated the gates, Ferdinand's forces had not been able to successfully make their way deep into Faldenheim. The open southern gate led them only eastward, toward the eastern gate and the river.

Despite the numbers of the Ferdinand forces, Faldenheim was giving little ground. Their collective effort seemed to revolve around keeping them held up against the gates. Kesara knew that they were tiring though, and that inevitably the fatigue would wear down their strength. She only worried how long that would take. For the better part of the day, Faldenheim fought with voracious intensity, leading them towards the east.

Something seemed strange about that, but Kesara was instead consumed with thoughts of her brother. She hadn't seen either of them, and she worried tremendously for their safety. *Perhaps this is how Ben often feels....* She saw as the Faldenheim forces gave their lives to stop the advance of the army at their gates. One of them with a war hammer particularly fought tirelessly. Each swing demonstrated his strength, each with unchanging speed and power, neither wavering nor diminishing.

The soldier with the war hammer struck another soldier on the steel plate of the armor, and through the shouting and the mayhem of war, Kesara heard the screeching sound of bones cracking and metal on metal. The soldier fell, crying in pain, as one of his comrades reacted with swift vengeance—attempting to return the caused pain. His attempt, however, failed, and the soldier was aided by his fellow soldiers, who blocked the crazed assailant.

The assailant went back to the fallen soldier, raising him off the ground and carrying him backwards as soldiers from Faldenheim and the army of Ferdinand continued their battle. Kesara was drawn to the soldier, who so obviously cared about the fallen soldier, speaking soothing words to him, and frantically rushing him back outside of Faldenheim, towards the tents for the injured.

Kesara followed the group who was being pushed eastward, but she evaded fighting as best she could, staying in the rear of the group and using primarily her shield to protect herself and other soldiers from the constant attacks thrown her way. Despite trying to evade the soldiers, she could not slip past all of them. One such man delivered a lazy blow, thinking himself superior and having confidence that Kesara would not pose a threat.

When Kesara countered with the skills she had acquired learning from her brothers, the man turned his attention to her with more care and caution. The man struck her raised shield, and she could feel the violent power behind it. She felt too young and incongruous with the soldiers around her. Still, she was a zalphic, and as such she had learned to protect herself. He changed his attack and directed it towards her sword rather than her shield. She gripped her sword with more force and parried the strike while simultaneously ramming her shield into his sword arm.

The soldier grabbed his arm and backed away a little, surprised at Kesara's skill. *They always underestimate me.* She grabbed her shield and backed away from an arrow. She briefly looked at the soldiers on the roof of the eastern gates, shooting arrows at the army.

She also noticed that the water that normally flowed through part of the castle was dry.

#

The dark spots blurring his vision eclipsed the light. Roy Rhapsados stared at an unknown direction, struggling to find life—or as he had been previously seeing, death. The spherical tiny bits of light floated away from his field of vision as he drifted further away into the recesses of the darkness. The weight of his body made itself present as he dragged further downwards into the depths of an unknown abyss.

He had no thoughts of anything but the small spherical lights, heading off at another direction, leaving him darkened and without something he knew was essential, but he had as yet been unable to determine what that might be. He grew tense in the immutable surroundings in which he was caught, and he struggled to keep mind of what he knew. The dark spots germinated, intensifying the little light that was left in an unfamiliar terrain.

The battle of the encompassing darkness and the remedial light wavered as he felt a pain near his throat. He struggled and clawed at the grimacing enemy, but his struggles did nothing to help with the crushing sensation, or the darkening scenery. He tried in vain to go upwards, but he couldn't as the weight of his armor anchored him to the ground. He clutched desperately at his throat as a greater concentration of spherical lights climbed away. He searched frenetically for the bindings in his armor, trying his best to undo them and be rid of the burden.

His strength diminished as he grabbed the first bindings and ripped it apart with ferocity.

More light.
More darkness.
More pain.

There was a nuance of blue, a spectrum of color darkened to hues and shades of one. The rushing feeling in his mind was crippling, and thoughts outside of his immediate predicament were foreign. The difference between the darkness and the abysmal black was deteriorating as the darkness and abysmal black converged into a singular pattern.

Another binding.
No light.
Pure darkness.
Absolute pain.

The frenzied head turned in all directions, hoping for respite from the grimacing enemy, finding only a deeper sensation of the crushing world around him. His woe was unutterable, and ineffable. The proliferating spheres travelled away from him as he fell, falling and falling, crushed from pressure and weight.

The armor fell around him as he released the final bindings. His weight relaxed as he continued plummeting towards the ground. Telekinesis, and Fire. Thunder, Earth, and Wood. He was forgetting one. No. He was forgetting two.

No gauntlets or armor, just greaves and weight. Roy kicked and jolted, jerking one way and another, trying desperately to remove the greaves as he touched the ground.

The pain in his throat demanded attention, and he saw the blackness consume his sight. His strength failed him—he angered at this thought. The blackness consumed. The darkness swallowed.

In his state of breathlessness and desperation, a fire inside him pushed forward—a fire not deterred by the waters around him, a fire that kept him conscious of what he needed to do, and a fire that kept him alive. The fire burned inside him, consuming the water as its fuel, flashing, and expanding and failing to wither. The flames arose, cleansing him more than water could do, and Roy felt a fiery impulse to live. The fires proceeded from him, consuming and burning whatever might lay in front. The fire burned everything down—his reservations, his fears, and his ineptitudes. The great fire gave him guiding light, showing him his path. The flames engulfed the skies, casting blazing shadows. The mountains blocking his way turned to ashes, and he could not be stopped.

The greaves fell to the ground in a soundless clamor, and his fatigue now overwhelmed him. He drew from his innermost strength a force to push him forward and upward. As the light blinded him, the grimacing enemy dissuaded, and his throat felt respite—if but for a moment.

Again he found himself submerged in darkness, but with a greater facility he emerged and faced the crippling brightness. He coughed and choked and closed his eyes as the pain slowly receded. He began regaining his senses as he heard the shouts of alarm and panic, of commands and a great whizzing of the air around him. He heard the coughs and cries of pain and heard the sound of crashing and rushing. His quick, deep, and desperate breaths diminished as they returned to regular intervals. His chest heaved less violently with each passing moment as he escaped the inundation that had previously held him.

He had not yet escaped danger.

Aurora Stephensen was alarmed at the sound of the violent crashing. It was the third day of the battle for Faldenheim. The second day had passed, with open gates to stand testament for the carnage. The third day had amassed a plethora of more lifeless bodies, as Ferdinand's army devastated the castle. It seemed indicative of Faldenheim's fall—its forces were pushed back and killed, giving way to the keep and to the eastern gates.

Despite the short time given to conquer the castle, Ferdinand's forces seemed to have made quick work of the defending forces. Aurora held no hope that Faldenheim would be saved before it fell. She wondered where this contention of siblings would lead. The war-stricken North had lost too numerous men, and war with Whaldo seemed imprudent.

These thoughts engulfed Aurora as she worried what it would be like under the rule of Ferdinand. Then she had heard the violent crashing. When she looked around, she saw she was not alone in her confusion. The wounded still continued some of their cries, but even *they* quieted after the piercing sound.

Though all were curious, they were instructed to stay in the tent and continue their efforts. Aurora continued with much chagrin, her natural inquisitiveness imploring persistently to determine the origin of the sound. When the Wise Ones resumed their work in the tents, the noiselessness subsided. The cries of wounded soldiers returned to their previous wailing, and Aurora tried focusing on the work, but found herself still too absorbed with the sound.

Eventually, she heard a persistent sound grow louder and louder, approaching with a diminished force, but undoubtedly making way towards the tent. Shouts from outside were indistinguishable, and she set down the syringe as the cold water entered the tent, flooding the tent's floors and forcing those laying on the floor to rise with flailing concern.

The Wise Ones instructed all those in the tent to remain. "I can help divert the waters. We can't let these conditions impede our efficiency," Aurora pleaded with one of the Wise Ones. The Elder assented, and sent her along with a group to divert the water. She exited the tent, first looking at Faldenheim, and the water pouring through the main gate. She turned to the others, who reflected her dismay and awe.

"How can that much water be exiting the castle?" Aurora didn't know the answer. She started creating a ditch around the tent, redirecting some of the water. Others joined her in her effort to make a ditch and others grabbed whatever they could and put it in front of the tent, trying to impede the progress of the water.

After having successfully diverted the waters, the others went back into the tent. Aurora instead went towards Faldenheim, slowly walking towards the chaotic pool of bodies. The water flowed steadily, and the soldiers could not get past the stream of water. The muddy floor made it too difficult to advance in full armor, and the ubiquitous water pushed constantly towards the opposite direction.

Off in the distance, arrows rained down like rain onto the water, making splashes and tainting the waters with crimson red— bodies sank to the bottom as the arrows took away their force, and the armor anchored them towards the ground. Aurora was in shock and awe as she saw the Faldenheim soldiers determinedly aiming their arrows at the drowning men, unperturbed by the waters that flooded their homes and destroyed their possessions.

Faldenheim had planned to flood their own castle to preclude Ferdinand from taking it. In these conditions, Ferdinand would be unable to conquer Faldenheim, and the Markai forces would arrive.

A chill went through Aurora as she saw Logan on a roof. He didn't need a bow and arrow. He was killing men by drowning them with the waters at his disposal.

###

"*Get on the roof.*" The imperious command had saved Kesara Hewley's life. Without need of an explanation, she confided in the familiar voice and climbed the stairs to the top. There, Max called off the soldiers, commanding them to let her up. The soldiers had shown confusion, but nonetheless laid aside to let her pass. Soldiers aimed downwards with drawn bows, searching the crashing waves for survivors.

Immediately, her face was against armor and she felt the tight squeezing of exuberant hands around her. Kesara smiled as she saw her brother Ben, and when Ben let go she saw her younger brother, Gideon, on the roofs, protected and well. She went over to him as they too hugged, glad and oblivious to the shouts around them.

Lost in the arms of her brothers, Kesara thought only of how great it was to be reunited at last. However, the screams echoing from the waves inevitably began their slow ascent and resonated in her ears, and she could only stand in a mix of horror and despondency as she saw the drowning soldiers picked off by arrows and weighed down to their deaths by the armor that was to protect them.

Ben yelled something Kesara didn't hear, but she saw as the men on the roof all released arrows to a same general direction. Even Gideon participated in the shooting, looking at his brother for encouragement. Kesara looked at the drowning bodies, horrified by what she saw but unable to avert her gaze.

Among the waters she saw countless bodies trying to float. She saw the droplets of water that protruded resultant from the countless arrows. She looked down, unable to identify the soldiers—all were miniscule animals, slaughtered for the benefit of those around her.

She looked at her brother, so certain of what he was doing. Kesara felt uncertain that she should do nothing more than stand there. She looked at the waters again, seeing lives shut off—water sealing the top of their eternal tombs. She saw a man flailing about in the water, desperate for breath, but the only thing that filled his lungs was water and metal and blood, an arrow now attaching itself to his throat. Kesara saw as a familiar face dived in the water to escape the volley of arrows. He couldn't seem to get back up, having expended already so much breath and strength. Kesara looked around the rooftop, seeing as all the others were concentrated with their arrows, shooting down the forces of Ferdinand.

She returned her attention to Agnar, as bubbles arose in his inability to hold his breath or reach the top of the waters. Kesara concentrated on the waters around Agnar and changed their direction, making them flow below Agnar, reducing the ferocity of the waters, and raising waves around him. Agnar arose to the top of the waters, drawing in sweet breath, and Kesara caused a wave as an arrow made way to shoot him down. The water absorbed the power of the arrow, and Agnar took off his remaining armor, took a deep breath, and dived under water to escape the raining death. Kesara moved the waves, propelling Agnar further and faster, and by the time he was out of view, Kesara was short of breath herself, and she sat down, exhausted from the effort.

Around her, the constant shouts continued, augmenting the surrounding chaos. Cries were shortened and waves were constant in their ferocity. Kesara questioned the war—the premise of it all. She saw a rapid collection of the scenes that featured death. She saw the great walls, she saw the open gate, soldiers filling the streets, bodies flooding the castle. Skies full of arrows, invisible shouts heard and lost, fiery pain and blood-stained swords—blood-stained *everything*. Hammers crushed steel, shields shattered, empty, white eyes stared back at their opponents. Love and limbs were split, and no color existed other than crimson red. The battle standards flapped with an intensity incongruous with the gentle breeze. Swords and skies fell, and the only thing left was death.

Roy Rhapsados had thought it strange that they were constantly pushed east. When in the third day, the vigor that Faldenheim had demonstrated the two days before dissipated, Roy thought that Faldenheim would fall. He saw no reason they should be unable to conquer the castle, and they had begun a massacre on their last day to conquer.

Despite this, despite the constant forward motion of their forces, they were pushed constantly to the east. Roy hadn't known why that was until the waters crashed and threatened to drown him. When he had escaped the weight of his armor, he reached the surface of the waters, only to see arrows from the sky falling, threatening to take bodies along with their downward trajectory. The waters absorbed many of the arrows, but this was true about bodies as well.

Roy caught his breath as best he could before diving again underwater. The arrows above him made contact with the water, but he turned and directed himself towards the shallow waters. His breath was escaping him, so he turned and turned until he entered an empty building by going through an open window. He gathered his breath with frantic inhalations, and he steadied himself in his breathing. As most of his comrades were not from Faldenheim, they could not have known that the building existed, but Roy remembered it from a time in his childhood. The memory made him rub his eyes, uncertain whether tears were forming or not.

He shot electricity out of his hands, troubled by what he could have done back then. As the reflected light from the lightning rippled across the waters, Roy returned his attention to the waters and Faldenheim. Roy swam back into some of the side streets, trying his best to look at the roofs to check for soldiers. When he didn't see any, he started climbing into a building, He broke into a window, going inside, and climbed the stairs to the roof. He saw most soldiers were looking down at the waters, searching for swimmers and letting loose their arrows. Roy looked around, got close to the ground, and teleported across a roof. He went to the edge, where a lone soldier had his arrow drawn, aiming downwards. Approaching silently and making sure no one was watching, he slit the soldier's throat and grabbed the bow and arrow.

Roy used his telekinetic powers to slowly drag the body down into the building, while he remained on the roof, arrow drawn, making sure no soldiers turned in his direction. After successfully

23. Faldenheim- 367

hiding the body, Roy drew an arrow and fired it at a soldier on the roof. He quickly drew another arrow and aimed downwards, and when he heard the cry of the soldier, the soldiers on the roof checked their fellow soldiers and searched the waters again. *The arrow is facing the wrong way.* Again Roy loosed an arrow at another soldier, this time using his telekinetic powers to redirect the trajectory of the arrow. The arrow shot upward at an angle at the soldier's throat, and he too cried as he stained the arrow with red and fell on the roof.

From another nearby roof, Roy used his telekinesis to knock a soldier down off the roof. The soldier fell on a side of the building, staining the building with a violent splatter of red, and filling the air with a sickening crunch. The cry of panic was heard by his comrades, who followed his dive into the water, accompanied by a spray of red, never to rise again.

The soldiers now were wary of what was happening to their companions. They backed up a little from the edge, questioning amongst themselves where the arrows were coming from. They looked at Roy's direction, but Roy knew that without his armor, the other soldiers wouldn't recognize him, as he didn't have the sigil engrained on his clothing.

The confused soldiers continued their search for the one who was killing. A soldier towards the bottom shot an arrow up towards the roof. Though he was tired from the effort, Roy once again redirected the trajectory of the arrow. As the arrow approached Roy, he used his telekinesis to rise the blood from the slit throat of the soldier he killed. He slowed the arrow immediately next to his side, though he pretended he was struck in a more central location. With his telekinesis, he spurted the blood to feign a more severe hit.

Having calculated the necessary distance, he stepped off the roof in a dive as the soldiers on the roof stared at him for a moment, and he dived into the waters, letting the current take him away, and escaped the soldiers of Faldenheim before they might realize what was happening.

#

Tadeus Banesworth was there, having removed some of his armor, his feet sinking in the mud due to his weight. Despite the mud, he traversed with rapidity towards the soldiers protecting access to the roof. The soldiers recognized him, and for a brief moment wavered. Tadeus would have been deadly even without the vacillating soldiers; Tadeus drove his sword through one soldier, blocked a second soldier's strike with his shield, and, leaving his sword in the first soldier, grabbed the first soldier's sword as he dropped it to the ground, using the first soldier's sword to slash a third soldier, whose blood blocked the second soldier's view just long enough for Tadeus to stab him with the shield spike.

He disappeared into the stairs before the bodies could all fall to the ground, and his entourage of soldiers were dumbfounded. Seeing a Bladesman fight was a rare sight—only a handful had the title of Bladesman. The step above Knight was not so easily achieved, and seeing Tadeus fight with such skill and swiftness only reinforced that idea for Aurora.

She knew that Faldenheim possessed only one Bladesman, Caspian Stoddard, from whom Maximillius and Benjamin had received their training and become Knights. Bravania had four— Prince Tadeus Banesworth, Melinda and Zachary Briar, and Garait Tiralus—and Vernatia had two—Kayton Drost and Jacob Victoriano. Arastaud and Garrisbrough led the castles with six each, whereas Markai had none. Three of the six in Garrisbrough were at the Capital, protecting King Whaldo. Garrisbrough, had Fredrick Bastion, leader of the Order of the Sword and lord of Garrisbrough. The most infamous of the Swordsmen, though, was Oliver, the Red, Alkarvan, heir to Arastaud and the Bladesman with the highest body count, said to be seen most often covered in the red blood of his enemies. Even if the general consensus was that Tadeus had more skill, Oliver was known to be the savage one. What a sight it would be to see *him* fight.

Aurora Stephensen went up to the soldiers, each of which had a death wound, and had expired before she reached them. Aurora heard as Tadeus and his men raced towards the roof. She disappeared into adjacent streets, still fearful of what Tadeus might do. She went underground and traversed the intricate tunnels, knowing where she needed to go through the countless hours she spent studying the tunnels at the Wise Ones, trying to decipher where a secret arsenal of Caster weapons would be stored.

Neither she nor Steven had ever divined where the treasure lay, but it was Steven who had gone through the logical steps that told them that the treasure had been found. He was always jealous he was not the one who had found it.

She traversed the deserted tunnels, undeterred by the shrilling echoes of animals scurrying. The intricate labyrinth diverged into many directions, but she travelled without difficulty, turning exactly where she needed to. The dark tunnels extended in many directions, heading off towards a gate or a landmark of Faldenheim. She went towards the direction of the western gate, wondering what might happen when she got there. She wondered if she would find a bloodbath, a constant flow of viscous red sliming in her direction, or an elated group of victors celebrating their defense, or perhaps a continual struggle of forces tearing and retreating and bursting apart. Her dejected pace only gave time for these things to happen, as she was forced to circle and travel through long corridors due to the intricate design.

The faint sound of shouts echoed lightly in the dungeon, and dark passageways hid imagined fears and exaggerated danger. She moved forward and came to a strange split in the tunnels. This had not been in any of the tunnel's plans. The tunnel was supposed to go straight, but the two passageways went forward and one slightly left, while the other one went slightly right. Aurora drew the schematics of the plan with her hand on the air, envisioning the tunnels as they were and should be. She saw in the schematics how she was supposed to go forward, take a left, then turn right almost immediately, and after a bit, another right. This path would turn slightly left until it met up with another tunnel. If she didn't turn right immediately, the left path would lead to a path that circled into itself.

Knowing the path on the right would take here where she needed to go, she went left. That would theoretically take her to the path that circled into itself. As she travelled the path, she found herself at another split. Aurora took the right tunnel, and went through it, going all around, until she found herself back at the main tunnel from which she had come. She again went around the tunnel in the same fashion, going through the right tunnel, searching. She wasn't certain for what she was searching, but with discerning eyes, she again circled the tunnel. There was something strange about it, how the split before had not been in the plans, why this tunnel circled into itself rather than ended, and why this part of the tunnel was slightly more illuminated than the rest of the underground paths.

    She decided to switch directions, this time entering from the left tunnel, and started circling once again. She observantly looked at the tunnels, scanning the walls. She then noticed a slight crevice in the wall. At first she thought it was a mirage, where the light appeared to be shining just a little more brightly. It was only a small piece of the wall, but as Aurora came closer to it, she saw it was no illusion. She brushed her hand on the wall, feeling a similar feel to the other parts of the wall. She hit the wall lightly, and noticed that it was hallow, something that was definitely different from the rest of the wall. She grabbed a rock that protruded from the wall, and pushed it. As a door opened inward into another tunnel, further underground, she looked around. Inside, strange sources of light illuminated the tunnel. No torches lined the wall, no fires glowed, but the tunnel was brightly lit by two long tubes that ran as far as she could see along the top of the tunnel.

    The tunnel did not twist nor turn, nor did it split into other tunnels. It simply went straight, in an unchanging direction. As Aurora walked the tunnel, she realized now why the tunnels went off in such strange directions, why they went underground and rose and turned in seemingly wild and haphazard directions. They circled this path, making sure not to intersect with it. This path was kept secret, not shown in the schematics. It also had been recently remodeled, as evidenced by the incongruence between the plans and the tunnels. The shining, tidy tunnel went undisturbed and unchanging. Aurora looked at the strange tubes that produced light, too small to reach and examine by hand, but viewing from a distance, walking along trying to see what exactly it might be.

23. Faldenheim- 371

She finally reached the end of the tunnel, and was met by a door. This time, the door was well-shut. She put her ear against the wall, trying to hear any voices beyond her sight. She heard faint voices, not from the room but another, so she pulled open the door and found herself in chambers on which she had not previously laid eyes. She noticed the lush decorations, the extravagant cloths, and the luxurious items all around. Her family was well off, but this was excessive to her taste. Certainly, only one man could possess such a chamber.

All the faint voices stopped, and she heard the sound of bodies collapsing onto the floor.

The Markai forces were arriving. They had little time to conquer Faldenheim. The only tactic Roy Rhapsados could imagine was a full frontal assault on the keep, regardless of the casualties. The water, however, made that impossible, and Roy found himself wondering what would happen now. Ferdinand had begun strong, but he now thought this would end in only a disastrous manner. A group of soldiers recognized Roy and asked him to follow as they took him to Prince Kingston.

As Roy approached Prince Kingston, he saw that the men they were with were all zalphics. Agnar, Javier, Miguel, and Joseph were waiting. He immediately recognized that whatever Argus would have them do would involve use of their zalphic powers, and would be inherently dangerous as there were countless people who could stand witness. Roy approached Argus as he conversed privately with Jacob. The two of them looked at the distant keep, turning often towards the horizon, from where the Markai forces were coming. Argus promptly dismissed the guards and invited Roy forward. When the guards had left their sights, he turned his attention back to Jacob. "So we get to the keep, and burn it down. As soon as we do, we exit through the same means, and escape. The keep will be ours before the Markai forces arrive."

Get to the keep? If only I had thought of that, I would have conquered the entire Kingdom already. Argus started walking away, not bothering to check if the others were following. Jacob stood still as the others followed Argus. Roy walked up to Jacob, to ask what the plan was, but Jacob walked towards a soldier who was itching at his sword. "Kayton. It is time." Roy looked at this man, at Kayton, observing immediately an inescapable fact: he was extremely skilled with a sword.

Jacob deferred respect to him, when Jacob was a Bladesman, and a friend of Prince Kingston. Kayton smiled at the simple statement, and started walking into Faldenheim, as Jacob followed. Roy, not knowing whether to follow Argus or to follow Jacob, asked Jacob through telepathy. *"What am I supposed to do?"*

As was his custom, Jacob did not answer Roy's question, and instead offered a simple, terse reply: *"Don't die."* *If you didn't want me to die, you wouldn't take me with you.* "Now hurry and come." Roy let out a sigh, and followed Jacob and Kayton as they went back to the vociferous cries of war. The two stuck to side roads, and advanced, while Roy followed, having very little use of Telekay as the two quickly disposed of enemy soldiers. Kayton expertly parried two swords and moved out of the way of a third coming from behind. As the soldier missed and was pushed forward by his momentum, Kayton again moved, spinning out of the way of the two previous soldiers, as their swords made to strike Kayton. Instead, they pierced their fellow soldier, and Kayton slashed another soldier, leaving only one standing. The soldier, perhaps realizing who he pretended to strike, started to retreat, but then Roy slit his throat.

Seeing Kayton use his sword worked to enhance his memory, knowing now from where he had heard the exploits of Kayton Drost. The two men in front of him were the only two members of the Order of the Sword in Vernatia with the rank of Bladesman. The mud left by the water was not optimal, but Jacob and Kayton kept going, undisturbed. They came across the keep, with its own set of walls, and plenty of more soldiers. The plethora of archers shot arrows at them as they came into view, and the three were forced to retreat behind whatever they could find. Roy realized these archers were well trained as, almost perfectly, arrows rained down at them, landing next to, and right in front of them. They raised their shields so they would not be pierced by the arrows.

Jacob turned at an inaudible sound, but as Roy waited, he heard footsteps coming towards them. Roy turned to Kayton and Jacob, who were already communicating silently with expressions and gesticulations. Kayton wasn't a zalphic, so that complicated things in Roy's view. In the least, it was an inconvenience. Roy let his shield down as the rain of arrows stopped. Soldiers were on their way to dispose of them, Roy knew, and the arrows stopped so that they might not inadvertently hit their own soldiers. A group of six soldiers appeared first. Upon seeing them clearly, he noticed as Jacob and Kayton slightly hesitated. The soldier leading the group stopped the fellow soldiers.

He drew a sword made of Caster metal, but Roy saw as he too was hesitant to move first. Roy looked at the sword, wondering how the soldier had come across a sword made of Caster metal. Jacob and Kayton recognized him, which was clear. Roy drew Telekay, which drew the soldier's attention. It occurred to Roy that he must have been wondering where *Roy* had gotten his sword. The soldier's gaze seemed to stick to the sword.

"Kayton, Jacob. I don't want to fight you."

"We don't want to fight you either," replied Jacob.

"Come with me." Jacob sheathed his sword, as did Kayton. Roy turned to them, confused as to why they were resigning themselves. The soldiers approached the three, swords still drawn. "You will be unable to do anything to those three—well, at least two of them, but I suppose you will not want to sheathe your swords."

The soldiers did not speak, but they looked among themselves, uncertain. "If swords calm your nerves, you need not sheathe them. Just don't think they can protect you." At that, the soldiers pressed their swords against Jacob all the more. Despite this, he walked towards the soldier, not seemingly worried. When the soldier turned around, Roy realized he had been focused on the wrong detail, as the blue cloak identifying him as a Bladesman swirled with the air. *Caspian.* Kayton and Jacob must have known their fellow Bladesman. The three followed him to the keep doors. Roy saw that the Faldenheim soldiers had all but abandoned their roofs, and congregated instead around the keep, protecting it guardedly. Other Faldenheim soldiers saw them approaching, talking amongst themselves, asking if it really was Jacob and Kayton who had been captured. The two Bladesmen of Vernatia, captured and taken to the keep in the climax of the war against Faldenheim. Their faces did not hide the pleasure and reassurance they felt. Roy walked past them, wondering what Jacob was doing. Caspian went up to the gate, demanding to be let in, something they did with utmost haste. They went straight to Lord Horus and Jackson, in the courtyard

"You may resume your work," Lord Horus told the soldiers. They hesitated, but obeyed their lord and walked back, leaving only Jackson and Caspain in charge to protect Lord Horus. Lord Horus turned to the soldier, and asked him to bring his brother and his companions to him. Before leaving, Caspian took Jacob and Kayton's swords. He went towards Roy, taking Telekay, but Roy noticed that Lord Horus fought back a scoff, knowing that it would be pointless to take his sword. *What does he know of it?*

Caspian took Telekay, and immediately examined it closely. Roy looked as the soldier left, watching as he turned the sword and touched it, feeling the weight of it. When the soldier had left, Jacob then addressed the lord. "You send the men protecting you away. How strange."

Lord Horus walked up to him, with a small dagger in hand. He reached out for Jacob's hand. With the dagger, he made a small cut on Jacob's arm. He repeated this process with Kayton, and walked up to Roy. "Jackson, bandage their arms," he said, before proceeding to Roy. Roy turned to Jacob, who seemed in a daze. He turned his attention back to the lord, and the dagger in his hand. It was no ordinary dagger, he recognized. His first thought was poison—the dagger was imbued with some sort of poison, causing Jacob to lose focus. Kayton seemed fine though, unperturbed by the dagger. Roy looked again at the dagger, as if he would somehow be able to detect what kind of poison it was. "For reasons known, and reasons not necessary to be stated, all the arrows of the archers protecting the keep are imbued with a certain...solution. This is only to protect ourselves." *Solution? What kind of poison is he using?* Lord Horus reached out to Roy, grabbed his arm, and Roy felt as the lord's hand was shaking. Roy felt his own arm shaking a little due to the hand that moved constantly in miniscule movements, back and forth. Lord Horus took shallow breaths, then Caspian came back. Lord Horus lowered his hand, turning his attention back to Caspian.

"My brother is coming."

"Very well," Lord Horus said, walking away from Roy.

"Father," Jackson started. "Roy needs it too." Lord Horus turned to Roy briefly, and he noticed something in the lord's eyes, something like pity.

"Yes, yes. Here, do it yourself," Lord Horus said, handing the dagger to Jackson. Jackson nodded, putting a hand on his father's shoulder. Jackson walked up to Roy, and without hesitation made the cut on his arm and put the dagger away. Roy felt his strength dissipate slightly, and as he turned to Jacob, he realized with frightening shock that the dagger had no poison on it.

He was powerless.

###

Kesara Hewley travelled alongside Gideon, heading towards the keep, where Max—and by extension her brother, Ben—were summoned. Kesara wondered what they wanted—surely summoning them to the keep was imperative, as there was a war to be fought. They were informed that the Lord had been in the courtyard, but had gone to the small dining hall where Lord Horus entertained special guests, adjacent to his chambers. They went through a plethora of soldiers, who guarded their doors and passageways fiercely, scrutinizing every soldier that passed. They looked at Kesara often, perhaps noticing her lack of armor identifying her as a soldier of Faldenheim. When they got there, Lord Horus was seated, looking a little pale. Jackson stood next to him, looking at their direction. The central table was not there, leaving an empty, strange opening before the Lord's chair.

"Brother," Max said, addressing Caspian. The two looked alike, though Caspian had sharper features than that of Max. "You called for me?"

"Lord Horus wished you to be here, so I set out to summon you." Everyone turned to Lord Horus as he rose empirically from his seat.

"How might I serve you, Lord?" Max asked.

"I thought it would be prudent to have the strongest soldiers in Faldenheim around. Your brother, Caspian, is a strong and noble soldier, the best we have, but even he cannot defeat armies on his own. That is why I have called you, knowing you and Benjamin would be both ready and able to protect the keep and the citizens of Faldenheim."

"You honor me, Lord. Despite the fame of both Jacob and Kayton, I would challenge them in solo sword combat in order to fulfill my duties."

"That will be unnecessary. I do, however, request something of you, Caspian. Show me first the swords you have confiscated from these three men." Caspian brought the three swords to Lord Horus. Lord Horus approached the swords, picking up Telekay. "This sword, made of Caster metal, was lost, stolen from a group of men, composed of both Benjamin and Maximillius. Tell me Roy Rhapsados, how is it that you came to possess this sword?"

"I found it," was all Roy said. Aurora had told Kesara that the sword had disappeared, teleported on its own accord to Roy. Clearly, that was not something he could say in front of Caspian and Kayton.

The Lord alternated his gaze, between Ben and Roy. He finally turned to Caspian. "Would you take Kayton elsewhere? It is with Jacob I wish to speak." Caspian nodded his head, and took Kayton out of the room, directing him to an unknown location.

"Something more foolish than sending my guards away in the presence of two Swordsmen is letting two Swordsmen be captured so easily. Obviously this is a stratagem, but despite what Allister might be planning, I am interested more in what Argus is planning. I was informed he called you and Roy, along with other zalphics. He is planning something, and knowing Argus, it is imprudent." Neither of them spoke, and Kesara noticed their appearance, which made them seem dazed and tired. The two of them were sweating now, with slightly inflamed eyes.

"Make it...make it stop," they pleaded. Jacob lifted his hand to his arm, but missed, and his hand fell dejectedly back to his side. Roy started swaying his head, with his eyes closed. Roy kneeled on the ground, still visibly weak.

"Roy, you can make this stop. All you have to do is tell me. What is Argus planning?"

"I don't know!" Roy shouted desperately. He started panting now, losing breath. "They never tell me. Stop it," he pleaded, almost inaudibly.

"The tunnels!" Jacob finally shouted. "That's where they are. Now stop this." Jackson went up to Jacob, with a syringe in his hand. He injected the vial into both Jacob and Roy.

"They're in the tunnels underneath Faldenheim? So you were to be captured on purpose, and use your teleporting powers to bring them inside the keep?" Jacob didn't say anything, but Kesara knew it was true. "Kayton and you, being Swordsmen, would boast that you two had fought off the Faldenheim forces, and you would conquer the keep." Still Jacob and Roy said nothing, recomposing themselves. "The vial won't return your powers, mind you. The engrims have been perfected, targeting only zalphics and giving them grossly unbearable symptoms. The vial simply minimizes your discomfort."

"Those engrims are monstrous," is all Jacob said.

"Yes, they are. Fitting only for monsters." Kesara turned to Lord Horus, alarmed. *Did he mean that zalphics were monsters? Or did he mean that Jacob was one?* "I must protect Faldenheim." Jacob didn't say anything, and Roy stood up. Before their eyes, Telekay materialized in his hand. Jackson immediately drew his sword.

"That sword has strange properties. Caster metal is something we were not able to study well, as the Lancasters owned all the metal. All the Caster metal is in the Lost Forest, far from our available reach. Even if we did sail, the Lancasters would fight us off. It is certain that it is not your own powers manipulating the sword, but the sword itself." Kesara didn't say anything, wondering about Telekay. Her brother had told her that the sword had energy within it, and that sometimes it would feed him energy, giving him more strength.

"I wonder why he has the sword, and why it has changed," Gideon said for the first time. "It was Steven's sword." Kesara wanted to turn to her brother, Gideon, alarmed at what he said. She also wanted to look at Roy, to see his reaction. Neither were possible, as the next thing she knew was darkness.

###

When Aurora heard the bodies collapse, she immediately put her ear against the door, trying to hear. No sounds came from the room, and as the beating of her heart returned to a normal state, she became convinced that no one was in the other room, something that conflicted with what she had been hearing just a few moments ago. She opened the door silently and slowly, looking through the cracks, seeing no shadows nor hearing sound that may have previously been absorbed. She looked around the chamber, trying to find something that might be useful. She grabbed a small mirror she found on a table and approached the slightly ajar door. She crouched, inching the mirror out of the door, near the floor. The mirror reflected an empty room, with various strange shapes on the floor. The shapes were too small for Aurora to see clearly, and her view of the mirror was not optimal. She opened the door, having seen no people around.

If the Lord himself was standing in front of her, with an army of soldiers, she would not have reacted as violently as she did when she saw the bodies on the floor. She let out a loud shriek and turned her head violently, seeing if anyone was still in the room. As her hair covered her eyes, she raced forward, and immediately fell to the ground next to the closest body, that of Lord Horus. She turned him around, so he would face the ceiling, and she checked for the vital signs of life. She felt no beat in his veins, heard no intake of breath, but also saw no signs of a wound. She rose, moving past the lord, and went towards Kesara, turning her around as well and pushing the hair out of her face. This time she found the beat from the vein, slowly pulsating with minimal strength. Aurora let out a breath of relief, turning to the others, checking the others. None of them had wounds, yet they were all on the ground, knocked out. She went up to Roy, turning his body over gingerly. *What's wrong with them?* She looked at Roy's face; he was the only one with visible signs of agitation—his face was pale, his heartbeat was faster than the others, and his expression reflected pain and confusion. Roy also had a cut on his arm and was injected with something.

Aurora stood up, heading towards the door, realizing that beyond this room she still heard nothing. She approached the door and opened it, seeing two soldiers next to the door knocked out on the floor, with another four soldiers on the floor down the hall.

What's wrong with everyone? She was confused, not knowing why all these soldiers were on the floor, powerless to do anything but lay on the floor. *No, that's not the right question,* Aurora realized. Her thought, becoming too powerful, could only be voiced. "What's wrong with *me*?" *Everyone...everyone except me. What's going on?* Aurora walked towards Jackson. He was the strongest one. She started shaking him. "Jackson, Jackson, wake up." He did not react, and her desperation was increasing, but her thoughts began to overcast them. She then moved on to Benjamin and Roy. No one woke up though.

I'm alone. Completely alone. So this is how it feels. I understand him better. Better than ever. Now, now when it doesn't matter.

Aurora stood now, not only bewildered, and lonely, but unknowing and longing...longing for longing itself. To be able to long for something, anything. Something to keep her chained to this world, something that she could live for, something she could fight for.

Steven had fought to seek knowledge. Always with him it was knowledge: understand this, comprehend that. He searched for the truth no one would tell him, and he died. Steven was her best friend. They never developed a romantic relationship, neither of them wanted one. They were friends beyond the realm of romanticism. She could tell him anything, talk about her problems without worrying that Steven would judge her. She had lost a crucial piece of herself, and she didn't think she could ever heal from the wound.

I want to understand, but...I can't. Roy lay on the floor, still unconscious. She wanted to know why she was the only one unaffected by whatever had just happened. She wanted to live for something, to have strength to push on. *I see now the obsession Steven had with it. It must have driven him crazy.* She wanted knowledge. She wanted to understand. That's what she needed.

Perhaps by keeping that search alive, she could keep him alive too. She needed Steven.

23. Faldenheim- 381

Chapter 24
Falling

"Roy."
"Yes?"
"Get up."
"I'm awake."
"Being awake is not getting up."
"Leave me alone."
"You need to get up."
"I don't want to."
"You never want to do *anything*."
"I want to lay down."
"Up is the only way down."
"That doesn't make sense."
"Because you're not up."
"Leave me alone."
"Why?"
"Because I want to lay down."
"Then who will pick you up?"
"Why do I need someone to pick me up?"
"Because you're down."
"I can pick myself up."
"That's what they all say."
"Who's 'they' and why do I care about them?"
"'They' are the people just like you."
"You're more confusing than all of them."
"Now who's 'them'?"
"Just, them. Everyone."
"Everyone is not confusing."
"Yes, they are."

"Then why aren't they the ones who are down?"
"You make no sense."
"They're not sad."
"I don't mean that kind of 'down'."
"Down as in drown then?"
"Yes, drown."
"Down as in fall?"
"Yes, a falling corpse."
"Who said anything about corpses?"
"Who said anything about drowning?"
"Do you know where you are Roy?"
"I'm down."
"Do you know what you're doing?"
"Talking to you."
"But who am I?"
"I don't know. I've never seen you before."
"Yes you have."
"No, I haven't. I'd remember."
"Like you remember Aurora?"
"But Aurora was familiar."
"That's not what you said when you were in the infirmary."
"She seemed familiar."
"Did she now?"
"At the time I didn't know, but now I know she was familiar."
"She's pretty, isn't she?"
"Yeah...she is."
"So why not talk to her?"
"I'm not good at talking."
"You're doing it right now."
"I don't know what to say."
"What is there to say?"
"Exactly. There is nothing to say."
"Why do you suppose there isn't?"
"Because I'm not good at conversing."
"But with anyone else, why would it be different?"
"I'm not good at talking with anyone else either."
"So why is she especially hard to talk with?"
"She...I don't know. She's a girl."

"Half the people are girls."
"She's a *pretty* girl."
"All girls are pretty in their own way."
"But only some in the way that matters."
"Why do the other ways not matter?"
"Because you give a chance to pretty girls."
"But you fall in love with their personality."
"Why approach an ugly girl rather than a pretty girl?"
"Personality."
"They have equal chances of having a nice personality."
"You have it all wrong."
"How am I wrong?"
"You're jaded."
"Why should that matter?"
"Wake up Roy."
"I *am* awake."
"Then get up."
"I don't want to."
"You never want to."
"I don't have to."
"You actually do."
"You can't boss me around."
"You're right; I'm not Argus or Jacob."
"I resent that. I'm my own man."
"Funny definition of a man."
"Who are you to question me?"
"The question is who are you to not question yourself?"
"Who are you?"
"That's the question you should start with."
"Are you not going to answer me?"
"You know the answer. It is my duty to help you get there."
"It seems simpler to tell me."
"How will you learn?"
"I know plenty."
"Then why don't you know who I am?"
"Because you won't tell me."
"It's because you won't learn."
"I need to be taught."

"Why does it have to be men who teach you?"
"I don't follow."
"Look around. What do the fellcondors teach?"
"How to chirp. Loudly"
"Is that all?"
"How to be annoying."
"Annoying?"
"With their constant chirpings."
"Is that so bad?"
"Yes."
"Annoying?"
"Yes. You seem to have learned from them."
"Why do you say I'm annoying?"
"Because you give only clues and hints."
"Is that what frustrates you?"
"You don't say what is on your mind."
"Like women?"
"Yes!"
"You're wrong."
"Then show me what's right."
"It's the opposite of left."
"That's not funny."
"Neither are you."
"Why are you doing this?"
"Because you need help."
"Help from what?"
"Help from yourself."
"What am I doing to myself?"
"It's what you are failing to do for yourself that is worrisome."
"Leave me alone."
"You're falling."
"Falling into what?"
"Into consciousness."
"Again, with your riddles and clues."
"Again, with your complaints and frustrations."
"Be clear."
"Be perceptive."
"Perspicacity is not my strength."

24. Falling- 385

"Stoicism and melancholy seem to be."
"I'm stoic and melancholy now?"
"You express no emotions, emotions that consume you."
"You're wrong about me."
"You're wrong about yourself. Most people are."
"You think you know me better?"
"I think you're more confused than I."
"I'm not confused."
"Then where are you?"
"I'm where I need to be."
"Who dictates where you need to be?"
"I do."
"Where are we then?"
"I don't know. But I've reason for being here."
"The Wise Ones really broke you, didn't they?"
"Shut up!"
"Can't handle the truth?"
"I will not fall for your tricks."
"They're not tricks."
"I hate you."
"I knew that already."
"How do you know?"
"You still haven't figured it out?"
"No."
"What do you see?"
"Fellcondors."
"Is that all?"
"Your silhouette."
"But not my face?"
"No."
"Nothing else?"
"There is nothing else."
"What about the shadowcat."
"Ah, yes. That shadowcat over there."
"Over where?"
"There—where...?"
"To my left?"
"Yes! Right there."

"No, *left* there."
"Not the direction."
"Why shouldn't you be referring to direction?"
"It wasn't important."
"Direction is always important."
"I only meant it was there."
"It left."
"I see that."
"It's actually there, on your sword."
"My sword? My sword...."
"What's wrong?"
"That's not Telekay."
"Not as you know it now, no."
"It's different."
"As were you."
"As was I before what?"
"Before you were broken."
"I'm not broken."
"Are we lying to one another now?"
"I'm not lying."
"You're just laying?"
"Yes."
"You're telling me you're not lying?"
"I'm not lying to you."
"This always happens between people and myself."
"What does that say about you?"
"That they lie to me?"
"Yes."
"Nothing. It says something about *them*."
"I don't understand."
"What does that say about you?"
"Mocking me now?"
"I'm most certainly not necessary to make a mockery of you."
"You're not as bright as you might think."
"Which makes me much darker. Jaded. Like you."
"Not what I meant with 'bright'."
"Exactly what I meant with 'darker'."
"Why are you pestering me?"

24. Falling- 387

"You won't stop."
"Stop what?"
"You won't stop your destructive path."
"I am not down a destructive path."
"You don't build. You destroy."
"I can build."
"All you will do is fall from what you build."
"I can do as I wish."
"You are not capable of it."
"Yes, I am."
"Then get up and prove me wrong."
"I will."
"Yet you're still here."
"I'm getting up."
"No you're not."
"I'm on my feet."
"Like I said, up is the only way down."
"You've been telling me to get up."
"What does it matter what I've been telling you?"
"I'm confused now."
"I thought you said you weren't confused."
"You confused me."
"You confused yourself."
"I'm pretty sure I didn't."
"Do you mean *ugly* sure you didn't?"
"You make no sense."
"I make more sense than you."
"You've been telling me to get up."
"That is true."
"When I get up, you tell me it doesn't matter what you told me."
"That is also true."
"You flippantly change your mind."
"My mind has not changed."
"Then why tell me to get up?"
"It doesn't matter what I *tell* you to do."
"What matters then?"
"What you *will* do."
"I hate you."

"I know."
"How do you know?"
"Because I'm you."

Chapter 25
Construct

Roy Rhapsados began waking, not able to recall what had happened. Before recovering consciousness and before opening his eyes to a bright world, he felt the touch of someone else, grabbing hold of his shoulder, shaking it slightly, while speaking softly and unintelligibly. The voice started getting slightly louder, but still he heard only a mess of sounds, far from the system of communication with which he was familiar. Clarity came to him as he slowly remembered he was with Jacob, in attendance to Lord Horus. The hands went to his forehead, then slightly on his cheek as soft hands turned his face. The voice did not stop, but despite being unable to hear what was being said, he knew to whom the voice belonged. Wanting desperately to see, he opened his eyes, seeing Aurora in front of him, with a worried expression. She smiled back and said more words he could still not decipher. Roy shook his head, lifting his hand to his ear, signaling he could not hear. He closed his eyes, still seeing Aurora in front of him. The noises around him stopped, and he heard haunting a silence.

"Aurora."

"Roy."

"It's good to see you." Aurora smiled at him a little. Roy looked around, looked at everyone else who was on the floor. He turned back to Aurora, in confusion. "What happened?"

"I was sort of hoping you could tell me."

"We were talking with Lord Horus. Then…I don't know."

"I heard you talking. Then I heard bodies collapsing, so I came to investigate and found all of you on the floor. Nearby guards were also knocked out."

"You weren't?"

"No, I am fine. Nothing happened to me. I...."

"You're the only one who seems not to have been affected by it."

"That's exactly right." Roy looked down at his hand. He made lightning appear in his hand, though was unable to hold it there as the energy drained him. He looked into Aurora's eyes, as she looked at him, probably trying to figure out what was wrong with him. Roy was relaxed by her gaze, convinced that despite the problems he may or may not have, that he could build something with her. Roy felt that she was the source of his drive to go forward. She made him want to achieve things he knew he wouldn't want without her.

"No one knows about this? No other guards have noticed?"

"No. Every guard in this part of the keep was knocked out." Roy looked around again at the people on the floor, wondering what had happened. Jacob was still down, something that worried him greatly. He was a Bladesman, he was stronger in his Telekinetic abilities, and yet he was on the floor, no signs of strength, while Aurora and him were standing, left wondering what had happened. Aurora was even more peculiar, not having suffered what everyone around her had. "What were you doing at the keep Roy? How did you get in here?" Roy recalled what Jacob had done, letting himself be captured along with Kayton, so that he could teleport Argus into the keep. Even if Roy wanted to, he wasn't strong enough to teleport Argus without touching him, as Jacob had managed.

"I was supposed to help bring Argus here." He saw as Aurora started judging him—or rather, judged his desire to do it. She was doing what he only knew to do: study people, trying to decipher their feelings through intuition rather than empathy. He wondered if that meant Aurora thought they were too different, that Aurora could not place herself in Roy's circumstances. Sometimes Roy forgot how different he was from others, but at times like these when he was trying to get intimate with people, when trying to express emotions, he failed and realized that perhaps he *was* jaded.

He knew in the depths of his suppressed emotions though, that if there was anyone with which he could build something, it was with Aurora. The fire in her eyes, the fire that he felt when he was with her, that was all he needed to continue forward.

"So why haven't you?" Aurora gazed deeply into his eyes, trying to find Roy's reasons. He stared back at those haunting eyes, asking himself continuously why he was doing it. In a moment of clarity, he realized why he was doing this. He was scared.

"I was a little kid. Lord Horus took me in, promising to help me. Instead, he broke me, tortured me, and now I desire to escape it. That is why I'm doing this." His anger welled up in him, and with strength of which he was unaware, he teleported Argus into the keep. Without feeling fatigue, without feeling drained, he stared into Aurora's eyes with determination. This was something he had to do before he could piece himself together.

"What happened here Roy? Jacob! What is Aurora doing here?"

"I was too strong for them. Get it over with Argus. After this, I am done with you. Done with the Wise Ones. I will live my days out in Farendor, or in Telkos. Anywhere so long as it is away from all of you." He looked at Aurora for reassurance. She, however, was caught up in the wrong part of his statement.

"I will not let you conquer Faldenheim. I will not let you do anything to the keep."

"Just kill her, Roy. If she wants to die alongside this place, it's her decision." Roy did not question whether or not he should kill her. He was determined to build something with her. He was not going to destroy that.

"No." He teleported Aurora behind him, and he blasted the Lord's chair with a telekinetic attack. The chair broke into pieces, its remnants not reflecting the luxury of the once intact chair. Argus set fire to the ground, while Aurora screamed at them to stop. Then Aurora stabbed Roy on his side with a dagger, and immediately he felt the same sensation he had been previously feeling.

"Stop this Argus!" Argus turned to Aurora, amused at what she was pretending to do. Roy was on his knees now, though, fighting to keep consciousness. Argus, confident that Aurora would be unable to do anything, let her approach. She lunged forward, quickly, and desperately, and nicked Argus on his arm. Argus grabbed hold of his arm, still not thinking too much of it. Aurora backed away from him, still defiantly looking at him. "You will not do this. I will not allow you to."

"You're going to stop me with that dagger?"

Aurora passed her hand over the syringes she kept at her sides. She must have known that the dagger was poisoned with something, and that the syringe was the antidote. Roy didn't think she realized which poison it was, and he found himself struggling to keep consciousness.

"Give me the syringe, Aurora," Roy started pleading, as he felt the effects of the engrims. "Please. I need it now."

"I won't let you destroy the keep, Roy."

"You don't understand what it is, Aurora. Please. I need the syringe." He could see in her eyes the unwillingness to give him the syringe, but he also saw that she was worried about his reaction.

"What is it Roy?" Argus inquired. Roy didn't pay Argus any attention as he felt the drugs introduce pain. He fell on the floor, his face against the cold and hard ground. He was still aware of his surroundings to a small extent, as of yet, still conscious. "Roy!" Despite what he knew ought to be a cold surface, he felt great heat, feeling feverish and weak. Droplets of water accumulated on the surface, as his face transferred the sweat onto the floor.

"Roy?" Aurora asked, worried. She ran up to him, turning him around. He saw her face above her, a beautifully haunting sight.

"What is this?" he heard Argus shout. He knew Argus must have started feeling the effects of the engrims.

"The syringe," pleaded Roy quietly. Aurora gathered the sweat on his brow.

"Will you destroy the keep?"

"I have to."

"You will get the syringe when I'm certain Faldenheim is safe."

"Give them to me!" Roy wasn't certain how loud his shout came out, or even if it did, but he could scarcely contain the pain as he let out a grimace of pain.

"I can't give it to you yet. I can't let you destroy my home. It's your home as well, you know."

This is not my home. This was my prison.

"Please."

"You will just destroy the keep."

25. Construct- 393

Desperate for the pain to stop, Roy lied. "I won't destroy it then. Just make it stop."

"Do you promise me?"

"Yes!"

"Promise me."

"Did you poison me?" He vaguely heard Argus shout. The realization seemingly shocked him.

"Upon my dead father's grave, upon the future grave of my mother, I promise not to destroy Faldenheim. Make it *stop!*"

The murmurs around him were drowned by the ringing in his ears, which continued in its solemn, shrilling, single note. The ringing reverberated throughout his body, leaving his arms and legs in an unchanging, motionless position. He would have thought the anger would be unable to manifest, as pain demanded all his attention. Surmounting the pain, he grew angry as Aurora would not give him the syringe, prolonging his pain and clouding his judgment. "Give me the *damn* syringe!" From the ground, Roy teleported onto his feet, pale and full of sweat, short of breath and overloaded by seeing three of the same things, while Telekay appeared menacingly in his hands. Without thinking, he acted, and teleported Aurora away from himself, while teleporting a syringe to his hand. He stuck his hand out at Aurora, levitating Telekay just in front of his hand, and a violent purple blast in the shape of a shadowcat engulfed the room, proceeding from both his hand and Telekay. He saw it, he saw Khisharat emerge from within the blast, sticking out its claw in upheaved anger. The blast was a white hot, purple shadowcat, making its way with the speed of a pouncing cat, lunging powerfully at Aurora. In that moment, Roy did not realize what he had done. He saw the blast slowly going towards her as everything around him seemed to stop. Past the shock, past the fear, Roy saw in Aurora's eyes her undying will. The purple eyes seemed only to reflect the light of the blast, no longer appearing to be her natural color.

He closed his eyes, time came back to reality, and the blast produced debris and crashing sounds, corroborating the violence of the blast as it hit with great ferocity.

###

Amidst shouts and worried faces, turmoil, and disarray, Kesara Hewley awoke whilst a frenetic rush of soldiers raced back and forth, gathering armaments and giving orders, desperately trying to control their fates. Looking around, she saw as other soldiers moaned, incapacitated by wounds. "Kesara," an all too familiar voice said, with worry. "Are you alright?" She looked up at her brother, Ben, as he put his hands on her face, trying to judge if she had a fever or some other condition. She nodded her head, and he visibly relaxed, his anxiety no longer overshadowing his features.

She could not pay attention to her brother as around her, soldiers shouted, turning constantly to the keep and the forces of Ferdinand. She turned to the keep, seeing the smoke rise ominously, blocking out the setting sun, filling the sky with unbreathable air. Around the keep, the men of Faldenheim were gathered, defending at all costs the keep that would determine the fate of the North. The soldiers of Ferdinand encircled them, fighting their way savagely through the streets, advancing towards the keep with desperate speed as news of the approaching Markai forces proliferated all through Faldenheim. The soldiers often spoke about this, constantly expressing their worry as the great force pushed forward. The forces were worried, seeing the smoke from the keep. They took it as an omen, possibly signifying the fall of Faldenheim. And just as the soldiers took it as a bad sign, the camp of Ferdinand thought it to mean their imminent victory. With this knowledge, a false zeal went through the camp, and they pushed forward, charging rather than planning their approach.

Soldiers called upon Ben, in response to this outbreak of fervor. "I'll see you soon," he said, turning his back to her before she could hug her brother. She stopped in her movement, feeling somehow silly. She turned to the wounded soldiers again, finding Gideon on the ground. Next to him were both Caspian and Maximillius, and there was something haunting about seeing the both of them on the ground, something that gave her more pause than seeing Gideon had. The Knight and the Bladesman showed no signs of life other than the slight movement of their chests as they took in life. Around them, other soldiers were is similar circumstances, but none of them had an effect as she stared at the two brothers, both strong warriors, one of them a strong zalphic.

She had assumed that Ben was strong, and had had time to get up and rest while she was unconscious. This assumption had relaxed her nausea at seeing her brother leave so soon after she had just awoken. However, seeing Caspian and Max, both still unconscious, forced Kesara to wonder if Ben was even fit for combat yet. She turned to her brother Gideon and, with the same motions that Ben had done on her, checked to see if her brother had a fever or some other alarming symptoms. Satisfied that no such symptoms existed, she stopped worrying about Gideon and concentrated on what had happened with Lord Horus. She remembered Jacob and Roy being there, but they were not anywhere among the unconscious soldiers. She wasn't surprised that Lord Horus nor Jackson were here—if they were unconscious, they would be treated separately.

Kesara vaguely remembered having a conversation about engrims. She remembered the syringe, saw the almost immediate reaction Jacob and Roy had, the viciousness of the drugs, and the helplessness of Jacob and Roy as they pleaded for the syringe. Jacob had told them what Argus had been planning. Slowly, it all came back to her, but she couldn't quite remember what had happened afterward. *Monstrous drugs for monstrous people,* she remembered with a chill. Lord Horus had been explaining something about Caster metal, but she couldn't quite remember. The vague conversation came to her in only small pieces—talk of Lancasters, and the Lost Forest, something about inherent properties. She couldn't recall, and after that there was certainly nothing—no cry of alarm, no pain, no confusion. Everything was nothing, and she had awaken among the soldiers.

Kesara fought the urge to run after her brother, to ask him for help, or ask him to rest. Instead, Kesara got up and armored herself. She picked up the sword, feeling for the first time in a while control over what might happen. She refused the offer one of the soldiers in charge gave her, of resting. She went towards the walls of the keep, determined to see that they stood firm against the invading force. She grabbed the arrows they provided her, and she joined archers as they sent volleys of arrows out towards the opposing forces.

Arrows flew towards her as well, falling or climbing or diverging from her path for the most, but stopped only by a shield for some. She noticed as an arrow grazed a nearby soldier, but he fell to the ground almost immediately, despite not sustaining any substantial wounds, and cried out in desperate pain. Alarmed, Kesara approached the soldier, examining the wound in closer detail. She could tell that the arrows were poisoned, and the eyes of the soldier grew distant as his cries of pain were silenced. Kesara continued shooting arrows as she moved out of the way of the incoming ones. Arrows flew, sometimes crashing into one another, stopped by shields or bodies, hitting stone and men. She shot an arrow, immediately losing sight of it as it was lost in a sea of arrows, becoming a miniscule drop in the imposing ocean.

She imagined that few of her arrows had hit anyone, if any. If the positions were reversed, Markai would be much better suited to defend the keep. They had the superior marksmanship, outnumbering every other castle combined with the amount of Deadeyes or Archerymen in the Order of the Bow. They, of course, would not have survived long in open combat, but at this point where Kesara could shoot only arrows, she thought of Markai, and their expert skill with bows.

The arrows weren't enough—Ferdinand's forces kept their forward march, slowly surrounding the castle. Kesara looked at the position of the sun, seeing that it was beginning to get late. She wondered how much longer the Markai forces would be. Faldenheim would be unable to maintain the keep for long. Perhaps she simply had doubts about Faldenheim—perhaps they *could* defend it, and they *could* fight off Ferdinand's forces, but Kesara worried about the inevitable fall. The smoke from the keep was still an ominous sight, and Ferdinand's forces were approaching with the conviction that they would conquer.

She moved out of the way as an arrow threatened to pierce her leg. Kesara lost her footing, almost unable to block another arrow approaching her arm, but with a quick movement of her shield, managed to bounce it off the side of the shield, passing it harmlessly past her right arm and onto the ground. The soldiers outside of the keep, those defending Faldenheim in sword-to-sword combat, were visibly tiring. Kesara wanted to be down there, fighting with them with her sword, perhaps secretly using her zalphic powers to slow their advance.

Kesara ran out of the arrows given her, and began picking up nearby arrows and shooting those. Above her, a shadow flew over, blocking the light from the sun. The dark spot that travelled on the ground went forward, consuming everything in its path, leaving it behind unperturbed as it kept its forward motion. It was like a wave, drowning everything underneath it, leaving heads bursting out of the waters behind it which were desperate for breath. She looked up as chirping began, not at all friendly in their tone, and in what sounded more like the howl of a ferocious beast, it advanced. The intonations of shock and marvel were heard as the giant birds flew past the gates, in an open sky, and dove down with frightening speed.

Arrows travelled towards the bird as it maneuvered with grace in the air, with sharp talons piercing enemy soldiers with sickening facility. Some soldiers stuck to its talons, flopping inertly with the movement of the bird and the gentle breeze. The giant fellcondor swooped down again, falling at high speeds towards the soldiers as they tried unsuccessfully to move out of the way. Soldiers were cut in half by the talons, splashing in pools of blood. The fellcondor landed, its talons crushing the stone beneath it, and it again chirped with violence, instilling awe, and fear. It reached out with its beak, snapping heads off of bodies and flapping its wings, knocking soldiers off their feet due to the great winds. Dust arose from the streets, blocking the eyes of some of the soldiers, who blindly brandished their swords, as if they expected to be rid of the bird in this manner. Arrows flew towards it, striking in various places but bouncing off or seemingly having no effect against a slim, dark coat around it.

The fellcondor flew back towards the keep, landing amidst soldiers in awe and duress. Perhaps some of them thought the fellcondor would attack them too, as they scrambled to get away. The bird, however, landed serenely, allowing soldiers to remove some of the arrows. Glistening with reflected light, the fellcondor seemed a manifestation of a bird of legend, shining with holy light and unscathed by their weapons. The light plate of armor did not preclude the bird from taking flight, nor did it seem to be a detriment to its capacity to maneuver. It chirped again, and Kesara almost felt the vibration of its squawk, imagining a shockwave travelling through the ground, to her feet, and up to her head. The bird took off again at some unheard command. The hysteria of Ferdinand's forces spread hastily as they saw not one, but three fellcondors rise into the sky with menacing speed and strength. They descended on the soldiers, with chirpings that compounded, amplifying the boisterous sound and propelling it throughout the camp of soldiers.

The poisonous arrows seemed to have no effect on the birds—perhaps the birds were immune to the poison. Kesara could not help but stare in awe as the birds took to the skies, circling, and then suddenly diving, as if the ground were not solid stone but water, which they could safely go through. Moments before striking the ground, they turned, descending with talons able to pierce even Khisharat. Despite their immense size, they were quick to change their direction; in a blink of the eye, they would turn and crush someone standing nearly behind them with their powerful beaks. Their plated armor provided them with brilliant splendor, blinding some of the soldiers as it reflected the light from the sun. One of the birds came back to the keep, landing relatively near Kesara. She approached the bird, better appreciating the armor that surrounded it.

Confounded with the idea that the armor would be thick and strong enough to protect the bird, and yet light enough to let it maneuver, she examined the color of the metal, which seemed eerily familiar. She had always seen it as an offensive metal—sturdier, able to pierce better and slash through stronger materials. For the first time, she saw it protecting rather than attacking, withstanding pummeling blows and a constant ocean of attacks. The Caster metal glowed with effervescent light; the bird prepared again to take off as Kesara stared at her reflection, which seemed to glow due to the metal, and she found in herself the determination to fight and reach strength similar to her brother's. She approached as a nearby soldier directed the

Faldenheim forces, instructing them that some would exit the keep and go on the offensive.

Kesara followed him, volunteering to be part of the group. The archers around readied their bows, and when part of the gates opened, she could see the soldiers who were attentively searching for any invading forces, wary not to let any soldiers into the keep. Kesara exited among other soldiers, and she joined them in their struggle to contain Ferdinand's forces. The fellcondors were excellent for the morale of the soldiers, but they still had a large force to fight, and she still was unsure how long the Markai forces would take to arrive. She again looked at the setting sun, feeling that it had not moved in the slightest since the last time she looked, overwhelmed by desire that the Markai forces might arrive soon. She had decided, though, that while the Markai forces arrived, she would fight with sword in hand and without fear.

She traversed the streets, still following the flight of the fellcondors as they continuously scrambled the opposing forces and drove talons through weak and unresisting skin and bones. While Ferdinand's forces were distracted by the fellcondors, the Faldenheim forces went forwards, trying to reduce their forces. Kesara drove her sword through an unsuspecting soldier. He tried to retaliate, almost immediately swinging his sword back at her. Presumably, the wound had slowed the soldier's speed, as Kesara parried the blow and backed away, letting the pain register and spread throughout the soldier. He collapsed on the ground, unable to recover from the gaping wound. Kesara took her eyes off him and focused on his countless allies, who were still shifty, constantly looking towards the sky and checking for the fellcondors. A soldier brought his sword down upon Kesara, who rather than try and parry it, moved, and dodged the attack. She tried striking him, but he parried and sent her a few steps back. Regardless of her training with her brother, she was not as strong as some of these men, something about which she could do nothing.

Instead, she had to rely on her speed and wit to prevail—and in a much more inconspicuous manner, her zalphic powers over water. The soldier struck again, but Kesara had no time to move out of the way, and so instead blocked with her shield. She felt his strength as her shield arm felt crushed by the force. She moved out of the way as he began to strike again, and she nicked his side quickly. He didn't seem to feel it, and he struck out against her, this time being hit by the sword on her left arm. The pain hastened to spread, and she consequently dropped her shield. He again made to strike Kesara, but she backed away quickly, though not without losing her footing. On the ground, she looked up as the soldier again raised his sword, ready to strike downwards. She heard the chirp of a bird, but that did little to distract him as the sword began its descent. What she needed was the power of earth, to cause a tremor which could change his footing and the direction of his sword. She, however, had the power of water. Kesara quickly tried to think of some sort of manner in which to utilize her powers.

The ground was wet from the waters of the eastern gate. She thought of using the puddle under the soldier's foot, to cause him to slip. She raised her sword, parrying as best she could the incoming blow. She pushed with all her strength, scarcely managing to prevent her own sword from slashing her. He slashed again from the side, which Kesara lamely blocked. He attacked from the sides another two times, keeping Kesara locked on the ground and not allowing her to get back up. He raised his sword and made to strike her again. A slight tremor shook them, and the soldier stopped his attack to regain his footing. In this moment of distraction, Kesara grabbed her sword and with her remaining force she threw herself forward, and drove the sword through the man, grabbing the soldier's sword from out of his hand and using it to cut his throat.

The soldier fell to the ground on top of Kesara, and the blood flowed onto her hair and face, smothering, and drowning her in an aqueous red. She managed to push him off of her long enough for her to escape the weight, and she got up, seeing a fellcondor flap its wings and hitting the soldiers with a gust. She wiped her face of the blood, though she could still feel the blood all over her face. The fellcondor flew back up, and she turned to her fellow soldiers, finding strength in their determination. Kesara opened and closed her left hand into a fist, as if the pain would heal her hand. She

25. Construct- 401

spun it around, hearing the bones crack. She grabbed her left wrist with her right and applied pressure, closing her hand and grimacing with pain as her fingers pressed down on the skin. She put her hand against her chest, keeping pressure on it with her other hand.

She went back towards the keep, turning in the side streets and passing soldiers who, although concerned with her wound, did not abandon their positions, and kept watch. She was weary, but she felt a sense of freedom from a weight inside her, a cry for justice which she answered, and a relief that dulled her senses. She walked the streets, almost oblivious to her surroundings, seeing arrows still shooting skyward, still seeing arrows land near and sometimes through soldiers. A shadow passed over her, circling around, before it went towards the keep and landed. It did not take her long to return to the walls of the keep, and she realized with a fright that the other soldiers were still advancing; she had not been aware while she fought, but they were undoubtedly closer to the keep.

The keep reverberated with some grand news, but Kesara didn't think about it. She followed very briefly the flight of a fellcondor as it disappeared from her sight into the boundless sky. Down the street, she saw as some of Ferdinand's soldiers approaching the keep. Kesara reached for an invisible arrow, suddenly realizing she didn't have her bow. She looked behind her, about to ask for aid, but there was no one. She turned back, and saw that the soldiers noticed Kesara down the street, and they shot arrows at her while escaping into a nearby street protected by the wall of a building. Knowing that no soldiers were around, she used her powers of water to form a shield in front of her. She felt tired from the attempt, and saw as the soldiers peered their head, seeing if Kesara had been hit. They retreated behind the walls of the building. Kesara looked at where the end of the street would be, which intersected with another street. Kesara could not let them get closer to the keep.

She thought first of a fire blocking their path, but she realized that would not happen. She also thought about the fellcondors descending, which would also not work. The street was too narrow for the fellcondors to swoop in and grab the men. She was about to start running forward, but felt a shortness of breath. Perhaps all her efforts in fighting had finally had a toll on her, as she could scarcely keep her footing. She advanced forward, seeing fellow soldiers in a side street to her left. She was about to yell at them, to ask for help, but the invading soldiers suddenly appeared from the street they were on, running away from where they were headed. They did not even bother to try and shoot Kesara, and without so much as directing their gaze to her direction, they continued running away from the keep. The soldiers went towards Kesara, possibly noticing her distress. They said something, but she was still so tired. She turned to them, but they pointed past her, and started running. Kesara confusedly turned her head, noticing smoke.

Kesara hurried after them, but to *her*, hurrying was much more taxing and very much slower than what the soldiers were doing. Regardless, she went after them, approaching the smoke. Before she got to the smoke, soldiers were running away from it, trying to get buckets of water, or trying to find other materials that could smother the flames. Behind her there was an uproar, but she went towards the flames. *Did they intend to burn the keep down?* That seemed unlikely unless the flame had the same properties as the last fire—so aptly named the Eastern Gate Fire. Perhaps they simply knew that the fire would generate too much attention, and their secretive objective was abandoned at the conspicuous fire. She saw the fire, blocking the intersection with the street from which the invading soldiers had escaped. Soldiers were dispersing, trying to get water. Kesara knew she could put the fire out with her powers, but such indiscretion would be folly. Instead, she approached the small fire, which produced an exorbitant amount of smoke. Some soldiers had already hurried back, pouring water and stones on the fire. The fire quickly died out, leaving scarcely more than a dark blotch.

When the fire had been extinguished, she travelled with the soldiers towards the keep. There was a general excitement amongst the Faldenheim soldiers, and Kesara noticed with a start that the fellcondors were no longer fighting the Ferdinand forces. There were also no soldiers with drawn bows, and no arrows rained down on them. Benjamin saw her, alarmed as to why she had been outside of the keep, fighting.

"Sis. What were you doing out there?"

"I was fighting, just as you were fighting."

"I...I was in the lord's room, with Jackson. We were trying to recall what happened. Kesara...you shouldn't have gone out there."

"What *did* happen?" She looked at her brother, inquiringly, but it was clear he did not know what had happened in that room. In the mutual understanding of siblings, they stayed quiet, Kesara looking around at the crowd around her. "Why is everyone celebrating?"

"The Markai forces are here. Ferdinand could not conquer Faldenheim."

It seemed strange to her, though, that they were celebrating despite the various circumstances of Faldenheim and just how close Ferdinand was to having successfully conquered the North; countless soldiers were lost, homes were flooded, the gates were still breached, and, undoubtedly, nothing had been resolved—to add to this, she was still concerned about Aurora, of whom she knew nothing of late, and what might have befallen her amongst the Vernatia lines.

#

Part III
Zertromium (1)

Telekay's blade was the color of midnight. This color, too, reflected Roy's soul in the particular circumstances in which he found himself. He had regained control of his senses, no longer feeling pain; his hands let go the objects in his grasps, leaving a syringe and Telekay on the floor, next to him. A new cloud of darkness, however, descended upon him as his senses took in what was around him. His breathing was short, and in a coughing fit, Roy turned away from the flames that Argus had previously set. He no longer felt heat, but Roy did not wonder if the flames were still alive. He turned his head again and looked straight at the smoke, in denial of what he did—what he *might* have done. Roy could not penetrate the thick smoke, and he simply stood there, no longer caring that he could not breathe properly.

I...I just killed her. I just killed Aurora. What have I done? I was going to build something. Aurora. "Aurora!" Roy had thought that his soul was no longer capable of genuine tears—that his capacity for such feelings had died alongside his father. Roy sobbed, seeing in his mind Aurora's body, placid and in place where Roy had placed her. She was angry. *Aurora. I'm sorry. Aurora. I...I loved you. But all I can do is destroy. Aurora. You didn't deserve this.* "She didn't deserve this Roy!" He fell to the floor, unable to stand the terrible weight of the guilt, ready to let himself suffocate here, or let someone take him away. *I just killed her, is this the remorse I should feel?* He no longer knew what to believe. He hadn't meant to do it, but his action was irrevocable, and his intentions could not change to outcome. *I didn't mean to. I would never harm you— I never thought I could. Aurora.* A cry of grief escaped his lips, causing him to gasp desperately for air. *What's wrong with me?*

More than just one thing. Everything is wrong with me. Every damn thing is wrong with me. What was going through my mind? Aurora forgive me, though I don't blame you if you don't. I still don't know my connection with you, maybe I'll never know. I'm sorry. He lifted his gaze, seeing how red his hands were. He had been slamming them on the floor without realizing. *I deserve to die for this. Aurora did not deserve this.* He slammed his fists against the floor again. The smoke still did not clear, and the nebulous sight made him stir with grief. His lamentations could never end, it seemed to him, as he continued to sob for Aurora. *You and Brandon were the only friends I've had. To the both of you, I've caused immeasurable pain. Aurora. I hate myself. Does that help?* He continued seeing Aurora; her hair was perfectly curled in her customary fashion, her eyes were still open, displaying her fierce will, her lips in a hauntingly beautiful frown, demonstrating her anger. Her lovely skin was unmarred by any sort of debris or smoke, and it was as clear as he was dark.

He could no longer stand to look in her direction, but the image followed his gaze as he turned around. He spotted Argus, who was much closer to him, and further away from the concentration of smoke. He was moving his lips, but Roy could not hear him. Perhaps Argus had been trying to communicate for some time now, but he did not care. Behind him all he could see was Aurora. Roy felt defeated, no longer with purpose. Aurora made him want to do something better; Roy now felt undetermined to change anything, fatalistically trapped in his servitude to Argus, and having no other recourse. He looked into his eyes, seeing desperation and pain, something that must have been manifesting in his own eyes with much stronger magnitude. *Aurora. I'm sorry. I can't do anything. I was too weak. I was too weak and I killed you. I'm sorry.*

Roy looked down on the floor, seeing a midnight blade and a holy needle. He levitated the syringe, and began moving it towards Argus, but teleported it instead. He injected Argus with the syringe, as his agony withered. Roy wished that there was some sort of syringe that could make his pain wither as well, but he suddenly became aware of the shouting and the pounding on the door. He also recognized that his telekinetic powers were draining his power, though he was not using them to inject Argus anymore.

The smoke was slowly starting to clear, but Argus shouted at him, informing them of their need to leave. Telekay teleported into his scabbard, and he teleported with both Jacob and Argus, back at the tunnels. His remorse seemed as endless as those tunnels. He could see Agnar talking, but Roy did not hear, and he remained silent, contemplating the pain of his decision. He saw himself on top of the keep, building the highest point of a tower, but the building collapsed onto itself, crushing everyone inside but managing to survive. Roy just stood there, letting his poisonous thoughts consume him as they grabbed Jacob and started walking away. Roy saw the shadows transform grotesquely, but when they left him, he looked only at his dark reflection. *I'm the one who should be dark, not my shadow.* He walked forward, moving synchronously with his light.

There was something special about Aurora, I could feel it. Those purple eyes, how beautiful they were. She.... Why did I do it? I could have stopped, I didn't need to. Why did I send that blast?

It was the pain. The pain. It was unbearable. I suppose, it doesn't even matter. She was dead the moment she came into the keep. Argus would have killed her. All I did was ensure she didn't survive to see his cruel punishment, or live in agony until the time of her death.

If it weren't for me, Argus might have done worse things. He could have tortured her. He could have done worse things to her and not care. I saved her from Argus.

When he looked up, Roy found that everyone was gone. He walked a solitary path, walking dejectedly, confusing the fragments of the path through his tears. *Aurora. I will now see your beautiful face only in my nightmares. Dreams will be tarnished, girls will not compare, and you will demand of me everything until the end of my days.* He stared at his hands, questioning his ability to control what they did. His hands seemed monsters of their own, each different in their attributes and their methods, but both just as deadly—permanent companions for his aching soul, there to constantly feed him and let his pain and sorrow and remorse fill again so that it might not run dry. The air around him constricted, his lungs desperate for breath, but he found that they were desperate to shut down, not to continue pumping air into his system. The pain was worse than anything a sword could make, even Telekay, even Khisharat.

The air, oh how desperate it was to escape!

% % %

His attack was not an easy one to pull off, it required great strength, such that he did not possess. He gathered force from an unseen source. It wasn't nearly enough strength, but with it, he was able to pull off a weaker version of the attack.

This, however, required great strength, so when this attack had been pulled off, no strength remained in him. He fell to the ground, pondering what would happen hence-forth, yet concerning himself more with others.

How did he manage to pull this off? He did not know, nor did the others. He used up another source of energy—that he shouldn't have possibly been able to find and use, but he did—and continued to send a message.

He had half a moment to determine who he would contact. His top five were obvious for him: Aurora, Benjamin, Gideon, Jennifer, and Kesara. But for some reason, Roy crawled into his mind, and so he took him into consideration.

He had feelings for Jennifer, but he felt that she didn't need the message, and so he eliminated her from the list. Though it was sad to admit, his relationship wasn't strong with his younger brother, so he eliminated him too. He would need to eliminate one more, he wouldn't be able to pull off a telepathy transmission of that size, try as he will. Aurora, his long-time friend, best friend really; Benjamin, his beloved brother who had always been there for him; Kesara, his sister who he loved more than anyone; and finally, Roy, who for some strange reason just happened to cross his mind—all were a part of his choice.

That choice seemed easy. Three people he cared for, ones who had been there for him his whole life, and some kid from school he had hung out with before, but not to the extent of the recent partnership. Yet, things were complicated for him. He knew not the reason of why his mind thought of Roy in sending his last message, but it did, and it must have done so for a reason.

Then he thought of the bond he had with him, through Telekay. He now knew who he had to contact.

"Roy, live on. Live both our lives. You too Aurora, I love you so much. You must live on as well, as only you can do. Kesara, sis, what can I say? I love you most of all. Tell Benjamin I love him, as well as my parents. I forgive them. ...Live on. ...live...on......."

Steven wondered why he had said he forgave *them*, when he was the one who needed forgiveness. Still, he said it, and had no strength to take it back, nor the strength to revise it.

His surroundings changed into limitless darkness. Yet, he was brightly illuminated, illuminated by a purple and bright white aura. The telepathy connected the minds of the four, and the lines connecting them were now illuminated. As he relayed his message, he could feel his weakness. He saw his light fade.

As his light faded evermore, the lines grew weaker, became more flimsy. He felt his powers dissipating; not his strength, but his *powers*. They were leaving him.

His brain continued to do its trick, slowing down time, yet it was the same.

He felt the lines connecting his brain, they were still flimsy, but now were inhabited by an unseen force.

Steven laughed. In the inside, he had no strength to actually laugh, but in the inside Steven thought and he laughed.

His last intelligent thought: *Hope is like the stars in the night sky. Each light has a glimmer of hope, which helps illuminate your world. The amount of stars—of hope—is innumerable. There are thousands, maybe millions.*

But just like the night, they are engulfed in darkness, and slowly, one by one, these lights must die. The darkness is ever present, a greater force. You just need to find that hope that shines brightest, that is closest to you, and that star will protect you from that darkness.

If I am correct in my assumption, that is exactly what the sun is, a star that shines closest and brightest to us. It can't protect all the time, but always it rises to engulf us in its embrace, saving us from the dark. You three are the ones that form this light of hope.

A line connected the mind of Steven Hewley with the minds of Roy Rhapsados, Aurora Stephensen, and Kesara Hewley. Steven was weak, his power had been consumed.

And then the line was no more....

* * *

Chapter 26
Castle of Stars

    The star-filled sky and the remaining water gave Faldenheim a magnificent color, and the shining moon was in the middle of the sky, full in its splendor.
    Roy had lost track of time, staring so intently at the sky, a myriad of thoughts passing through his mind, one thought for each star. Roy was on the roof, staring at the stars, still pensive and all too aware of the day's events. *They're beautiful. Aurora would love the stars, surely. If she were here, what would she say? Would she remark the apparent shift of the light, or would she speak of the formations visible in the stars?* He sighed, feeling empty and insignificant, haunted by thoughts of Aurora's body and the loneliness *that* produced. He wanted to go home, to his mother and his brother, but Farendor was now only a town to him, run by Wyatt Stephensen, whom would be indignant against him. Isolated from his home, Roy lay on the roof, staring at the light of the moon and wondering what feelings it produced in others—in the shadowcats, the fellcondors, the dogs or the creatures of the night. The stars around the moon twinkled faintly, but despite the countless sources of light, he was intrigued by the darkness that surrounded them, staring at the empty ether, absent of any life.
    What if each of those stars are suns in their own right? What if they each possess worlds of their own, each with lives like ours?
    Roy lay on the roof, observing the stars. He wondered about their secrets, wondered how life may be in other places. Roy tried suppressing his thoughts about Aurora, preferring to think of a life elsewhere. He did not care to think more about Aurora, though she

inevitably crossed his mind. Aurora stood next to him, looking up at the stars, saying nothing. Roy looked at her, finding more beauty in her than he did in the night sky. She would not turn to him, so that her face was looking elsewhere and denying him attention. Afraid to address the issue, Roy stood silent for a long while. The silence was not broken, so finally Roy asked Aurora about the stars. "They're beautiful, aren't they? Do you have a favorite one?" Still, she offered no reply. "Mine is the star over there," he pointed, as if Aurora would be able to follow his gaze towards the star representing the banner on the wall of the castle constellation. Roy did not know what else he could say, and he stayed silent, with the ghostly body of Aurora next to him, staring at the sky. Oblivious to his surroundings, he fell asleep, where, in accordance with his previous thoughts, Aurora haunted his dreams.

    He awoke with a start, but he couldn't remember the dream, only that Aurora had been in them. The cold air gently flowed, stirring with a placid breeze while beneath the building, men rushed to kill Ferdinand's army. With the arrival of the Markai forces, their army was now in retreat, trying to escape being trapped between the Faldenheim and the Markai forces, and being forced onto the banks of the river. Roy just lay there, closing his eyes again. Aurora was no longer appearing next to him, though sometimes she flashed into his vision past his closed eyes. Soldiers fortified the keep and fortified the parts of the castle the Ferdinand forces abandoned. Roy opened his eyes, looking around, and finding nothing but darkness and the light from the stars. He stood up, slowly levitating himself off the ground and returning to a vertical position. Roy went to the edge of the roof, seeing some soldiers on the street. He grabbed Telekay, stretched his right hand out, and dropped the sword. As it fell, it reflected the light from the moon, shining light on a soldier's helm, which refracted the light, flashing momentarily into another soldier's eye. Before Telekay landed on the soldier, Roy teleported the sword back into his hand. His eyes smiled wickedly at his power, but his face remained unchanged, and his arms hung loosely on his side, only just holding Telekay backhandedly with his left hand.

His telekinetic powers were manifesting quickly, and he had control of his abilities. In his humble arrogance, he thought Jacob was still stronger, still possessing powers in both thunder and telekinesis that he had yet to imagine. Despite it all, he knew he couldn't take back what he had done with his powers, so when he gripped Telekay, he felt disdain for the power within the sword. He sheathed it, wanting desperately to feel the warmth of Aurora's hair, or skin, or hands, rather than the cold hilt of the Caster metal sword. He backed away from the edge of the roof, looking to the horizon at the walls of Faldenheim and the general direction of the Capital. He could see the army in retreat. There were a lot more arrows now—he had thought they were plentiful, but the arrows from Markai's soldiers made the previous concentration of arrows seem like a spark, while now they thundered with murderous malice. Lost in the ever-darkening world, Roy absent-mindedly descended onto a platform, from which he proceeded to go down some stairs. He walked amongst the Faldenheim soldiers, heading towards Ferdinand's army, and having nothing on his mind but Aurora.

###

Kesara Hewley was trying to rest, but she was much too anxious to sleep. Most of the Faldenheim forces were resting, taking care of the wounded, and rebuilding Faldenheim by removing the debris. It was the Markai forces that were now on the offensive, shooting arrows and chasing the army. She was with Gideon, who had awoken after whatever had happened in the keep, and Ben. The three were in the room, in silence, trying to sleep. Kesara didn't think any of them had been able to do it, but she wanted to make no noise in the chance that they *were* resting. Kesara looked at the dark room in which they were located—courtesy of Jackson Horus. She wanted instead to be in her home, at Farendor, but then, if she had her way, a lot of things would be different.

"I assume none of us can sleep," said Ben silently. She turned to his direction, though she would not be able to see him.

"Too much stuff," she replied even more softly.

Gideon feigned a snore and an exaggerated exhale, at which both Kesara and Ben chuckled lightly. "I don't know about you two, but nothing puts me more at ease than a war that can potentially destroy my home," Gideon continued.

"I can sleep better than the dead soldiers," they said in unison. Ben got up from his bed, lighting his face with a small flame he procured on his hand. The fire gently flickered, shining light and casting shadows on Ben's face.

"This war soon will be over, but that does not mean we are free from service. I am to join Mr. Stephensen to Bravania—he will be there to limit the Banesworths, while the terms of their defeat are negotiated. I want you two to join me."

"Will Aurora be there as well?"

"I don't know. I haven't heard from her, nor has Mr. Stephensen addressed me about her. She might just stay in Farendor with her mother. In any case, in Bravania I will make a trip to our grandfather's piece of land. I assume the war sort of got in your way of visiting it, Kesara."

"Something like that happened...." Ben turned to Gideon, who now got up.

"I am sleepwalking, don't mind me," Gideon said in a light tone. Kesara smiled at her brother, who went towards the door. He opened it, looked outside, and then closed the door and came back inside. "We still don't know what happened at the keep, with Lord Horus. Did Jacob do something?"

"I don't know yet. I am confident, though, that the engrims would not be so easily overcome. Even Jacob would have trouble manifesting any of his zalphic powers under the effects of the engrims—for him to manifest a blast of that proportion, to render us all unconscious, is unthinkable. The only thing that could have happened is if another Telekinetic zalphic was nearby. Most Telekinetic zalphics were either indisposed, or not inclined to knock us out."

"Perhaps it was Kayton? It seems odd that Kayton was with Jacob and Roy," offered Gideon.

"Kayton didn't have telekinetic abilities, I couldn't feel it."

"You said that Jacob was very strong. Is it at all possible that he could manage to disguise his powers?"

Ben seemed to consider it. "Perhaps...Jackson was able to disguise Pierre's telekinetic presence. But I think that had to do more with the fact that there wasn't much of a mental presence to feel. But I do suppose it is possible. Kayton certainly had the swordsmanship to get through any guards. The only problem would be Caspian."

"But Caspian is not a zalphic," offered Kesara. "If Kayton *does* have powers, he could have used those to overwhelm Caspian. Then he could have snuck up on all of us."

"No," Ben suddenly realized. "The Lord administered engrims to the three of them as soon as they entered the keep. He only gave the antidote to Jacob and Roy, which only eliminated the pain and not the effects of the engrims. If Kayton were a zalphic, he would have suffered the absolute effects of the engrims."

"So Kayton, he had nothing to do with it?"

"He was simply a Bladesman, a distraction for what they would do. Lord Horus suspected that, with Jacob and Kayton being both Bladesmen, they would claim to have fought their way through the keep."

"So we've reached no conclusions is what you're telling us."

"Nothing." The flame on Ben's hand died out, but he seemed to be pensive and oblivious to the withered flame that had produced light in the room. The silence took hold of the siblings, each reluctant to communicate. Kesara was curious about the event in the keep, but she was more interested in going to Bravania, and the terms of the negotiation. To her, the keep was an event in the past that, although curious, was unimportant when compared to the settlement of the war, and the future decisions, and the length of time they would prolong another conflict. Kesara sat in thought, still too anxious to sleep.

"Should we start packing?" asked Gideon. Kesara absent-mindedly got up, prepared to start packing, and not bothering to wait for her brother's response. When she thought about packing for Bravania, she realized that she wasn't home, in Farendor. She was with her brothers, but nothing around her belonged to them. "Should we go home?" Kesara wanted to go home, to see her parents, to gather her belongings, and to feel at home after being so long apart. Immediately, Ben agreed and started heading towards the door. Gideon and Kesara followed, exiting the room, and going down the keep hallways. The soldiers did not bother them, letting them pass freely and giving them no more than a curious glance. When they exited the keep, they saw as the moon glowed, only faintly visible past the walls of Faldenheim as it was already three fourths through its descent. They walked continuously until they arrived at Farendor when the sun was beginning its ascent. They went to their home, not making any noise so that they would not wake their parents. When they opened the doors though, they found their parents there, waiting, frightened—this lasted only for a moment; when their parents saw the three of them enter the house, all well and without visible wounds, they immediately relaxed and smiled, getting up so fast that they seemed to have already been standing.

Their distant figures soon grew into giants as they approached them quickly. Cries of relief escaped their mouths as tears of happiness started flowing. Her mother grabbed and kissed each of the siblings, happy to finally know what had become of her children, and exuberant to see the three were well. "Kesara, I'm glad to see you."

"I'm sorry I haven't been home. Truly, I wanted to visit you as soon as I could."

"What's important is that you're here now, and that you found your way to your brothers."

"I'm sorry to have worried you."

"We all are," Gideon added.

"My son," their father began, "I grew fretful at seeing you be a man, racing off towards the war. I am glad to have you back at home. I should have been there to protect you."

"It is not your fault," started Ben. "Were it up to you, you would have been in the front lines if it meant protecting us, we know that. Your illness is progressing though—certainly, we could not allow you to fight when your strength has been so impaired."

"For my sons, it would not matter if I had but a finger—I would use that finger to grip a weapon and fight."

"Please, you must rest. Have you slept?" Their father gave a slight scoff.

"I could not sleep knowing you three were there."

"You seem ill. Have you taken your medication?"

"Remembering to take my medication was the least of my worries, child." Kesara went to the bottle in which his medication was stored, grabbing water to accompany it. She walked to her father, gently putting it in his hand as he took it. "You three go off to war, and the three of you are concerned that I didn't take my medication. You're a special lot, you three."

"Kesara, is your arm okay?" her mother asked, worried. Kesara noticed that she had unconsciously grabbed hold of her hand, which still stung with pain from before.

"It's nothing, just an ache." Their mother, though, insisted that they sit and rest. Kesara felt at peace with her family there. Still, surrounded by the four living people who loved her most, she thought of the one that no longer lived, of Steven, and how at a moment like this she would be in his arms. The melancholy was furrowed in her heart, though being with her family kept it buried, and unable to surface in all its grievous potential. The family sat there, relating their state of fatigue, and settling their worries. Ben told their parents about their forthcoming trip to Bravania alongside of Wyatt Stephensen, and explicitly declaring that there would be no danger, as the war would no longer continue. Their parents expressed their concerns and asked them to be wary and to be sensible about problems over which they had no control. The siblings calmed their parents' anxiety, promising to follow all their stipulations.

After conversing with their parents, they gathered some of their clothing and headed off for the Stephensen's household. They arrived, where Lily, Aurora's mother, attended them and asked them to step inside while Wyatt finished gathering some of his things. They patiently waited in the room, talking amongst themselves while Lily went upstairs, presumably informing her husband that they had arrived. She did not descend, while Kesara reminisced with Gideon about the first time he had successfully landed a hit on Ben while they sparred; it had been an accident— he had taken a step forward, ready to slash with his sword, but he lost his grip in mid-step. When he paused, Ben had turned to the side and jabbed forward with his sword where Gideon would have been. Instead, he had struck only air, and Gideon recovered his grip and quickly got Ben on the shoulder and part of his chest. Ben admitted with humility that, although that wasn't what Gideon was trying to do, he had reacted quickly and hit him before he could retaliate in any form. The topic of their father arose, to which Kesara then addressed Ben, wanting to learn of their father's condition.

"Tell us truly, Ben, how is father? His condition has obviously been accelerating as of late. Is he alright."

"Kesara. Now is not the time to talk about it."

"Ben. We're his children as well. We ought to know."

Ben was reluctant. "This is not the place to talk about it."

"Why is he getting worse? Is his sickness accelerating?" asked Gideon.

"He's been taking the medication for too long. They are losing their efficiency. The Wise Ones can devise a better medication. There is nothing to worry about."

"You're not telling us something." But at that moment, Wyatt Stephensen descended, and the siblings silenced their discussion. Wyatt was dressed finely, certainly looking the part of envoy and official representative of Faldenheim. He approached them, politely addressing each of them and asking if there was something he could provide for them, such as food or vaccines. They all respectfully declined.

"There is something I must ask of you Kesara."

"How might I serve you?"

"You and Aurora were both headed towards Bravania when we first heard of the war. Since then, I have been unable to learn anything of Aurora—I could not even be certain that they had killed her or taken her captive. I see you are fine, so my wife and I must implore you to share any information you have regarding our daughter."

"Unfortunately, I do not know where she is currently. However, I can tell you that we were both treated well enough. In Vernatia, she and I were together, hiding from the Banesworths and the Kingstons. I was amongst the soldiers, the recruits who joined their army on the second day of battle. When my battalion headed to Faldenheim, we were separated."

"Still I know naught of my daughter."

"While I was training with the soldiers, she was amongst the Wise Ones, healing the wounded and helping dispose of the dead. She was to go to Faldenheim to help take care of the soldiers. She did not see combat. She must still be with the Wise Ones, in the tents.

"That calms my nerves slightly, but you understand that this does not dissuade our worries."

"Aurora is a strong person and extremely bright. I'm certain she can handle herself. Even if she cannot currently escape the Wise Ones and the camps, she will formulate a strategy. Undoubtedly, when she hears that you will be going to Bravania, to act as an envoy, she will follow the Wise Ones back there, so that she might be reunited with you."

"Thank you Kesara," was the only thing Lily could offer as she struggled not to audibly cry in front of the group. There was a knock on the door, which Wyatt promptly went to open, putting his hand on his wife to stop her from doing it. The man at the door told him something Kesara didn't quite hear.

Wyatt turned around, instructing them to help load the carriage. He went towards an accumulation of bags, and picked up a few, exiting the door. The man went inside towards the bag, and the siblings picked up some of the bags on top of the belongings they would take and headed towards the carriage. The man gathered the remaining bags, and Kesara loaded them into the carriage with the help of Wyatt. Immediately, they headed towards Faldenheim, Now that it was bright outside, Kesara could better see the Markai forces that had arrived. They were certainly numerous. They were travelling much too fast to be able to count them—the mounts they were riding were travelling quickly, taking the individuals to Faldenheim and leaving the carriage straggling behind.

When they arrived at Faldenheim, they were joined by another group of soldiers. Among these soldiers were the warrior brothers, Caspian and Maximillius. The finest soldiers Faldenheim had were going to Bravania with Wyatt Stephensen, it seemed. Kesara was curious as to what they would do about Vernatia, and who might be there. Certainly Jackson could go, but if he did, Caspian should be defending *him,* and not Wyatt. The group did not stop to talk and instead continued forward, towards some unknown destination for Kesara.

Her mount followed Wyatt's mount, so Kesara rode it, taking in the destruction and the damage she had previously been unable to see. The encampment had destroyed much of the foliage, leaving a barren land in sight, stomped, and molded by an array of men in full armor. They pressed forward, approaching an encampment surrounded by guards. They grew attentive at their approach, but upon seeing Wyatt amongst the ones approaching, they readily dispersed, allowing him to go through. She tried to follow, but they let only Wyatt through, and stopped them, instructing them to wait while he talked with Lord Horus. Ben went with Max immediately, discussing something at length. Kesara waited while they spoke, thinking about her family while they surely discussed other families, namely the Banesworths, Kingstons, and the Alexanders. A rider came from the east, with white banners and nothing but a parchment on his hand. The guards set out to stop him, forcing him off his mount and walking him towards the tent with swords focused on him. The rider was young, as young as she was, but he showed no fear and walked unconcerned with the soldiers around him. Kesara realized with a start that she knew who that was.

At that moment, the lord exited the tent, having heard news of the rider. Jackson, Wyatt, and two other people Kesara didn't know walked out as well. "Ferdinand, I cannot say I am surprised at the circumstances in which our paths cross once again."

"Lord Horus, admittedly this is not how I envisioned it."

"You walk unarmed into enemy lines. Why?"

"I want to speak with you. Clearly, I do not care to play the role of assailant nor will I gain anything by attempting to intimidate."

"Of what would we speak?"

"There is no need for this fighting to continue while there are better, more viable options."

"What would those options be?"

"For one, you stop your advance. Yours and the Markai forces, they go back to Faldenheim, and we go back to ours."

"Your forces are in retreat. Why should we stop and allow you to organize yourselves?"

"You will gain nothing from attacking. We want you to stop advancing, go back to Faldenheim, and no more men have to die."

"It is *your* men that will do the dying. We have a stronger force."

"We had already sent letters to the Capital, demanding the Wise Ones to reconvene and settle a peace between the North and my brother's kingdom."

"You had sent letters in anticipation? It seems you were a bit too arrogant in thinking you could conquer Faldenheim so easily."

"On the contrary, I knew it would be difficult. If we had successfully conquered it, we would have lost many men, and would be in no condition to fight. If we lost, well we certainly would not have been in the condition to fight against the full of my brother's forces."

"So you admit that you would not be able to fend off King Whaldo, yet you still want a peace treaty in which, if I am not mistaken, you would demand to be left alone with the territories you had conquered thus far."

"Something like that. As I said, the message had already been sent. The reply should arrive at any moment now."

"You think King Whaldo will want to negotiate with you?"

"I made no mention of my brother. I said the Wise Ones should reconvene. That means, among yourself, Lord Kingston, and the Wisest One, you would conceive a treaty."

"Why not just run you down with our forces?"

"Because as soon as I heard that the Markai forces were marching towards Faldenheim, I sent messages to my uncle to amass soldiers in Whaldo's Port and stay behind the Markai forces. They will be here shortly. They might not be enough men to turn the tide of the war, or maybe there are exactly the amount of fresh soldiers we need. In either case, it will mean much more meaningless deaths, something which neither one of us wants, surely."

"We have forces from the Capital."

"And we have forces from the Korscher Mountains. The Bender's have accepted my terms to reinstate them in Andros. They have been settling in Chordica while we were freeing the North of my brother's control. But I don't need to kill off so many of my people when my reign has just begun."

"You consider it a "reign" now, do you? It seems to me more like a starry-eyed boy who thinks he can play at king."

"Surely even *you*, Lord Horus, cannot think my brother has done and will continue doing a grand job administering the kingdom."

"I have faith in my friend in the Capital."

"So do I, but the Wise Ones will not have the power to continue running the kingdom as it has attempted to do. My brother grows restless with the power he is denied, and soon he will discard any attempts to make sensible decisions. He will outgrow the chains you have tried using, and when he no longer heeds your friend, he will cause the ruination of this great kingdom."

"The only thing he will ruin is all your hopes of being king."

"So you would have us kill each other nonsensically?"

"No. You will have your convening of the Wise Ones. I will travel to the Capital, alongside Allister, and we will discuss. While we make that trip, you will abandon all of Faldenheim's lands, you will go to Vernatia, and Wyatt Stephensen will go to Bravania, where he will administer the region alongside Neister. The lord and the prince both go to the Capital, leaving you in charge of Vernatia. As for Chordica, the Korschers are not to leave the Desert Lands of Chordola until after we have decided what will be done. So that we are ensured you will do nothing to cross us, we shall take a hostage: your wife, Fayrah."

"I shall amuse you and accept all your conditions. Contrary to what you seem to believe, I only want the best for all of Andros. I hope you find your voyage to the Capital enjoyable. You must take care of my dear wife. If Fayrah should be harmed, no amount of Caster metal and forces from the Capital will help you. I will send word right away to Whaldo's Port to allow you to use the port to sail down. If you do not trust me still, and would prefer to walk, I will not take it as an insult," Ferdinand said with a smile as the lord audibly scoffed. With those words, Ferdinand turned around and began towards his mount. He got on his mount with expert ease and galloped away, taking the white banner with him. The lord said a few private words to Wyatt before turning around and heading towards Faldenheim. The soldiers around them followed their lord, protecting him as was their duty. Kesara remained in place, sticking to her brother and to Wyatt Stephensen as they watched the soldiers and the lord leave.

"Ben, go to Haernaveh. Let the people know they should not retaliate against Ferdinand Alexander. Let them know we will reach peace. I will follow you, but I need to stop by various cities and towns on the way, to let them know what is happening." Ben nodded, and signaled Kesara to follow him. He told Gideon to follow him as well, and the three of them rode their mounts, quickly passing through the outskirts of Faldenheim. They raced forward, heading towards Haernaveh.

Roy Rhapsados was with Argus, awaiting the return of their King anxiously, wondering if they would have to continue the war. In the distance, he saw Ferdinand coming back, with the white flag. *That's a good sign.* Ferdinand went to the camp, joining his wife Fayrah before addressing them. "Lord Horus has agreed to go to the Capital. Lord Allister and his son, Prince Argus, will go to the Capital as well, where the Wise Ones will convene and determine a treaty. Until that time, we will go back to our lands. I will take control of Vernatia while the Kingstons go to the Capital, and the Banesworths will go back to Bravania."

"Is that all?" asked Lord Kingston. He seemed to know something, or at least knew Lord Horus well enough that he knew there was more.

"Wyatt Stephensen, of Farendor, will go to Bravania, to regulate our actions."

"*Regulate?* He has no right—I'm the Lord." The name, however, had instilled fear in Roy. While Lord Banesworth argued with Ferdinand, Roy thought of Aurora. *He expected her to die of zalphia—maybe the shock was not too painful.* He felt suddenly a chill in his being, as if the blood water coursing through him were freezing, or boiling. The feeling was all the same to him. He looked at Argus, who was paying careful attention to Ferdinand and did not give him as much as a glance. He was glad to know that he would not be going to Bravania, and that he would not have to face Mr. Stephensen. Roy knew that perhaps he should speak with him—it was his right to know what had happened to his daughter—his right to know who had caused her pain. Roy would want to know if anything happened to his brother or his mother, and he would be restless until he found out who had hurt them. He was also reluctant to speak with him and being confronted with the decisions for which he cursed himself constantly.

In the distant horizon, three riders approached rapidly. They held no white flag, and rather seemed to be three soldiers racing forward. Kayton, Jacob, Zachary, and Melinda all drew their swords and stood in front of the king. The other soldiers grew wary as well, and they all had their sight set on the riders. They continued, not slowing down at the sight of the soldiers. The king addressed them, expressing his doubt that they were coming to cause the king trouble. They diverged their straight trajectory, and started leaning towards the right, away from the group. Ferdinand instructed the soldiers to let them pass. As they got closer, galloping with speed, Roy recognized familiar faces, and as they passed in a blur, his eyes briefly came into contact with those of Kesara Hewley.

Chapter 27
Safe Harbor

The waters receded in gentle, almost still waves. The water seemed unbroken in its vast blue sheet, extending far into a horizon that was inviting. The soft sound of the birds resounded through the harbor, silencing the cries of dogs and stomping feet. The placid breeze moved no more than a strand of hair as it flowed, gently cascading through the top layers of the earth. No frenetic rush accompanied the soldiers—instead, citizens lay their errands to rest. A dog circled wildly around the beach, lost in a fervor for something unknown, while other dogs lazily lie on the ground, following the dog with their eyes. The dog inevitably slowed, walking in small circles slowly before laying down. The sand under its paw contracted, almost melting around the dog. Its tail gently rested on the sand—the tail did not disturb the sand, and instead the tail seemed to lightly hover over it, moving nothing about from the sand particles. The boats were docked, visually bristling with life but audibly resembling a crypt. No shouts could be heard, nor did men argue about prices and shipments. They went about their business, harboring no ill feelings and finding no necessity to argue. The men walked forward, approaching the harbor in which ships were aplenty, seemingly outnumbering the birds keeping a watchful eye from the sky. The birds were observing the land, guarding them almost silently, with only occasional cries breaking their silence.

Then, a guardian broke the placid pool of water, diving violently, creating a splash in the form of a rising circle of spears. Quickly enough, the bird arose with a fish splashing desperately in its beak, with an even more impressive catch of two similar fish clasped in its talons. The spears broke apart, with a shield of water being left behind as the guardian ascended. The effect manifested as if it had been a direhawk, raining down from above and snapping its prey in half. The once still waves rippled with violent disturbance, while the cries of the bird augmented, crashing with one another, and intensifying the squalor. This resulted in an outcry from the merchants on their ships, whose voices came to the fore and sounded with unmistakable bartering. They argued prices and communicated the jolly of living while the guardians watching over them dove and communicated their hunger. The restlessness of a port city reestablished at that infinitesimal moment in time when the bird emerged from the water, with the lives of its prey resting in its talons—a god over death. The direhawks floated in the sky, the fellcondors descended, but what arose were the ashes of a fortress yet to be destroyed, a fortress stronger than Garrisbrough, and more resilient than Caster metal armor.

    The port, founded by the first Whaldo, seemed indicative of the first settlement in Andros outside of the Lancaster Lands—the Lost Forest was said to contain two great cities, while the Lancaster Forest that still remained attached to Andros had one: Timbergrove. While these cities in these forested lands were hidden, not traversed by the Androsii, Whaldo's Port was a prime harbor for the North, and the biggest port city in all the land. The countless ships corroborated this fact, as well as the presence of two men: Yaric Bihr and Xyliander Dicray. The former owned a shipping company which held possession of a majority of the boats used in trading. The latter was captain to the *Xycray*, a ship renowned for its absolute speed. The two gave standing to both Irvine Jeram, and Whaldo's Port, of which Jeram was in charge. Ferdinand's uncle, if the stories were to be believed, was standing to lose whether or not his nephew was named king of the North. Becoming a separate kingdom would mean that Bloodpool and Aquareus would now belong to another kingdom, and trade would be in the very least, more complex. If Ferdinand was defeated, he was not likely to receive a pardon, and would have to abandon his post in Whaldo's Port, assuming a pair of assassin's did not liberate him from his worries.

Strangely enough, Whaldo's Port did not seem to be worried about the war, nor was it preoccupied with how it might continue. Ships were being prepared to voyage to other ports, and plenty of shipments were still in transit, evidenced by the collection of civilians at the port anxiously awaiting their loved ones' return. It almost seemed as though no one had informed them about the war, but the anchored warships and surveillance ships demonstrated that it was not so. Regardless, the chatter of mates and civilians was heard throughout the port. In the horizon, one of the ships became clear, and civilians looked at the ship, as if expecting the ship to magnify instantaneously before their eyes and reveal the passengers and the cargo it held.

While the civilians who lacked power, who lacked control of their lives, and who lacked wealth or fame looked at the incoming boat, the men of importance, of power, and of influence were focused on another boat which lay resting on the waves that rippled constantly and suddenly with unexpected activity—upon which already lay much of the cargo to be taken to the Capital—upon where men were working tediously in their necessity to receive pay, but who weren't immune to the grasps of curiosity as it physically tore at them, turning their head to the other boat so that they weren't paying attention to the boat just under their feet; against the preconceived expectations of its condition, the boat conceptualized niggardliness (the imaginative lushness of the boat, which was intended to carry the lord's possessions, ruined the appearance of the fair boat, and the high standards expected of the boat made it seem rather underwhelming and seemingly inconsequential in comparison to the non-existent luxury boat) albeit in a sense where simultaneously it was as a beggar in the King's palace yet it was a proud, old lady with exhausted funds who carried her head high whilst the rich ladies reacted in their particular forms: they murmured, questioning what sort of blasphemy she was committing with her poor appearance, they laughed, denigrating her person with their indifference, and they pointed, indicting her with charges of regicide—for with her behavior, she would have been seen with more favorable eyes if she had killed the king rather than perform this sacrilege, disdainfully staining his name with her indecency—but through all this she undoubtedly managed to garner respect with her determination and fortitude, and it was this eccentric characteristic, which she exuded alongside that of the scrounging vagrant, that manifested itself in the ignored fair boat wherein a transcription of some sort was written, a name for the boat, that had been rendered illegible by the constant bashing of the waters and had failed as of yet to be restored, perhaps speaking volumes of the quality of the boat or the profit in its utilization...whatever the case may be, the boat certainly did not meet with the unsubstantiated expectance with which it was scrutinized.

On top of the aforementioned boat was the aforementioned cargo and the aforementioned workers who carried the last of the cargo onto the boat, so that it might head off to the Capital. The boat was to be accompanied by two other boats, because of course the Lord's possessions were much more precious than the cargo of any other men, and certainly more than the lives of some commoner sailor. As the group of men arrived at the specified boat, they examined it, discerning any and every flaw in the make of the boat. They were greatly disappointed at the current condition of the boat, expecting still only the best boat for the possessions of Lord Horus, but they swallowed their reprimands and ensured that, if not aesthetically pleasing, it was seaworthy and capable. It was.

The fair boat had no name as a result of its travels, but on the portside of the boat, the marking of *BIHR Shipping* and its insignia of *Better, Intelligent, Hasty, Reliable,* with a castle floating on still waves, flying a white banner, were easily observable. The boat had no spectacular colors—it had been painted blue, as all other standard ships belonging to Bihr Shipping. The ship had no broken oars nor were any of its sails tattered in any form. All the time, Yaric Bihr defended the quaint ship, guaranteeing that it was more than capable of transporting the Lord's possessions, and that it would arrive at the Capital with no complications resulting from the vessels themselves. He made no promises about possible storms or pirates, but he maintained that his vessels could appropriately manage any sort of obstacles. The boat was quickly filled with all its cargo, and immediately set out, accompanied by two other warships. Other ships became visible, approaching the harbor, while other ships still were making preparations to leave, and to head to another port. Of the company of twenty men, six went on each of the warships, while one of them went on the boat with all the possessions—his job, of course, to make sure none of the Lord's possessions went missing. The other seven would stay with Roy and Jacob, who rather than go by ship to the Capital, would travel by land to Markai, from where they would meet with Lord Kingston and his company, and continue the voyage to the Capital. They came with Lord Horus as a sign of good faith—Jacob was the valuable hostage though, being a Bladesman. Roy and Jacob would wait for Lord Kingston's possessions, which would also travel by ship. They would head to Markai after the possessions left harbor.

Kesara Hewley was in Haernaveh, speaking with a man who was telling her an interesting tale about herself. The man spoke to Kesara about her previous stay at Haernaveh, how she had aroused suspicion being alone "travelling" and having the outfit of a warrior. The man expressed in earnest that he had thought her a zalphic, and that she was running away from her home because they had discovered her abilities.

Kesara laughed at that, almost scoffing at the man, and asking if the man was serious about these suspicions. "Truly, I did. Understand, it was not out of malice but out of curiosity that I mention it. Originally I hadn't thought you a zalphic, but another traveler mentioned something to those lines."

"Another visitor?"

"Yes, shortly after meeting you another young lady was inquiring about the town in general, asking about zalphics as well. Perhaps she wanted to see our reaction. Her words made me paranoid."

"Well, sometimes you have to believe the fantastical to keep yourself cemented in reality."

"Precisely. Can you imagine though? You, a zalphic. How preposterous," the man laughed once again. "Seeing you with your group and hearing the message you brought from

Faldenheim absolutely dissolved any lingering doubts I had. I must truly apologize for thinking such vile things."

"Oh, you do not need to apologize. Everyone must entertain thoughts out of the realm of possibility. Sometimes those are the things that will become true."

"You have a kind soul. Is that characteristic of people from Farendor?"

"You remember that?" asked Kesara.

"I certainly do. You said you were going east to find your brother and I said that most visitors travelled west, to Faldenheim. You replied that you were coming from there. I believe your exact words were: 'That's actually where I'm coming from—well, from Farendor, a nearby village.'"

"Wow, and I thought you were too busy to notice."

"We're always busy, but that doesn't mean we shouldn't remember."

"Well I've kept you much too long from your work."

"It was my pleasure to speak with you. Again, I'm terribly sorry for what I might have thought."

"You caused no harm to anyone. It's perfectly fine." With those words, Kesara excused herself and went to find her brother Gideon, who she found near some debris. He was helping the people clean it up, moving it away from where it was disturbing passage. Vernatia soldiers stood around, keeping a watchful eye on those from Haernaveh, looking at the debris and looking past it at the citizens working hard to reinstate their livelihoods. They remained undeterred by the circumstances, having most likely already killed for the war. They were spread throughout the city—one wasn't far from sight wherever Kesara turned. Haernaveh was, after all, still part of Ferdinand's conquered lands until he got to Haernaveh and took his troops away and back to Vernatia.

In the interim, the soldiers still walked the streets, keeping the conquered land in their constraint and ensuring the shattered peace of the land. The civilians did not have a dejected pace, and rather than seeming defeated and conquered, they seemed restless, ready to take up arms at any point. It was probably this attitude that kept the guards so focused, and so constant in their vigilance. Gideon moved the debris, clearing it, while the Vernatia soldiers looked at him, as if offended that Gideon were removing the work they had accomplished. Kesara approached Gideon as one of the soldiers approached the group, guardedly watching them. The citizens glanced at his direction, trying to ignore his presence. The soldier looked at them still.

"Those are nice boots you all have there." The citizens turned to the soldier, completely paying attention to the soldier. Some looked down at their boots, others just continued staring. "We soldiers have it hard, you know. Lay down our lives for others, work, and fight, with little luxury. I think my fellow soldiers and I would enjoy having boots such as those." Still, no one said anything, nor did they make any movements. Kesara stopped walking towards them, and Gideon slowly reached his hand towards the sword on his hip. "Seems unfair that we soldiers have to live so miserably. Don't you think that's true?" the soldier asked no one in particular.

Other soldiers gathered around the first soldier. "Is there trouble?" they asked.

"I was commenting on the injustice of our service, and the lack of appreciation we receive. They do not even bother to supply us with boots."

"It truly is," they agreed. "It seems to me that one would be wise to show appreciation to the soldier's circumstances. A soldier needs some good working boots."

"Yes, but we have no money to pay with, or show any form of appreciation," the first soldier replied sarcastically.

"Steel can buy many things in the right hand."

"That is precisely what I was thinking." The soldiers, done pontificating, now turned on the group of people, including Gideon, who were cleaning the debris. Some reached their hands to their boots, ready to offer them rather than the alternative. Some still didn't reach for anything, standing firmly against them. Gideon had his hand on the hilt of his sword, ready to strike. Others also had their hands on their swords. One of the men was slowly drawing his sword, and in response the soldier who had begun accosting them drew his, demanding that the man sheathe his sword. The man stopped drawing his sword, raising his hand to the air defensively, but then he violently threw something with his left hand. The soldier cried out in pain, grabbing the dagger that had been thrown and stabbed into his side. All the soldiers drew their swords, but only the one man drew his. The soldier who had been struck by the dagger lifted his hand in protest to his fellow soldiers, telling them that he would handle the miscreant himself. The soldier approached the man, sword in his right hand and dagger in his left. The man grabbed his sword with both hands and lunged quickly towards the soldier, who side stepped and parried the blow as the man tried changing directions with his strike. The soldier stood still as the man turned and charged once again. This time, the soldier did not move, and instead parried the blow. The soldier used the dagger to cut one of the man's arm, but he was still pushed back by the strength of the strike.

The soldier brought his arm to his side, while the other man wiped the blood from his hand on his shirt. The man now held his sword with his right hand, keeping his left hand close to his side. The man attacked the soldier once again, who side stepped and slashed with his sword. The man parried the soldier's strike, then brought his hand towards the soldier and cut him. When the soldier distanced himself from the man, he saw a dagger in the man's hand. The soldier looked at his hand, examining the wound, and looked back at the man, threateningly. The man dropped the dagger to the ground and attacked the soldier again. The soldier held his ground and struck back, parrying his attacks, and striking. He was, however, unable to land a strike. The soldier went to strike the man on his side, but the man quickly stepped to a side and plunged his sword into the soldier just under his heart. The soldiers around him were alarmed as the soldier fell to the ground, putting pressure on the wound and grimacing in pain. "To be fair, I *did* have properly good boots," the man mocked.

Enraged, the soldier jumped to his feet, lunging quickly towards the man, and shot lightning from his hands. The thunder shocked the man, paralyzing him where he stood, while the soldier stabbed his sword through him. The man fell to the ground, and the soldier looked down on him, if only for a moment. The other soldiers had already encircled him, and he looked around violently before falling to the ground due to exhaustion. In that moment, he realized what he had done—that his ill temperament had caused him his life. He quickly grabbed his sword and brought it to his throat. Before the soldier could do anything, another soldier knocked the sword out of his hand, maiming off his arm. The sword bounced off the soldier harmlessly and fell to the ground as the soldier began his cries of pain. Kesara continued looking, unable to avert her gaze to what she knew would happen next: one of three things. Perhaps, if it had been solely Haernaveh, rather than people of Vernatia, the soldier would not have met such gruesome a reply. The soldiers, without a moment's hesitation, lifted him off the ground and removed his armor and cut off his shirt. On his body, the soldiers drew a mountain with red blood. *The crumbling mountain.* One of the soldiers grabbed the dagger, ready to make it crumble. He approached the soldier, while the other soldiers grabbed his arms, stopping him from flailing. The soldier cried in pain, wanting to escape the pain already. The one with the dagger carved various patches of skin off, all inside the boundary of the drawn mountain. Various patches were cut, representing chunks of the mountain falling off, to the ground. The soldier's innards could be seen behind rivers of red. "On the day of the Great Shaking, the mountains crumbled." The soldier dug the dagger into the outline of the mountain, cutting and carving into the mountain. The cries of pain stopped, but that did nothing to the horrid sight. Finally, the skin outlining the mountain was removed.

Chapter 28
Tears

Kesara Hewley heard only a few words: "Make your enemies cry, and drown them with their tears."

With those words, Maximillius had left. Kesara was not certain which enemies Ben was referring to when he said that. She looked at her brother, whom she didn't want to leave. Ben was going to stay in Vernatia with Gideon for a while. Lord Horus had decided to send some of his possessions—some of his notes and some of his riches, among other things—to Whaldo's Port, where they would transport their things to the Capital to have it ready for him when he arrived. Lord Kingston prepared his voyage, as did Roy. Kesara had learned from Ben that Jacob and Roy would become temporary hostages, and would travel to Whaldo's Port and ensure the safety of the Lord's possessions. The two of them were on their way to Faldenheim.

Kesara was going to Bravania with Maximillius and the party joining Mr. Stephensen. Caspian was never far-off from his person, being the strongest and the commander of the regiment of soldiers. Ben had wanted Kesara to join him, but Caspian had insisted Kesara go to Bravania for some reason or other. Having walked amongst complete strangers in her march towards Faldenheim, Kesara thought that she would feel at ease travelling in an occasion that would not require her to raise arms, and in which she was surrounded by others she knew. Instead, she felt out of place—she felt lost among the people she knew and yearned instead for the solace of strangers. She wanted to be surrounded by strangers, so that she could feel alone in peace.

Travelling along Maximillius, she found herself unable to speak with him. She had never had problems communicating with him before, but now, she struggled to think of any topic that might be suitable. Around their group, those who lived past Vernatia, and on towards Bravania, travelled alongside them. They were returning home, though Kesara figured they knew too well that their service was still not over, and those swords would need to continue being sharpened with whet stones. The armor would have to last, the shields would have to remain intact, and their strength would need to withstand any sort of withering. She knew that the tears would not stop—that continually, more soldiers would die and more families would shed tears in their lamentations. She still wasn't done shedding hers, and though the time had decreased their consistency, she still found herself thinking of her brother Steven and resulting unable to hold back the tears. She felt she was being drowned in those tears those days, but she had learned to live—as he had told her to do. Every tear she shed was another tear he wouldn't want her to waste, and she knew the only way to remember him was to gather the strength to continue living. He would hate it if he were a form of trepidation for her, so she learned to be strong because of him, and to fight until she joined him in death.

Until that time—which she hoped was long away—she would fight and live on, and keep in mind that Steven would never part from her heart. She might not have his warmth to feel in embrace, but she had his strength, and his courage, his wit and his determination—all this things helped her drive forward. Sporadically, emotions of desolation, loneliness and anger consumed her, and the tears would not stop their ceaseless march. These times, though, helped Kesara keep perspective, and the pain helped her remember the wound, and what she needed to do in accordance. It reminded her she needed to be strong. As his memory caressed her soul, she grew the will to continue.

"Why is it that all of you do that?"

Kesara turned towards Maximillius, startled. "Do what?"

"You, Ben, Steven. The three of you are always so pensive. Gideon is the only normal one from the lot of you."

"We're pensive?"

"Only a little," teased Maximillius.

"I would have thought Ben would not shut up with you around. That's how it seems when all of us are together."

"That's because all of us are together. It's much easier to enjoy silence with an intimate friend than for there to be silence in a group."

"Well, I suppose overthinking runs in the family."

"Ben will have conversations, but then he just trails off, getting somewhat oblivious. You just tend to stay quiet and become oblivious. Steven would just talk nonsense and be oblivious. Gideon is normal. He'll become pensive when he's alone, when you're supposed to be pensive."

"I'm sorry for the pain my family has caused in our pensiveness," replied Kesara amiably.

"You don't have to do it—think I mean. You don't need to analyze everything and find meaning to every emotion and event."

"I find it helps."

"Helps with the sadness?"

"Yeah."

"It doesn't. It makes you miserable. Some people like being miserable though, and that is their choice."

"Misery is not something I experience by choice."

"I'm not saying you do. You feel misery in the right circumstances. Others are not as strong as you."

"Who is miserable?"

"Aurora, for one. She analyzes everything, and she cannot find a rational explanation, so it drives her crazy. Roy. He wants to know everything, which causes him to raise a shield to protect himself. Jackson. He is driven crazy still by his mother's death, and the illnesses consume him."

"And you? You are one of the people who don't look for explanations for everything?"

"The only explanations I need are for those that concern me directly."

"Aren't all our concerns ones that directly affect us?"

"Are yours? I see you looking around at the soldiers. Are theirs the same as your concerns?" asked Max.

"I can empathize with them. That is not a flaw."

Maximillius shrugged. "To some it could be. I'm not saying you're flawed." Kesara began thinking about that, seeing if she truly overthought things. Clearly, Maximillius had already had this discussion with Ben, and he knew her pretty well. Perhaps it was something they all got from Ben. Regardless, there was always a pensive nature to their family—along with things that didn't necessarily have to be expressed in words. She knew that Ben and Maximillius were good friends, and that they had learned swordsmanship together—but the bond between them, Kesara suspected, was due to being zalphics.

Whether it was truly a flaw to be a zalphic or not, the powers were both a detriment and a blessing. Even past that awe and excitement of powers, the common disdain of the people united them, and kept them strong together. Ben and Max perhaps would not have been friends had it not been for their common powers. Ben had met Maximillius after they were both already part of the Guardians of Peace. Doubtless, Ben knew most zalphics in all the Faldenheim territory, and this was something that kept them strong, and together. Only those who chose to isolate themselves, not wanting to draw attention, were truly lonely, but that was a personal decision, not something forced on them. It made them stronger and more resourceful, and more cautious.

Even past the awe and excitement of powers, it was also a curse. The fear of their powers, that they could cause harm with something that perhaps should not be controlled, was frightening. Whenever Kesara used her powers, she always kept in mind that these actions she used them for were not to be irresponsible. It was fearful that she should have so much power over a certain force, and that she could utilize that force to cause ill to other beings. Coupled with that was the harm she was causing herself in using the powers, feeling it drain her energy and poison her body. It was known that zalphics, living out their lives peacefully and away from war, died younger than non-Zalphics. The constancy with which they used their powers made them die even quicker, as the Wise Ones had also collected data from those who had lived during times of war and died from no perceivable fatal illness.

Everyone hated them—that was also something of strife. Even though Kesara knew she was like the other Androsii, sometimes the continual verbal affronts to zalphics made her question herself. She spent some nights crying over them, hating herself and wanting to be the same, to be like all those other "normal" people. She grew angry at their impertinence. She pitied their fallaciousness. Still, she never killed any of them, and she never unleashed her powers to instill fear—nor did she ever refrain from thinking these thoughts of instilling fear and death. She never diverged markedly from the standards of all the others, and she never did anything that any typical Androsii would not do. The only aberrant behavior she manifested was that of empathy.

The journey to Bravania seemed long. It was exhaustive. The march forward was relatively slow. Despite this, the battle weary warriors were passing along dejectedly. The tedious pace of the march imprinted in their mind. *Right.* The monotonous pace of the march imprinted in their being. *Left.* Cities grew from faint, almost imperceptible spots in the background to cities. *Right.* Cities shrank from grand, encompassing cities in the foreground to spots. *Left.* The sound on the roads was stomping feet. *Right.* The sound in the cities didn't matter. *Left.* Their feet wandered. *Right.* Their minds wondered. *Left.* The mounted soldiers wanted to walk, to stretch out their feet and escape the discomfort of the saddle. *Right.* The soldiers walking on foot wished to climb on a mount and ride easily through the roads and escape the pain on the soles of their feet, so that they may rest. *Left.*

Kesara momentarily wished that Telekinetic zalphics could simply teleport all of them instantaneously to the Bravania gates. This ephemeral thought and wish vanished when she recalled the absolute terror of teleporting and feeling every part of the body fall into nothingness and then stop without warning. Even recalling the feeling was enough to stifle the thought. Countless times she had thought that the memory of teleporting exaggerated in her mind, and countless times she had been proven wrong. She was still not used to teleporting, and it was not something she wanted to get used to. Her brothers had teleported her a few times, and those times sufficed for a lifetime. She wondered if all the recruits were forced to accustom themselves to teleporting. None of her powers over water paralleled the feeling of teleporting; she wondered if there was perhaps one with which she was simply unfamiliar. *Right.*

She wanted to know more about her fellow zalphics, and their array of powers. She wanted to know why she had water, and others fire or wood. Apart from whatever determined which power they received, she wanted to know how the strength of the power was determined, how *many* powers, and why Invincibility was so rare, so much rarer than Telekinesis was rare when compared to Fire. Most of all, why her family was cursed to have zalphics. She didn't want Gideon to have to suffer through the pains of being a zalphic. She didn't want her already sick father to worry any further about his children, who were *all* zalphics. *Left.*

Bravania was not as close to Vernatia as Vernatia was to Faldenheim, but the distance was not too long, even if the trip there felt as much. Kesara yearned to be in Bravania, so she could go to the Lancaster Forest and visit in peace, without the distraction of having to prevent a war. Lord Horus and Lord Kingston were headed towards the Capital, where they would discuss a treaty. Kesara would reach Bravania before the lords even arrived at Markai, though, and she did not favor the idea of being in Bravania with Prince Tadeus for so long while the lords travelled to the Capital. Their belongings hadn't even reached Whaldo's Port yet, she knew. It seemed that waiting while the others negotiated peace was ineffective. There was little she could do though, having no power over the land and having been added as an afterthought to the protective regiment for Wyatt Stephensen. Certainly, a temporary truce would arrive. How long that would last, though, was entirely up to Ferdinand, who did not seem the type that would wait too long before presenting another affront. *Right.*

The hooves seemed to take a personality on their own, as they clanked cantankerously against the ground. The mounts stepped onward, carrying the weight of armored men, and hauling carriages full of supplies and belongings. The mounts slowly advanced, step after step, careful not to anger their riders. They turned right at the smallest sign, and they travelled at speeds according to the riders' wishes. The mounts registered the change in height from Vernatia to the Bravania lands. They also noticed the slightly warmer air, and they adjusted and travelled just slightly slower as a result. Through their hooves, they registered that the road was somewhat less travelled than the road on which they were previously. All this, they noticed as the mounts continued forward with weight on their backs and reins connecting to their mouths. The saddles they wore were an accustomed discomfort, which weighed them down additionally to the other weights. *Left.*

Kesara looked at the Order of the Wise Ones, and marveled at their obvious power. They had countless mounts hauling supplies for them, and carrying their elite members. They were all rich, accustomed to "necessities" that were luxuries to most people. *All of them probably learned to ride mounts while the rest of us were working to help our parents.* She didn't know how to ride them, and she had been relying on the mount to do what was needed. Her mount had followed the lead of the mounts in front of them, whose riders *did* know how to ride mounts. The Wise Ones were compromised of the wealthy and their children. Steven had been admitted only through Jackson and Ben—without either of them, Steven would have never been able to join, even if he was smarter and better suited than the lot of them. *They aren't all bad,* she had to remind herself, remembering Aurora. *Right.*

King Ferdinand had insisted that Bravania open its gates to the Wise Ones. As a great castle, he argued, they ought to demand excellence, not only physically, but mentally as well. At the request of Ferdinand Alexander, some members of the Wise Ones at Vernatia travelled to Bravania to help establish the order. They were travelling luxuriously, though Kesara supposed that she was travelling under those exact circumstances, and she was considerably miserable. Her goal, though, for the trip was considerably different than those of the Wise Ones. She turned, seeing Caspian and Max talking about something, but up until that point she hadn't been paying attention. *Left.*

"I was afraid that if we stayed there any longer the people would revolt. They're a proud people, and more resilient than any others I know." Kesara vaguely recognized that they were talking about

Haernaveh. It was true; when the zalphic soldier had been killed, the people began shouting that the soldiers were probably all zalphics, and that their oppression was a manifestation of their ill being. In the case of the zalphic soldier, he had grown cruel because those around him were cruel to who he was. They suppressed zalphics, and they harmed them and ridiculed them, called them monsters, and tortured them. No living zalphic had experienced the physical aspect of the torture, but the mental abuse was strong, and even the strongest of them could be disconcerted by it. The soldier had unleashed his frustrations on others, treating them as inferiors to calm his insecurities. *Right.*

"I hate to imagine where we would be now if no one had stopped the men from attacking the soldiers." After the thunder had shot out of the zalphic soldier's hand, the people of Haernaveh and the soldiers of Vernatia had gathered around. After the soldier had been killed through the crumbling mountain, the soldiers had stopped accosting the citizens. They, however, had still felt offended and threatened. The men had drawn swords and brandished them at the soldiers. The soldiers, in turn, did not react to the aggression and rather tried to calm the anxieties of the people. They had backed away and even kept their swords sheathed. Though the soldiers reacted commendably, their actions had had little effect on the group. Serenity was not characteristic of a gathering. The men had gathered around the soldiers, as the soldiers tried to back away. Gideon and Kesara went to the side, where they had watched as the fragile temporary peace between Vernatia and Faldenheim was about to end. Voices of reason had tried to calm the people with soothing words, promising peace, and respite. The group, though, had had no desire to listen, and they had demanded satisfaction from the soldiers. *Left.*

"If it hadn't been for Wyatt...." The brothers turned towards Wyatt Stephensen, who rather than pay attention to the conversation, seemed lost in thought and anxious about his duties. Wyatt had been the one who was able to calm the group, expressing his deepest desire to protect his daughter, and his desire to protect everyone else he loved. He made them see that this explosion of anger could cause the lives of countless brothers and sons and fathers. He made them see the repercussions of their future actions, and he promised them that Vernatia and Bravania would receive their comeuppance—and that it was precisely for this reason that he was travelling to Bravania. Hearing his appeal, and seeing his genuine concern for his daughter, the men of Haernaveh managed to calm themselves enough to see reason. They halted their advance and, though with chagrin, sheathed their swords. Wyatt had precluded Haernaveh from revolting prematurely and threatening the peace that they would make. *Right.*

It was a game of patience—they had to wait, and make sure they did not make any brash decisions. They had to wait for the Committee of the Wise Ones to take place, and for them to determine a sort of peace between Ferdinand and his brother. Kesara realized with a start that she had confided too much in the Wise Ones. She had assumed that they would be able to forge, in the minimum, a temporary alliance. She thought, suddenly, what would happen if they could not satisfy King Whaldo and they could not successfully forge a peace. King Whaldo would look weak if he did not take action against his brother. If King Whaldo waited, Ferdinand could gather more allies and further his goals. She reminded herself that the three smartest people in all the land would converse, and keeping this in mind helped her assuage her doubts. She was nervous about what would happen if she was caught at an unfavorable time in Bravania. This had already happened to her once, and she only managed to escape the Banesworths because of Ferdinand's sympathy. *Left.*

There was still so much fear in the future, so much tears yet to be shed, so much pain that still had to be inflicted and received—Kesara was prepared. She wanted no longer to shed tears of pain, and she was done with the tears of memory. She wanted only tears of happiness and relief. She rode atop the saddle of her mount, and nothing could stop her full gallop. She was done with her tears. *Halt.*

###

Chapter 29
Power

On the outskirts of Markai, Jacob and Roy reunited with Lord Kingston and his party. They heard that Lord Horus had yet to make it to Markai—which indicated that they would get to the Capital before them. The party that came from Markai to bring Lord Kingston into the castle was made up of countless soldiers, with bows that, although were not aimed at them, were in each soldiers hands, ready to take action with an arrow held by soldiers' fingers on the taut sting. Roy followed Jacob, who was now wearing his blue cloak, and easily traversed the men who split apart at the sight of the Bladesman to let him pass. The people waited anxiously as Jacob and Roy approached Lord Kingston and Prince Argus. Neither the lord nor the prince had any weapons, but the guards surrounding them were cautious to look for any threats to their lord and prince. Jacob, being the strongest soldier in the party, would now be entrusted to head the group of soldiers protecting Lord Kingston and Prince Argus. Roy wasn't sure what his role would be, but he didn't doubt that Jacob and Argus had already planned something.

"Lord Kingston, Prince Argus. Welcome to Markai."

"Not the best welcome I've received," started Argus.

Lord Kingston turned to his son, and with an invisible signal, quieted him. "Lady Leisiter, I am honored to once again be in the pleasure of your company. I thank you wholeheartedly for the hospitality that you are giving us."

"Always so wise, aren't you Lord Kingston?"

"I would hope that is characteristic of any member of the Wise Ones, and especially so of, not only an Elder, but a member of the Committee."

"Yes, I would hope so as well. Members of the Committee should demonstrate adequate sense, as I do."

"I've told you before; I have no power to add or exclude anyone from the Committee. That decision is based solely on the wishes of the Wisest One."

"I'm sure if you truly wanted, you could get someone in."

"I am but one of the three members of the Committee. I, myself, can do nothing for you alone. Rest assured, if the Wisest One were to decide on adding an additional member, you would be a primordial candidate." Lady Leisiter didn't seem to believe Lord Kingston, but nonetheless she expressed her thanks and invited them to enter Markai. Next to her, The Disgraced, Mayrah Leisiter turned contemptuously away, and walked without addressing the Kingstons. The greater part of the bowmen put their arrows away and the bows on their backs, but a small group still maintained their bows in their hands.

"Go talk to the girls," Jacob told him. Roy looked around, startled by the sudden request. He turned to Jacob, and followed his gaze to a group of men with bows in their hands.

"Talk to what girls?"

"The three girls. Talk to them."

"Where?"

Jacob shifted his gaze elsewhere, and Roy followed it to a group of girls with bows and arrows. None of them particularly stood out, but Roy knew there must have been a reason for the request. Again he paid attention to the girls, and could think of only one reason for the request. He used his telekinetic abilities, and identified two zalphics—one with thunder, and one with wood. He felt more inclined to talk with the Thunder zalphic, as she and he shared a common power. The other one produced a strange sensation in Roy. He knew he could have never known her, but he felt as if he had known her, and that she had been someone special. He could have only seen her around in Faldenheim, if she had been visiting, but Roy had no idea what to think of her. A certain familiarity lingered. *Who is the third one?* He looked around at the group, wondering who Jacob could possibly have meant. The two were the only zalphics.

They walked into Markai, where people were clearly awaiting Lord Kingston and the men that accompanied him. Roy tried inching closer to the zalphic girls, but the Markai soldiers were careful to keep their distance, and so he could not get very close to them without drawing too much attention to himself. He walked along, seeing the two pay him no attention at all. "Elisa," Jacob called out. Roy looked at his direction, and saw as one of the Markai soldiers stopped, and turned to him. She was breaking formation, so she continued walking as Jacob walked towards her. He then addressed the captain of the soldiers. "Could Elisa accompany me to the keep?" The captain at first said no, but upon seeing his blue cloak and his disinterest in his reply—Jacob had in fact signaled Elisa to follow him and had already begun to walk back towards the Kingstons—the captain agreed to comply with his request. Roy saw as the Thunder zalphic stared after him, mesmerized for some strange reason at the scene. The other zalphic paid them no mind.

Was that the third person of which Jacob spoke? Roy wondered. Elisa followed him with chagrin. Roy approached the same captain, to converse with him. "I'm sorry about his attitude. He tends to be terse, and obviously a man who takes action rather than speak." The captain readily agreed with Roy. "The lord wondered if he could take advantage of your hospitality and ask if two other of your soldiers could join us. You, of course, will be recompensed for the inconvenience." When he mentioned recompense, the captain changed his face from one of disdain to one of pleasure.

"Did you have two specific ones in mind?"

"Those two over there," Roy pointed to the two zalphics.

"Miss Whittiker, Miss Flores. Go with Miss Kelvinly to the keep." By the reaction to the names, the Thunder zalphic was Miss Whittiker, and the other was Miss Flores. They were both of similar age—some twenty four or twenty five years. Whittiker was better trained than Flores, and consequently was slightly more imposing in her physique. The latter had some Telk traits—brown hair, but still the blue eyes of the typical Androsii. Whittiker was an Androsii with dirty blond hair and pinkish eyes. Flores was a little darker skinned than Whittiker.

"What are your names?" Roy asked them as they approached him.

"You asked for us specifically. I would think you knew already. Who are you, and what do you want with us?" asked the Whittiker girl.

"*I simply asked for the two zalphics,*" Roy transmitted telepathically. Both Whittiker and Flores stopped walking, in shock. They turned around, wondering if any ill would befall them. The others continued walking forward, taking no note of them. Roy was amused as the two looked at each other, discovering for the first that they were each zalphics. Their shock didn't seem too great, so Roy figured they must have suspected each of them was a zalphic. Asking such a question was very compromising however, so neither of them had decided to ask the question.

"I ask again, what are your names? I obviously will do you no harm."

"I am Tori Whittiker," said the Thunder zalphic.

"Jackie Flores," said the Wood zalphic.

"Have I seen you before, Jackie? Where are you from?"

"I'm from Markai. I can't say we've met. I've never been around your area. Why?"

"You seem familiar. Sorry," Roy said, shaking his head. There was still something about this girl that caught Roy's attention. He had an odd sense that he knew her, though he couldn't imagine from where, and certainly she didn't know him either. Roy now understood that he would have to train and recruit them—this would give him the time to decipher why he felt this strange sensation, assuming he succeeded. He didn't want to alienate Tori Whittiker, so he quickly asked about her. "What of you, Tori? Have you lived in Markai all your life?"

"Yes, I've spent my life here. I've been a member of the Order of the Bow since I can remember."

"What rank are you?"

"Marksman."

"Really? That's quite impressive. What of you, Jackie? Are you a member as well?"

She nodded her head. "I am an Archer."

"Well, you don't have to accept anything yet, but as you might have noticed, I have ties with the leaders of Vernatia." *"I can protect you—no one will know your secret—and I can help you control and develop your powers. I have thunder as well."* "If you momentarily agree to come with us to the keep, I can show you something. You will not be obligated to accept anything, and you may leave as you wish."

Jackie seemed disinterested in the proposal, but nonetheless she did not leave, and instead continued walking with them. Tori seemed much more open to the idea. "I thought Vernatia hated...them."

"Lord Kingston and Prince Argus protect them." *"My name is Roy Rhapsados, Working under Jacob Victoriano, I am trying to teach fellow zalphics how to use their powers, and to escape being their victims."*

"Jacob?" Tori asked with interest. "You mean, he's a...he knows you?"

"Yeah. He is a zalphic too. He is good friends with Argus, and that is one of the reasons they protect us."

"That is quite interesting," interjected Jackie.

"You know our secret, just as we know yours. We will not expose you, nor shall we harm you." They both nodded. Roy knew from personal experience that they would trust no one but a zalphic—which meant exposing himself as well, and for good measure, Jacob. Lady Leisiter took the party of men to where they would rest. Lord Kingston and Prince Argus would be received at the keep, along with some of the members of the Wise Ones. This included Jacob, but not Roy, who would stay with the rest of the adjoining party. Although he would not be staying at the keep, Roy would go to the keep with Lord Kingston and Prince Argus, and along with Tori and Jackie, would train the two zalphics. Lord Kingston and Prince Argus abandoned the party at their place of stay and continued walking towards the keep. Roy followed them, bringing Tori and Jackie with him. Jacob was conversing all the time with the girl, Elisa. Tori looked at their direction constantly, perhaps wondering how a zalphic could get so close to the prince—Roy didn't exactly know. Elisa seemed to be holding back

a certain bitterness, while Jacob undoubtedly expressed concern, and undoubtedly did not care. Roy walked with them towards the keep, where Lady Leisiter left them to rest from their voyage.

Tori kept looking at Jacob's direction. *Does she know him?* Roy thought. Something troubled her, Roy knew that much—he was an expert when troubled people were concerned—but now was not the time to bring that up. Instead, Roy mentioned nothing, and didn't make any movements to imply he noticed something strange. He looked ahead, identifying with Tori, and taking note of both hers, and Jackie's movements.

"*Go in that room,*" Jacob told him, signaling towards a door not too far away from the chambers. Roy did as he was told and entered the room—which he discovered to be the armory. Swords and bows aplenty lined the walls and racks, but the weapons were dull with misuse for the most part. Roy thought that it really should be Jacob who was training at least Tori, who could learn a lot about thunder from him. Despite this, both Jackie and Tori were left to Roy, while Jacob kept talking and seemingly arguing with Elisa. Jacob delegated the responsibility of teaching the recruits to him—though Roy suspected he simply didn't want to do it. Jacob would probably have him teach Telekinetic zalphics as well, but that thought was pointless as no such recruits were among the order.

Roy called Tori forward to spar with him. She was older than him, and Roy could see that Tori had clearly gone through harsh times, and knew how to handle herself, even if relatively it was an easier life than his. The girl approached the weapons laid out in front of her. Whereas some of the weapons were dull, some of the others were well tended, and especially the bows were masterfully kept. She grabbed some of the blunted arrows, but she did not reach for any of the fine bows that were there. She instead reached for the bow she was carrying—a bow with an inscription of a thunderbolt. The bow was not as big as the others he was used to. She was a short girl, and the bow seemed tailored to her. There were a couple of other inscriptions on the bow—underneath the thunderbolt were the letters T.W. (which Roy took to stand for Tori Whittiker) and on the bottom a sword piercing a shield, which Roy couldn't comprehend.

Roy was intrigued by her choice of weapon. "Normally, we don't carry weapons dealing with range. A bow and arrow or a spear may be good for normal warriors, but we of course are far from normal. Our powers allow us to use long range attacks, while dealing short range attacks with swords and daggers." Roy had understood that swords were all but imperative; if an enemy got in close range, a bow and arrow would have little use, and he would be unable to use his thunder powers to the fullest.

"Our powers work to enhance our attacks," Tori said with a smile. Roy knew that she felt comfortable with a bow and arrow—she was, after all, a Marksman, but her desire to use only her bow would be problematic. Regardless, Roy assented and grabbed a blunted sword from the armory. The weight of it felt strange as he was so used to the lightness of Caster metal. He briefly considered a shield. He confided in his swordsmanship skills to parry normal blows, and his shield was a necessary part of protecting himself from the blows. Bow and arrows were different from swords though, and he would need the extra protection against them. Tori, however, had nothing to protect her from his sword, so Roy decided to use only a sword. They went into an adjacent room, which was completely empty.

Tori quickly drew an arrow, and in an unbroken, fluid motion, she shot an arrow at him. Roy blocked the arrow with his sword, making it bounce off without too much force. To his surprise, he felt a surge of electricity, which, for the briefest moment, paralyzed him in his spot. *Tori's using her powers to shock the arrows,* he realized with a start. This was a creative tactic—he certainly hadn't seen it before. Roy could think of doing little more before he found himself moving out of the way of another incoming arrow. This time, rather than block the arrow, he knew to move out of the way. Tori kept her distance, using her powers to shock the arrows and firing them with great precision and speed. She was incredibly fast, though Roy still thought she could better utilize her powers. She shot another arrow at Roy, but Roy struck the arrow with his sword and used his zalphic powers to redirect the electricity from the arrow into an electric stream of his own. He launched the attack towards her. She side-stepped and shot another arrow to Roy's side. At that instant, Roy changed the direction of the stream, and hit her on her side as the arrow travelled dangerously fast towards him. If Roy had been any less experienced, he would have moved into the way of the incoming arrow. Instead, Roy remained in place. He was certainly intrigued by Tori's skill.

Naturally, Roy would be more adept in hand-to-hand combat, so by maintaining her distance, she crippled that advantage. Attacking from afar also kept her in her preferred method of fighting—ranged weaponry, with the bows and arrows with which she was so familiar. Roy knew she had a place amongst the more advanced pupils. She would certainly give Agnar trouble. If she learned from Roy and from Jacob, she could become even stronger, and adept at her abilities. Roy knew he would have to try harder to beat her.

In quick succession, she loosed three arrows. Roy side-stepped one of them and turned his sword in order to block the other two. Before the arrows hit the sword, he let go of his sword, thereby preventing himself from being shocked, and then used the thunder to attack a fourth arrow that Roy hadn't seen her draw nor fire. The arrow fell to the ground. She shot another arrow, but Roy shot a lightning bolt at the tip of the arrow, making it spin rapidly and fall to the ground, where it continued spinning some more. Roy used his telekinesis to lift it up, and made it spin faster. Tori shot another arrow. Roy moved the spinning arrow towards where the incoming arrow was coming. The incoming arrow hit the spinning arrow as it was spinning, causing it to spin faster, while the incoming arrow cruised past Roy without hitting him. Roy shot thunder at the spinning arrow and launched it forward with great speed, something that had caught her off guard. Roy stopped the arrow just before it hit the girl. Roy congratulated her excellent performance and let the arrow fall powerlessly on the ground.

Roy went to the armory again so that Jackie could choose her weapons. Without apparently having met her, Roy know that she would choose a light sword and a light bow. Jackie went up to the sword rack, and grabbed a sword which she swung a couple of times to get a feel for it. She put it back and grabbed another one, that was a little smaller, and again she swung it, this time going faster. She grabbed the sword and a scabbard and wore it on her hip. She stopped by the bows, where she spent no time deliberating. She seemed accustomed to bows, and knew exactly what she needed. After choosing her weapons, and grabbing some arrows, she went to the adjacent room. Roy followed her there, with the same sword he had had before.

Jackie quickly shot an arrow at Roy, though without the same grace as Tori. She was not as skilled with the bow, but she was still skilled with it. Roy side stepped the arrows, and tried not coming in contact with them. Roy realized though that this was not Tori with her thunder powers. Jackie would be unable to do anything, even if the arrows hit his sword. He blocked the next arrow with his sword, and started moving closer to her. She did not back away, but instead grabbed a few arrows and put them all on the string of her bow. The arrows shot at him, scattering wildly. Roy side stepped and blocked an arrow with his sword, but another arrow managed to just graze him.

A poison entered his system, slowing down his speed and blurring his vision. Another arrow came towards him, but he didn't know whether to go right or left to escape it. The arrow came rushing towards him, but Roy used his telekinetic abilities to stop it, and drop it to the floor. Jackie grew bigger in size before him, and before he realized what he was doing, Telekay appeared in his hand, blocking the attack from Jackie. She seemed disconcerted slightly by the sudden appearance of the sword, but she continued with her attack.

Right, left, right-right, center, right-right, right, left, wood. She struck towards his left, which Roy blocked with the sword from the armory. She then attacked towards his right, almost unbalancing him. She again changed the direction of the strike and attacked to his left. Roy blocked, but she quickly made another attack to the same side. Roy blocked the attack again, and she once again switched directions. She feigned to attack to his right, but halfway through she quickly stabbed towards his center. He blocked the attack with Telekay. In rapid motions, she made two more attacks to his left, which Roy only just managed to parry. She made a movement to his right, but once again struck him on his left. Roy had not been fast enough to stop the strike on the shoulder. Jackie made the same movement, but this time she went towards Roy's right. This one, Roy managed to block. She sheathed her sword, and Roy teleported behind her. He turned around to see Jackie start to turn her head towards him, but before she could do that the wood she had summoned slammed into her and knocked her to the ground.

###

Chapter 30
Direhawk

Kesara Hewley was bored, much like she was on her last visit. Bravania was a big castle, the biggest one of the North, yet she found there was nothing to do but wait. Her days at the keep extended as she trained and thought. The anxiety of doing nothing, while Andros was on the brink of war, was frustrating. There was no word from the Capital, so Kesara was forced to wait, taking turns to protect Wyatt. In her long wait, very little was of interest. There was only the one event that was remotely remarkable: the visit of some of the Bastions.

It seemed strange that at a time like this, the Bastions would visit Bravania. Obviously, this trip had been planned and undertaken with much anticipation. Lord Fredrick Bastion travelled North, with his son, Prince Elsamar. They had gone to Bloodpool, where they had gone by ship to Kervin Port. When Whaldo's Port opened its port, they travelled to Alk Harbor to restock, then headed to the Port. From there, they had gone due east, towards Bravania. Lord Bastion was accompanied by members of the Order of the Sword, and two Elders from the Wise Ones. No Bladesman accompanied the lord, as the two remaining Bladesmen—Uracli Cristem and Roger Weiracle—were left in Garrisbrough to protect the remaining Bastions. The party was made up almost completely of red cloaks—Knights—including his son, Prince Elsamar. Lord Bastion had his blue cloak, as was customary of most Bladesmen. There was one black cloak, a Warrior, who accompanied Prince Elsamar, as a friend and companion. Lord Bastion and Prince Elsamar's friend, along with the two Elders, were the only four who did not sport a red cloak.

The party had made their way to Bravania. This, at first, alarmed some of the citizens of Bravania. They had not known that the Bastions were coming, and at the sight of them, the citizens quickly rose in outcry that King Whaldo had ordered an attack on them, and that the Garrisbrough Army had been summoned to fight. They had abandoned hope, shattered by the thought of fighting the Bastions so soon and unexpectedly. The Bastions did not even enter Bravania. They waited outside the gates, asking to speak with Lord Banesworth. The Lord and his son quickly went to meet them. The Prince did not come back with the Lord. Lord Banesworth did not address the issue that his son had not returned to Bravania. He simply mentioned that the Bastions were going a little north, and on the outskirts of the Lancaster Forest. That was the only thing he offered about his talk with Lord Bastion.

Speculations arose amongst the Bravania people—anywhere from the Bastions had abandoned King Whaldo and sided with King Ferdinand, to the Bastions *did* come to attack Bravania with its army, but were waiting to strike at a better time. These wild rumors spread, withstanding critiques that demonstrated their great folly with outstanding robustness. Whether someone mentioned that no party outside of the one that came to Bravania was present, or whether they mentioned that the Bastion's females were still in Garrisbrough, the rumors kept the attention of the castle. As they waited, and no significant events occurred, the people slowly started losing interest, though some were still worried about the mysterious visit. They attributed the lack of fighting to the fact that Tadeus was no longer in Bravania—some of them maintained that Lord Banesworth had given the Bastions his son and heir as a hostage to placate them, and to hold off the fighting.

Eventually, Tadeus *did* come back to Bravania, with the Bastion party. Again, Lord Banesworth went to the gates of Bravania and conversed with Lord Bastion. No one knew of what they spoke, but Lord Bastion left all the same, leaving Tadeus back in Bravania with, if the rumors were true, a Caster metal sword and gravely gaping wounds. Tadeus was immediately rushed to the keep. There, the Wise Ones who had come along with them from Vernatia attended the prince's wounds. She had seen Tadeus inside the keep, walking stiffly as if he had been in battle. He did have wounds on him, but she saw him carrying no Caster metal sword.

Not much was known, which of course meant that everyone knew what had occurred. Their differing views meant little—only Tadeus could know exactly what had happened. Kesara certainly wouldn't ask Tadeus what had happened. She felt strange being in the same room with him. She was still afraid of Prince Tadeus. Incidentally, on an occasion in which she was in the same room, Prince Tadeus had pulled her aside.

"Kesara, might I speak with you? In private?" Kesara knew that Prince Tadeus remembered her name due to only one reason: her brother had killed his brother, and Tadeus hated her by extension. No amount of war and other such distractions could dissipate or distract him from his hatred. Still deathly afraid of him, Kesara hopelessly turned towards Max.

"I'll be right outside."

"Yeah," Kesara replied. "Certainly, Prince Tadeus. Whatever you require."

Tadeus pulled her to another room. He paced around a little, as if he didn't know how to word his next phrase. In the end, he turned to Kesara, looked her in the eyes, and began: "I wanted to apologize to you Kesara." *Wait...did he just say he wanted to apologize?* Kesara thought, confused. "I'm sorry. I should be more thorough in what I say. When I found out that your brother was the culprit who had killed my brother, I grew enraged. I hated you, and I hated Aurora, and I hated everyone near him. I was blinded by the rage, lost in grievance over my little brother. When I found out you were his brother, I wanted to have you killed for what your brother did. I'm sorry I called you a zalphic. I'm sorry for any ill words I might have spoken. I'm sorry for my behavior, and treating you as if you were the criminal."

"I...I don't know what to say," Kesara started.

"You do not need to say anything. It is I who is apologizing. I still feel anger at him, at your brother. I wouldn't change what befell him if I had the chance, but I know he is your brother, and you love him as I love mine. And if I did have the choice, I wouldn't want you to suffer from the same pain I lived through. So, I'm sorry. I should not have treated you in the way that I did. I needed to tell you that."

"I...Prince, you do not need to apologize. I know all too well the pain you felt."

"Yet you didn't demonstrate anger towards others." This attempt of reassurance had a strange effect as Kesara thought deeply about her feelings towards Argus, and the hatred she had felt for those who served him. When she had come from Haernaveh, and fought some of the people in the group, she had been reacting in much the same way as Tadeus had. In the end, she hadn't killed them, but the thought had crossed her mind, and she looked at Tadeus, unsure what to say.

"If you still harbor ill feelings, I understand, but it is this which I wanted to tell you." With those words, Tadeus exited the room and walked outside. After a few moments, Max entered the room.

"Is everything fine, Kesara?"

"I'm not sure anymore," she responded.

Kesara Hewley headed deeper and deeper into the Lancaster Forest, worrying little about turning back, or fighting a war, or Tadeus. She travelled along with Max, who was accompanying her in the forest, as she went to visit the place she had been unable to visit since her brother's death—so long, yet so vividly recent, ago. She traversed the Lancaster Forest expertly, heading exactly where she wanted. As she walked further into the depths of the forest, she gradually took respite in the relaxation she felt there.

She then saw the trees in front of her grow, and the flowers blossom. The land took on a lusher nuance of the green of life, and the flowers were being arranged in a pattern. The flowers bloomed and grew, each its own assortment of color. The blue and red and green and yellow hues all mixed and exalted the lack of difference in colors. They all grew together to accentuate their beauty and created an impossible exquisiteness. The different colors served as a means in the grander color scheme, each surrounded by different colors, but none crashing in intensity or brightness. Each was the perfect shade, the perfect shine. Vines in the surrounding trees accumulated together, out of sight. Leaves and branches seemed to move, to allow just the right amount of light through, shining majestically atop the flowers. She looked around as the grass grew slightly, and the grass surrounding the flowers seemed to be combed, or bowing down to the flowers. Once every flower had been positioned, and every color had been intensified, the arrangement spelled out Kesara.

She knew it could have only been the work of one person: Gideon. Kesara kept looking at the flowers, mesmerized. Ben thought the use of this power was a waste, and that Gideon should not use them for such a trivial matter. The arrangement was beautiful, and she kept looking as her brother appeared from the nearby trees. Gideon came out from the trees.

"Gideon!" Kesara exclaimed, while going towards her brother. Gideon moved towards his sister as well; too long had it been since last they saw each other.

"Hey. I haven't seen you in quite a while Kesara. Is this where you've been hiding from me? Bad choice, I *do* have powers over these forests you know." By the time he had finished, they were already hugging.

"It's good to see you. Where's Ben? I thought he would be with you."

"Oh, you know our brother; he's out there protecting us and ensuring our safety and all that." Kesara laughed at that, though Max looked a little annoyed.

"Gideon you shouldn't have troubled yourself in coming all the way here. But I'm so very glad to see you. What are you doing here?"

"Ben and I stayed behind at Vernatia, to keep an eye on Ferdinand. It had not been part of the arrangement, but Wyatt knew we needed to make sure Ferdinand wasn't planning anything."

"So if you are keeping an eye on Ferdinand, why are you here?"

"Ferdinand came here, and he's meeting with Prince Tadeus. They're going to discuss something. I don't know."

"Where's Ben?"

"He's following Ferdinand. He told me you were here, so he sent me towards you."

"Why not use his telepathy to have us go there?"

"He wants me to *stay* with you."

"Typical Ben."

"Yeah," Gideon smiled. "Max, I haven't seen you since the last time I saw you. Have you missed me so much that you wanted to go to the Lancaster Forest to find me?"

"I came at Kesara's request you little arrogant bastard."

"Yeah, I'm sure it just all worked out for you."

"There are Wise Ones who specialize in arrogant bastards, you know."

"Oh, I'm sure your parents and your brother sent you there as soon as they could. You can give me the shortened version, yes?" Max laughed at that, messing with his hair.

"I suppose we should be going."

"Going where?" asked Kesara.

"Wherever you want."

Suddenly, Kesara felt a strange impulse. She wanted to be far away from all this—the war, the fighting, the plots, and royal disagreements. She wanted to escape, to head off somewhere where she wouldn't worry about the war. "Have you ever wanted to visit Timbergrove?"

"Timbergrove?" asked Max in surprise.

"Why don't we go there? We can visit it, leave behind our worries of King Ferdinand and Prince Tadeus and King Whaldo. What do you say?"

"Do you know how to get there, Kesara?" asked Gideon. She shook her head. No, she didn't. It had been a sudden thought, and it occurred to her before she could think of a plan to get there. "So you plan to learn the location of Timbergrove by asking the trees?" Gideon laughed a little. He then added: "I studied the Lancasters thoroughly. I thought it appropriate to learn about that particular civilization. When the Great Shaking split the Lancaster Lands into that of the Lancaster Forest and the Lost Forest, it is said that the two sister cities were split—one connected still to Andros, and the other floating away in the Lost Forest. The sister cities were reportedly close, so Timbergrove has to be on the outer reaches of the forest."

"So we should head east? And from there travel accordingly?" Both Max and Gideon nodded their heads. "But first...." Kesara started.

Gideon laughed. "You don't even have to mention it." They walked, heading towards their destination. Just then, they heard as voices ordered them to stop, and men in armor stepped out to prevent them from getting closer. In the distance, Kesara saw Prince Tadeus and King Ferdinand. She hadn't known they were so close. The sight of them frightened Kesara. The guards called for the King, who went to the group of three.

"I recognize you," Ferdinand said, pointing at Kesara. "You were the girl from last time right? The sister of Steven. Kesara, right?"

Kesara felt a slight relief that he remembered. Perhaps he would demonstrate the same kindness, and let her go. "King Ferdinand. Yes, I am Kesara. This is my brother Gideon, and a friend, Max. We are heading towards Timbergrove."

"If only you could stay there. You are protecting Wyatt Stephensen. As soon as you get back, you will tell him you saw me here, and that would put me in a *very* compromising position."

"King Ferdinand. We wish only to go to Timbergrove."

"You've seen me. I cannot permit you to ruin the plans I have worked so hard to forge."

"We will do nothing to inconvenience you, King."

"Is that what Wyatt told you to say when he sent you to spy on me?"

"No my King. We aren't following anyone. I simply want to go to Timbergrove."

"I'm not a Wise One, and certainly no expert in the locations of places, but Timbergrove is *that* way," he said, pointing to the east. "Guards, kill them."

"My King!" Kesara shouted.

"You can't!" shouted Gideon at the same time.

"Behind me," Maximillius told Kesara and Gideon.

"Wyatt knows we're here," said Ben, from behind some other trees. Ferdinand turned to him, as Ben walked slowly towards his siblings, and his friend. "If we do not return, Wyatt will know something has occurred."

"So we have yet another spy."

"Yes. I know you are going to Chordica, to meet the Korschers that are coming from the east. You are also very far away from

Vernatia, something that will be hard to explain. I've already sent word."

"There seems to be no reason then," Ferdinand said. "Guards, stand down." Kesara was surprised by the ease of the matter. "It occurs to me, though, that I only recently discussed my plan with Prince Tadeus here. So that you could sneak past us, and hear my discussion, *and* send word seems unlikely. Interesting, isn't it?"

Ben didn't know what to say to that. "Tadeus, back when you had asked me to allow you to do as you willed with Kesara and Aurora, I should have let you. It was truly a mistake. Go now, and take revenge for your brother."

"My King. I was lost in grievance. I do not care to kill them. I will, however, do as you say."

"Tadeus, do you know what will happen if they discover I am here? They will try to hurt me, they will try to find me. They will invade Vernatia, and they will invade Bravania. They will kill you— or at least kill enough of your people that it doesn't matter. All these people, I wouldn't expect you to care for. But remember that they also have my wife, your sister, Fayrah. If they discover I broke the temporary treaty, would you like to wait and see what they might choose to do with her?" Tadeus seemed to react to this strongly.

Tadeus turned to them and drew a sword, which he threw to the ground. "Bring me Guardiana." Two men scurried to him, carrying something surrounded in cloth. Tadeus removed the cloth and held the sword in his hand, a sword that glowed with the luster of Caster metal. "Leave them to me," he told the men. They scattered away from him, finally revealing something other than his face. On his back, a cloak lay resting. The calm, unmoving cloak, unfazed by the gentle breeze worked to rise a great panic through the small group. They stared, unable to comprehend and believe what was in front of them. As Tadeus gripped the Caster metal, Kesara thought that it was a pointless extravagance. Tadeus didn't need the Caster metal sword. They stared in horror at the ungodly scene, as the godly cloak rested on his back. Green, Brown, Black, Red, Blue. That was the way of the cloaks. The Order of the Sword had specific rules for their members. Rather than wear a blue cloak, Oliver the Red wore a red cloak. He was the only member to wear a color cloak that wasn't fitting with his rank. Oliver was a Bladesman though, and chose to wear the outfit of a Knight. Oliver Alkarvan regressed in color. This...this was something different, hauntingly chilling. Tadeus stirred, moving his cloak as he moved towards them. The cloak itself seemed to have power and strength. The cloak was gold.

"Prince Tadeus...." Ben trailed off, unable to speak.

"The honorary title is Prince Tadeus-Raze, now. Until I become lord of Bravania of course."

"Prince Tadeus-Raze, how did you...you're so young." Max started. Indeed, it was so. Prince Tadeus was no more than thirty, and just a few years older than Max. It took years of practice for even the most adept of Bladesmen to acquire the skill and talent of the prince. Bladesmen were forced to perfect their techniques with countless years of practice. By the time the techniques were perfected, most were too old to maintain the necessary vigor for long. The youngest one at par with this particular Banesworth had been some thirty eight already, while the oldest had been fifty three.

Kesara realized the tremendous trouble in which they found themselves. In no conceivable reality did she imagine they could escape now. It was impossible. It *should* be impossible. Even if he demonstrated enormous skills with a sword—such that she hadn't seen before. She thought of the Razed City of Serenity, and how power similar to his was responsible for it. This was the origin of the honorary title.

"You're a...you're a Swordsmaster." Swordsmasters were legendary swordsmen—the last Swordsmaster had been around some three hundred years ago. Seeing Tadeus with the Caster metal sword and the gold cloak was intimidating. It made it seem as if he alone could win Ferdinand the war. Kesara looked at the guards, in panic. She looked around, seeing her brothers and Max, alone. She tried desperately thinking of something. They would never beat him in sword combat. They needed to use their powers. They needed to use them to escape—if all the soldiers saw that they were zalphics, though, their odds of escaping would be worse. They had to be able to use their powers without the soldiers seeing or interrupting them. To prevent them from seeing, Kesara and Ben could create smoke with their powers, but they would also be unable to see. If they made the smoke only where the soldiers were, they would just walk out of the area. They needed to stop them from seeing.

"Take care of them Tadeus," Ferdinand said, leaving with some of the soldiers.

Some of the soldiers left with him, but some others remained. Kesara wished Tadeus would send them off as well.

"All of you, leave them to me. You are not to strike them, you are not to "protect" me. I'm sorry. I'll make this quick." Ben and Max drew their swords, Infernus and Azure. Kesara turned to the guards, who seemed excited to see Tadeus fight. Under different circumstances, she would be excited as well. "I have to make it look like an accident. Only precise cuts will do." Kesara thought those words were directed at the soldiers, to prevent them from interfering. "I'll bring back the carcass of some strong animal—say it was *it* that killed you and that all I could do was kill one of them before the pack went away."

"We will not rest to die so easily," Ben said with irritation.

"That cloak would have turned red after I finished—regardless of what color it was before. Rest or fight, the result will be the same."

Ben and Max went towards Tadeus, who waited for their attacks. Ben and Max attacked at the same time. Tadeus stepped aside and slipped through both their attacks, the struck them in the face with his hands. Ben and Max backed away, gripping their swords tighter. Ben went forward, trying to strike four separate times before Tadeus pushed him back. Max circled around and went for his back. Tadeus turned around rapidly and parried his attack, then kicked him away. Ben tried striking to cover Max, but Tadeus parried his attack. Ben tried again, but Tadeus stepped forward, brought the flat of his sword towards Ben's back, and pushed him towards Max with the blade. Ben looked at Max, and disconcertedly turned back towards Tadeus.

Max tried striking Tadeus, but he parried the attacks with ease. Ben went low while Max aimed higher, but Tadeus side stepped, brought his sword towards Max's, and forced the sword to accelerate towards Ben's sword with his sword behind. Max lost his footing, and almost tripped forward. He regained his footing, but this had come after moving a few steps forward and exposing himself—he was between Ben and Tadeus. The prince put his foot in front of Max and tripped him. Tadeus backed away as Ben went to pick up Max.

"Prince Tadeus-Raze," began one of the soldiers. "We've lost sight of the King's party. You have been toying too long with them."

"If it makes you so uneasy, you can run and catch them." Despite these words, the soldiers stood put, waiting. Kesara drew her sword and started approaching Tadeus.

"No," Ben demanded. Kesara had taken only a couple of steps before she was frozen in place by her brother's word. Kesara knew she had to do something—that Ben and Max would be unable to defeat Tadeus. She needed to create a wall between the guards and them.

Tadeus stood put, seemingly toying with the two Knights. It occurred to Kesara that this was simply his method of fighting. He stood his ground, allowing his enemy to attack. She looked at Guardiana, his Caster metal sword. The sword seemed tailored to him somehow, even if the sword was ancient, and some four-hundred years old. Ben and Max struck, but Tadeus expertly parried and moved out of the way. Suddenly, he grabbed at his side and threw a dagger at Kesara. Kesara shrank in fear, only to hear a cry of pain behind her. She turned around to see a soldier with sword in hand, and a cut on his arm. Tadeus yelled at the soldier, almost in fury. "I told you to leave them alone. *Leave.*" The soldier didn't know what to say to the prince, so he started walking away. "All of you, *leave.*" The soldiers were greatly disconcerted, and turned towards one another. "Go meet the King's party. I shall handle this myself." Begrudgingly, they left. Mercifully, they had gone.

Kesara worked quickly, and steam arose. The steam shrouded the trees surrounding their fight. Tadeus seemed to turn to the steam, as if he noticed it was rising. Kesara didn't think he would be able to see though, and Tadeus quickly turned his attention to Ben and Max, who had not stopped attacking. Ben and Max turned to each other briefly, when they seemed to notice the stream, then struck at Tadeus. Prince Tadeus parried both strikes simultaneously and asked what the steam was. Kesara saw as the greenery began to thrive, and she saw vegetation starting to die. Kesara recognized that Gideon was killing some of the greenery to make it look like the path led elsewhere in case the soldiers decided to come back. He was disorienting them. Kesara added more mist into the fogged area. The steam grew bigger and thicker, and she could feel the moist heat. Gideon raised vines and shrubs, masking their location.

Tadeus seemed to have deciphered what was happening. He gripped his sword and started on the offensive. He went towards Max and Ben and struck with amazing speed. It took both Max and Ben alternating to block his quick flurry of attacks. They were being pushed back easily. Tadeus lunged towards Max, who only just managed to block. Tadeus parried Ben's attack, which attempted to protect Max from the subsequent onset. Tadeus slashed again at Max, who was visibly struggling to keep up with Tadeus, even with Ben trying to protect him at the same time. Tadeus struck to Max's left, but Max was not fast enough to block the attack. The Caster metal sword Guardiana drew crimson blood from his side. With no hesitation, Tadeus did not stop to marvel at the landed hit but rather continued attacking. Max retreated rapidly while Ben tried blocking most of the hits. They could not keep up with Tadeus though. Tadeus slipped past Ben and struck Max again on his hand.

Tadeus turned and struck Ben on his leg before stopping unexpectedly. Tadeus spun his sword around his hand, caught it by the hilt again, and aimed for Ben's heart. Ben teleported behind Tadeus and struck at his back. Tadeus turned around violently and parried the blow with a backhanded defensive move, striking again only to find Max blocking the attack, but Max fell on the ground as well.

"Telekinetic zalphic." Tadeus almost spit the words out. "Just like your brother, right?" He turned to Kesara. "Was I right when I said you were a zalphic as well?" Kesara didn't know what to say. She couldn't turn away from him. "You're all zalphics." Max teleported to Ben. Ben's left hand blazed with fire as Max's hand swam with water. "Fire and telekinesis? Water and telekinesis" This seemed to anger Tadeus even more. Ben shot the fire, but

Tadeus jumped out of the way. None of the flames singed him. Max shot water, but Tadeus struck with his sword, splitting the water into two streams that passed by him harmlessly. Tadeus started towards Max, but Kesara wet the ground they were on. Tadeus stopped, almost slipping, but then quickly pushed forward, sliding on the wet grass, and propelled himself quickly towards Max. Max could not move out of the way fast enough, and was struck on the side. Ben shot fire, forcing Tadeus to abandon Max. He went towards Ben, using the same technique.

No matter what I do, he will adapt, thought Kesara. She lifted the moisture from the water, forcing him to stop sliding before he got close to Ben. Gideon sent various needles of poison towards Tadeus, who crouched towards the ground and stopped some with his sword. Gideon rose vines with thorns at his feet, but Tadeus cut them down seamlessly and went towards Ben, striking him with great fury. Ben tried shooting fire as he approached, but Tadeus moved out of the way and jumped back towards the fire as Ben stopped, anticipating that Ben would shoot another stream of fire where he was. Tadeus struck with his sword, and almost disarmed Ben, but he teleported and gripped his sword better. Max went to strike Tadeus, but Tadeus ducked, dousing him with the stream of water Kesara had launched at him. Gideon made wood rise as Ben fired telekinetic energy at Tadeus. Tadeus jumped onto the wood and used it to jump over the telekinetic energy. He then struck backwards, cutting the wood that was to hit him from the back. Tadeus turned to his right, where Max started slowly towards Tadeus. Max created water in front of him, and hardened the water and turned it to ice. He teleported forward, making himself closer to Tadeus, and launched the ice towards him. Max's hope had undoubtedly been to give Tadeus less time to react, but Tadeus stopped the ice with the flat of his blade and with a flicking motion sent it back towards Max. Max, now, was too close to Tadeus to react in time, and he got hit with the ice and fell to the ground.

Kesara raised water from the ground, trying to hit Tadeus, but he moved out of the way and used his sword to redirect it towards a blast of fire that Ben sent. Gideon again sent poisoned needles to Tadeus, but he moved out of the way and approached Max. Ben teleported and struck at Tadeus, but Tadeus blocked his attack and spun around. Max hit Ben on his side, as Tadeus pushed Ben into Max.

Ben created fire in front of him, trying to create a barrier between him and Tadeus. The fire expanded rapidly, making too much fire for Tadeus to simply jump through without getting burned. "Four zalphics, two with two powers, the same two Knights, yet still not a single hit landed on me. I'm a little disappointed, you know."

"This will not end so easily."

"I promised I would make it quick. But that was before I knew you were zalphics." Kesara and Gideon went towards Tadeus, swords in hand. Tadeus did not turn around as Gideon and Kesara approached. He waited, then turned around, stepped towards Gideon, and moved out of the way of his sword. Rather than strike him down, Tadeus moved to his side and with great strength he pushed Gideon towards the flames. As Gideon entered the flames, and his cries of anguish rang out, Kesara stopped, shocked and disturbed. Tadeus lunged towards the flames which quickly died away as Ben stopped the fire, afraid of what he might have done to Gideon. From the back, Gideon looked to have suffered from the burns. Ben crawled in pain towards Gideon, but Tadeus then stabbed Ben under his heart.

"Not quite the heart, so you are not quite dead. You had the option of making this quick, and you denied. You've yourself to blame." Kesara, enraged at what Tadeus did to her brothers, lunged towards Tadeus. He parried the blow, and grabbed Kesara's sword arm with his other hand. Kesara kicked at him, but he stopped her with his feet. Max rose, trying to stop Tadeus, but Tadeus spun and pushed Kesara forward. She did not let go of her sword, and she tried to turn around and strike him, but his push had sent her forward, and she found herself shuffling forward, and then tripping. The sword she held outright in front of her stabbed Max on his face, just underneath his eye. Max cried in pain, as Kesara turned towards the looming figure of Tadeus.

"Not where I was hoping you would have struck him," said Tadeus. He grabbed his sword and struck Max in his stomach region. Kesara tried striking Tadeus, but he parried and disarmed her. She shot water, desperately trying to do something against

Tadeus. He used his sword and diverted the water. Kesara thought his strength should be impossible. Desperate, Kesara outstretched her arm again. Tadeus moved out of the way, almost shocked. The thunder passed dangerously close to him. "Water and Thunder zalphic? So you have two as well?" Kesara looked at her arm, not sure what to say. *Thunder?* She turned around, as if expecting some other zalphic with thunder to be around.

    She tried stirring, tried doing something on the ground. She didn't have her sword, but she still had her powers. She wanted desperately to try something, knowing full well that if Ben, Max, Gideon and her *combined* had not done anything, she wouldn't either. The anger built up, manifesting itself in a tremor, before Tadeus struck her head with the hilt of his sword, knocking her out.

###

Chapter 31
Unhappy Reunion

Roy Rhapsados walked along with Tori, who had decided to join them. As he had suspected, Jackie had not been interested in joining Argus, but she amiably thanked Roy for the proposal. Tori walked, excited to be a part of this group of zalphics, but she forgot her rank. Too quickly, she tried talking to Jacob. Roy asked her to give him time, as the impending war demanded most of his time. Tori accepted this, recognizing that it certainly would be a time-heavy task. Regardless, she expressed her disappointment, but nonetheless remained optimistic and followed Roy. They travelled to the Capital, where the Wise Ones would finally convene. He didn't know what role he would have to play at the Capital—if he had to play a role at all. It was the Capital, so recruiting zalphics might be a little dangerous. He certainly wasn't of rank to be with the lords and the Wisest One as they conversed. Perhaps Roy would be stuck talking with people. Suddenly, the war didn't seem so bad.

He thought about the Wise Ones at the Capital, and at how grand the building would be. It was strange to think that the biggest order in all of Andros was run by three people, all in different places: The Wisest One, in the Capital, Allister Kingston, in Vernatia, and Hal Horus, in Faldenheim. Those three minds were at the front of learning about the mysteries of the world. Their interest in all things, from the zalphics, to the geometric properties of a hyperbola, pushed progress in knowledge. The three of them were good friends—most took it as fact that they had known each other much before joining the Wise Ones. Roy knew that at the time of the birth of both Argus and Jackson, the three lived in the Capital. Argus and Jackson had grown up together, and both Argus and Jackson knew this man before they had even registered his importance, or how much knowledge and power he had.

Argus told Jacob, who in turn told Roy, about the Wisest One, and how he would tell Argus stories about his land of origin. He would tell Argus about their exploits, and give him fantastical stories and improvements on what they were accustomed to. Though Roy didn't know name of his birthplace, it was always said to be a land far away. The Wisest One had always treated them like his own children, supposedly. Roy thought about this men, who certainly ought to be so consumed with his thirst for knowledge. The idea of him taking time from that to dedicate to the two boys seemed strange.

After some time, Argus and Jackson moved. In a period of some years after the Firion Calamity, Hal Horus went to Faldenheim and became lord, and Allister Kingston went to Vernatia, and became lord. Allister Kingston went to Vernatia after the last of the Kaines died, and left no living heirs. Through his connection with the Wisest One, he was appointed lordship of the castle. Lord Hal Horus got Faldenheim in a similar manner. Lord Horus travelled to Faldenheim, as one of the leading Elders, to cure the Spinozahs of Faldenheim. The disease that infected the lord and his family was resilient, and unlike anything Lord Horus had seen before. They all died, leaving no heirs. Lord Horus had been unable to cure them, but he was then appointed lord of Faldenheim.

Once again, they made for the Capital, where they would see their old friend. Roy almost forgot he was a member of the Wise Ones. It had been too long since he sat in a room and discussed with them. He had been so preoccupied trying to fight a war.

Roy reminisced on his past, at how he had become a member of the Wise Ones.

& & &

He had been a little kid, around seven or eight. He was the youngest brother of three siblings. One day, the entire family had gone to Faldenheim. Roy couldn't remember what they were doing. They lived in Farendor, and they seldom visited the nearby castle. It was such a tragic event; he could only remember the negative aspects.

The family was approached by some soldiers. Roy had become scared. The guards kept looking at Roy and questioning his father, Ronald. Even then, Roy knew why that was. He had developed powers, the power of Thunder. And he was young.

It was only years later that Roy realized why this was an important detail. Most develop their powers during the years of adolescence. Roy however, developed these powers at an earlier age—when he was but five. The guards recognized that he was a zalphic. They were angered.

The guards and Ronald had started shouting at each other, and afterwards, the situation had escalated. The guard drew his sword. Roy's father had had no weapon on him, no armor, and absolutely no chance to win the fight. Roy had grown scared. He wanted to use his powers to help his father, but he was paralyzed by fear. His parents had told him and warned him not to use his powers. He didn't know what to do. Raymond, the eldest brother, showed no fear. He stood by his father and readied to fight alongside him. He had sent his little brother, Francis, to get someone's attention, anyone who could help them. Roy stood there with his mom, scared, and confused. Felicity was crying and holding her scared and confused son.

The guards warned him, but they weren't going to let Roy go. They pushed Ronald, and he struck back. The guard then stabbed Ronald. Roy remembered clearly how his dad had fallen to the ground. He remembered the piercing cry from his mother and his brother. He remembered standing there, dumbfounded. Anger arose inside him. Still, he didn't use his powers. He was scared. Raymond went crazy. He attacked the guards. They did nothing to him. They walked towards Roy. Felicity was shouting things now—shouting obscenities perhaps, or indignation. Roy no longer heard what was around him. His ears stopped hearing, his nose stopped smelling. His feet could no longer run, and his arms could do little to protect him.

The only things that worked were his eyes and his brain. His eyes saw them, and his brain perceived the threat. They were going towards him. Everything was happening slowly. He couldn't believe what was going on.

Francis came back. Roy didn't know who he came with, but the man was important enough to give the guards pause. They grew nervous, and they received a scolding.

Roy didn't pay attention to this. His thoughts were with his father. They were all lamenting. His dad was already dead. They all cried.

The next day, they had received a visit. Roy didn't know the man, but he had sensed something wrong. Something was off about the man. Roy was scared of him. The man talked to his mother and offered his condolences. Roy didn't remember exactly what he said, and not because it wasn't important, but because what he said next had claimed his memory of that day. "I know this fails to compare to your loss, but I'd like you to move to the castle. I can provide quarters, and food. You shall not need anything. There is only one condition."

His mother had grown nervous. Roy grew more so. He didn't know why, but he did not trust that man. He did not trust what his condition would be.

"Roy ought to join the Wise Ones. He seems a bright lad, and if he were to serve the Wise Ones and learn with us, it would give us reason to provide for you."

With those words, the man left, allowing them to lament and consider his proposal. Naturally, they left this decision for a later time. They had a family member to remember.

Roy knew though that he would have to accept. He had no choice. The family had been going through a lot, and his cowardice allowed it. Had he only used his powers, Roy thought he could have kept his father alive. There was no point now in wishing he could have done something else.

He knew his mother needed this, and he knew he would have to accept. He didn't trust that man, but surely his mom would see only benefits: a place to live, food to eat, necessities met, and a free education for Roy. He had to accept, and so when it came to make the decision, Roy announced he would gladly oblige.

That was the decision he came to regret more.

31. Unhappy Reunion- 471

His first day of studies sealed his fate. The Wise Ones took him to a separate room and injected him with something he did not recognize.

The side effects were almost immediate. Roy felt nauseated, and his vision blurred. He started sweating profusely. He looked up and saw the man. He was the head Wise One of the castle, the newly appointed Lord.

"The subject fell to the ground immediately upon consuming the drugs." Roy could see from the corner of his eye that someone was writing down what he said. "The subject apparently is burning up. His visual capabilities are intact. Can you hear me boy?"

Roy could say nothing.

"His vocal skills seem impaired, though he seems to be able to hear me. This is only observation; it has yet to be confirmed."

Roy was scared. He lifted his hand, and tried to use his powers to shock this man. Tried.

"The subject tried using his powers on me. It did not work. Whether this is the effect of induced fatigue or the drug is still unclear. The subject is resilient and has not passed out like the others have. The subject is a little boy, of perhaps eight. Perhaps the more the powers develop, the stronger the effects of the drugs." The man went up to Roy and put his hand on his head. He put his hand on his heart. He could do nothing to push him away.

"The subject has a slowed down heartbeat." That was the only thing he had heard before he passed out. When next he awoke, the Wise One said "The subject has regained consciousness." He stood up, feeling his regained strength. He tried to shock the man.

"It is now confirmed: the drugs have effectively interfered with the subject's ability to use his power. The engrims work." That was the story of how the engrims came to be.

* * *

Arriving at the Capital, Jacob approached Roy and Tori. He did not address Tori, even though she introduced herself and greeted him. Instead, Jacob turned to Roy and told him to go with Argus. When Roy asked why, Jacob simply said he didn't know. Roy tried once again to get Jacob to speak with Tori, but Jacob cut him off:

"This time, don't promise to recompense anyone." As if there was nothing wrong with this sort of conversation, he walked away, signaling to Tori to follow. Tori walked away quickly, following Jacob wherever he was going. Before Jacob walked too far away, he thought he heard Jacob ask her "weren't there supposed to be two of you?" Roy turned to Prince Argus, who was with his father. The two were at the head of the entire group—they were visibly anxious to enter the Capital and see their friend.

Roy hurried towards the group, but they were not concerned with Roy getting to them. They continued inside the Capital, where guards led them to the King's Tower—the keep in the Capital and the center of the Wise Ones. The order received only the highest honors, as the well-respected order founded by the king and father of Andros. King Whaldo Alexander had tasked his wisest men with discovering the properties and origins of Caster metal, after the Lancasters had used such weaponry to push the Telk forces back. They had done their research, explained their findings, and took their normal, minimal role again. However, King Whaldo had established the Wise Ones, and they grew bigger and collected more knowledge. Towards the end of his days, King Whaldo grew sick, dying from some strange illness. Fearing his death, King Whaldo called upon the Wise Ones once again, who were successful in determining what illness befell their King. After curing him, and extending his life for another thirteen years, King Whaldo demonstrated his gratitude by elevating their strength and influence.

The Wise Ones consequently were established in any big city and formed part of the circle of advisors for most lords. The greatly respected order was very powerful, and the eternally grateful King Whaldo poured money into the order. His descendants never failed to go against the established amity between the order and the kingdom. Recently, leaders of the Wise Ones were given positions as lords. Though before they had formed part of the nobility, and historically has been so, non-nobility leaders of the Wise ones were soon given positions of power—namely Lord Horus and Lord Kingston, appointed to lordship of Faldenheim and Vernatia, and the Victoriano family, entitled to property and power in Vernatia. Even without such titles, leaders of the Wise

Ones resided in keeps and places of prestige, with luxuries akin to nobility.

King Whaldo III had not changed this strong relationship, and had relied on the Wisest One to be his foremost advisor in matters of the Kingdom. Most stipulated that, if not for the Wisest One, the kingdom would have gone through revolt and elected a new King long ago. Most spoke about the Wisest One with the utmost respect, and any descriptions of him and his efforts made him sound as a man of another time. One inescapable fact reminded everyone he was not infallible: almost in every account, the Wise Ones agreed that the Wisest One was sick. The idea that the smartest man in all of Andros, who was in charge of curing all others, was sick seemed inherently disconcerting. The disease, however, was unknown, and the only people that might have a clue—that is, the Wisest One, Lord Horus, Lord Kingston, Jackson and Argus—offered no comment as to the nature of the sickness, nor did they comment on whether or not the Wisest One was actually sick.

Roy approached Argus, wondering what his task would be. "You are coming with me."

"Where?" Roy asked, confused.

"With the Wisest One."

"With the Wisest One?" Roy was now even more confused.

"You have to present and talk about a topic he knows nothing about." Roy looked at Argus, worried and lost. Argus just let out a good laugh. "You are too serious Roy. You will accompany us because the Wisest One likes us to bring a member of the Wise Ones before him. You will see shortly."

Lord Kingston and Prince Argus walked confidently through the King's Chamber. Roy had to pause and remind himself that this was where they grew up, and these pathways were imprinted in their minds. Lord Kingston went through a set of double doors, which led into a great antechamber. This room was protected by various soldiers, all paying close attention to intruders. Lord Kingston and Prince Argus approached the guards, who opened the doors for them. Roy wondered how the guards knew it was them for whom the Wisest One was waiting. Regardless, they opened the doors and stepped aside as the lord and his prince son went inside.

Roy got a glance for the first time—and he thought potentially the last—of the Wisest One. He was wearing a robe, but he seemed to be of average height, and moving slowly, but not with the gait of old age, but rather of sickness. Perhaps he was reading into his movements. Roy felt a certain strangeness protruding from him. This man seemed different in some fundamental way, but Roy couldn't quite discern the discrepancy. His appearance showed no deviation of what Roy might have expected, so he couldn't quite describe the sense.

When the Wisest One saw the three, he took his robe off, revealing a set of fair hair and dark-brown—almost black—eyes. The features of his face and body were not just that of an Androsii, but of an original Lancaster—the only difference being that he had dark-brown rather than blue eyes. Now Roy understood why it was said that the Wisest One hailed from the Lancaster Lands. This seemed contradictory to what he had heard: that his native land was some far-off land. Roy wondered how a foreigner had taken control of the Wise Ones, one of the most important establishments in the entire kingdom. Roy looked upon this man, but still something seemed wrong.

Roy dismissed this thought. Though his curiosity was peaked, he knew not to stare too long and ask too many questions.

Prince Argus kneeled before the Wisest One. "How long it has been, Wisest One. Too long, I say."

"It has been indeed. My dear boy, it is with great joy that I look upon your face." He signaled Argus to rise, and implied with an offended manner that Argus did not need to show him such respect. "It is one of my blessings to see you grow into the strong man you are."

Roy stood awkwardly while the prince, lord, and the Wisest One exchanged pleasantries. Roy was the only one who didn't know the Wisest One, and he consequently felt out of place. No other person was there to endure his discomfort with him. The Lord hugged the Wisest One and spoke and laughed with him about old times. The process of their salutations seemed exorbitantly long, so Roy tormented himself with thoughts of Aurora. He thought, as they spoke, that it should be Aurora who was meeting the Wisest One—that she was who Jackson should have and would have taken to see. He thought about her demeanor, and how with her gracefulness she would have joined their conversation and laughed among them. She would make a joke about the Wise Ones, or about some current situation, while all Roy could think of saying was a derivation of "why not kill Whaldo and make Ferdinand king by default?" This brilliant line would be followed by "Then, at least, King Whaldo will be remembered for something—as the one who got killed."

As this internal dialogue went on inside Roy, he envisioned Aurora at his side, laughing at his stupidity, but loving him for it. She laughed, playfully hit him, and laughed some more. Roy would then recognize that it was more likely she would laugh at him, hit him, and laugh some more. While the dialogue was running its course, he finally recognized that Lord Kingston was introducing Roy. "Wisest One, this is Roy Rhapsados. He is an advancing member in the organization, currently a Scholar."

"It is always great to see young men who are interested in more than swinging a sword and shooting thunder from their hands."

Roy was surprised by this, turning immediately to Argus. He turned back to the Wisest One, still shocked. "Wisest One, how is it that you know I am a Thunder zalphic?" Roy then realized that he shouldn't have said that. Even there, in the Capital, the people were little fond of his kind. Roy became nervous, thinking it might have been a simple figure of speech. *He didn't mean it literally. How are you a member of the Wise Ones?* He wanted desperately to turn around, to look at the soldiers who would stab him and kill him for being a zalphic. He wanted to run. He wanted to teleport.

"You think I should be scared?" Still, he was not calm. He was on edge, thinking that this was merely a ruse to keep him from fleeing. Try as he might, he could not move. The glaring eyes of the Wisest One kept him in place.

"I am different. Isn't that what makes people afraid?" His secret was out. He would die here, in the Capital. He would never ask for forgiveness. Suddenly, he felt the desire to see Wyatt Stephensen, and admit what he did.

"Those who are afraid of change and difference have no business being alive. Is it not the steps of life to be borne into a new world, one where you learn and appreciate your surroundings? If I were afraid of others, I had no business coming to this land." These words calmed him down as he recognized his sincerity. He was not afraid of him. He was not afraid of zalphics. Did he know Argus and Jackson were zalphics? Roy didn't know. He understood that their parents knew them to be zalphics—sometimes even *that* was too risky.

Roy pondered the Wisest One's words. His thoughts were then interrupted. "Lord Allister has been telling me about you. He had decided adamantly that you would be the one who joined us today. He tells me that you lived in Faldenheim, learning under the Wise Ones under Hal over there."

"You have the right of it, Wisest One. I learned under Lord Horus's institution, but when I joined the Protectors, I began learning under the tutelage of Lord Kingston."

"It is not strange you decided to stop being under Lord Horus's power. I encourage you to continue your studies. Often knowledge is pushed aside as frivolous and unimportant with daily aspects of life."

"I want to be the best I can be—and that entails both intellectual and physical advancement," Roy replied. He wasn't sure if that was true, but he figured it was something that he would want to hear, and it seemed appropriate.

"So you're telling me you want to be the best there can be?"

Roy nodded.

"There is an old fable in my land. I'd like for you to hear it.

"There was a man, a sculptor, who hammered away at rocks and stone and created works of beauty. He toiled away day after day in this profession, under the sun and the rain, cold and heat; weariness or no, he worked. The labor became too much for him, as he could no longer persist in the laborious effort. Then he looked upon the King and thought: 'If only I were King. I would have subjects to do as I wish, and would have no need to work under such conditions.' And so he tried and tried, and eventually became King.

"The King now, enjoyed his days. He had laborers and sculptors making grand pieces for him. He didn't have to work, and enjoyed respite in his servants. They cared for him. One day, during the zenith of the heat, in the summer, he grew hot and irritable. His servants fanned him, and he had shade, but it was not enough. Then he looked upon the Sun and thought: 'If only I were the Sun. I would be above all, producing light and giving off heat to anyone, and no one would bother me.' And so he tried and tried, and eventually became the Sun.

"The Sun now, enjoyed his days. He produced brilliant light and no one could bother him. He did as he wished and went about his life merrily. One day, he was shining upon the world, when a cloud covered him. Despite his efforts to shine, the cloud blocked his brilliance. Then he looked upon the Clouds and thought: 'If only I were the Cloud. I would block the light of stars and produce darkness if so I desire, and I could block anything and rain down at my whim.' And so he tried and tried, and eventually became the Cloud.

"The Cloud now, enjoyed his days. He blocked off any light, and he rained upon anything and everything. He didn't need permission to rain, or to cover, and he kept upon his life, content. One day, a mighty gust moved him, and he was powerless to do anything but go along with him. He couldn't stay where he wanted, being pushed around. Then he looked upon the Wind and thought: 'If only I were the Wind. I could move clouds around to my liking, causing them to block the sun, pushing anything I want around. I could cause hurricanes of wind, and nothing could stop me.' And so he tried and tried, and eventually became the Wind.

"The Wind now, enjoyed his days. He pushed things around and was pleasantly entertained by all the things that flew according to his orders. He pushed this, and pushed that, and blew tremendously. One day, trying to move everything, he came upon stone. Where the sand and dirt and clouds and all else flew around, he couldn't move the stone. Then he looked upon the

Stone and thought: 'If only I were the Stone. I could stand firm, undeterred and infallible, unable to be moved.' And so he tried and tried, and eventually became the Stone.

"The Stone now, enjoyed his days. No one could move him, he was an immovable object, unable to be scathed by wind or sun. He stood proudly, having no fear. One day, standing firmly in place, immovable, a sculptor approached the stone, and to his horror, the sculptor hammered away at him and toiled furthermore, until he broke a piece of the stone, and shaped it to his will."

Roy nodded weakly. "We will never be content—we always want more. Don't try to hold in your possession things that cannot and will not pertain to you." Again, Roy didn't know what to say, so he stayed quiet. "Do you know why Lord Kingston wanted me, specifically, to meet you today?" Roy shook his head. "For one, so that I could see how you think. You really have shown me a side to you, even if you don't think you have. You have much to learn, and still ample space in which to grow. You, however, will continue learning—I'm certain of that. It is for that reason that you are promoted to Instructor now." Roy could scarcely believe the words he was speaking. This praise, from so wise and powerful a man instilled a drive for him, to grow smarter and stronger.

"You honor me greatly," is all Roy could think to say.

"Do not obsess with what you cannot have. All the knowledge in the world will destroy you, as it has done to countless others. Instead, learn what is needed to make this world better. Might I ask you: when did you develop your powers Roy?"

"Around the age of 5," he said, trying not to sound weak.

"And your telekinetic ones?"

Roy didn't know what to say to that. He honestly did not know. "Some time after the fourteenth day of the fifteenth month, of the 545th year."

"That is oddly specific," is all he said back. After a time of silence, he amiably added: "I like something odd, and certainly specificity." He then took a pill he had hidden somewhere in his clothes and swallowed it. Roy thought he recognized them, but with a shudder he rejected the thought. *He would already be dead, regardless.* "It has been a pleasure meeting you, Instructor Roy. Keep learning, and the knowledge will help you face your fears." Roy almost couldn't leave. He was at a loss for words, wanting to say more to him but having no clue what might be of interest.

"The pleasure was certainly mine, Wisest One."

"I suppose it is time for our dues. Enough of these pleasantries. There are dark times ahead."

"Wisest One, you are correct. The days are shortening and nighttime approaches sooner."

"That is not what I meant Lord Allister, and you know it. Enough of this folly, we know what we must discuss."

"Wisest One, surely we could converse at a more appropriate time."

"Lord Hal is not yet here, but that does not delay the arrival of my brother. When would you have us decide? In months, when they will be upon us searching for blood and gold?"

"Wisest One, these are your kin. It ill befits us to discuss what we will do."

"You fail to see the gravity of this threat. I've alerted the king; he readies the army."

"Will this army help?"

"I'm afraid it won't Allister."

"Surely you could negotiate with them. They would listen to you."

"I'm afraid I can do no such thing. Nevil is a leader, and if he has to sacrifice one of his own to sustain his kingdom, he would make the sacrifice himself and shine with glee as he cut my throat."

"Surely this man is no monster."

"I may exaggerate his glee—of course he would be troubled, but nonetheless, my throat he would slit."

Roy was confused. He thought the entire point of convening the Committee of the Wise Ones was to forge a treaty. The Wisest One was talking about an invasion.

"He will be thrilled to see you."

"He will be thrilled that it was not him who indirectly killed me. Apart from that, he will *lead*. You must stop this nonsensical war.

Wars have been fought for much less, and have failed to begin for notions which it merited. Now we must decide our strategy."

"I agree," began Prince Kingston. "We will do what we must to protect this land. We must kill them."

"It is not so simple."

"You would kill your own people?" Lord Kingston asked.

"Do not be mistaken. I do not choose to kill them because that is what I've decided. They intend to kill us, profit from us, and enslave us, so we must anticipate their actions and defend ourselves."

"You would be killing your brother."

"Your King Ferdinand attempts to do the same thing."

"He doesn't want to kill him."

"No other event will unite them."

"Not even the invasion of your people?"

"Especially not that. I have studied people all my life. They will try to take advantage of this situation."

"How?"

"One of them will not do enough to fight them. The other will make a derision out of his brother's actions."

"If you were the one negotiating, I'm certain your people can come to rational decisions."

"Rationality is a joke where we are from. What I've told you about our people and their customs are true. They are not ones to simply negotiate. They will take what they want and make it feel like a bargain when they give us crumbs. They will not fail to exercise their power—they never have."

"But if what you have told us is true, about the power they possess, we cannot possibly win."

"For those same reasons, we cannot possibly risk failure."

###

Chapter 32 Thunder

Roy Rhapsados was in the antechamber, waiting to talk with Argus. Argus was talking with Jacob at the time, and Roy wanted to discuss the assignment he was to carry out. King Whaldo would take part of his army and travel east, going around the Desert Lands of Chordola. To the east of Chordica, King Ferdinand would meet King Whaldo to hear the terms of treaty which the Wise Ones had determined. The Wisest One had adamantly insisted that the treaty be read in the presence of the two kings, and he refused to tell King Whaldo what they had decided. As the army went east, Garrisbrough would go north and meet with those of the Capital. Roy knew—or at least assumed—that he would not be part of the army heading east. Argus was going to make him go elsewhere. Suddenly, the doors opened and Jacob exited. Jacob signaled Roy to join them. Roy was intrigued as to what they would tell him. Fortunately, Argus and Jacob weren't ones to squander time.

"You will take a recruit of your choosing to Highstorm. You can choose one of those who joined us, or some of the ones we picked up on the way. You will go with Jacob, who will accompany you to retrieve something. The three of you will leave immediately; Jacob will expand on the details of the voyage as you travel."

Argus dismissed them and Jacob turned to him. "You know who you're going to take?"

"Yeah, I'm taking Tori. Can you get her while I gather my stuff?"

"I don't know her. Go on Roy, you're wasting time." *He doesn't know her? But she's a promising pupil, his most adept one. How could he have failed to notice? He had spent time with her while they were at the Capital, hadn't he?*

Roy used his telepathy and told Tori that they were leaving immediately. When he had gathered some supplies and Telekay, he loaded his belongings onto the wagon and waited. Shortly after, Tori came with her belongings. He knew the food and money would be taken care of by the Wise Ones, so all he needed now was to wait for Jacob.

This was something that took much longer than he thought it would. Jacob did not appear as Roy and Tori stood, then sat, then stood again, waiting. "What are we waiting for? I thought we were leaving immediately?"

"Apparently Jacob and I have different views of the meaning of the word."

"Jacob's coming with us?" Tori said, sounding startled or enthusiastic. Roy wasn't sure which.

"Yeah, the three of us are going to Highstorm." Tori looked eager now, and he noticed her bow. It was still an odd weapon, but she had proven herself with the bow, and she was really good with it. She also had the power of thunder, and she was travelling with Roy and Jacob—both of whom had a lot of knowledge on that particular subject. Perhaps Roy would show Jacob just how much potential Tori had. He still couldn't believe Jacob hadn't known who she was.

Jacob approached, and Roy noticed Tori stand up straighter—more alert and...he didn't know. She had a look similar to one someone else he knew at some point or another, though he couldn't quite pinpoint it.

Jacob, terse as ever, greeted them with a "Let us make haste," and departed all the same without looking at either of them. Roy looked at Tori, a bit annoyed by his rudeness, but Tori lingered her gaze on Jacob.

Tori then looked at Roy and quickly took off as well. *What is wrong with everyone?* Roy abandoned his hope that Jacob would inform him what they were doing. Roy had a feeling Jacob wouldn't be particularly predisposed to parley. He looked at Tori who, with great determination, went forward, decidedly wanting to converse with Jacob. She remarked about his rank as a Bladesman, and she expressed her desire to see his skill. "It would be grand to see you fight; I just know it would be an amazing sight."

32. Thunder- 483

"As far as Bladesmen are concerned, I am ranked about twelve. An amazing sight to see would be observing Prince Oliver the Red fight someone like Lord Bastion."

"You are a Bladesman, like they are. Do not be so modest. I know you are a strong warrior." Jacob didn't remark, and rather looked into the distant horizon. Roy wasn't sure what Jacob was looking for, but he stared long and hard. It was clear by his elevated head that he was looking, rather than thinking.

"Back in the Capital, three Bladesmen lived there, protecting King Whaldo: Valadiar Helmsdan, Horaclys Naeia, and Orton Eridan. With Lord Bastion, that makes four from Garrisbrough, all of which are stronger than me. In Arastaud, the Red, Oleander Lyrad, Ivan Skar, and Quade Glenna are stronger than I am. In Faldenheim you have Caspian Stoddard, who is stronger than I am."

"From what I've seen," started Roy, "you two are quite evenly matched."

"I still maintain that he is slightly better—not something I will allow for long, but for now it holds true. Then there is Kayton Drost of Vernatia, who is stronger than I am. Finally, in Bravania, as far as Bladesmen go, there is Melinda Briar, who is stronger than I am. That makes eleven people who are stronger than me who are Bladesmen in the Order of the Sword—that doesn't include those who are not members of the order and therefore have no rank.

"But being able to *number* the people that are stronger than you is impressive," started Tori. "I could not number all the people that are betters Marksmen than I am—the number would be too great."

"Wait," began Roy. "For Bravania, you said Melinda Briar was stronger than you. But what about Prince Tadeus? We have all heard tales of his strength."

"I said as far as Bladesmen went, Melinda was stronger. Tadeus is no longer a Bladesmen."

Roy was confused. "Was Tadeus demoted? He is a strong warrior, they couldn't possibly reduce his rank to a Knight."

"No Roy. That is not what happened."

"Was he expelled from the order?"

"No Roy. That is not what happened."

"What else is there?"

"Prince Banesworth is now a Swordsmaster."

Neither Tori nor Roy could believe they heard right, as they turned to each other in shock and confusion. "A Swordsmaster? That's impossible," said Roy.

"There hasn't been a Swordsmaster in some three hundred years," added Tori.

"All of Andros would know already if Prince Tadeus were a Swordsmaster," argued Roy, thinking this could only be a lie. The skills of Swordsmasters were legendary.

"Understandably, King Whaldo does not want his Kingdom knowing that Prince Tadeus is a Swordsmaster, so they have kept the information quiet. Even in Bravania, the word has not spread. Lord Bastion sent letters only to the Capital, informing them that Tadeus Banesworth was promoted to Swordsmaster after having successfully completed the test in front of Lord Bastion and others. They are not in Garrisbrough, as they are only just returning from the voyage."

"But, Bravania is in revolt against the Kingdom. Why would Lord Bastion travel to Bravania and promote someone?"

"The Order of the Sword is an entity of its own, established throughout Andros. It is not necessarily restricted inside the Kingdom. It is just about finding strong warriors. All those under Ferdinand who were members of the Order of the Sword continue being so. They enjoy the same membership, just as you and I are still members of the Wise Ones."

Roy turned to Tori, seeing that they were both still shocked and confused. A Swordsmaster, after so many years. Everyone knew the names of the Swordsmasters: Lexifer Mortison, Mikiah Alexander, Fernando Bastion, Kirrivor Elsavar, and Yarimir Spinozah. To imagine that Tadeus would form part of these names seemed strange. They kept asking Jacob questions about Tadeus: whether he had seen him fight, whether he had fought him himself, whether Tadeus was truly that strong. Clearly, Jacob was tiring of the topic, so Roy slowly stopped asking questions and walked in silence. At that point, Tori was the only one talking, while Jacob and Roy offered only occasional responses. Tori told them about the Order of the Bow. Roy was amazed she found something to say to them. He thought it unnatural that people would continually converse throughout the trip. They travelled quickly towards Highstorm, where Roy still did not know what they would do. Jacob had still failed to tell him.

Heading towards Highstorm, a group of travelers intersected their line of sight. Roy turned to Jacob, who had immediately grabbed his sword, but who then proceeded to let go and turned to Tori. Tori still did not know what was happening, so the strange look Jacob gave her disconcerted her some. She asked Jacob what was wrong. "The travelers have no supplies, nor anything to carry back what they set out to do." Tori, having understood what Jacob meant, went to grab her bow, but Jacob stopped her with his hand. She turned to Jacob, lingering her gaze and hands on him. "Instructor Roy, *instruct* her."

Roy nodded his head, even if no one was looking in his direction. Roy turned around, making sure no other travelers were nearby. He saw no one, so then he searched with his mind, still seeing no one, and seeing that none of the bandits were zalphics. "Thunder is a fairly common power, but that doesn't make it a weak power. Knowing how to use Thunder influences its effectiveness greatly. It is like a bow. Some are alright at using it, some haven't a clue, and then there are those Deadeye which have mastered it. Its power can change drastically." Tori nodded her head, while they approached the group. "Thunder happens to be one of the faster powers. Fire and water are behind thunder in quickness, and behind them are earth and wood. Before the bandits realize it, I will have been able to strike them down. You, however, will be the one who will use your powers."

Tori seemed confident, but Roy did not think she should be. She was relying too much on the alternative—that if she failed, Jacob could dispose of the bandits, or even Roy. Roy needed Tori to realize that she had to be able to do this by herself. "We will not always be with you, so it is important for you to develop the necessary strength. There are various things to keep in mind. Thunder can pass on to its environments—this you already know. If you shock your arrow, and I block with a sword, it can course through the sword and still shock me. Same holds true for people. Being next to someone who is being shocked will cause you to be shocked as well."

"Yeah," she said. She stepped forward faster, making sure she was the closest one to them. As the bandits approached, trying to seem harmless, they congregated together in the center, so Roy, Jacob and Tori would have to separate to go around them. Now that they were closer, Roy could see that there were five bandits. Tori went up to them, running. Roy turned to Jacob, alarmed at what she was doing. She began speaking with the group of bandits, trying to keep her voice soft. Jacob and Roy continued walking, until they reached Tori and the bandits. Tori turned to Jacob and Roy, and told them that they would be going on their way.

"You are quite close to the Capital," Jacob mentioned.

"In my experience, they safer people think they are, the more money they carry without the proper skill to protect it," replied the bandits.

"That is quite interesting. I enjoy a challenge." Jacob walked forward, grabbing Tori, and pushing her forward as they walked. "Certainly, even better than having control of your powers is catching the enemy off guard." Jacob turned, shooting thunder before he could finish turning. The group of bandits had their swords out, prepared to attack, and they were all shocked violently by Jacob's attack. The bandits all fell to the ground. "Zalphics!" they yelled.

Bandits! Roy thought mockingly. "You anticipated something would go wrong, and it is that why you had your bow so close at hand, isn't that right?" Jacob said pointedly. Tori nodded weakly. "You have good reactions. You would never have thought your old bandit friends would attack you so suddenly." Again, Tori nodded weakly, agreeing with Jacob.

Roy, a little annoyed, didn't direct any words to her. *Those bandits were supposed to deal with us?* Tori turned, looking at the bandits on the ground. "No one feels sympathy for their attackers," Jacob mentioned. Tori quickly turned her head forward, visibly struggling to not turn around again.

"Aren't you afraid that they know you're a zalphic?"

"Are people going to believe them over me? I am in good standing with the lord of Vernatia, and I have two witnesses who will testify that, after humiliating them with my skill, we left them on the ground, where afterward they surely conceived of a rumor they could spread to tarnish my name."

"Next time," Roy began, "they should choose their marks more carefully. It's almost insulting to think they thought they could catch us unaware." Roy didn't know why he was continuing this game that Jacob had started, but accusations were scarcely beneficial. They continued their voyage in silence now. Tori no longer spoke endlessly, and now Jacob kept close to Tori. Roy continuously thought about Aurora, wishing she was there to keep him company, or wishing he could look forward to seeing her again. He was still haunted by the memory of a purple cat going towards her, while his senses came back to him in time to feel the pain and repulsiveness of his actions. A thunderous storm continually assaulted his mind. Try as he might to calm the anger, the tempest flashed brilliantly. He attempted to relieve the gales of wind caused by Aurora by keeping busy among the Protectors, and learning from the Wise Ones. When that failed, he tried to stop thinking, not knowing that this only made him think more. He wished the war could continue, so that he could fight and be distracted by its horrors. He wanted nothing more than to feel control as metal pierced flesh and the cries for the fallen resounded. War reminded him that everyone could die, so he ought to kill and remain standing.

When the group had arrived at Highstorm, they left their supplies outside of the city. Dark clouds rained from above, and the collection of Water zalphics and Thunder zalphics exercised their power, hitting anything inanimate or living. Their immense strength resonated throughout the desolate city, as its inhabitants had abandoned it long ago to escape the fury of these zalphics. They did not tire, and they did not feel the power of the poison course through them as they continuously fought with unwavering strength. Violent sounds of thunder bursting and water smashing the ground indicated the zalphics gift for their power. The Water zalphics rained down their sweat with unison, not letting anything escape their downward gaze. The Water zalphics teamed together, collecting the water in massive floods, and hitting every part of the group's bodies.

The Thunder zalphics did not stay behind, as they decided jointly that they would attack a certain specific point in the city. Remaining customary to their power, the Thunder zalphics unleashed quick bolts across the expansion, lighting the city section by section. The city glowed with their power. The Thunder zalphics could only be sacrificing parts of their bodies with the constant assault and use of their powers. The Thunder zalphics pointed them to a horizon, where the travelers went. The Thunder zalphics lit the Water zalphics, making them shine with angered fits. Together, their noise pierced the weary travelers.

Tori covered her ears. She was unable to withstand the constant bashing of the rain and the thunder. Her body shivered underneath the storm, craving heat, and wanting to escape the rain. Her hair was wet, her feet were wet, her face was wet, and in all the wetness, she could not summon any strength past what she was doing to move forward. Roy tried using his telekinetic powers to deviate the water. Momentarily, the rain water fell to either side of him, but the constant flood of water drained his strength. Rapidly, Roy felt tired from the effort, unable to contain the water. He stopped using his powers, allowing the water to bathe him. The powerful water seemed to push him to the ground. Roy remained on his feet, striving forward as his boots sunk to the ground, halting his progress. Jacob was having a hard time as well, evidenced by his attempt to cover his face from the rain and his jittering movements upon hearing thunder strike and seeing it come too closely. Jacob pushed forward, seemingly knowing where he was going.

When Roy had been told they would be going to Highstorm, he had assumed it was at a point when the tireless storms weren't pounding the city. Jacob navigated the city, leading them towards the concentration of the thunder. The storm raged, trying to hold them back with gales of wind, floods of water, and a rampage of thunder. None of these stopped the group as they pushed forward. He turned to Tori, who was having the hardest time of the three in the storm. He was glad she was at least receiving some sort of comeuppance for her actions, but even then Roy felt pity for her. If Argus hadn't told him to take a recruit, he wouldn't have. At that moment, this seemed preferable. There must have been a reason Argus sent another recruit with them, though, so Roy kept following Jacob.

The journey across the city was slow. They stopped various times underneath any edifice they could find, and enjoyed momentary respite from the pounding water. The wind and water worked to continue to splash them despite their refuge under a roof. They rested but did not stay idling long, and soon after would go forward until they reached another formation that would protect them from the worst of the storm. This continued slowly. The wind pushed back, and the strength of the storm attacked their strength. There was nothing they could do against the strength of the storm, so they rested and continued. Roy noticed they were getting ever-closer to the concentration of the thunder. Worried, Roy wanted to communicate through telepathy. This required strength that he wanted to concentrate on getting through the storm. Figuring there must be good reason for Jacob's commitment to wither the worst of the storm, he continued. Tori had no choice after her previous attempt, so she followed zealously behind. She struggled but she fought to keep up.

Finally, Roy could see the thunder striking down towards the ground. In sharp turns, the thunder redirected towards some object at the top of a building. The building was lit by the thunder, but it was otherwise indistinguishable. They went inside the edifice and went towards the roof. The stairs croaked in aggravation and the interior of the building was extremely dilapidated. They got as far as they could from inside of the building, so they went out on a balcony and grabbed the ladder. The ladder was flimsy and did not seem adequate. Roy held the ladder in place as best he could, but the storm still made it too difficult to keep in place. Tori went to the other side of the ladder, helping Roy hold it in place, while Jacob climbed. When Jacob reached the top, he held the ladder from the top, and Tori then started climbing. When Tori was close to the top, Jacob extended his hand, and helped Tori up. He held her in place at the top, helping her orientate herself. They both held the ladder to allow Roy to climb. When he got to the top, Jacob walked away, not bothering to help Roy up the final bits of the ladder.

Roy saw as the thunder went towards him, but then quickly and sharply turned, hitting something on the roof. The metal shone if but for a moment before returning to its shade of black which kept it camouflaged. More thunder went to strike the sword, and this time the sword radiated thunder to its surroundings. Roy was shocked by some of the thunder. *"Roy, that sword is a Caster metal sword. We need it. I need you to divert the storm."*

"What do you mean by divert *the storm? What am I supposed to do?"*

"Use your powers to prevent the thunder from striking the sword. Redirect the thunder elsewhere."

"You make it sound simple."

"You only need to do it until I can sheathe the sword in a scabbard immune to the bolts." Roy turned his head up, struggling to see through the countless spheres of water falling on him. He tried emptying his mind, so that he could concentrate on the task. Thunder struck the sword again, making a loud noise and again lighting the sword. The sword radiated some of the thunder, but none of it hit Roy. Roy took a deep breath and waited. When he saw light, he turned his head to the sky.

"Now." The light lit the sword, and Roy prepared for the next bolt of thunder. Jacob approached the sword when thunder came angrily shooting at the sword. Roy quickly used his powers, trying to send it elsewhere. As the thunder descended, the task was much harder, as the thunder seemed to be attracted to the Caster metal. Mustering his strength, Roy managed to push away the single bolt of thunder. Without waiting, more bolts of thunder appeared, threatening to fry Jacob in the process.

Diverting the thunder was an immense, indescribable feeling. His entire body felt pain—from the bones in his fingers to the inside entrails that few knew anything about. He could only feel pain, and could register nothing else. He saw pain, and heard pain, and felt pain, tasted pain, and smelled it. Pain, pain, and more pain. He saw the pain in the form of a mighty hammer striking him, releasing sparks as Roy was being crushed under its immense weight. He heard the pain breaking him, shattering his armor, crunching his body, heard the shrieking of his body and the scream being produced by every member of his being. The taste of pain was eerily similar to the taste of remedies prepared by apothecaries, filled with the foulest, most unimaginable ingredients, and he tasted its wretchedness, with an electrifying and completely foreign taste. He smelled the burnt power of the force, the smell of finality, of crypts and sweat. The lightning coursing through his body circulated pain. He could not think; the pain was too much. He felt the pain above all—felt the mighty jolts reverberate his entire being. He felt as the pain coursed throughout his body, making every possible stop to introduce pain. He was on the ground, and even the floor felt the pain, as the pain pushed Roy's body downward.

    Jacob entered his mind and stopped his attempt. Roy did not fight back, nor could he if he wanted to. He accepted Jacob into his mind, and did nothing to fight him off. Roy, with no energy left, let the nothingness engulf him....

###

Chapter 33
Fallen Castle

The zalphic, who was alarmed at the sight of a young burned boy, two Knights suffering from sword wounds, and especially the girl, who, like the rest of them, was unconscious, stirred with panic. The zalphic had heard some sort of trouble from afar. She went to the familiar opening in the forest, and saw them, on the ground and wounded. She had expected another day of peace, where she would go through the familiar lands, and relax and think. Instead, she saw the wounds of the nearly dead group. She immediately raced towards another nearby zalphic. She was scared, and did not know what to do.

"Allison, you have to help them!" Allison turned to the zalphic. "There's a wounded party." The zalphic's anguish stirred Allison, and she went with the zalphic to examine the wounds. The group had nasty wounds, all of which were fatal.

"Is this what was causing so much noise not five minutes ago?" The zalphic nodded her head. Allison approached them, sensing they were all zalphics. "They are all zalphics." The zalphic knew this already, and she turned to Allison. "Is that why you are so desperate to help them? Because they are like you?"

"Please Allison. Help them." Allison examined the wounds. "These are quite nasty. Whoever did this wanted to make it look like some animal did it. Look at how the cuts are in groups of three. Some of the wounds are deeper than the others."

"Please. I don't care what the wounds look like." The zalphic was almost in tears now.

"These wounds are fatal. The Wise Ones would be unable to help them." Allison looked at the zalphic, who seemed horrified. "Not even the Wisest One could help them now—not with what he has at his disposal, anyway."

"You need to help them Allison." The two zalphic girls in the forest looked around, and Allison went up first to the burned boy. "I can do nothing for burns. Those are external problems. I need you to gather something to protect his burn wounds." The zalphic girl quickly went to look in the forest. Allison knew she was a smart girl, and she would gather the necessary ingredients. The zalphic went to the forest, knowing exactly where to look. She had learned what plants were good for burns. She gathered them with utmost haste, spending long only because she needed so much of the plants to cover all the burns. After which, she returned to Allison while preparing the remedy for the burns.

Allison was focusing on the girl. The zalphic went towards the burned boy, and with shaky hands she administered the rough remedy for the burns she had prepared. "This one is special," Allison told the zalphic. "Can you tell?"

"I can't tell, not with my powers, but I know," replied the zalphic. Allison worked on the otherwise impossible task, while the zalphic stared at the group, and stared at Allison. She wanted to be like Allison. She wanted to learn her power, so that she could help as well—not just protect herself from attacks, but protect others as well. Protecting others after they had been attacked was immediately useful, and she wanted to learn. With a calm demeanor, Allison took care of the zalphics.

The zalphic took them to the nearby room with which she was familiar. There was nothing much else she could do. She began preparing food, arguing to herself that they would be hungry. Making enough food for six helped her feel better, as it reinforced the idea that they would actually live and eat. She confided in Allison, and she knew Allison could do amazing things, but she saw the wounds of the group. Looking at them made her imagine the worst: that they would all die, and their parents wouldn't know. Perhaps that is the fate her own father was suffering while she idled around in the Lancaster Forest.

"Not even the Wisest One could help them now." The zalphic wished Allison had lied, or not mentioned the severity of the wounds. She questioned what Allison could do compared to the Wisest One. She also knew that each had their own particular skills. The zalphic still worried. She tried to hide the tears, trying to hide how much she cared. She was terrified. Perhaps there was something she could do for them. She could think of nothing. She only looked at Allison. *That is what I've done for them. I've given them the best healer I know.* With futility, she tried envisioning all of them waking up, seeing her, thanking her and in merriment, all of them joining together to eat food and converse. She looked at Allison. She saw her fiery character represented in her fiery hair, and she saw her determination in her slender body. Her immaculate skin reflected her knowledge in healing, and her youth spoke power about her skills. But she was scared, like any zalphic. She understood that fear now.

###

Roy Rhapsados awoke in a daze. The last thing he remembered was the terrible storm, and now there was no city around. They were headed...somewhere. Roy was still disoriented. He was on the wagon—the unusually empty wagon they had taken with them to Highstorm. Roy wondered if it was planned. With someone as smart as Lord Kingston and his son, it was. Roy was still too weak to stand up, and all he heard was the noise of mounts going forward. He knew he was still much too out of his senses, as he heard Jacob *laugh.* It was an unnatural sound, and he wondered where his mind could have imagined such a laughter. Roy closed his eyes, not able to stare any longer at the blinding light. Despite this, he was glad it was no longer thunder he saw. Roy rested, his body rising lightly with every breath he took. He heard voices talking, but Roy focused on the sound of his beating heart. *One, two three...*the beats continued steadily.

With a sudden surge, he felt the pain course through his body. He could not speak nor transmit the idea that he was in pain. He tried using telepathy, but he seemed to have forgotten how to use it. The pain was too much, but Roy could not move. His body was

33. Fallen Castle- 495

still, rising emphatically with the rapid beating of his heart. He tried to calm himself, but as ever, this failed. He felt electricity surge through him. He recalled that this had happened already—that it was not a new sensation. He tried thinking back, seeing only ominous clouds raining down on him and thunder constantly shooting in various directions.

Roy could no longer hear the voices, and instead heard his rapid and shallow breaths. There was no strength in him to cry out for help. He thought about the engrims, knowing he had suffered attacks much worse than what he was feeling now. Despite this knowledge, and despite the real sensation of the pain of the engrims, he felt weak and disoriented and in pain at the surging electricity. He found no respite from the pain. He felt like digging his hands into something like stone, but he had no control over his body. *The engrims made this look like a nice nap,* he thought, but still nothing saved him from the pain. He wanted to fall unconscious, so that he might awake in another state where he was not in so much pain.

In an instant, he felt no more pain. It was not as bright as it was before. He opened his eyes, seeing less food around him than was there before. Roy wondered where they were, or how long ago they had been in Highstorm. Roy listened intently to Jacob, who, to his surprise, was conversing with Tori. He immediately recognized he was talking about the Fallen Castle of Alexander. The fall of the castle was due to the Firion Calamity, as it was so named, which had occurred in Roy's infancy. Though he had been too little to remember, he vicariously lived it. Everything had stopped—all news revolved around the event. People stopped working, children stopped playing, and all lamented the tragic loss of life. People were in turmoil, wondering what would happen to the kingdom. Roy still remembered the day in the Wise Ones where they reviewed the events of the Firion Calamity.

The Alexander Castle had been the first—and only—castle to support zalphics. There had been outrage from many people, while others defended it. The castle's owner died shortly after. His heir did not change the stance of the castle, and they continued protecting zalphics. Refugees went into the castle—too many for their resources. Eventually, they had to pass a tax to all those entering the castle—that didn't work well.

There were refugee zalphics trying to come in, where their lives were in danger anywhere else. When it came down to it, killing a simple tax collector, or a guard or two, was much simpler than continuing life as an exile—especially when you could shoot fire from your hands and thunder from your fingers.

The castle was struggling, and their opponents ridiculed their every move. They critiqued their stance on zalphics; they scoffed at the tax and the poor handling of the killings. Most of all, though, they kept quiet and expressed only solemnity. Roy knew they laughed at their next attempt: eradication.

When it had been too much, and the lord of the Alexander Castle had no more power to hold the people back, the people revolted. They took up arms and fought against them. Even the lord of the castle tried to take them down. The others were not going to die so easily though, and they had a natural leader, who was adept at fire and knowledgeable of the properties of the world. Their leader led the people to the nearby Firion Volcano. This was the largest volcano in the entire world, and what the leader did next would attract the attention of everyone of this land.

He did what little thought possible.

He demonstrated his strength and determination.

He erupted that volcano.

The Firion Volcano erupted with tremendous force, sending lava spewing across the castle and nearby land. The leader dedicated his life to liberating the zalphics, and, using all his life force, expired erupting the volcano. Roy still remembered the words of the speaker: "Firion Volcano brought wrath upon those who thought could control it. Nothing could have saved them. The volcano let out a mighty menacing roar, as the heat of its indignation scorched the will of the heathens. The volcano cried its tears of lava, and the land felt its sadness. All those who pretended to use it received only a fiery retribution.

"But it did not spare the others of its wrath, for it was they who let them live with them. It was the people of the Alexander Castle who embraced them with open arms and allowed them their treacherous stay. For this, they too felt the volcano's wrath. Let us remember this day, and prevent this from happening another time, for with vigilance and determination, we can prevent a similar disaster."

At the time, Faldenheim was not so kind to zalphics, as Hal Horus had not yet become lord of Faldenheim. Now, the Fallen Castle of Alexander serves as a constant reminder that zalphics are dangerous, and not to be trusted. The Alexanders offered them a home, and they burnt it to the ground. That lava from the Firion Volcano still envelops the land around the castle. The Fallen Castle of Alexander perished that day, as did their family line—all but two.

The final Alexander had remained in the Capital—remained in the stomach of his mother, who was in the Capital. King Raymond Alexander had left the Capital and went to the Alexander Castle to help appease the rioting people. There, he had met his doom along with his kin. The expecting queen was the only Alexander left, and she had in her belly the next King of Andros, Whaldo Alexander.

No one knew, though, about Ferdinand. King Raymond had had a wife before the queen. He had married her without consideration for his standing and his betrothal to one of the Leisiter girls. He married Urimé Jeram, who lived in Aquareus, and gave birth to a son, Ferdinand Alexander. Urimé had another daughter with some other man, though Roy knew nothing about her, and Ferdinand had made no mention of her name, even if he admitted to having a sister.

King Raymond's father, King Giovani, silently put this aside, and married his son to one of the Leisiters. Surely King Giovani sent someone to deal with the...inconvenience. The boy was young, and could have appeared to be of no consequence. Ferdinand claims the kingdom, as the firstborn. He has no proof that King Raymond and Urimé Jeram had actually married though, so he was considered a bastard—still the firstborn, but not the son of Queen Serinah.

The leader gave his life erupting the volcano, killing all those people—all those Alexanders. He gave his life to protect the zalphics. Roy suspected that some zalphic would at least attempt to save him from the aftermath.

Roy Rhapsados listened intently to Jacob's words, as he was unable to do much more.

"If you had to destroy a city to save a land, what would you do? Destroying the city guaranteed the land peace; that city could have caused abundant grief, but there was also a chance things would be alright without its destruction.

"The Alexander family, as you know, has held the reigns of leadership since the Telks, Korschers, and Lancasters decided to live together. They wanted more though. Their leadership was being undermined by the Lancasters. The Lancasters were in charge of everything else—most of the ports, most of the cities and castles and keeps. They had control of the Wise Ones.

"The Telks recognized this. In their desperate attempt to retain control, they tried assassinating the three leaders of the Wise Ones: Hal Horus, Allister Kingston, and the Wisest One. They, of course, failed. They had underestimated the sagacity of the Wisest One, and they did not expect Lord Horus and Kingston's sons to be zalphics. Argus and Jackson identified the assassins and killed them before they could approach.

"The Alexanders knew that they were no longer safe. They tried to kill the three most prominent members of the land's most influential organization. They knew that soon, the people would rise up against them. They assumed that this would logically occur in the form of an armed revolution.

"Preparing for this, they invited zalphics to their keep. They wanted to attract the attention of strong warriors that would protect them. They would accomplish this by giving them a place to stay. It was their hope that with these powers, the people would fight to keep their new home safe.

"It's a little tragic really. The Lancasters were planning to win favor with the Bastion's. After which, when the king died, the Lancasters would demand the new king to be chosen in a manner similar to how Queen Abigail Alexander first came to power.

"With the support of the Bastion's, they would get rid of the Alexander control. There was no armed revolution coming, just a lot of plotting. Regardless of the true circumstances, the

Alexanders now had to worry about the unrest in their castle. The Alexanders decided to get rid of those that would not fight for the castle. Of course, by doing this, those who *were* going to fight for them abandoned their homes and joined their zalphics. In fighting them, Lord Alexander sealed his people's fate. They would lose power, and they wouldn't win the revolution that hadn't even begun.

"Argus had gone to the Alexander Castle, not to flee, but to get revenge for what they tried to do to his father. How convenient for him, then, when the Alexanders opened their doors for his kind. He smeared his face with dirt and practiced to rid himself of his mannerisms and idiosyncrasies. He entered the castle under the guise of someone fleeing and tried to find the best way to King Raymond Alexander, and his brother the lord of the castle.

"I suppose he was destined to kill King Raymond, as everything fell into place without having to instigate much. Lord Alexander's decision to target zalphics unified them, and he closely followed an emerging leader: Heramyr Mortison."

"Heramyr *Mortison?* As in, *Lexifer* Mortison?"

"Yes. Heramyr was a descendant of Lexifer Mortison."

"But Lexifer was one of the three original Swordsmasters, who destroyed Serenity to help the Alexanders keep the crown. Why would Heramyr destroy them?"

"I am not certain. Likely because he was a zalphic. I *do* know that it was Heramyr Mortison who led the zalphics then. Argus learned under him. Argus had an army and a means to kill the lord. It was Heramyr's decision what to do with them, but Argus could persuade him.

"They gathered all those with power over fire and headed to the Firion Volcano. With the help of the acolytes, Heramyr erupted the Firion Volcano. Those with the power of earth made trenches in the volcano to aid the magma into their desired location: the Alexander Castle. The lava travelled along these trenches, though it also overflowed. Those with telekinesis then teleported them to safety, though some could not be spared from the excess lava. Many zalphics were lost that day. Even to us, the Firion Calamity was a disastrous event. The lives of many good men were lost that day, and it ended with an Alexander being crowned anyway. The

Lancasters did not think it prudent to resist the Alexander reign after the tragic event. Foreseeing that the baby King would be unable to do anything but follow their wisdom, they did not make to subvert the kingdom.

"Many of the survivors took off on their own, agreeing among themselves that it was not safe for them to congregate in one place. Some however, did not enjoy the prospect of returning to their former lives. That is where Argus came up with a solution and offered them something better. He told them to join him. They would gather together and protect one another. They would help zalphics and aid their progress.

"Heramyr had expressed a wish of that sort: a union between zalphics where they protected one another against the others. He gave his life for that wish, and Argus took the commission to heart. To shorten an otherwise lengthy tale, this was the beginning of the Protectors. Argus has been aiding us since that time to grow our powers. Unfortunately, many of the senior members who had joined him have passed away due to the detrimental effects of the power. The young ones who joined him were often brash, and carelessly got killed or went their own way."

There was a long pause now. Jacob didn't seem quite finished with his story—as if there was something he still wanted to say. Tori did not speak a word, as if she knew that doing otherwise would somehow deter Jacob's sudden extroversion. Roy also stood quiet, allowing Jacob to gather his thoughts and choose his words, though he suspected he would still be unable to vocalize his thoughts.

"Heramyr decided to destroy the city, and Argus agreed with his decision and moved to take action. Though he had had a personal vendetta against the place, it was clearly something bigger than revenge. Had he opted for revenge, killing the lord would have sufficed. This had been something entirely different.

"He doesn't speak about it often. Heramyr was a good friend to him. With the Alexander Castle destroyed, only King Whaldo Alexander was left to succeed, a baby that was not even born. The expecting mother, Serinah, ruled as Queen Regent until Whaldo grew of age.

"Some of the zalphics still wanted to strike the entire Alexander name. They attempted to kill Serinah with the expecting baby. Argus knew about this plot, and mentioned it to Jackson. The Wisest One, however, overheard this, and protected the queen from the attempt. Argus was surprised at his actions—the Alexanders had attempted to kill him, yet he was protecting her. The Wisest One saw past the attempts of hiding the murder, and kept her safe.

"This of course all caused trouble for Argus, and zalphics. The Firion Calamity, the death of King Raymond, Queen Serinah's attempted murder, and how they indicted us zalphics for all of it, all of it made our lives more difficult. We were further targeted and suppressed. Argus took the people that had decided to join him to the Capital, but with the increased hunt of those with fire, he did not think it prudent to stay.

"The Wisest One was a friend to Lord Horus and Lord Kingston, and understood their situation. He convinced Queen Serinah to send Hal Horus to Faldenheim to help the sick lord, and convinced her to name Allister Kingston lord of Vernatia. Not everyone accompanied Argus to Vernatia, so some remained in the Capital. They found though, that it was much too dangerous there, with the Queen Regent hunting them, so they moved elsewhere. A great lot of them chose to go to Arastaud, where the Alkarvan's were famous for their neutrality to most matters. Some went to Bloodpool, some went to Markai, and some went to Garrisbrough. Most opted to escape the discerning eyes of the Capital."

Roy had been intent on following the conversation, so when next he looked at the roof of the wagon, with Jacob looking in on him, and with a strong noise in the background, Roy was startled. Jacob said something, but now his ears were focusing on the noise he was hearing: it was the sound of countless voices, clamoring, and yelling, and of feet stomping and mounts neighing. Looking past Jacob, he saw men walking around, none of them paying any attention to them.

"Are you fine Roy?"

"Just a little tired. Where are we? What are we doing?"

Jacob pulled out the sword. It was made of Caster metal. It was Spark. *"You did well. We got the sword. We've been travelling to Chordica since leaving Highstorm. These are the men from Garrisbrough. We're going to join Argus. They're going to meet with Ferdinand there."*

Roy was a little disoriented. It seemed like only moments ago, he had been in Highstorm, feeling the surging thunder through him.

There was a beautiful garden. The greenery was a lushness that seemed only possible by a strong Wood zalphic. The green seemed much more lush and grand than to what she was accustomed. It was the beautiful green of the Lancaster Forest, with its assortment of trees and bushes and flowers which made it so magnificently desirable. The flowers were an appealing spectrum of colors, beautifying each other with their splendor. The trees rose like gentle giants, protecting the garden from the outside. They provided shade and grew their respective fruits. They lined her sight, providing the barrier and filling the garden with vivaciousness.

Animals lined the garden, moving and singing and flying all over. The cats walked gently on the grass, leaving no more than a slight imprint as they neared the shade of one of the trees. The birds flew, filling the air with their songs of joy and pleasantry. The poisonous insects climbed on the non-reactive cats. The insects passed them, wishing them no harm, and proceeded towards the trees. The animals were peaceful towards one another and did not fight amongst themselves for shade or fruit. They passed each other lazily, no longer wary of the danger of others.

The bright light shone immaculately on the garden. The gentle clouds had already receded from the sky, allowing the sun to stay lustrously in the clear skies. The gentle breeze pushed the leaves on the trees ever so slightly, and gave the life a nice and refreshing breath. The place was desirable, and in no place was there excrement or filth, or any tainting view.

The rivers watered the land, lending it the green gloss. The rivers spread throughout the garden—two rivers crossed, flowing with blue liquid. The current was not rapid. The current gently followed its course, watering everything and anything. The pure water shone splendidly, and the cleanliness was a marvel.

Kesara looked up at the sky. She was almost blinded by the immense light, but it did her no harm and was no inconvenience. She reached for a fruit, but could not reach it on account of her height. She turned, trying to find something with which to climb, but none of the worldly artifacts with which she was familiar were around. A bird from up high descended, grabbing the fruit with its talon and gently landing towards Kesara. The bird dropped the fruit onto her hand. The fruit was blue with some red splotches, unlike any fruit she had seen, and it was in perfect condition: it was round, plump, with no signs of damage from the talons nor any sort of worm burrowing inside. The fruit felt smooth and clean. Kesara looked up to the bird as it flew away. "Thank you," Kesara said to the bird aloud.

"You're welcome," a voice replied. The voice was that of a young lady, some years older than her. Kesara was startled as the garden ceased to be, and she saw only red lines and spherical lights in front of the dark background. She opened her eyes, only to see the same red lines on the head of a young lady. The lady looked back at her compassionately. "How are you feeling?"

"Disoriented," Kesara said. "Tired." She tried getting up, but felt pain in her sides.

"You should rest."

"Who are you? Where am I? What happened? Tadeus...."

"My name is Allison. You are in the Lancaster Forest. You were wounded by someone, presumably Tadeus and his group."

"I...my brothers." Kesara turned, trying to find them. "Where are my brothers?"

"They will be fine. You need to rest."

"How did you find us? I thought we were alone. I thought Tadeus would...."

"You were on the ground, each suffering from serious wounds. Did you do something to someone? Or did they find out you were all zalphics?"

Kesara stiffened. "We...are not zalphics. We were travelling to Timbergrove. They assaulted us."

Allison smiled at her. "I healed you. You needn't worry. I know you're zalphics." Kesara still did not say something. *Who is she? Allison? Why does she have red hair...?* "I also know that these men made it look like some sort of beast killed you. They did a very good job, as well. That is not something that happens often." Kesara still did not say anything, even if Allison had saved their lives. Well, hers—she still hadn't seen the others. "You seemed to have the least severe wounds. You were also...untouched let's say." Kesara parted her gaze, embarrassed."

"Why did you help us?"

"My friend seemed bent on saving you. She tried her best to hide her emotions from me, but I could tell seeing you had a particular toll on her."

"Your friend?"

"Yes, she's another zalphic. She grew largely distressed when she saw you, so she brought me to you, and then I healed you."

"Did you study with the Wise Ones?" Kesara asked.

"I was taught, not necessarily to heal, by the best. He *is* part of the Wise Ones. I am simply a long-time friend of his."

"Why did your zalphic friend care so much?"

"She has her reasons. It is not my part to interrogate her."

"Is it because she thinks we're zalphics?"

"That's what she would like me to believe. She obviously didn't think too far ahead. I think she doubted I could help you. When you see her, you can ask her."

"Where are we?"

"Remember that long-time friend of mine I just mentioned? This place belonged to him."

"Belonged?"

"He passed it on."

"But we're...." Kesara stood silently, finally realizing where they were. What was Allison doing here? How did she get in? Who was this long-time friend?

"My friend should be here soon. Just rest."

#

33. Fallen Castle- 505

Chapter 34
Lancaster

The company from Garrisbrough marched steadily forward until they had met with the army from the Capital. They were to head east, going around the Desert Lands of Chordola, until they were between Chordica and the Korscher Mountains. King Ferdinand Alexander would leave his jail in Vernatia and travel to Bravania, from where he was to go south towards the same midpoint between Chordica and the Korscher Mountains. No one knew why the Wisest One had chosen this location, but no one questioned him and listened obediently. The Wisest One travelled in a glorious wagon, where only Lord Horus and Lord Kingston were allowed. When Lord Kingston wasn't visiting the Wisest One in the wagon, he was confined to the party escorting the Lord, towards the right and front of the entire army. No one expected a fight, but that did not mean King Whaldo had not made preparations and armed all his men with sharpened swords and fine arrows.

Roy was still weary, but he was walking afoot with Lord Kingston's party. Jacob Victoriano was in charge of defending Lord Kingston, while Valadiar Helmsdan was protecting the Wisest One—even if he was unable to enter the tent and talk with him. Lord Bastion and King Whaldo travelled together, but Orton Eridan was in charge of protecting both of them. Horaclys Naeia stayed at the Capital, to protect King Whaldo's mother, Serinah. Roger Weiracle was spared to protect Lord Horus. With Uracli Cristem in Garrisbrough, protecting Lady Elana Bastion and the princesses, all the Bladesmen of Garrisbrough were accounted for.

It was now that certain moment where Lord Kingston was to visit the Wisest One. Lord Horus went to the tent at the same time. Jacob accompanied Lord Kingston, and Roy went as well. He was not allowed anywhere close to the king, but he thought a locked chest mattered little when compared to a mansion of riches. Valadiar Helmsdan stood haughtily in front of the tent. Jacob lowered his head, showing respect for the Bladesman. *Jacob mentioned Valadiar was one of the strongest Bladesmen, bested only by Prince Oliver and Lord Bastion.* Although Valadiar knew Jacob, he did not let him pass. Only Lord Kingston passed, as Valadiar watched carefully. Roger Weiracle also lowered his head to both Valadiar and Jacob. Jacob had called Roger the weakest Bladesman in the order. *And he would still leave you in the dust,* he had added. He wondered how Jacob would fare against Valadiar if he would be able to use his zalphic powers.

It did not matter. Jacob would never be able to.

Lord Kingston and Lord Horus saluted each other and disappeared into the tent. Nothing could be heard. The Wisest One had not even allowed King Whaldo to demand an audience with him—the power he must have held over him was astounding.

Roy dreamed of a world in which he wielded so much power. Roy wore a gold cloak and talked down to the king. His advice was sought all over the land. His enormous skill with a sword and his vast knowledge over everything made him famous in the world. Even then, he knew it wasn't enough. All the most beautiful ladies in all of Andros wished to be with him. Roy would walk past his adoring fans, mad with an idea. Being the smartest man in all known history, he discovered the key to life: an herb that cured death, and even reversed its effects. He sought and found the most beautiful girl in all the land: a girl with short, curly hair, purple eyes, a slender build, supple skin, and a radiant smile. *Aurora.* He saw her rise from the grave, and the tears made way through and from the hardiness of the Caster metal wall he called his heart. Aurora was grateful to be resurrected, but she didn't cling to Roy and ask to be his. She had respect for herself, and she recognized that it was he who killed her. She turned away from him, and lived her life in contentedness while Roy fought with the skill of a Swordsmaster and thought with the acuity of the Wisest One. He tried winning Aurora's favor—and only after countless years did he win her heart, and they had a child together.

As a family, they rode on their pet fellcondor. He flew around all of Andros, bringing peace to the land. The King, ever so grateful for his tireless efforts to improve the circumstances of the land, named him heir. The heir showed up in all the various keeps of the land and inspired the people. He did not speak, and it was instead Aurora. He sat next to her, content to stay quiet while Aurora worked her endless charm and won over the masses. He was content. He did not need to lead. He did not need to act. He just needed to be with Aurora. They travelled to Arastaud and met the auburn-haired Alkarvans. They went to Telkos and met the dark-haired and medium-toned Telks. He flew to the Lost Forest and met the original Lancasters: the fair-haired and fair-skinned dwellers of the forest. He flew across the Korscher Mountains, and met the dark-eyed and darker-skinned Korschers that inhabited the rocky terrain. He met so much other people, but he didn't really meet any of them, and he was happy.

He saw his daughter grow into a young lady, beautiful, smart, and talented. When the king passed away, he was named King of Andros. King Wisest One-Raze raised a campaign for the acceptance of zalphics. He made the people realize that they were all people—that they were all the same. The only truly important differences were those that they fabricated. zalphics did not merit all the disdain they received. After successfully turning the masses to accept the zalphics, Roy killed all the Telks. They were the cause for all the suffering of the Androsii. It was the Telks who had invaded the peaceful Lancasters in their forest. The Lancasters, in retaliation, were forced to defend themselves with their powerful weapons. The Telks had instigated everything. The Lancasters would not have left their forests. Even with the Great Shaking, they would have remained in whatever forest remained and lived peacefully. The Telks were the ones who came and destroyed parts of it. Roy Rhapsados killed every single remaining Telk. He killed and exterminated the race, finally bringing peace and acceptance in the land. With the Telks gone, the conquered Redimer people rose to power. Those from which descended the Alkarvans came to power.

The Alkarvans had come to Andros after the Great Shaking. The Redimer people were slaves, and they had been defeated, so upon hearing that the Alexanders had landed on a place they called Andros, they made preparations to embark on a voyage. They crossed the seas after what seemed like years, but was truly a month. Since they had little to lose, they travelled and left their lives behind. The former slaves landed in Whaldo's Port and were forced to join the fight against the Lancasters. The Lancasters killed many of the Alkarvan people. When they were allowed to travel south, they settled primarily in three places: Arastaud, Kervin Port, and Alk Harbor. Unlike in Telkos, where they were suppressed and killed, the Alkarvans thrived. They became extremely strong, but refused to support their former captives, the Telk Alexanders, nor did they wish to support those that had killed them upon landing, the Lancaster Banesworths. No one knew why they did not join the Korschers, but they had chosen to stay neutral in most matters.

With the Redimer people in the reins of power in Telkos, some of the Alkarvans started returning to their original lands. A mass exodus occurred, and the majority of the Alkarvan family returned to the conquered lands of the Telks, and resettled their land. Soon, the Alkarvans all went back. They had some considerable power in Andros, but in Telkos, they were kings. The power called them back with a lulling song, amplified vociferously by kinship. There was nothing they could do against the call, and the Alkarvans left, abandoning the only other castle except Bravania whose rulers had not changed since the beginning of Androsii history.

The King established himself and his progeny as future kings and queens of Andros. With the Alkarvans gone, he named the Sullivans as Lords of Arastaud, and his friend Brandon Sullivan was now Lord of Arastaud along with his other privilege as member of the Committee of the Wise Ones. The Sullivans now ruled Arastaud, and Whaldo's Port was under the command of Jackie Flores. He questioned shortly why he had chosen her, but he disregarded the thought and allowed it. Then there were only the Korschers.

The Benders had come at the request of Ferdinand Alexander. When Roy Rhapsados killed all the Telks in Andros, the Korschers had zealously helped to eradicate their kind. After the war against them, Roy sentenced them back to the Desert Lands of Chordola. As the Wisest One, he had discovered a method in which to grow even the most delicate flowers in the harshest terrains, such as the Desert Lands. With this newfound method, Roy transformed the Desert Lands of Chordola into a veritable oasis. When their lands were tampered with, the Korschers had decided to abandon the lands and go east, back to the Korscher mountains. Roy had accomplished a dream.

The Lancasters retook the land of Andros.

Kesara Hewley awoke with much of her strength regained. Whoever Allison was, she was undoubtedly good at attending wounds. She relived constantly the battle with Tadeus, and saw the horrible wounds inflicted on all of them. She saw Gideon yelling out in pain as he burned alive, and saw as his skin turned black with fire and pain. His cry rang out, piercing her. She saw as the flames around him receded, with Ben using his powers to remove them. The fire might have disappeared, but his burns were unmistakable. His face was almost unrecognizable. Grief stretched Ben's features as he approached Gideon, desperate to see that he would be alright. Then Guardiana cut through Ben with sickening ease. With no resistance, the Caster metal sliced through his body. Max's body offered a similar lack of resistance. She had gazed into his eyes. Tadeus hated zalphics. At that moment, he had hated her for being one. He had hated that she was a zalphic, but not *because* she was a zalphic.

She tried using thunder again, but to no avail. She could not recreate the thunder. She was unable to use her water either, leading her to believe she was still too weak, or Allison had done something to her when she was "healing" her. This made her wary of Allison. She hadn't explained who she was, or how she knew they were zalphics, nor who her zalphic friend was. Kesara rose, going towards another room. There, she saw some fruits on a platter. She felt weak, and thought perhaps it was due to a lack of food. She grabbed a fruit and bit into it. She went towards a room, where she saw her brother, Ben, resting. Allison had said that

Kesara had suffered the least severe wounds, but she could not see any such wounds on her brother. He rested, continuously breathing lightly, and rising his chest infinitesimally. Kesara went up to him, feeling the warmth of his skin. She felt Ben's skin, and felt where his wound should be. Miraculously, she felt nothing—only skin. Ben didn't wince when she touched it, it had no bruising or any other discoloration, nor did it feel any different from the rest of his body.

Next to him was Max, who seemed in a similar condition to Ben. His face did not show where Kesara accidentally stabbed him. His wounds seemed to have disappeared as well. He serenely lay next to Ben. Both their red cloaks lay on the ground, stained darkly by something. The two seemed content, at rest. Kesara wanted desperately to wake them up and talk with them, but she was afraid to deprive them of their rest. She wanted to ask her brother for help, but it was she who needed to help her brother now, and it troubled her. She went towards Gideon, where Allison had her hand on his face. Kesara stood silently and gazed, watching her brother for a long time. "He will be alright Kesara," she said without turning.

"How did you know it was me?"

"I could just tell. Your brother Ben should be up soon, as should Max."

"How do you know our names?"

"I talked with my friend. She knew who you were."

"How do you know about this place? It belongs to my brother."

"*Belonged.*" *How does she know us?* Kesara wondered. Kesara was slightly angered. *She shouldn't know about this place.*

"Who are you? Why do you know so much about us?"

"Your brother got up. I'm sure you would rather talk to him," she said, still not diverting her gaze from Gideon. Kesara turned around, hearing someone moving. Kesara turned back towards Allison, wondering how she knew that. Kesara went with her brother, asking him immediately if he was feeling well.

"I'm fine. Kesara, did you take us all here? What happened?" Kesara expressed her similar confusion. She didn't exactly know. Ben turned to Max, and after seeing that Max had no visible wounds, he went towards Gideon. Allison was still working on him. His burns were not as bad as Kesara remembered. She knew that she remembered the burns vividly, so seeing him in that state was a relief.

"Who are you?"

"You all seem to think that by continuously asking me that question that my answer will change. My name is Allison, I am a zalphic travelling with another friend of mine in the Lancaster Forest. My friend found you on the ground with severe wounds, and she implored me to help you. We went here, where I cured your wounds. As for your brother Gideon, I could not do too much about the external wounds, as I can only fix the internal problems."

"You have red hair."

"Everyone always points that out."

"Are you an Alkarvan?"

"Yes. I am."

"I've never heard of you. There's Lady Dalia, Prince Oliver, Princess Samantha, Princess Alice, and the Princelings May and Oskar."

"Sweet Dalia. She was only fifteen when I left."

"*Fifteen?* Lady Dalia was fifteen almost fifty years ago. You are no more than thirty."

"Is that what you think, Ben?" Ben turned to Kesara, confused. "I can know you are zalphics, I can heal deadly wounds which no one, not even Trevor could cure, and I can be here, red hair and all, but you can't believe that I'm not sixty-eight years old?"

"Sixty-eight? That's not possible."

"I did not lie. My name is Allison Alkarvan, rightful Lady of Arastaud, denounced and denied my birthright after being discovered to be a zalphic. After I left, my sister Dalia was named heir to Arastaud. She married the man I was supposed to marry, Greymont. I don't hold a grudge against her. It wasn't her idea nor her doing."

"That's impossible. You are young." She lifted her finger, and a strong gust started blowing inside the room. The fruits all started falling to the ground, but they stopped just short of the floor and circled around in the air. The fruits were then positioned back on the plate. She turned around.

"There is so much you still don't know. I'm a zalphic with powers you've never seen—not truly anyway. Try and shoot me with your fire, Ben." Ben stared at her, not sure what to do. "Nothing will happen. Shoot me with your fire." Ben shot a slight ember at her. The ember stopped in the air, where it circled around again, forming a ring of fire. Allison put her hand inside the ring, and then the flames constricted, but they disappeared before burning Allison's wrist. "I was hoping for something a little stronger. Max. Water."

Kesara turned around, startled to see Max standing behind them. Max rose his hand, but nothing came out. He tried again, this time looking at his hand in wonder. "Do not worry Max. You haven't lost your powers, nor have I given you anything. This is simply me stopping you with my powers. Kesara. You can choose what you wish to send at me. Thunder perhaps?"

"She doesn't have thunder," Ben replied.

"Amazing how much you think you know because of your telekinesis. Tell me, could you tell what power I have? Even with your abilities?" Ben didn't say anything, and rather stood silent. "Even telekinesis is flawed. You can only see one of the powers."

"How can you prevent someone from using their powers?" Max asked.

Allison turned to him. "The Z1 mutation, as they call it, is very special. Just as telekinesis offers you a plethora of powers, my powers also are numerous." Kesara raised her hand. *Thunder.* She unleashed a jet of water which swirled around an imaginary center. When the water was halfway to Allison, thunder shot from her hand, occupying the center of the jet. The water and the thunder shot off in a different direction as it approached Allison, and then circled around Allison. Both disappeared, leaving behind no trace.

"You really are Allison Alkarvan," Ben said, amazed.

"I suppose I don't blame you for doubting me. It is a lot to take in."

"So you healed us? With your powers?"

"Yes."

"And you brought us here? To keep us safe while you healed us?"

"Something like that."

"But how did you know about this place?" asked Kesara. "How did you know this was here?"

"My long-time friend. It was his. This is where I met him."

"Your long-time friend?"

"I would tell you about him, but it is not my life to share. He wishes to remain anonymous."

"Why are you helping us?"

"Is it not enough that I helped you? I need a reason?"

"We are grateful for what you've done, Allison. I am just curious as to why you helped us."

"My friend was the one who decided you needed to live. I would have left you." Kesara stared blankly at their strange savior. "Understandably, I do not want it known I am here."

"Where is this friend of yours?"

"She went to gather supplies for your brother. As I mentioned, burns are not something I have too much power over."

"We are grateful for what you've done Allison. I'm sorry to ask you so much, but we are confused. How is it you know our names then? That can't be part of your powers as well."

"No, that is my friend. But she's coming right now. Perhaps you would like to ask her yourselves."

Kesara turned toward Allison's gaze, where she heard nothing for a while before hearing someone running and breathing hard. Hurriedly, the zalphic descended into the room. Even before seeing the zalphic, Kesara could tell the person cared. They ran, in hurry to help them, and they were breathing hard, which meant they had been running for a long while now. When Kesara glimpsed the zalphic who was apparently friends with Allison, she almost jumped out of glee. She no longer mistrusted Allison, and now she didn't care about everything about which she had worried.

"Aurora!" Kesara exclaimed in glee.

###

514 - The Midnight War

Chapter 35
Bend

Roy Rhapsados marched complacently with Whaldo's army, and among the ranks of Lord Kingston's party. They were now entering between the Desert Lands of Chordola and the Fallen Castle of Alexander. To either side, they had deserts and lava heating the air around them. Roy felt suffocated by the heat, and their ceaseless march did nothing to help. King Whaldo had separated slightly from his army. He and a small party went to the edge of the land enveloped by the lava from the Firion Volcano. Roy could see it clearly, towering high above the rest of the flat land. He had no wish to get any closer to it, nor imagine what the Alexanders must have felt upon seeing it erupting. The sight was strange—it was his first glimpse of the Firion Volcano. Always it had appeared in his mind as an enormous volcano, continuously spewing lava and burning with the fiery red of its lava. It would always cause tremors and provide excessive heat. The Firion Volcano would always burst with energy. The real Firion Volcano seemed almost complacent. It stood calm and did not spurt with energy. No lava escaped the top of the Firion Volcano, and instead it simply stood in a field of an aqueous red.

Tori spent her time walking around, not really doing much. Roy recognized with chagrin that he was doing much of the same thing. He simply marched with them. Tori accompanied Jacob while he took Lord Kingston to the Wisest One's enormous wagon. Lord Kingston entered, alone. Roy wondered how anyone could suffer staying inside the wagon. It was more of a roaming room—it was big enough to sleep in, and bring some visitors inside. Roy imagined himself being trapped in there, and felt glad that he was walking. He felt respite in the soft pain in his feet as he took another step. He stirred with anxiety at thinking of being in the wagon, never stepping out or seeing the sun, but rather staying in there, eating, drinking, resting, while some of his friends visited.

Lord Kingston stayed inside the wagon long, and Roy was disinterested, but noticed Prince Argus standing next to Valadiar Helmsdan. It was strange, seeing Prince Argus just outside of the wagon. He recalled that the instructions were no one with the exception of Lord Kingston and Lord Horus could enter the tent, but Roy wondered why Prince Argus and Jackson were not allowed inside. The Wisest One demonstrated love for those two, and Roy thought they too would be able to enter. It was the first time Roy saw Argus waiting outside of the wagon. Argus must have known he would be unable to enter, so Roy thought it strange he should be there, waiting.

Would Argus be able to defeat Valadiar in sword combat? Probably not, if Jacob is to be believed. But what about Jacob? Could Prince Argus beat him? Jacob was his subordinate, and Jacob followed Argus and his instructions, but Roy wondered how Argus would fare if he were a member of the Order of the Sword. Jacob was talking with Tori, while Argus just seemed to look inside. When Lord Kingston exited, Argus immediately turned and waited patiently for his father to join him. He seemed pensive, and began talking quickly to his father while they walked back towards their party. Roy followed back, noticing how distressed Argus was. They continued talking, separating themselves from everyone else while they continued walking. Roy could see a rider racing towards Whaldo's army. Roy wondered what the rider could have possibly seen, as he galloped quickly towards them. Without stopping, he went through the army as some of them scattered to move out of the way.

Men started rushing to the front with their swords drawn. Continuing their march, they eventually saw a group of people, waiting. Roy turned to Lord Kingston and Argus, who seemed to have stopped arguing. Lord Kingston walked towards the front of the group, and instructed the entire party to follow him. They all went forward, but the men in the front instructed them to stop. Lord Bastion went towards the group. Orton Eridan was not near him, which meant that he was with King Whaldo, and King Whaldo was not going to approach the group. Lord Bastion set out to talk to the group, while King Whaldo's army slowed their advance. From the distance, it was observable that the group consisted of Korschers. They waited, but observably were not looking to fight Whaldo's army.

Lord Kingston went towards the Korschers and Lord Bastion, so consequently Argus and Jacob went with him. Roy followed closely by as well. When Lord Kingston reached the group, Lord Bastion turned to him, telling him that he should not be there.

"King Ferdinand has sent me to ensure Lord Kingston's safety."

"Lord Kingston is perfectly safe with Whaldo's army surrounding him."

"I want you to repeat what you just said, and think about that."

"*Nothing* will befall him," Lord Bastion answered.

"King Ferdinand would feel more at ease if Lord Kingston was with us."

"It is not up to Ferdinand to decide. He comes with us, as was agreed by Ferdinand when he first sent him here."

"Lord Bastion," began Lord Kingston, "King Ferdinand instructed me to go to the Capital, in your company, so that I may partake in the Committee of the Wise Ones, and to put an end to the war. I have met with that obligation, as I have been among your party, and I have deliberated with Lord Horus and the Wisest One on a treatise to end the war."

"King Whaldo will not allow you to take him."

"Lord Bastion," began the Korscher, "we realize the required delicacy of the situation, but Lord Kingston is not your captive. He is not a prisoner, and belongs next to King Ferdinand."

Lord Bastion didn't know what to say to that, as he turned towards the direction of the army. "Cyrus, this isn't so simple that I can simply hand Lord Kingston to you and continue our march. I must speak to the King."

"Talk to your King all you want. Lord Kingston is not your hostage, and has every right to leave the party and join us and the army."

Lord Bastion turned, signaling Lord Kingston to follow suit. He headed back towards the army. Roy wondered if Lord Bastion should have more power, being lord to the mightiest of the castles, and a Bladesman and leader of the Order of the Sword, or if it should be Lord Kingston, who was an Elder, and a member of the Committee of the Wise Ones, an order above all others in the land. Regardless, Lord Kingston followed Lord Bastion towards King Whaldo. Roy stayed put, not rejoining those that went back. Cyrus Bender stood complacently. Next to him was Jennifer, and the guy that never seemed to leave her side, an Earth zalphic, Jon. There was another swordsman close to them. *Jennifer Bender. Daughter of Cyrus Bender*, he assumed, which meant that the swordsman was in charge of protecting her. Jennifer looked at Roy, but turned around quickly upon meeting his gaze. Roy looked at her abashed face, confused. Roy wondered why she looked at him so strangely, and tried recalling anything he could. She was a Bender, descendant of Chordric, and she was an Earth zalphic. Her twin sister Amy was killed by...someone. She was the daughter of Jessica and...*Patrick* Bender. *So she is the niece,* Roy corrected himself. She had a Caster metal sword, *Smasher,* and she was the Chordun.

    Still, Roy could not place where he would know her. Her uncle moved to Vernatia, but her dad and mother were in Faldenheim. *Perhaps I met her there,* thought Roy. *She meant something to someone.* Roy stood there in silence while in another location, away from Roy's vision, King Whaldo and Lord Bastion discussed what they would do. He awaited, standing awkwardly as elsewhere they were deciding. Roy wanted to go up to Jennifer and talk with her, and try to recollect his memory. Instead, he watched as Jon and Jen laughed, and as the other swordsman stood sternly. Roy thought of Aurora, thought of both of them talking, of the both of them laughing at jokes only funny to them. He could almost smell her hair and imagine the smoothness of her skin as they held hands and huddled up close to each other. Aurora would say something witty, and Roy would reply with something equally as witty.

    He wanted to be with Aurora, and was tormented by the pain and suffering he had caused himself. Aurora was gone. He would never see her again. But he couldn't accept that. He wanted there to be hope—some sort of manner in which he would see her again. He could not accept that she was gone. He saw Jennifer, and was envious of Jon. He wanted to be in their position, and be with someone who he could love.

But you could never love anyone, he thought to himself.

Aurora Stephensen was overwhelmed with happiness upon seeing the three of them roaming about. When she had seen them, on the floor and suffering gaping wounds, she was afraid that she would be the last one to see them alive. She was thankful that this was not the case, and she owed a great debt to Allison for treating them. Aurora looked appreciatively at Allison as she explained some of her powers to the others.

"So do you protect yourself only with your powers?"

"Primarily yes. But sometimes I have need of a sword."

"Where is it?"

"I can summon it at command." Allison opened her hand, and a sword materialized out of the encircling winds. *Talon* appeared in her hand, shining with the familiar Caster metal glow.

"That's a Caster metal sword. I've only seen certain people do that."

"It's a manifestation of the power, both of the sword and of the person. For me it is a manifestation of air. This one is special though. It appears at my whim. To summon other swords, I have to actively summon it." Again, a whirlwind appeared in her other hand, but this time the winds were stronger, and she took longer. With some visible effort, another Caster metal sword appeared in her hand. This one gleaned with a special green hue, while Talon glowed with an immaculate white.

"Do you have so much Caster metal swords just lying to be summoned?" Allison shook her head. "How incredible—this metal is extremely rare. Can you summon my sword?"

Allison stood for a while before shaking her head. "No, I can't. Your sword is like mine. Like Talon," she said, raising the Caster metal sword glowing with white. "I can't summon yours either, Max." Maximillius took his sword out with the manifestation of his powers. A small stream of water proceeded from his hands, circling, and converging until it finally came to look like a sword.

The water ceased to be, and Azure took its place, firmly grasped by Max's hand. Upon seeing this, Ben did the same with Infernus: a fire took root in the palm of his hands, and spread to the air above it. The flames flickered and expanded, gradually making their way upwards. The fires seemed to be setting ablaze a sword hidden underneath, and when the flames vanished, Infernus glowed quickly with red.

"Any idea why you can't do it with our swords?"

"Yeah. My friend mentioned something of the sort—a long time ago. There are swords pertaining to some strange beasts. The Khisharat. The Okran. The Chordun."

"I thought those were just stories," said Kesara.

"They are quite real. Well, at least the Okran. I've seen it."

"You've *seen* it. The Okran?" Gideon asked.

"Yes. Or at least, one of its children. That is where I got this sword," Allison said, pointing to the other Caster metal sword. "It is the fabled sword from its back: Forester."

"That's *Forester?* How is that possible? If the Okran is real, you would never be able to find it because it can use its power to hide. And even if you found it, it would strike you with its tail or kill you with its roar," Ben said incredulously.

"My powers allowed me to find it. Something else about Air."

"Does it really appear as the stories mention it?" asked Maximillius.

"I met one of its daughters. She was quite intimidating. But I trust it now. She even helped me recover a book I lost once."

"*She?*"

"Yes. The Okran with which we are familiar was a female. She is no longer living, but when the Great Shaking separated the Okran from its native lands, she was pregnant. Her children roam the lands. They prefer to be much deeper in the forests though."

"This is a lot to take in."

"More than learning that I cured your wounds, I'm an Air zalphic, or that Aurora was with me?"

"Something like that," said Kesara. Suddenly, she seemed to have realized something. She looked at Aurora, with a confused gaze. She turned to Allison and back to Aurora, then turned around to her brothers and Maximillius. "Allison. You kept saying that Aurora was the one who convinced you to help us."

"Yes," admitted Allison. "That is true."

"But you didn't call her by name. You said your zalphic friend. zalphic." Ben and Gideon and Maximillius and Kesara all turned to Aurora. She had thought they had known, or that they had understood. She smiled at their shock, though felt their awe was misplaced. Perhaps this is what she had done to them when she had learned that they were all zalphics.

"Yes. I am an Air zalphic. Just like Allison. Just as Steven was. I have the power."

"Aurora...." Kesara could not say much past her shock.

"When did you...," began Ben, but he could not finish.

"Is that why you managed to survive zalphia?" asked Kesara.

Aurora didn't know, but she had considered the possibility. "I don't know. Perhaps. I can think of no other reason why I could have survived zalphia."

"Could you...could you *cure* zalphia?" Ben asked. Aurora turned to Allison. She was not certain—neither of them were. Aurora had spoken with Allison about her zalphia, and they had discussed at length the possibility, but they had no manner to determine.

"I do not think so. In any case, I've not met anyone with zalphia. They tend to stay home and rest, not venture out to the Lancaster Forest."

"There was another Air zalphic," began Aurora, "but he developed zalphia and died. For me, it was the opposite: I had zalphia, then developed my powers over air. Clearly, having the powers of an Air zalphic does not absolutely cure zalphia, but my circumstances seem to suggest it could have some effect." Aurora thought about that other boy. He was already an Air zalphic, and had already manifested some of his powers over Air before he got sick of zalphia. *Two extremely unlikely diseases, and he was struck with both of them. How unlucky for him,* thought Aurora. Of course, to her, it was not a disease, but to him it must have seemed that way. *It's not a matter of aptitude, since I had no powers before recovering from zalphia. I proved that zalphia is not deadly without fail—or perhaps I simply relapsed. But Allison has found nothing wrong with me. The only thing that separates me*

35. Bend- 521

apart from everyone else is my powers. She was not familiar if other zalphics had also developed zalphia, but she was certain it would have had to happen before.

"Allison, I hate to ask you this, but I must." Aurora turned to Ben. "I don't imagine Aurora has developed curing powers, since you were the one who helped us. The only thing the Wise Ones seem to be able to do is prolong his symptoms. Could you...come to Farendor with us? It's next to Faldenheim." Aurora saw Ben's gaze, full of misery and frustration. *One of his parents is sick.* Steven's words came rushing back to her. *I forgive them.* Aurora considered briefly what those words could have meant. *He was angered because he discovered that one of them was a zalphic. His dad was dying because he was a zalphic.* "My father is dying. He is sick. Could you help him?"

"Ben. I know it must not have been easy to ask this of me. However, I cannot help you. I cannot leave the Lancaster Forest. I have to stay here."

"Why?" Ben asked, fighting to hold back his anger. Aurora knew he was desperate.

"I cannot leave. I will not. But that does not mean I cannot help him. My friend, he can help your dad. He will not let your father die."

"Who is your friend then, so that I might seek him out?"

"It is not my life, so it is not my story to share with you. But he will help."

"How can he help if I don't know him, and he doesn't know who my father is?" Ben asked, now failing to stop his voice from rising.

"My friend will not let your father die. He will help him. Trust in the Wise Ones to help him." That was not the first time Aurora had heard someone tell the other to confide in the Wise Ones. Aurora looked at Ben.

She wouldn't trust them either.

The Wise Ones knew too much, showing just how little they knew.

Chapter 36
Air

Aurora Stephensen was walking with Allison Alkarvan, Maximillius Stoddard, and Ben, Kesara, and Gideon Hewley. They were heading towards the edge of the Lancaster Forest. From there, the latter three would head back to Bravania, and meet with Wyatt Stephensen and Caspian Stoddard. Allison would not join them, and nor would Aurora, who planned to stay and learn more about her powers alongside Allison. Kesara had tried to convince her to go with them, insisting that her father was worried about her and that he would be glad to see her again. Aurora still refused, wanting to learn more still about Air. She asked Kesara to speak with her father, and inform him that she was in the forest, with friends who would protect her, and that he shouldn't worry. Kesara had been reluctant to do so, but Aurora convinced Kesara to do it for her.

They walked silently, no longer asking each other questions to satisfy their curiosity. No one directed any question to Allison regarding the power of air, nor did they address the same issue to Aurora. Ben and Maximillius walked together in silence. Perhaps they were communicating through telepathy, but neither of them voiced anything. Their expressions, too, remained unchanged, as they walked to the outskirts of the forest. Soon, they would be going to Bravania, and Aurora did not know how much longer it would be before she saw them again. It seemed as if she should care and want to converse, but she felt only like giving herself into introspection.

She thought about Steven. He had had the power of air, and this power gave him the ability to use telekinesis efficiently. Though his powers had not finished developing, it was his powers over air which allowed him to further his telekinetic abilities. Without the proper training, teleporting was limited to only what one could see. Very few inherently had the ability to teleport without such limitations, but his powers aided him in doing so. He knew naught of it, and was ignorant to the powers granted to him. He manifested an attack which no one ought to be able to use. In comparison to its full strength, it was relatively weak, but the attack was much too strong for him. In the process of the attack, he sealed Argus and Jackson's power. The power coursed through him, incapacitating him.

If only he had met Allison before, he would have known that his power of air would keep him alive. Instead, thinking it the end, he had used his remaining strength to send a message, and bless three people with the key to a locked potential. He contacted Roy and unlocked his power of Telekinesis. Roy learned the powers of Telekinesis and learned to control it through Steven—both when they shared minds and when Steven sent him the message. He transferred his powers and soon, Roy will be unparalleled in his telekinetic abilities. That is why Telekay is Roy's. To Kesara he unlocked her sealed powers as well, allowing her other powers to manifest. Kesara is just as special as Steven, and soon her powers will manifest and amaze the most adept—and demand jealousy from all else. To me...to me he gave me this. The power to live, and to survive my zalphia. I am here only because of him.

Steven left a visible inheritance. Roy had Telekay, Kesara had thunder, and Aurora was still alive—and this was only the beginning of the inheritance. Already, Roy had grown strong, managing to overcome the crippling effects of engrims. Kesara was only just manifesting her powers. Aurora still had a plethora of information to learn about air. But she also knew that Steven didn't have to die. If he had only known about his powers, he wouldn't have had to make the sacrifice. Aurora would have rather risked her fate with zalphia than the finality of his sacrifice. *A useless sacrifice.* That was the worst part for Aurora.

Of what she knew of air, Aurora knew the power was adept for protecting oneself. She could protect herself, and with the proper training, she could protect others as well. This is what had protected her from Roy at the keep in Faldenheim—what had protected her both times: when all else around had lost consciousness, and when Roy had unleashed his attack out of desperation from the engrims. She could not be hurt. She was invincible.

Why, then, do I feel so vulnerable? Aurora looked at Kesara. Kesara had determination to live on, while she had broken down with the death of Steven. Aurora didn't know how to deal with him gone. She could not get over it. Kesara continued on, and Aurora was stuck reminiscing. Steven was her best friend. She just didn't know how to get over it. *How can you live without your best friend? He was always there for me. He held me when I cried, comforted me when I was sad, and made me laugh when I wanted to scream. He listened patiently, and he cared so much about me. Now he's gone. What am I supposed to do about it?*

He is gone, and I cannot replace him. People may love me, and I love them, but it will never compare. It will never be the same. He is gone and I've no hope to see him again. Aurora's eyes grew watery. She wondered what she would do. Steven had been an important part of her. Now he was gone, and that gaping hole would only be filled by sadness and bitterness.

She could still recall when she had first met Steven:

The people were rejoicing. Festivities were all around, and the people had gone to the castle to have fun and dance and eat and drink. Aurora was with her friends. They were dancing and having fun. She hardly noticed that it was getting dark. The torches were lit, but it didn't provide much light. From behind her she heard, "Kesara, there you are!" She felt arms wrap around her. Then the strange boy asked "Are you enjoying yourself?"

The boy must have felt something was wrong. Perhaps it was the strange look her friends were giving him, or he could finally discern her features through the light of the torch. She didn't know. All she knew was that the boy awkwardly let go and backed away a little.

Aurora turned around and asked, "Who are you?"

The boy's reaction was hilarious. "Oh crap...I'm so sorry, I thought you were...oh man, sorry. I'm going to go now and hide in a corner. I'm sorry, I didn't mean to...Sorry."

Aurora laughed and asked, "Who is Kesara?"

36. Air- 525

"She's my sister. I thought you were her. I'm sorry. I didn't know...sorry."

"That's quite alright. You thought I was your sister? Either I really look like her or you really don't know your sister," she said with a grin, doing her best to contain her laughter.

"Sorry. It's dark and you have a similar stature, your hair is similar. You had your back to me. I'm sorry. I'll leave you alone now, forever."

Aurora couldn't help but laugh. This boy had mistaken her for his sister and felt an embarrassment that made her want to laugh more. The more she wanted to laugh, the more embarrassed he seemed. "What's your name 'boy who confuses girls for his sister'?"

"I'm Steven. Steven Hewley. I...this has never happened before. I'm sorry. This is awkward."

Aurora laughed a little and said "You gave me a good laugh. It's quite alright. I'm Aurora Stephensen. But now I have to meet this sister of yours, Steven Hewley." She could see the discomfort of Steven and his wish to literally hide in a corner. So of course, there was only one thing Aurora could say. "Come dance with me."

"Wha-what? Dance with you? I...um...I don't know what to say. I...uh...al-alright."

They went to the patch of area that was used for dancing. They danced to songs while Aurora got to know Steven. Now that he had composed himself more, he could better communicate. "What village are you from?"

"I'm from Farendor. I am going to start my studies here, under the Wise Ones."

"I'm from Farendor too, but I haven't seen you around. In any case, Steven, it seems like you will be seeing more of me, since I too will be studying with the Wise Ones."

After having danced with Steven, Aurora went with her friends. They were questioning her, asking her if she thought he was cute, wanting to know what they talked about. Aurora laughed and gave vague answers to their specific questions.

When it was time to leave, she saw Steven. She couldn't help but tease him one last time. "Goodbye brother. Oh, sorry, that isn't you." Steven looked at her. First he laughed at her taunt, but he looked down, clearly still embarrassed by what had happened.

"I'll see you soon I suppose. At the Wise Ones."

"Yeah. You're not getting rid of me *that* easily. I still have to meet your sister. I'm beginning to think you don't even have one."

Again, Steven turned a bright red. Aurora said farewell one more time and left.

#

Roy Rhapsados waited with the Korschers as the King's men were dispersing the supplies they had received which were sent from Bloodpool. Lord Kingston did not bother to pay attention, and instead went once again to visit the Wisest One. Jacob and some of the Korschers went with Lord Kingston to the wagon. The decision that had been made consisted of Lord Kingston being with the Korscher party, going towards Chordica. While Lord Kingston was permitted to go with them, and away from the army, the group was to stay close to the army. In other words, the Korschers were allowed to enter as part of Lord Kingston's party, expanding his forces and giving him just a few more liberties.

Roy wondered if Lord Kingston had insisted to stay, as the Wisest One had charged both him and Lord Horus to speak with him to discuss whatever matters they discussed in that wagon. There was, however, an equally plausible explanation: Lord Kingston was held against his will trapped around Whaldo's Army, and that despite his desires to leave with the Korscher party, he had been instructed to maintain pace with the army. The Korschers around him spoke only of going to Chordica. They were anxious, as was Whaldo, to meet up with Ferdinand and hear their fate. The Korschers did not have the same confidence in the Wisest One as all the Androsii, and they worried about continuing the war, and whether they would serve as the fodder which happened to lie between Whaldo's army and Ferdinand's army.

The men routed the supplies evenly, giving the important people supplies equivalent to their stature, and giving the future corpses that would simply serve as an obstruction supplies equal to their importance. The egalitarian nature of this distribution was amazing; first the supplies headed to those of import. The supply wagons crossed with the wagon of the Wisest One. There, they waited as Lord Kingston exited to take their message and determine what supplies the Wisest One would need. Lord Kingston dismissed them, and they proceeded to go towards other members of the Wise Ones. Another wagon had simultaneously travelled towards King Whaldo, who took a good portion of the supplies on the wagon, and then they proceeded to others. No man received more than he was worth, and their worth was predetermined by a set of rules that naturally separated them. Those that would only be food for the avian creatures of death were given minimal supplies. They continued their march without the proper boots and food. It seemed only fair if they were to be food, there would be less of them for the avian creatures to pick off. The equality of the supplies was so great that, even when the supplies were distributed completely, the equality still spread to those that had not received the supplies.

Roy turned to the Korschers around him. None of them seemed to like the idea of being surrounded by Whaldo's army. *If I were a Korscher, I'd* want *them to kill me,* thought Roy briefly. *If only Brandon were here,* he thought. He was bored of walking and waiting. They all were. Roy slowly was being poisoned by his thoughts. With nothing to distract him, he was ever-more engulfed in thoughts of Aurora, of the keep, of the Wise Ones. He wanted to kill. He considered exposing Tori as a zalphic, but the temporary satisfaction would result in prolonged consequences—assuming that Tori did not take him down with her.

Lord Kingston made his way back to the Korschers, and Jacob escorted him before retiring from his post. Jacob walked away from Lord Kingston, towards Tori, who was waiting impatiently, just as Roy did. The two, however, differed in their reason for waiting, and Tori walked off with Jacob to some unknown place. *Don't let her bandit friends kill you,* thought Roy. Then he considered whether that would be the worst thing that could happen. Jacob did not teach him how to be a strong warrior as he had hoped he would. Jacob did not seem to care to teach Roy about thunder and how to better control it. He especially had no interest in teaching him telekinesis, and it was only through watching others that he got a grasp on the power.

It was a simple power, despite all the complicated methods in which to use it. Roy had wanted to test his telekinetic powers, and see what he could accomplish. Whenever this happened, he remembered sourly that he had accomplished all this the final day of the attack on Faldenheim. The thought made him reluctant to further push his powers. He wanted no part in it. At that moment, Argus crossed into his field of vision. He recalled the power that Argus had manifested: even with his power somehow capped, he had caused the Eastern Gate Fire in Faldenheim. He thought of Heramyr Mortison and the Firion Calamity. Such power was possible, he only need to achieve the strength. Inane as it was, the thought that an Earth zalphic caused the Great Shaking crossed his mind. He wanted to be invincible.

They headed towards Chordica and the Korscher Mountains.

He wanted desperately to go to war.

Aurora Stephensen said farewell to Kesara Hewley upon reaching the outskirts of the Lancaster Forest. They hugged, as old friends did, but Aurora wanted to leave and learn about air. Her obsession with the knowledge seemed to worry Allison, who suggested they relax, or go to Timbergrove before they continue their training. Aurora immediately rejected the proposal. "Knowledge is the difference between eating a viable plant, and dying of poison. It is the difference between living your days with certainty, and hoping nothing will go wrong. ...It is the difference between giving your life with folly, and preserving it so that you might help others."

"No obsession is healthy, however reasonable it may seem."

"Obsessions stem from the fear of what we do not know."

"If you wish to continue, we shall continue." Aurora nodded her head and turned to the fruit on the high tree. She used her powers to create wind that would knock down a single fruit. The wind blew gently, ruffling the leaves of the tree. Aurora knew that more strength was required. She used her force to make a stronger wind. The wind quickly spanned the distance to the tree, striking it with metallic strength. Multiple fruits fell, splattering on the floor in a wasteful rain. Allison watched, not bothering to use her powers to stop the falling fruit. The new power took its toll, quickly and degenerately draining her energy. When Aurora reached towards one of the fallen fruits, Allison used her powers to crush the fruit to juice on the ground. Aurora looked up at Allison, who was staring again at the top of the tree. "You must be able to concentrate your powers, so that you only knock one of the fruits down."

Aurora wanted to reply that it did not matter if she could knock them all down. She then remembered as Roy unleashed a purple cat at her, who intended to claw at her fragile body. She knew that controlling the power was equally as important. She breathed deeply and tried again. This time, three fruits fell. Aurora attempted to catch one, but Allison used the wind to shoot the three at Aurora's direction. Aurora quickly and easily diverted the incoming fruits. She could protect herself—that was the first thing she had managed to do. Allison still liked testing Aurora, but the protective nature of her powers was strong. It had manifested before she had realized she had the power, and it continued to grow stronger. From behind her, the fruits sped towards her. Aurora spun them around her and pushed them forward. Again they were redirected, but this time they were headed towards the tree. Aurora tried to push the fruit aside, but she could not, and they crashed into the tree and splattered on its trunk. She had still not managed to protect others from anything—only herself. Seeing Aurora fail to divert the fruits from the tree, Allison walked up to her. She grabbed Aurora's hand and opened her palm. She grabbed Aurora's other hand and made her left hand grab her right wrist. Allison let Aurora's hands go, and used her powers to put a fruit on her palm. "Without moving your right hand, you need to lift the fruit."

To Aurora, this seemed a simple test. She could move something without her hand. It was quite easy. Without thinking, she tried moving the fruit. Her left hand kept her right hand in place, which in turn kept the fruit in place. Aurora was confused by this, and again tried moving the fruit, but to no avail. She

530 - The Midnight War

wondered if Allison was pushing down on the fruit, but Aurora knew that it wasn't a force pushing it down—there was just no force pushing it *up*. Aurora briefly let go of her right hand and saw as the fruit seamlessly rose as her right hand slightly rose with it. She stopped using her strength, and let the fruit fall back into her hand. She again grabbed her right hand and tried lifting the fruit. Again, she could not lift it. "Let's try something else. Let go of your hand."

Aurora let go, and Allison lifted the fruit with her powers. "Make it rest gently onto your palm." Allison stopped using her powers and let the fruit fall. Aurora slowed down its descent, where it landed lightly in her hand. "Again. This time, hold your wrist." Aurora grabbed her wrist, and Allison let go of the fruit. Try as she did, Aurora could not slow the fruit. It landed on her hand with a slight thud. "You rely too much on your hands to control your powers. The first rule of a zalphic is not to be caught." *Quite the expert, aren't you?* Aurora thought. She discarded the thought, thinking it petty to displace her frustration on her. "If you use your hands, people will see. If people see, they will assume you are a zalphic, regardless if they've ever seen your power before."

Aurora nodded her head. She knew Allison was right. She could not risk moving her hands to cause a gust of wind. It was much too conspicuous. She forced her hands to maintain still. After practicing longer, she succeeded in completing the small tasks Allison had been having her do. Aurora knew that her progress must have seemed slow to Allison, but Aurora confided in her ability to learn and apply what she learned. That skill, at least, she knew she had from the Wise Ones. She and Steven both had been the sharpest of the group.

Aurora kept learning from Allison. "You really are good at this, even if you don't realize it," Allison said. Aurora did not know what to say to Allison. To her, her progress in air was slow. She needed to learn what she could, and use it to protect herself, and protect her friends. "It took me months to learn what you have learned in weeks, and what took me multiple days, you've accomplished in but a few hours. My attempts to protect myself were flawed at best, and you manage to protect yourself with an ease you seem to think is inherent."

"It doesn't matter how much I learn in a given amount of time if I don't learn the important things—like protecting my friends and dissuading all doubts about my not have powers."

"You expect too much of yourself Aurora." Aurora wondered if she did. Allison could have valid observations; Aurora had never been satisfied with what sufficed. She had given herself the task to learn all there was about air with too short a time. *But you cannot compare yourself to others. The sharpest of swords are still dull in comparison to Caster metal.* Steven had taught her she was special. Whether others classified it as arrogance or confidence, Steven was smarter than most, and consequently he held himself to more demanding criteria.

"The only criterion I can use to judge my progress is my ability to manifest my powers in order to pass whatever test is coming."

###

Chapter 37
Raze

King Ferdinand's army and King Whaldo's army finally stood in front of each other. King Ferdinand Alexander was in the front lines of his army, accompanied by Lord Neister Banesworth, Prince Tadeus-Raze, Kayton Drost, and Garait Tiralus. Upon seeing the army, the Korscher party quickly went to join their allies, stepping aside and trying to avoid being in the middle of the two armies. Cyrus Bender went towards the King, where he joined them as the rest of the army positioned themselves. Lord Allister Kingston did not hurry to join Ferdinand, and instead stayed behind next to the wagon of the Wisest One. Lord Hal Horus and Valadiar Helmsdan remained at the wagon as well, zealously waiting for the Wisest One to exit. While the three stayed motionless next to the wagon, the others mobilized towards the front of the army. King Whaldo III Alexander was joined by Lord Fredrick Bastion, Orton Eridan, and Roger Weiracle. Caspian Stoddard walked towards King Whaldo's army, escorting Wyatt Stephensen, and a group of others containing Benjamin, Kesara, and Gideon Hewley, and Maximillius Stoddard. Caspian joined Orton Eridan and Roger Weiracle in protecting the King and Lord.

Roy Rhapsados accompanied Jacob Victoriano and the group and walked towards King Ferdinand's army, where Jacob Victoriano took his side next to Kayton Drost. Both Jacob and Roy wanted to see Tadeus-Raze and see his gold cloak for themselves, but Tadeus-Raze had it covered with some sort of cloth. King Whaldo and King Ferdinand did not stir, and they waited for the Wisest One to come out of his wagon to read the stipulated terms of the treatise. The tense armies stared constantly at the wagon's direction, where Lord Horus and Lord Kingston had now entered.

They tried waiting patiently for the three to exit, but the silence was louder than anything they could have said.

Finally, Lord Kingston and Lord Horus exited the wagon with a letter. They walked to the area between the two armies and looked around quickly before briefly talking quietly amongst themselves. "You must all be wondering where the Wisest One is, and this is understandable," began Lord Horus.

"We are all anxious to hear how Whaldo and Ferdinand will cohabitate on Andros, and what the Wisest One has determined to be the most beneficial for all the land," finished Lord Kingston.

Lord Kingston grabbed the letter and opened it up. "'Citizens of Andros, subjects of King Whaldo, subjects of King Ferdinand, and all the good people of lands far and close, I am terribly contrite for my inability to speak with you directly. For reasons known to me and circumstances beyond my control, I was forced to travel elsewhere rather than meet you all.'" A great murmur arose between both armies. They began suspecting the worse—that the Wisest One had been unable to forge a peace. King Whaldo's army especially, were confused and the Wisest One's wagon was opened, revealing no one was inside. They questioned what the point of the wagon had been, and why Lord Kingston and Lord Horus had continually entered the wagon.

Lord Kingston and Lord Horus waited as the noise subsided, so that they could continue reading. This time, Lord Horus retook the lecture. "'This façade with the wagon, and implying that I was in the wagon heading towards Chordica, was necessary for various reasons—some yet to be explained, and others withheld. I resolutely believe that this was necessary, and consequently asked Lord Kingston and Lord Horus to maintain this farce.

"'When I was in the Capital, reunited with Lord Kingston and Lord Horus for the Committee of the Wise Ones, we discussed at length the impending war, and the resolution to this. While we discussed possible tactics and methodologies, I could not find an acceptable alternative to my original plan—which I admit is fraught with fallacies, potentially false assumptions, and rational fear which propagated a certain theory of fighting.'" The murmurs arose again. Everyone feared that the intended meaning was that there would be a war. Wild speculations about a secret attack circulated, and that the Wisest One had not attended in fear that he could be killed in the fighting. *Good idea—that's why he's the smart one,* thought Roy. Roy hoped he would have the same sense to distance himself from the danger, but he also enjoyed the idea of fighting, and would never avoid it. While some thought the Wisest One was showing cowardice, others, a majority, still confided in the Wise Ones and in the Wisest One. They denied the speculations, and were convinced that they were interpreting his words wrong. *He is the smartest in all of the land; if he were to decide to fight, he would have handled this with much more care. He still has something planned,* thought Kesara.

Prince Jackson Horus and Prince Argus Kingston were close to their fathers, waiting patiently to hear the entire letter the Wisest One had left. *"They still haven't a clue,"* Jackson told Argus. Argus did not reply anything, but rather looked at Jackson and communicated through his expression that they could not possibly fathom what the Wisest One could mean. As the speculations finally died down, Lords Horus and Kingston again consulted the letter. Lord Kingston retook reading the letter.

"'Back when the Firion Calamity could not be imagined, before the Alexander Castle fell—back when Chordica was still populated, and Highstorm had not been abandoned, and back when the waters of Bloodpool were not yet stained with red, the city of Serenity stood in the furthest reaches of all the land. After Queen Abigail Alexander died after ruling for so many years, some wanted the next King to be decided in the similar fashion to Abigail's coronation. The Alexanders, however, maintained that they maintained the rights to rule. Serenity was one of the cities with the view that the Alexanders should not rule. Consequently, three Bladesmen of the Order of the Sword went to Serenity: Mikiah Alexander, Fernando Bastion, and Lexifer Mortison. In response to the cities outcry against the Alexanders, the three decided to act against it. Mikiah Alexander was the son of Abigail, and next in line to rule. The Brogues, then-rulers of Garrisbrough were disloyal to the Alexander crown, and the Alexanders constantly were accusing the Brogues of treason. When the Alexanders learned that Garrisbrough had sent men to Serenity, to keep it safe from the Alexanders, Mikiah Alexander decided to travel to Serenity. He promised Fernando Bastion power, and the childhood friends set out. Lexifer Mortison had a grudge against the Brogues, and volunteered to join the two to Serenity, not sure what they would do.

"'When the three arrived in Serenity, they were promptly received by the men of Garrisbrough. No documentation survives of the encounter, and only what the three men had to say served as evidence for what occurred. The men aggravated the three, threatening to have them killed, and the three acted with ferocity only seen five times since. The three Bladesmen, Mikiah Alexander, Fernando Bastion, and Lexifer Mortison, laid waste to the city, destroying the structures, desolating its lands, and decimating Serenity. Mikiah Alexander fought with the Caster metal sword Redimure, killing all men in sight. Fernando Bastion protected them with the Caster metal sword Guardiana, blocking any attempt to stop them. Lexifer Mortison blocked and attacked with his Caster metal sword, Dreadmort. The three displayed such an extravagant amount of skill, the Order of the Sword found it necessary to create another rank for these three legendary swordsmen: Swordsmaster.

"'News of the destruction of Serenity quickly spread throughout Andros, and it was then that Serenity became known as the razed city, and the Swordsmasters received the honorary title of Raze.'" Many stood, anxiously awaiting where this story was headed. Almost everyone had heard the legendary tale of the Swordsmasters, and their feat of destroying an entire city by themselves. To most, these swordsmen of the past were unparalleled, and none of them imagined seeing such skill in their life. Most of them did not know that Prince Tadeus Banesworth had been recently promoted to Swordsmaster.

"'Garrisbrough surrendered promptly after hearing this, and the Bastions were given control over the castle. They are now staunch allies to the Alexander crown. I share this story, not to educate, but to remind you. Power we would have thought impossible exists. Three Swordsmasters were able to destroy a city. Despite their small numbers, and despite the apparent impossibility of the task, they had powers and skills not seen before then. Perhaps we might be shocked by what is to come, but I must assure you the threat is real. Just as only three Swordsmasters were able to destroy the city, it will not take much of them to destroy us.

"'Even the Alkarvans will be unable to maintain neutrality. Powers such as the Swordsmasters will strike, and we must retaliate against them. The Brothers' War must come to an end. There is great folly in arguing about pay when Firion is erupting. The Swordsmasters approach, but if you want to kill each other and make their task easier, there is nothing I can do to stop you. Wait until the end of the day before shedding more blood.'" The strange letter from the Wisest One understandably troubled both armies. Some still hoped that there was more to the letter, but Lord Kingston and Lord Horus put it away and walked towards their respective armies. They did not understand all the talk of Swordsmasters, but they had not heard any plans for a treaty, and they knew war was coming. Both armies bristled with activity, and both kings were angered at the colossal waste of time. They began separating, and retiring to their corners of the land, but Lord Kingston and Lord Horus told them to wait, insisting that, according to the demands of the Wisest One, they should stay.

Neither army held a positive view of the Wisest One, but nonetheless they assented. Nighttime was quite a ways away. The somber faces of Ferdinand's army matched those from Whaldo's army. They waited ignorantly for the Wisest One's words to be understood. His description of something that would arrive seemed at the very least eerie. Some would finally understand the threat, and for the first time, the information would be revealed. They maintained that they would go to war, and this thought engulfed them. The tense air was stretched taut into a string, ready to snap and break apart at any time. Most did not know what would transpire, so they waited anxiously, as the Wisest One had instructed.

Argus Kingston knew that the Kingdom of Seville had gained control of a man's land. It proved to be one of the most successful governances, and now they were coming to invade. The Wisest One had warned them of this, but he did not heed his words. He hadn't given weight to the words, but seeing the Wisest One do all this, just for Nevil, made him realize that he had been mistaken to think no harm could come from him.

The empty field was a collection of the armies' hopes. No hills lined the sight, and the flat, consistent land stretched into the Desert Lands of Chordola and the Korscher Mountains. The vegetation grew meekly; instead, the color of dead leaves and parched vegetation surrounded them. Sand dunes were visible, and the heat was exhaustive. No animals were around; surely they would have picked a better location to search for water, since clearly there was none here. Water failed to bring life to the barren land. It rather appeared as the remnants of a fire. The stomping of feet was heard as the crunching of dead vegetation, which filled the still air even if feet were only stomped ever so often. Aside from that, no sound was heard. No one spoke. The silence added to their anxiety, and the anxiety propagated silence.

Prince Jackson Horus stood with the members of the Order of the Guardians of Peace that accompanied him: Dart Derinsky, Logan Osterous, and Brandon Sullivan. Jonathon Kinsley and Jennifer Bender stood with the Korschers, next to Claudius Atkinson and other Korschers. Jackson was nervous. He had indoctrinated the members of the order. Jackson wanted to treat with Nevil and prosper from a mutual agreement. How will they react to Nevil and his people though? Will they accept him and continue to wish to treat with them?

On the other hand, Argus Kingston worried not about the convictions of the members of the Protectors. Rather, he worried about the impending fight against Nevil. Argus looked around at the members of his group: Jacob Victoriano, Roy Rhapsados, Joseph Cameron, Javier Lunaer, Agnar Nostic, Miguel Garrington, and David Uriah. He knew that upon seeing Nevil and his people, they would rise up against them. The impending battle would result much more difficult to predict. It was imperative to battle against them, but because it was so important, it would be far from simple. Both Argus and Jackson stood worrying about the future events. The heat caused beads of sweat to course down their brow, and they wished for some action. They were helpless, stuck waiting for some movement.

Aurora Stephensen was still in the Lancaster Forest, desperately learning from Allison how to manifest her defensive powers, leaving Kesara, Gideon, and Benjamin Hewley, and

Maximillius Stoddard alone within King Whaldo's army. They waited as everyone else, in complete silence and disturbed by the heat. As opposed to most, who simply wondered why they were waiting, the three of them knew something important was going to happen. Aurora had told Kesara that only something dire could have made Jackson and Argus work together for so long. They wanted different things, but Jackson was helping Argus, and Argus, albeit inadvertently, was helping Jackson. *This won't end until Nevil and his people are gone, whether they are killed, or they go back to their land and treat with us.*

Kesara still didn't know quite what to do. She hadn't truly understood what Aurora was saying, and she hadn't asked. She wondered what could possibly keep the Wisest One away, rather than being between these two armies. The Wisest One had implied that something was coming. Someone. With a lot of power. She thought that, even if they had a lot of power, it did not mean they would exert it. But then she remembered what Steven once told her: *those with power want to show it, for what is power if no one recognizes that you have it?*

Nothing happened for a while.

They waited and waited, and finally, they heard something.

No one knew what sound it was, for they had never heard it before. Quickly, the armies stopped moving and talking, and held their breaths in order to hear the sound. They whispered quietly, trying to determine what the noise was. The Wisest One had told Argus and Jackson about tales of their people, but they didn't know what to expect. They had never seen them before. Even the Wisest One had always kept his secret. Argus and Jackson, Hal and Allister, all looked around, confused. They didn't know what they would see. For a brief moment, Argus worried that the tales of Nevil and his people were not the descriptions he had dismissed as a dying old man's crazy ramblings. He had grown fond of the Wisest One, but he had thought he might have exaggerated his people's achievements; it had seemed too fanciful.

The sound grew louder, causing the nerves of those waiting to grow ever-more. There was a sort of humming coming from afar, but they could not make it out. No one had heard this sound before; no one knew what was coming, not even Hal and Allister, with their growing suspicions. Up in the sky, something peculiar could be discerned. With time, it was more noticeable. It didn't look like one of the many avian animals, it was something different. It was much too big to be a fellcondor or a direhawk, but this left all of them confused. There was nothing bigger than these two massive beasts they called birds simply because they could fly. Apart from its size, its sound, too, was different from what they were accustomed. The sound it was producing was growing louder, a sort of humming and what sounded like fire or some great crackling of some sort. No one knew what to think about it.

The distant object approached. Though it was still too far to see clearly, the sound was growing louder. All eyes were now on the sky. No longer did any of them care about the Wisest One's words, or the army in front of them. While they were distracted was the perfect time to strike the opposing army, but they did not consider the option. They cared only about identifying this strange object in the sky they had not seen before. The sound was far from familiar, which tensed the groups even more. No one could answer what this was; it was far from their capacity to rationalize. This was nothing they had seen before. Some of them thought, *Perhaps it is a bird of legend?* None of them knew of any civilization that venerated some kind of avian beast, and they were no closer to identifying it.

The object grew closer, and they could see it more clearly. It was strange. It was silver in color, it seemed to be made of metal, but they couldn't understand. It somewhat resembled a bird, but this strange thing was not alive. The sound grew louder, and the fire was hotter. It was descending. The bright object was descending, and it was going towards them. Panic was arising, but all were too panic-stricken to move. Instead, they observed as this strange object came closer to them, and grew louder. The metal aspect was more visible. The metal bird object had a couple of wheels in the bottom, and the fires produced from some massive wings grew hotter, and it seemed to slow the metal bird's descent. They backed away from this strange object, in fear and awe, having no clues what to think of these events. The air around them was shifting. Now the once still air was crashing against their faces and clothes, attacking their eyes with dust from the barren land. A chill arouse inside those congregated around the metal bird.

Finally, the metal bird landed, and the fires ceased to burn. A strange hissing sound came from the metal object. What were they to do? What was happening? They were ready to fight against an army and die, but they weren't ready for this. A ramp of sorts descended from within the metal bird, revealing an inside made of metal as well. There were strange lights from inside, and strange noises they couldn't pinpoint. It was like the growling of wild animals, but these animals did not sound like they were distressed. And as if this weren't all weird enough, something came out of the metallic object. It was a weird creature, very strange looking. This was all too strange for them.

More creatures came, all with some distinct features, but they all shared some characteristics. They varied in height, but all of them were short. These things were dwarves, not something you would expect to come out of a giant metallic bird—though this was at a point where the standard for a norm was a giant metallic bird. The creatures were quite short, they varied in their tone, some were dark brown, others a lighter brown, some black, and others a tan color. Their hair was black and brown for the most part, though there were some with yellowish hair, and one with reddish hair. They had two legs, but these legs were quite short. Their arms too, were not long, of which they also possessed two. There were some similarities between these creatures and them, but that didn't make them any less hostile, or strange.

In each hand they had an extra finger, another striking feature. They had two eyes, a nose, and mouth, just like them. They walked and made strange sounds. More and more climbed down, until about fifty of these creatures were on the land in front of them, each holding a strange silver thing. It was composed of two rectangles, with a rectangular opening from an extremity of the larger rectangle. Some presumed that it was some sort of crossbow weapon that shot something at the enemy. That could be the only explanation, since they clearly would not be able to fight them in sword to sword combat. The strange creatures were standing there, while one of them moved around.

This was too much for them all. Under instructions of the Wisest One, they had travelled here, around Chordica. The Wisest One had told them that some sort of Swordsmasters would approach there. Some had quickly deduced that they could only come from the East, since from the North would be Ferdinand's Army, from the South would be Whaldo's Army, and the West was filled with desert lands. They had assumed somehow they would come from the East, from somewhere in the Korscher Mountains.

These came from the sky.

Nevil Da Real moved around, not caring much about the things in front of him. He went back inside to get the translator. His men were slacking. When he came out of the spaceship again, he noticed Elizabeth Prior examining these creatures, making hypotheses. He simply went towards the center of the field. The things in front of Elizabeth were tall creatures. They were humanoid, but their feet and hands were long. Logically, if the creatures were taller, their feet and hands would be longer as well, but these creatures' ratio of their feet and hands compared to their height was bigger than that of Elizabeth and her people. Elizabeth looked around at the groups of creatures around her.

There were two different groups, which seemed strange to her. She would have thought that their appearance would cause uproar and a panic. *Why were all these people here? Did they know we were coming? How could that be possible?* Elizabeth concluded that these creatures must be very observant, since the only way they could know of their impending presence would be by observing the stars and noticing a strange disturbance in the light of the stars they blocked. Still, this made no sense. The life forms should have put aside their differences and come together against them, their race against hers, so why should they be divided like that? She knew she could later use this against the group of creatures.

After having examined the creatures individually, she looked around at the surroundings. The land in which they had landed was barren—Nevil had chosen the spot assuming that no creatures traversed the place. Though they were not expecting to be surrounded by them upon landing, it was great to finally see them with their own eyes. They had done research on them with their satellites, but observing them like this was better.

The environment, she knew, varied much like their own planet did. There were barren lands, forests, lands filled with vegetation, oceans, and plateaus. The place they were currently at was barren and deserted, the beginning of the desert land. The skies were a shade of green, turning a dark purple with the setting star. Elizabeth had analyzed the star that gave this planet light; the star was a class 01IV star. This particular star's spectrum of light was maroon, blue, violet, green, and yellow. Elizabeth assumed that green was its shortest wavelength since the sky had a greenish hue to it. The atmosphere was filled with more Oxygen and less Nitrogen, and it had more heavy metals due to the star's enormous use of fusion. Elizabeth had not been able to produce conclusive data from afar, but now that she was here, she could analyze this planet some more. She grew confused upon picking up remnants of an anti-electromagnetic explosion. The explosions produced heat, but did not interact normally with its surroundings past a small radius. She had thought the energy waves the old satellite had registered were resultant from a malfunction, which they consequently had to crash and explode. The new evidence seemed to indicate the satellite had not malfunctioned. The technology was much too advanced, even for most species. She wondered what could have happened. She could not think of a natural incidence of this type of explosion.

Before Elizabeth could continue formulating her thoughts, Nevil began speaking into the translator he had taken out. The translator would mimic the sounds of the natives and communicate with them.

"My name is Nevil Da Real. I come as a representative of the Kingdom of Seville. We have come, in the name of God, may He bless you all, to communicate and exchange resources. We both can greatly benefit from one another. We want some of your metals. We are not here to fight, but should you resist, imminent chaotic destruction awaits you. This doesn't have to be an invasion."

The Earthlings had arrived on the planet Andros.

37. Raze- 543

Epilogue

Five years shy of a lifetime ago, my father killed me.

I was but a little kid, so I had no idea as to what was going on. Instead, like any other kid, I confided that my father knew what was best, and it would be beneficial to trust him. That was also the day my naïveté was no more.

I was much too little to recall the conversations I had with my father, or the reasons he gave me. I trusted him since he was my father, and yet he killed me.

What I do recall from those conversations is that my father was trying to explain why I needed to die. Their enemy needed to break apart. They needed me as their reason. This wasn't the only day he talked to me. He began telling me, getting me ready for my death. Throughout this whole process, I couldn't understand the information he was telling me, nor could I perceive the "critical" situations of which he spoke.

Nevertheless, the day came. My father told me and my two brothers to go play outside. In reality, my father was simply getting things ready. He was preparing the death of his son. He was getting ready to kill me.

I remember being outside, awaiting my end. My two brothers were in the sandbox playing with some toys. The younger of my older brothers didn't have his favorite toy with him.

There I was, ready to die, and I was obsessing over this insignificant absence of my brother's favorite toy. Perhaps this is just the nature of a child's mind. He cares only about fun and toys. I was too young to register that I was about to die. I couldn't understand it. I didn't know what it entailed.

Then everything became darker. Undoubtedly, this was just a trick of my mind. I do not recall the weather. It was day time, that's all I know. Whether it was sunny or raining, I could not say.

There I was, ready to die, and in retrospect, I obsess over the weather. Perhaps nothing abnormal happened to the sun, but my world grew much darker at that point.

It was the exact same point I saw my father come outside. It was about to be time. I ran towards him, not because I was glad to see him, or I wanted to play, but because that is what he would expect of me. He picked me up and whispered in my ear to go inside. It was now time.

I went towards my mother and told her I was going to go to the bathroom. She and I had always shared a special bond. I recall that specifically. It went past that of a relationship between a mom and her son—even a mom and her *youngest* son. She seemed to understand me. She felt like a part of me, not simply someone who cared for me or loved me.

I mention this because, upon telling her this, she looked at me knowingly, and weakly nodded. She knew I was lying. She knew I didn't have to go to the bathroom. She understood.

I walked towards the house, step by little step. Each step felt heavy. I could no longer enjoy the outside, and the mysteries of the world would go unanswered. I would never find out why the sky was blue. I would not understand the greenness of the grass. Why should I ever understand the flight of birds, or the barks of dogs?

I opened the door and felt a cold wind from inside. The house was a cold empty crypt. I could feel the absence of heat throughout my body. My feet registered the ice that was the tiles of the floor. My hands went into my pockets to feel respite from the attacking chill.

I closed the door, trapping myself in this crypt. I glanced outside. I do not trust this was my actual sense of sight, but I saw my brother get his missing favorite toy, only to be smacked on the head by my mother. She had warned him after all, but he had simply continued.

The eldest brother then hit my dad on the leg to retaliate. Then my other brother's toy was lost. He looked at me, and began walking towards me.

I turned around, rejecting this image, and went deeper into the house. To this day I remember what was outside: the tree, the

Epilogue- 545

sandbox, the grill, the lamp, and the hose. I could delineate the place if so I desired. Yet, the door leading to the kitchen ends my memory of the place. I do not recall the deeper parts of the house. I do not recall the physical appearance of the place.

I remember smelling the same aroma the home had had since I was born. It was a distinct smell of cherry—my mother loved cherries. To my dismay, there was also another smell. As a kid I couldn't pinpoint its distinct aroma. I realize that thinking back on the smell isn't reliable, but in retrospect, the aroma was that of death. There was decay, something rotting in the kitchen.

I felt small. I felt powerless. I *was* small and powerless. I do not recall what I may have passed—perhaps a picture—but I then felt sad. The only people I remember of that world are my mother, father, and my two brothers. I distinctly remember being sad that I wouldn't be with them anymore though. This is why I conclude it was a picture. Nonetheless, I felt melancholy. The room seemed to be getting darker. Finally, my father came.

He had waited outside. Now was the time though. There was no going back. I cannot yet recall the conversation. He mentioned something about a hard life.

Perhaps my brain developed a defense mechanism. I can't recall. I do not remember the physical world. I remember only the emotions I felt: confusion, ambivalence, gloom, and anger—though that last one is a result of looking back. I didn't feel anger back then. I instead felt fright.

How absurd. I can't remember what he said. I can hardly recall what he looked like. The house is a blur to me, my brothers' faces only appear in half remembered dreams.

I felt a cold object in my hand. The object was distinctly spherical; I kept rolling it in my hands. My father continued talking, but I rolled this spherical object. He then gave me a cubic storage unit. The only thing from my memory is a cubic feeling container the size of my hand.

He finished his speech, and I felt relief. Perhaps I felt this because I would finally have done it. I would no longer worry about this grand weight.

I've tried to remember what he told me that day. I can't though; it was too long ago, perhaps my mind was even blocking the event.

Absurdly, I envision my father giving his speech. When he finally finishes, I yell at him. It's always the same words: "No, I don't thank you for this." I know not why these are the words that come to mind.

Back then, I felt relief when he finished his speech. The coffin would close; the door would be shut tight. I didn't have to look back. I didn't have to worry; I had no choice in the matter. My naïveté died that day, and so did I.

The last sound I heard was the shot from a gun.

Appendix

Faldenheim:

The first great castle established by the Telks in the first year after the Great Shaking. Originally ruled by Orville Falden, the distant relative of King Andros abandoned Faldenheim when the Lancasters drove them out, never to return. Consequently, the Lancasters gave the castle to the Farrens, who ruled Faldenheim for the next 200 years. The Swordsmaster Yarimir Spinozah, suffering from their cruelty, overthrew the lord and established his brother as lord, and the Spinozah family as rulers. They ruled for 300 years, but they all were poisoned, and became ill. Hal Horus went to "cure" them but secretly let them die so that he may take control of the castle.

Lord Hal Horus: 59, Lord of Faldenheim, Elder and member on the Committee of the Wise Ones.

Lady Malena Horus: Deceased (from zalphia), married with child to Hal before his appointment of Lordship.

(Prince) Jackson Horus: 36, Son of Lady Horus, Telekinesis Zalphic, grew up in the Capital.

Wyatt Stephensen: 56, Would-Be Lord of Faldenheim, lives in Farendor with his blood money. Has dull-orange eyes.

Lily Stephensen: 54, Wife of Wyatt, mother to Aurora.

Aurora Stephensen: 22, Daughter of Wyatt, Steven's best friend. A descendant of the Vibrants; she has lilac eyes.

Leonardo Hewley: 49, Father to Ben, suffers from an unknown disease.

Veronica Hewley: 47, Married to Leonardo, mother to Ben.

Benjamin Hewley: 27, Eldest son of Leonardo and Veronica, Fire/Telekinesis Zalphic. He is a Knight in the Order of the Sword and is the elder brother of Steven.

Steven (Hewley) Mc.Roy: 23, Second son of Leonardo, Telekinesis/Invincibility Zalphic. A Scholar.

Kesara Hewley: 17, Only daughter to Leo and Veronica, Water Zalphic.

Gideon Hewley: 14, Youngest son of Leonardo and Veronica, Wood Zalphic.

Maximillius Stoddard: 26, Best friends with Benjamin, Water/Telekinesis Zalphic.

Caspian Stoddard: 33, The only Bladesman of Faldenheim. Trained Maximillius and Benjamin.

Brandon Sullivan: 22, Former friends with Roy, Fire Zalphic.

Logan Osterous: 31, Second-in-Command of Peacekeeps. Water Zalphic.

Dart Derinsky: 28, Third-in-Command of Peacekeeps. Thunder Zalphic.

Devin Gallious: 21, Wood Zalphic.

Ronald Rhapsados: Deceased, Father of Roy.

Felicity Rhapsados: 54, Mother of Roy.

Raymond Rhapsados: 29, Eldest son of Ronald and Felicity.

Francis Rhapsados: 27, Second son of Felicity.

Roy Rhapsados: 23, Youngest son of Ronald and Felicity. Telekinesis/Thunder Zalphic.

Erim Falden: 19, member of the Wise Ones

Vernatia:

Established in the second year, after the Great Shaking, the second great castle was ruled originally by the Navers. When the Lancasters took control of the castle, the Navers had children with the Lancasters, who proceeded to rule. 150 years later, they were betrayed by their allies in the castle, the Valdens. The Valdens were killed 130 years later by the Kaines. They ruled until all of them died, and Allister Kingston was named lord.

Lord Allister Kingston: 62, Lord of Vernatia, Elder and member of the Committee of the Wise Ones.

Prince Argus Kingston: 36, Prince to Vernatia, a Fire Zalphic.

Sinehvar Victoriano: 53, Captain of the guards.

Jacob Victoriano: 32, Bladesman, 2nd of the Protectors. Telekinesis/Thunder Zalphic. An Instructor in the Wise Ones.

Austin Drost: 26, Skilled warrior. Brother of Kayton.

Kayton Drost: 35, Strongest Bladesman in Vernatia.

Miguel Garrington: 20, Wood Zalphic.

Agnar Nostic: 24, Thunder Zalphic.

Javier Lunaer: 23, Best friend to Joseph, Water Zalphic.

Joseph Cameron: 23, Best friend to Javier, Wood Zalphic.

David Uriah: 25, Wood Zalphic.

Bravania:

Third castle established by the Telks, in the fourth year, in order to make a settlement closer to the forest. The castle never went through the formal process of choosing a lord before the Lancasters invaded. They took control of the castle, and Theobald Banesworth took the reins of the castle. They never abandoned the castle, even after the Telks had seemingly left, and the Banesworths have been unchanging in their lords. Along with Arastaud, Bravania is the only castle that has never changed the family lines that govern them.

Lord Neister Banesworth: 57, Lord of Bravania.

Lady Melisa Banesworth: 56, Lady of Bravania.

Prince Tadeus Banesworth: 31, Heir to Bravania. The most skilled swordsman on the continent.

Prince Maekor Banesworth: 26, Youngest son of Neister and Melisa.

Princess Fayrah Banesworth: 18, Only daughter, and youngest child to Lord Neister and Lady Melisa.

Melinda Briar: 34, Bladesman.

Zachary Briar: 37, Bladesman.

Garait Tiralus: 39, Bladesman.

Valerie Landral: 22, Young guard.

Markai:

Established in the eighth year by the Telks and Lancasters, the castle was given to the Elimaves. They ruled until Merril Alexander killed the lord. The successor, the Arcay family, ruled afterward for seventy years before the Reimers took control. After 170 years, Giovani Alexander made a pact with the Leisiters, to instill them in the castle, and promised marriage between the houses. The Leisiters currently rule Markai.

Lady Callisto Leisiter: 47, Lady of Markai, a Deadeye.

Queen Serinah (Leisiter) Alexander: 38, Sister to Callisto, married to King Raymond.

Princess Mayrah (The Disgraced) Leisiter: 26, Lost her maidenhood.

Tori Whittiker: 25, Marksman, Thunder Zalphic.

Elisa Kelvinly: 27, Marksman.

Kevin Kelvinly: 23, Travelled to Faldenheim for opportunity.

Jacquelyn Flores: 24, Daughter of Urimé. Wood Zalphic.

Iriadine Bellozo: 28, Sharpshooter, with Jacquelyn.

Sarayi Flores: 21, Lives in Meliserah. Befriends Jacquelyn.

Paul Dune: 28, a Captain in Markai. Mayrah's lover.

Aaron Herbert: 36, Captain of Jacquelyn and Sarayi's platoon.

Sezekiah Urai: 29, Second cousin to Elizar, who is the Sword of Baroth. A Telk, and Deadeye.

Franciska Selmira: 33, Deadeye.

Chordica:

Established by Chordric Bender in the second year, the Korscher chose the desert lands and established themselves in the almost inhospitable land. The isolationist people lived in the land, enduring hardships, while keeping trade at a minimum. Consequently, Korscher blood is still strong in them, and little Androsii inheritance has established itself. They blocked access between the mountains and the desert lands, so Sebastian Alexander drove them out. They willingly left, as the "Great Shaking became no more than a story".

Cyrus Bender: 48, Older brother of Patrick, leader of the Korscher people.

Patrick Bender: 44, Younger brother of Cyrus, left the Korscher Mountains.

Jessica Bender: 45, Married Patrick.

Kenneth Bender: 26, Eldest son of Patrick and Jessica. Thunder Zalphic.

Kyler Bender: 16, Brother of Kenneth.

Jennifer Atkinson: 22, Twin sister of Amy. Earth Zalphic.

Amy Atkinson: Deceased, twin sister of Jennifer. Non-Zalphic.

Claudius Atkinson: 27, Childhood friend of Jennifer. Bodyguard of the Benders.

Jonathon Kinsley: 22, In love with Jennifer. Earth Zalphic.

Nikko Zerkin: 20, Wood Zalphic, hired by the Benders.

Pierre Lepis: 24, Telekinesis Zalphic.

Arastaud:

After the Lancasters fought the Telks back to its shore, the Alkarvans and their red-haired people, the Redimer people, travelled south, and established Arastaud in the eleventh year. From thence, they have remained in control of the castle. They are known for evading conflict and remaining neutral to almost all matters. When Barrymore Alexander declared war on Arastaud, Kirrivor Elsavar killed the fellcondors sent towards them, and fought back against the crown, withstanding their own. They were left alone after, and when Ian Alexander proposed joining houses in marriage, the Alkarvans resolutely refused.

Lord Greymont Alkarvan: 66, Lord of Arastaud.

Lady Dalia Alkarvan: 63, Lady of Arastaud, younger sister to Allison.

(Lady) Allison Alkarvan: 68, Rightful Lady of Arastaud. Invincibility Zalphic

Prince Oliver (The Red) Alkarvan: 43, Bladesman, infamous blood shedder.

Princess Samantha Alkarvan: 41, Eldest daughter of Greymont and Dalia.

Princess Alice Alkarvan: 39, Youngest daughter of Greymont and Dalia.

May Alkarvan: 16, Daughter of Oliver.

Oskar Alkarvan: 13, Son of Oliver. Desert Cloak—Fighter in the Order of the Sword.

Oleander Lyrad: 40, Bladesman.

Ivan Skar: 37, Bladesman.

Quade Glenna: 41, Bladesman, red-haired bastard; The Red's wife.

Nora Elsavar: 24, Bladesman, The Beauty of Arastaud.

Larah Heim: 42, Bladesman.

Garrisbrough:

Established in the thirteenth year, Garrisbrough is considered the greatest castle of Andros. Originally ruled by the Brogues, the Alexanders constantly fought with Garrisbrough, accusing them of all manner of perversions. Mikiah Alexander declared war on one of its cities, Serenity, and then defeated the Garrisbrough army. The Brogues were removed from leadership, and the Bastions were cemented in its place. Since that change in rulers in the year ninety, the Bastions have been staunch allies of the Alexanders, and have enjoyed considerable power.

Lord Fredrick Bastion: 44, Lord of Garrisbrough, Bladesman.

Lady Elana Bastion: 42, Lady of Garrisbrough, married to Fredrick.

Prince Elsamar Bastion: 21, Son of Fredrick, heir to Garrisbrough. Knight.

Princess Hellen Bastion: 16, Daughter of Fredrick.

Princess Priah Bastion: 12, Youngest daughter of Fredrick

Valadiar Helmsdan: 42, Bladesman, protecting King Whaldo.

Orton Eridan: 46, Bladesman, protecting King Whaldo.

Horaclys Naeia: 44, Bladesman, protecting King Whaldo.

Roger Weiracle: 51, Bladesman, oldest with the rank.

Uracli Cristem: 46, Bladesman.

Giovani Ignat: 19, Prince Elsamar's friend, a Fighter.

Lacy Kurama: 23, Known as Jewel. A thief.

Aquareus:

The temporary port is so-called due to its location in the Detrimental Shores. When the waters rain in and flood the city, it becomes desolate except for a few floating platforms. When the waters retreat and leave it barren, ships can do little to get to its port. However, for a great part of the year, it thrives as a major port, where ships from all over, and especially from Whaldo's Port come and trade. Aquareus, despite its strange geography and its temporal existence, is a thriving port.

Irvine Jeram: 39, Runs the ports of Aquareus, brother of Urimé.

Urimé Jeram: 36, Sister of Irvine, a mother.

Xyliander Dicray: 44, Captains the fastest ship in the known world, the *Xycray*.

Yaric Bihr: 53, Owns many of the ships in Aquareus, of *Bihr Shipping*.

Darrien Kormund: 39, Water Zalphic.

Tristam Eris: 36, Protecting the Jerams.

Refia Abengane: 17, Befriended a blue-green lizard, who she affectionately refers to as Scales.

Alexander Castle:

The Alexander Castle was established in the fourteenth year by Whaldo Alexander, and housed Telks and a majority of the Alexander family, with the exception of the King or Queen who would reside in the Capital. The Alexander Castle has always had an Alexander in its reigns. In the year 527, Heramyr Mortison erupted the Firion volcano, along with other Fire Zalphics, and caused the Firion Calamity, extinguishing all the Alexanders in one fell swoop—all but Whaldo and Ferdinand Alexander. The Fallen Castle of Alexander is enveloped to this day with the remaining lava and is inhospitable and abandoned.

King Raymond Alexander: Deceased, died during the Firion Calamity.

King Whaldo III Alexander: 15, Son of Late King Raymond and Queen Serinah.

Ferdinand Flores: 17, Travelling to Faldenheim, a bastard.

Lyrus Flores: 31, Travelling with Ferdinand, a bastard.

Korey (Youngblood) Weirack: 16, Young warrior.

Rhema Farren: 32, Travelling with Ferdinand.

Seville:

Citizens of the Kingdom of Seville, the invaders originally were part of the ULA. When Adam sent his youngest son, Trevor, to Andros and accused the ULA of killing his son, he began a revolution which eventually led to the establishment of the Kingdom of Seville, headed by Seville Da Real. The Kingdom of Seville currently rules the ESE, though they are meeting resistance. They have been rivaled only by the Atlers but their superior weaponry could do nothing against the hard nature of the invaders, who chose to kill them without showing the same mercy showed unto them.

Adam Da Real: (Deceased) Father of Nevil. Overthrew the ULA and enthroned Seville.

Evelyn Da Real: Married Adam. Mother of Trevor.

Seville Da Real: (Deceased) Eldest son of Adam and Evelyn. Former King.

Nevil Da Real: 66, Leader of the Kingdom of Seville's forces.

Trevor Da Real: 63, Youngest son of Adam.

Seville II Da Real: Son of Seville. King of Seville.

Elizabeth Prior: 62, Alternatively known as Abigail, keeper of peace, maker of rulers.

Bryan Sect: 69, Cautious warrior wary of inadvertently spreading war secrets.

Levi Langston: 66, Third commander of the invading forces.

Isaiah Rayel: 59, the Priest. Preaches to the Androsii about their religion.

Telkos:

From the lands in the West, Telk is an umbrella term for all the inhabitants of the Telk continent. Many people have inhabited the Telk lands, such as the Teltecs, Redimers, Madaites, Cyrs, and Nahbens, and is the continent with the most history. The Telk continent is mostly under the power of Queen Rama Lizer. It is also home to Glavaus, which is widely considered to be the most important city in the world.

"Duskman": Member of Assassin's Dawn.

Kain Traire: 37, Strongest Telk swordsmen. Telekinetic Zalphic. Telk Royal Guard.

Rama Lizer: 54, Queen of the Telk Lands.

Merren Rhand: 43, Captain of the Royal Fleet.

Selvia Hoffen: 29, Telk Royal Guard. Emissary.

Paramin Alexander: 36, Sword of Mada, part of the "6 Swordsmen of Paths"

Cseyah Orophus: 39, Sword of Heif, part of the "6 Swordsmen of Paths"

Elizar Urai: 42, Sword of Baroth, part of the "6 Swordsmen of Paths"

Ryke Irae: 36, Sword of Mhorov, part of the "6 Swordsmen of Paths"

Jezehmar Marcus: 33, Sword of Krall, part of the "6 Swordsmen of Paths"

"Laihs": Sword of Rhyne, part of the "6 Swordsmen of Paths"

Taraki Rodrick: 28, Training under Kain

Historical Figures:

Argus: Telk soldier sent to accompany the settlers. Protected the city from cruelty.

Jack: Hero to the peasants. Protected the common people in Whaldo's Port

Arjen Elsavar: Telk Royal Guard that was sent to Andros to accompany the settlers.

King Whaldo Alexander: First King of Andros. Established the Wise Ones.

Queen Abigail Alexander: Queen of Andros, chosen by election, successor to Whaldo.

Chordric Bender: Led the Korschers to desert lands and founded a city.

Theobald Banesworth: Managed the Lancaster forces outside of the forest.

Heramyr Mortison: Fire Zalphic, the most infamous zalphic. Caused the Firion Calamity.

Lexifer Mortison: One of the original 3 Swordsmasters. Desolated Serenity.

Mikiah Alexander: One of the original 3 Swordsmasters. Decimated Serenity.

Fernando Bastion: One of the original 3 Swordsmasters. Destroyed Serenity.

Kirrivor Elsavar: Swordsmaster, protected Arastaud from the Alexanders.

Yarimir Spinozah: Swordsmaster, conquered Faldenheim and installed brother as lord.

The Kings and Queens of Andros:

0-14 Lancasters. The original Lancasters ruled the land at this time.

15-40 Whaldo Alexander: First to cross the sea. Established the Wise Ones.

40-90 Abigail Alexander: Longest ruler. Elected by vote. A fair queen.

90-103 Mikiah Alexander: Legendary Swordsmaster. Forged alliance with the Bastions.

103-107 Carroll Alexander: Inept ruler, with no strength.

107-114 Meredith Alexander: Inept ruler, with no determination.

114-119 Marrah Alexander: Inept ruler, with no intelligence.

119-132 Sebastian Alexander: Drove the Korschers out of Andros.

132-158 Sebastian II Alexander: Abandoned his help of those in Highstorm.

158-169 Barrymore Alexander: War with Arastaud; died in battle. *Kirrivor Elsavar*

169-184 Irene Alexander: Surrendered Arastaud to the Alkarvans.

184-203 Mellissa Alexander: Attempted to settle Chordica.

203-227 Daniel Alexander: Abandoned Desert Lands.

227-244 Merrill Alexander: Fought Markai. Defeated them. *Yarimir Spinozah.*

244-278 Serena Alexander: Made peace among the land.

278-302 Zachary Alexander: Bloodied Bloodpool. Died from contracted disease.

302-302 Mary Alexander: Died of illness.

302-302 June Alexander: Died of illness.

302-315 Whaldo II Alexander: Survived illness. Ruled justly.

315-346 Korey Alexander: Fought with the North.

346-370 Ergon Alexander: Fought the Telks.

370-402 Remy Alexander: Fought the Telks.

402-428 Warren Alexander: Drove the Telks further west.

428-436 Lazard Alexander: Abandoned the conquered lands. Returned to Andros.

436-461 Tristan Alexander: Deposed by the Wise Ones for killing his wife.

461-487 Ian Alexander: Failed attempt to join the Alkarvans in marriage; died childless.

487-503 Farah Alexander: Poisoned by a heart-struck lover.

503-526 Giovani Alexander: Searched in vain for the Lost Forest.

526-527 Raymond Alexander: Died in the Firion Calamity, with the other Alexanders.

528- Whaldo III Alexander: Young lad, too young to rule.

Order of the Sword: Centered in Garrisbrough, with subsidiaries in every major castle, this order puts an emphasis on sword-to-sword combat. The sword is the key weapon of choice of members in the order.

> Squire, the green cloaks
> Fighter, the desert cloaks
> Warrior, the black cloaks
> Knight, the red cloaks
> Bladesman, the blue cloaks
> Swordsmaster, the gold cloaks

Order of the Bow: Centered in Markai, the order puts emphasis on the bow, in a world where swords are ever-present.

> Bowman, the desert strings
> Archer, the black strings
> Marksman, the red strings
> Sharpshooter, the blue strings
> Deadeye, the gold strings

Order of the Wise Ones: Centered in the Capital, the Order of the Wise Ones is the most important order in all of Andros. They teach knowledge and serve as mentors.

> Acolyte
> Scholar
> Instructor
> Elder

Assassin's Dawn: A legendary assassin order from across the Sehrin Sea. In the Telk Lands, the assassin order is known throughout the land to have the most fearsome assassins.

Zalphic Hunters: Specialized group of soldiers that hunt zalphics. Due to the low number of zalphics, these hunters are very rare, but this only adds to their prestige. There are trackers who specialize in following rumors and finding zalphics, while their warriors specialize in fighting and killing them. Faldenheim has a group that notably has long since idled and become lethargic, but the other castles boast a strong group.

The Ten Representatives: Believed to be the key in an upcoming war, the ten each wield a Caster metal sword. The identity of all ten has yet to be determined, but significant progress has been made to find them.

[Redacted]: Known internally as [redacted] this organization [redacted].

Members of the order are limited to the following 10 members:
[Redacted]
[Redacted]
[Redacted]
[Redacted]
[Redacted]
[Redacted]
[Redacted]
[Redacted]
[Redacted]
[Redacted]

Made in the USA
Las Vegas, NV
28 February 2024

86451061R00315